Books by TONY HILLERMAN

 *FICTION*

Coyote Waits

Talking God

A Thief of Time

Skinwalkers

The Ghostway

The Dark Wind

People of Darkness

Listening Woman

Dance Hall of the Dead

The Fly on the Wall

The Blessing Way

The Boy Who Made Dragonfly *(for children)*

 *NONFICTION*

The Great Taos Bank Robbery

Rio Grande

New Mexico

The Spell of New Mexico

Indian Country

TONY HILLERMAN

LEAPHORN & CHEE

THREE CLASSIC HILLERMAN MYSTERIES

SKINWALKERS
A THIEF OF TIME
TALKING GOD

HarperCollins*Publishers*

Skinwalkers was originally published by Harper & Row, Publishers, in 1987.

A Thief of Time was originally published by Harper & Row, Publishers, in 1988.

Talking God was originally published by Harper & Row, Publishers, in 1989.

ISBN 0-06-018789-1

CONTENTS

SKINWALKERS

This book is dedicated to Katy Goodwin, Ursula Wilson, Faye Bia Knoki, Bill Gloyd, Annie Kahn, Robert Bergman, and George Bock, and all the Medicine People, Navajo and belagana, *who care for The People—and about them. My thanks to Dr. Albert Rizzoli for his kindness and his help, and a tip of my hat to the good work of the too often unappreciated Indian Health Service.*

AUTHOR'S NOTE

Those who read these Navajo mysteries with a map of the Big Reservation beside them should be warned that Badwater Wash, its clinic, and its trading post are as fictional as the people who inhabit them. The same is true of Short Mountain. Finally my good friend Ernie Bulow correctly reminds me that more traditional shamans would disapprove of both the way Jim Chee was invited to do the Blessing Way mentioned in this book (such arrangements should be made face-to-face and not by letter) and of Chee practicing a sandpainting on the ground under the sky. Such sacred and powerful ritual should be done only in the hogan.

We Navajo understand Coyote is always waiting out there, just out of sight. And Coyote is always hungry.

—ALEX ETCITTY,
born to the *Water Is Close* People

No character in this work of fiction is based upon
any real person, living or dead.

WHEN THE CAT CAME THROUGH the little trapdoor at the bottom of the screen it made a *clack-clack* sound. Slight, but enough to awaken Jim Chee. Chee had been moving in and out of the very edge of sleep, turning uneasily on the narrow bed, pressing himself uncomfortably against the metal tubes that braced the aluminum skin of his trailer. The sound brought him enough awake to be aware that his sheet was tangled uncomfortably around his chest.

He sorted out the bedclothing, still half immersed in an uneasy dream of being tangled in a rope that he needed to keep his mother's sheep from running over the edge of something vague and dangerous. Perhaps the uneasy dream provoked an uneasiness about the cat. What had chased it in? Something scary to a cat—or to this particular cat. Was it something threatening to Chee? But in a moment he was fully awake, and the uneasiness was replaced by happiness. Mary Landon would be coming. Blue-eyed, slender, fascinating Mary Landon would be coming back from Wisconsin. Just a couple of weeks more to wait.

Jim Chee's conditioning—traditional Navajo—caused him to put that thought aside. All things in moderation. He would think more about that later. Now he thought about tomorrow. Today, actually, since it must be well after midnight. Today he and Jay Kennedy would go out and arrest Roosevelt Bistie so that Bistie could be charged with some degree of homicide—probably with murder. Not a complicated job, but unpleasant enough to cause Chee to change the subject of his thinking again. He thought about the cat. What had driven it in? The coyote, maybe. Or what? Obviously something the cat considered a threat.

The cat had appeared last winter, finding itself a sort of den under a juniper east of Chee's trailer—a place where a lower limb, a boulder, and a rusted barrel formed a closed cul-de-sac. It had become a familiar, if suspicious, neighbor. During the spring, Chee had formed a habit of leaving out table scraps to feed it after heavy snows. Then when the snow melt ended and the spring drought arrived, he began leaving out water in a coffee can. But easy water attracted other animals, and birds, and sometimes they turned it over. And so, one afternoon when there was absolutely nothing else to do, Chee had removed the door, hacksawed out a cat-sized rectangle through its bottom frame, and then attached a plywood flap, using leather hinges and Miracle Glue. He had done it on a whim, partly to see if the ultracautious cat could be taught to use it. If the cat did, it would gain access to a colony of field mice that seemed to have moved into Chee's trailer. And the watering problem would be solved. Chee felt slightly uneasy about the water. If he hadn't started this meddling, nature would have taken its normal course. The cat would have moved down the slope and found itself a den closer to the San Juan—which was never dry. But Chee had interfered. And now Chee was stuck with a dependent.

Chee's interest, originally, had been simple curiosity. Once, obviously, the cat had been owned by someone. It was skinny now, with a long scar over its ribs and a patch of fur missing from its right leg, but it still wore a collar, and, despite its condition, it had a purebred look. He'd described it to the woman in the pet store at Farmington—tan fur, heavy hind legs, round head, pointed ears; reminded you of a bobcat, and like a bobcat it had a mere stub of a tail. The woman had said it must be a Manx.

"Somebody's pet. People are always bringing their pets along on vacations," she'd said, disapproving, "and then they don't take care of them and they get out of the car and that's the end of them." She'd asked Chee if he could catch it and bring it in, "so somebody can take care of it."

Chee doubted if he could get his hands on the cat, and hadn't tried. He was too much the traditional Navajo to interfere with an animal without a reason. But he was curious. Could such an animal, an animal bred and raised by the white man, call up enough of its hunting instincts to survive in the Navajo world? The curiosity gradually turned to a casual admiration. By early summer, the animal had accumulated wisdom with its scar tissue. It stopped trying to hunt prairie dogs and concentrated on small rodents and birds. It learned how to hide, how to escape. It learned how to endure.

It also learned to follow the water can into Chee's trailer rather than make the long climb down to the river. Within a week the cat was using the flap when Chee was away. By midsummer it began coming in when he was at home. At first it had waited tensely at the step until he was away from the door, kept a nervous eye on him while it drank, and bolted through the flap at his first motion. But now, in August, the cat virtually ignored him. It had come inside at night only once before—driven in by a pack of dogs that had flushed it out of its den under the juniper.

Chee looked around the trailer. Far too dark to see where the cat had gone. He pushed the sheet aside, swung his feet to the floor. Through the screened window beside his bed he noticed the moon was down. Except far to the northwest, where the remains of a thunderhead lingered, the sky was bright with stars. Chee yawned, stretched, went to the sink, and drank a palmful of water warm from the tap. The air smelled of dust, as it had for weeks. The thunderstorm had risen over the Chuskas in the late afternoon, but it had drifted northward over the Utah border and into Colorado and nothing around Shiprock had gotten any help. Chee ran a little more water, splashed it on his face. The cat, he guessed, would be standing behind the trash canister right beside his feet. He yawned again. What had driven it in? He'd seen the coyote's tracks along the river a few days ago, but it would have to be terribly hungry to hunt this close to his trailer. No dogs tonight, at least he hadn't heard any. And dogs, unlike coyotes, were easy enough to hear. But probably it was dogs, or the coyote. Probably a coyote. What else?

Chee stood beside the sink, leaning on it, yawning again. Back to bed. Tomorrow would be unpleasant. Kennedy said he would be at Chee's trailer at 8 A.M. and the FBI agent was never late. Then the long drive into the Lukachukais to find the man named Roosevelt Bistie and ask him why he had killed an old man named Dugai Endocheeney with a butcher knife. Chee had been a Navajo Tribal Policeman for seven years now—ever since he'd graduated from the University of New Mexico—and he knew now he'd never learn to like this part of the job, this dealing with sick minds in a way that would never bring them back to harmony. The federal way of curing Bistie would be to haul him before a federal magistrate, charge him with homicide on a federal reservation, and lock him away.

Ah, well, Chee thought, most of the job he liked. Tomorrow he would endure. He thought of the happy times stationed at Crownpoint. Mary Landon teaching in the elementary school. Mary Landon always there. Mary Landon always willing to listen. Chee felt relaxed. In a moment he would go back to bed. Through the screen he could see only a dazzle of stars above a black landscape. What was out there? A coyote? Shy Girl Beno? That turned his thoughts to Shy Girl's opposite. Welfare Woman. Welfare Woman and the Wrong Begay Incident. That memory produced a delighted, reminiscent grin. Irma Onesalt was Welfare Woman's name, a worker in the tribal Social Services office, tough as saddle leather, mean as a snake. The look on her face when they learned they had hauled the wrong Begay out of the Badwater Clinic and delivered him halfway across the reservation was an image he would treasure. She was dead now, but that had happened far south of the Shiprock district, out of Chee's jurisdiction. And for Chee, the shooting of Irma Onesalt didn't do as much as it might have to diminish the delight of the Wrong Begay Incident. It was said they'd never figure out who shot Welfare Woman because everybody who ever had to work with her would be a logical suspect with a sound motive. Chee couldn't remember meeting a more obnoxious woman.

He stretched. Back to bed. Abruptly he thought of an alternative to the coyote-scared-the-cat theory. The Shy Girl at Theresa Beno's camp. She had wanted to talk to him, had hung on the fringes while he talked to Beno, and Beno's husband, and Beno's elder daughter. The shy one had the long-faced, small-boned beauty that seemed to go with Beno women. He had noticed her getting into a gray Chevy pickup when he was leaving the Beno camp, and when he had stopped for a Pepsi at the Roundtop Trading Post, the Chevy had driven up. Shy Girl had parked well away from the gasoline pumps. He'd noticed her watching him, and waited. But she had driven away.

Chee moved from the sink and stood by the screen door, looking out into the darkness, smelling the August drought. She knew something about the sheep, he thought, and she wanted to tell me. But she wanted to tell me where no one could see her talking to me. Her sister's husband is stealing the sheep. She knows it. She wants him caught. She followed me. She waited. Now she will come up to the door and tell me as soon as she overcomes her shyness. She is out there, and she frightened the cat.

It was all, of course, a silly idea, product of being half asleep. Chee could see nothing through the screen. Only the dark shape of the junipers, and a mile up the river the lights that someone had left on at the Navajo Nation Shiprock Agency highway maintenance yards, and beyond that the faint glow that attempted to civilize the night at the town of Shiprock. He could smell dust and the peculiar aroma of wilted, dying leaves—an odor familiar to Chee and to all Navajos, and one that evoked unpleasant boyhood memories. Of thin horses, dying sheep, worried adults. Of not quite enough to eat. Of being very careful to take into the gourd dipper no more of the tepid water than you would drink. How long had it been since it had rained? A shower at Shiprock at the end of April. Nothing since then. Theresa Beno's shy daughter wouldn't be out there. Maybe a coyote. Whatever it was, he was going back to bed. He ran a little more water into his palm, sipped it, noticing the taste. The reservoir on his trailer would be low. He should flush it out and refill it. He thought of Kennedy again. Chee shared the prejudices of most working policemen against the FBI, but Kennedy seemed a better sort than most. And smarter. Which was good, because he would probably be stationed at Farmington a long time and Chee would be working . . .

Just then he became aware of the form in the darkness. Some slight motion, perhaps, had given it away. Or perhaps Chee's eyes had finally made the total adjustment to night vision. It was not ten feet from the window under which Chee slept, an indistinct black-against-black. But the shape was upright. Human. Small? Probably the woman at Theresa Beno's sheep camp. Why did she stand there so silently if she had come all this way to talk to him?

Light and sound struck simultaneously—a white-yellow flash which burned itself onto the retina behind the lens of Chee's eyes and a boom which slammed into his eardrums and repeated itself. Again. And again. And again. Without thought, Chee had dropped to the floor, aware of the cat clawing its way frantically over his back toward the door-flap.

Then it was silent. Chee scrambled to a sitting position. Where was his pistol? Hanging on his belt in the trailer closet. He scrambled for it on hands and knees, still seeing only the white-yellow flash, hearing only the ringing in his ears. He pulled open the closet door, reached up blindly and fumbled until his fingers found the holster, extracted the pistol, cocked it. He sat with his back pressed against the closet wall, not daring to breathe, trying to make his eyes work again. They did, gradually. The shape of the open door became a rectangle of black-gray in a black-black field. The light of the dark night came through the window above his bed. And below that small square, he seemed to be seeing an irregular row of roundish places—places a little lighter than the blackness.

Chee became aware of his sheet on the floor around him, of his foam-rubber mattress against his knee. He hadn't knocked it off the bunk. The cat? It couldn't. Through the diminishing ringing in his ears he could hear a dog barking somewhere in the distance toward Shiprock. Awakened by the gunshots, Chee guessed. And they must have been gunshots. A cannon. Three of them. Or was it four?

Whoever had fired them would be waiting out there. Waiting for Chee to come out. Or trying to decide whether four shots through the aluminum skin of the trailer into Chee's bed had been enough. Chee looked at the row of holes again, with his vision now clearing. They looked huge—big enough to stick your foot through. A shotgun. That would explain the blast of light and sound. Chee decided going through the door would be a mistake. He sat, back to the closet wall, gripping the pistol, waiting. A second distant dog joined the barking. Finally, the barking stopped. Air moved through the trailer, bringing in the smells of burned gunpowder, wilted leaves, and the exposed mud flats along the river. The white-yellow blot on Chee's retina faded away. Night vision returned. He could make out the shape of his mattress now, knocked off the bed by the shotgun blasts. And through the holes punched in the paper-thin aluminum walls, he could see lightning briefly illuminate the dying thunderhead on the northwest horizon. In Navajo mythology, lightning symbolized the wrath of the *yei*, the Holy People venting their malice against the earth.

2

LIEUTENANT JOE LEAPHORN HAD GONE to his office early. He'd awakened a little before dawn and lay motionless, feeling Emma's hip warm against his own, listening to the sound of her breathing, feeling a numbing sense of loss. He had decided, finally, that he would force her to see a doctor. He would take her. He would tolerate no more of her excuses and delays. He had faced the fact that he had humored Emma's reluctance to see a *belagana* doctor because of his own fear. He knew what the doctor would say. Hearing it said would end his last shred of hope. "Your wife has Alzheimer's disease," the doctor would say, and his face would be sympathetic, and he would explain to Leaphorn what Leaphorn already knew too well. It was incurable. It would be marked by an episodic loss of function of that territory of the brain which stored the human memory and which controlled other behavior. Finally, this loss would be so severe that the victim would simply forget, as it seemed to Leaphorn, to remain alive. It also seemed to Leaphorn that this disease killed its victim by degrees—that Emma was already partly dead. He had lain there, listening to her breathing beside him, and mourned for her. And then he had gotten up, and put on the coffeepot, and dressed, and sat at the kitchen table and watched the sky begin to brighten behind the upthrust wall of stone that gave the little town of Window Rock its name. Agnes had heard him, or smelled the coffee. He had heard water running in the bathroom, and Agnes joined him, face washed, hair combed, wearing a dressing gown covered with red roses.

Leaphorn liked Agnes, and had been happy and relieved when Emma had told him—as her headaches and her forgetfulness worsened—that Agnes would come and stay until health returned. But Agnes was Emma's sister, and Agnes, like Emma, like everyone Leaphorn knew in their branch of the Yazzie family, was deeply traditional. Leaphorn knew they were modern enough not to expect him to follow the old way and take another wife in the family when Emma died. But the thought would be there. And thus Leaphorn found himself uneasy when he was alone with Agnes.

And so he'd finished his coffee and walked through the dawn to the tribal police building, moving away from fruitless worry about his wife to a problem he thought he could solve. He would spend some quiet time before the phone began to ring, deciding, once and for all, whether he was dealing with a coincidence in homicides. He had three of them. Seemingly, absolutely nothing connected them except the exquisite level of frustration with which they confronted Joe Leaphorn. Everything in Leaphorn's Navajo blood, bones, brains, and conditioning taught him to be skeptical of coincidences. Yet for days he had seemed stuck with one—a problem so intractable and baffling that in it he was able to find shelter from the thought of Emma. This morning he intended to take a preliminary step toward solving this puzzle. He would leave the phone off the hook, stare at the array of pins on his map of the Navajo Reservation, and force his thinking into some sort of equal order. Given quiet, and a little time, Leaphorn's mind was very, very good at this process of finding logical causes behind apparently illogical effects.

A memo lay in his in-basket.

FROM: *Captain Largo, Shiprock.*

TO: *Lieutenant Leaphorn, Window Rock.*

"Three shots fired into trailer of Officer Jim Chee about 2:15 A.M. this date," the memo began. Leaphorn read it quickly. No description of either the suspect or the escape vehicle. Chee unharmed. *"Chee states he had no idea of the motive,"* the memo concluded.

Leaphorn reread the final sentence. Like hell, he thought. Like hell he doesn't. Logically, no one shoots at a cop without a motive. And logically, the cop shot at knows that motive very well indeed. Logically, too, that motive reflects so poorly upon the conduct of the policeman that he's happy not to remember it. Leaphorn put the memo aside. When the more normal working day began, he'd call Largo and see if he had anything to add. But now he wanted to think about his three homicides.

He swiveled his chair and looked at the reservation map that dominated the wall behind him. Three pins marked the unsolved homicides: one near Window Rock, one up on the Arizona-Utah border, one north and west in the empty country not far from Big Mountain. They formed a triangle of roughly equal sides—some 120 miles apart. It occurred to Leaphorn that if the man with the shotgun had killed Chee, the triangle on his map would become an oddly shaped rectangle. He would have four unsolved homicides. He rejected the thought. The Chee business wouldn't be unsolved. It would be simple. A matter of identifying the malice, uncovering the officer's malfeasance, finding the prisoner he had abused. It would not, like the three pins, represent crime without motive.

The telephone rang. It was the desk clerk downstairs. "Sorry, sir. But it's the councilwoman from Cañoncito."

"Didn't you tell her I won't get in until eight?"

"She saw you come in," the clerk said. "She's on her way up."

She was, in fact, opening Leaphorn's door.

And now the councilwoman was sitting in the heavy wooden armchair across from Leaphorn's desk. She was a burly, big-bosomed woman about Leaphorn's middle age and middle size, dressed in an old-fashioned purple reservation blouse and wearing a heavy silver squash blossom necklace. She was, she informed Leaphorn, staying at the Window Rock Motel, down by the highway. She had driven in all the way from Cañoncito yesterday afternoon following a meeting with her people at the Cañoncito Chapter House. The people of the Cañoncito Band were not happy with Navajo Tribal Police. They didn't like the police protection they were getting, which was no protection at all. And so she had come by the Law and Order Building this morning to talk to Lieutenant Leaphorn about this, only to find the building locked and only about two people at work. She had waited in her car for almost half an hour before the front door had been unlocked.

This discourse required approximately five minutes, giving Leaphorn time to think that the councilwoman had actually driven in to attend the Tribal Council meeting, which began today, that the Cañoncito Band had not been happy with the tribal government since 1868, when the tribe returned from its years of captivity at Fort Stanton, that the councilwoman unquestionably knew it wasn't fair to expect more than a radio dispatcher and a night staffer to be on duty at dawn, that the councilwoman had gone over this complaint with him at least twice before, and that the councilwoman was making a lot of her early rising to remind Leaphorn that Navajo bureaucrats, like all good Navajos, should be up at dawn to bless the rising sun with prayer and a pinch of pollen.

Now the councilwoman was silent. Leaphorn, Navajo fashion, waited for the signal that would tell him whether she had finished with what she had to say or was merely pausing to collect her thoughts. The councilwoman sighed, and shook her head.

"Not no Navajo police at all," she summarized. "Not one on the whole Cañoncito Reservation. All we got is a Laguna policeman, now and then, part of the time." She paused again. Leaphorn waited.

"He just sits there in that little building by the road and he doesn't do nothing. Most of the time he's not even there." The councilwoman, aware that Leaphorn had heard all this before, wasn't bothering to look at him while she recited it. She was studying his map.

"You call on the telephone and nobody answers. You go by there and knock, nobody home." Her eyes drifted from map to Leaphorn. She was finished.

"Your Cañoncito policeman is an officer of the Bureau of Indian Affairs," Leaphorn said. "He's a Laguna Indian, but he's actually a BIA policeman. He doesn't work for the Lagunas. He works for you." Leaphorn explained, as he had twice before, that since the Cañoncito Band lived on a reservation way over by Albuquerque, so far from the Big Reservation, and since only twelve hundred Navajos lived there, the Judicial Committee of the Tribal Council had voted to work out a deal with the BIA instead of keeping a full shift of the NTP stationed there. Leaphorn did not mention that the councilwoman was a member of that committee, and neither did the councilwoman. She listened with patient Navajo courtesy, her eyes wandering across Leaphorn's map.

"Just two kinds of pins on the Cañoncito," she said when Leaphorn had finished.

"Those are left over from before the Tribal Council voted to give jurisdiction to the Bureau of Indian Affairs," Leaphorn said, trying to avoid the next question, which would be What do the pins mean? The pins were all in shades of red or were black, Leaphorn's way of marking alcohol-related arrests and witchcraft complaints. The two were really Cañoncito's only disruptions of the peace. Leaphorn did not believe in witches, but there were those on the Big Reservation who claimed everybody at Cañoncito must be a skinwalker.

"Because of that decision by the Tribal Council, the BIA takes care of Cañoncito," Leaphorn concluded.

"No," the councilwoman said. "The BIA don't."

The morning had gone like that. The councilwoman finally left, replaced by a small freckled white man who declared himself owner of the company that provided stock for the Navajo Rodeo. He wanted assurance that his broncos, riding bulls, and roping calves would be adequately guarded at night. That pulled Leaphorn into the maze of administrative decisions, memos, and paperwork required by the rodeo—an event dreaded by all hands in the Window Rock contingent of the tribal police. Before he could finish the adjustments required to police this three-day flood of macho white cowboys, macho Indian cowboys, cowboy groupies, drunks, thieves, con men, Texans, swindlers, photographers, and just plain tourists, the telephone rang again.

It was the principal of Kinlichee Boarding School, reporting that Emerson Tso had reopened his bootlegging operation. Not only was Tso selling to any Kinlichee student willing to make the short walk over to his place; he was bringing bottles to the dorm at night. The principal wanted Tso locked up forever. Leaphorn, who detested whiskey as ardently as he hated witchcraft, promised to have Tso brought in that day. His voice was so grim when he said it that the principal simply said thank you and hung up.

And so finally, just before lunch, there was time for thinking about three unsolved homicides and the question of coincidence. But first Leaphorn took the telephone off the hook. He walked to the window and looked out across the narrow asphalt of Navajo Route 27 at the scattered red-stone buildings that housed the government bureaucracy of his tribe, at the sandstone cliffs behind the village, and at the thunderclouds beginning to form in the August sky, clouds that in this summer of drought would probably not climb quite high enough up the sky to release any moisture. He cleared his mind of Tribal Council members, rodeos, and bootleggers. Sitting again, he swiveled his chair to face the map.

Leaphorn's map was known throughout the tribal police—a symbol of his eccentricity. It was mounted on corkboard on the wall behind his desk—a common "Indian Country" map published by the Auto Club of Southern California and popular for its large scale and its accurate details. What drew attention to Leaphorn's map was the way he used it.

It was decorated in a hundred places with colored pins, each color representing its own sort of crime. It was inscribed in a hundred places with notes written in Leaphorn's cryptic shorthand. The notes reminded Leaphorn of information he'd accumulated in a lifetime of living on the reservation and half a lifetime of working it as a cop. The tiny *q* west of Three Turkey Ruins meant quicksand in Tse Des Zygee Wash. The *r* beside the road to Ojleto on the Utah border (and beside dozens of other such roads) recalled spots where rainstorms made passage doubtful. The *c*'s linked with family initials marked the sites of summer sheep camps along the mountain slopes. Myriad such reminders freckled the map. *W*'s marked places where witchcraft incidents had been reported. *B*'s marked the homes of bootleggers.

The notes were permanent, but the pins came and went with the ebb and flow of misbehavior. Blue ones marked places where cattle had been stolen. They disappeared when the cattle thief was caught driving a truckload of heifers down a back road. Gaudy rashes of scarlet, red, and pink ones (the colors Leaphorn attached to alcohol-related crimes) spread and subsided inside the reservation with the fate of bootleggers. They made a permanent rosy blotch around reservation border towns and lined the entrance highways. Markers for rapes, violent assaults, family mayhem, and other, less damaging, violent losses of control tended to follow and mingle with the red. A few pins, mostly on the reservation's margins, marked such white-man crimes as burglary, vandalism, and robbery. At the moment, Leaphorn was interested only in three brown pins with white centers. They marked his homicides.

Homicides were unusual on the reservation. Violent death was usually accidental: a drunk stumbling in front of a passing car, drunken fights outside a bar, an alcohol-primed explosion of family tensions—the sort of unpremeditated violence that lends itself to instant solutions. When brown-and-white pins appeared, they rarely remained more than a day or two.

Now there were three. And they'd been stuck in Leaphorn's corkboard, and in his consciousness, for weeks. In fact, the oldest had been there almost two months.

Irma Onesalt was her name—pin number one. Leaphorn had stuck it beside the road between Upper Greasewood and Lukachukai fifty-four days ago. The bullet that killed her was a 30-06, the second most popular caliber in the world and the one that hung on the rifle rack across the rear window of every third pickup truck on the reservation, and around it. Everybody seemed to own one, if they didn't own a 30-30. And sometimes even if they did. Irma Onesalt, born to the Bitter Water Clan, born for the Towering House People, daughter of Alice and Homer Onesalt, thirty-one years old, unmarried, agent of the Navajo Office of Social Services, found in the front seat of her overturned Datsun two-door, hit in the jaw and throat by a bullet that smashed through the driver's-side window and, after destroying her, lodged in the opposite door. They had found a witness, more or less and maybe. A student from the Toadlena Boarding School had been en route home to visit her parents. She had noticed a man—an old man, she'd said—sitting in a pickup truck parked about where the shot would have been fired from. That theory presumed that Irma Onesalt had lost control of the Datsun the moment she'd been hit. Leaphorn had seen the body. It seemed a safe presumption.

Pin two, two weeks later, represented Dugai Endocheeney, born to the Mud People, born for the Streams Come Together Clan. Maybe seventy-five, maybe seventy-seven, depending on whom you believed. Stabbed (the butcher knife left in his body) at the sheep pen behind his hogan on the Nokaito Bench, not far from where Chinle Creek runs into the San Juan River. Dilly Streib, the agent in charge, had said there was an obvious connection between pin one and pin two. "Onesalt didn't have any friends, and Endocheeney didn't have any enemies," Dilly had said. "Somebody is working from both ends. Going to keep knocking off good ones and bad ones until there's nothing left but the middle."

"Just us average ones," Leaphorn said.

Streib had laughed. "I think he'll get to you pretty quick, on the obnoxious end."

Delbert L. Streib wasn't your usual FBI agent. It had always seemed to Leaphorn, who had spent a tour at the FBI Academy and half his life running errands for the Agency, that Streib was smarter than most. He had a quick, innovative intelligence, which had made him a terrible misfit in the J. Edgar Hoover years and got him exiled to Indian country. But Streib, whose case it was since it was a homicide committed on a federal reservation, had drawn a blank on Onesalt. And on Endocheeney. And so had Leaphorn.

When he had seen Leaphorn's map, Streib had argued that pin two should be pin three. And maybe he was right. Leaphorn had assigned the third pin to Wilson Sam, born to the One Walks Around Clan, and born for the Turning Mountain People. The late Mr. Sam was fifty-seven, a herder of sheep who sometimes worked on Arizona Highway Department grader crews. He had been hit on the back of the neck with the blade of a shovel, so very, very hard that there was no question he had died instantly. But there was a question of when he had been hit. Sam's nephew had found the victim's sheepdog, voiceless from howling and half dead from thirst, sitting on the rim of Chilchinbito Canyon. Wilson Sam's body was on the canyon floor below—apparently dragged to the edge and tumbled over. The autopsy suggested a time of death about the same as Endocheeney's. So who died first? Anyone's guess. Again, no witnesses, no clues, no apparent motive, not much of anything except the negative fact that if the coroner was right, it would have been very difficult for the same man to have killed them both.

"Unless he was a skinwalker," Dilly Streib had said, looking somber, "and you guys are right about skinwalkers being able to fly, and outrun turbocharged pickup trucks, and so forth."

Leaphorn didn't mind Streib kidding him, but he didn't like anyone kidding him about witches. He hadn't laughed.

Remembering it now, he still didn't laugh. He sighed, scratched his ear, shifted in the chair. Staring at the map today took him exactly where it had taken him the last time he tried it. One pin was a Window Rock pin, relatively speaking. The first one. The next two were out-in-the-boondocks pins.

The first victim was a bureaucrat, younger, female, more sophisticated. Shot. The last two were men who had followed their flocks, traditional people, probably spoke little English, killed at close quarters. Did he have two separate cases? So it would seem. In the Window Rock case, premeditation—rarity of rarities on the reservation—was obvious. In the boondocks cases, it was possible but didn't look probable. A shovel hardly seemed a likely weapon of choice. And if you were determined to kill someone, most Navajos Leaphorn knew could take along an easier weapon than a butcher knife.

Leaphorn thought about his cases separately. He got nowhere. He thought about them as a trio. Same results. He isolated the Onesalt killing, considered everything they had learned about the woman. Mean as a snake, it seemed. People hesitated to badmouth the dead, but they had trouble finding good to say about Irma. No, Irma was a busybody. Irma was a militant. Irma was an angry young woman. Irma made trouble. As far as he could learn, she had no jilted lovers. In fact, the only one who seemed to mourn her aside from her immediate family was a longtime and apparently devoted live-in boyfriend—a schoolteacher at Lukachukai. Leaphorn always suspected devoted boyfriends in homicide cases. But this one had been standing in front of twenty-eight students talking about math when Onesalt was killed.

The mail arrived. Without breaking his concentration on the

problem, idly, he sorted through it, mind still on Onesalt. Two telexes from the FBI were on top of the stack. The first one contained the details of the Jim Chee affair. He read the telex quickly. Nothing much new. Chee had not given chase. Chee said he had no idea who might have fired the shots. Tracks left by size seven rubber-soled running shoes had been found adjoining the trailer. They led about four hundred yards to a point where a vehicle had been parked. Tracks indicated worn tires. Drippage where vehicle had parked indicated either a lengthy stay or a serious oil leak.

Leaphorn set the message aside, expression glum. Again, no motive. But there was a motive, of course. When someone tries to ambush a cop there is a strong motive, and the motive tends to be unpleasant. Well, Chee was Captain Largo's boy, and finding out what Officer Chee was doing to provoke such a reaction would be Largo's problem.

The second telex reported that Agent Jay Kennedy of the Farmington office would this date locate and interrogate subject Roosevelt Bistie in connection with the Dugai Endocheeney homicide. Two witnesses had been located who placed a vehicle owned by Bistie at the Endocheeney hogan at the time of the killing. Another witness indicated that the driver of the vehicle had said he intended to kill Endocheeney. Any officer with any information about subject Roosevelt Bistie was asked to contact Agent Kennedy.

Leaphorn turned the paper over and looked at the back. Blank, of course. He glanced at the map, mentally removing the Endocheeney pin. The triangle of unsolved crimes became a line—two dots and no real reason to link them. It looked suddenly as if his rash of homicides were, in fact, coincidences. Two unsolved was a hell of a lot better than three. And perhaps Bistie would also prove to be the Wilson Sam killer. That seemed logical. The lives of the two men might be linked in many ways. Leaphorn felt much better. Order was returning to his world.

The telephone buzzed.

"This is your day for politicians, Lieutenant," the desk clerk said. "Dr. Yellowhorse wants to talk to you."

Leaphorn tried to think of some workable reason to justify not seeing Dr. Yellowhorse, who was a tribal councilman representing the Badwater Chapter and a member of the Tribal Council Judiciary Committee, as well as a doctor. And who, as a doctor, was founder and chief of medical staff of the Badwater Clinic.

No reason occurred to Leaphorn. "Tell him to come up," he said.

"I think he's already up," the clerk said.

Leaphorn's office door opened.

Dr. Bahe Yellowhorse was a barrel of a man. He wore a black felt reservation hat with a silver-and-turquoise band and a turkey feather. A closely braided rope of hair hung, Sioux fashion, behind each ear, the end of each tied with a red string. The belt that held his jeans over his broad, flat belly was two inches wide, studded with turquoise and buckled with a sand-cast silver replica of Rainbow Man curved around the symbol of Father Sun.

"*Ya-tah,*" said Yellowhorse, grinning. But the grin looked mechanical.

"*Ya-tah-hey,*" Leaphorn said. "Have a ch—"

"Going to have a meeting of Judicial Committee this afternoon," Yellowhorse said, easing himself into the chair across from Leaphorn's desk. "My people want me to talk to the committee about doing something to catch that fellow that killed Hosteen Endocheeney."

Yellowhorse dug in the pocket of his denim shirt and dug out a package of cigarets, giving Leaphorn an opportunity to comment. Leaphorn didn't. Old Man Endocheeney had been a resident of that great sprawl of Utah-Arizona borderlands included in the Badwater Chapter. Leaphorn didn't want to discuss the case with Tribal Councilman Bahe Yellowhorse.

"We're working on it," he said.

"That means you're not getting nowhere," said Yellowhorse. "You having any luck at all?"

"The FBI has jurisdiction," Leaphorn said, thinking that this was his day for telling people what they already knew. "Felony committed on federal trust land comes under—"

Yellowhorse held up a huge brown hand. "Save it," he said. "I know how it works. The feds don't know anything unless you guys tell 'em. You finding out who killed Endocheeney? I need to know something to tell my people back at the chapter house."

He leaned back in the wooden chair, extracted a cigaret from the package, and tapped its filtered end uselessly against his thumbnail, eyes on Leaphorn.

Leaphorn considered his police academy conditioning against ever telling anybody anything about anything, weighed it against common sense. Yellowhorse was sometimes an unusually severe pain in the ass, but he did have a legitimate interest. Beyond that, Leaphorn admired the man and respected what he was trying to do. Bahe Yellowhorse, born to the Dolii Dinee, the Blue Bird People of his mother. But he had no paternal clan. His father was an Oglala Sioux. Yellowhorse had founded the Bad Water Clinic mostly with his own money. True, there was a big Kellogg Foundation grant in it, and some other foundation money, and some federal funds. But from what Leaphorn knew, most of the money, and all of the energy, had come from Yellowhorse himself.

"You can tell them we have a suspect in the Endocheeney homicide," Leaphorn said. "Witnesses put him at the hogan at the right time. Expect to pick him up today and talk to him."

"You got the right fellow?" Yellowhorse asked. "He have a motive?"

"We haven't talked to him," Leaphorn said. "We're told he said he wanted to kill Endocheeney, so you can presume a motive."

Yellowhorse shrugged. "How about the other killing? Whatever his name was?"

"We don't know," Leaphorn said. "Maybe they're connected."

"Your suspect," Yellowhorse said. He paused, put the cigaret between his lips, lit it with a silver lighter, and exhaled smoke. "He another one of my constituents?"

"Seems to live up in the Lukachukais. Long way from your country."

Yellowhorse stared at Leaphorn, waiting for further explanation. None came. He inhaled smoke again, held it in his lungs, let it trickle from his nostrils. He extracted the cigaret and came just close enough to pointing it at Leaphorn to imply the insult without delivering it. Navajos do not point at one another.

"You guys s'posed to be out of the religion business, aren't you? Since the court cracked down on you for hassling the peyote people?"

Leaphorn's dark face turned a shade darker. "We haven't been arresting anyone for possession of peyote for years," Leaphorn said. He had been very young when the Tribal Council had passed its ill-fated law banning the use of hallucinogens, a law openly aimed at suppressing the Native American Church, which used peyote as a sacrament. He hadn't liked the law, had been glad when the federal court ruled it violated the First Amendment, and he didn't like to be reminded of it. He especially didn't like to be reminded of it in this insulting way by Yellowhorse.

"How about the Navajo religion?" Yellowhorse asked. "The tribal police got any policies against that these days?"

"No," Leaphorn said.

"I didn't think you did," Yellowhorse said. "But you got a cop working out of Shiprock who seems to think you have."

Yellowhorse inhaled tobacco smoke. Leaphorn waited. Yellowhorse waited. Leaphorn waited longer.

"I'm a crystal gazer," Yellowhorse said. "Always had a gift for it, since I was a boy. But only been practicing for the last few years. People come to me at the clinic. I tell 'em what's wrong with 'em. What kind of cure they need."

Leaphorn said nothing. Yellowhorse smoked, exhaled. Smoked again.

"If they have been fooling with wood that's been struck by lightning, or been around a grave too much, or have ghost sickness, then I tell them whether they need a Mountaintop sign, or an Enemy Way, or whatever cure they need. If they need a gallstone removed, or their tonsils out, or a course of antibiotics to knock a strep infection, then I check them into the clinic for that. Now, the American Medical Association hasn't approved it, but it's free. No charge. And a lot of the people out there are getting to know about me doing it, and it brings 'em in where we can get a look at 'em. The sick ones come in. Wouldn't have come in otherwise. They'd have gone to some other medicine man instead of me. And that way we catch a lot of early diabetic cases, and glaucoma, and skin cancer, blood poisoning, and God knows what."

"I've heard about it," Leaphorn said. He was remembering what else he'd heard. He'd heard that Yellowhorse liked to tell how his mother had died out there in that empty country of a little cut on her foot. It had led to an infection, and gangrene, because she never got any medical help. That, so the story went, was how Yellowhorse was orphaned, and got stuck in a Mormon orphanage, and got adopted into a large amount of Midwestern farm machinery money, and inherited a way to build himself a clinic—sort of a perfect circle.

"Sounds like a good idea to me," Leaphorn said. "We damn sure wouldn't have any policy against it."

"One of your cops does," Yellowhorse said. "He's telling people I'm a fake and to stay away from me. I hear the little bastard is trying to be a *hataalii* himself. Maybe he thinks I'm unfair competition. Anyway, I want you to tell me how what he's doing squares with the law. If it doesn't square, I want it stopped."

"I'll check into it," Leaphorn said. He reached for his notepad. "What's his name?"

"His name's Jim Chee," Yellowhorse said.

ROOSEVELT BISTIE WASN'T AT HOME, his daughter informed them. He had gone into Farmington to get some medicine yesterday, and was going to spend the night with his other daughter, at Shiprock, and then drive back this morning.

"When do you expect him?" Jay Kennedy asked. The relentless high desert sun of the reservation had burned the yellow out of Kennedy's short blond hair and left it almost white, and his skin was peeling. He looked at Chee, waiting for the translation. Bistie's Daughter probably understood English as well as Kennedy, and spoke it as well as Chee, but the way she had chosen to play the game today, she knew only Navajo. Chee guessed she was a little uneasy—that she hadn't seen many sunburned blond white men up close before.

"That's the kind of questions *belagana* ask," Chee told her in Navajo. "I'm going to tell him you expect your father when you see him. How sick is he?"

"Bad, I think," Bistie's Daughter said. "He went to a crystal gazer down there at Two Story and the crystal gazer told him he needed a Mountaintop sing. I think he's got something wrong with his liver." She paused. "What do you policemen want him for?"

"She says she expects him when he gets here," Chee told Kennedy. "We could start back and maybe meet him on the road. Or we could just wait here. I'll ask her if she knows where the old man went—what was it—two weeks ago?"

"Just a minute." Kennedy motioned Chee over toward the Agency's carryall. "I think she can understand some English," he said in just above a whisper. "We have to be careful of what we say."

"I wouldn't be surprised," Chee said. He turned back to Bistie's Daughter.

"Two weeks ago?" she asked. "Let's see. He went to see the crystal gazer the second Monday in July. That's when I go in and get all my laundry done down at Red Rock Trading Post. He took me down there. And then it was . . ." She thought, a sturdy young woman in an "I Love Hawaii" T-shirt, jeans, and squaw boots. Pigeon-toed, Chee noticed. He remembered his sociology professor at the University of New Mexico saying that modern dentistry had made crooked teeth an identifying mark of those who were born into the bottommost fringe of the American socioeconomic classes. Unstraightened teeth for the white trash, uncorrected birth defects for the Navajo. Or, to be fair, for those Navajos who lived out of reach of the Indian Health Service. Bistie's Daughter shifted her weight on those bent ankles. "Well," she said, "it would have been about a week later. About two weeks ago. He took the truck. I didn't want him to go because he had been feeling worse. Throwing up his food. But he said he had to go find a man somewhere way over there around Mexican Hat or Montezuma Creek." She jerked her chin in the general direction of north. "Over by Utah."

"Did he say why?"

"What you want to see him about?" Bistie's Daughter asked.

"She says Bistie went to see a man over by the Utah border two weeks ago," Chee told Kennedy.

"Ah," Kennedy said. "Right time. Right place."

"I don't think I will talk to you anymore," Bistie's Daughter said. "Not unless you tell me what you want to talk to my father about. What's wrong with that *belagana*'s face?"

"That's what sunshine does to white people's skin," Chee said. "Somebody got killed over there around Mexican Hat two weeks ago. Maybe your father saw something. Maybe he could tell us something."

Bistie's Daughter looked shocked. "Killed?"

"Yes," Chee said.

"I'm not going to talk to you anymore," Bistie's Daughter said. "I'm going into the house now." And she did.

Chee and Kennedy talked it over. Chee recommended waiting awhile. Kennedy decided they would wait one hour. They sat in the carryall, feet hanging out opposite doors, and sipped the cans of Pepsi-Cola that Bistie's Daughter had given them when they arrived. "Warm Pepsi-Cola," Kennedy said, his voice full of wonder. This remark caught Chee thinking of the way the buckshot had torn through the foam rubber of his mattress, fraying it, ripping away chunks just about over the place where his kidneys would have been. Thinking of who wanted to kill him. Of why. He had thought about the same subjects all day, interrupting his gloomy ruminations only with an occasional yearning thought of Mary Landon's impending return to Crownpoint. Neither produced any positive results. Better to think of warm Pepsi-Cola. For him, it was a familiar taste, full of nostalgia. Why did the white culture either cool things or heat them before consumption? The first time he had experienced a cold bottle of pop had been at the Teec Nos Pos Trading Post. He'd been about twelve. The school bus driver had bought a bottle for everyone on the baseball team. Chee remembered drinking it, standing in the shade of the porch. The remembered pleasure faded into the thought that anyone with a shotgun in any passing car could have mowed him down. Someone now, on the ridgeline behind Bistie's hogan, could be looking over a rifle sight at the center of his back.

Chee moved his shoulders uneasily. Took a sip of the Pepsi. Turned his thoughts back to why whites always iced it. Less heat. Less energy. Less motion in the molecules. He poked at that for a cultural conclusion, found himself drawn back to the sound of the shotgun, the flash of light. What had he, Jim Chee, done to warrant that violent reaction?

Suddenly, he badly wanted to talk to someone about it. "Kennedy," he said. "What do you think about last night? About . . ."

"You getting shot at?" Kennedy said. They had covered that question two or three times while driving out from Shiprock, and Kennedy had already said what he thought. Now he said it again, in slightly different words. "Hell, I don't know. Was me, I'd been examining my conscience. Whose lady I'd been chasing. Anybody's feelings I'd hurt. Any enemies I'd made. Anybody I'd arrested who just recently got out of jail. That sort of thing."

"The kind of people I arrest are mostly too drunk to remember who arrested 'em. Or care," Chee said. "If they have enough money to buy shotgun shells they buy a bottle instead. They're the kind of people who have eaten a lot of shaky soup." As for whose lady he had been chasing, there hadn't been any lady lately.

"Shaky soup?" Kennedy asked.

"Local joke," Chee said. "Lady down at Gallup runs her own soup line for drunks when the cops let 'em out of the tank. They're shaking, so everybody calls it shaky soup." He decided not to try to explain another reason it was called shaky soup: the combination of Navajo gutturals used to express it was almost identical to the sounds that said penis—thereby producing the material for one of those earthy puns Navajos treasure. He had tried once to explain to Kennedy how the similarity of Navajo words for rodeo and chicken could be used to produce jokes. Kennedy hadn't seen the humor.

"Well," Kennedy said, "I'd examine my conscience, then. Somebody shoots at a cop . . ." Kennedy shrugged, let the sentence trail off without finishing the implication. Captain Largo had not bothered to be so polite this morning in Largo's office. "It's been my experience," the captain had rumbled, "that when a policeman has got himself in a situation where somebody is coming after him to kill him, then that policeman has been up to something." Captain Largo had been sitting behind his desk, examining Chee pensively over his tented fingers, when he said it, and it hadn't angered Chee until later, when he was back in his patrol car remembering the interview. Now the reaction was quicker. He felt a flush of hot blood in his face.

"Look," Chee said. "I don't like—"

Just then they heard a vehicle clanking and groaning up the track.

Kennedy removed the pistol from the holster under his jacket on the seat, put on the jacket, dropped the pistol into the jacket pocket. Chee watched the track. An elderly GMC pickup, rusty green, emerged from the junipers. A 30-30 lever-action carbine was in the rack across the back window. The pickup eased to a slow, almost dustless stop. The man driving it was old and thin, with a black felt reservation hat pushed back on his head. He looked at them curiously while the engine wheezed to a stop, sat for a moment considering them, and then climbed out.

"Ya-tah-hey," Chee said, still standing beside the carryall.

Bistie responded gravely with the Navajo greeting, looking at Chee and then at Kennedy.

"I am born for Red Forehead People, the son of Tessie Chee, but now I work for all of the Dinee. For the Navajo Tribal Police. This man"—Chee indicated Kennedy Navajo fashion, by shifting his lips in Kennedy's direction—"is an FBI officer. We have come here to talk to you."

Roosevelt Bistie continued his inspection. He dropped his ignition key in his jeans pocket. He was a tall man, stooped a little now by age and illness, his face the odd copper color peculiar to advanced jaundice. But he smiled slightly. "Police?" he said. "Then I guess I hit the son-of-a-bitch."

It took Chee a moment to digest this—the admission, then the nature of the admission.

"What did he—" Kennedy began. Chee held up his hand.

"Hit him?" Chee asked. "How?"

Bistie looked surprised. "Shot the son-of-a-bitch," he said. "With that rifle there in the truck. Is he dead?"

Kennedy was frowning. "What's he saying?"

"Shot who?" Chee asked. "Where?"

"Over there past Mexican Hat," Bistie said. "Over there almost to the San Juan River. He was a Mud Clan man. I forget what they call him." Bistie grinned at Chee. "Is he dead? I thought maybe I missed him."

"Oh, he's dead," Chee said. He turned to Kennedy. "We have a funny one here. He says he shot Old Man Endocheeney. With his rifle."

"Shot?" Kennedy said. "What about the butcher knife? He wasn't—"

Chee stopped him. "He probably speaks some English. Let's talk. I think we should take him back over there. Have him show us what happened."

Kennedy's face flushed under the peeling epidermis. "We haven't read him his rights," he said. "He's not supposed—"

"He hasn't told us anything in English yet," Chee said. "Just in Navajo. He's still got a right to remain silent in English until he talks to a lawyer."

Bistie told them just about everything on the long, dusty drive that took them out of the Lukachukais, and back through Shiprock, and westward into Arizona, and northward into Utah.

"Navajo or not," Kennedy had said, "we better read him his rights." And he did, with Chee translating it into Navajo.

"Better late than never, I guess," Kennedy said. "But who would guess a suspect would walk right up and tell you he shot the guy?"

"When he didn't," Chee said.

"When he stuck him with a butcher knife," Kennedy said.

"Why is the white man talking all this bullshit about a knife?" Bistie asked.

"I'll explain that," Chee said. "You haven't told us why you shot him."

And he didn't. Bistie continued his account. Of making sure

the 30-30 was loaded. Of making sure the sights were right, because he hadn't fired it since shooting a deer last winter. Of the long drive to Mexican Hat. Of asking people there how to find the Mud Clan man. Of driving up to the hogan of the Mud Clan man, just about this time of day, with a thunderstorm building up, and taking the rifle down off the rack, and cocking it, and finding nobody at the hogan, but a pickup truck parked there, and guessing that the Mud Clan man would be around somewhere. And hearing the sound of someone hammering, and seeing the Mud Clan man working on a shed back in an arroyo behind the hogan—nailing on loose boards. And then Bistie described standing there looking over the sights at the Mud Clan man, and seeing the man looking back at him just as he pulled the trigger. And he told them how, when the smoke had cleared, the man was no longer on the roof. He told them absolutely everything about the chronology and the mechanics of it all. But he told them absolutely nothing about why he had done it. When Chee asked again, Bistie simply sat, grimly silent. And Chee didn't ask why he was claiming to have shot a man who had been knifed to death.

While Roosevelt Bistie talked, describing this insanity in a calm, matter-of-fact, old man's voice, Chee found other questions forming in his mind.

"You were in Shiprock last night? At your daughter's house? Tell me her name. Where she lives."

Chee wrote the name and place in his notebook. It would have taken Old Man Bistie ten minutes to drive from that Shiprock address to Chee's trailer.

"What are you writing?" Kennedy asked.

Chee grunted.

"Do you have a shotgun?" he asked Bistie.

There is no Navajo word for shotgun and Kennedy caught the noun.

"Hey," he said. "What are you getting into?"

"Just the rifle," Bistie said.

"I'm getting into who tried to shoot Jim Chee," Jim Chee said.

AWAKENING WAS ABRUPT. An oblong of semi-blackness against the total darkness. The door of the summer hogan left open. Through it, against the eastern horizon, the faint glow of false dawn. Had the boy cried out? There was nothing but silence now. No air moved. No night insect stirred. Anxiety alone seemed to have overcome sleep. There was the smell of dust, of the endless, sheep-killing drought. And the smell, very faint, of something chemical. Oil, maybe. More and more, the truck engine leaked oil. Where it stood in the yard beside the brush arbor, the earth was hard and black with the drippings. A quart, at least, every time they drove it. More than a dollar a quart. And not enough money, not now, to get it fixed. All the money had gone with the birth of the boy, with the time they had had to spend at the hospital while the doctors looked at him. Anencephaly, the doctor had called it. The woman had written the word on a piece of paper for them, standing beside the bed in a room that seemed too cold, too full of the smell of white-man medicines. "Unusual," the woman had said. "But I know of two other cases on the reservation in the past twenty years. It happens to everybody. So it happens to Navajos too."

What did anencephaly mean? It meant Boy Child, the son, would live only a little while. "See," the woman had said, and she had brushed back the thin hair on the top of Boy Child's head. But it had already been apparent. The top of the head was almost flat. "The brain has not formed," the woman had said, "and the child cannot live long without that. Just a few weeks. We don't know what causes it. And we don't know anything to do about it."

Well, there were things that the *belagana* doctors didn't know. There was a cause, for this and for everything. And because there was a cause, something could be done about it. The cure lay in undoing that cause, restoring the harmony inside the small, fragile skull of Boy Child. The skinwalker had caused it, for some reason lost in the dark heart of malicious evil. Thus the skinwalker must die. His brain must shrivel so the brain of Boy Child could grow. And quickly. Quickly. Quickly. Kill the witch. The anxiety rose into something close to panic. Stomach knotted. Despite the predawn chill, the blanket roll against the cheek was damp with sweat.

The shotgun had seemed a good idea—fired through the thin skin of the trailer into the bed where the witch was sleeping. But skinwalkers were hard to kill. Somehow the skinwalker had known. It had flown from the bed and the bone had missed.

Boy Child stirred now. Sleep for him was always momentary, a fading out of consciousness that rarely lasted an hour. And then the whimpering would start again. A calling out to those who loved him, were bone of his bone and flesh of his flesh. The whimpering began, the only sound in the darkness. Just a sound, like that the newborn young of animals make. It seemed to say: Help me. Help me. Help me.

There would be no more sleep now. Not for a while. No time to sleep. Boy Child seemed weaker every day. He had already lived longer than the *belagana* woman at the hospital had said he would. No time for anything except finding the way to kill the witch. There had to be a way. The witch was a policeman, and hard to kill, and being a skinwalker, he had the powers skinwalkers gain—to fly through the air, to run as fast as the wind can blow, to change themselves into dogs and wolves and maybe other animals. But there must be a way to kill him.

The rectangle of the door frame grew lighter. Possibilities appeared and were considered, and modified, and rejected. Some were rejected because they might not work. Most were rejected because they were suicidal: The witch would die, but there would be no one left to keep Boy Child from starving. There must be a way to escape undetected. Nothing else was a useful solution.

In the cardboard box where he was kept, Boy Child whimpered endlessly—a pattern of sound as regular and mindless as an insect might make. A faint breeze moved the air, stirring the cloth that hung beside the hogan doorway—Dawn Girl awakening to prepare the day. About then the thought came: how it could be done. It was simple. It would work. And the witch they called Jim Chee would surely die.

5

LIEUTENANT JOE LEAPHORN nosed his patrol car into the shade of the Russian olive tree at the edge of the parking lot. He turned off the ignition. He eased himself into a more comfortable position and considered again how he would deal with Officer Chee. Chee's vehicle was parked in a row of five patrol cars lined along the sidewalk outside the entrance of the Navajo Tribal Police Station, Shiprock subagency. Unit 4. Leaphorn knew Chee was driving Unit 4 because he knew everything officially knowable about Chee. He had called the records clerk at 9:10 this morning and had Chee's personnel file sent upstairs. He'd read every word in it. Just a short time earlier, he had received a call from Dilly Streib. Streib had bad news.

"Weird one," Streib had said. "Kennedy picked up Roosevelt Bistie, and Roosevelt Bistie said he shot Endocheeney."

It took only a millisecond for the incongruity to register. "Shot," Leaphorn said. "Not stabbed?"

"Shot," Streib said. "Said he'd gone over to Endocheeney's hogan, and Endocheeney was fixing the roof of a shed, and Bistie shot him, and Endocheeney disappeared—fell off, I guess—and Bistie drove on home."

"What do you think?" Leaphorn asked.

"Kennedy didn't seem to have any doubt Bistie was telling the truth. Said they were waiting at Bistie's house, and he drove up and saw they were cops, and right away said something about shooting Endocheeney."

"Bistie speak English?"

"Navajo," Streib said.

"Who'd we have along? Who interpreted?" What Streib was

telling him seemed crazy. Maybe there had been some sort of mis-understanding.

"Just a second." Leaphorn heard papers rustling. "Officer Jim Chee," Streib said. "Know him?"

"I know him," said Leaphorn, wishing he knew him better.

"Anyhow, I'll send you the paperwork on it. Thought you'd want to know it turned funny."

"Yeah. Thanks," Leaphorn said. "Why did Bistie want to kill Endocheeney?"

"Wouldn't say. Flatass refused to talk about it at all. Kennedy said he seemed to think he might have missed the man, and then he was glad when he found out the guy was dead. Wouldn't say a word about what he had against him."

"Chee did the questioning?"

"Sure. I guess so. Kennedy doesn't speak Navajo."

"One more thing. Was it Chee on this from the beginning? Working with Kennedy, I mean, back when the investigation opened?"

"Just a sec," Streib said. Papers rustled. "Here it is. Yeah. Chee."

"Well, thanks," Leaphorn said. "I'll look for the report."

He clicked the receiver cradle down with a finger, got the file room, and ordered Chee's folder.

While he waited for it, he pulled open the desk drawer, ex-tracted a brown pin with a white center, and carefully stuck it back in the hole where the Endocheeney pin had been. He looked at the map a minute. Then he reached into the drawer again, took out another brown-and-white pin, and stuck it at the *p* in "Shiprock." Four pins now. One north of Window Rock, one on the Utah border-lands, one on Chilchinbito Canyon, one over in New Mexico. And now there was a connection. Faint, problematical, but something. Jim Chee had investigated the Endocheeney killing before some-one had tried to kill Chee. Had Chee learned something that made him a threat to Endocheeney's killer?

Leaphorn had been smiling, but as he thought, the smile thinned and disappeared. He could see no possible way this helped. Getting old, Leaphorn thought. He had reached the ridge and now the slope was downward. The thought didn't depress him, but it gave him an odd sense of pressure, of time moving past him, of things that needed to be done before time ran out. Leaphorn con-sidered this, and laughed. Most un-Navajo thinking. He had been around white men far too long.

He picked up the phone and called Captain Largo at Shiprock. He told Largo he wanted to talk to Jim Chee.

"What's he done now?" Largo said. And he sounded relieved, Leaphorn thought, when Leaphorn explained.

The short route from Window Rock to Shiprock, through Crystal and Sheep Springs, is a 120-mile drive over the hump of the Chuska Mountains. Leaphorn, who rarely broke the speed limit, drove it far too fast. It was mostly a matter of nerves.

And sitting here in the parking lot at Shiprock, he was still tense. Cumulus clouds climbing the sky over the Chuskas were tall enough to form the anvil tops that promised rain. But here the August sun glared off the asphalt beyond the small shade of Leaphorn's olive. He'd told Largo he'd be here by one, almost forty-five minutes away. Largo had said he'd have Chee on hand at one. Now Largo would be out to lunch. Leaphorn considered lunch for himself. A quick hamburger at the Burgerchef out on the highway. But he wasn't hungry. He found himself thinking of Emma, of the appointment he'd made with the neurologist at the Indian Health Service hospital in Gallup.

("Joe," Emma had said. "Please. You know how I feel about it. What can they do? It's headaches. I am out of *hozro*. I will have a sing and be well again. What can the *belagana* do? Saw open my head?" She'd laughed then, as she always laughed when he wanted to talk about her health. "They would cut open my head and let all the wind out," she'd said, smiling at him. He had insisted, and she had refused. "What do you think is wrong with me?" she asked, and he could see that she was, for once, half serious. He had tried to say "Alzheimer's disease," but the words wouldn't form, and he had simply said, "I don't know, but I worry," and she had said, "Well, I'm not going to have any doctor poking around in my head." But he had made the appointment anyway. He inhaled, exhaled. Maybe Emma was right. She could go to a listener, or a hand trembler, or a crystal gazer like Yellowhorse pretended to be, and have a curing ceremonial prescribed. Then call in the singer to perform the cure, and all the kinfolks to join in the blessing. Would that make her any worse than she'd be when the doctors at Gallup told her that something they didn't understand was killing her and there was nothing they could do about it? What would Yellowhorse tell her if she went to him? Did he know the man well enough to guess? What did he know about him? He knew Yellowhorse was pouring his inherited money and his life into Badwater Clinic, feeding an obsession. He knew he was hiring foreign-trained refugee doctors and nurses—a Vietnamese, a Cambodian, a Salvadoran, a Pakistani—because he could no longer afford the domestic brand. So maybe the money was smaller than the obsession. He knew Yellowhorse was an adept politician. But he didn't know him well enough to guess what his prescription would be for Emma. Would he leave her to the singers or to the neurologists?)

The door of the station opened and three men in the khaki summer uniforms of Navajo Policemen emerged. One was George Benaly, who long ago had worked with Leaphorn out of Many Farms. One was a jolly-looking, plump young man with a thin mustache whom Leaphorn didn't recognize. The other was Jim Chee. The round brim of Chee's hat was tilted, shading his face, but Leaphorn could see enough of it to match the photo in Chee's personnel file. A longish, narrow face fitting a longish, narrow body—all shoulders and no hips. The "Tuba City Navajo," as some anthropologist had labeled the type. Pure Athabaskan genetics. Tall, long torso, narrow pelvis, destined to be a skinny old man. Leaphorn himself fell into the "Checkerboard type." He represented—according to this authority—a blood/gene mix with the Pueblo peoples. Leaphorn didn't particularly like the theory, but it was useful ammunition when Emma pressed him to get his weight and belt size down a bit.

The three officers, still talking, strolled toward their patrol cars. Leaphorn watched. The plump officer had not noticed Leaphorn's car parked under the olive tree. Benaly had seen it without registering any interest. Only Chee was conscious of it, instantly, aware that it was occupied, that the occupant was watching. Perhaps that alertness was the product of being shot at two nights earlier. Leaphorn suspected it was permanent—a natural part of the man's character.

Benaly and Plump Cop climbed into their cars and drove out of the lot. Chee extracted something from the back seat of his vehicle and strolled back toward the station, conscious of Leaphorn's watching presence. Why wait? Leaphorn thought. He would check in with Largo later.

At Leaphorn's suggestion, they took Chee's police car to Chee's trailer. Chee drove, erect and nervous. The trailer, battered, dented, and looking old and tired, sat under a cluster of cottonwoods not a dozen yards from the crumbling north bank of the San Juan River. Cool, Leaphorn thought. Great spot for someone who wasn't bothered, as Leaphorn was, by mosquitoes. He inspected the three patches of duct tape Chee had used to heal the shotgun wounds in the aluminum skin of his home. About evenly spaced, he noticed. About two feet apart. Each a little more than hip high. Nicely placed to kill somebody in bed if you knew exactly where the bed was located in such a trailer.

"Doesn't look random," Leaphorn said, half to himself.

"No," Chee said. "I think some thought went into it."

"Trailer like this . . . Any trouble for anyone to find out where the bed would be located? How far off the floor?"

"How high to shoot?" Chee said. "No. It's a common kind. When I bought it in Flagstaff there were three just about like it on the used lot. See 'em all the time. Anyway, I think they're all pretty much alike. Where they put the beds."

"I think we'll ask around, anyway. See if somebody who sells them at Farmington, or Gallup, or Flag, can remember anything." He glanced at Chee. "Maybe a customer came in and asked to see this particular model, and pulled out a tape measure and said he had to measure the bed off to see where to hold the shotgun to get himself a Navajo Policeman."

Chee's expressionless face eased into what might have been a smile. "I'm not usually that lucky."

Leaphorn's fingers were on the tape that covered the hole nearest the front of the trailer. He glanced at Chee again.

"Pull it off," Chee said. "I've got more tape."

Leaphorn peeled off the patch, inspected the ragged hole punched through the aluminum, then stooped to peer inside. He could see only blue-and-white cloth. Flowers. Chee's pillow slip. It looked new. Hole torn in the old one, Leaphorn guessed. He was impressed that a bachelor would put a pillowcase on his pillow. Pretty tidy.

"You were lucky when this happened," said Leaphorn, who was always skeptical about luck, who was always skeptical about anything that violated the orderly rules of probability. "The report said your cat woke you up. You keep a cat?"

"Not exactly," Chee said. "It's a neighbor. Lives out there." Chee pointed upstream to a sun-baked slope of junipers. But Leaphorn was still looking thoughtfully at the shotgun hole—measuring its width with his fingers. "Lives out there under that juniper," Chee added. "Sometimes when something scares it, it comes in."

"How?"

Chee showed him the flap he'd cut in the trailer door. Leaphorn examined it. It didn't look new enough to have been put there after the shooting. He noticed that Chee was aware of his examination, and of the suspicion it suggested.

"Who tried to kill you?" Leaphorn asked.

"I don't know," Chee said.

"A new woman?" Leaphorn suggested. "That can cause trouble." Chee's expression became totally blank.

"No," Chee said. "Nothing like that."

"It could be something mild. Maybe just talking too often to a woman with a boyfriend who's paranoid."

"I've got a woman," Chee said slowly.

"You've thought all this out?" Leaphorn asked. He motioned toward the holes in the side of the trailer. "It's your ass somebody's after."

"I've thought about it," Chee said. He threw his hands apart, an angry gesture aimed at himself. "Absolutely damned nothing."

Leaphorn studied him, and found himself half persuaded. It was the gesture as much as the words. "Where did you sleep last night?"

"Out there," Chee said, gesturing toward the hillside. "I have a sleeping bag."

"You and the cat," Leaphorn said. He paused, dug out his pack of cigarets, offered one to Chee, took one himself. "What do you think about Roosevelt Bistie? And Endocheeney?"

"Funny," Chee said. "That whole thing's odd. Bistie's . . ." He paused, hesitated. "Why not come on in," Chee said. "Have a cup of coffee."

"Why not," Leaphorn said.

It was left-over-from-breakfast coffee. Leaphorn, made an authority on bad coffee by more than two decades of police work, rated it slightly worse than most. But it was warm, and it was coffee, and he sipped it appreciatively while Chee, sitting on the bunk where he had so nearly died, told him about meeting Roosevelt Bistie.

"I don't believe he was faking anything," Chee concluded. "He didn't act surprised to see us. Seemed pleased when he heard Endocheeney was dead, and then the whole business about shooting at Endocheeney on the roof, thinking he'd killed him, not really wondering about it until he got home, not going back to make sure because he figured if he hadn't killed him, Endocheeney wouldn't have stuck around to give him a second chance at it." Chee shrugged, shook his head. "Genuine satisfaction when he heard Endocheeney was dead. I just don't think he could have been faking any of that. No reason to. Why not just deny everything?"

"All right," Leaphorn said. "Now, tell me again exactly what he said when you asked him why he wanted to kill Endocheeney."

"Just like I said," Chee said.

"Tell me again."

"He wouldn't say anything. Just shut his mouth and looked grim and wouldn't say a word."

"What do you think?"

Chee shrugged. The light through the window over the trailer sink dimmed slightly. The shadow of the thunderhead over the Chuskas had moved across the Shiprock landscape. With the shadow, the cloud's advance guard of breeze sighed through the window screen. But it wouldn't rain. Leaphorn had studied the cloud. Now he was considering Chee's face, which wore a look of uneasy distaste. Leaphorn felt his own face beginning a smile, a wry one. Here we go again, he thought.

"Witchcraft?" Leaphorn asked. "A skinwalker?"

Chee said nothing. Leaphorn sipped the stale coffee. Chee shrugged. "Well," he said. "That could explain why Bistie wouldn't talk about it."

"That's right," Leaphorn said. He waited.

"Of course," Chee added, "so could other things. Protecting somebody in the family."

"Right," Leaphorn said. "If he tells us his motive, it's also the motive for the guy with the butcher knife. Brother. Cousin. Son. Uncle. What relatives does he have?"

"He's born to the Streams Come Together Dinee," Chee said, "and born for the Standing Rock People. Three maternal aunts, four uncles. Two paternal aunts, five uncles. Then he's got three sisters and a brother, wife's dead, and two daughters and a son. So not even counting his clan brothers and sisters, he's related to just about everybody north of Kayenta."

"Anything else you can think of? For why he won't talk?"

"Something he's ashamed of," Chee said. "Incest. Doing something wrong to some relative. Witchery."

Leaphorn could tell Chee didn't like the third alternative any better than he did.

"If it's witchcraft, which one is the skinwalker?"

"Endocheeney," Chee said.

"Not Bistie," Leaphorn said, thoughtfully. "So if you're right, Bistie killed himself a witch, or intended to." Leaphorn had considered this witch theory before. Nothing much wrong with the idea, except proving it. "You pick up anything about Endocheeney to support it? Or try it on Bistie?"

"Tried it on Bistie. He just looked stubborn. Talked to people up there on the Utah border who knew Endocheeney. Got nothing." Chee was looking at Leaphorn, judging the response.

He's heard about me and witches, Leaphorn thought. "In other words, everybody just shut up," he said. "How about Wilson Sam. Anything there?"

Chee hesitated. "You mean any connection?"

Leaphorn nodded. It was exactly what he was driving at. They were right. Chee was smart.

"That's out of our jurisdiction here," Chee said. "Where he was killed, that's in Chinle's territory. The subagency at Chinle has that case."

"I know that," Leaphorn said. "Did you go out there and look around? Ask around?" It was exactly what Leaphorn would have done under the circumstances—with two killings almost the same hour.

Chee looked surprised, and a little abashed. "On my day off," he said. "Kennedy and I hadn't gotten anything helpful on the Endocheeney thing yet, and I thought—"

Leaphorn held up his palm. "Why not?" he said. "You seeing anything that links them?"

Chee shook his head. "No family connections. Or clan connections. Endocheeney ran sheep, used to work when he was younger with that outfit that lays rails for the Santa Fe railroad. He got food stamps, and now and then sold firewood. Wilson Sam was also a sheepherder, had a job as a flagman on a highway construction job down near Winslow. He was fifty-something years old. Endocheeney was in his middle seventies."

"Did you try Sam's name on people who knew Endocheeney? To see if . . ." Leaphorn made a sort of inclusive gesture.

"No luck," Chee said. "Didn't seem to know the same people. Endocheeney's people didn't know Sam. Sam's people never heard of Endocheeney."

"Did you know either one of them? Ever? In any way? Even something casual?"

"No connection with me, either," Chee said. "They're not the kind of people policemen deal with. Not drunks. Not thieves. Nothing like that."

"No mutual friends?"

Chee laughed. "And no mutual enemies, as far as I can learn."

The laugh, Leaphorn thought, seemed genuine.

"Okay," he said. "How about the shooting-at-you business."

Chee described it again. While he talked, the cat came through the flap in the screen.

It was a large cat, with short tan hair, a stub of a tail, and pointed ears. It stopped just inside the screen, frozen in the crouch, staring at Leaphorn with intense blue eyes. Quite a cat, Leaphorn thought. Heavy haunches like a bobcat. The hair was matted on the left side of its head, and what looked like a scar distorted the smoothness of its flank. Some *belagana* tourist's pet, he guessed. Probably taken along on a vacation and lost. Leaphorn listened to Chee with half of his mind, alert only for some variation in an account he had already read twice in the official report, and heard from Largo over the phone. The other half of his consciousness focused on the cat. It still crouched by the door—judging whether this strange human was a threat. The flap probably had made enough noise when the cat came in to waken a man sleeping lightly, Leaphorn decided. The cat was thin, bony; its muscles had the ropy look of wild predators. If it had, in fact, been a pampered pet, it had adapted well. It had got itself in harmony with its new life. Like a Navajo, it had survived.

Chee had finished his account, without saying anything new. Or anything different. The metal seat of the folding chair was hard against Leaphorn's tailbone. He felt more tired than he should have felt after nothing much more than the drive from Window Rock. Chee was said to be smart. He seemed smart. Largo insisted he was. A smart man should have some idea who was trying to kill him. And why. If he wasn't a fool, was he a liar?

"When it got light, you looked outside," Leaphorn prompted. "What did you find?"

"Three empty shotgun shells," Chee said. His eyes said he knew Leaphorn already knew all this. "Twelve gauge. Center fire. Rubber sole tracks of a small shoe. Size seven. Fairly new. Led off up the slope to the road up there. Top of the slope, a vehicle had been parked. Tires were worn and it leaked a lot of oil."

"Did he come in the same way?"

"No," Chee said. The question had interested him. "Tracks down along the bank of the river."

"Past where this cat has its den."

"Right," Chee said.

Leaphorn waited. After a long silence, Chee said, "It seemed to me that something might have happened there. To spook the cat out of his hiding place. So I looked around." He made a deprecatory gesture. "Ground was scuffed. I think somebody had knelt there behind the juniper. It's not far from where people dump their trash and there's always a lot of stuff blowing around. But I found this." He got out his billfold, extracted a bit of yellow paper, and handed it to Leaphorn. "It's new," he said. "It hadn't been out there in the dirt very long."

It was the wrapper off a stick of Juicy Fruit gum. "Not much," Chee said, looking embarrassed.

It *wasn't* much. Leaphorn couldn't imagine how it would be useful. In fact, it seemed to symbolize just how little they had to work on in any of these cases. "But it's something," he said. His imagination made the figure squatting behind the juniper, watching the Chee trailer, a small figure holding a pump shotgun in his right hand, reaching into his shirt pocket with his left hand, fishing out a package of gum. No furious emotion here. Calm. A man doing a job, being careful, taking his time. And, as an accidental by-product, giving the cat crouched under the juniper a case of nerves, eroding its instinct to stay hidden until this human left, sending it into a panicky dash for a safer place. Leaphorn smiled slightly, enjoying the irony.

"We know he chews gum. Or she does," Chee said. "And what kind he sometimes chews. And that he's . . ." Chee searched for the right word. "Cool."

And I know, Leaphorn thought, that Jim Chee is smart enough to think about what might have spooked the cat. He glanced at the animal, which was still crouched by the flap, its blue eyes fixed on him. The glance was enough to tilt the decision. Two humans in a closed place were too many. The cat flicked through the flap, *clack-clack,* and was gone. Loud enough to wake a light sleeper, especially if he was nervous. Did Chee have something to be nervous about? Leaphorn shifted in the chair, trying for a more comfortable position. "You read the report on Wilson Sam," Leaphorn said. "And you went out there. When? Let's go over that again."

They went over it. Chee had visited the site four days after the killing and he'd found nothing to add significant data to the original report. And that told little enough. A ground-water pond where Wilson Sam's sheep drank was going dry. Sam had been out looking for a way to solve that problem—checking on his flock. He hadn't returned with nightfall. The next morning some of the Yazzie outfit into which Sam was married had gone out to look for him. A son of his sister-in-law had remembered hearing a dog howling.

They found the dog watching the body in an arroyo that runs into Tyende Creek south of the Greasewood Flats. The investigating officers from Chinle had arrived a little before noon. The back of Sam's head had been crushed, just above where head and neck join. The subsequent autopsy confirmed that he'd been struck with a shovel that was found at the scene. Relatives agreed that it wasn't Sam's shovel. The body apparently had fallen, or had rolled, down the bank and the assailant had climbed down after it. The nephew had driven directly out to the Dennehotso Trading Post, called the police, and then followed instructions to keep everybody away from the body until they arrived.

"There were still some pretty good tracks when I got there," Chee said. "Been a little shower there the day before the killing and a little runoff down the arroyo bottom. Cowboy boots, both heels worn, size ten, pointed toes. Heavy man, probably two hundred pounds or over, or he was carrying something heavy. He walked around the body, squatted beside it." Chee paused, face thoughtful. "He got down on both knees beside the body. Spent a little time, judging from the scuff marks and so forth. I thought maybe they were made by our people when they picked up the body. But I asked Gorman, and he said no. They were there when he'd checked originally."

"Gorman?"

"He's back with us now," Chee said. "But he was loaned out to Chinle back in June. Vacation relief. He was that guy who was walking out in the parking lot with me at noon. Gorman and Benaly. Gorman is the sort of fat one."

"Was the killer a Navajo?" Leaphorn asked.

Chee hesitated, surprised. "Yes," he said. "Navajo."

"You sound sure," Leaphorn said. "Why Navajo?"

"Funny. I knew he was Navajo. But I didn't think about why," Chee said. He counted it off on his fingers. "He didn't step over the body, which could have just happened that way. But when he walked down the arroyo, he took care not to walk where the water had run. And on the way back to the road, a snake had been across there, and when he crossed its path he shuffled his feet." Chee paused. "Or do white men do that too?"

"I doubt it," Leaphorn said. The don't-step-over-people business grew out of families living in one-room hogans, sleeping on the floor. A matter of respect. And the desert herders' respect for rain must have produced the taboo against stepping in water's footprints. Snakes? Leaphorn tried to remember. His grandmother had told him that if you walk across a snake's trail without erasing it by shuffling your feet, the snake would follow you home. But then his grandmother had also told him it was taboo for a child to keep secrets from grandmothers, and that watching a dog urinate would cause insanity. "How about the killer at Endocheeney's place? Another Navajo? Could it have been the same person?"

"Not many tracks there," Chee said. "Body was about a hundred yards from the hogan, with the whole family milling around after he was found. And we hadn't had the rain there. Everything dry."

"But what do you think? Another Navajo?"

Chee thought. "I don't know," he said. "Couldn't be absolutely sure. But when we eliminated what everybody who lived there was wearing, I think it was a boot with a flat rubber heel. And probably a smallish hole worn in the right sole."

"Different suspect, then," Leaphorn said. "Or different shoes." In fact, three different suspects. In fact, maybe four different suspects, counting Onesalt. He shook his head, thinking of the implausible, irrational insanity of it. Then he thought of Chee. An impressive young man. But why didn't he have at least an inkling of who had tried to kill him? Or why? Could he possibly not know? Leaphorn's back hurt. Sitting too long always did it these days. Easing himself out of the chair, he walked to the window over the sink and looked out. He felt something gritty under his boot sole, leaned down, and found it. The round lead pellet from a shotgun shell.

He showed it to Chee. "This one of them?"

"I guess so," Chee said. "I swept up, but when they went through the bedclothes, they bounced around. Got into everything."

Into everything except Jim Chee, Leaphorn thought. Too bad he had so much trouble learning to believe in luck. "Did you see anything at all that would connect the Endocheeney and Sam things? Anything at all? Anything to connect either one of them to this?" Leaphorn gestured at the three patched shotgun holes.

"I've thought about that," Chee said. "Nothing."

"Did the name Irma Onesalt turn up either place?"

"Onesalt? The woman somebody shot down near Window Rock? No."

"I'm going to ask Largo to take you off of everything else and have you rework everything about Endocheeney and Sam," Leaphorn said. "You willing? I mean talk to everybody about everything. Who people talked to. Who people saw. Try to get a fix on whatever the killers were driving. Just try to find out every damn thing. Work on it day after day after day until we get some feeling for what the hell went on. All right?"

"Sure," Chee said. "Fine."

"Anything else about this shooting of your own here that didn't seem to fit on the FBI report?"

Chee thought about it. His lips twitched in a gesture of doubt or deprecation.

"I don't know," he said. "Just this morning, I found this. Might not have anything to do with anything. Probably doesn't." He pulled out his wallet again and extracted from it something small and roundish and ivory-colored. He handed it to Leaphorn. It was a bead formed, apparently, from bone.

"Where was it?"

"On the floor under the bunk. Maybe it fell out when I changed the bedding."

"What do you think?" Leaphorn asked.

"I think I never had anything that had beads like that on it, or knew anybody who did. And I wonder how it got here."

"Or why?" Leaphorn asked.

"Yes. Or why."

If you believed in witches, Leaphorn thought, as Chee probably did, you would have to think of a bone bead as a way witches killed—the bone being human, and the fatal illness being "corpse sickness." And if you loaded your own shotgun shells, or even if you didn't, you would know how simple it would be to remove the little plug from the end, and the wadding, and add a bone bead to the lead pellets.

6

THE WIND BLEW OUT OF THE SOUTHWEST, hot and dry, whipping sand across the rutted track in front of Jim Chee's patrol car. Chee had backed the car a hundred yards up the gravel road that led to Badwater Wash Trading Post. He'd parked it under the gnarled limbs of a one-seed juniper—a place that gave him a little shade and a long view back down the road he had traveled. Now he simply sat, waiting and watching. If anyone was following, Chee intended to know it.

"I'm going to go along with the lieutenant," Captain Largo had told him. "Leaphorn wants me to rearrange things and let you work on our killings." As usual when he talked, Captain Largo's hands were living their separate life, sorting through papers on the captain's desk, rearranging whatever the captain kept in the top drawer, trying to reshape a crease in the captain's hat. "I think he's wrong," Largo said. "I think we ought to leave those cases to the FBI. The FBI's not going to break them, and neither are we, but the FBI's getting paid for it, and nobody's going to do any good on them until we have some luck—and taking you off your regular work isn't going to make us lucky. Is it?"

"No, sir," Chee had said. He wasn't sure Largo expected an answer, or wanted one, but being agreeable seemed a good policy. He didn't want the captain to change his mind.

"I think that Leaphorn thinks you getting shot is connected with one or the other of those killings, or maybe both of them. He didn't say so, but that's what I think he thinks. I can't see any connection. How about it?"

Chee shrugged. "I don't see how there could be."

"No," Largo agreed. His expression, as he looked at Chee, was skeptical. "Unless you're not telling me something." The tone of the statement included a question mark.

"I'm not not telling you anything," Chee said.

"Sometimes you haven't," Largo said. But he didn't pursue it. "Real reason I'm going along with this is I want you to stay alive. Just getting shot at is bad enough." Largo pointed to the folder on his desk. "Look at that, and it's not finished yet. If somebody kills you, think how it would be." Largo threw out his arms in a gesture encompassing mountains of forms. "When we had that man killed over in the Crownpoint subagency back in the sixties, they were doing reports on that for two years."

"Okay," Chee said. "That's okay with me."

"What I mean is, poke around on Endocheeney and Wilson Sam and see what you can hear, but mostly I want you out where it would be hard for anybody to get a shot at you. In case they're still trying. Let 'em cool off. Be careful."

"Good," Chee had said, meaning it.

And while he was out there, Largo had added, he might as well get some useful work done. For instance, the people at the refinery over at Montezuma Creek were sore because somebody was stealing drip gasoline out of the collector pipeline. And somebody seemed to be hanging out around the tourist parking places at the Goosenecks, and other such places, and stealing stuff out of the cars. And so forth. The litany had been fairly long, indicating that the decline of human nature on the Utah part of the reservation was about the same as it was in Chee's usual New Mexico jurisdiction. "I'll get you the paperwork," Largo said, shuffling papers out of various files into a single folder. "Xerox copies. I wish we could put a stop to this getting into people's cars," he added. "People raise hell about it, and it gets to the chairman's office and then he raises hell. Be careful. And get some work done."

And now, parked here out of sight watching his back trail, Chee was being careful, exactly as instructed. If the man (or the woman) with the shotgun was following, it would have to be down this road. The only other way to get to the trading post at Badwater Wash was to float down the San Juan River, and then take one of the tracks that connected it to the hogans scattered where terrain allowed along the river. Badwater wasn't a place one passed through by accident en route to anywhere else.

And now the only dust on the Badwater road was wind dust. The afternoon clouds had formed over Black Mesa, far to the south, producing lightning and air turbulence. As far as Chee could estimate from thirty miles away, no rain was falling. He studied the cloud, enjoying the range of blues and grays, its shapes and its movement. But he was thinking of more somber things. The hours of thinking he had done about who would want to kill him had depressing effects. His imagination had produced an image in his mind—himself standing at the face of a great cliff of smooth stone, as blank as a mirror, feeling hopelessly for fingerholds that didn't exist. There was a second unpleasant effect. This persistent hunt for malice, for ill will, for hatred—examining relationships with friends and associates with cynical skepticism—had left him gloomy. And then there was Lieutenant Leaphorn. He'd gotten what he wanted from the man—more than he'd expected. But the lieutenant hadn't trusted him when they'd met, and he hadn't trusted him when they'd parted. Leaphorn hadn't liked the bone bead. When Chee had handed it to him, the lieutenant's face had changed, expressing distaste and what might have been contempt. In the small universe of the Navajo Police, total membership perhaps less than 120 sworn officers, Lieutenant Leaphorn was a Fairly Important Person, and somewhat of a legend. Everybody knew he hated bootleggers. Chee shared that sentiment. Everybody also knew Leaphorn had no tolerance for witchcraft or anything about it—for those who believed in witches, or for stories about skinwalkers, corpse sickness, the cures for same, and everything connected with the Navajo Wolves. There were two stories about how Leaphorn had acquired this obsession. It was said that when he was new on the force in the older days he had guessed wrong about some skinwalker rumors on the Checkerboard. He hadn't acted on what he'd heard, and a fellow had killed three witches and got a life term for murder and then committed suicide. That was supposed to be why the lieutenant didn't like witchcraft, which was a good enough reason. The other story was that he was a descendant of the great Chee Dodge and had inherited Dodge's determination that belief in skinwalkers had no part in the Navajo culture, that the tribe had been infected with the notion while it was held captive down at Fort Sumner. Chee suspected both stories were true.

Still, Leaphorn had kept the bone bead.

"I'll see about it," he'd said. "Send it to the lab. Find out if it is bone, and what kind of bone." He'd torn a page from his notebook, wrapped the bead in it, and placed it in the coin compartment of his billfold. Then he'd looked at Chee for a moment in silence. "Any idea how it got in here?"

"Sounds strange," Chee had said. "But you know you could pry out the end of a shotgun shell and pull out the wadding and stick a bead like this in with the pellets."

Leaphorn's expression became almost a smile. Was it contempt? "Like a witch shooting in the bone?" he asked. "They're supposed to do that through a little tube." He made a puffing shape with his lips.

Chee had nodded, flushing just a little.

Now, remembering it, he was angry again. Well, to hell with Leaphorn. Let him believe whatever he wanted to believe. The origin story of the Navajos explained witchcraft clearly enough, and it was a logical part of the philosophy on which the Dinee had founded their culture. If there was good, and harmony, and beauty on the east side of reality, then there must be evil, chaos, and ugliness to the west. Like a nonfundamentalist Christian, Chee believed in the poetic metaphor of the Navajo story of human genesis. Without believing in the specific Adam's rib, or the size of the reed through which the Holy People emerged to the Earth Surface World, he believed in the lessons such imagery was intended to teach. To hell with Leaphorn and what he didn't believe. Chee started the engine and jolted back down the slope to the road. He wanted to get to Badwater Wash before noon.

But he couldn't quite get Leaphorn out of his mind. Leaphorn posed a problem. "One more thing," the lieutenant had said. "We've got a complaint about you." And he'd told Chee what the doctor at the Badwater Clinic had said about him. "Yellowhorse claims you've been interfering with his practice of his religion," Leaphorn said. And while the lieutenant's expression said he didn't take the complaint as anything critically important, the very fact that he'd mentioned it implied that Chee should desist.

"I have been telling people that Yellowhorse is a fake," Chee said stiffly. "I have told people every chance I get that the doctor pretends to be a crystal gazer just to get them into his clinic."

"I hope you're not doing that on company time," Leaphorn said. "Not while you're on duty."

"I probably have," Chee said. "Why not?"

"Because it violates regulations," Leaphorn said, his expression no longer even mildly amused.

"How?"

"I think you can see how," Leaphorn had said. "We don't have any way to license our shamans, no more than the federal government can license preachers. If Yellowhorse says he's a medicine man, or a hand trembler, or a road chief of the Native American Church, or the Pope, it is no business of the Navajo Tribal Police. No rule against it. No law."

"I'm a Navajo," Chee said. "I see somebody cynically using our religion . . . somebody who doesn't believe in our religion using it in that cynical way . . ."

"What harm is he doing?" Leaphorn asked. "The way I understand it, he recommends they go to a *hataalii* if they need a ceremonial sing. And he points them at the white man's hospital only if they have a white man's problem. Diabetes, for example."

Chee had made no response to that. If Leaphorn couldn't see the problem, the sacrilege involved, then Leaphorn was blind. But that wasn't the trouble. Leaphorn was as cynical as Yellowhorse.

"You, yourself, have declared yourself to be a *hataalii,* I hear," Leaphorn said. "I heard you performed a Blessing Way."

Chee had nodded. He said nothing.

Leaphorn had looked at him a moment, and sighed. "I'll talk to Largo about it," he said.

And that meant that one of these days Chee would have an argument with the captain about it and if he wasn't lucky, Largo would give him a flat, unequivocal order to say nothing more about Yellowhorse as shaman. When that happened, he would cope as best he could. Now the road to Badwater had changed from bad to worse. Chee concentrated on driving.

It was the policy of the Navajo Tribal Police, as a matter of convenience, to consider Badwater to be in the Arizona portion of the Big Reservation. Local wisdom held that the store itself was actually in Utah, about thirty feet north of the imaginary line that marked the boundary. One of the local jokes was that Old Man Isaac Ginsberg, who built the place, used to move out of his room behind the trading post and into a stone hogan across the road one hundred yards to the south because he couldn't stand the cold Utah winters. Nobody seemed to know exactly where the place was, mapwise. Its location, in a narrow slot surrounded by the fantastic, thousand-foot, red-black-blue-tan cliffs, made pinpointing it on surveys mostly guesswork. And nobody cared enough to do more than guess.

Historically, it had been a watering place for herdsmen. In the immense dry badlands of Casa del Eco Mesa, it was a rare place where a reliable spring produced pools of drinkable water. Good water is a magnet anywhere in desert country. In a landscape like Caso del Eco, where gypsum and an arsenal of other soluble minerals tainted rainwater almost as fast as it fell, the stuff that seeped under the sandy arroyo bottoms was such a compound of chemicals that it would kill even tumbleweeds and salt cedar. Thus, the springs in Badwater Wash were a magnet for all living things. They attracted those tough little mammals and reptiles which endure in such hostile places. Eventually it attracted goats that strayed from the herds the Navajos had stolen from the Pueblo Indians. Then came the goatherders. Next came sheepherders. Finally, geologists discovered the shallow but persistent Aneth oil deposit, which brought a brief, dusty boom to the plateau. The drilling boom left behind a little refinery at Montezuma Creek, a scattering of robot pumps, and a worn-out spiderweb of truck trails connecting them with the world. Sometime in this period between boom and dust, it had attracted Isaac Ginsberg, who built the trading post of slabs of red sandstone, earned the Navajo name Afraid of His Wife, and died. The wife to whom Ginsberg owed his title was a Mud Clan Navajo called Lizzie Tonale, who had married Ginsberg in Flagstaff, had converted to Judaism, and, it was locally believed, had persuaded Ginsberg to establish his business in such an incredibly isolated locale because it was the hardest possible place for her relatives to reach. It would have been a sensible motive. Otherwise, the trading post would have been bankrupt in a month, since Lizzie Tonale could refuse no kin who needed canned goods, gasoline, or a loan, and maintain her status as a respectable woman. Whatever her motives, the widow Tonale-Ginsberg had run the post for twenty years before her own death, steadfastly closing on the Sabbath. She had left it to their daughter, the only product of their union. Chee had met this daughter only twice. That was enough to understand how she had earned her local name, which was Iron Woman.

Now, as he rolled his patrol car down the final slope and into the rutted yard of Badwater Wash Trading Post, he saw the bulky form of Iron Woman standing on the porch. Chee parked as much of the car as he could in the scanty shade of a tamarisk and waited. It was a courtesy learned from boyhood in a society where modesty is prized, privacy is treasured, and visitors, even at a trading post, are all too rare. "You don't just go run up to somebody's hogan," his mother had taught him. "You might see something you don't want to see."

So Chee sat, without giving it a thought, to allow the residents of Badwater Wash to get in harmony with the idea of a visit from a tribal policeman, to button up and tidy up, or to do whatever was required by Navajo good manners. While he sat, perspiring freely, he looked in his rearview mirror at the people on the porch. Iron Woman had been joined by another woman, as thin and bent as Iron Woman was stout and ramrod rigid. Then two young men appeared in the front door, seeming, in the dusty rearview glass, to be dressed exactly alike. Each wore a red sweatband around the forehead, a faded red plaid shirt, jeans, and cowboy boots. Iron Woman was saying something to the bent woman, who nodded and looked amused. The two young men, standing side by side, stared with implacable rudeness at Chee's car. An old Ford sedan was parked at the corner of the building, a cinder block supporting the right rear axle. Beside it, perched high on its backcountry suspension, was a new GMC four-by-four. It was black with yellow pinstripes. Chee had priced a similar model in Farmington and couldn't come close to affording it. He admired it now. A vehicle that would go anywhere. But richer than anything you expected to see parked at Badwater Wash.

Through his windshield, beyond the thin screen of Russian olive leaves, the red mass of the cliff rose to the sky, reflecting the sun. The patrol car was filled with dry heat. Chee felt uneasiness stirring. He was getting used to it, finding the anxiety familiar but not learning to like it. He got out of the car and walked toward the porch, keeping his eyes on the men, who kept their eyes on him.

"Ya-tah-hey," he said to Iron Woman.

"Ya-tah," she said. "I remember you. You're the new policeman from Shiprock."

Chee nodded.

"Out here the other day with the government officer seeing about the Endocheeney business."

"Right," Chee said.

"This man is born to the Slow Talking People and born for the Salts," Iron Woman told the bent woman. She named Chee's mother, and his maternal aunt, and his maternal grandmother, and then recited his father's side of the family.

Bent Woman looked pleased. She faced Chee with her head back and her eyes almost closed, looking at him under her lids, a technique the descending blindness of glaucoma and cataracts taught its victims. "He is my nephew," Bent Woman said. "I am born to the Bitter Water People, born for the Deer Spring Clan. My mother was Gray Woman Nez."

Chee smiled, acknowledging the relationship. It was vague—the Bitter Waters being linked to the Salt Clan and thereby to his father's family. The system meant that Chee, and all other Navajos, had wholesale numbers of relatives.

"On business?" Iron Woman asked.

"Just out poking around," Chee said. "Seeing what I can see."

Iron Woman looked skeptical. "You don't get out here much," she said. "Nobody gets out here except on purpose."

Chee was aware of the two men watching him. Barely men. Late teens, he guessed. Obviously brothers, but not twins. The one nearest him had a thinner face, and a half-moon of white scar tissue beside his left eye socket. Under the old rules of Navajo courtesy, they would have identified themselves first, since he was the stranger in their territory. They didn't seem to care about the old rules.

"My clan is Slow Talking People," Chee said to them. "Born for the Salt Dinee."

"Leaf People," the thinner one said. "Born for Mud." His face was sullen.

Chee's efficient nose picked up a whiff of alcohol. Beer. The Leaf Clan man let his eyes drift from Chee to study the police car. He gestured vaguely toward the other man. "My brother," he said.

"What's happening over your way?" Iron Woman asked. "I heard on the radio they had a knifing at a wedding over at Teec Nos Pos. One of the Gorman outfit got cut. Anything to that?"

Chee knew very little about that one—just what he'd overheard before the morning patrol meeting. Normally he worked east and south out of Shiprock—not this mostly empty northwestern area. He put the beer (possession illegal on the reservation) out of his mind and tried to remember what he had heard.

"Didn't amount to much," Chee said. "Fella was fooling with a girl and she had a knife. Stuck him in the arm. I think she was a Standing Rock girl. Not much to it."

Iron Woman looked disappointed. "It got on the radio, though," she said. "Lot of people around here related to the Gorman outfit."

Chee had gone to the battered red pop cooler just inside the front door, inserted two quarters, and tried to open the lid.

"Takes three," Iron Woman said. "Costs too much to get that stuff hauled way out here. And icing it down. Now everybody wants it cold."

"No more change," Chee said. He fished out a dollar and handed it to Iron Woman. It was dark inside the store and much cooler. At the cash register, Iron Woman handed him four quarters.

"Last time you were with that FBI man—asking about the one that got killed," she said, respecting the Navajo taboo of not speaking the name of the dead. "You find out who killed that man?"

Chee shook his head.

"That fellow that came through here looking for him the day he was killed. Sounded to me like he did it."

"That's a crazy thing," Chee said. "We found that man at his hogan over in the Chuskas. A man they call Roosevelt Bistie. Bistie told us he came over here to kill that man who got killed. And the man Bistie was after was up on his roof fixing something, and Bistie shot at him and he fell off. But whoever killed the man did it with a butcher knife."

"That's right," Iron Woman said. "Sure as hell, it was a knife. I remember his daughter telling me that." She shook her head, peered at Chee again. "Why would that fellow tell you he shot him?"

"We can't figure that out, either," Chee said. "Bistie said he wanted to kill the man, but he won't say why."

Iron Woman frowned. "Roosevelt Bistie," she said. "Never heard of him. I remember when he stopped in here asking directions, I never had seen him before. The man's kinfolks, do they know this Bistie?"

"None of them we've talked to," Chee said. He was thinking of how disapproving Kennedy would be if he could hear Chee discussing this case with a layman. Captain Largo too, for that matter, Largo having been a cop long enough to start acting secretive. But Kennedy was FBI to the bone, and the first law of the Agency was, Say nothing to nobody. If Kennedy were here, listening to this Navajo talk, he'd be waiting impatiently for a translation—knowing that Chee must be telling this woman more than she needed to know. However, Kennedy wasn't here, and Chee had his own operating theory. The more you tell people, the more people tell you. Nobody, certainly no Navajo, wants to be second in the business of telling things.

Chee dropped in quarters and selected a Nehi Orange. Cold and wonderful. Iron Woman talked. Chee sipped. Outside, noonday heat radiated from the packed earth of the yard, causing the light to shimmer. Chee finished his soda pop. The four-by-four drove away with a roar, dust spurting from its wheels. Beer in the four-by-four, Chee guessed. Unless the boys had bought it here. But if Iron Woman was a bootlegger, he hadn't heard it, and he hadn't remembered seeing this place on the map Largo kept of liquor sources in his subagency territory. Beer in the morning, and an expensive rig to drive. Iron Woman had said the two were part of the Kayonnie outfit, which ran goats down along the San Juan to the north and sometimes worked in the oil fields. But Iron Woman obviously did not want to discuss the Kayonnie boys, her neighbors, with a stranger. The local murder victim was another matter. She couldn't understand who would do it. He was a harmless old man. He stayed at home. Since his wife had died, he rarely came even as far as the trading post. Maybe two or three times a year, sometimes riding in on a horse, sometimes coming with a relative when a relative came to see him. No Endocheeney daughters to bring home their husbands, so the old man had lived alone. Only thing important she could remember happening involving him was a Red Ant Way sing done for him six or seven years ago to cure him of something or other after his woman died. In all the years she'd been at Badwater, which was all her life, she couldn't remember him getting into any kind of trouble, or being involved in bad problems. "Like getting your wood on somebody else's wood-gathering place, or getting into some other family's water, or running his sheep where they shouldn't be, or not helping out somebody that needed it. Never heard anything bad about him. Never been in any trouble. Always helping out at sheep dippings, always tried to take care of his kinfolks, always there when somebody was having a sing."

"I don't know if I ever told you that I have studied to be a *hataalii* myself," Chee said. "I do the Blessing Way and some others." He got out his billfold, extracted a card, and handed it to Iron Woman. The card said:

THE BLESSING WAY
and other ceremonials sung
by a singer who studied with Frank Sam Nakai
Contact Jim Chee

The next lines provided his address and telephone number at the Shiprock Police Station. He had mentioned this to the dispatcher, thinking he would square it with Captain Largo if the captain ever learned about it. So far, the risk seemed small. There had been no calls, and no letters.

Iron Woman seemed to share the general lack of enthusiasm. She glanced at the card and laid it on the counter.

"Everybody liked him," Iron Woman said, getting back on the

subject. "But now he's dead, some people are saying he was a skin-walker." Her face reflected distaste. "Sons-a-bitches," she added, clarifying that the distaste was not for skinwalkers but for the gossips. "When you live by yourself, people say things like that."

Or when you get stabbed to death, Chee thought. Violent death always seemed to provoke witch talk.

"If everybody around here liked him," Chee said, "then who-ever killed him must have come from someplace else. Like Bistie. Did he know anybody anywhere else?"

"I don't think so," Iron Woman said. "Long as I been here, he only got one letter."

Chee felt a stir of excitement. Something at last. "You remem-ber anything about it? Who it was from?" Of course she would remember. The arrival of any mail on this isolated outpost would be something to talk about, especially a letter to a man who never received letters and who couldn't read them if he did. It would lie in the little shoebox marked MAIL on the shelf above Iron Woman's cash register, the subject of conjecture and speculation until Endo-cheeney came in, or a relative showed up who might be trusted to deliver it to him.

"Wasn't from anybody," Iron Woman said. "It was from the tribe. There in Window Rock."

The excitement evaporated. "One of the tribal offices?"

"Social Services, I think it was. One of those that are always messing around with people."

"How about his pawn?" Chee asked. "Anything unusual in that?"

Iron Woman led him behind the counter, fished a key out of the folds of her voluminous reservation skirt, and unlocked the glass-topped cabinet where she kept the pawn.

The Endocheeney possessions held hostage for credit in-cluded one belt of heavy, crudely hammered conchas, old-fash-ioned and heavily tarnished; a small sack containing nine old Mex-ican twenty-peso coins, their silver as tarnished as the belt; two sand-cast rings; and a belt buckle of sand-cast silver. The buckle was beautiful, a simple geometric pattern that Chee favored, with a single perfect turquoise gem set in its center. He turned it in his hand, admiring it.

"And this," Iron Woman said. She thumped a small deerskin pouch on the countertop and poured out a cluster of unset turquoise nuggets and fragments. "The old man made some jewelry now and then. Or he used to. Guess he got too old for it after the old woman died."

There was nothing remarkable about the turquoise. It was worth maybe two hundred dollars. Add another two hundred for the belt and maybe one hundred for the buckle and probably fifteen or twenty dollars each for the old pesos. They were once standard raw material for belt conchas on the reservation, and cheap enough, but Mexico had long since stopped making them, and the price of silver had soared. Nothing remarkable about any of this, except the beauty of the buckle. He wondered if Endocheeney had cast it himself. And he wondered why some of his kin had not claimed these belongings. Once, tradition would have demanded that such personal stuff be disposed of with the body. But that tradition was now often ignored. Or perhaps Endocheeney's relatives didn't know about this pawn. Or perhaps they didn't have the cash to redeem it.

"How much do you have on the old man's bill?" Chee asked.

Iron Woman didn't have to look it up. "One hundred eighteen dollars," she said. "And some cents."

Not much, Chee thought. Far less than the stuff was worth. Someone without any cash could raise that much by selling a few goats.

"And then there's them," Iron Woman said. She tilted her head toward a corner behind the counter. There stood a posthole digger, two axes, a pair of crutches, a hand-turned ice cream freezer, and what seemed to be an old car axle converted into a wrecking bar.

Chee looked puzzled.

"The crutches," Iron Woman said impatiently. "He wanted to pawn them too, but hell, who wants crutches? They loan 'em to you free, up there at the Badwater Clinic, so I didn't want to get stuck with 'em as pawn. Anyway, he just left 'em there. Said give him half if I could sell 'em."

"Was he hurt?" Chee asked, thinking as he did that he could have found a smarter way to ask the question.

Iron Woman seemed to think so too. "Broke his leg. Fell off of something and they had to put a cast on it over at the clinic and he came back with the crutches."

"And then he climbed right back on the roof," Chee said. "Sounds like he was a slow learner."

"No, no," Iron Woman said. "Broke his leg way last autumn doing something else. Think he fell off of a rail fence. Leg caught."

Iron Woman broke an imaginary stick with her fingers. "Snap," she said.

Chee was thinking of relatives who didn't come in and collect pawn. "Who buried the old man?" he asked.

"They got a man that works on those old well pumps out there." Iron Woman made a sweeping gesture with both hands to take in the entire plateau. "White man. He does that sometimes for people. Doesn't mind about corpses."

"This witch talk. You hear that a long time or just now?"

Iron Woman looked uneasy. From what Chee had heard about her, she had gone to school over at Ganado, at the College of Ganado, a good school. And she was a Jew, more or less, raised in that religion. But she was also a Navajo, a member of the Halgai Dinee, the People of the Valley Clan. She didn't like talking about witches in any specific way with a stranger.

"I heard about it just now," she said. "Since the killing."

"Was it just the usual stuff? What you'd expect when somebody gets killed?"

Iron Woman licked her lips, caught the lower lip between her teeth, looked at Chee carefully. She shifted her weight and in the silence the creak of the floorboard plank under her shoe was a loud groaning sound. But her voice was so faint when she finally spoke that, even in the silence, he had to strain to hear.

"They say that when they found him, they found a bone in the wound—where the knife had gone in."

"A bone?" Chee asked, not sure that he'd heard it.

Iron Woman held her thumb and forefinger up—an eighth of an inch apart. "Little corpse bone," she said.

She didn't need to explain it more than that. Chee was remembering the bone bead he'd found in his trailer.

DR. RANDALL JENKS HELD a sheet of paper in his fist. Presumably it was the laboratory report on the bead, since Jenks's office had called Leaphorn to tell him the report was ready. But Jenks gave no sign he was ready to hand it over.

"Have a seat," Dr. Jenks said, and sat down himself beside the long table in the meeting room. He wore a headband of red fabric into which the Navajo symbol of Corn Beetle had been woven. His blond hair was shoulder length and under his blue laboratory jacket Leaphorn could see the uniform—a frayed denim jacket. Leaphorn, who resented those who stereotyped Navajos, struggled not to stereotype others. But Dr. Jenks fell into Leaphorn's category of Indian Lover. That meant he irritated Leaphorn even when he was doing him favors. Now Leaphorn was in a hurry. But he sat down.

Jenks looked at him over his glasses. "The bead is made out of bone," he said, checking for reaction.

Leaphorn was not in the mood to pretend surprise. "I thought it might be," he said.

"Bovine," Jenks said. "Modern but not new, if you know what I mean. Dead long enough to be totally dehydrated. Maybe twenty years, maybe a hundred—more or less."

"Thanks for the trouble. Appreciate it," Leaphorn said. He got up, put on his hat.

"Did you expect it to be human?" Jenks asked. "Human bone?"

Leaphorn hesitated. He had work to do back at Window Rock—a rodeo that would probably be causing problems by now and a meeting of the Tribal Council that certainly would. Getting that many politicians together always caused some sort of problem. He wanted to confirm Emma's appointment before he left the hospital, and talk to the neurologist about her if he could. And then there were his three homicides. Three and a half if you counted Officer Chee. Besides, he wanted to think about what he had just learned—that the bone wasn't human. And what he had expected was none of Jenks's business. Jenks's business was public health, more specifically public health of the Navajos, Zunis, Acomas, Lagunas, and Hopis served by the U.S. Indian Service hospital at Gallup. Jenks's business, specifically, was pathology—a science that Lieutenant Leaphorn often wished he knew more about so he wouldn't be asking favors of Jenks.

"I thought it might be human," Leaphorn said.

"Any connection with Irma Onesalt?"

The question startled Leaphorn. "No," he said. "Did you know her?"

Jenks laughed. "Not exactly. Not socially. She was in here a time or two. Wanting information."

"About pathology?" Why would the Onesalt woman want information from a pathologist?

"About when a bunch of people died," Jenks said. "She had a list of names."

"Who?"

"I just glanced at it," Jenks said. "Looked like Navajo names, but I didn't really study it."

Leaphorn took off his hat and sat down.

"Tell me about it," he said. "When she came in, everything you can remember. And tell me why this bone bead business made you think of Onesalt."

Dr. Jenks told him, looking pleased.

Irma Onesalt had come in one morning about two months earlier. Maybe a little longer. If it was important, maybe he could pin down the date. He had known her a little bit before. She had come to see him way back when the semiconductor plant was still operating at Shiprock—wanting to know if that kind of work was bad for the health. And he had looked stuff up for her a couple of times since.

Jenks paused, getting his thoughts in order.

"What kind of stuff?" Leaphorn asked.

Jenks's long, pale face looked slightly embarrassed. "Well, one time she wanted some details about a couple of diseases, how they are treated, if hospitalization is needed, how long, so forth. And one time she wanted to know if an alcohol death we had in here might have been beaten."

Jenks didn't say beaten by whom. He didn't need to say. Irma Onesalt would have been interested, Leaphorn suspected, only if police, and preferably Navajo Tribal Police, had been the guilty party. Irma Onesalt did not like police, particularly Navajo Police. She called them Cossacks. She called them oppressors of The People.

"This time she had a sheet of paper with her—just names typed on it. She wanted to know if I could go back through my records and come up with the date each one had died."

"Could you?" Leaphorn asked.

"A few of them, maybe. Only if they had died in this hospital, or if we did the postmortem workup for some reason. But you know how that works. Most Navajo families won't allow an autopsy and usually they can stop it on religious grounds. I'd have a record of it only if they died here, and then only if there was some good reason—like suspicious causes, or the FBI was interested, or something like that."

"She wanted to know cause of death?"

"I don't think so. All she seemed to want was dates. I told her the only place I could think of she could get them all was the vital statistics offices in the state health departments. In Santa Fe and Phoenix and Salt Lake City."

"Dates," Leaphorn said. "Dates of their death." He frowned. That seemed odd. "She say why?"

Jenks shook his head, causing the long blond hair to sway. "I asked her. She said she was just curious about something." Jenks laughed. "She didn't say what, but that little bone bead of yours made me think of her because she was talking about witchcraft. She said something about the problem with singers and the health situation. People getting scared by the singers into thinking a skin-walker has witched them, and then getting the wrong medical treatment, or treatment they don't need because they're not really sick. So when I saw your little bead I made the connection." He studied Leaphorn to see if Leaphorn understood. "You know. Witches blowing a little piece of bone into somebody to give 'em the corpse sickness. But she never said that had anything to do with her list of names and what she was curious about. She said it was too early. She shouldn't talk about it yet—not then, she meant—and she said if anything came of it she would let me know."

"But she didn't come back?"

"She came back," Jenks said. He looked thoughtful, running the tip of his thumb under the headband, adjusting it. "Must have been a couple of weeks before she got killed. This time she wanted to know what sort of treatment would be indicated for two or three diseases, and how long you'd be hospitalized. Things like that."

"What diseases?" Leaphorn asked, although when he asked it he couldn't imagine what the answer would mean to him.

"One was TB," Jenks said. "I remember that. And I think one was some sort of liver pathology." He shrugged. "Nothing unusual. Sort of routine ailments we deal with around here, I remember that."

"And did she tell you then? I mean tell you why she wanted the dates those people died?" He was thinking of Roosevelt Bistie— the man who tried to kill Endocheeney—the man they had locked up at Shiprock, with not much reason to keep him, according to Kennedy's report. Roosevelt Bistie had something wrong with his liver. But so did a lot of people. And what the hell could that mean, anyway?

"I was in a hurry," Jenks said. "Two of our staff were on vacation and I was covering for one of them and I was trying to get my own operation caught up so I could go on vacation myself. So I didn't ask any questions. Just told her what she wanted to know and got rid of her."

"Did she ever explain it to you? In any way at all?"

"When I got back from vacation—couple of weeks after that— somebody told me somebody had shot her."

"Yeah," Leaphorn said. Shot her and left Leaphorn to guess why, since nobody else seemed to care a lot. And here might be the motive—this further example of Irma Onesalt in the role of busybody, to use the *belagana* term for it. His mother would have called her, in Navajo, a "one who tells sheep which weed to eat." Onesalt's job in the Navajo Office of Social Services, obviously, had no more to do with death statistics than it did with the occupational hazards of the semiconductor plant or, to get closer to Leaphorn's own emotional scar tissue, with punishing bad judgment in the Navajo Tribal Police.

"Do you think what she was working on had anything to do with why . . ." Jenks didn't complete the sentence.

"Who knows," Leaphorn said. "FBI handles homicides on Indian reservations." He heard himself saying it, his voice curt and unfriendly, and felt a twinge of self-disgust. Why this animus against Jenks? It wasn't just that he felt Jenks's attitude was patronizing. It was part of a resentment against all doctors. They seemed to know so much, but when he gave them Emma, the only thing that mattered, they would know absolutely nothing. That was the principal source of this resentment. And it wasn't fair to Jenks, or to any of them. Jenks had come to the Big Reservation, as many of the Indian Health Service doctors did, because the federal loans that had financed his education required two years in the military or the Indian Health Service. But Jenks had stayed beyond the two-year obligation, as some other IHS doctors did—delaying the Mercedes, the country club membership, the three-day work week, and the winters in the Bahamas—to help Navajos fight the battle of diabetes, dysentery, bubonic plague, and all those ailments that follow poor diets, bad water, and isolation. He shouldn't resent Jenks. Not only wasn't it fair; showing it would hurt his chances of learning everything Jenks could tell him.

"However," Leaphorn added, "we know something about it. And from what we know, the FBI hasn't a clue about motive." Nor do I, Leaphorn thought. Not about motive. Not about anything else. Certainly not about how to connect three and a half murders whose only connection seems to be an aimless lack of motive. "Maybe this list Irma had would help. All Navajo names, you said. Right? Could you think of any of them?"

Jenks's expression suggested he was probing his brain for names. All the homicide victims were still alive when Jenks had seen the list, Leaphorn thought, but wouldn't it be wonderful and remarkable if . . .

"One was Ethelmary Largewhiskers," Jenks said, faintly amused. "One was Woody's Mother."

Leaphorn rarely allowed his face to show irritation, and he didn't now. These were exactly the sort of names he'd expect Jenks to remember: names that were quaint, or cute, that would provoke a smile at a cocktail party somewhere when Dr. Jenks had become bored with Navajos—when too few of them drove wagons, and hauled drinking water forty miles, and slept in the desert with their sheep, and too many drove station wagons and got their teeth straightened by the orthodontist.

"Any others?" Leaphorn asked. "It might be important."

Jenks put on the expression of a man trying hard for a recall. And failing. He shook his head.

"Would you remember any, if you heard?"

Jenks shrugged. "Maybe."

"How about Wilson Sam?"

Jenks wrinkled his face. Shook his head. "Isn't he that guy who got killed early this summer?"

"Right," Leaphorn said. "Was his name on the list?"

"I don't remember," Jenks said. "But he was still alive then. He didn't get killed until after Onesalt. If I remember it right, and I think I do because they did the autopsy at Farmington and the pathologist there called me about it."

"You're right. I'm just fishing around. How about Dugai Endo-cheeney?"

Jenks produced the expression that signifies deep thought. "No," he said. "I mean no, I can't remember. Been a long time." He shook his head. Stopped the gesture. Frowned. "I've heard the name," he said. "Not on the list, I think, but . . ." He paused, adjusted the headband. "Wasn't he a homicide victim too? The other one that was killed about then?"

"Yes," Leaphorn said.

"Joe Harris did the autopsy too, at Farmington," Jenks said. "He told me he got a dime out of one of the wounds. That's why I remembered it, I guess."

"Harris found a dime in the wound?" Harris was the San Juan County coroner working out of the Farmington hospital. Pathologists, like police, seemed to know one another and swap yarns.

"He said Endocheeney got stabbed a bunch of times through the pocket of his jacket. In knifings we're always finding threads and stuff like that in the wound. Whatever the knife happens to hit on the way in through the clothing. Buttons. Paper. Whatever. This time it hit a dime."

Leaphorn, whose memory was excellent, recalled reading the autopsy report in the FBI file. No mention of a dime. But there had been mention of "foreign objects," which would cover a dime as well as the more usual buttons, thread, gravel, and broken glass. Could a knife punch a dime into a wound? Easily enough. It seemed odd, but not unreasonable.

"But Endocheeney wasn't on the list."

"I don't think so," Jenks said.

Leaphorn hesitated. "How about Jim Chee?" he asked.

Dr. Jenks thought hard again. But he couldn't remember whether or not Jim Chee's name was on the death date list.

8

IT WAS ALMOST DARK when Chee pulled into the police parking lot in Shiprock. He parked where a globe willow would shade the car from the early sun the next morning and walked, stiff and weary, toward his pickup truck. He had left it that morning where another of the police department willows would shade it from the afternoon sun. Now the same tree hid it from the dim red twilight in a pool of blackness. The uneasiness Chee had shaken off at Badwater Wash and on the long drive home was suddenly back in possession. He stopped, stared at the truck. He could see only its shape in the shadows. He turned abruptly and hurried into the Police Building.

Nelson McDonald was working the night shift, lounging behind the switchboard with the two top buttons of his uniform shirt open, reading the sports section of the Farmington *Times*. Officer McDonald glanced up at Chee, nodded.

"You still alive?" he asked, with no hint of a smile.

"So far," Chee said. But he didn't think it was funny. He would later, perhaps. Ten years later. Crises past, in police work, tended to transmute themselves from fear into the stuff of jokes. But now there was still the fear, a palpable something affecting the way Chee's stomach felt. "I guess nobody noticed anyone tinkering around with my truck?"

Officer McDonald sat up a little straighter, noticing Chee's face and regretting the joke. "Nobody mentioned it," he said. "And it's parked right out there where everybody could see it. I don't think . . ." He decided not to finish the sentence.

"No messages?" Chee asked.

McDonald sorted through the notes impaled on a spindle on

the clerk's desk. "One," he said, and handed it to Chee.

"Call Lt. Leaphorn as soon as you get in," it said, and listed two telephone numbers.

Leaphorn answered at the second one, his home.

"I want to ask you if you learned anything new about Endocheeney," Leaphorn said. "But there's a couple of other loose ends. Didn't you say you met Irma Onesalt just recently? Can you tell me exactly when?"

"I could check my logs," Chee said. "Probably in April. Late April."

"Did she say anything to you about a list of names she had? About trying to find out what date the people on that list died?"

"No, sir," Chee said. "I'm sure I'd remember something like that."

"You said you went to the Badwater Clinic and picked up a patient there and took him to a chapter meeting for her and they gave you the wrong man. And she was sore about it. That right?"

"Right. Old man named Begay. You know how it is with Begays." How it was with Begays on the reservation is how it is with Smiths and Joneses in Kansas City or Chavezes in Santa Fe. It was the most common name on the reservation.

"She said nothing about names? Nothing about a list of names? Nothing about how to go about finding out dates of deaths? Nothing that might lead into that?"

"No, sir," Chee said. "She just said a word or two when I got to the chapter house. She was waiting. Wanted to know why I was late. Then she took the old man in to the meeting. I waited because I was supposed to take him back after he had his say. After a while, she came out and raised hell with me for bringing her the wrong Begay, and then he came out and got in and I took him back to the clinic. Not much of a chance for chatting."

"No," Leaphorn said. "I had some dealing with the woman myself." Chee heard the sound of a chuckle. "I imagine you learned a few new dirty words?"

"Yes, sir," Chee said. "I did."

A long silence. "Well," Leaphorn said. "Just remember that a little while before she was shot she showed up at the pathologist's office at the Gallup hospital with a list of names. She wanted to know how to find out when each of them died. If you hear anything that helps explain that, I want to know about it right away."

"Right," Chee said.

"Now. What did you learn out around Badwater?"

"Not much," Chee said. "He had several hundred dollars' worth of pawn left at the post there—a lot more than he owed for—and his kinfolks haven't picked it up. And he broke a leg last summer falling off a fence. Nothing much."

Silence again. Then Leaphorn said, in a very mild voice: "I've got a funny way of working. Instead of telling me 'Not much,' I like people to tell me all the details and then I'll say, 'Well, that's not much,' or maybe I'll say, 'Hey, that part about the pawn explains something else I heard.' Or so forth. What I'm saying is, give me all the details and let me sort it out."

And so Chee, feeling slightly resentful, told Leaphorn of the bent woman, and the Kayonnie brothers with morning beer on their breath, and the letter from Window Rock, and the crutches which Iron Woman wouldn't accept as pawn and couldn't sell, and all the other details. He finished, and listened to a silence so long that he wondered if Leaphorn had put down the telephone. He cleared his throat.

"That letter," Leaphorn said. "From Window Rock. But what agency? And when?"

"Navajo Social Services," Chee said. "That's what Iron Woman remembered. It came back in June."

"That's who Irma Onesalt worked for," Leaphorn said.

"Oh," Chee said.

"Where'd he get the crutches?"

"Badwater Clinic," Chee said. "They set his leg. Guess they loan out their crutches."

"And don't get them back," Leaphorn said. "You learn anything else you're not telling me?"

"No, sir," Chee said.

Leaphorn noticed the tone. "You can see why I need the details. You haven't been working on the Onesalt case, so you had no way of knowing—or giving a damn—who she worked for. Now we have a link. Victim Onesalt wrote a letter to victim Endocheeney. Or somebody in her office did."

"That help?"

Leaphorn laughed. "I don't see how. But nothing else helps, either. You figured out yet why you got shot at?"

"No, sir."

Another pause. "Something I want you to think about." Silence. "I'm going to bet you that when we find out who did it and why, it's going to be based on something you know. You're going to say, 'Hell, I should have thought of that.'"

"Maybe," Chee said. But he thought about it as he put down the telephone. And he doubted it. Leaphorn was a hotshot. But Leaphorn was wrong about this.

He glanced at McDonald, immersed again in the *Times.* Chee had come in mostly to get the station's portable spotlight out of the storeroom and shine it on his truck. But now, in this well-lit room with his friend waiting behind the newspaper, curious and embarrassed, doing that seemed ridiculous. Instead he went to his typewriter and pounded out a note to Largo.

TO: Commanding Officer

FROM: Chee

SUBJECT: Investigation thefts from vehicles at tourist parking
sites and theft of drip gasoline in Aneth field.
At Badwater Wash Trading Post ran into two
young men, Kayonnie family, driving a new GMC
4 × 4 and drinking in the morning. Am told they are
unemployed. Will check more out there again.

He initialed the memo and handed it to Officer McDonald. "Going home," he said, and left.

He stood a moment in the darkness beyond the entrance until his eyes adjusted enough to make his pickup visible. By then the fear had reestablished itself, and the thought of walking up to that truck in the darkness, and then of driving into the darkness surrounding his trailer, was more than he wanted to handle. He'd walk. It was less than two miles from the station down along the river to his homesite under the cottonwoods. An easy walk, even at night. It would work out the stiffness of a day spent mostly in his patrol car. He trotted across the asphalt of U.S. 666 and found the path that led toward the river.

Chee was a fast walker and normally this trip took less than thirty minutes. Tonight, moving soundlessly, he took almost forty and used another ten carefully scouting, pistol in hand, the places around his trailer where someone with a shotgun might wait. He found nothing. That left the trailer itself.

He paused behind a juniper and studied it. Light from a half-moon made the setting a pattern of cottonwood shadows. The only sound on the breezeless air was a truck changing gears on the highway far behind him, growling up the long slope out of the valley en route to Colorado. As to whether someone with a shotgun was waiting in the trailer, Chee could think of no safe way to answer that question. He'd left the door locked, but the lock would be easy to pick. He slipped the pistol out of its holster again, thinking that this was a hell of a way to live, thinking that he might give up on the trailer, walk back to the station, get his patrol car, and spend the night in a motel, thinking that he might just say to hell with it and walk up to the door, pistol cocked, and unlock it, and go in. Then he remembered the cat.

The cat was probably out hunting the nocturnal rodents it had lived on until Chee began supplementing its diet with his table scraps. But maybe not. Maybe it was still a little early for rodents and the predators that hunt them. More than once when he had risen early he'd seen Cat returning to its den about dawn. So perhaps it slept early and hunted late. The juniper under which Cat made its home was along the slope to Chee's left. He picked up a handful of dirt and gravel and threw it into the bush.

Later, he thought that the cat must have been crouched, alert, under the juniper listening to his prowling. It shot from the bush, moving almost too fast to be seen in the poor light for its refuge in the trailer. He heard the *clack-clack* of the cat door. He relaxed. No one would be waiting for him inside.

But now he knew he couldn't sleep in the trailer. He got out his sleeping bag, packed his toothbrush and a change of clothing, and walked back to the police station. He was tired now, and the incident of the cat had broken the tension. The fear that had lived in his truck was gone now. It was simply a friendly, familiar vehicle. He unlocked the door, climbed in, and started the engine. He drove across the San Juan and then west on 504, with the dark shape of the Chuskas looming in the moonlight to the south. Just past Behclahbeto, he pulled onto the shoulder, turned off his lights, and waited. The car lights he'd noticed miles behind him turned out to belong to a U-Haul truck, which roared past him and disappeared over the hill. He restarted his engine and turned onto a dirt road that jolted through the dusty sagebrush and dipped into an arroyo. Up the arroyo, he parked and rolled out his sleeping bag. He lay on his back, looking up at the stars, thinking about the nature of fear and how it affected him, and about what Iron Woman had told him of the bone being found in Dugai Endocheeney. It could be false, one of those witch rumors that spring up like tumbleweeds after rain when bad things happen. Or it could be true. Perhaps someone thought he had been witched by Endocheeney, and had killed him and returned the bone of corpse poison to reverse the witching. Or it could be that a witch had killed

Dugai Endocheeney and left the bone as its marker. In either case, how would the people at Badwater Wash have learned of it? Chee considered that and found an answer. The bone would have shown up in the autopsy. The surgeon would have seen it only as a piece of foreign matter lodged in the wound. But it was odd, and he would have mentioned it. The word would have spread. A Navajo would have heard it—a nurse, an orderly. To a Navajo, any Navajo, the significance would have been apparent. The word of the bone would have reached Badwater Wash with the speed of light.

So why hadn't he mentioned the bone gossip to the lieutenant who insisted on knowing every detail? Chee examined his motives. It was too vague to mention, he thought, but the real reason was his expectation of Leaphorn's reaction to anything associated with witchery. Ah, well, perhaps he would mention it to Leaphorn the next time he saw him.

Chee rolled onto his side, seeking comfort and sleep. Tomorrow he would go to the Farmington jail, where Roosevelt Bistie was being held until the federals could decide what to do with him. He would try to get Bistie to talk about witchcraft.

9

"I THINK YOU'RE TOO LATE," the officer on the jail information desk telephone said. "I think his lawyer's coming to get him."

"Lawyer?" Chee asked. "Who?"

"Somebody from DNA," the deputy said. "Some woman. She's driving over from Shiprock."

"So am I," Chee said, checking his memory for the name to go with the deputy's voice, and finding it. "Listen, Fritz, if she gets there first, maybe you could stall around a little. Take some time getting him checked out."

"Maybe so, Jim," Fritz said. "Sometimes people say we're slow. Can you be here by nine?"

Chee glanced at his watch. "Sure," he said.

From the police station in Shiprock to the jail in Farmington is about thirty miles. While he drove it, Chee considered how he would deal with the lawyer, or try to deal with her. DNA was the popular acronym for Dinebeiina Nahiilna be Agaditahe, which translates roughly into "People Who Talk Fast and Help the People Out," and which was the Navajo Nation's version of Legal Aid Society/public defender organization. Earlier in its career it had attracted mostly young militant social activists whose relationship with the Navajo Tribal Police had ranged from icy to hostile. Things had improved gradually. Now, generally, the iciness had modified to coolness, and the hostility to suspicion. Chee expected no trouble.

However . . .

The young woman in the white silk shirt sitting against the wall in the D Center reception room was looking at him with something stronger than suspicion. She was small, skinny, a Navajo, with short black hair and large angry black eyes. Her expression, if not hostile, showed active distaste.

"You're Chee," she said, "the arresting officer?"

"Jim Chee," Chee said, checking his reflex offer of a handshake in midmotion. "Not the arresting officer, technically. The federal—"

"I know that," said Silk Shirt, getting to her feet with a graceful motion. "Did Agent Kennedy explain to you . . . did Agent Kennedy explain to Mr. Bistie . . . that a citizen, even a Navajo citizen, has a right to consult with an attorney before he undergoes a cross-examination?"

"We read him—"

"And do you know," Silk Shirt asked, forming each word with icy precision, "that you have absolutely no legal right to hold Mr. Bistie here in this jail with no charge against him whatsoever, and knowing that he didn't commit the homicide you arrested him for, just because you 'want to talk to him'?"

"He's being held for investigation," Chee said, aware that his face was flushed, aware that Officer Fritz Langer of the Farmington Police Department was standing there behind the reception desk, watching all this. Chee shifted his position. From the corner of his eye he could see Langer was not only listening, he was grinning. "He admitted taking a shot—"

"Without advice of counsel," Silk Shirt said. "And now, just at your request and without any legal grounds at all, Mr. Bistie is being held here by the police while you take your time driving over from Shiprock so you can talk to him. Just a favor from one good old boy to another."

The grin disappeared from Langer's face. "The paperwork," he said. "It takes time when the federals are involved."

"Paperwork, my butt," Silk Shirt snapped. "It's the good old boy network at work." She pointed a thumb in Chee's direction, something one polite Navajo did not do to another. "Your buddy here calls you and says keep him locked up until I can get around to talking to him. Stall around all day if you have to."

"Naw," Langer said. "Nothing like that. You know how the Federal Bureau of Investigation is about crossing all the *t*'s and dotting the *i*'s."

"Well, Mr. Chee is here now. Can you get the *i* dotted and release Mr. Bistie?"

Langer made a wry face at Chee, lifted the telephone, and talked to someone. "He'll be out in a minute," he said. He reached under the counter, extracted a brown paper grocery bag, and put it on the countertop. It bore the legend R. BISTIE, WEST WING in red Magic Marker. Chee felt a yearning to explore that paper sack. He should have thought of it earlier. Much earlier. Before Silk Shirt arrived. He smiled at Silk Shirt.

"All I need is just a few minutes. Just some information."

"About what?"

"Well," Chee said, "if we knew why Bistie wanted to kill Endocheeney—and he says he wanted to kill him," he inserted hastily, "then maybe we'd know more about why someone else did kill Endocheeney. Stabbed Endocheeney. Later."

"Make an appointment," Silk Shirt said. "Maybe he'll want to talk to you." She paused, looking at Chee. "And maybe he won't."

"I guess we could pick him up again," Chee said. "As a material witness. Something like that."

"I guess you could," she said. "But it better be legal this time. Now he'll be represented by someone who understands that even a Navajo has some constitutional rights."

Roosevelt Bistie came through the door, trailed by an elderly jailer. The jailer patted him on the shoulder. "Come see us," he said, and disappeared back through the doorway.

"Mr. Bistie," Silk Shirt said. "I am Janet Pete. We were told you needed legal counsel and the DNA sent me over to represent you. To be your lawyer."

Bistie nodded to her. *"Ya-tah-hey,"* he said. He looked at Chee. Nodded. Smiled. "I don't need no lawyer," he said. "They told me somebody else killed the son-of-a-bitch. I missed him." Bistie chuckled when he said it, but to Chee he still looked sick.

"You need a lawyer to tell you to be careful what you say," Janet Pete said, glancing at Chee. And then, to Langer: "And we need a place where my client and I can talk. In private."

"Sure," Langer said. He handed Bistie the sack and pointed. "Down the hall. First door to the left."

"Miss Pete," Chee said. "When you're talking to your client, would you ask him if I can talk to him for a minute or two? Otherwise . . ."

"Otherwise what?"

"Otherwise I'll have to drive all the way up into the Lukachukais to his place and talk to him there," Chee said meekly. "And just to ask three or four questions I forgot to ask him earlier."

"I'll see," Janet Pete said, and disappeared down the hall after Bistie.

Chee looked out the window. The lawn needed water. What was it about white men that caused them to plant grass in places where grass couldn't possibly grow without them fiddling with it all the time? Chee had thought about that a lot, and talked to Mary Landon about it. He'd told Mary he thought it represented a subconscious need to remind themselves that they could defy nature. Mary said no, it wasn't need for remembered beauty. Chee looked at the lawn, and at the desert country visible across the San Juan beyond it. He preferred the desert. Today even the fringe of tumbleweeds along the sidewalk looked wilted. Dry heat everywhere and the sky almost cloudless.

"I didn't tell her you'd asked me to stall," Langer said, apologetically. "She figured that out for herself."

"Oh, well," Chee said. "I don't think she likes cops, anyway." A thought materialized abruptly. "You remember what was in Bistie's sack?"

Langer looked surprised at the question. He shrugged. "Usual stuff. Billfold. Keys to his truck. Pocket knife. One of those little deerskin sacks some of you guys carry. Handkerchief. Nothing unusual."

"Did you look in the billfold?"

"We have to inventory the money," Langer said. He sorted through papers on a clipboard. "Had a ten and three ones and seventy-three cents in change. Driver's license. So forth."

"Anything else you remember?"

"I didn't check him in," Langer said. "Al did. On the evening shift. Says here: 'Nothing else of value.'"

Chee nodded.

"What you looking for?"

"Just fishing," Chee said.

"Speaking of which," Langer said, "can you get a permit for fishing up there at Wheatfields Lake? Free, I mean."

"Well," Chee said. "I guess you know—"

Janet Pete appeared at the hall door. "He says he'll talk to you."

"I thank you," Chee said.

The room held a bare wooden table and two chairs. Roosevelt Bistie sat in one of them, eyes half closed, face sagging. But he returned Chee's salutation. Chee put his hand on the back of the other chair, glanced at Janet Pete. She was leaning against the wall behind Bistie, watching Chee. The paper sack was under Bistie's chair.

"Could we talk in private?" Chee asked her.

"I'm Mr. Bistie's legal counsel," she said. "I'll stay."

Chee sat down, feeling defeated. It had never been likely that Bistie would talk. He hadn't, after all, in the past. It was even less likely that he would talk about the subject Chee intended to raise, which was witchcraft. There was a simple enough reason for that. Witches hated to be talked about—to even have their evil business discussed. Therefore the prudent Navajo discussed witchcraft, if at all, only with those known and trusted. Not with a stranger. Certainly not with two strangers. However, there was no harm in trying.

"I have heard something which I think you would like to know," Chee said. "I will tell you what I heard. And then I will ask you a question. I hope you will give me an answer. But if you won't, you won't."

Bistie looked interested. So did Janet Pete.

"First," Chee said, speaking slowly, intent on Bistie's expression, "I will tell you what the people over at the Badwater Wash Trading Post hear. They hear that a little piece of bone was found in the body of that man you took a shot at."

There was a lag of a second or two. Then Bistie smiled a very slight smile. He nodded at Chee.

Chee glanced at Janet Pete. She looked puzzled. "Understand that I do not know if this is true," Chee said. "I will go to the hospital where the body of that man was taken and I will try to find out if it was true. Should I tell you what I find out?"

No smile now. Bistie was studying Chee's face. But he nodded.

"Now I have a question for you to answer. Do you have a little piece of bone?"

Bistie stared at Chee, face blank.

"Don't answer that," Janet Pete said. "Not until I find out what's going on here." She frowned at Chee. "What's this all about? It sounds like an attempt to get Mr. Bistie to incriminate himself. What are you driving at?"

"We know Mr. Bistie didn't kill Endocheeney," Chee said. "Somebody else killed him. We don't know who. We aren't likely to find out who until we know why. Mr. Bistie here seems to have had a good reason to kill Endocheeney, because he tried to do it. Maybe it was the same reason. Maybe it was because Endocheeney was a skinwalker. Maybe he witched Mr. Bistie. Put the witch bone into him. Maybe Endocheeney witched somebody else. If what I heard at Badwater Wash isn't just gossip, maybe Mr. Endocheeney had a bone put in him because that other person, the one who knifed Endocheeney, put it in him when he stabbed Endocheeney to turn the witching around." Chee was talking directly to Janet Pete, but he was watching Bistie from the corner of his eye. If Bistie's face revealed any emotion, it was satisfaction.

"It sounds like nonsense to me," Janet Pete said.

"Would you recommend to your client that he answer my question, then?" Chee asked. "Did he believe Mr. Endocheeney was a witch?"

"I'll talk to him about this," she said. "There are no charges against him. None. He's not accused of anything. You're just holding him to satisfy your curiosity."

"About a murder," Chee said. "And there may be a charge filed by now. Attempted homicide."

"Based on what?" Janet Pete asked. "On what he told you and Kennedy before consulting with his attorney? That's absolutely all you have."

"That, and some other stuff," Chee said. "Witnesses who put him where it happened. His license number. The ejected shell from his rifle." Which, as far as Chee knew, hadn't been found and wasn't being looked for. Why look for a shell casing from a shot that missed when they had a butcher knife, which didn't miss? But Janet Pete wouldn't know they hadn't found it.

"I don't think there's any basis for charges," Janet Pete said.

Chee shrugged. "It's not up to me. I think Kennedy—"

"I think I will call Kennedy," Janet Pete said. "Because I don't believe you." She walked to the door, stopped with her hand on the knob, smiled at Chee. "Are you coming?"

"I'll just wait," Chee said.

"Then my client is coming," she said. She motioned to Bistie. He got up, steadied himself with a hand on the tabletop.

"This interview is over," Janet Pete said, and she closed the door behind them.

Chee waited. Then he went to the door and glanced down the hall. Janet Pete was using the telephone in the pay booth. Chee closed the door again, picked up Bistie's sack, sorted quickly through it. Nothing interesting. He extracted Bistie's billfold.

In it, in the corner of the currency pocket that held a ten and three ones, Chee found a bead. He turned it over between thumb and first finger, examining it. Then he put it back where he had found it, put the wallet back in the sack, and the sack back on the floor under Bistie's chair. The bead seemed to be made of bone. In fact, it looked exactly like the one he'd found on the floor of his trailer.

10

THE TURBULENCE CAUSED BY THE THUNDERHEAD was sweeping across the valley floor toward them. It kicked up an opaque gray-white wall of dust which obscured the distant shape of Black Mesa and spawned dust devils in the caliche flats south of them. They were standing, Officer Al Gorman and Joe Leaphorn, beside Gorman's patrol car on the track that led across the sage-brush flats below Sege Butte toward Chilchinbito Canyon.

"Right here," Gorman said. "Here's where he parked his car, or pickup, or whatever."

Leaphorn nodded. Gorman was sweating. A trickle of it ran down his neck and under his shirt collar. It was partly the heat, and partly that Gorman should lose a few pounds, and partly, Leaphorn knew, because he made Gorman nervous.

"Tracks lead right back here." Gorman pointed. "From over there near the rim of Chilchinbito Canyon, where he killed Sam, and down that slope there, where the shale outcrops are, and then across the sagebrush right up to here."

Leaphorn grunted. He was watching the dust storm moving down the valley with its outrider of whirlwinds. One of them had crossed a gypsum sink, and its winds had sucked up that heavier mineral. The cone changed from the yellow-gray of the dusty earth to almost pure white. It was the sort of thing Emma would have noticed, and found beauty in, and related in some way or other to the mythology of The People. Emma would have said something about the Blue Flint Boys playing their games. They were the *yei* personalities credited with stirring up whirlwinds. He would de-scribe it to her tonight. He would if she was awake and aware—and not in that vague world she now so often retreated into.

Beside him, Gorman was describing the sign he had followed from killing scene to car, and the sign the car had left, and his conclusion that the killer had raced away. "Spun his wheels in the grass," Gorman was saying. "Tore it up. Threw dirt. And then, right down there, he backed around and drove on back toward the road."

"Where was the killing?"

"See that little bunch of juniper? Look across the shale slope, and then to the right. That man . . ." Gorman stopped, glanced at Leaphorn for a reading of whether the lieutenant would allow him to avoid "wearing out the name" of a dead man. He made his decision and restated the sentence. "That's where Wilson Sam was, by the juniper. Looked like it was a regular stopping place for him when he was out with the sheep. And the killer got him about twenty-five, thirty yards to the right of those junipers."

"Looks like he took sort of a roundabout way to get back here, then," Leaphorn said. "If he circled all the way around and came down that shale."

"Looks that way," Gorman said. "But it's not. It fools you. You can't see it from here because of the way the land folds, but if you try to go straight across, then over that ridge there—the ridge that shale is in—over that there's an arroyo. Cut deep. To get across it you got to skirt way up, or way down, where there's sheep crossing. So the short way—"

Leaphorn interrupted him. "Did he go the same way he came back?"

Gorman looked puzzled.

Leaphorn rephrased the question, partly to clarify his own thinking. "When he drove along here, we'll say he was looking for Sam. Hunting him. He sees Sam, or maybe just the flock of sheep Sam was watching, over there across the flats by the junipers. This is as close as he can get a vehicle. So he parks here. Gets out. Heads for Sam. You say the fastest way to get there is angling way to the right, and then up that shale slope over there, and across the ridge, and then across an arroyo at a sheep crossing, and then swing left again. Long way around, but quickest. And that's the way he came back. But is that the way he went?"

"Sure," Gorman said. "I guess so. I didn't notice. I wasn't looking for that. Just tracking him to see where he went."

"Let's see if we can find out," Leaphorn said. It wouldn't be easy, but for the first time since he'd awakened that morning, with the homicides instantly on his mind, he felt a stirring of hope. This might be a way to learn whether or not the person who'd killed

Wilson Sam was a stranger to Sam's territory. Small though that would be, it would satisfy Leaphorn's quota for this unpromising day.

Leaphorn had given himself the quota as he'd eaten his breakfast: Before the day was done, he would add one single hard fact to what he knew about his unsolved homicides. He'd eaten a bowl of cornmeal mush, a piece of Emma's fried bread, and some salami from the refrigerator. Emma, who for all the almost thirty years of their marriage had risen with the dawn, was still asleep. He'd dressed quietly, careful not to disturb her.

She'd lost weight, he thought. Not eating. Before Agnes had come to help, she would simply forget to eat when he wasn't home. He would make her a lunch before he left for the office and find it untouched when he came home at the end of the day. Now she would sometimes forget to eat even when the food was on her plate in front of her. "Emma," he would say. "Eat." And she would look at him with that embarrassed, confused, disoriented smile and say, "It's good, but I forget." He had looked down at her as he buttoned his shirt, seeing an unaccustomed hollowness below the cheekbones, under the eyes. When he was away from her, her face would always have the same smooth roundness he'd noticed that day he first saw her—walking with two other Navajo girls across the campus at Arizona State.

Arizona State. His mother had buried his umbilical cord at the roots of a piñon beside their hogan—the traditional Navajo ritual for binding a child to his family and his people. But for Leaphorn, Emma was the tie. A simple physical law. Emma could not be happy away from the Sacred Mountains. He could not be happy away from Emma. He had frowned down at her, studying her, seeing the flatness of her cheek, the lines under her eyes and at the corners of her mouth. ("I'm feeling fine," she would say. "I never felt better. You must not have any work to do down at the police to be worrying about me all the time.") But now she would admit the headaches. And there was no way she could hide the forgetfulness, nor those odd blank moments when she seemed to be awakening, confused, from some bad dream. Day after tomorrow was the appointment. At 2 P.M. They would leave early, and drive to Gallup, and check her in at the Indian Health Service hospital. And then they would find out. Now there was no reason to think about it, about what it might be. No reason to let his mind reexamine again and again and again all he had heard and read of the horrors of Alzheimer's disease. Maybe it wasn't that. But he knew it was. He'd called the toll-free number of the Alzheimer's Disease and Related Disorders Association, and they had sent him a package of information.

> . . . initially a patient with AD exhibits the following symptoms:
> 1. Forgetfulness.
> 2. Impairment of judgment.
> 3. Inability to handle routine tasks.
> 4. Lack of spontaneity.
> 5. Lessening of initiative.
> 6. Disorientation of time and place.
> 7. Depression and terror.
> 8. Disturbance of language.
> 9. Episodic confusional states.

He had read it in the office, checking them off. The suddenly faltering unfinished sentences, the business of always thinking today was his day off, the lethargy, the trouble with getting the garbage bag installed in the garbage can, the preparation for Agnes's arrival two days after Agnes had arrived. Worst of all, his awakening in the night to find Emma clutching at him, frantic with some nightmare fear. He had, as was his fashion, made notes in the margin. Emma had scored nine for nine.

Leaphorn had every reason to think of something else.

And so that morning he had thought, first, of Irma Onesalt's list of the dead, and why death dates would be important to her. As he left Emma still sleeping he heard Agnes stirring in her room. He drove to his office in the clear, sunrise light of another day of heat and drought. Dust was already rising from the rodeo grounds down at the highway intersection—the dust of stock feeding. Sometime today he would think of the rodeo and the myriad of problems it always brought. Now he wanted to think of his homicides.

At the office, he composed a letter to go to the various county health departments in Arizona, New Mexico, and Utah that would have been contacted by Onesalt if she followed the advice of Dr. Randall Jenks. It was too complicated, and too sensitive, to be handled by the half-dozen telephone calls it would require. And there was no real urgency. So he put the letter together—very carefully. He explained who he was, explained that the investigation of the murder of Irma Onesalt was involved, described the list as best he could, trying to recall for them the question she might have asked.

Finally, with these needed preliminaries out of the way, he inquired if anyone in the department had received a letter or a telephone call from Ms. Onesalt concerning these names, asking death dates. If so, could he have a copy of the letter, or the name of the person who had handled the telephone call, so he could question that person more closely.

He wrote a clean copy of the final draft and a cover memo for the clerk, listing to whom copies should be sent. That done, he considered what Jenks had told him about Chee's bone bead. It was made of cow bone. A witch, if one believed bona fide witches existed, would have used human bone, presuming the bona fide witch believed Navajo witchcraft mythology in a literal meaning. So if a real witch was involved, presuming such existed, said witch had been swindled by his bone supplier. On the other hand, if someone was merely pretending to be a witch, such things didn't matter. Those who believed witches magically blew bone particles into their victims would hardly subject said bone to the microscope. And of course, cow-bone beads would be easy to get. Or would they? It seemed likely. Every slaughterhouse would produce mountains of cattle bones. Raw material for mass producing beads for the costume jewelry market. Leaphorn found his thought process leading him into the economics of producing bone beads as opposed to molding plastic beads. Chee's bone beads would certainly be old, something from old jewelry, or perhaps clothing. Jenks had said the bead was fairly old. Perhaps the FBI, with its infinite resources, could track down the source. But he couldn't imagine how. He tried to imagine Delbert Streib phrasing the memo about corpse poison and witches to touch off such an effort. Streib would simply laugh at the idea.

Leaphorn wrote another memo, instructing Officer Jimmy Tso, who handled liaison with the Gallup police department, to check suppliers for jewelry makers, pawnshops, and wherever else he could think of, to learn how a Navajo/Zuni/Hopi jewelry maker might obtain beads, and particularly bone beads. He dropped that memo in his out-basket atop the drafted letter. Then he extracted his homicide folders from the cabinet, put them on his desk, and looked at them.

He pushed the Onesalt file aside. Onesalt had been the first to die. Something in his instinct told him she was the key, and he knew her file by heart. It baffled him. It seemed as lacking in purpose as death by lightning—as cruel and casual as the malicious mischief of the Holy People. He picked up the file labeled

WILSON SAM, opened it, and read. He saw nothing that he hadn't remembered. But when he'd first read it, he hadn't noticed that the tribal policeman working with Jay Kennedy on this investigation was Officer Al Gorman. The name then had meant nothing to him. It had simply identified a new, probably young, officer whom Leaphorn did not know. Now the name carried with it a visual image.

Leaphorn put the file on the desk and looked out his window at the early morning sunlight on the scattered roofs of Window Rock village. Gorman. The plump cop walking across the Shiprock parking lot with Chee and Benaly. Chee instantly conscious of the parked car, of what car it was, of its occupant, all with hardly a glance. But the walk became a little stiffer, the shoulders a little straighter, knowing he was watched. Benaly becoming aware of Chee's awareness, noticing the car, not being interested. And Gorman, talking, noticing nothing. Oblivious. Blind to everything except the single thought that occupied him. Officer Gorman had never noticed Leaphorn sitting in the shade in his car. If he missed that, what had he missed at the scene of Wilson Sam's death? Maybe nothing, but it was worth checking. To be honest, perhaps he should say it gave him an excuse.

It was nine minutes until eight. In nine minutes his telephone would start ringing. The world of the troublesome rodeo, the Tribal Council meeting, indignant school principals, bootleggers, too few men and too many assignments, would capture him for another day. He looked past the clock at the world outside the window, the highway leading away over the ridge toward everywhere but Window Rock, the world in which his job had once allowed him to pursue his own curiosity and to hell with the paperwork. He picked up the telephone and called the Shiprock station. He asked for Officer Al Gorman.

Now it was early afternoon. Gorman had met him, as requested, at the Mexican Water Trading Post. They'd made the bone-jarring drive back into the Chilchinbito Canyon country. Rather quickly, Officer Gorman had proved he was the sort of man who—as Leaphorn's grandmother would have said—counted the grass and didn't see the grazing.

Gorman was sitting now in Leaphorn's car, waiting (uneasily, Leaphorn hoped) for Leaphorn to finish whatever the hell Leaphorn was doing. What Leaphorn was doing was looking past the grass at the grazing. They had established by two hours of dusty work that the route the killer had taken to reach the growth of junipers where Wilson Sam was waiting was very different from his return route. Broken twigs here, dislodged rocks there, a footprint sheltered enough to survive two months of rainless days, showed them that he had headed in an almost straight line through the sagebrush toward the junipers. He had crossed the ridge, maintaining that direction except when heavy brush forced a detour, until he reached the arroyo. He had walked down its bank perhaps a hundred yards, presumably looking for a crossing point. Then he had reversed direction almost a quarter mile, to cross at a sheep trail—the same trail he'd used on his return trip.

Leaphorn spent the remainder of the morning having Gorman shown him just what he had found, and where he had found it, when Gorman had worked this scene for Kennedy early in the summer. Gorman had shown him where Wilson Sam's body had been found on the bottom of the narrow wash draining into Chilchinbito. He had pointed out the remains of the little rock slides that showed Sam had been tumbled down from above. The rainless summer had left the sign pretty much undisturbed. Ants had carried away most of the congealed blood from the sand where the body had lain, but you could still find traces. In this protected bottom, the winds had only smoothed the tracks of those who had come to carry Sam away.

Above, the scouring had been more complete. Gorman had shown Leaphorn where Sam had been and where the killer had come from. "Easy enough to tell 'em apart," Gorman said. "The ground was softer then. Sam had boots on. Flat heels. Easy to match them with his tracks. And the other fellow had on cowboy boots." He glanced at Leaphorn. "Bigger. Maybe size eleven."

All that had been in Kennedy's report. So had the answer to the question Leaphorn had decided to ask. But he wanted to hear it for himself.

"And they didn't stand and talk at all? No sign of that?"

"No, sir," Gorman said. "No sign of that. When I tracked the suspect back, it showed he started running about forty yards out there." Gorman had pointed into the sparse sagebrush to the south. "No more heel prints. He was running."

"And Sam? Where did he start running away?"

Gorman showed him. Sam had not run far. Perhaps twenty-five yards. Old men are poor runners, even when they are running for their life.

Back at the car, Leaphorn stood where the killer had parked and stared across the broken landscape toward the junipers where this person must have seen Sam, or Sam's sheep. He stood with his lower lip held between his teeth, nibbling thoughtfully, trying to recreate what the killer must have been thinking, retracing with his eyes the route the man had taken.

"Let's make sure we agree—that I'm not overlooking anything," Leaphorn said. "He's driving along here. He sees Sam, or maybe Sam's flock, over there by the junipers. He parks. He heads directly toward Sam." Leaphorn glanced at Gorman, saw no sign of disagreement. "In a hurry, I'd say, because of the way he crashed through the sagebrush. He didn't know the arroyo was there behind the ridge, and couldn't get across it there, so he had to skirt upstream to where the banks get lower."

"Not too smart," Gorman said.

"Could be that," Leaphorn said, although being smart had nothing to do with it. "And when he got close to Sam he was in such a hurry to kill him that he started running. Right?"

"I'd say so," Gorman said.

"Why did Sam start running?"

"Scared," Gorman said. "Maybe the guy was yelling at him. Or waving that shovel he killed him with."

"Yeah," Leaphorn said. "That's what I'd guess. When we catch him, who do you think it will turn out to be?"

Gorman shrugged. "No way of telling," he said. "It'd be a man. Big, man-sized feet. Probably some kinfolks or other." He looked at Leaphorn, smiling slightly. "You know how it is. It's always some sort of fight with some of his wife's folks, or some fight with some neighbor over where he's grazing his sheep. That's the way it always is."

It was, in fact, the way it always was. But this time it wasn't. "Think about him not knowing the arroyo was there. Not knowing where to find the sheep crossing," Leaphorn said. "That tell you anything?"

Gorman's pleasant round face looked puzzled. He thought. "I didn't think about that," he said. "I guess it wasn't a neighbor. Anybody lives around here, they'd know how the land lays. How it drains."

"So our man was a stranger."

"Yeah," Gorman said. "That's funny. Think it will help any?"

Leaphorn shrugged. He couldn't see how. It did form a sort of crazy harmony with the Endocheeney affair. Bistie and Endocheeney seemed to have been strangers. What did that mean? But he'd met his quota. He'd added one fact to his homicide data. Wilson Sam had been killed by a stranger.

11

AFTER MANY PAINSTAKING RECONSIDERATIONS, Jim Chee
finally decided he didn't know what the hell to do about the bone
bead in Roosevelt Bistie's billfold. He had walked out of the visiting
room and closed the door behind him, leaving Bistie's paper sack
of belongings on the floor beside the chair, exactly where Bistie
had put it. Then he stood by the door, looking at Bistie with a
curiosity intensified by the thought that Bistie had tried to blast
him out of bed with a shotgun. Bistie was sitting on the hard bench
against the wall looking out of the window at something, his face
in profile to Chee. Chee memorized him. A witch? Why had this
man fired the shotgun through the skin of his trailer? He looked no
different from any other human, of course. None of those special
characteristics that the white culture sometimes gives its witches.
No pointy nose, sharp features, broomstick. Just another man
whose malice had led him to try to kill. To shoot Dugai Endocheeney, a stranger, on the roof of his hogan. To shoot Jim Chee,
another stranger, asleep in his bed. To butcher Wilson Sam amid
his sheep. As Bistie sat now, slumped on the bench, Chee had no
luck relating his shape to the shape he had seen, or dreamed he
had seen, in the darkness outside his trailer. His only impression
had been that the shape had been small. Bistie seemed a little
larger than the remembered shape. Could Bistie actually be the
man?

Bistie lost interest in whatever he'd been watching through
the window and glanced down the hall toward Chee. Their eyes
met. Chee read nothing in Bistie's expression except a mild and
guarded interest. Then the door of the phone booth pushed open
and Janet Pete emerged. Chee walked down the hall, away from

her, and out the exit into the parking lot and to his car, away from all the impulsive actions his instinct urged. He wanted to rearrest Bistie. He wanted to take the wallet and confront Bistie—in front of witnesses—with the bone bead. He wanted to make Bistie's possession of the bone a matter of record. But keeping a bone bead in one's billfold was legal enough. And Chee had absolutely no right to know it was there. He'd found it in an illegal search. There was a law against that. But not against bone possession or—for that matter—against being a skinwalker.

Having thought of nothing he could do, he sat in his car waiting for Pete and Bistie to emerge. Maybe they would leave without Bistie's sack. Simply forget it. If that happened, he would go to the jail, tell Langer that Bistie had left his belongings behind, get Langer to make another, more complete inventory, which would include all the billfold's contents. But when Pete and Bistie emerged, Bistie had the sack clutched in his hand. They drove out of the jail lot, turning toward Farmington. Chee turned west, toward Shiprock.

His mind worked on it as he drove. Reason told him that Bistie might not have been the shape in the darkness that had fired the shotgun into his trailer. Bistie had used the 30-30 on the rack across the back window of his pickup to shoot at Endocheeney. Or said he did. Not a shotgun. There had been no reason to search Bistie's place for a shotgun. Maybe he didn't have one. And the complex mythology of Navajo witchcraft, which Chee knew as well as any man, usually attached a motive to the malice of the skinwalkers. Bistie had no conceivable motive for wanting to kill Chee. Perhaps Bistie was not the one who had tried to kill him.

But even as he thought this, he was aware that his spirit was light again. The dread had lifted. He was not afraid of Bistie, as he had been afraid of the unknown. He felt an urge to sing.

The in-basket on his desk held two envelopes and one of the While You Were Out memos the tribal police used to record notes and telephone calls. One envelope, Chee noticed with instant delight, was the pale blue of Mary Landon's stationery. He put it in his shirt pocket and looked at the other one. It was addressed to Officer Chee, Police Station, Shiprock, in clumsy letters formed with a pencil. Chee glanced at the telephone memo, which said merely: "Call Lt. Leaphorn immediately," and tore open the envelope.

The folded letter inside had been written on the pulpy lined tablet paper schoolchildren use, in the format students are taught in grade school.

In the block where one is taught to put one's return address, the writer had printed:

> Alice Yazzie
> Sheep Springs Trading Post
> Navajo Nation 92927

Dear Nephew Jim Chee:

I hope you are well. I am well. I write you this letter because your Uncle Frazier Denetsone is sick all this summer and worst sick about this month. We took him to the Crystal Gazer over at the Badwater Clinic and the Crystal Gazer said he should let the belagana doctor there give him some medicine. He is taking that green medicine now but he is still sick. The Crystal Gazer said he should take that medicine but that he needs a sing too. That will get him better faster, having the sing. And the sing should be a Blessing Way. I heard that you did the Blessing Way sing for the Niece of Old Grandmother Nez and everybody said it was good. Everybody said you got it all right and the dry paintings were right. They said the Niece of Old Grandmother Nez got better after that.

We want you to talk about it. We want you to come to the place of Hildegarde Goldtooth and we will talk to you about having the sing. We have about $400 but maybe there could be more.

Chee read with intense satisfaction. The Blessing Way he had conducted last spring had been his first job as a *hataalii*. And his last. The niece of Old Grandmother Nez was a niece by the broad Navajo definition—the daughter of a first cousin on the maternal side of Chee's family—and hiring him as singer had been family courtesy. In fact, the event had been a trial balloon—as much to inform the north central slice of the Big Reservation that Chee had begun his practice as to cure the girl of nothing more serious than the malaise of being sixteen.

Now, finally, a summons had come. Alice Yazzie called him nephew, but the title here reflected good manners and not ties of either clan or family. Frazier Denetsone was probably some sort of uncle, as Navajos defined such things, through linkage with his father's paternal clan. But a call for a *hataalii* didn't come from the patient. It came from whoever in the patient's circle of family took responsibility for such things. Chee glanced at Alice Yazzie's signature, which included, in the custom of old-fashioned Navajos, her clan. Streams Come Together Dinee. Chee was born to the Slow Talking People, and for the Salt Clan. No connections with the Streams Clan. Thus her invitation was the first clue that Jim Chee was becoming accepted as a singer outside his own kinfolk.

He finished the letter. Alice Yazzie wanted him to come to Hildegarde Goldtooth's place the next Sunday evening, when she and the patient's wife and mother could be there to work out a time for the ceremony. "We want to hold it as soon as we can because he is not good. He is not going to last long, I think."

That pessimistic note diminished Chee's jubilation. It was much better for a *hataalii* to begin his career with a visible cure—with a ceremony that not only restored the patient to harmony with his universe but also returned him to health. But Chee would tolerate nothing negative today. It would be better still to effect a cure on a hopeless case. If Frazier Denetsone's illness was indeed subject to correction by the powers evoked by the Blessing Way ritual, if Jim Chee was good enough to perform it precisely right, then all things were possible. Chee believed in penicillin and insulin and heart bypass surgery. But he also believed that something far beyond the understanding of modern medicine controlled life and death. He folded Alice Yazzie's letter into his shirt pocket. With his thumbnail he opened the letter from Mary Landon.

Dearest Jim:

I think of you every day (and even more every night). Miss you terribly. Can't you get some more leave and come back here for a while? I could tell you didn't enjoy yourself on your visit in May, but now we are having our annual two weeks of what passes for summer in Wisconsin. Everything is beautiful. It hasn't rained for two or three hours. You would like it now. In fact, I think you could learn to love it—to live somewhere away from the desert—if you would give it a chance.

Dad and I drove down to Madison last week and talked to an adviser in the College of Arts and Sciences. I will be able to get my master's degree—with a little luck—in just two more semesters because of those two graduate courses I took when I was an undergraduate. Also found a cute efficiency apartment within walking distance of the university and picked up the application papers for graduate admission. I can start taking classes on nondegree status while they process the grad school admission. The adviser said there shouldn't be any problem.

Classes will start the first week of September, which means that, if I enroll, I won't have time to come back out to see you until semester break, which I think is about Thanksgiving. I'm going to hate not seeing you until then, so try to find a way to come. . . .

Chee read the rest of it without much sense of what the words meant. Some chat about something that had happened when he'd visited her in Stevens Point, a couple of sentences about her mother. Her father (who had been painfully polite and had asked Chee endless questions about the Navajo religion and had looked at him as Chee thought Chee might look at a man from another planet) was well and thinking about retirement. She was excited about the thought of returning to school. Probably she would do it. There were more personal notes too, tender and nostalgic.

He read the letter again, slowly this time. But that changed nothing. He felt a numbness—a lack of emotion that surprised him. What did surprise him, oddly, he thought, was that he wasn't surprised. At some subconscious level he seemed to have been expecting this. It had been inevitable since Mary had arranged the leave from the teaching job at Crownpoint. If he hadn't known it then, he must have learned it during that visit to her home—which had left him on the flight back to Albuquerque trying to analyze feelings that were a mixture of happiness and sorrow. He glanced at the opening salutation again. "Dearest Jim . . ." The notes she'd sent him from Crownpoint had opened with "Darling . . ."

He stuffed the letter into his pocket with the Yazzie letter and picked up the memo.

It still said: "Call Lt. Leaphorn immediately."

He called Lt. Leaphorn.

12

THE TELEPHONE ON Joe Leaphorn's desk buzzed.

"Who is it?"

"Jim Chee from Shiprock," the switchboard said.

"Tell him to hold it a minute," Leaphorn said. He knew what to learn from Chee, but he took a moment to reconsider exactly how he'd go about asking the questions. He held the receiver lightly in his palm, going over it.

"Okay," he said. "Put him on."

Something clicked.

"This is Leaphorn," Leaphorn said.

"Jim Chee. Returning your call."

"Do you know any of the people who live out there around Chilchinbito Canyon. Out there where Wilson Sam lived?"

"Let me think," Chee said. Silence. "No. I don't think so."

"You ever worked anything out there? Enough to be familiar with the territory?"

"Not really," Chee said. "Not my part of the reservation."

"How about the country around Badwater Wash? Around where Endocheeney lived?"

"A lot better," Chee said. "It's not what Captain Largo has me patrolling, but I spent some time out there trying to find a kid who got washed down the San Juan last year. Several days. And then I handled the Endocheeney business. Went out there twice on that."

"I'm right that Bistie wouldn't say anything about whether he knew Endocheeney?"

"Right. He wouldn't say anything. Except he was glad Endocheeney was dead. He made that plain. So you guess he knew the man."

You do, Leaphorn thought. But maybe you guess wrong.

"Did he say anything that would give you an idea whether he knew that Badwater country? Like about having trouble finding Endocheeney's place? Anything like that?"

"You mean beyond stopping at the trading post to ask directions? He did that."

"That was in Kennedy's report," Leaphorn said. "What I meant was did you hear anything from him, or from the people you talked to at Badwater, that would tell you he was totally strange to that country? Afraid of not finding the road? Getting lost? Anything like that?"

"No." The word was said slowly, indicating the thought wasn't finished. Leaphorn waited. "But I didn't press it. We just got his description, and a make on his truck. Didn't look for that sort of information."

Obviously it wouldn't have seemed to have any meaning at that stage of the game. Perhaps it didn't now. He waited for Chee to make unnecessary excuses. None materialized. Leaphorn began phrasing his next question, but Chee interrupted the thought.

"You know," he said slowly, "I think the fellow who knifed Endocheeney was a stranger too. Didn't know the country."

"Oh?" Leaphorn said. He'd heard Chee was smart. He'd heard right. Chee was saving him his question.

"He came down out of the rocks," Chee said. "Have you seen that Endocheeney place? It's set back from the San Juan maybe a hundred yards. Cliffs to the south of it. The killer came down off of those. And went back the same way to get to where he'd left his car. I spent some time looking around. There were two or three easier ways to get down to Endocheeney. Easier than the way he took."

"So," Leaphorn said, half to himself. "Two strangers show up the same day to kill the same man. What do you think of that?"

There was silence. Through his window Leaphorn watched an unruly squadron of crows flying in from the cottonwoods along Window Rock Ridge toward the village. Lunchtime for crows in the garbage cans. But he wasn't thinking of crows. He was thinking of Chee's intelligence. If he told Chee now that the man who killed Wilson Sam was also a stranger, and how he knew it, Chee would quickly detect the reason for his first question. They had established that Chee, too, was a stranger to Wilson Sam's landscape. They established Leaphorn's suspicions. But to hell with that. A cop who got himself shot at from ambush should expect to be under close scrutiny. Chee might as well. He would tell Chee what he'd learned.

"It's possible," Chee was saying, slowly, "that there weren't two strangers coming to find Endocheeney. Maybe there was just one."

"Ah," said Leaphorn, who had the very same thought.

"It could be," Chee went on, "that Bistie knew he missed Endocheeney when he shot at him on the roof. So he drove away, parked up on the mesa, climbed down, and killed Endocheeney with the knife. And then—"

"He confesses to shooting Endocheeney," Leaphorn concluded. "Pretty smart. Is that what happened?"

Chee sighed. "I don't think so," he said.

Neither did Leaphorn. It violated what he'd learned of people down the years. People who prefer guns don't use knives, and vice versa. Bistie had preferred a rifle. He still had the rifle. Why not use it on the second attempt?

"Why not?" Leaphorn asked.

"Different tracks. I don't think Bistie would have brought along a change of footwear, and what few tracks I found at Endocheeney's didn't match Bistie's boots. Anyway, why would he do that? And why not shoot him on the second attempt? Why use a knife? It gave him an alibi, sure. And fooled us. But think of the advance planning it would take to make it all work out like that. And the things that could go wrong. It doesn't match my impression of Bistie."

"Okay," Leaphorn said. "Do you know anything from talking to Bistie, or from anything, that would suggest that Bistie might have known Wilson Sam?"

"No, sir. Nothing."

"Well, we seem to have another strange situation, then." He told Chee what he'd learned at Chilchinbito Canyon.

"Doesn't make much sense," Chee said. "Does it?"

"That bone bead in your trailer," Leaphorn said. "It turned out to be bovine. Made out of old cow bone."

Chee made a noncommittal sound.

"Anything else happened with you? Anything suspicious?"

"No, sir."

"You learning anything?"

"Well . . ." Chee hesitated. "Nothing much. I heard gossip at Badwater Trading Post. They say a bone was found in Endocheeney's corpse."

Leaphorn exhaled, surprised. "Like he had been witched?"

"Yeah," Chee said. "Or like he'd witched somebody else and they put it back into him."

And this was, in Leaphorn's thinking, the very worst part of a sick tradition—this cruel business of killing a scapegoat when things went wrong. It was what Chee Dodge had railed against when he tried to stamp it out. It was what had made Joe Leaphorn, young then and new to the Navajo Tribal Police, responsible for the deaths of four people. Two men. Two women. Three witches and the man who killed them. He had heard the gossip. He had laughed at it. He had collected the bodies—three murders and a suicide. That was twenty years ago. It had converted Leaphorn's contempt for witchcraft into hatred.

"Nothing about any foreign bone fragment showed up in the autopsy," Leaphorn said. But even as he said it, he knew it wasn't necessarily true. The pathologist might not list—probably wouldn't list—such odds and ends. When the cause of death was so obvious—a butcher knife blade driven repeatedly through clothing into the victim's abdomen and side—why list the threads and buttons, lint and gum wrappers, the blade might drive through the skin?

"I thought it might be worth asking about," Chee said.

"It is," Leaphorn said. "I will."

"Also," Chee said. And then paused.

Leaphorn waited.

"Also, Bistie had a bone bead in his wallet. Just like the one I found in my trailer. Looked like it, anyway."

Leaphorn exhaled again. "He did? What did he say about it?"

"Well, nothing," Chee said. He explained what had happened at the jail. "So I just put it back where I found it."

"I think we better go talk to Bistie again," Leaphorn said. "In fact, I think we better pick him up, and lock him up until we get this sorted out a little better." Leaphorn imagined trying to persuade Dilly to file the complaint. Dilly Streib would be hard to persuade. Dilly had been FBI too long not to care about his batting average. The Agency didn't like cases it didn't win. Still . . .

Leaphorn swiveled in his chair and looked at his map. A line of bone beads now connected two of his dots. And Roosevelt Bistie must know how they connected. And why.

"We can charge him with attempted murder, or attempted assault, or hold him as a material witness."

"Umm," Chee said. A sound full of doubt.

"I'll call the feds," Leaphorn said. He glanced at his watch. "Can you meet me in an hour at . . ." He looked at the map again, picking the most practical halfway point between Window Rock and Shiprock for their drive into the Chuskas. "At Sanostee," he concluded. "Sanostee in an hour?"

"Yes, sir," Chee said. "Sanostee in an hour."

13

SANOSTEE WAS HARDLY A HALFWAY POINT, but it was convenient for where they were going. For Chee it was fast—twenty miles south on the worn pavement of U.S. 666 to Littlewater, and then nine miles westward, into the teeth of the gusting, dusty wind, up the long slope of the Chuska range to the trading post. For Leaphorn it was triple that distance—from Window Rock to Crystal and over Washington Pass to Sheep Springs, then north to the Littlewater intersection. When Leaphorn reached Sanostee it was sundown, the copper-colored twilight of one of those days when the desert sky is translucent with hanging dust.

Chee was sitting under his steering wheel, feet out the door, drinking an orange crush. They left Leaphorn's car and took Chee's. Leaphorn asked questions. Chee drove. They were astute questions, intended to duplicate as much of Chee's memory in Leaphorn's as was possible. At first the focus was on Bistie, on everything he'd said and how he'd said it, and then on Endocheeney, and finally on Janet Pete.

"I had a little mixup with her last year," Leaphorn said. "She thought we'd roughed up a drunk—or said she did."

"Had we?"

Leaphorn glanced at him. "Somebody had. Unless the officer was lying about it, it was somebody else."

The road that wandered northward from Sanostee had been graded once, and graveled at some time in the dim past when this part of the Chuskas had elected an unusually fierce advocate to the Tribal Council. The perpetual cycle of January snows and April thaws had swallowed the gravel long ago, and the highway superintendent for that district had solved the problem by erasing the road from his map. But it was still passable in dry weather and still used by the few families who grazed their sheep in this part of the highlands. Chee drove it carefully, skirting washouts and avoiding its washboard pattern of surface erosion when he could. Sunrays from below the curve of the planet lit cloud banks on the western horizon and reflected red now, converting the yellow hue of the universe into a vague pink tint.

"I've been wondering who called her in on this," Chee said. "When we told Bistie he could call a lawyer, he wasn't interested."

"Probably his daughter," Leaphorn said.

"Probably," Chee agreed. He remembered the daughter standing in the yard of Bistie's house. Would she have thought of calling a lawyer? Driven back to Sanostee to make the call? Known whom to call? He amended the "probably." "Maybe so," he said.

That concluded the conversation. They rode in silence. Leaphorn sat back straight against the seat, his eyes memorizing what he could see of the landscape in fading yellow light, his mind drawn to the intolerable problem of Emma's illness and then flinching away from that to escape into the merely frustrating puzzle of the four pins on his map. Chee rode slumped against the door, right hand on the wheel, a taller man and slender, thinking of the bone bead in Bistie's wallet, of what questions he might ask to cause the stubborn Bistie to talk about witchcraft to hostile strangers, of whether Leaphorn would allow him any questions, of how Leaphorn, the famous Leaphorn, the Leaphorn of tribal police legends, would handle this. And thinking of Mary Landon's letter. He found he could see the words, dark blue ink against the pale blue of the paper.

"Dad and I drove down to Madison last week and talked to an adviser in the College of Arts and Sciences. I will be able to get my master's degree—with a little luck—in just two more semesters . . ."

Just two semesters. Only two semesters. Only two. Or, put another way, I will only take two long steps away from you. Or, I promised I would come back to you at the end of summer, but now I am going away. Or, rephrased again, former lover, you are now a friend. Or . . .

The patrol car slanted up into the thicket of piñon and stunted ponderosa. Chee shifted into second gear.

"Just over this ridge," he said.

Just over the ridge, the light became visible. It was below them, still at least half a mile away, a bright point in the darkening twilight. Chee remembered it from the afternoon they had arrested Bistie. A single bare bulb protected by a metal reflector atop a forty-foot ponderosa pine stem. Bistie's ghost light. Would a witch be worried about ghosts? Would a witch keep a light burning to fend off the *chindi* which wandered in the darkness?

"His place?" Leaphorn asked.

Chee nodded.

"He's got electricity out here?" Leaphorn sounded surprised.

"There's a windmill generator behind the house," Chee said. "I guess he runs that light off batteries."

Bistie's access route required a right turn off the road, bumped over a rocky hummock and past a scattering of piñons, to drop again down to his place. In the harsh yellow light it looked worse than Chee had remembered it—a rectangular plank shack, probably with two rooms, roofed with blue asphalt shingles. Behind it stood a dented metal storage shack, a brush arbor, a pole horse corral, and, up the slope by the low cliff of the mesa, a lean-to for hay storage. Beyond that, against the cliff, the yellow light reflected from a hogan made of stacked stone slabs. Beside the shack, side by side and with their vanes turned away from the gusting west wind, were Bistie's windmill and his wind generator.

Chee parked his patrol car under Bistie's yard light.

There was no sign of the truck and no light on in the house.

Leaphorn sighed. "You know enough about him to do any guessing about where he might be?" he said. "Visiting kinfolks or anything?"

"No," Chee said. "We didn't get into that."

"Lives here with his daughter. Right?" Leaphorn said.

"Right."

They waited for someone to appear at the door and acknowledge the presence of visitors, delaying the moment when they'd admit the long drive had been for nothing. Delaying what would be either a return trip to Sanostee or a fruitless hunt for neighbors who might know where Roosevelt Bistie had gone.

"Maybe he didn't come back here when the lawyer got him out," Chee said.

Leaphorn grunted. The yellow light from the bare bulb above them lit the right side of his face, giving it a waxy look.

No one appeared at the door.

Leaphorn got out of the car, slammed the door noisily behind him, and leaned against the roof, eyes on the house. The door wouldn't be locked. Should he go in, and look around for some hint of where Bistie might be?

The wind gusted against him, blowing sand against his ankles above his socks and pushing at his uniform hat. Then it died. He heard Chee's door opening. He smelled something burning—a strong, acrid odor.

"Fire," Chee said. "Somewhere."

Leaphorn trotted toward the house, rapped on the door. The smell was stronger here, seeping between door and frame. He turned the knob, pushed the door open. Smoke puffed out, and was whipped away by another gust of the dry wind. Behind him, Chee yelled: "Bistie. You in there?"

Leaphorn stepped into the smoke, fanning with his hat. Chee was just behind him. The smoke was coming from an aluminum pot on top of a butane stove against the back wall of the room. Leaphorn held his breath, turned off the burner under the pan and under a blue enamel coffeepot boiling furiously beside it. He used his hat as a potholder, grabbed the handle, carried it outside, and dropped it on the packed earth. It contained what seemed to have been some sort of stew, now badly charred. Leaphorn went back inside.

"No one's here," Chee said. He was fanning the residual smoke with his hat. A chair lay on its side on the floor.

"You checked the back room?"

Chee nodded. "Nobody home."

"Left in a hurry," Leaphorn said. He wrinkled his nose against the acrid smell of burned meat and walked back into the front yard. With the butt of his flashlight, he poked into the still-smoking pan, inspected the residue it collected.

"Take a look at this," he said to Chee. "You're a bachelor, aren't you? How long does it take you to burn stew like this?"

Chee inspected the pot. "The way he had the fire turned up, maybe five, ten minutes. Depends on how much water he put in it."

"Or she," Leaphorn said. "His daughter. When you were here with Kennedy, they just have one truck?"

"That's all," Chee said.

"So they must be off somewhere in it," Leaphorn said. "One or both. And they drove off the other way from the way we were coming. But if it was that way, why didn't we see their headlights? They would have just left." Leaphorn straightened, put his hands on his hips, stretched his back. He stared into the deepening twilight, frowning. "Just one plate on the table. You notice that?"

"Yeah," Chee said. "And the chair turned over."

"Five or ten minutes," Leaphorn said. "If you know how long it takes to incinerate stew, then we didn't scare him off. The truck was already gone. And the stew was already burning before we got here."

"I'll go in and look around again," Chee said. "A little closer."

"Let me do it," Leaphorn said. "See if you can find anything out here."

Leaphorn stood at the doorway first, not wishing to further disturb any signs that might have been left. He suspected Chee might be good at this, but he knew he was good. The floor was covered with dark red linoleum, seamed near the middle of the room. It was fairly new, which was good, and dusty, which was almost inevitable considering the weather, and absolutely essential considering what Leaphorn hoped to do. But before he did anything, he looked. This front room was used for cooking, eating, general living, and the woman's bedroom. One corner of the bed, a single wooden frame neatly made up, was visible behind a curtain of blankets which walled off a corner. Shelves loaded with canned goods, cooking utensils, and an assortment of boxes lined the partition wall. Except for the overturned chair, nothing seemed odd or out of place. The room showed the habitual neatness imposed by limited living space.

But the floor was dusty.

Leaphorn squatted on the step and inspected the linoleum with his eyes just an inch or so above its surface. The pattern of dust newly disturbed by his footsteps, and Chee's, was easy enough to make out. He could easily separate the treads of Chee's bigger feet from his own. But the angle of light was wrong. Walking carefully, he went in and pulled the chain to turn off the light bulb. He clicked on his flashlight. Working the light carefully, squatting at first and then on his stomach with his cheek against the floor, he studied the marks left in the dust.

He ignored the fresh scuffs he and Chee had made—looking for other marks. He found them. Dimmer but fairly fresh and plain enough to an eye as experienced at this as Leaphorn's. Waffle marks left by the soles of someone who had apparently sat beside the table, someone who had pulled his feet back under the chair, leaving the drag marks of the toes. Also under the table, and near the fallen chair, another pattern, left by a rubber sole. Some sort of jogging or tennis shoes, perhaps. Smaller than the big-footed person who wore the waffle soles. Bistie and daughter? If so, Bistie's Daughter had large feet.

Leaphorn emerged from under the table, whacking his ear in the process. Behind the curtain of blankets, on a chest beside the bed, stood two pair of shoes. Worn tan squaw boots and low-heeled black slippers. They were narrow and about size six. He took a left slipper back to the table, relocated the track, and made the comparison. The slipper was far too small. Bistie had been entertaining a visitor not long before Leaphorn and Chee arrived.

But where the devil had they gone? And why had they left the stew to burn and the coffee to boil away?

He found nothing interesting in the back room. Against the wall, a bedroll on which Bistie apparently slept was folded neatly. Bistie's clothing hung with equal neatness from a wire strung taut along the wall—two pairs of well-worn jeans, a pair of khaki trousers with frayed cuffs. A plaid wool jacket, four shirts, all with long sleeves and one with a hole in the elbow. Leaphorn clicked his tongue against his teeth, thinking, studying the room. He pushed his forefinger into the enamel washbasin on the table beside Bistie's bedroom, testing water temperature without thinking why. It was tepid. Exactly what one would expect. He picked up the crumpled washcloth beside the basin. It was wet. Leaphorn looked at it, frowning. Not what one would expect.

The cloth had been used to clean something. Leaphorn studied it in the flashlight beam. In three places the cloth was heavily smudged with dirt—as if to clean spots from the dusty floor. He held one of the spots to his nose and smelled it.

"Chee!" he shouted. "Chee!"

He examined the floor, moving the flash beam methodically back and forth, looking for a wiped place and seeing none. Perhaps it had been done in the front room. He squatted, holding the flash close to the linoleum, looking for tracks. He saw, instead, a path. It was fairly regular, possibly eighteen inches wide—a strip of the plastic surface wiped clean of dust. A pathway leading from the doorway into the front room, down the center of this back room, to the back door.

The back door opened and Chee looked in. "I think somebody, or maybe something, got dragged out of here," Chee said. "Drag marks leading up toward the rocks."

"Through here too," Leaphorn said. He drew the flashlight beam along the polished, dust-free path. "To the back door. But look at this." He handed Chee the damp cloth. "Smell it," he said.

Chee smelled.

"Blood," Chee said. "Smells like it." He glanced at Leaphorn. "Wonder what was in that stew. Fresh mutton, you think?"

"I doubt it," Leaphorn said. "I think we ought to find where those drag marks take us. I want to know what's being dragged."

"Or who's being dragged," Chee said.

Bare earth that has been lived on for years and as dry as drought can make it becomes almost as hard as concrete. From the back door, Leaphorn saw nothing until Chee's flashlight beam, held close to the earth, created shadows where something even harder had been pulled across its surface. Scratches. The scratches led past the windmill tower, past the metal storage building, and beyond. On the slope, where the earth was less pounded, the scratches became scuff marks between the scattering of wilted weeds and clumps of grass.

"Up toward the hogan," Leaphorn said. "It leads that way."

Even in the less compacted earth the drag marks were hard to follow. The twilight had faded into almost full dark now, with only a flush of dark red in the west. The wind had risen again, kicking up dust in front of Leaphorn. He walked with his flashlight focused on the ground, picking up the sign of dislodged earth and crushed weeds.

Even in retrospect, Leaphorn didn't remember hearing the shot—being aware first of pain. Something that felt like a hammer struck his right forearm and the flashlight was suddenly gone. Leaphorn was sitting on the ground, aware of Chee's voice yelling something, aware that his forearm hurt so badly that something must have broken it. The sound of Chee's pistol firing, the muzzle flash, brought him out of the shock and made him aware of what had happened. Roosevelt Bistie, that son-of-a-bitch, had shot him.

14

THE "OFFICER DOWN" CALL provokes a special reaction in each police jurisdiction. In the Shiprock subagency of the Navajo Tribal Police, Captain A. D. Largo commanding, it produced an immediate call to Largo himself, who was home watching television, and almost simultaneous radio calls to all Navajo Police units on duty in the district, to the New Mexico State Police, and the San Juan County Sheriff's Office. Then, since the Chuska Mountains sprawl across the New Mexico border into Arizona, and Sanostee is only a dozen or so miles from the state boundary, and neither the dispatcher at Shiprock nor anyone else was quite sure in which state all this was happening, the call also went out to the Arizona Highway Patrol and, more or less out of courtesy, to the Apache County Sheriff's Office, which might have some legitimate jurisdiction even though it was a hundred miles south, down at St. Johns.

The Farmington office of the Federal Bureau of Investigation, which had ultimate jurisdiction when such a lofty crime is committed on an Indian reservation, got the word a little later via telephone. The message was relayed to Jay Kennedy at the home of a lawyer, where he was engaged in a penny-a-point rotating-partner bridge game. Kennedy had just won two consecutive rubbers and was about to make a small slam, properly bid, when the telephone rang. He took the call, finished the slam, added up the score, which showed him to be ahead 2,350 points, collected his $23.50, and left. It was a few minutes after 10 P.M.

A few minutes after 10:30, Jim Chee got back to the Bistie place. He had met the ambulance from Farmington at Littlewater on U.S. 666. While Leaphorn was being tucked away in the back, Captain Largo had arrived—Gorman riding with him—and had taken charge. Largo asked a flurry of questions, sent the ambulance on its way, and made a series of quick radio checks to ensure roadblocks were in place. He'd hung up the microphone and sat, arms folded, looking at Chee.

"Too late for roadblocks, probably," he said.

It had been a long day for Chee. He was tired. All the adrenaline had drained away. "Who knows," he said. "Maybe he stopped to fix a flat. Maybe he didn't even have a car. If it was Bistie himself, maybe he just went back to his house. If—"

"You think it might be somebody besides Bistie?"

"I don't know," Chee said. "It's his place. He shoots at people. But then maybe somebody doesn't like him any better than he likes other people, and they came and shot him and dragged him off into the rocks."

Largo's expression, which had already been sour, suggested he didn't like Chee's tone. He stared at Chee.

"How did it happen?" he asked. "One old man, sick, and two cops with guns?"

Largo obviously didn't expect an answer and Chee didn't attempt one.

"You and Gorman go back up there and see if you can find him," Largo said. "I'll have the state police and the sheriff's people follow you. Don't let 'em get lost."

Chee nodded.

"I'm meeting Kennedy here," Largo said. "Then we'll come along and join you."

Chee headed for his car.

"One more thing," Largo shouted. "Don't let Bistie shoot you."

And now, at 10:55, Chee parked beside Bistie's now-dark light pole, got out, and waited for the entourage to finish its arrival. He felt foolish. Bistie's truck was still absent. Bistie's shack was dark. Everything seemed to be exactly as they had left it. The chance of Bistie's hanging around to await this posse simply didn't exist.

There was a general slamming of doors.

Chee explained the layout, pointed up into the darkness to the hogan from which the shots had come. They moved up the slope, weapons drawn, the state policeman carrying a riot gun, the deputy carrying a rifle. What had happened here two hours before already seemed unreal to Chee, something he had imagined.

No one was at the hogan, or in it.

"Here's some brass," the state policeman said. He was an old-timer, with red hair and a freckled, perpetually sunburned face.

He stood frowning down at a copper-colored metal cylinder which reflected the beam of his flashlight. "Looks like thirty-eight caliber," he said. "Who'll be handling the evidence?"

"Just leave it there for Kennedy," Chee said. "There should be another one." He was thinking that the empty cartridge certainly wasn't from a 30-30. It was shorter. Pistol ammunition. And, since it had been ejected, probably from an automatic—not a revolver. If Bistie had fired it, he seemed to have quite an arsenal.

"Here it is," the state policeman said. His flashlight was focused on the ground about a long step from where the first cartridge lay. "Same caliber."

Chee didn't bother to look at it. He considered asking everyone to be careful of where they walked, to avoid erasing any useful tracks. But as dry and windy as it was, he couldn't imagine tracking as anything but a waste of time. Except for the drag marks. Whatever had been dragged up here should be easy to find.

It was.

"Hey," Gorman shouted. "Here's a body."

It was half hidden in a clump of chamiso, head downhill, feet uphill, legs still spraddled apart as if whoever had dragged it there had been using them to pull the body along and had simply dropped them.

The body had been Roosevelt Bistie. In the combined lights of Chee's and Gorman's flashlights, the yellow look of his face was intensified—but death had done little to change his expression. Bistie still looked grim and bitter, as if being shot was only what he'd expected—a fitting ending for a disappointing life. The dragging had pulled his shirt up over his shoulders, leaving chest and stomach bare. The waxy skin where the rib cage joined at the sternum showed two small holes, one just below the other. The lower one had bled a little. Very small holes, Chee thought. It seemed odd that such trivial holes would let out the wind of life.

Gorman was looking at him, a question in his face.

"This is Bistie," Chee said. "Looks like the guy who shot Lieutenant Leaphorn had shot this guy. I guess he was dragging him up here when we drove up, the lieutenant and me."

"And after he shot the lieutenant he just took off," Gorman said.

"And got clean away," Chee added.

Four flashlights now were illuminating the body. Only the San Juan County deputy was still out in the darkness, doing his fruitless job.

Down in Roosevelt Bistie's yard below, two more vehicles parked. Chee heard doors slam, the voice of Kennedy, the sound of Kennedy and Captain Largo coming up the slope. Chee's flashlight now was focused above the bullet wounds at a place on Bistie's left breast—a reddish mark, narrow, perhaps a half-inch long, where a cut was healing. It would seem, normally, an odd place for such a cut. It made Jim Chee think of Bistie's wallet, and the bone bead he had seen in it, and whether the wallet would have been dragged out of Bistie's hip pocket on his heels-first trip up this rocky slope, and whether the bone bead would still be in it when it was found.

He squatted beside Bistie, taking a closer look, imagining the scene at which this little healing scar had been produced. The hand trembler (or stargazer, or listener, or crystal gazer, or whatever sort of shaman Bistie had chosen to diagnose his sickness) explaining to Bistie that someone had witched him, telling Bistie that a skinwalker had blown the fatal bone fragment into him. And then the ritual cut of the skin, the sucking at the breast, the bone coming out of Bistie, appearing on the shaman's tongue. And Bistie putting the bone in his billfold, and paying his fee, and setting out to save himself by killing the witch and reversing the dreaded corpse sickness.

Chee moved the beam of his light up so that it reflected again from the glazed, angry eyes of Roosevelt Bistie. How did Bistie know the witch was Endocheeney, the man who all at Badwater agreed was a mild and harmless fellow? The shaman would not have known that. And if the two men even knew each other, Chee had seen no sign of it.

Behind him, the state policeman was shouting to Largo, telling him they'd found a body. The wind kicked up again, blowing a flurry of sand against Chee's face. He closed his eyes against it, and when he reopened them, a fragment of dead tumbleweed had lodged itself against Bistie's ear.

Why was Bistie so certain the witch who was killing him was Endocheeney? He had been certain enough to try to kill the man. How had their paths crossed in this fatal way? And where? And when? Now that Bistie was also dead, who could answer those questions? Any of them?

Largo had joined the circle now, and Kennedy. Chee sensed them standing just behind him, staring down at the body.

"There's what killed him," the state policeman said. "Two gunshots through the chest."

Just on the edge of the circle of illumination, Chee could see the healing cut on Bistie's breast. Those two bullets had completed the death of Roosevelt Bistie. But the little wound high on his breast above them had been where Roosevelt Bistie's death had started.

15

THE INDIAN HEALTH SERVICE HOSPITAL at Gallup is one of the prides of this huge federal bureaucracy—modern, attractive, well located and equipped. It had been built in a period of flush budgeting—with just about everything any hospital needs. Now, in a lean budget cycle, it was enduring harder times. But the shortage of nurses, the overspent supplies budget, and the assortment of other fiscal headaches that beset the hospital's bead counters this particular morning did not affect Joe Leaphorn's lunch, which was everything a sensible patient should expect from a hospital kitchen, nor the view from his window, which was superb. The Health Service had located the hospital high on the slope overlooking Gallup from the south. Over the little hump in the sheet produced by his toes, Leaphorn could see the endless stream of semitrailers moving along Interstate 40. Beyond the highway, intercontinental train traffic rolled east and west on the Santa Fe main trunk. Above and beyond the railroad, beyond the clutter of east Gallup, the red cliffs of Mesa de los Lobos rose—their redness diminished a little by the blue haze of distance, and above them was the gray-green shape of the high country of the Navajo borderlands, where the Big Reservation faded into Checkerboard Reservation. For Joe Leaphorn, raised not fifty miles north of this bed in the grass country near Two Gray Hills, it was the landscape of his childhood. But now he looked at the scene without thinking about it.

He had been awake only a minute or two, having been jarred by the arrival of his lunch tray from a hazy, morphine-induced doze into a panicky concern for the welfare of Emma. He remembered very quickly that Agnes was there, had been there for days, living in the spare bedroom and playing the role of concerned younger sister. Agnes made Leaphorn nervous, but she had good sense. She'd take care of Emma, make the right decisions. He needn't worry. No more than he normally did.

Now he had finished the wit-collection process that follows such awakenings. He had established where he was, remembered why, quickly assessed the unfamiliar surroundings, checked the heavy, still cool and damp cast on his right arm, moved his thumb experimentally, then his fingers, then his hand, to measure the pain caused by each motion, and then he thought about Emma again. Her appointment was tomorrow. He would be well enough to take her, no question of that. And another step would be taken toward knowing what he already knew. What he dreaded to admit. The rest of his life would be spent watching her slip away from him, not knowing who he was, then not knowing who she was. In the material the Alzheimer's Association had sent him, someone had described it as "looking into your mind and seeing nothing there but darkness." He remembered that, as he remembered the case report of the husband of a victim. "Every day I would tell her we'd been married thirty years, that we had four children. . . . Every night when I got into bed she would say, 'Who are you?'" He had already seen the first of that. Last week, he had walked into the kitchen and Emma had looked up from the carrots she was scraping. Her expression had been first startled, then fearful, then confused. And she had clutched Agnes's arm and asked who he was. That was something he'd have to learn to live with—like learning to live with a dagger through the heart.

He groped clumsily with his good left hand for the button to summon an attendant, found it, pressed it, glanced at his watch. Outside the glass, the light was blinding. Far to the east, a cloud was building over Tsoodzil, the Turquoise Mountain. Rain? Too early to tell, and too far east to fall on the reservation if it did develop into a thunderstorm. He swung his legs over the edge of the bed and sat, slumped, waiting for the dizziness to subside, feeling an odd, buzzing sense of detachment induced by whatever they'd given him to make him sleep.

"Well," a voice behind him said. "I didn't expect to find you out of bed."

It was Dilly Streib. He was wearing his FBI summer uniform, a dark blue two-piece suit, white shirt, and necktie. On Streib, all of this managed to look slept in.

"I'm not out of bed yet," Leaphorn said. He gestured toward

the closet door. "Look around in there and see if you can find my clothes. Then I'll be out of bed."

Streib was holding a manila folder in his left hand. He dropped it at the foot of Leaphorn's bed and disappeared into the closet. "Thought you'd like to take a look at that," he said. "Anybody tell you what happened?"

It occurred to Leaphorn that he had a headache. He took a deep breath. His lunch seemed to consist of a bowl of soup, which was steaming, a small green salad, and something including chicken which normally would have looked appetizing. But now Leaphorn's stomach felt as if it had been tilted on its side. "I know what happened," Leaphorn said. "Somebody shot me in the arm."

"I meant after that," Streib said. He dumped Leaphorn's uniform at the foot of his bed and his boots on the floor.

"After that I'm blank," Leaphorn said.

"Well, to get to the bottom line, the guy got away and he left behind Bistie's body."

"Bistie's body?" Leaphorn reached for the folder, digesting this.

"Shot," Streib said. "Twice. With a pistol, probably. Probably a thirty-eight or so."

Leaphorn extracted the report from the folder. Two sheets. He read. He glanced at the signature. Kennedy. He handed the report back to Streib.

"What do you think?" Streib asked.

Leaphorn shook his head.

"I think it's getting interesting," Streib said. That meant, Leaphorn understood from half a lifetime spent working with the federals, that people with clout and high civil service numbers were beginning to think they had more bodies than could be politely buried. He took off his hospital gown, picked up his undershirt, and considered the problem of how to get it on without moving his right arm around more than was necessary.

"I think we should have kept that Indian locked up a while," Streib said. He chuckled. "I guess that's belaboring the obvious." The chuckle turned into a laugh. "I'm sure his doctor would have recommended it."

"You think we could have got him to change his mind? Tell us what he had against Endocheeney?" Leaphorn asked. He thought a moment. If they had taken Bistie back into custody, Leaphorn had planned to try an old, old trick. The traditional culture allows a lie, if it does no harm, but the lie can be repeated only three times. The fourth time told, it locks the teller into the deceit. He couldn't have worked it on Bistie directly, because Bistie would have simply continued to refuse to say anything about Endocheeney, or bone beads, or witchcraft. But maybe he could have worked around the edges. Maybe. Maybe not.

"I'm not so sure," Leaphorn said. He was even less sure he could have talked Streib into signing his name on the sort of complaint they would have needed. This was a notably untidy piece of work, this business of a man who seemed to think he'd shot a man who'd actually been stabbed. And the FBI hadn't fooled the taxpayers all these years by getting itself involved with the messy ones. Streib was a good man, but he hadn't survived twenty years in the Agency jungle without learning the lessons it taught.

"Maybe not," Streib said. "I defer to you redskins on that. But anyhow . . ." He shrugged, letting it trail off. "This is going to put the heat on. Now we don't just have a bunch of singles. Now we got ourselves a double. And maybe more than a double. You know how that works."

"Yeah," Leaphorn said. Doubling homicides didn't double the interest—it was more like squaring it. And if you had yourself genuine serial killings, nicely mysterious, the interest and the pressure and the potential for publicity went right through the roof. Publicity had never been an issue with Navajo Tribal Police—they simply never got any—but for federals, good press brought the billions pouring in and kept the J. Edgar Hoover Building swarming with fat-cat bureaucrats. But it had damned sure better be good press.

Streib had seated himself. He looked at the report and then at Leaphorn, who was pulling on his pants with left-handed awkwardness. Streib's round, ageless, unlined face made it difficult for him to look worried. Now he managed. "Trouble is, among the many troubles, I can't see how the hell to get a handle on this. Doesn't seem to have a handle."

Leaphorn was learning how difficult it can be to fasten the top button of his uniform trousers with his left-hand fingers after a lifetime of doing it with right-hand fingers. And he was remembering the question Jim Chee had raised. ("I heard gossip at Badwater Trading Post," Chee had said. "They say a bone was found in Endocheeney's corpse.") Had the pathologist found the bone?

"The autopsy on Old Man Endocheeney up at Farmington," Leaphorn said. "I think somebody should talk to the pathologist about that. Find out every little thing they found in that stab wound."

Streib put the report back in the folder, the folder on his lap, pulled out his pipe, and looked at the No Smoking sign beside the door. Beside the sign, Little Orphan Annie stared from a poster that read: "Little Orphan Annie's Parents Smoked." Beside that poster was another, a photograph of rows and rows of tombstones, with a legend reading "Marlboro Country." Streib sniffed at the pipe, put it back in his jacket pocket.

"Why?" he asked.

"One of our people heard rumors that a little fragment of bone was found in the wound," Leaphorn said. He kept his eyes on Streib. Would that be enough explanation? Streib's expression said it wasn't.

"Jim Chee found a little bone bead in his house trailer along with the lead pellets after somebody shot the shotgun through his wall," Leaphorn said. "And Roosevelt Bistie was carrying a little bone bead in his wallet."

Understanding dawned slowly, and unhappily, causing Streib's round face to convert itself from its unaccustomed expression of worry to an equally unaccustomed look of sorrow and dismay.

"Bone," he said. "As in skinwalking. As in witchcraft. As in corpse sickness."

"Bone," Leaphorn said.

"Lordy, lordy, lordy," Streib said. "What the hell next? I hate it."

"But maybe it's a handle."

"Handle, shit," Streib said, with a passion that was rare for him. "You remember way back when that cop got ambushed over on the Laguna-Acoma. You remember that one. The agent on that one said something about witchcraft when he was working it, put it in his report. I think they called him all the way back to Washington so the very top dogs could chew him out in person. That was after doing it by letters and telegrams."

"But it was witchcraft," Leaphorn said. "Or it wasn't, of course, but the Lagunas they tried for it said they killed the cop because he had been witching them, and the judge ruled insanity, and they—"

"They went into a mental hospital, and the agent got transferred from Albuquerque to East Poison Spider, Wyoming," Streib said, voice rich with passion. " 'The judge ruled' don't cut it in

Washington. In Washington they don't believe in agents who believe in witches."

"I'd do it myself. Look into it, I mean. But I think you'd have more luck talking to the doctor," Leaphorn said. "Getting taken seriously. I go in there, a Navajo, and start talking to the doc about witch bones and corpse sickness and—"

"I know. I know," Streib said. He looked at Leaphorn quizzically. "A bone bead, you said? Human?"

"Cow."

"Cow? Anything special about cow bones?"

"Damn it," Leaphorn said. "Cow or giraffe, or dinosaur or whatever. What difference does it make? Just so whoever we're dealing with thinks it works."

"Okay," Streib said. "I'll ask. You got any other ideas? I got a sort of a feeling that the one at Window Rock—the Onesalt woman—could be some sort of sex-and-jealousy thing. Or maybe the Onesalt gal nosed into some sort of ripoff in the tribal paperwork that caused undue resentment. We know she was a sort of full-time world-saver. Usually you just put her type down as a pain in the ass, but maybe she was irritating the wrong fellow. But I sort of see her as one case and those others as another bag. And maybe now we toss that Chee business in with 'em. You have any fresh thinking about it?"

Leaphorn shook his head. "Just the bone angle," he said. "And probably that leads no place." But he was doing some fresh thinking. Nothing he wanted to talk to Streib about. Not yet. He wanted to find out if Onesalt's agency knew anything about the letter that office had mailed to Dugai Endocheeney. If Onesalt had written it, Dilly might be dead wrong about Onesalt not being linked to the other homicides. And now he was thinking that Roosevelt Bistie fell into a new category of victim. Bistie had been part of it, part of whatever it was that was killing people on the Big Reservation. Thus the killing of Bistie was something new. Whatever it was, this lethal being, now it seemed to be feeding on itself.

16

THE CAT WAS THERE when Chee awakened. It was sitting just inside the door, looking out through the screen. When he stirred, rising onto his side in the awkward process of getting up from the pallet he'd made on the floor, the cat had been instantly alert, watching him tensely. He sat, completed a huge yawn, rubbed the sleep from his eyes, and then stood, stretching. To his mild surprise, the cat was still there when he finished that. Its green eyes were fixed on him nervously, but it hadn't fled. Chee rolled up the sleeping bag he'd been using as a pad, tied it, dumped it on his unused bunk. He inspected the irregular row of holes the shotgun blasts had punched through the trailer wall. One day, when he knew who had done it, when he knew it wouldn't be happening again, he would find himself a tinsmith—or whomever one found to patch shotgun holes in aluminum alloy walls—and get them patched more permanently. He peeled off the duct tape he'd used to cover them and held out his hand, feeling the breeze sucking in. Until the rains came, or winter, he might as well benefit from the improved ventilation.

For breakfast he finished a can of peaches he'd left in the refrigerator and the remains of a loaf of bread. It wasn't exactly breakfast, anyway. He'd got to bed just at dawn—thinking he was too tired, and too wired, to sleep. Even though night was almost gone, he avoided the bunk and used the floor. He had lain there remembering the two black holes in the skin of Roosevelt Bistie's chest, remembering the healing cut higher on Bistie's breast. Those vivid images faded away into a question.

Who had called Janet Pete?

Unless she was lying, it had not been Roosevelt Bistie's daughter. The daughter had driven up just behind the ambulance. She had been following it, in fact—coming home from Shiprock with four boxes of groceries. She had emerged from Bistie's old truck into the pale yellow light of police lanterns, with her face frozen in that expression every cop learns to dread—the face of a woman who is expecting the very worst and has steeled herself to accept it with dignity.

She had looked down at the body as they carried it past her and slid the stretcher into the ambulance. Then she had looked up at Captain Largo. "I knew it would be him," she'd said, in a voice that sounded remarkably matter-of-fact. Chee had watched her, examining her grief for some sign of pretense and thinking that her prescience was hardly remarkable. For whom else could the ambulance have been making this back-road trip? Virtually no one else lived on this particular slope of this particular mountain—and no one else at all on this particular spur of track. The emotion of Bistie's Daughter seemed totally genuine—more shock than sorrow. No tears. If they came, they would come later, when her yard was cleared of all these strangers, and dignity no longer mattered, and the loneliness closed in around her. Now she talked calmly with Captain Largo and with Kennedy—responding to their questions in a voice too low for Chee to overhear, as expressionless as if her face had been carved from wood.

But she had recognized Chee immediately when all that was done. The ambulance had driven away, taking with it the flesh and bones that had held the living wind of Roosevelt Bistie and leaving behind, somewhere in the night air around them, his *chindi.*

"Did Captain Largo tell you where he died?" Chee had asked her. He spoke in Navajo, using the long, ugly guttural sound which signifies that moment when the wind of life no longer moves inside a human personality, and all the disharmonies that have bedeviled it escape from the nostrils to haunt the night.

"Where?" she asked, at first puzzled by the question. Then she understood it, and looked at the house. "Was it inside?"

"Outside," Chee said. "Out in the yard. Behind the house."

It might be true. It takes a while for a man to die—even shot twice through the chest. No reason for Bistie's Daughter to believe her house had been contaminated with her father's ghost. Chee had evolved his own theology about ghost sickness and the *chindi* that caused it. It was, like all the evils that threatened the happiness of humankind, a matter of the mind. The psychology courses he'd taken at the University of New Mexico had always seemed to

Chee a logical extension of what the Holy People had taught those original four Navajo clans. And now he noticed some slight relaxation in the face of Bistie's Daughter—some relief. It was better not to have to deal with ghosts.

She was looking at Chee, thoughtfully.

"You noticed when you and the *belagana* came to get him that he was angry," she said. "Did you notice that?"

"But I don't know why," Chee said. "Why was he so angry?"

"Because he knew he had to die. He went to the hospital. They told him about his liver." She placed a hand against her stomach.

"What was it? Was it cancer?"

Bistie's Daughter shrugged. "They call it cancer," she said. "We call it corpse sickness. Whatever word you put on it, it was killing him."

"It couldn't be cured? Did they tell him that?"

Bistie's Daughter glanced around her, looked nervously past Chee into the night. The state policeman's car—on its way back to paved highways—crunched through the weeds at the edge of the yard. Its headlights flashed across her face. She raised her hand against the glare. "You can turn it around," she said. "I always heard you could do that."

"You mean kill the witch and put the bone back in him?" Chee said. "Is that what he was going to do?"

Bistie's Daughter looked at him silently.

"I talked to them already," she said finally. "To the other policemen. To the young *belagana* and the fat Navajo."

Largo would hate hearing that "fat Navajo" description, Chee thought. "Did you tell them that's what your father was doing? When he went to the Endocheeney place?"

"I told them I didn't know what he was doing. I didn't know that man who got killed. All I know is that my father was getting sicker and sicker all the time. He went to see a hand trembler over there between Roof Butte and Lukachukai to find out what kind of cure he would need to have. But the hand trembler had gone off someplace and he wasn't home. He went over on the Checkerboard Reservation, someplace over there by the Nageezi Chapter House, and talked to a listener over there. He told him he had been cooking food over a fire made out of wood struck by lightning and he needed to have a Hail Chant." Bistie's Daughter looked up at Chee with a strained grin. "We burn butane to cook on," she said. "But he charged my father fifty dollars. Then he went to the Badwater Clinic to see if they would give him some medicine. He didn't come back until the next day because they kept him in the hospital. Made X-rays, I think. Things like that. When he came back he was angry. Said they told him he was going to die." Bistie's Daughter stopped talking then, and looked away from Chee. Tears came abruptly but without sound.

"Why angry?" Chee asked, his voice so low she might have thought he meant the question only for himself.

"Because they told him he could not be cured," Bistie's Daughter said in a shaky voice. She cleared her throat, wiped the back of her hand across her eyes. "That man was strong," she continued. "His spirit was strong. He didn't give up on things. He didn't want to die."

"Did he say why he was angry at Endocheeney? Why he blamed Endocheeney? Did he say he thought Endocheeney had witched him?"

"He didn't say hardly anything at all. I asked him. I said, 'My Father, why—'" She stopped.

Never speak the name of the dead, Chee thought. Never summon the *chindi* to you, even if the name of the ghost is Father.

"I asked that man why he was angry. What was wrong. What had they told him at the Badwater Clinic? And finally he told me they said his liver was rotten and they didn't know how to fix it with medicine and he was going to die pretty quick. I told the other policemen all this."

"Did he say anything about being witched?"

Bistie's Daughter shook her head.

"I noticed that he had a cut place on his breast." Chee tapped his uniform shirt, indicating where. "It was healing but still a little sore. Do you know about that?"

"No," she said.

The answer didn't surprise Chee. His people had adopted many ways of the *belagana,* but most of them had retained the Dinee tradition of personal modesty. Roosevelt Bistie would have kept his shirt on in the presence of his daughter.

"Did he ever say anything about Endocheeney?"

"No."

"Was Endocheeney a friend?"

"I don't think so. I never heard of him before."

Chee clicked his tongue. Another door closed.

"I guess the policemen asked you if you know who came here to see your fath— to see him tonight?"

"I didn't know he was home. I was away since yesterday. In

Gallup to visit my sister. To buy things. I didn't know he was back from being in jail."

"After we arrested him, did you go and get the lawyer to get him out?"

Bistie's Daughter looked puzzled. "I don't know anything about that," she said.

"You didn't call a lawyer? Did you ask anyone else to call one?"

"I don't know anything about lawyers. I just heard that lawyers will get all your money."

"Do you know a woman named Janet Pete?"

Bistie's Daughter shook her head.

"Do you have any idea who it might have been who came here and shot him? Any idea at all?"

Bistie's Daughter was no longer crying, but she wiped her hand across her eyes again, looked down, and released a long, shuddering sigh.

"I think he was trying to kill a skinwalker," she said. "The skinwalker came and killed him."

And now, as Jim Chee finished the last slice of peach and mopped the residue of juice from the can with the bread crust, he remembered exactly how Bistie's Daughter had looked as she'd said that. He thought she was probably exactly correct. The Mystery of Roosevelt Bistie neatly solved in a sentence. All that remained was another question. Who was the skinwalker who came and shot Bistie? Behind that, how did the witch know Bistie would be home instead of safely jailed in Farmington?

In other words, who called Janet Pete?

He would find out. Right now. The very next step. As soon as he finished breakfast.

He unplugged his coffeepot, filled his coffee cup with water, swirled it gently, and drank it down.

("I never saw anybody do that before," Mary Landon had said. "What?"

"That with the water you rinsed your cup with." Empty-handed, she had mimicked the swirling and the drinking.

It still had taken him a moment to understand. "Oh," he had said. "If you grow up hauling water, you don't ever learn to pour it out. You don't waste it, even if it tastes a little bit like coffee."

"Odd," Mary Landon said. "What the old prof in Sociology 101 would call a cultural anomaly."

It had seemed odd to Chee that not wasting water had seemed odd to Mary Landon. It still seemed odd.)

He put the pot under the sink. "Look out, Cat," he said. And the cat, instead of diving for the exit flap as it normally did when he came anywhere near this close, moved down the trailer. It sat under his bunk, looking at him nervously.

It took a millisecond for Jim Chee to register the meaning of this.

Something out there.

He sucked in his breath, reached for his belt, extracted his pistol. He could see nothing out the door except his pickup and the empty slope. He checked out of each of the windows. Nothing moved. He went through the door in a crouched run, holding the pistol in front of him. He stopped in the cover of the pickup.

Absolutely nothing moved. Chee felt the tension seep away. But something had driven in the cat. He walked to its den, eyes on the ground. In the softer earth around the juniper there were paw prints. A dog? Chee squatted, studying them. Coyote tracks.

Back in the trailer, the cat was sitting on his bedroll. They looked at each other. Chee noticed something new. The cat was pregnant.

"Coyote's after you, I guess," Chee said. "That right?"

The cat looked at him.

"Dry weather," Chee said. "No rain. Water holes dry up. Prairie dogs, kangaroo rats, all that, they die off. Coyotes come to town and eat cats."

The cat got up from the bedroll, edged toward the doorway. Chee got a better look at it. Not very pregnant yet. That would come later. It looked gaunt and had a new scar beside its mouth.

"Maybe I can fix something up for you," Chee said. But what? Fixing something that would be proof against a hungry coyote would take some thought. Meanwhile he looked through the refrigerator. Orange juice, two cans of Dr. Pepper, limp celery, two jars of jelly, a half-consumed box of Velveeta: nothing palatable for a cat. On the shelf above the stove, he found a can of pork and beans, opened it, and left it on a copy of the Farmington *Times* beside the screen door. When he got back from finding out who called Janet Pete, he'd think of something to do about the coyote. He backed his pickup away from the trailer. In the rearview mirror he noticed that the cat was gulping down the beans. Maybe Janet Pete would have an idea about the cat. Sometimes women were smarter about such things.

But Janet Pete was not at the Shiprock DNA office, a circumstance that seemed to give some satisfaction to the young man in the white shirt and the necktie who answered Jim Chee's inquiry.

"When do you expect her?" Chee asked.

"Who knows?" the young man said.

"This afternoon? Or has she left town or something?"

"Maybe," the man said. He shrugged.

"I'll leave her a message," Chee said. He took out his notebook and his pen and wrote:

"Ms. Pete—I need to know who called you to come and get Roosevelt Bistie out of jail. Important. If I'm not in, please leave message." He signed it and left the tribal police telephone number.

But on the way out, he saw Janet Pete pulling into the parking area. She was driving a white Chevy, newly washed, with the Navajo Nation's seal newly painted on its door. She watched him walk up, her face neutral.

"*Ya-tah-hey,*" Chee said.

Janet Pete nodded.

"If you have just a minute or two, I need to talk to you," Chee said.

"Why?"

"Because Roosevelt Bistie's daughter told me she didn't call a lawyer for her father. I need to know who called you."

And I need to know absolutely everything else you know about Roosevelt Bistie, Chee thought, but first things first.

Janet Pete's expression had shifted from approximately neutral to slightly hostile.

"It doesn't matter who called," she said. "We don't have to have a request for representation from the next of kin. It can be anybody." She opened the car door and swung her legs out. "Or it can be nobody, for that matter. If someone needs to have his legal rights protected, we don't have to be asked."

Janet Pete was wearing a pale blue blouse and a tweed skirt. The legs she swung out of the car were very nice legs. And Miss Pete noticed that Chee had noticed.

"I need to know who it was," Chee said. He was surprised. He hadn't expected any trouble with this. "There's no confidentiality involved. Why be—"

"You have another homicide to work on now," she said. "Why not just leave Mr. Bistie alone. He didn't kill anyone. And he's sick. You should be able to see that. I think he has cancer of the liver. Another homicide. And no arrest made. Why don't you work on that?"

Janet Pete was leaning on the car door while she said this, and smiling slightly. But it wasn't a friendly smile.

"Where did you hear about the homicide?"

She tapped the car. "Radio," she said. "Noon news, KGAK, Gallup, New Mexico."

"They didn't say who was shot?"

" 'Police did not reveal the identity of the victim,' " she said, but the smile faded as she said it. "Who was it?"

"It was Roosevelt Bistie," Chee said.

"Oh, no," she said. She sat down on the front seat again, wrinkled her face, closed her eyes, shook her head against this mortality. "That poor man." She put her hands across her face. "That poor man."

"Somebody came to his house last night. His daughter was gone. They shot him."

Janet Pete lowered her hands to listen to this, staring at Chee. "Why? Do you know why? He was dying, anyway. He said the doctor told him the cancer would kill him."

"We don't know why," Chee said. "I want to talk to you about it. We're trying to find out why."

They left Janet Pete's clean Chevy and got into Chee's unwashed patrol car. At the Turquoise Cafe, Janet Pete ordered iced tea and Chee had coffee.

"You want to know who called me. That's funny, because the man who called lied. I found out later. He said his name was Curtis Atcitty. Spelled with the *A*. Not *E*. I had him spell it for me."

"Did he say who he was?"

"He said he was a friend of Roosevelt Bistie's, and he said Bistie was being held without bond and without any charges being filed against him, and that he was sick and didn't have any lawyer and he needed help." She paused, thinking about it. "And he said that Bistie had asked him to call DNA about a lawyer." She looked at Chee. "That's where he lied. When I told Bistie about it, he said he hadn't asked anybody to call. He said he didn't know anybody named Curtis Atcitty."

Chee clicked his tongue against his teeth, the sound of disappointment. So much for that.

"When you left the jail, I saw you driving back into Farmington. Where did you go? When was the last time you saw him?"

"Down to the bus station. He thought one of his relatives might be there, and they'd give him a ride home. But nobody he knew was there, so I took him back to Shiprock. He saw a truck he recognized at the Economy Washomat and I left him out there."

"Did he ever tell you why he tried to kill Old Man Endo-cheeney?"

Janet Pete simply looked at him.

"He's dead," Chee said. "No lawyer-client confidentiality left. Now it's try to find out who killed him."

Janet Pete studied her hands, which were small and narrow, with long, slender fingers, and if her fingernails were polished it was with the transparent, colorless stuff. Nice feminine hands, Chee thought. He remembered Mary Landon's hands, strong, smooth fingers intertwined with his own. Mary Landon's finger-tips. Mary Landon's small white fist engulfed in his own. Janet Pete's right hand now gripped her left.

"I'm not stalling," she said. "I'm thinking. I'm trying to re-member."

Chee wanted to tell her it was important. Very important. But he decided it wasn't necessary to say that to this lawyer. He watched her hands, thinking of Mary Landon, and then her face, thinking of Janet Pete.

"He said very little altogether," she said. "He didn't talk much. He wanted to know if he could go home. We talked about that. I asked him if he knew exactly what he was accused of doing. What law he was supposed to have broken." She glanced at Chee, then turned her eyes away, gazing out the street window through the dusty glass on which THE TURQUOISE CAFE was lettered in reverse. Beyond the glass, the dry wind was chasing a tumbleweed down the street. "He said he had shot a fellow over in the San Juan Canyon. And then he sort of chuckled and said maybe he just scared him. But anyway the man was dead and that was what you had him in jail for." She frowned, concentrating, right hand grip-ping the left. "I asked him why he had shot at the man and he said something vague." She shook her head.

"Vague?"

"I don't remember. Something like 'I had a reason,' or 'good reason,' or something like that—without saying why."

"Did you press him at all?"

"I said something like 'You must have had a good reason to shoot at a man,' and he laughed, I remember that, but not like he thought it was funny, and I asked him directly what his reason was and he just shut up and wouldn't answer."

"He wouldn't tell us anything, either," Chee said.

Janet Pete had taken a sip from her glass. Now she held it a few inches from her lips. "I told him I was his lawyer—there to help him. What he told me would be kept secret from anyone else. I told him shooting at somebody, even if you missed them, could get him in serious trouble with the white man and if he had a good reason for doing it, he would be smart to let me know about it. To see if we could use it in some way to help keep him out of jail."

She put down the glass and looked directly at Chee. "That's when he told me about being sick. It was easy enough to see anyway, with the way he looked. But anyway, he said the white man couldn't give him any more trouble than he already had, because he had cancer in his liver." She used the Navajo phrase for it—"the sore that never heals."

"That's what his daughter told me," Chee said. "Cancer of the liver."

Janet Pete was studying Chee's face. It was a habit that Chee had learned slowly, and come to tolerate slowly, and that still sometimes made him uneasy. Another of those cultural differences that Mary found odd and exotic.

("That first month or two in class I was always saying: 'Look at me when I talk to you,' and the kids simply wouldn't do it. They would always look at their hands, or the blackboard, or anywhere except looking me in the face. And finally one of the other teachers told me it was a cultural thing. They should warn us about things like that. Odd things. It makes the children seem evasive, deceptive."

And Chee had said something about it not seeming odd or evasive to him. It seemed merely polite. Only the rude peered into one's face during a conversation. And Mary Landon had asked him how this worked for a policeman. Surely, she'd said, they must be trained to look for all those signals facial expressions reveal while the speaker is lying, or evading, or telling less than the truth. And he had said . . .)

"You needed to know who called me," Janet Pete was saying, "because you suspect that whoever called is the one who killed Roosevelt Bistie. Isn't that it?"

Like police academy, Chee thought, law schools teach interrogators a different conversational technique than Navajo mothers. The white way. The way of looking for what the handbook on interrogation called "nonverbal signals." Chee found himself trying to keep his face blank, to send no such signals. "That's possible," he said. "It may have happened that way."

"In fact," Janet Pete said, slowly and thoughtfully, "you think this man used me. Used me to get Mr. Bistie out of jail and home. . . ." Her voice trailed off.

Chee had been looking out past the window's painted lettering. The wind had changed direction just a little—enough to pull loose the leaves and twigs and bits of paper it had pinned against the sheep fence across the highway. Now the gusts were pulling these away, sending them skittering along the pavement. Changing winds meant changing weather. Maybe, finally, it would rain. But the new tone in Janet Pete's voice drew his attention back to her.

"Used me to get him out where he could be killed."

She looked at Chee for confirmation.

"He would have gotten out, anyway," Chee said. "The FBI had him, and the FBI didn't charge him with anything. We couldn't have—"

"But I think that man wanted Mr. Bistie out before he would talk to anyone. Doesn't that make sense?"

It was exactly the thought that had brought him looking for Janet Pete.

"Doubtful," Chee said. "Probably no connection at all."

Janet Pete was reading his nonverbal signals. Rude, Chee thought. No wonder Navajos rated it as bad manners. It invaded the individual's privacy.

"It's not doubtful at all," she said. "You are lying to me now." But she smiled. "That's kind of you. But I can't help but feel responsible." She looked very glum. "I am responsible. Somebody wants to kill my client, so they call me and have me get him out where they can shoot him." She picked up her glass, noticed it was empty, put it down again. "He didn't even particularly want to be my client. The guy who wanted to shut him up just put me on the job."

"It probably wasn't that way," Chee said. "Different people, probably. Some friend called you, not knowing that this madman was coming along."

"I'm getting to be a jinx," Janet Pete said. "Typhoid Mary. A sort of curse."

Chee waited for the explanation. Janet Pete offered none. She sat, her square shoulders slumped a little, and looked sadly at her hands.

"Why jinx?" Chee said.

"This is the second time this happened," Janet Pete said, without looking at Chee. "Last time it was Irma. Irma Onesalt."

"The woman who got killed over by . . . You knew her?"

"Not very well," Janet said. She produced a humorless laugh. "A client."

"I want to hear about it," Chee said. Leaphorn seemed to think there might be some connection between the Onesalt killing and the Sam and Endocheeney cases. The lieutenant had been very interested when Chee had told him about the letter Endocheeney received from Onesalt's office. It didn't seem likely, but maybe there was some sort of link.

"That's how I heard about Officer Jim Chee," Janet Pete said, studying him. "Irma Onesalt said you did her a favor, but she didn't like you."

"I don't understand," Chee said. And he didn't. He felt foolish. The only time he'd met Onesalt, the only time he could remember, had been that business about picking up the patient at the clinic—the wrong Begay business.

"She told me you were supposed to deliver a witness to a chapter meeting and you showed up with the wrong man and screwed everything all up. But she said she owed you something. That you'd done her a favor."

"What?"

"She didn't say. I think it must have been some sort of accident. I remember she said you helped her out and you didn't even know it."

"I sure didn't," Chee said. "And don't." He waved at the man behind the counter, signaling a need for refills. "How was she your client?"

"That's pretty vague too," Janet Pete said. "She called one day and made an appointment. And when she came by, she mostly just asked a lot of questions." She paused while her glass was refilled and then stirred sugar into her tea—two teaspoons.

How did she keep so slim? Chee wondered. Nervous, he guessed. Runs it off. Mary was like that. Always moving.

"I don't think she trusted me. Asked a lot of questions about our relationship at DNA with the tribal bureaucracy and the BIA and all that. When we got that out of the way, she had a lot of questions about what I could find out for her. Financial records, things like that. What was public. What wasn't. How to get documents. I asked her what she was working on, and she said she would tell me later. That maybe it wasn't much of anything and then she wouldn't bother me. Otherwise, she would call me back."

"Did she?"

"Somebody shot her," Janet Pete said. "About ten days later."

"Did you report talking to her?"

"Probably no connection, but finally I did. I checked to find out who was handling the case and then called him and told him—Streib I think it was." She shrugged. "The fed at Gallup."

"Dilly Streib," Chee said. "What did he say?"

She made a wry face. "You know the FBI," she said. "Nothing."

"How about you? Any idea what she was after?"

"Not really." She sipped the tea, slim fingers around the tall glass.

A Navajo complexion, Chee thought. Perfect skin. Smooth, glossy. Janet Pete would never have a freckle. Janet Pete wouldn't have a wrinkle until she was old.

"But she said something that I remembered. It made me curious. Let's see if I can remember just how she put it." She raised a slim hand to her cheek, thinking. "I asked what she would want to look for and she said maybe some answers to some questions, and I said what questions and she said . . . she said how people can look so healthy after they're dead. And then I asked her what that meant. Didn't really ask her exactly, you know. Just looked puzzled, raised my eyebrows or something like that. And she just laughed."

"How people can look healthy after they're dead?"

"That's it," she said. "Maybe not the exact words, but that was the sense of it. Mean anything to you?"

"Absolutely nothing," Chee said, thinking about it so hard that he forgot the refill, and gulped scalding coffee, and spilled it on his uniform shirt—which was not at all what Jim Chee wanted to do in front of Janet Pete.

17

THE FIRST THING Joe Leaphorn noticed when he rolled Emma's old Chevy sedan to a halt in the yard of the Short Mountain Trading Post was that McGinnis had repainted his Sale sign. The sign had been there the first time Leaphorn had seen the place, coming on some long-forgotten assignment when he was a green new patrolman working in the Tuba City subagency. He sat assessing the pain in his forearm. And remembering. Even then the sign had been weather-beaten. Then, as now, it proclaimed in large block letters:

> THIS ESTABLISHMENT
> FOR SALE
> INQUIRE WITHIN

Around Short Mountain, they said that the store on the rim of Short Mountain Wash had been established sometime before the First World War by a Mormon who, it was said, noticed the lack of competition without noticing the lack of customers. It was also said that he had been convinced that the oil prosperity he saw far to the north around Aneth and Montezuma Creek would spread inexorably and inevitably south and west—that the Just Creator must have blessed this area somehow with something. And since the surface itself offered nothing but scanty grass, scarce wood, and a wilderness of erosion, there surely must be a bountiful treasure of oil below those sterile rocks. But his optimism had finally faltered with the Aneth field, and when his church ruled against multiple wives, he'd opted to join the polygamist faction in its trek to tolerant Mexico. Everyone around Short Mountain Wash seemed to remember the legend. No one remembered the man himself, but those who knew McGinnis marveled at the Mormon's salesmanship.

McGinnis now appeared in his doorway, talking to a departing customer, a tall Navajo woman with a sack of cornmeal draped over her shoulder. While he talked he stared at Emma's Chevy. A strange car out here usually meant a stranger was driving it. Among the scattered people who occupied the emptiness of Short Mountain country, strangers provoked intense curiosity. In Old Man McGinnis, almost anything provoked intense curiosity. Which was one reason Leaphorn wanted to talk to Old Man McGinnis, and had been talking to him for more than twenty years, and had become in some odd way his friend. The other reason was more complicated. It had something to do with the fact that McGinnis, alone, without wife, friend, or family, endured. Leaphorn appreciated those who endured.

But Leaphorn was in no hurry. First he would give his arm a chance to quit throbbing. "Don't move it," the doctor had told him. "If you move it, it's going to hurt." Which made sense, and was why Leaphorn had decided to drive Emma's sedan—which had automatic transmission. Emma had been delighted to see him when he'd come home from the hospital. She had fussed over him and scolded and seemed the genuine Emma. But then her face had frozen into that baffled look Leaphorn had come to dread. She said something meaningless, something that had nothing at all to do with the conversation, and turned her head in that odd way she'd developed—looking down and to her right. When she'd looked back, Leaphorn was sure she no longer recognized him. The next few moments formed another of those all too familiar, agonizing episodes of confusion. He and Agnes had taken her into the bedroom, Emma talking in a muddled attempt to communicate something, and then lying on the coverlet, looking lost and helpless. "I can't remember," she'd said suddenly and clearly, and then she'd fallen instantly asleep. Tomorrow they would keep their appointment with the specialist at the Gallup hospital. Then they would know. "Alzheimer's," the doctor would say, and then the doctor would explain Alzheimer's, all that information Leaphorn had already read and reread in "The Facts About Alzheimer's Disease" sent him by the Alzheimer's Association. Cure unknown. Cause unknown. Possibly a virus. Possibly an imbalance in blood metals. Whatever the cause, the effect was disruption of the cells on the outer surface of the brain, destroying the reasoning process, eroding the memory until only the moment of existence remains, until—in merciful finality—there is no longer a signal to keep the lungs breathing, no longer the impulse to keep the heart beating. Cure unknown. For Emma, he had watched this process of unlearning begin. Where had she left her keys? Walking home from the grocery with the car left parked in the grocery lot. Being brought home by a neighbor after she'd forgotten how to find the house they'd lived in for years. Forgetting how to finish a sentence. Who you are. Who your husband is. The literature had warned him what would be coming next. Fairly early, all speech would go. How to talk. How to walk. How to dress. Who is this man who says he is my husband? Alzheimer's, the doctor would say. And then Leaphorn would put aside pretense and prepare Emma, and himself, for whatever would be left of life.

Leaphorn shook his head. Now he would think of something else. Of business. Of whatever it was that was killing the people he was paid to protect.

He had the cast propped against the steering wheel, letting the pain drain away, sorting what he hoped to learn from this visit to Old Man McGinnis. Witchcraft, he guessed. Much as he hated to admit it, he was probably involved again in the sick and unreal business of the skinwalker superstition. The bits of bone seemed to link Jim Chee, and Roosevelt Bistie, and Dugai Endocheeney. Dilly Streib's call had confirmed that.

"Jim Chee's gossip had it right," Streib had said. "They found a little bead down in one of the knife wounds. Thread, little dirt, and a bead. I've got it. I'll have it checked to see if it matches the first one." And then Streib had asked Leaphorn what it meant, beyond the obvious connection it made between the Endocheeney and Bistie killings and the attempt on Chee. Leaphorn had said he really didn't know.

And he didn't. He knew what it might mean. It might mean that the killer thought Endocheeney was a witch. He might have thought that Endocheeney, the skinwalker, had given him corpse sickness by shooting the prescribed bit of bone into him. Then, instead of relying on an Enemy Way ritual to reverse the witchcraft, he had reversed it himself by putting the lethal bone back into the witch. Or it might mean that the killer in some crazy way thought himself to be a witch and was witching Endocheeney, putting the bone into him at the very moment he killed him with the knife. That seemed farfetched, but then everything about Navajo witchcraft seemed farfetched to Leaphorn. Or it might mean that the killer inserted the notion of witchcraft into this peculiar crime simply to cause confusion. If that had been the goal, the project had succeeded. Leaphorn was thoroughly confused. If only Chee had wormed it out of Bistie. If only Bistie had told them why he was carrying the bone bead in his wallet, what he planned to do with it, why he wanted to kill Endocheeney.

The pain in his arm had subsided. He climbed out of the Chevy, and walked across the hard-packed earth toward the sign that proclaimed the willingness of McGinnis to leave Short Mountain Wash for a better world, and stepped through McGinnis's doorway—out of the glare and heat and into the cool darkness.

"Well, now," the voice of McGinnis said from somewhere. "I wondered who it was parked out there. Who sold you that car?"

McGinnis was sitting on a wooden kitchen chair, its back tilted against the counter beside his old black-and-chrome cash register. He was wearing the only uniform Leaphorn had ever seen him wear, a pair of blue-and-white-striped overalls faded by years of washings, and under them a blue work shirt like those that convicts wear.

"It's Emma's car," Leaphorn said.

" 'Cause it's got automatic shift and you got your arm hurt," McGinnis said, looking at Leaphorn's cast. "Old John Manymules was in here with his boys a little while ago and said a cop had got shot over in the Chuskas, but I didn't know it was you."

"Unfortunately it was," Leaphorn said.

"The way Manymules was telling it, old fella got killed up there at his hogan and when the police came to see about it, one of the policemen got shot right in the middle."

"Just the arm." Leaphorn was no longer surprised by the dazzling speed with which McGinnis accumulated information, but he was still impressed.

"What brings you out here to the wrong side of the reservation?" McGinnis said. "Broke arm and all."

"Just visiting," Leaphorn said.

McGinnis eyed him through his wire-rimmed bifocals, expression skeptical. He rubbed his hand across the gray stubble on his chin. Leaphorn remembered him as a smallish man, short but with a barrel-chested strength. Now he seemed smaller, shrunken into his overalls, the sturdiness missing. The face, too, had lost the remembered roundness, and in the dimness of the trading post, his blue eyes seemed faded.

"Well, now," McGinnis said. "That's nice. I guess I ought to offer you a drink. Be hospitable. That is, if my customers can spare me."

There were no customers. The tall woman was gone and the only vehicle in the yard was Emma's Chevy. McGinnis walked to the door, limping a little and more stooped than Leaphorn remembered. He closed it, slipped the bolt lock. "Got to lock her up, then," he said, half to Leaphorn. "Goddam Navajos they'll steal the panes outta the windows if they need it." He limped toward the doorway into his living quarters, motioning Leaphorn to follow. "But only if they need it. White man, now, he'll steal just for the hell of it. I've known 'em to steal something and then just throw it away. You Navajos, now, if you steal a sack of my meal I know somebody's hungry. Screwdriver's missing, I know somebody lost his screwdriver and has a screw that needs driving. I think it was your granddaddy that first explained that to me, when I was new out here."

"Yeah," Leaphorn said. "I think you told me that."

"Get so I repeat myself," McGinnis said, with no sound of repentance in his voice. "Hosteen Klee, they called him before he died. Your mother's father. I knew him when they was still calling him Horse Kicker." McGinnis had opened the door of a huge old refrigerator. "I ain't offering you a drink because you don't drink whiskey, or at least you never did, and whiskey's all I got," he said into the refrigerator. "Unless you want a drink of water."

"No, thanks," Leaphorn said.

McGinnis emerged, holding a bourbon bottle and a Coca Cola glass. He carried these to a rocking chair, sat, poured bourbon into the glass, examined it, then, with the glass close to his eyes, dripped in more until the level reached the bottom of the trademark. That done, he set the bottle on the floor and motioned Leaphorn to sit. The only place open was a sofa upholstered with some sort of green plastic. Leaphorn sat. The stiff plastic crackled under his weight and a puff of dust arose around him.

"You're here on business," McGinnis declared.

Leaphorn nodded.

McGinnis sipped. "You're here because you think old McGinnis knows something about Wilson Sam. He'll tell you, and you'll put it with what you already know and figure out who killed him."

Leaphorn nodded.

"Outta luck," McGinnis said. "I've known that young fella since he was a buck Indian and I don't know anything about him that's going to help."

"You've been thinking about it," Leaphorn said.

"Sure," McGinnis said. "Fella you've known gets killed, you think about it." He sipped again. "Lost a customer," he said.

"Anything in that?" Leaphorn said. "Unusual, I mean. Like him coming in with money to pay off his pawn. Or buying anything unusual. People coming to ask where to find him."

"Nothing," McGinnis said.

"He make any trips? Go anyplace? Been sick? Any ceremonials for him?"

"Nothing like that," McGinnis said. "He used to come in now and then to do his buying. Sell me his wool. Things like that. Get his mail. I remember he cut his hand bad way back last winter and he went into that clinic that Sioux Indian opened there at Badwater Wash and they sewed it up for him and gave him a tetanus shot. But no sickness. No sings for him. No trips anyplace, except he told me couple of months ago he went into Farmington with his daughter to get himself some clothes." McGinnis took another sip of bourbon. "Too damn fashionable to buy his clothes from me anymore. Everybody's wearing designer jeans."

"How about his mail? Do you write his letters for him? He get anything unusual?"

"He could read and write," McGinnis said. "But he ain't bought no stamps this year. Not from me, anyway. Or mailed any letters. Or got any unusual mail. Only thing unusual, couple of months ago he got a letter in the middle of the month." He didn't explain that, or need to. On the far reaches of the reservation, mail consists primarily of subsistence checks, from the tribal offices in Window Rock or some federal agency. They arrive on the second day of the month, in brown stacks.

"In June was it?" That was when Chee had said Endocheeney received his letter from Irma Onesalt's office. "About the second week?"

"That's what I said," McGinnis said. "Two months ago."

Leaphorn had managed to find a way to be fairly comfortable on the sofa. He had been watching McGinnis, who in turn had kept his watery eyes focused on the bourbon while he talked. And while he talked, he rocked, slowly and steadily, coordinating a motion in his forearm with the motion of his chair. The net result of this was that while the bourbon glass seemed to move, the liquid in it remained level and motionless. Leaphorn had noticed this lesson in hydraulic motion before, but it still intrigued him. But what

McGinnis had said about the letter regained his full attention. He leaned forward.

"Don't get excited," McGinnis said. "You gonna expect me to tell you that inside that envelope there was a letter from somebody telling Wilson Sam to hold still because he was coming to kill him. Something like that." McGinnis chuckled. "You got your hopes up too high. It wasn't from anybody. It was from Window Rock."

Leaphorn wasn't surprised McGinnis had noticed this, or that he remembered it. A midmonth letter would have been an oddity.

"What was it about?"

McGinnis's placid expression soured. "I don't read folks' mail."

"All right then, who was it from?"

"One of them bureaus there in Window Rock," McGinnis said. "Like I said."

"You remember which one?"

"Why would I remember something like that?" McGinnis said. "None of my business."

Because everything out here is your business, Leaphorn thought. Because the letter would have lain around somewhere for days while you waited for Wilson Sam to come in, or for some relative to come in who could take it to him, and every day you would look at it and wonder what was in it. And because you remember everything.

"I just thought you might," Leaphorn said, overcoming a temptation to tell McGinnis the letter was from Social Services.

"Social Services," McGinnis said.

Social Services. Exactly. He wished he had found time to check. If the letter wasn't in the file, if no one there remembered writing to Endocheeney, or to Wilson Sam, it would be fair circumstantial evidence that Onesalt had done the writing, and that the letters were in some way unofficial. Why would Social Services be writing to either man?

"Did it have a name on it? I mean on the return address. Or just the office?"

"Come to think of it, yeah." McGinnis sipped again and inspected the bourbon level with watery eyes. "That might be of some interest to you," he said, without taking his eyes off the glass. "Because that woman who had her name on the return address, she was the one that got shot a little later over there in your part of the reservation. Same name, anyway."

"Irma Onesalt," Leaphorn said.

"Yessir," McGinnis said. "Irma Onesalt."

The circle was thus complete. The bone beads linked Wilson Sam and Endocheeney and Jim Chee and Roosevelt Bistie. The letters linked Onesalt into the pattern. Now he had what he needed to solve this puzzle. He had no idea how. But he knew himself. He knew he would solve it.

18

IT WAS A DAY OFF FOR CHEE, and in a little while it would be time to leave for the long drive to the place of Hildegarde Goldtooth, to meet with Alice Yazzie. Ninety miles or so, some of it on bad roads, and he intended to leave early. He planned to detour past the Badwater Clinic to see if he could learn anything there. And he didn't want to keep Alice Yazzie waiting. He wanted to do her Blessing Way. Now Chee was passing the time in what Captain Largo called his "laboratory." Largo had laughed about it. "Laboratory, or maybe it's your studio," Largo had said when he found Chee working there. In fact, it was nothing but a flat, hard-packed earthen surface up the slope from Chee's trailer. Chee had chosen it because a gnarled old cottonwood shaded the place. He had prepared it carefully, digging it up, leveling it, raking out bits of gravel and weed roots, making it an approximation of the size and shape of a hogan floor. He used it to practice dry painting the images used in the ceremonials he was learning.

At the moment, Chee was squatting at the edge of this floor. He was finishing the picture of Sun's Creation, an episode from the origin story used in the second night of the Blessing Way. Chee was humming, mouthing the words of the poetry that recounted this episode, letting a controlled trickle of blue sand sift between his fingers to form the tip of the feather that was hung from Sun's left horn.

> Sun will be created—they say it is planned to
> happen.
> Sun will be created—they say he has planned it all.
> Its face will be blue—they say he has planned it all.

Its eyes will be yellow—they say he planned it all.
Its forehead will be white—they say he planned it
all.

Feather finished, Chee rocked back on his heels, poured the surplus blue sand from his palm into the coffee can that held it, wiped his hand on the leg of his jeans, and surveyed his work. It was good. He had left off one of the three plumes that should have extended eastward from the headdress of Pollen Boy, standing against Sun's face—thus not completing the power of the holy image at this inappropriate time and place. Otherwise, the dry painting looked perfect. The lines of sand—black, blue, yellow, red, and white—were neatly defined. The symbols were correct. The red sand was a bit too coarse, but he would fix that by running a can of it through the coffee grinder again. He was ready. He knew this version of the Blessing Way precisely and exactly—every word of every song, every symbol of the dry paintings. It would cure for him. He squatted, memorizing again the complicated formula of symbols he had created on the earth before him, feeling its beauty. Soon he would be performing this old and holy act as it had been intended, to return one of his people to beauty and harmony. Chee felt the joy of that rising in him, and turned away the thought. All things in moderation.

The cat was watching him from the hillside above its juniper. It had been in sight much of the morning, vanishing down the bank of the San Juan for a while but returning after less than an hour to lie in the juniper's shade. Chee had put the shipping case under the tree the previous evening—fitting it beneath the limbs as near to the cat's sleeping place as he could force it. In it he'd put an old denim jacket, which the cat sometimes sat on when it came into the trailer. He had added, as lure, a hamburger patty from his refrigerator. He'd been saving the patty for some future lunch, but the edges had curled and turned dark. This morning he noticed the meat was missing and he presumed the cat had gone into the case to retrieve it. But he could see no sign that the cat had slept there. No problem. Chee was patient.

The case was really a cage with a carrying handle and had cost Chee almost forty dollars with taxes. It had been Janet Pete's idea. He had brought up the problem of cat and coyote as they left the Turquoise Cafe, trying to extend the conversation—to think of something to say that would prevent Miss Pete from getting into her clean white official Chevy sedan and leaving him standing there on the sidewalk.

"I don't guess you'd know anything about cats?" Chee had said, and she'd said, "Not much, but what's the problem?" And he'd told her about the cat and the coyote. Then he'd waited a moment while she thought about it. While he waited (Janet Pete leaning, gracefully, against her Chevy, frowning, lower lip caught between her teeth, taking the problem seriously), he thought about what Mary Landon would have said. Mary would have asked who owned the cat. Mary would have said, Well, silly, just bring the cat in, and keep it in your trailer until the coyote goes away and hunts something else. Perfectly good solutions for a *belagana* cat in a *belagana* world, but they overlooked the nature of Jim Chee, a Navajo, and the role of animals in Dine' Bike'yah, where Corn Beetle and Bluebird and Badger received equal billing when the Holy People emerged into this Earth Surface World.

"I don't guess you'd want a cat," Janet Pete said, looking at Chee.

Chee grinned.

"Can you fix up something out there? So the coyote can't get to it?"

"You know coyotes," Chee said.

Janet Pete smiled, looked wry, brightened. "I know," she said. "Get one of those airline shipping cages." She described one, cat-sized, with her hands. "They're tough. A coyote couldn't get her in that."

"I don't know," Chee said, doubting the cat would get into such a thing. Doubting it would foil a coyote. "I don't think I've ever seen one. Where can you get 'em? Airport?"

"Pet store," Janet Pete said. And she'd driven him to the one in Farmington. The shipping cage Chee eventually bought had been designed for a small dog. It was made of stiff steel wire that looked coyote-proof. And it was large enough, in Chee's opinion, to seem hospitable to the cat. Janet Pete had remembered an appointment and hurried him back to his car at the courthouse.

Even as he was driving to Shiprock with the cage on the seat beside him it was seeming less and less of a good idea. He'd have to narrow the doorway to make it just big enough for the cat and too small for the coyote's head. That looked simple enough. In fact, it had been merely a matter of using some hay baling wire. But there was still the question of whether the cat would accept it as a bedroom, and whether she would be smart enough to recognize the safety it offered when the coyote was stalking her.

Chee thought about that as he swept up the sand, using the feathered wand from his *jish* bundle for the task. After she had created the first of the Navajo clans, Changing Woman had taught them how to perform their curing ceremonials. She'd made the first dry paintings out of the clouds, blowing each away with her breath as its purpose was completed. And she'd taught the first of the Navajos to scatter their painting sand to the winds, just as Chee did now—collecting it on a dustpan and then throwing it into the air to drift away. He brushed the last traces of the picture away and collected the coffee cans in which he kept his supply of unused sands. No use thinking about the cat now. Time would tell. Perhaps the cat would use the cage. If it didn't, there would be the time to seek another solution. And there were other, tougher problems. How would she fare when she grew big with pregnancy? How would the litter survive? Worse, she was hunting less now—or seemed to be. Relying more on the food he provided her. That was exactly what he couldn't allow to happen. If the cat was to make the transition—from someone's property to self-sufficient predator—it couldn't rely on him, or on any person. To do so was to fail. Chee had been surprised when he first realized that he cared how this struggle ended. Now he accepted it. He wanted the cat to tear itself free. He wanted *belagana* cat to become natural cat. He wanted the cat to endure.

Chee stacked the cans of sand back into the outside storage compartment in the wall of his trailer, where he kept all his ceremonial regalia. He would take with him, he decided, his *jish* just in case the circumstances at his meeting with Alice Yazzie required some sort of blessing. Besides, the *jish* case itself and the ceremonial items in it were impressive. In this, Chee was a perfectionist. His prayer sticks were painted exactly right, waxed, polished, with exactly the right feathers attached as they should be attached. The bag that held his pollen was soft doeskin; labeled plastic prescription bottles held the fragments of mica, abalone shell, and the other "hard jewels" his profession required. And his Four Mountain bundle—four tiny bags contained in a doeskin sack—included exactly the proper herbs and minerals, which Chee had collected from the four sacred mountains exactly as the *yei* had instructed. Chee would take his *jish.* He would hope that the opportunity would arise to get it out and open it.

Inside the trailer, he exchanged his dusty jeans for a pair he'd just bought in Farmington. He put on the red-and-white shirt he saved for special occasions, his polished "go-to-town" boots, and his black felt hat. Then he checked himself in the mirror over his washbasin. All right, he thought. Better if he looked a lot older. The Dinee liked their *hataalii* to be old and wise—men like Frank Sam Nakai, his mother's brother. "Don't worry about it," Frank Sam Nakai had told him. "All the famous singers started when they were young. Hosteen Klah started when he was young. Frank Mitchell started when he was young. I started when I was young. Just pay attention and try to learn."

Now, finally, he would be beginning to use what Frank Sam Nakai had been teaching him for so many years. As he drove up the slope away from the river, he noticed that the cloud formation that built every afternoon over the slopes behind Shiprock was bigger today, dark at the bottom, forming its anvil top of ice crystals earlier than usual in this dry summer. Howard Morgan, the weatherman on Channel 7, had said there was a 30 percent chance of rain in the Four Corners today. That was the best odds of the summer so far. Morgan said the summer monsoon might finally be coming. Rain. That would be the perfect omen. And Morgan was often right.

When he turned west on 504, it looked as if Morgan was right again. Thunderheads had merged over the Carrizo range, forming a blue-black wall that extended westward far into Arizona. The afternoon sun lit their tops, already towering high enough to be blowing ice crystals into the jet stream winds. By the time he turned south beyond Dennehotso across Greasewood Flats, he was driving in cloud shadow. Proximity winds were kicking up occasional dust devils. But Chee had been raised with the desert dweller's conditioning to avoid disappointment. He allowed himself to think a while about rain, sweeping its cool, wet blessing across the desert, but not to expect it. And now he needed to think of something else. The Badwater Clinic was over the next ridge.

The quirky wind generated by the thunderstorms' great updrafts bounced a tumbleweed across the unpaved clinic parking lot just as he pulled his truck to a stop. He turned off the engine and waited for the gust to subside. The place had been built only five or so years ago—a long one-story, flat-roofed rectangle set in a cluster of attendant buildings. A cube of concrete housing the clinic's water well was just behind the building, surmounted by a once-white storage tank. Beyond that stood a cluster of those ugly frame-and-brown-plaster housing units that the Bureau of Indian Affairs had scattered by the thousands across Indian reservations from Point Barrow to the Pagago Reservation. New as the clinic compound was, the reservation had already touched it, as it seemed to touch all such unnatural shapes imposed upon it, with an instant look of disrepair. The white paint of the clinic building was no longer white, and blowing sand had stripped patches of it from the concrete-block walls. None of this registered on the consciousness of Chee, who, Navajo fashion, had looked at the setting and not the structures. It was a good place. Beautiful. A long view down the valley toward the cliffs that rose above Chilchinbito Canyon and Long Flat Wash, toward the massive shape of Black Mesa—its dark green turned a cool blue by cloud shadow and distance. The view lifted Chee's spirits. He felt exultant—a mood he hadn't enjoyed since reading Mary Landon's letter. He walked toward the clinic entrance, feeling a gust of sand blown against his ankles and guessing that today it would finally rain and he would be lucky.

He was. The person sitting behind the counter-desk in the entrance foyer was the Woman from the Yoo'l Dinee, the Bead People. Chee's excellent Navajo-trained memory also produced her name—Eleanor Billie. She had been the receptionist on duty that cold late-spring day when he had come with the Onesalt woman to collect the wrong Begay. Her memory seemed to be as good as Chee's.

"Mister Policeman," she said, smiling very slightly. "Who can we get for you today? Do you need another Begay?"

"I just need you to help me understand something," Chee said. "About the time we got the wrong one."

Mrs. Billie had nothing to say to that. That smile, Chee realized, had not been a warm one. Maybe he wasn't so lucky.

"What I need to know is whether the woman who was with me—that woman from Window Rock—if she ever contacted anybody about that. Wrote a letter. Telephoned. Anything like that. Did she have any questions? Who would I ask about that?"

Mrs. Billie looked surprised. She produced an ironic chuckle. "She raised hell," she said. "She came in here the next day and acted real nasty. Wanted to see Dr. Yellowhorse. I don't know how she acted with him. She acted nasty with me."

"She came back?" Chee laughed. "I guess I shouldn't act surprised. She was mad enough to kill somebody." He laughed again. Mrs. Billie smiled, and now, he noticed, it seemed genuine. In fact, it was spreading into a broad grin.

"I always wondered what happened. To get that bitch in such a rage," Mrs. Billie said.

"Well, we took Begay to the chapter house over at Lukachukai. They were having a meeting—trying to settle whether a family from the Weaver Clan or an outfit from the Many Hogans Dinee had a right to live on some land over there. Anyway, Irma Onesalt had found out that this old Begay man had lived over there for about a thousand years and he was supposed to tell the council that the Many Hogans family had lived there first, and had the grazing and the water and all that. I didn't see all of it, but what I heard was that when they called on that Begay you gave us to talk about it, he gave them this long speech about how he never had lived there at all. He was born to the Coyote Pass People, and born for the Monster People, and him and his outfit lived way over east on the Checkerboard Reservation."

Chee was grinning as he finished, remembering Irma Onesalt's incoherent rage as she stomped out of the chapter house and back to his patrol car. "You should have heard what she said to me," he said. What Irma Onesalt had said would translate precisely from Navajo to English. It was the equivalent of: "You stupid son-of-a-bitch, you got the wrong Begay."

Mrs. Billie's grin showed an array of very white teeth in a very round face.

"I'd like to have seen that," Mrs. Billie said, with Chee now firmly established as a fellow victim. "You should have heard what she said to me. I just reminded her she'd called and said she was picking up Frank Begay to take him to the hearing, and we gave her the only Begay we had. Franklin Begay. Pretty damn close."

"Pretty close," Chee agreed.

"And the only Begay we had," Mrs. Billie said. "Still is, for that matter."

"Wonder what caused her to get the wrong name—or whatever happened."

"Oh, Frank Begay used to be here. He was diabetic, with all sorts of complications. But he died way back in the winter. Earlier than that. It was in October. He was the one from Lukachukai."

"I wonder if that's what caused the confusion," Chee said. "She didn't seem like a woman who'd get confused much."

Mrs. Billie nodded, agreeing. She looked thoughtful. "What she said was that we had our records all screwed up. Said we had him on our list as a patient. I looked, and told her we didn't. And she said, Damn it, yes we did. Maybe not today, she said, but a couple of weeks ago." Mrs. Billie was showing her white teeth in another joyful grin, remembering. "That's why I know just when Frank Begay died. October three. I went back into the files and found it."

Chee allowed himself to imagine for a moment how much pleasure Mrs. Billie had attained by giving that news to Irma Onesalt. He remembered his own discomfort at the chapter house, with the woman leaning on the door of his patrol car, staring at him contemptuously, bombarding him with questions about why he had delivered Franklin Begay when she had told him to deliver Frank Begay. An unusually arrogant woman, Irma Onesalt. He wondered, half seriously, if Dilly Streib, or whoever was working her homicide for the FBI, had considered that as a motive for her murder. Someone might simply have got tired of suffering Irma Onesalt's bad conduct.

"What else did Onesalt say?" Chee asked.

"Wanted to see the doctor to argue about it."

"Dr. Yellowhorse?"

"Yeah. So I sent her on in."

Yellowhorse and Onesalt, Chee thought. Two tough coyotes. For different reasons, he didn't like either of them—but Yellowhorse he respected. His differences with the doctor were purely philosophical—the believer and the agnostic exploiting the belief. Onesalt was, or had been, simply an obnoxious jerk. "I wish I could have seen those two," Chee said. "What happened?"

Mrs. Billie shrugged. "She went in. Maybe five minutes she came out."

The telephone at Mrs. Billie's plump elbow buzzed. "Badwater Clinic," she said. "What? Okay. I'll tell him." She hung up. "Came out steaming," she continued, grinning again. "Pure rage now. The doctor, he can be rough, you get him stirred up."

Chee was remembering what Janet Pete had told him—of Irma Onesalt's remark about the wrong Begay business tipping her off to something. This conversation hadn't opened any doors to what that might be. Or had it?

"She say anything else? Any remarks or anything?"

"No," Mrs. Billie said. "Well, not much. She got almost to the door and then she turned around and came back and asked me what that date was when Frank Begay died."

"You told her October third?"

"No. I hadn't looked it up yet. I told her last fall, I guess. And then she asked me if she could see a list of the patients we had in here." Mrs. Billie's face expressed disapproval of this remembered outrage. "Imagine that kind of brass!" she said. "And I said she'd have to ask the doctor about that and she said to hell with it then, she'd get it another way." Mrs. Billie looked even more disapproving. "Actually she said a little worse than that. Rough-talking woman."

A middle-aged black woman in a nurse's uniform came down the hall with a young Navajo who was pushing a wheelchair. The wheelchair contained a woman with her leg in a cast. "Now tell her again that it will itch, but she's not supposed to scratch it. Just let it itch. Think about something else." The Navajo said, "Don't scratch," in Navajo, and Woman in Cast said, in English, "Don't scratch. You told me that before."

"She speaks English," Mrs. Billie told the nurse. "Better than I do."

"That was it? Nothing else?" Chee asked, getting Mrs. Billie's attention again.

"Just walked out after that," Mrs. Billie said.

"She said she could get the list of patients another way?"

"Yeah," Mrs. Billie said. "I guess she could, too. They'd all be on some sort of medical-cost reimbursement list. Medicare, or Medicaid, or some insurance claim if they had insurance. Most of them wouldn't."

"Just have to go through the red tape?"

"Probably no big deal. She worked in Window Rock with all the other bureaucrats. Probably just get somebody in the right accounting office to get her a Xerox, or let her take a peek."

Chee had been remembering Leaphorn in his trailer, putting the list on his countertop. Leaphorn watching his face as he looked at the list. Leaphorn asking if he knew any of them. Looking disappointed when he didn't. Asking if the names suggested anything to him. They had suggested nothing. But now they did. Now they seemed terribly important.

"I haven't got any friends among the bureaucrats at Window Rock. Any way I could find out who was here that day?"

"You could ask Dr. Yellowhorse."

"Good," Chee said. "Can I get in to see him?"

"He's not here," Mrs. Billie said.

Chee looked as disappointed as possible. He shrugged, made a wry face.

"You're a policeman. I guess you could say it was police business."

"It's police business," Chee said.

"It will take a while," Mrs. Billie said, getting up. "Call me if the telephone rings."

It took about ten minutes and the telephone didn't ring. "I just copied them off for that date," Mrs. Billie said. "I hope you can read my writing."

Mrs. Billie's writing was a beautiful, clear, symmetrical script—a script that would win penmanship competitions, if there were still penmanship competitions. Chee noticed that before he looked at the names.

Ethelmary Largewhiskers

Addison Etcitty

Wilson Sam

This was the list Leaphorn had told him about. The names for which Irma Onesalt was seeking death certificate dates. Wilson Sam's name was third. And second from the bottom Chee saw Dugai Endocheeney.

"Thanks," he said. He folded the paper absently and put it into his billfold, thinking: Sam and Endocheeney were alive when Onesalt was hunting their death certificates. Endocheeney had been into the clinic for that broken leg Iron Woman had told him about, and Sam for God knows what. But they were still alive. What was Onesalt . . . ?

His mind answered the question even before he completed it. He knew why Irma Onesalt had died, and almost all the rest of it. All that remained of the puzzle was why someone had tried to kill him. He glanced at his watch. He'd spent more time here than he'd intended.

"Need to use your telephone," he told Mrs. Billie.

He would call Leaphorn and tell him what he'd learned. Then he had to hurry. He'd been hearing thunder and it seemed to be getting closer. He'd have to leave a little time in case it got muddy. After he made a deal with Alice Yazzie to conduct a Blessing Way, he'd see if he could figure out why Jim Chee's ghost was supposed to join the *chindis* of Onesalt, Sam, and Endocheeney. Now was not the time to be thinking such unpleasant thoughts.

19

THE TELEPHONE WAS BUZZING when Leaphorn came through his office door. "You just missed a call," the operator told him. "I took the message for you."

"Okay," Leaphorn said. He was tired. He wanted to clean off his desk in a hurry, go home, take a shower, try to relax for a few minutes, and then drive back to Gallup. Emma had to stay overnight for the tests they were making, for the things they do when something is wrong inside the head. Why? Leaphorn didn't understand that. Uncharacteristically for him, he hadn't insisted on an explanation. Everything about Emma's illness left him feeling helplessly out of control. Things were happening to them that would change their lives—devastate his life—and there was nothing he could do that would affect it. He felt surrounded by inevitability—something new for Joe Leaphorn. It made him feel as he'd heard people felt when caught in earthquakes, with the solid earth no longer solid.

He worked quickly through the "Immediate Action" memos, and found none that required immediate action. The most urgent two concerned the rodeo. First, a bootlegger, a woman in a blue Ford 250 pickup, seemed to be selling more or less openly, according to the complaints, but hadn't been arrested. Second, a problem with traffic management had developed at points where the rodeo grounds access routes tangled with mainstream flow on Navajo Route 3. Leaphorn wrote the necessary order to deal with the traffic first. The bootlegger required thought. Who would the woman be? He sorted through a career-long accumulation of bootlegger knowledge, studied his map briefly. Usually five or six bootleggers would work an event as popular as the rodeo, two or three of them female. One of these women was sick, Leaphorn knew, maybe even in the hospital. Of the other two, the one who lived down at Wide Ruins drove a big pickup. Leaphorn conjured up her family connections. She was born to the Towering House Clan, born for the Rock Gap People? He compared this mentally with the clans of the policemen he had working the rodeo—following the simple and true theory that no one is going to arrest his own clan sister if he can avoid it. He found what he expected to find. The sergeant in charge of internal order was a Towering House man.

Leaphorn tore up the order he'd written to deal with the access problem and wrote another, switching the Towering House sergeant to traffic control and replacing him with the corporal who had been handling traffic. Then he looked at his telephone messages.

The call he had just missed was from Jim Chee.

Lieutenant Leaphorn: Irma Onesalt came back to Badwater Clinic the day after I picked up Franklin Begay there. She was angry. She found out that Frank Begay had died last October. She asked for a list of patients in the clinic, went to see Dr. Yellowhorse about it, got a turndown, said she could get the names elsewhere. I got a list of the names on list on the date Onesalt was there. The list included both Endocheeney and Wilson Sam. I remember hearing that Endocheeney had been in the clinic about then with a broken leg.

The remainder of the message was a listing of all those who had been patients in the Badwater Clinic that April day. They included the names Dr. Jenks had remembered, the quaint names.

Leaphorn read the note again. Then he let it drop from his fingers and picked up the telephone.

"Call Shiprock and get me Chee," he said.

"Doubt if we can," the dispatcher said. "He was calling from the Badwater Clinic. Said he was just leaving. Going over toward Dinebito Wash and he'd be out of touch for a while."

"Dinebito Wash?" Leaphorn said. What the hell would he be doing there? Even on the reservation, where isolation was the norm, Dinebito country was an empty corner. There the desert rose toward the northern limits of the Black Mesa highlands. Leaphorn told the switchboard to get Captain Largo at Shiprock.

He waited, standing by the window. The entire sky, south and west, was black with storm now. Like all people who live a lot out of doors and whose culture depends upon the weather, Leaphorn was a student of the sky. This one was easy enough to read. This storm wouldn't fade away, as storms had been doing all this summer. This one had water in it, and force. It would be raining hard by now across the Hopi mesas, at Ganado and on the grazing country of his cousins around Klagetoh and Cross Canyons and Burntwater. By tomorrow they'd be hearing of the flash floods down Wide Ruins Wash, and the Lone Tule, and Scattered Willow Draw, and those dusty desert-country drains that converted themselves into roaring torrents when the male rains came. Tomorrow would be a busy day for the 120 men and women of the Navajo Tribal Police.

Leaphorn watched the lightning, and the first cold drops splattering themselves across the glass, and did not think of Emma sleeping in her hospital room. Instead he let the links offered in Chee's message click into place. Onesalt's motivation? Malice, of course. Leaphorn thought about it. It was unproductive thought, but it was better than thinking of Emma. Better than thinking about what he would learn tomorrow when the tests were finished.

The telephone rang.

"I've got Captain Largo," the operator said, with Largo's voice behind him saying something about quitting time.

"This is Leaphorn," Leaphorn said. "Do you know where Jim Chee was going today?"

"Chee?" Largo laughed. "I do. Son-of-a-bitch finally got himself a sing. He was going out to see about it. All excited."

"I need to talk to him," Leaphorn said. "Is he working tomorrow? Could you call in and check for me?"

"I am in," Largo said. "I don't have any better luck getting away from the office than you do. Just a minute."

Leaphorn waited, hearing Largo's breathing and the sounds of papers shuffling. "It raining down there yet?" Largo asked. "Looks like we might finally get some up here."

"Just starting," Leaphorn said. He drummed his fingertips against the desktop. Through the rain-streaked window he saw a triple-flash lightning.

"Tomorrow," Largo said. "No, Chee's off."

"Well, hell," Leaphorn said.

"But let's see now. He was supposed to keep in touch. Because of somebody trying to shoot him. I told him, and sometimes Chee does what he's told. Let's see if there's a note on that."

More rustling of papers. Leaphorn waited.

"Be damned. He did it for once." Largo's tone changed from man talking to man reading. " 'Will go today to the place of Hildegarde Goldtooth out near Dinebito Wash to meet with her and Alice Yazzie about doing a sing for a patient.' " Largo's voice switched back to normal. "He got invited to do that sing last week. Real proud of it. Going around showing everybody the letter."

"Nothing about when he'll be back?"

"With Chee, that'd be asking too much," Largo said.

"I haven't been out there since I worked out of Tuba City," Leaphorn said. "Wouldn't he have to go past Piñon?"

"Unless he's walking," Largo said. "That's the only road."

"Well, thanks," Leaphorn said. "I'll call our man there and get him to catch him going in or out."

The policeman assigned to work out of the Piñon Chapter House was a Sleep Rock Dinee named Leonard Skeet. Leaphorn had worked with him in his younger days at Tuba City and remembered him as reliable if you weren't in a hurry. The voice that said "Hello" was feminine—Mrs. Skeet. Leaphorn identified himself.

"He's gone over to Rough Rock," the woman said.

"When you expect him?"

"I don't know." She laughed, but the storm, or the distance, or the way the telephone line was tied to miles of fence posts to reach this outpost, made it difficult to tell whether the sound was amused or ironic. "He's a policeman, you know."

"I'd like to leave a message for him," Leaphorn said. "Would you tell him Officer Jim Chee will be driving through there. I need your husband to stop Chee and tell him to call me." He supplied his home telephone number. It would be better to wait there until it was time to go back to Gallup.

"About when you think he'll come by? Lenny's going to ask me that."

"It's just a guess," Leaphorn said. "He's gone out somewhere around Dinebito Wash. Out to see Hildegarde Goldtooth. I don't know how far that is."

There was something as close to silence as the crackling of the poorly insulated line allowed.

"You there?" Leaphorn asked.

"That was my father's sister," Mrs. Skeet said. "She's dead. Died last month."

And now it was Leaphorn's turn to produce the long silence. "Who lives out there now?"

"Nobody," Mrs. Skeet said. "The water was bad, anyway. Alkaline. And when she died, there was nobody left but her daughter and her son-in-law. They just moved away."

"The place is empty, then."

"That's right. If anybody moved in, I'd know it."

"Can you tell me exactly how to get there from Piñon?"

Mrs. Skeet could. As Leaphorn sketched out her instructions on his notepad, his mind was checking off other Navajo Police subagency offices that might be able to get someone to Piñon quicker than he could get there himself from Window Rock. Many Farms would be closer. Kayenta would be closer. But who would be working at this hour? And he could think of nothing he could tell them—nothing specific—that would instill in them the terrible sense of urgency that he felt himself.

He could be there in two hours, he thought. Perhaps a little less. And find Chee, and be back here in time to get to Gallup by midnight or so. Emma would be asleep, anyway. He had no choice.

"You taking off for home?" the desk officer asked him when he came down the stairs.

"Going to Piñon," Leaphorn said.

20

IN ALBUQUERQUE, in the studio of KOAT-TV, Howard Morgan was explaining it. The newscast was picked up and relayed by drone repeater stations to blanket the Checkerboard Reservation and reach into the Four Corners country and into the eastern fringes of the Navajo Big Reservation. Had Jim Chee been at home in his trailer with his battery-powered TV turned on, he would have been seeing Morgan standing in front of a projection of a satellite photograph, explaining how the jet stream had finally shifted south, pulling cool, wet air with it, and this mass was meeting more moisture. The moisture coming up from the south was serious stuff, being pushed across Baja California and the deserts of northwest Mexico by Hurricane Evelyn. "Rains at last," said Morgan. "Good news if you're growing rhubarb. Bad news if you're planning picnics. And remember, the flash flood warnings are out for all of the southern and western parts of the Colorado plateau tonight, and for tomorrow all across northern New Mexico."

But Chee was not at home watching the weathercast. He was more or less racing the storm front—driving through the cloud-induced early twilight with his lights on. Just past Piñon he had run into a quick and heavy flurry of rain—drops the size of peach stones kicking up spurts of dust as they struck the dirt road ahead of him. Then came a bombardment of popcorn snow which moved like a curtain across the road, reflecting his headlights like a rhinestone curtain. That lasted no more than a hundred yards. Then he was in dry air again. But rain loomed over him. It hung over the northeast slopes of Black Mesa like a wall—illuminated to light gray now and then by sheet lightning. The smell of it came through the pickup vents, mixed with the smell of dust. In Chee's desert-trained nostrils it was heady perfume—the smell of good grazing, easy water, heavy crops of piñon nuts. The smell of good times, the smell of Sky Father blessing Mother Earth.

Chee drove with the map Alice Yazzie had drawn on the back of her letter spread on his lap. The volcanic outcrop rising like four giant clenched fingers just ahead must be the place she'd marked to watch for a left turn. It was. Just beyond it, two ruts branched from the dirt road he'd been following.

Chee was early. He stopped and got out to stretch his muscles and kill a little time, partly to check if the track was still in use and partly for the sheer joy of standing under this huge, violent sky. Once the track had been used fairly heavily, but not recently. Now the scanty weeds and grass of a dry summer had grown on the hump between the ruts. But someone had driven here today. In fact, very recently. The tires were worn, but what little tread marks they left were fresh. Jagged lightning streaked through the cloud and repeated itself—producing a thunderclap loud as a cannon blast. A damp breeze moved past, pressing the denim of his trousers against his legs and carrying the smell of ozone and wet sage and piñon needles. Then he heard the muted roar of the falling water. It moved toward him like a gray wall. Chee climbed back into the cab, as an icy drop splashed against the back of his wrist.

He drove the final 2.3 miles that Alice Yazzie had indicated on her map with his windshield wipers lashing and the rain pounding on the roof. The track wandered up a wide valley, rising toward the Black Mesa highlands, becoming increasingly rocky. Chee had been worried a little, despite the mud chains he always carried. The rockiness eliminated that worry. He wouldn't get stuck on this. Abruptly, the sky lightened. The rain eased—one of those brief respites common to high-altitude storms. The tracks climbed a ridge lined with eroded granite boulders, followed it briefly, and then turned sharply downward. Below him Chee saw the Goldtooth place. A round stone hogan with a domed dirt roof, a peak-roofed frame house, a pole corral, a storage shed, and a lean-to of poles, planks, and tarpaper, built against the wall of a low cliff. Smoke was coming from the hogan, hanging in the wet air and creating a blue smudge across the narrow cul-de-sac where the Goldtooth outfit had built its place. An old truck was parked beside the plank house. From behind the house, the back end of an ancient Ford sedan was visible. Chee could see a dim light, probably a kerosene lamp, illuminating one of the side windows of the house. Except for that, and the smoke, the place had an abandoned look.

He parked a polite distance from the house and sat for a moment with his headlights on it, waiting. The front door opened and the light outlined a shape, wearing the voluminous long skirt and long-sleeved blouse of the traditional Navajo woman. She stared out into Chee's headlights, then made the traditional welcoming motion and disappeared into the house.

Chee switched off the lights, opened the door, and stepped out into the resuming rain. He walked toward the house, past the parked truck. He could see now that the Ford had no rear wheels. The damp air carried the thousand smells aroused by rain. But something was missing. The acrid smell that fills the air when rain wets the still-fresh manure of corrals and sheep pens. Where was that? Chee's intelligence had its various strengths and its weaknesses—a superb memory, a tendency to exclude new input while it focused too narrowly on a single thought, a tendency to be distracted by beauty, and so forth. One of the strengths was an ability to process new information and collate it with old unusually fast. In a millisecond, Chee identified the missing odor, extracted its meaning, and homogenized it with what he had already noticed about the place of the Goldtooth outfit. No animals. The place was little used. Why use it now? Chee's brain identified an assortment of possible explanations. But all this changed him, midstride, from a man happily walking through the rain toward a long-anticipated meeting, to a slightly uneasy man with a memory of being shot at.

It was just then that Chee noticed the oil.

What he saw was a reflection in the twilight, a slick blue-green sheen where rainwater had washed under the truck and picked up an oil emulsion. It stopped him. He looked at the oily spot, then back at the house. The door was open a few inches. He felt all those odd, intense sensations caused when intense fear triggers the adrenaline glands. Maybe nothing, one corner of his brain said. A coincidence. Leaky oil pans are usual enough among the old trucks so common on the reservation. But he had been foolish. Careless. And he turned back toward his pickup, walking at first, then breaking into a trot. His pistol was locked in the glove compartment.

He was not conscious of any separation between the boom of the shotgun and the impact that staggered him. He stumbled against the hogan, catching the edge of the door lintel for support. Then the second shot hit him, higher this time, the feel of claws tearing against his upper back and neck muscles and the back of his head. It knocked him off balance and he found himself on his knees, his hands in the cold mud. Three shots, he remembered. An automatic shotgun legally choked holds three shells. Three holes torn through the aluminum skin of his trailer. Another shot would be coming. He slammed against the hogan door, pushed his way through it, just as he heard the shotgun again.

He pushed the door shut, sat against it, trying to control the shock and the panic. The hogan was empty, stripped bare and lit by flickering coals of a fire built on the earthen floor under the smoke hole. His ears were ringing with the sound of the shots, but through that he could hear the splashing sound of someone running through the rain. His right side felt numb. With his left hand he reached behind him and slid the wooden latch.

Something pushed, tentatively, against the door.

He pressed his shoulder against it. "If you open the door, I'll shoot you," Chee said.

Silence.

"I am a police officer," Chee said. "Why did you shoot me?"

Silence. The ringing in his ears diminished. He could distinguish a pinging noise—the sound of the rain hitting the metal shield placed over the smoke hole to keep the hogan dry. The sound of feet moving on muddy ground. Metallic sounds. Chee strained to hear them. The shotgun was being reloaded. He thought about that. Whoever had shot him hadn't bothered to reload before running after him. He had seen Chee had been hit, knocked down. Apparently it was presumed the shots had killed him. That Chee was no danger.

The pain was fierce now—especially the back of his head. He touched it gingerly with his fingers and found the scalp slick with blood. He could also feel blood running down his right side, warm against the skin over his ribs. Chee looked at his palm, tilted it so that the weak glow from the coals would reach it. In that light the fresh blood looked almost black. He was going to die. Not right away, probably, but soon. He wanted to know why. This time he shouted.

"Why did you shoot me?"

Silence. Chee tried to think of another way to get an answer. Any response. He tried his right arm, found he could move it. The worst pain was the back of his head. A teeth-gritting ache in what seemed to be twenty places where shotgun pellets had struck the skull bone. Overlying that was the feeling that his scalp was being scalded. The pain made it hard to think. But he had to think. Or die.

Then the voice: "Skinwalker! Why are you killing my baby?"

It was a woman's voice.

"I am not," Chee said, slowly and very plainly.

No reply. Chee tried to concentrate. In not very long, he would bleed to death. Or, before that happened, he would faint, and then this crazy woman would push open the hogan door and kill him with her shotgun.

"You think I'm a witch," he said. "Why do you think that?"

"Because you are an *adan'ti*," she said. "You shot a bone into me before my baby was born, or you shot a bead into my baby, and now it is dying."

That told him just a little. In the Navajo world, where witchcraft is important, where daily behavior is patterned to avoid it, prevent it, and cure it, there are as many words for its various forms as there are words for various kinds of snow among the Eskimos. If the woman thought he was *adan'ti,* she thought he had the power of sorcery—to convert himself into animal form, to fly, perhaps to become invisible. Very specific ideas. Where had she gotten them?

"You think that if I confess that I witched your baby, then the baby will get well and pretty soon I will die," Chee said. "Is that right? Or if you kill me, then the witching will go away."

"You should confess," the woman said. "You should say you did it. Otherwise, I will kill you."

He had to keep her here. Had to keep her talking until he could make his mind work. Until he could learn from her what he had to learn to save his life. Maybe that was impossible. Maybe he was already dying. Maybe his life wind was already blowing out of him—out into the rain. Maybe there was nothing he could learn that would help him. But Chee's conditioning was to endure. He thought, frowning with concentration, willing away the pain and the dreadful consciousness of the blood running down his flanks and puddling under his buttocks. Meanwhile he had to keep her talking.

"It won't help your baby if I confess, because I am not the witch. Can you tell me who told you I was the witch?"

Silence.

"If I were a witch . . . if I had the power of sorcery, did someone teach you what I could do?"

"Yes, I was taught." The voice was hesitant.

"Then you know that if I was a witch, I could turn myself into something else. Into a burrowing owl. I could fly out the smoke hole and go away into the night."

Silence.

"But I am not a witch. I am just a man. I am a singer. A *hataalii*. I have learned the ways to cure. Some of them. I know the songs to protect you against a witching. But I am not a witch."

"They say you are," the woman said.

"Who are they? They who say this?" But he already knew the answer.

Silence.

The back of Chee's head was on fire, and beneath the fire the shattering pain in the skull was beginning to localize itself into a dozen spots of pain—the places where shotgun pellets had lodged in the bone. But he had to think. This woman had been given him as her witch just as Roosevelt Bistie must have been given Endocheeney as his scapegoat. Bistie had been dying of a liver disease. And this woman was watching her infant die. A conclusion took its shape in Chee's mind.

"Where was your baby born?" Chee asked. "And when it got sick, did you take it to the Badwater Clinic?"

He had decided she wouldn't answer before the answer came. "Yes."

"And Dr. Yellowhorse told you he was a crystal gazer, and that he could tell you what caused your baby to be sick, is that right? And Dr. Yellowhorse told you I had witched your child."

It was no longer a question. Chee knew it was true. And he thought he might know how to stay alive. How he might talk this woman into putting down her shotgun, and coming in to help stop his bleeding and to take him to Piñon or someplace where there would be help. He would use what little life he had left telling this woman who the witch really was. Chee believed in witchcraft in an abstract way. Perhaps they did have the power, as the legends claimed and the rumors insisted, to become were-animals, to fly, to run faster than any car. On that score, Chee was a skeptic willing to accept any proof. But he knew witchcraft in its basic form stalked the Dinee. He saw it in people who had turned deliberately and with malice from the beauty of the Navajo Way and embraced the evil that was its opposite. He saw it every day he worked as a policeman—in those who sold whiskey to children, in those who bought videocassette recorders while their relatives were hungry, in the knife fights in a Gallup alley, in beaten wives and abandoned children.

"I am going to tell you who the witch is," Chee said. "First I am going to throw out the keys to my truck. You take 'em and unlock the glove box in the truck, and you will find my pistol there. I said I had it in here with me because I was afraid. Now I am not afraid any more. Go and check, and see that I don't have my pistol with me. Then I want you to come in here where it is warm, and out of the rain, and where you can look at my face while I tell you. That way you can tell whether I speak the truth. And then I will tell you again that I am not a witch who harmed your child. And I will tell you who the witch is that put this curse on you."

Silence. The sound of gusting rain. And then a metallic clack. The woman doing something with the shotgun.

Chee's right arm was numb again. With his left hand he extracted his truck keys, slid back the latch, and eased the door toward him. As he tossed the keys through the opening, he waited for the shotgun. The shotgun didn't fire. He heard the sound of the woman walking in the mud.

Chee exhaled a gust of breath. Now he had to hold off the pain and the faintness long enough to organize his thoughts. He had to know exactly what to say.

21

THE PATROL CAR of Officer Leonard Skeet, born to the Ears Sticking Up Clan, the man in charge of law and order in the rugged vacant places surrounding Piñon, was parked in the rain outside the subagency police station. The station, a double-width mobile home, stood on the bank of Wepo Wash. It also served as home for Leonard Skeet and Aileen Beno, his wife. Leaphorn pulled off the asphalt of Navajo Route 4 and into the mud of Skeet's yard, tapped on Skeet's door, and collected him.

Skeet had seen no sign of Chee's pickup. His house was located with a view of both Navajo 4 and the road that wandered north-westward toward the Forest Lake Chapter House and, eventually, to the Goldtooth place. "He was probably already past here long before I got home," Skeet said. "But he hasn't come back through. I would have seen his truck."

At Emma's car, Skeet hesitated. "This isn't good for mud, and maybe I oughta drive," he said, looking at Leaphorn's cast. "You probably oughta give that arm some rest."

Under the cast, the arm arched from wrist to elbow. Leaphorn stood in the rain, common sense wrestling with his conditioned instinct to be in control. Common sense won. Skeet knew the road. They switched to Skeet's patrol car, left the tiny scattering of buildings that was Piñon behind, left asphalt for gravel, and soon, gravel for graded dirt. It was slick now and Skeet drove with the polished skill of an athletic man who drives the bad back roads every working day. Leaphorn found himself thinking of Emma and turned away from that. Skeet had asked no questions and Leaphorn's policy for years had been to tell people no more than they needed to know. Skeet needed to know a little.

"We may be wasting our time," Leaphorn said. He didn't have to tell Skeet anything about the attempt on Chee's life—everyone in NTP knew everything about that and everyone, Leaphorn guessed, had a theory about it. He told Skeet about Chee being invited to the Goldtooth place to talk about doing a sing.

"Uh huh," Skeet said. "Interesting. Maybe there's some explanation for it." He concentrated on correcting a rear-end skid on the muddy surface. "He didn't know nobody lives there," Skeet said. "No way he could have, I guess. Still, if somebody was shooting at me . . ." He let the statement trail off.

Leaphorn was riding in the back, where he could lean against the driver-side door and keep the cast propped along the top of the backrest. Despite the cushioning, the jolts and jarring of the bumpy road communicated themselves to the bone. He didn't feel like talking, or like defending Chee. "No IQ test required for the job," he said. "But maybe I'm just overnervous. Maybe there's an explanation for having the meeting there."

"Maybe so," Skeet said. His tone was skeptical.

Skeet slowed at an oddly shaped outcrop of volcanic basalt. "If I remember right, the turnoff's here," he said.

Leaphorn retrieved his arm from the backrest. "Let's take a look," he said.

On a clear evening, this lonely landscape would still have been lit by a red afterglow. In steady rain, the dark was almost complete. They used their flashlights.

"Some traffic," Skeet said. "One out pretty recently."

The rain had blurred the track of the tires without erasing them. And the depth of the rut in the softer earth at the juncture showed the vehicle had passed after the moisture had soaked in. And these fresher tracks had partly overlapped earlier, shallower tracks which the rain had almost smoothed away.

"So maybe he's come and gone," Skeet said. But as he said it he doubted it. At least two vehicles had gone in. One had come out since the rain became heavy.

Their headlights reflected first from the rain-slick roof of a truck, then they picked up the windows of the Goldtooth house. No lights visible anywhere. Skeet parked fifty yards away. "Leave 'em on?" he said. "What do you think?"

"Turn 'em off for now," Leaphorn said. "Until we make sure that's Chee's truck. And find out who's here."

They found a wealth of half-erased, rain-washed tracks but no sign of anyone outside. "Check the truck," Leaphorn said. "I'll take the house."

Leaphorn pointed his light at the building, holding it gingerly in his left hand, as far from his body as was practical. "Kicked once, double careful," his mother would have told him. And in this case, they might be dealing with a shotgun. Leaphorn thought, wryly, that he should have a telescoping arm, like Inspector Gadget in the television cartoon.

The house door was open. The beam of Leaphorn's light shined through it into emptiness. In front of the door, on the wet, packed earth, it lit a small red cylinder. Leaphorn picked it up, an empty shotgun shell. He switched off the light, sniffed the open end of the cartridge, inhaled the acrid smell of freshly burned powder. "Shit," Leaphorn said. He felt bleak, defeated, conscious of the cold rainwater against his ribs.

Skeet splashed up behind him.

"Truck unlocked," Skeet said. "Glove box open. This was on the seat." He showed Leaphorn a .38 caliber revolver. "That his?"

"Probably," Leaphorn said. He checked the cylinder, sniffed the barrel. It hadn't been fired. He shook his head, showed Skeet the empty shotgun shell. They would find Jim Chee's body and they would call it a homicide. Maybe they should call it suicide. Or death by stupidity.

The house was empty. Absolutely empty. Of people, of furniture, of anything except a scattered residue of trash. They found small footprints around the door, damp but not muddy. Whoever had been here had come before the rain turned heavy. Had left. Hadn't returned.

From the front door, Leaphorn shined his flash on the hogan. Its door was half open.

"I'll check it," Skeet said.

"We will," Leaphorn said.

They found Jim Chee just inside the door, slumped against the wall just south of the entrance—the correct place for a proper Navajo to be if he had entered the hogan properly "sunwise"— which was from east to south to west to north. In the light of the two flashes, the back of his head and his side seemed clotted with grease. In the reflected light, Skeet's long face was pinched and stricken.

Grief? Or was he conscious that he was standing in a ghost

hogan, being infected with the virulent ghost of Officer Jim Chee? Leaphorn, who had long since come to terms with ghosts, stared at Skeet's face, trying to separate out the sorrow and find the fear.

"I think he may be alive," Skeet said.

22

AS IT USUALLY DOES on the Colorado Plateau, night defeated the storm. It drifted northeastward, robbed of the solar power that had fed it, and exhausted its energy in the thin, cold air over the Utah canyons and the mountains of northern New Mexico. By midnight there was no more thunder; the cloud formation had sagged into itself, flattening to a vast general rain—the sort Navajos call female rain—which gently drenched an area from the Painted Desert northward to Sleeping Ute Mountain.

From the fifth-floor windows of the Indian Health Service hospital in Gallup, Joe Leaphorn saw the deep blue of the newly washed morning sky—cloudless except for scraps of fog over the Zuni Mountains to the southeast, and the red cliffs stretching eastward toward Borego Pass. By afternoon, if moisture was still moving in from the Pacific, the towering thunderheads would be building again, bombarding earth with lightning, wind, and rain. But now the world outside the glass where Leaphorn stood was brilliant with sun—clean and calm.

He was hardly aware of it. His mind was full of what the neurologist had told him. Emma did not have Alzheimer's disease. Emma's illness was caused by a tumor pressing against the right front lobe of her brain. The doctor, a young woman named Vigil, had told Leaphorn a great deal more, but what was important was simple enough. If the tumor was cancerous, Emma would probably die, and die rather soon. If the tumor was benign, Emma would be cured by its removal through surgery. "What are the odds?" Dr. Vigil didn't want to guess. This afternoon she would call a doctor she knew in Baltimore. A doctor she had studied with. Cases like this were his field. He would know.

"I want to discuss it with him before I do any guessing." Dr. Vigil was in her early thirties, Leaphorn guessed. One of those who went to medical school with a government grant and worked it off in the Indian Health Service. She stood, hands on desk, waiting for Leaphorn to leave. "Leave word where I can get in touch with you," she said.

"Call now," Leaphorn said. "I want to know."

"He does his surgery in the mornings," she said. "He won't be in."

"Try it," Leaphorn said. "Just try."

Dr. Vigil said, "Well, now, I don't think . . ." Then her eyes met Leaphorn's. "No harm trying," she said.

He'd waited in the hall, just outside the doctor's door, staring out at the morning, digesting this new data. The news was good. But it left him off balance, trying to live again with hope. It was a luxury he had given up weeks before. The exact moment, he thought, was when he sat at his desk reading the literature the Alzheimer's organization had sent him and seeing Emma's awful confusion described in print. It had been a terrible morning—the worst pain he'd ever endured. Now all his instincts cried out against enduring it again—against reentering that door which hope held open for him. But there was the ultimate fact: Emma might be well again. He wanted to celebrate. He wanted to shout for joy. But he was afraid.

So he waited. To avoid the trap of hope, he thought of Jim Chee. Specifically he thought of what Jim Chee had told them when the ambulance unloaded him at the Badwater Clinic. Just a few words, but a lot of information in them if only Leaphorn knew how to read it.

"Woman," Chee had said, in a voice so weak that Leaphorn had heard it only because he was leaning with his face just inches from Chee's lips.

"Who shot you?" Leaphorn had asked while attendants shifted the stretcher onto the hospital cart. Chee had moved his head. "Do you know?" Chee had moved his head again, a negative motion. And then he had said: "Woman."

"Young?" Leaphorn had asked, and got no response.

"We'll find her," Leaphorn had said, and that had provoked the rest of the information Chee had provided.

"Baby dying," Chee said. He said it clearly, in English. And then he repeated it in mumbled Navajo, his voice fading away.

So it would seem that the person who had shot Chee at the

Goldtooth place was a woman with a fatally ill infant. Probably the same person had fired the three shotgun blasts through Chee's trailer wall. When Chee came out of surgery it would be easy enough to find her. He would be able to identify the vehicle she was driving, probably even give them the license number if he had been halfway alert before the shooting. And if he knew she had a sick child, he had to have talked to her face to face. They would also have a physical description. But even if Chee didn't survive to describe her, they could find her. A young woman with a critically ill child who knew about the Goldtooth place, about it being abandoned. That would give them all the narrowing they needed.

They would find the woman. She would tell them why she wanted Jim Chee dead. Then all this insane killing would make sense.

Below Leaphorn, a flock of crows moved toward the center of Gallup, their cawing muted by the glass. Far beyond, an endless line of tank cars moved eastward down the Santa Fe mainline.

Or, Leaphorn thought, they wouldn't find the woman. Or they would find her dead. Or she, like Bistie, would tell them absolutely nothing. And he would be exactly where he was now. And where was that?

The crows disappeared out of his line of vision. The freight crawled inexorably eastward. Leaphorn considered why he was nagged with the feeling that these homicides made perfect sense, that Chee had somehow, in those three words, put the key in the lock and turned it.

"Woman," Chee had said. A woman Chee didn't know. How did that help? Of the victims, only Irma Onesalt was female. She had been killed with a rifle shot, not a shotgun. No apparent connection there. "Baby dying," Chee had said. Presumably the baby of the woman who had shot him. Presumably she had told Chee about it. Why?

"Mr. Leaphorn?" a woman's voice said at Leaphorn's elbow. "She asked me to get you. Dr. Vigil."

Dr. Vigil had come to the door to meet him. "I can give you the statistics now," she said, smiling slightly. "Recovery from the actual surgery, close to ninety-nine percent. Nature of tumor: malignant twenty-three-plus percent, benign seventy-six-plus percent."

And so Joe Leaphorn allowed himself again the heavy risk of hope. He went to Emma's room to tell her, found her sleeping, and left her a note. It told her what Dr. Vigil had told him, and that he loved her, and that he would be back as soon as he could be.

Then he left on the long drive to the Badwater Clinic. He wanted to be there when Chee recovered from the anesthesia. And he wanted to talk to Yellowhorse about Irma Onesalt's list, and learn what Onesalt had said to Yellowhorse about it; specifically if she had told him why she wanted the dates of death of people who had not yet died. The Cambodian doctor who had been in charge when they'd brought Chee in had said Yellowhorse was in Flagstaff—that he would be driving back today, that he should be back by early afternoon.

Leaphorn stopped for gas at Ganado and called the clinic while his tank was being filled. Yes, Chee had survived the surgery. He was still in the recovery room. No, Yellowhorse was not back from Flagstaff yet. But he'd called and they expected him sometime after lunch.

Leaphorn was finding it difficult to think about homicides. He was preoccupied, indeed fascinated, by his own emotions. He had never felt quite like this before—this immeasurable joy. This relief. Emma, who had been lost forever, was found again. She would live. She would be herself again. He thought of Dr. Vigil, watching him receive her hopeful news. Doctors must see a lot of such violent emotional reaction—even more than policemen do. Understanding the intensity love can produce would be a by-product of that profession. Dr. Vigil would understand how a dying infant could motivate a murder. If not yet, she would when she was older. Leaphorn was thinking this as he passed the turnoff to Blue Gap. He moved from that into analyzing his own emotions. Watching what was happening to Emma had caused everything else to recede into triviality. Other values ceased to exist for him. Had there been anything he could do to help her, anything, he would have done it. Beyond the turnoff to Whippoorwill School, his thoughts moved back to a question that had intrigued him earlier. Why had the woman told Chee her baby was dying? He seemed to know the answer. She had told Chee to explain why she was killing him. She was killing him to reverse the witchcraft that was killing her baby. Logical. Why did something keep tugging him back to this?

Just then, Leaphorn saw how it all had worked. All the pins on his map came together into a single cluster at the Badwater Clinic. Four and a half homicides became a single crime with a single motive. His car fishtailed on the muddy road as he jammed down the accelerator. If he didn't reach the clinic before Dr. Yellowhorse, the four and a half homicides would become five.

23

IT WAS ALL VERY VAGUE to Chee. The nurse who moved him down the hall from the recovery room had shown him a paper cup containing a spoonful of shot. "What Dr. Wu dug out of your back and your neck and your head," she explained. "Dr. Wu thought you'd want to keep it."

Chee, woozy, could think of nothing to say to that. He raised his eyebrows.

"Sort of a souvenir," she explained. "To help you remember." And then she had added something about Dr. Wu being Chinese, but actually a Cambodian Chinese, as if this would clarify why he thought Chee would want a souvenir.

"Um," Chee said, and the nurse had looked at him quizzically and said, "Only if you want to."

The nurse had talked a lot more, but Chee remembered little of it. He recalled wanting to ask her where he was, and what had happened, but he didn't have the energy. Now the back of his head was helping him remember. Whatever painkiller they had used to numb it was wearing off and Chee could isolate and identify about seven places where the surgeon had dug a piece of shot out of the thick bone at the back of his skull. It reminded Chee of a long time ago when a yearling horse they were branding had kicked him squarely on the shinbone. Bruised bone seemed to issue a peculiarly painful protest to the nervous system.

But he kept the pain at bay by celebrating being alive. It surprised him. He could only dimly remember the woman coming hesitantly into the hogan, the shotgun pointing at him. He remembered the seconds when he had thought she would simply shoot him again and that would be the end of it. Perhaps that was what she'd intended to do. But she had let him talk, and he had forced himself into a kind of coherence. Now it was all hazy, much of it simply blank. The medics called it temporary post-trauma amnesia, and Chee had seen it in enough victims of knife fights and traffic accidents to recognize it in himself. He didn't try to force his memory. What was important, obviously, was that the woman had believed him. She seemed to have brought him here, although Chee couldn't remember that happening, or imagine how she had gotten him from the hogan to her truck. The last he remembered was describing for her what must have happened, relying on his recollection of the time he himself had been taken to a crystal gazer as a child, remembering the old man's eye, immensely magnified and distorted, looking into his own eye, remembering his own fear.

"I think I know what happened," Chee had told her. "Yellowhorse pretends to be a crystal gazer. I think you took your sick baby to the Badwater Clinic and Yellowhorse looked at it, and then Yellowhorse got out his crystal, and pretended to be a shaman, and he told you that the baby had been witched. And then he did the sucking ceremony, and he pretended to suck a bone out of your baby's breast." Chee remembered that at this point he began to run out of strength. His eyes were no longer focusing and it was difficult to generate the breath to form the guttural Navajo words. But he had gone on. "Then he told you that I was the skinwalker who had witched your baby and that the only way to cure it was to kill me. And he gave you the bone and told you to shoot it into me."

The woman, hazy and distant, had simply sat there, holding the shotgun. He couldn't see well enough to know if she was listening.

"I think he wants to kill me because I have told people that he is not really a shaman. I told people he had no real powers. But maybe there is some other reason. That doesn't matter. What matters is that I am not the skinwalker. Yellowhorse is the skinwalker. Yellowhorse witched you. Yellowhorse turned you into someone who kills." He had said a lot more, or he thought he had, but maybe that was part of the dream that he had drifted into as he fell asleep. He couldn't separate it.

The nurse was back in the room. She put a tray on the table beside his bed—a white towel, a syringe, other paraphernalia. "You need some of this by now," she said, glancing at her watch.

"First I need to do some things, know some things," Chee said. "Are there any policemen here?"

"I don't think so," the nurse said. "Quiet morning."

"Then I need to make a call," Chee said.

She didn't bother to look at him. "Fat chance," she said.

"Then I need somebody to make a call for me. Call the tribal police headquarters at Window Rock and get a message to a Lieutenant Leaphorn."

"He's one of them who brought you in. With the ambulance," she said. "If you want to tell him who shot you, I'll bet that can wait until you're feeling a little better."

"Is Yellowhorse here? Dr. Yellowhorse?"

"He's in Flag," the nurse said. "Some sort of meeting at the Flagstaff hospital."

Chee felt dizzy, and a little nauseated, and vastly relieved. He didn't understand why Yellowhorse wanted to kill him—not exactly, anyway. But he knew he didn't want to be sleeping in his hospital when Yellowhorse was here.

"Look," he said. Trying to sound like a policeman when your head and your arm and shoulder and side were encased in bandages and you were flat on your back wasn't easy. "This is important. I have to tell Leaphorn some things or a murderer might get away. Might kill somebody again."

"You're serious?" the nurse asked, still doubting it.

"Dead serious."

"What's the number?"

Chee gave her the number at Window Rock. "And if he's not in, call the substation at Piñon. Tell 'em I said we need a policeman out here right away." Chee tried to think of who was stationed at Piñon now, and drew a blank. He was conscious only that his eyes were buzzing and that his head hurt in at least seven places.

"You know that number?"

Chee shook his head.

The nurse went out the door, leaving the tray. "Here he comes now," she said.

Leaphorn, Chee thought. Great!

Dr. Yellowhorse came through the door, moving fast.

Chee opened his mouth, began a yell, and found Yellowhorse's hand clamped across his jaws, cutting off all sound.

"Keep quiet," Yellowhorse said. With his other hand he was pressing something hard against Chee's throat. It was another source of pain—but no competition for the back of his head.

"Struggle and I cut your throat," Yellowhorse said.

Chee tried to relax. Impossible.

Yellowhorse's hand came off his mouth. Chee heard it fumbling in the tray.

"I don't want to kill you," Yellowhorse said. "I'm going to give you this shot so you'll get some sleep. And remember, you can't yell with your windpipe cut."

Chee tried to think. Whatever was pressing against his throat was pressing too hard to make yelling practical. Almost instantly he added the feel of the needle going into his shoulder to the battery of other pains. And then Yellowhorse's hand was over his mouth again.

"I hate to do this," Yellowhorse said, and his expression said he meant it. "It was that damned Onesalt woman. But in the long run, it more than balances out."

Chee's expression, as much as Yellowhorse could see of it around his smothering hand, must have seemed skeptical.

"It balances way out in favor of saving the clinic," Yellowhorse said, voice insistent. "Four lives. Three of them were men past their prime and one of them was dying fast anyway. And on the balance against that, I know for sure we've saved dozens of lives already, and we'll save dozens more. And better than that, we're stopping birth defects, and catching diabetes cases early." Yellowhorse paused, looking into Chee's eyes.

"And glaucoma," he said. "I know we've caught a dozen cases of that early enough to save good vision. That Onesalt bitch was going to put an end to all that."

Chee, who was in no position to talk, didn't.

"You feeling sleepy?" Yellowhorse said. "You should be by now."

Chee was feeling—despite an intense effort of will—very sleepy. There was no question at all that Yellowhorse was going to kill him. If there were any other possibility, Yellowhorse would not be telling him all this, making this apology. Chee tried to gather his strength, tense his muscles for a lunge against the knife. All he had to muster was a terrible weakness. Yellowhorse felt even that and tightened his grip.

"Don't try it," he said. "It won't work."

It wouldn't. Chee admitted it to himself. Time was his only hope, if he had a hope. Stay awake. He made a questioning sound against Yellowhorse's palm. He would ask him why Onesalt and the rest had to be killed. It was to cover up something at the clinic, clearly, but what?

Yellowhorse eased the grip on Chee's mouth.

"What?" he said. "Keep it low."

"What did Onesalt know?" he asked.

The hand gripped again. Yellowhorse looked surprised. "I thought you had guessed," he said. "That day when you came and got the wrong Begay. Onesalt guessed. I figured you would. Or she would tell you."

Chee mumbled against the palm. "You gave us the wrong Begay. I wondered what had happened to the right one. But I didn't guess you were keeping him on your records."

"Well, I thought you were guessing," Yellowhorse said. "I always knew you would guess sooner or later. And once you did, it would take time but it would be inevitable. You would find out."

"Overcharging?" Chee asked. "For patients who weren't here?"

"Getting the government to pay its share," Yellowhorse said. "Have you ever read the treaty? The one we signed at Fort Sumner. Promises. One schoolteacher for every thirty children, everything else. The government never kept any promises."

"Charging for people after they were dead?" Chee mumbled. He simply could not keep his eyes open any longer. When they closed, Yellowhorse would kill him. Not immediately, but soon enough. When his eyes closed they would never open again. Yellowhorse would keep him asleep until he could find a way to make it look normal and natural. Chee knew that. He must keep his eyes open.

"Getting sleepy?" Yellowhorse asked, his voice benign.

Chee's eyes closed. He went to sleep, a troubled sleep, dreaming that something was hurting the back of his head.

24

LEAPHORN PARKED RIGHT AT THE DOOR, violating the blue handicapped-only zone, and trotted into the clinic. He'd made his habitual instant eyeball inventory of the vehicles present. A dozen were there, including an Oldsmobile sedan with the medical symbol on its license plate, which might be Yellowhorse's car, and three well-worn pickup trucks, which might include the one driven by the woman determined to kill Chee. Leaphorn hurried through the front door. The receptionist was standing behind her half-round desk screaming something. A tall woman in a nurse's uniform was standing across the desk, hands in her hair, apparently terrified. Both were looking down the hallway that led to Leaphorn's right, down a corridor of patients' rooms.

Leaphorn's trot turned into a run.

"She has a gun," the receptionist shouted. "A gun."

The woman stood in the doorway four rooms down, and she did, indeed, have a gun. Leaphorn could see only her back, a traditional dark blue blouse of velvet, the flowing light blue skirt which came to the top of her squaw boots, her dark hair tied in a careful bun at the back of her head, and the butt of the shotgun protruding from under her arm.

"Hold it," Leaphorn shouted, digging with his left hand for his pistol.

Aimed as the shotgun was into the room and away from him, the sound it made was muted. A boom, a yell, the sound of someone falling, glass breaking. With the sound, the woman disappeared into the room. Leaphorn was at the door two seconds later, his pistol drawn.

"The skinwalker is dead," the woman said. She stood over

Yellowhorse, the shotgun dangling from her right hand. "This time I killed him."

"Put down the gun," Leaphorn said. The woman ignored him. She was looking down at the doctor, who sprawled face-up beside Jim Chee's bed. Chee seemed to be sleeping. Leaphorn shifted his pistol to the fingers that protruded from his cast and lifted the shotgun from the woman's hand. She made no effort to keep it. Yellowhorse was still breathing, unevenly and raggedly. A man in a pale blue hospital smock appeared at the door—the same Chinese-looking doctor who had been on duty when they delivered Chee. He muttered something that sounded like an expletive in some language strange to Leaphorn.

"Why did you shoot him?" he asked Leaphorn.

"I didn't," Leaphorn said. "See if you can save him."

The doctor knelt beside Yellowhorse, feeling for a pulse, examining the place where the shotgun blast had struck Yellowhorse's neck at point-blank range. He shook his head.

"Dead?" the woman asked. "Is the skinwalker dead? Then I want to bring in my baby. I have him in my truck. Maybe now he is alive again."

But he wasn't, of course.

It took Jim Chee almost four hours to awaken and he did so reluctantly—his subconscious dreading what he would awaken to. But when he came awake he found himself alone in the room. Sunset lit the foot of his bed. His head still hurt and his shoulder and side ached, but he felt warm again. He removed his left hand from under the covers, flexed the fingers. A good strong hand. He moved his toes, his feet, bent his knees. Everything worked. The right arm was another matter. It was heavily bandaged elbow to shoulder and immobilized with tape.

Where was Yellowhorse? Chee considered that. Obviously he had guessed wrong about the doctor. The man hadn't killed him, as common sense said he should have. Apparently Yellowhorse had run for it, or turned himself in, or went to talk to a lawyer, or something. It seemed totally unlikely that Yellowhorse would come back now to finish off Chee. But just in case, he decided he would get up, put on his clothes, and go somewhere else. Call Leaphorn first. Tell him about all this.

Just about then it also occurred to Chee how he would solve the problem of the cat. He would put the cat in the forty-dollar case, and take it to the Farmington airport and send it off to Mary Landon. But first he would write her and explain it all—explain how this *belagana* cat simply wasn't going to make it as a Navajo cat. It would starve, or be eaten by the coyote, or something like that. Mary was a very smart person. Mary would understand that perfectly. Probably better than Chee.

Carefully, slowly, he turned himself onto his good side, swung his feet off the bed, pushed himself upright. Almost upright. Before he completed the move, weakness and faintness overcame him. He was on his side again, the back of his head throbbing, and a metal tray he'd tumbled from the bedside stand still clattering on the floor.

"I see you're awake," a female voice said. "Tell the lieutenant that Officer Chee is awake."

Lieutenant Leaphorn's expression, when he came through the door behind the nurse, could best be described as blank. He sat on the chair beside Chee's bed, resting his cast gingerly on the cover.

"Do you know her name? The woman who shot you?"

"No idea," Chee said. "Where is she? Where's Yellowhorse? Do you know—"

"She shot Yellowhorse," Leaphorn said. "Right here. Did a better job on him than she did on you. We have her in custody, but she won't tell us her name. Anything else, for that matter. Just wants to talk about her baby."

"What's wrong with it?"

"It's dead," Leaphorn said. "The doctors say it's been dead for a couple of days." Leaphorn shifted his cast, which was generally grimy and had a streak of dried blue-black mud on its bottom side.

"She thought it was witched," Chee said. "That's why she wanted to kill me. She thought I was the witch and she could turn the witching around."

Leaphorn looked disapproving. "It had something they call Werdnig-Hoffmann disease," Leaphorn said. "Born with it. The brain never develops properly. Muscles never develop. They live a little while and then they die."

"Well," Chee said. "She didn't understand that."

"No cure for it," Leaphorn said. "Not even by killing skinwalkers like you."

"Do you know why Yellowhorse was doing all this?" Chee asked. "He told me he was trying to get the government to pay its share, or something like that, and Onesalt found out about it, or was finding out, and he figured sooner or later I would understand it too, because of what I knew." Chee paused, slightly abashed by the admission he would be making. "I guess he figured I'm smarter than I am. I guess I was supposed to figure out that he was turning in hospitalization claims on patients after they were dead. I guess that's why Onesalt was looking for those death dates."

"About right," Leaphorn said. "After they died, or long after they'd checked out and gone home. Dilly Streib is in the business office now. They're going through the billing records."

"I began to see how he was doing it," Chee said. "I couldn't see why. Wasn't he using a lot of his own money to run this place?"

"Yeah," Leaphorn said. "Mostly his own money. Through his foundation. And he had other private foundation money. And some tribe support. Medicare. Medicaid. Guess it wasn't enough. Not even with hiring immigrant doctors."

"I understand how he killed Endocheeney and Wilson Sam. How about why?"

"Streib thinks he's going to find they were out of here for months before Yellowhorse stopped billing for them," Leaphorn said. "I guess there were a lot of them like that. But they were the only two on Onesalt's list. After he shot Onesalt, it took the pressure off. No rush anymore. But I guess he figured that since you were with Onesalt, you'd know about the list and sooner or later you'd just naturally find out about it. Or if you didn't, somebody else would. So he decided to get rid of Sam and Endocheeney, and you too."

"He told me it balanced out," Chee said. "Onesalt was going to put an end to the clinic and it was saving more lives than those he had to kill."

Leaphorn had nothing to say to that. He raised his cast off the bed, grimaced, put it down again. *"Anti'll,"* he said sourly, using the Navajo word for witchcraft.

Jim Chee just nodded.

"Pretty smart, really," Leaphorn added. "No hurry, so he could pick his people carefully. From desperate people. Like Bistie, who was dying. Or the woman he sent after you. People won't talk about witches, so there wasn't much risk of tracking anything back here."

"I guess he sent two after Endocheeney. Maybe Bistie was too slow and he thought he wasn't going to do it."

"Apparently," Leaphorn said. "And then he found out we'd arrested Bistie, so he had to kill him—just in case we did trick him into talking."

"I guess we could find them now," Chee said. "The one who killed Endocheeney. The one who killed Wilson Sam. Just work down through the records of the caseload here, looking at them the way Yellowhorse would have looked."

"I guess we could," Leaphorn said.

Chee considered that answer awhile. It was, after all, a federal problem.

"You think Streib will think of it?"

"I doubt it," Leaphorn said. He laughed a humorless laugh. "People say I hate witchcraft. Dilly, he hates to even think about witches."

"Doesn't matter, anyway," Chee said. "It's finished."

A THIEF OF TIME

This story is dedicated to Steven Lovato, firstborn son of Larry and Mary Lovato. May he always go with beauty all around him.

With special thanks to Dan Murphy of the U.S. Park Service for pointing me to the ruins down the San Juan River, to Charley and Susan DeLorme and the other river lovers of Wild River Expeditions, to Kenneth Tsosie of White Horse Lake, to Ernie Bulow, and to the Tom and Jan Vaughn family of Chaco Culture National Historical Park. All characters in this book are imaginary. True, Drayton and Noi Vaughn actually do make the sixty-mile bus ride to school each morning but they are even classier in real life than the fictitious counterparts found herein.

AUTHOR'S NOTE

While most of the places in this volume are real, Many Ruins Canyon has had its name changed and its location tinkered with to protect its unvandalized cliff ruins.

THE MOON HAD RISEN just above the cliff behind her. Out on the packed sand of the wash bottom the shadow of the walker made a strange elongated shape. Sometimes it suggested a heron, sometimes one of those stick-figure forms of an Anasazi pictograph. An animated pictograph, its arms moving rhythmically as the moon shadow drifted across the sand. Sometimes, when the goat trail bent and put the walker's profile against the moon, the shadow became Kokopelli himself. The backpack formed the spirit's grotesque hump, the walking stick Kokopelli's crooked flute. Seen from above, the shadow would have made a Navajo believe that the great *yei* northern clans called Watersprinkler had taken visible form. If an Anasazi had risen from his thousand-year grave in the trash heap under the cliff ruins here, he would have seen the Humpbacked Flute Player, the rowdy god of fertility of his lost people. But the shadow was only the shape of Dr. Eleanor Friedman-Bernal blocking out the light of an October moon.

Dr. Friedman-Bernal rested now, sitting on a convenient rock, removing her backpack, rubbing her shoulders, letting the cold, high desert air evaporate the sweat that had soaked her shirt, reconsidering a long day.

No one could have seen her. Of course, they had seen her driving away from Chaco. The children were up in the gray dawn to catch their school bus. And the children would chat about it to their parents. In that tiny, isolated Park Service society of a dozen adults and two children, everyone knew everything about everybody. There was absolutely no possibility of privacy. But she had done everything right. She had made the rounds of the permanent housing and checked with everyone on the digging team. She was driving into Farmington, she'd said. She'd collected the outgoing mail to be dropped off at the Blanco Trading Post. She had jotted down the list of supplies people needed. She'd told Maxie she had the Chaco fever—needed to get away, see a movie, have a restaurant dinner, smell exhaust fumes, hear a different set of voices, make phone calls back to civilization on a telephone that would actually work. She would spend a night where she could hear the sounds of civilization, something besides the endless Chaco silence. Maxie was sympathetic. If Maxie suspected anything, she suspected Dr. Eleanor Friedman-Bernal was meeting Lehman. That would have been fine with Eleanor Friedman-Bernal.

The handle of the folding shovel she had strapped to her pack was pressing against her back. She stopped, shifted the weight, and adjusted the pack straps. Somewhere in the darkness up the canyon she could hear the odd screeching call of a saw-whet owl, hunting nocturnal rodents. She glanced at her watch: 10:11, changing to 10:12 as she watched. Time enough.

No one had seen her in Bluff. She was sure of that. She had called from Shiprock, just to make doubly sure that no one was using Bo Arnold's old house out on the highway. No one had answered. The house was dark when she'd arrived, and she'd left it that way, finding the key under the flower box where Bo always left it. She'd done her borrowing carefully, disturbing nothing. When she put it back, Bo would never guess it had been missing. Not that it would matter. Bo was a biologist, scraping out a living as a part-timer with the Bureau of Land Management while he finished his dissertation on desert lichens, or whatever it was he was studying. He hadn't given a damn about anything else when she'd known him at Madison, and he didn't now.

She yawned, stretched, reached for her backpack, decided to rest a moment longer. She'd been up about nineteen hours. She had maybe two more to go before she reached the site. Then she'd roll out the sleeping bag and not get out of it until she was rested. No hurry now. She thought about Lehman. Big. Ugly. Smart. Gray. Sexy. Lehman was coming. She'd wine him and dine him and show him what she had. And he would have to be impressed. He'd have to agree she'd proved her case. That wasn't necessary for publication—his approval. But for some reason, it was necessary to her. And that irrationality made her think of Maxie. Maxie and Elliot.

She smiled, and rubbed her face. It was quiet here, just a few insects making their nocturnal sounds. Windless. The cold air settling into the canyon. She shivered, picked up the backpack, and struggled into it. A coyote was barking somewhere over on Comb Wash far behind her. She could hear another across the wash, very distant, yipping in celebration of the moonlight. She walked rapidly up the packed sand, lifting her legs high to stretch them, not thinking of what she would do tonight. She had thought long enough of that. Perhaps too long. Instead she thought of Maxie and Elliot. Brains, both. But nuts. The Blueblood and the Poorjane. The Man Who Could Do Anything obsessed by the woman who said nothing he did counted. Poor Elliot! He could never win.

A flash of lightning on the eastern horizon—much too distant to hear the thunder and the wrong direction to threaten any rain. A last gasp of summer, she thought. The moon was higher now, its light muting the colors of the canyon into shades of gray. Her thermal underwear and the walking kept her body warm but her hands were like ice. She studied them. No hands for a lady. Nails blunt and broken. The skin tough, scarred, callused. Anthropology skin, they'd called it when she was an undergraduate. The skin of people who are always out under the sun, working in the dirt. It had always bothered her mother, as everything about her bothered her mother. Becoming an anthropologist instead of a doctor, and then not marrying a doctor. Marrying a Puerto Rican archaeologist who was not even Jewish. And then losing him to another woman. "Wear gloves," her mother had said. "For heaven's sake, Ellie, you have hands like a dirt farmer."

And a face like a dirt farmer too, she'd thought.

The canyon was just as she remembered from the summer she had helped map and catalog its sites. A great place for pictographs. Just ahead, just beyond the cottonwoods on the sheer sandstone wall where the canyon bottom bent, was a gallery of them. The baseball gallery, they called it, because of the great shaman figure that someone had thought resembled a cartoon version of an umpire.

The moon lit only part of the wall, and the slanting light made it difficult to see, but she stopped to inspect it. In this light, the tapered, huge-shouldered shape of the mystic Anasazi shaman lost its color and became merely a dark form. Above it a clutter of shapes danced, stick figures, abstractions: the inevitable Kokopelli, his humped shape bent, his flute pointed almost at the ground; a heron flying; a heron standing; the zigzag band of pigment representing a snake. Then she noticed the horse.

It stood well to the left of the great baseball shaman, mostly in moon shadow. A Navajo addition, obviously, since the Anasazi had vanished three hundred years before the Spanish came on their steeds. It was a stylized horse, with a barrel body and straight legs, but without the typical Navajo tendency to build beauty into everything they attempted. The rider seemed to be a Kokopelli— Watersprinkler, the Navajos called him. At least the rider seemed to be blowing a flute. Had this addition been there before? She couldn't remember. Such Navajo additions weren't uncommon. But this one puzzled her.

Then she noticed, at each of three feet of the animal, a tiny prone figure. Three. Each with the little circle representing the head separated from the body. Each with one leg cut away.

Sick. And they hadn't been here four years ago. These she would have remembered.

For the first time Eleanor Friedman-Bernal became aware of the darkness, the silence, her total isolation. She had dropped her backpack while she rested. Now she picked it up, put an arm through the carry strap, changed her mind. She unzipped a side pocket and extracted the pistol. It was a .25 caliber automatic. The salesman had shown her how to load it, how the safety worked, how to hold it. He had told her it was accurate, easy to use, and made in Belgium. He had not told her that it took an unusual ammunition that one always had to hunt for. She had never tried it out in Madison. There never seemed to be a place to shoot it safely. But when she came to New Mexico, the first day when there was enough wind to blow away the sound, she'd driven out into the emptiness on the road toward Crownpoint and practiced with it. She had fired it at rocks, and deadwood, and shadows on the sand, until it felt natural and comfortable and she was hitting things, or getting close enough. When she used up most of the box of cartridges, she found the sporting goods store in Farmington didn't have them. And neither did the big place in Albuquerque, and finally she had ordered them out of a catalog. Now she had seventeen bullets left in the new box. She had brought six of them with her. A full magazine. The pistol felt cold in her hand, cold and hard and reassuring.

She dropped it into the pocket of her jacket. As she regained the sandy bottom of the wash and walked up it, she was conscious of the heaviness against her hip. The coyotes were closer, two of them somewhere above her, on the mesa beyond the clifftops. Sometimes the night breeze gusted enough to make its sounds in the brush along the bottom, rattling the leaves on the Russian olives and whispering through the fronds of the tamarisks. Usually it was still. Runoff from the summer monsoons had filled pools along the rocky bottom. Most of these were nearly dry now, but she could hear frogs, and crickets, and insects she couldn't identify. Something made a clicking sound in the darkness where dead tumbleweed had collected against the cliff, and from somewhere ahead she heard what sounded like a whistle. A night bird?

The canyon wound under the cliff and out of the moonlight. She turned on her flash. No risk of anyone seeing it. And that turned her thoughts to how far the nearest human would be. Not far as the bird flies—perhaps fifteen or twenty miles as the crow flew. But no easy way in. No roads across the landscape of almost solid stone, and no reason to build roads. No reason for the Anasazi to come here, for that matter, except to escape something that was hunting them. None that the anthropologists could think of—not even the cultural anthropologists with their notorious talents for forming theories without evidence. But come they had. And with them came her artist. Leaving Chaco Canyon behind her. Coming here to create more of her pots and to die.

From where Dr. Friedman-Bernal was walking she could see one of their ruins low on the cliff wall to her right. Had it been daylight, she remembered, she could have seen two more in the huge amphitheater alcove on the cliff to her left. But now the alcove was black with shadow—looking a little like a great gaping mouth.

She heard squeaking. Bats. She'd noticed a few just after sundown. Here they swarmed, fluttering over places where runoff had filled potholes and potholes had bred insects. They flashed past her face, just over her hair. Watching them, Ellie Friedman-Bernal didn't watch where she was walking. A rock turned under her foot, and she lost her balance.

The backpack cost her enough of her usual grace to make the fall hard and clumsy. She broke it with her right hand, hip, and elbow and found herself sprawled on the stream bottom, hurt, shocked, and shaken.

The elbow was most painful. It had scraped over the sandstone, tearing her shirt and leaving an abrasion that, when she touched it, stained her finger with blood. Then her bruised hip got her attention, but it was numb now and would punish her later. It was only when she scrambled back to her feet that she noticed the cut across the palm of her hand. She examined it in the light of her flash, made a sympathetic clicking sound, and then sat down to deal with it.

She picked out a bit of the gravel imbedded in the heel of her hand, rinsed the cut from her canteen, and bandaged it with a handkerchief, using left hand and teeth to tighten the knot. And then she continued up the wash, more careful now, leaving the bats behind, following a turn back into the full moonlight and then another into the shadows. Here she climbed onto a low alluvial ledge beside the dry streambed and dumped her pack. It was a familiar place. She and Eduardo Bernal had pitched a tent here five summers ago when they were graduate students, lovers, and part of the site-mapping team. Eddie Bernal. Tough little Ed. Fun while it lasted. But not much fun for long. Soon, surely before Christmas, she would drop the hyphen. Ed would hardly notice. A sigh of relief, perhaps. End of that brief phase when he'd thought one woman would be enough.

She removed a rock, some sticks, smoothed the ground with the edge of her boot sole, dug out and softened an area where her hips would be, and then rolled out the sleeping bag. She chose the place where she had lain with Eddie. Why? Partly defiance, partly sentiment, partly because it was simply the most comfortable spot. Tomorrow would be hard work and the cuts on her palm would make digging difficult and probably painful. But she wasn't ready for sleep yet. Too much tension. Too much uneasiness.

Standing here beside the sleeping bag, out of the moonlight, more stars were visible. She checked the autumn constellations, found the polestar, got her directions exactly right. Then she stared across the wash into the darkness that hid what she and Eddie had called Chicken Condo. In the narrow stone alcove, Anasazi families had built a two-story dwelling probably big enough for thirty people. Above it, in another alcove so hidden that they wouldn't have noticed it had Eddie not wondered where an evening bat flight was coming from, the Anasazi had built a little stone fort reachable only by a precarious set of hand- and footholds. It was around the lower dwelling that Eleanor Friedman-Bernal first had found the peculiar potsherds. If her memory didn't fool her. It was there, when it was light enough tomorrow, that she would dig. In violation of Navajo law, of federal law, and of professional ethics. If her memory only had not fooled her. And now she had more evidence than just her memory.

She couldn't wait until daylight. Not now. Not this near. Her flashlight would be enough to check.

Her memory had been excellent. It took her unerringly and without a misstep on an easy climb up the talus slope and along the natural pathway to the rim. There she paused and turned her light onto the cliff. The petroglyphs were exactly as she had stored them in her mind. The spiral that might represent the *sipapu* from which humans had emerged from the womb of Mother Earth, the line of dots that might represent the clan's migrations, the wide-shouldered forms that the ethnographers believed represented kachina spirits. There, too, cut through the dark desert varnish into the face of the cliff, was the shape Eddie had called Big Chief looking out from behind a red-stained shield, and a figure that seemed to have a man's body but the feet and head of a heron. It was one of her two favorites, because it seemed so totally unexplainable even by the cultural anthropologists—who could explain anything. The other was another version of Kokopelli.

Wherever you found him—and you found him everywhere these vanished people carved, and painted, their spirits into the cliffs of the Southwest—Kokopelli looked about the same. His humpbacked figure was supported by stick legs. Stick arms held a straight line to his tiny round head, making him seem to be playing a clarinet. The flute might be pointed down, or ahead. Otherwise there was little variation in how he was depicted. Except here. Here Kokopelli was lying on his back, flute pointed skyward. "At last," Eddie had said. "You have found Kokopelli's home. This is where he sleeps."

But Eleanor Friedman-Bernal hardly glanced at Kokopelli now. The Chicken Condo was just around the corner. That was what had drawn her.

The first things her eyes picked up when the beam of her flash lit the total darkness of the alcove were flecks of white where nothing white should be. She let the flash roam over the broken walls, reflect from the black surface of the seep-fed pool below them. Then she moved the beam back to that incongruous reflection. It was exactly what she had feared.

Bones. Bones scattered everywhere.

"Oh, shit!" said Eleanor Friedman-Bernal, who almost never used expletives. "Shit! Shit! Shit!"

Someone had been digging. Someone had been looting. A pot hunter. A Thief of Time. Someone had gotten here first.

She focused on the nearest white. A human shoulder bone. A child's. It lay atop a pile of loose earth just outside a place where the wall had fallen. The excavation was in the hump of earth that had been this community's trash heap. The common place for burials, and the first place experienced pot hunters dug. But the hole here was small. She felt better. Perhaps not much damage had been done. The digging looked fresh. Perhaps what she was hunting would still be here. She explored with the flash, looking for other signs of digging. She found none.

Nor was there any sign of looting elsewhere. She shined the light into the single hole dug in the midden pile. It reflected off stones, a scattering of potsherds mixed with earth and what seemed to be more human bones—part of a foot, she thought, and a vertebra. Beside the pit, on a slab of sandstone, four lower jaws had been placed in a neat row—three adult, one not much beyond infancy. She frowned at the arrangement, raised her eyebrows. Considered. Looked around her again. It hadn't rained—at least no rain had blown into this sheltered place—since this digging had been done. But then when had it rained? Not for weeks at Chaco. But Chaco was almost two hundred miles east and south.

The night was still. Behind her, she heard the odd piping of the little frogs that seemed to thrive in this canyon wherever water collected. Leopard frogs, Eddie had called them. And she heard the whistle again. The night bird. Closer now. A half-dozen notes. She frowned. A bird? What else could it be? She had seen at least three kinds of lizards on her way from the river—a whiptail, and a big collared lizard, and another she couldn't identify. They were nocturnal. Did they make some sort of mating whistle?

At the pool, her flashlight reflected scores of tiny points of light—the eyes of frogs. She stood watching them as they hopped, panicked by her huge presence, toward the safety of the black water. Then she frowned. Something was strange.

Not six feet from where she stood, one of them had fallen back in midhop. Then she noticed another one, a half-dozen others. She squatted on her heels beside the frog, inspecting it. And then another, and another, and another.

They were tethered. A whitish thread—perhaps a yucca fiber—had been tied around a back leg of each of these tiny black-green frogs and then to a twig stuck into the damp earth.

Eleanor Friedman-Bernal leaped to her feet, flashed the light frantically around the pool. Now she could see the scores of panicked frogs making those odd leaps that ended when a tether jerked them back to earth. For seconds her mind struggled to process this crazy, unnatural, irrational information. Who would . . . ? It would have to be a human act. It could have no sane purpose. When? How long could these frogs live just out of reach of the saving water? It was insane.

Just then she heard the whistle again. Just behind her. Not a night bird. No sort of reptile. It was a melody the Beatles had made popular. "Hey, Jude," the words began. But Eleanor didn't recognize it. She was too terrified by the humped shape that was coming out of the moonlight into this pool of darkness.

2

"ELEANOR FRIEDMAN HYPHEN BERNAL." Thatcher spaced the words, pronouncing them evenly. "I'm uneasy about women who hyphenate their names."

Lieutenant Joe Leaphorn didn't respond. Had he ever met a hyphenated woman? Not that he could remember. But the custom seemed sensible to him. Not as odd as Thatcher's discomfort with it. Leaphorn's mother, Leaphorn's aunts, all of the women he could think of among his maternal Red Forehead clan, would have resisted the idea of submerging their name or family identity in that of a husband. Leaphorn considered mentioning that, and didn't feel up to it. He'd been tired when Thatcher had picked him up at Navajo Tribal Police headquarters. Now he had added approximately 120 miles of driving to that fatigue. From Window Rock through Yah-Ta-Hey, to Crownpoint, to those final twenty jarring dirt miles to the Chaco Culture National Historical Park. Leaphorn's inclination had been to turn down the invitation to come along. But Thatcher had asked him as a favor.

"First job as a cop since they trained me," Thatcher had said. "May need some advice." It wasn't that, of course. Thatcher was a confident man and Leaphorn understood why Thatcher had called him. It was the kindness of an old friend who wanted to help. And the alternative to going would be to sit on the bed in the silent room and finish sorting through what was left of Emma's things—deciding what to do with them.

"Sure," Leaphorn had said. "Be a nice ride."

Now they were in the Chaco visitors' center, sitting on the hard chairs, waiting for the right person to talk to. From the bulletin board, a face stared out at them through dark sunglasses.

A THIEF OF TIME, the legend above it said. POT HUNTERS DESTROY AMERICA'S PAST.

"Appropriate," Thatcher said, nodding toward the poster, "but the picture should be a crowd scene. Cowboys, and county commissioners, and schoolteachers and pipeline workers, and everybody big enough to handle a shovel." He glanced at Leaphorn, looking for a response, and sighed.

"That road," he said. "I've been driving it thirty years now and it never gets any better." He glanced at Leaphorn again.

"Yeah," Leaphorn said. Thatcher had called them ceramic chugholes. "Never gets wet enough to soften 'em up," he'd said. "Rains, the bumps just get greasy." Not quite true. Leaphorn remembered a night a lifetime ago when he was young, a patrolman working out of the Crownpoint subagency. Melting snow had made the Chaco chugholes wet enough to soften the ceramic. His patrol car had sunk into the sucking, bottomless caliche mud. He'd radioed Crownpoint but the dispatcher had no help to send him. So he'd walked two hours to the R.D. Ranch headquarters. He'd been a newlywed then, worried that Emma would be worried about him. A hand at the ranch had put chains on a four-wheel-drive pickup and pulled him out. Nothing had changed since then. Except the roads were a lifetime older. Except Emma was dead.

Thatcher had said something else. He had been looking at him, expecting some response, when he should have been watching the ruts.

Leaphorn had nodded.

"You weren't listening. I asked you why you decided to quit."

Leaphorn had said nothing for a while. "Just tired."

Thatcher had shaken his head. "You're going to miss it."

"No, you get older. Or wiser. You realize it doesn't really make any difference."

"Emma was a wonderful woman," Thatcher had told him. "This won't bring her back."

"No, it won't."

"She were alive, she'd say: 'Joe, don't quit.' She'd say, 'You can't quit living.' I've heard her say things just like that."

"Probably," Leaphorn had said. "But I just don't want to do it anymore."

"Okay," Thatcher drove awhile. "Change the subject. I think women who have hyphenated names like that are going to be rich.

Old-money rich. Hard to work with. Stereotyping, but it's the way my mind works."

Then Leaphorn had been saved from thinking of something to say to that by an unusually jarring chughole. Now he was saved from thinking about it again. A medium-sized man wearing a neatly pressed U.S. Park Service uniform emerged from the doorway marked PERSONNEL ONLY. He walked into the field of slanting autumn sunlight streaming through the windows of the visitors' center. He looked at them curiously.

"I'm Bob Luna," he said. "This is about Ellie?"

Thatcher extracted a leather folder from his jacket and showed Luna a Bureau of Land Management law enforcement badge. "L. D. Thatcher," he said. "And this is Lieutenant Leaphorn. Navajo Tribal Police. Need to talk to Ms. Friedman-Bernal." He pulled an envelope from his jacket pocket. "Have a search warrant here to take a look at her place."

Luna's expression was puzzled. At first glance he had looked surprisingly young to Leaphorn to be superintendent of such an important park—his round, good-humored face would be perpetually boyish. Now, in the sunlight, the networks of lines around his eyes and at the corners of his mouth were visible. The sun and aridity of the Colorado Plateau acts quickly on the skin of whites, but it takes time to deepen the furrows. Luna was older than he looked.

"Talk to her?" Luna said. "You mean she's here? She's come back?"

Now it was Thatcher's turn to be surprised. "Doesn't she work here?"

"But she's missing," Luna said. "Isn't that what you're here about? We reported it a week ago. More like two weeks."

"Missing?" Thatcher said. "Whadaya mean missing?"

Luna's face had become slightly flushed. He opened his mouth. Closed it. Inhaled. Young as he looked, Luna was superintendent of this park, which meant he had a lot of experience being patient with people.

"Week ago last Wednesday. . . . That would be twelve days ago, we called in and reported Ellie missing. She was supposed to be back the previous Monday. She hadn't showed up. Hadn't called. She'd gone into Farmington for the weekend. She had an appointment Monday evening, back out here, and hadn't showed up for that. Had another appointment Wednesday. Hadn't been here for that, either. Totally out of character. Something must have happened to her and that's what we reported."

"She's not here?" Thatcher said. He tapped the envelope with the search warrant in it against the palm of his hand.

"Who'd you call?" Leaphorn asked, surprised at himself even as he heard himself asking the question. This was none of his business. It was nothing he cared about. He was here only because Thatcher had wanted him to come. Had wheedled until it was easier, if you didn't care anyway, to come than not to come. He hadn't intended to butt in. But this floundering around was irritating.

"The sheriff," Luna said.

"Which one?" Leaphorn asked. Part of the park was in McKinley County, part in San Juan.

"San Juan County," Luna said. "At Farmington. Anyway, nobody came out. So we called again last Friday. When you showed up, I thought you'd come out to start looking into it."

"I guess we are now," Leaphorn said. "More or less."

"We have a complaint about her," Thatcher said. "Or rather an allegation. But very detailed, very specific. About violations of the Antiquities Preservation Protection Act."

"Dr. Friedman?" Luna said. "Dr. Friedman a pot hunter?" He grinned. The grin almost became a chuckle, but Luna suppressed it. "I think we better go see Maxie Davis," he said.

Luna did the talking as he drove them up the road along Chaco Wash. Thatcher sat beside him, apparently listening. Leaphorn looked out the window, at the late afternoon light on the broken sandstone surface of the Chaco cliffs, at the gray-silver tufts of grama grass on the talus slope, at the long shadow of Fajada Butte stretching across the valley. What will I do tonight, when I am back in Window Rock? What will I do tomorrow? What will I do when this winter has come? And when it has gone? What will I ever do again?

Maxie is Eleanor Friedman's neighbor, Luna was saying. Next apartment in the housing units for temporary personnel. And both were part of the contract archaeology team. Helping decide which of the more than a thousand Anasazi sites in Luna's jurisdiction were significant, dating them roughly, completing an inventory, deciding which should be preserved for exploration in the distant future when scientists had new methods to see through time.

"And they're friends," Luna said. "They go way back. Went to school together. Work together now. All that. It was Maxie who called the sheriff." Today Maxie Davis was working at BC129, which was the cataloging number assigned to an unexcavated Anasazi site. Unfortunately, Luna said, BC129 was on the wrong side of Chaco Mesa—over by Escavada Wash at the end of a very rocky road.

"BC129?" Thatcher asked.

"BC129," Luna repeated. "Just a tag to keep track of it. Too many places out here to dream up names for them."

BC129 was near the rim of the mesa, a low mound that overlooked the Chaco Valley. A woman, her short dark hair tucked under a cap, stood waist-deep in a trench watching. Luna parked his van beside an old green pickup. Even at this distance Leaphorn could see the woman was beautiful. It was not just the beauty of youth and health, it was something unique and remarkable. Leaphorn had seen such beauty in Emma, nineteen then, and walking across the campus at Arizona State University. It was rare and valuable. A young Navajo man, his face shaded by the broad brim of a black felt hat, was sitting on the remains of a wall behind the trench, a shovel across his lap. Thatcher and Luna climbed out of the front seat.

"I'll wait," Leaphorn said.

This was his new trouble. Lack of interest. It had been his trouble since his mind had reluctantly processed the information from Emma's doctor.

"There's no good way to tell this, Mr. Leaphorn," the voice had said. "We lost her. Just now. It was a blood clot. Too much infection. Too much strain. But if it's any consolation, it must have been almost instantaneous."

He could see the man's face—pink-white skin, bushy blond eyebrows, blue eyes reflecting the cold light of the surgical waiting room through the lenses of horn-rimmed glasses, the small, prim mouth speaking to him. He could still hear the words, loud over the hum of the hospital air conditioner. It was like a remembered nightmare. Vivid. But he could not remember getting into his car in the parking lot, or driving through Gallup to Shiprock, or any of the rest of that day. He could remember only reviving his thoughts of the days before the operation. Emma's tumor would be removed. His joy that she was not being destroyed, as he had dreaded for so long, by the terrible, incurable, inevitable Alzheimer's disease. It was just a tumor. Probably not malignant. Easily curable. Emma would soon be herself again, memory restored. Happy. Healthy. Beautiful.

"The chances?" the surgeon had said. "Very good. Better than ninety percent complete recovery. Unless something goes wrong, an excellent prognosis."

But something had gone wrong. The tumor and its placement were worse than expected. The operation had taken much longer than expected. Then infection, and the fatal clot.

Since then, nothing had interested him. Someday, he would come alive again. Or perhaps he would. So far he hadn't. He sat sideways, legs stretched, back against the door, watching. Thatcher and Luna talked to the white woman in the trench. Unusual name for a woman. Maxie. Probably short for something Leaphorn couldn't think of. The Navajo was putting on a denim jacket, looking interested in whatever was being said, the expression on his long-jawed face sardonic. Maxie was gesturing, her face animated. She climbed out of the trench, walked toward the pickup truck with the Navajo following, his shovel over his shoulder in a sort of military parody. In the deep shadow of the hat brim Leaphorn saw white teeth. The man was grinning. Beyond him, the slanting light of the autumn afternoon outlined the contours of the Chaco Plateau with lines of darkness. The shadow of Fajada Butte stretched all the way across Chaco Wash now. Outside the shadow, the yellow of the cottonwood along the dry streambed glittered in the sun. They were the only trees in a tan-gray-silver universe of grass. (Where had they found their firewood, Leaphorn wondered, the vanished thousands of Old Ones who built these huge stone apartments? The anthropologists thought they'd carried the roof beams fifty miles on their shoulders from forests on Mount Taylor and the Chuskas—an incredible feat. But how did they boil their corn, roast venison, cure their pottery, and warm themselves in winter? Leaphorn remembered the hard labor each fall—his father and he taking their wagon into the foothills, cutting dead piñon and juniper, making the long haul back to their hogan. But the Anasazi had no horses, no wheels.)

Thatcher and Luna were back at the van now. Thatcher slammed the door on his coat, said something under his breath, reopened it and closed it again. When Luna started the engine the seat belt warning buzzed. "Seat belt," Thatcher said.

Luna fastened the seat belt. "Hate these things," he said.

The green pickup pulled ahead of them, raising dust.

"We're going down to look at what's-her-name's stuff,"

Thatcher said, raising his voice for Leaphorn. "This Ms. Davis doesn't think hyphenated could be a pot hunter. Said she collected pots, but it was for her work. Scientific. Legitimate. Said Ms. . . . . Ms. Bernal hated pot hunters."

"Um," Leaphorn said. He could see the big reservation hat of the young man through the back window of the pickup ahead. Odd to see a Navajo digging in the ruins. Stirring up Anasazi ghosts. Probably someone on the Jesus Road, or into the Peyote Church. Certainly a traditional man wouldn't be risking ghost sickness—or even worse, the reputation of being a witch—by digging among the bones. If you believed in the skinwalker traditions, bones of the dead made the tiny missiles that the witches shot into their victims. Leaphorn was not a believer. Those who were were the bane of his police work.

"She thinks something happened to Ms. Bernal," Thatcher said, glancing in the rearview mirror at Leaphorn. "You ought to have that seat belt on."

"Yeah," Leaphorn said. He fumbled it around him, thinking that probably nothing had happened to the woman. He thought of the anonymous call that had provoked this trip. There would be a connection, somewhere. One thing somehow would link Dr. What's-Her-Name's departure from Chaco with the motive for the call. The departure had led to the call, or something had happened that provoked both.

"What do you think?" he would have asked Emma. "Woman takes off for Farmington and drops off the world. Two days later somebody nasty turns her in for stealing pots. It could be she'd done something to make him sore, and knew he'd find out about it and turn her in. So she took off. Or she went to Farmington, made him sore there, and took off. So what you think?"

And Emma would have asked him three or four questions, and found out how little he knew about the woman, or about anything else to do with this, and then she would have smiled at him and used one of those dusty aphorisms from her Bitter Water Clan.

"Only yearling coyotes think there's just one way to catch a rabbit," she'd say. And then she'd say, "About next Tuesday the woman will call and tell her friends she ran away and got married, and it won't have anything to do with stealing pots." Maybe Emma would be right and maybe she'd be wrong, and that didn't really matter. It was a game they had played for years. Emma's astute mind working against his own intelligence, honing his thinking, testing his logic against her common sense. It helped him. She enjoyed it. It was fun.

Had been fun.

Leaphorn noticed it immediately—the cold, stagnant air of abandoned places. He was standing beside Thatcher when Thatcher unlocked the door to the apartment of Dr. Friedman-Bernal and pushed it open. The trapped air flowed outward into Leaphorn's sensitive nostrils. He sensed dust in it, and all that mixture of smells which humans leave behind them when they go away.

The Park Service calls such apartments TPH, temporary personnel housing. At Chaco, six of them were built into an L-shaped frame structure on a concrete slab—part of a complex that included maintenance and storage buildings, the motor pool, and the permanent personnel housing: a line of eight frame bungalows backed against the low cliff of Chaco Mesa.

"Well," Thatcher said. He walked into the apartment with Maxie Davis a step behind him. Leaphorn leaned against the door. Thatcher stopped. "Ms. Davis," he said, "I'm going to ask you to wait outside for a while. Under this search warrant here . . . well, it makes everything different. I may have to take an oath on what was in here when I opened the door." He smiled at her. "Things like that."

"I'll wait," Maxie Davis said. She walked past Leaphorn, smiling at him nervously, and sat on the porch railing in the slanting sunlight. Her face was somber. Again, Leaphorn noticed her striking beauty. She was a small young woman. Cap off now, her dark hair needed combing. Her oval face had been burned almost as dark as Leaphorn's. She stared toward the maintenance yard, where a man in coveralls was doing something to the front end of a flatbed truck. Her fingers tapped at the railing—small, battered fingers on a small, scarred hand. Her blue work shirt draped against her back. Under it, every line of her body was tense. Beyond her, the weedy yard, the maintenance shed, the tumbled boulders along the cliff, seemed almost luminous in the brilliant late-afternoon sunlight. It made the gloom inside Dr. Friedman-Bernal's apartment behind Leaphorn seem even more shadowy than it was.

Thatcher walked through the living room, pulled open the drapes and exposed sliding-glass doors. They framed Fajada Butte and the expanse of the Chaco Valley. Except for a stack of books on the coffee table in front of the bleak brown institutional sofa, the room looked unused. Thatcher picked up the top book, examined it, put it down, and walked into the bedroom. He stood just inside the doorway, shaking his head.

"It would help some," he said, "if you knew what the hell you're looking for."

The room held a desk, two chairs, and two double beds. One seemed to be for sleeping—the covers carelessly pulled back in place after its last use. The other was work space—covered now with three cardboard boxes and a litter of notebooks, computer printouts, and other papers. Beyond this bed other boxes lined the floor along the wall. They seemed to hold mostly broken bits of pottery. "No way on God's green earth of telling where she got any of this stuff," Thatcher said. "Not that I know of. It might be perfectly legal."

"Unless her field notes tell us something," Leaphorn said. "They might. In fact, if she collected that stuff as part of some project or other, they should tell exactly where she picked up every bit of that stuff. And it's going to be legal unless she's been selling the artifacts."

"And of course if she's doing it for a project, it's legal," Thatcher said. "Unless she doesn't have the right permit. And if she's selling the stuff, she sure as hell ain't going to write down anything incriminating."

"Nope," Leaphorn said.

A man appeared at the apartment door. "Finding anything?" he asked. He walked past Leaphorn without a glance and into the bedroom. "Glad to see you people getting interested in this," he said. "Ellie's been missing almost three weeks now."

Thatcher put a fragment of pot carefully back into its box. "Who are you?" he asked.

"My name's Elliot," he said. "I work with Ellie on the Keet Katl dig. Or did work with her. What's this Luna's been telling me? You think she's stealing artifacts?"

Leaphorn found himself interested—wondering how Thatcher would deal with this. It wasn't the sort of thing anticipated and covered in the law enforcement training Thatcher would have received. No chapter covering intrusion of civilian into scene of investigation.

"Mr. Elliot," Thatcher said, "I want you to wait outside on the porch until we get finished in here. Then I want to talk to you."

Elliot laughed. "For God's sake," he said, in a tone that canceled any misunderstanding the laugh might have caused. "A woman vanishes for almost a month and nobody can get you guys off your butts. But somebody calls in with an anonymous . . ."

"Talk to you in a minute," Thatcher said. "Soon as I'm done in here."

"Done what?" Elliot said. "Done stirring through her potsherds? If you get 'em out of order, get 'em mixed up, it will screw up everything for her."

"Out," Thatcher said, voice still mild.

Elliot stared at him.

Maybe middle thirties or a little older, Leaphorn thought. A couple of inches over six feet, slender, athletic. The sun had bleached his hair even lighter than its usual very light brown. His jeans were worn and so were his jean jacket and his boots. But they fit. They had been expensive. And the face fit the pattern—a little weather-beaten but what Emma would have called "an upper-class face." A little narrow, large blue eyes, nothing crooked, nothing bent, nothing scarred. Not the face you'd see looking out of a truckload of migrant workers, or in a roofing crew, or the cab of a road grader.

"Of course this place is full of pots." Elliot's voice was angry. "Studying pots is Ellie's job. . . ."

Thatcher gripped Elliot at the elbow. "Talk to you later," he said mildly, and moved him past Leaphorn and out the door. He closed the door behind him.

"Trouble is," Thatcher said, "everything he says is true. Her business is pots. So she'll have a bunch of 'em here. So what the hell are we looking for?"

Leaphorn shrugged. "I think we just look," he said. "We find what we find. Then we think about it."

They found more boxes of potsherds in the closet, each shard bearing a label that seemed to identify it with the place it had been found. They found an album of photographs, many of them snapshots of people who seemed to be anthropologists working at digs. There were three notebooks—two filled and one almost half filled—in which little pencil drawings of abstract patterns and pots were interposed with carbon rubbings of what they agreed must be the surface patterns of potsherds. The notes that surrounded these were in the special shorthand scientists develop to save themselves time.

"You studied this stuff at Arizona State," Thatcher said. "Can't you make it out?"

"I studied anthropology," Leaphorn admitted. "But mostly I

studied cultural anthropology. This is a specialty and I didn't get into it. We went on a few digs in a Southwestern Anthro class, but the Anasazi culture wasn't my thing. Neither were ceramics."

Among the papers on the bed were two Nelson's catalogs, both auctions of American Indian art, African art, and Oceanic art. Both facedown, both open to pages that featured illustrations of Mimbres, Hohokam, and Anasazi pots. Leaphorn studied them. The appraised prices ranged from $2,950 to $41,500 for a Mimbres urn. Two of the Anasazi ceramics had been circled in red in one catalog, and one in the other. The prices were $4,200, $3,700, and $14,500.

"Heard of Nelson's all my life," Thatcher said. "Thought they were just a London outfit. Just auctioned art, masterpieces, the *Mona Lisa,* things like that."

"This is art," Leaphorn said.

"A painting is art," Thatcher said. "What kind of nut pays fourteen grand for a pot?" He tossed the catalog back on the bed.

Leaphorn picked it up.

The cover picture was a stylized re-creation of a pictograph—stick-figure Indians with lances riding horses with pipestem legs across a deerskin surface.

Across the top the legend read:

NELSON'S

FOUNDED 1744

Fine American Indian Art
New York
Auction May 25 and 26

It opened easily to the pottery pages. Ten photographs of pots, each numbered and described in a numbered caption. Number 242 was circled in red. Leaphorn read the caption:

242. Anasazi St. John's Polychrome bowl, circa
A.D. 1000–1250, of deep rounded form, painted on the
interior in rose with wavy pale "ghost lines." Has a
geometric pattern enclosing two interlocked spirals.
Two hatched, serrated rectangles below the rim. Interior
surface serrated. Diameter 7¼ inches (19 cm).
$4,000/$4,200.

Resale offer by an anonymous collector.
Documentation.

Inside the scrawled red circle, the same pen had put a question mark over "anonymous collector" and scribbled notations in the margin. What looked like a telephone number. Words that seemed to be names. "Call Q!" "See Houk." Houk. The name made a faint echo in Leaphorn's mind. He'd known someone named Houk. The only notation that meant anything to him was: "Nakai, Slick." Leaphorn knew about Slick Nakai. Had met him a time or two. Nakai was a preacher. A fundamentalist Christian evangelist. He pulled a revival tent around the reservation in a trailer behind an old Cadillac sedan, putting it up here and there—exhorting those who came to hear him to quit drinking, leave off fornication, confess their sins, abandon their pagan ways, and come to Jesus. Leaphorn scanned the other names, looking for anything familiar, read the description of a Tonto Polychrome olla valued at $1,400/ $1,800. He put the catalog back on the bed. On the next page, a Mimbres black-on-white burial pot, with a "kill hole" in its bottom and its exterior featuring lizards chasing lizards, was advertised for $38,600. Leaphorn grimaced and put down the catalog.

"I'm going to make a sort of rough inventory," Thatcher said, sorting through one of the boxes. "Just jot down some idea of what we have here, which we both know is absolutely nothing that is going to be of any use to us."

Leaphorn sat in the swivel chair and looked at the 365-day calendar on the desk. It was turned to October 11. "What day was it they said Dr. Hyphenated left here? Wasn't it the thirteenth?"

"Yeah," Thatcher said.

Leaphorn flipped over a page to October 13. "Do it!" was written under the date. He turned the next page. Across this was written: "Away." The next page held two notes: "Be ready for Lehman. See H. Houk."

H. Houk. Would it be Harrison Houk? Maybe. An unusual name, and the man fit the circumstances. Houk would be into everything and the Houk ranch—outside of Bluff and just over the San Juan River from the north side of the reservation—was in the heart of Anasazi ruins country.

The next page was October 16. It was blank. So was the next page. That took him to Wednesday. Across this was written: "Lehman!!! about 4 P.M. dinner. sauerbraten, etc."

Leaphorn thumbed through the pages up to the present. So far

Dr. Friedman-Bernal had missed two other appointments. She would miss another one next week. Unless she came home.

He put down the calendar, walked into the kitchen, and opened the refrigerator, remembering how Emma liked to make sauerbraten. "It's way too much work," he would say, which was better than telling her that he really didn't like it very well. And Emma would say: "No more work than Navajo tacos, and less cholesterol."

The smell of soured milk and stale food filled his nostrils. The worse smell came from a transparent ovenware container on the top shelf. It held a Ziploc bag containing what seemed to be a large piece of meat soaking in a reddish brown liquid. Sauerbraten. Leaphorn grimaced, shut the door, and walked back into the room where Thatcher was completing his inventory.

The sun was on the horizon now, blazing through the window and casting Thatcher's shadow black against the wallpaper. Leaphorn imagined Eleanor Friedman-Bernal hurrying through the sauerbraten process, getting all those things now shriveled and spoiled lined up on the refrigerator shelves so that fixing dinner for Lehman could be quickly done. But she hadn't come back to fix that dinner. Why not? Had she gone to see Harrison Houk about a pot? Leaphorn found himself remembering the first, and only, time he'd encountered the man. Years ago. He'd been what? Officer Leaphorn working out of the Kayenta substation, obliquely involved in helping the FBI with the manhunt across San Juan.

The Houk killings, they had called them. Leaphorn, who forgot little, remembered the names. Della Houk, the mother. Elmore Houk, the brother. Dessie Houk, the sister. Brigham Houk, the killer. Harrison Houk, the father. Harrison Houk had been the survivor. The mourner. Leaphorn remembered him standing on the porch of a stone house, listening intently while the sheriff talked, remembered him climbing up from the river, staggering with fatigue, when it was no longer light enough to search along the bank for Brigham Houk. Or, almost certainly even then, Brigham Houk's drowned body.

Would it be this same H. Houk now whom Eleanor Friedman-Bernal had noted on her calendar? Was Harrison Houk some part of the reason for the uneaten banquet spoiling in the refrigerator? To his surprise Joe Leaphorn found his curiosity had returned. What had prevented Eleanor Friedman-Bernal from coming home for her party with a guest whose name deserved three exclamation points? What caused her to miss a dinner she'd worked so hard to prepare?

Leaphorn walked back into the closet and recovered the album. He flipped through it. Which one was Eleanor Friedman-Bernal? He found a page of what must have been wedding pictures—bride and groom with another young couple. He slipped one of them out of the corners that held it. The bride was radiant, the groom a good-looking Mexican, his expression slightly stunned. The bride's face long, prominent bones, intelligent, Jewish. A good woman, Leaphorn thought. Emma would have liked her. He had two weeks left on his terminal leave. He'd see if he could find her.

3

IT HAD BEEN A BAD DAY for Officer Jim Chee of the Navajo Tribal Police. In fact, it had been the very worst day of an abysmal week.

It had started going bad sometime Monday. Over the weekend it had dawned upon some dimwit out at the Navajo Tribal Motor Pool that a flatbed trailer was missing. Apparently it had been missing for a considerable time. Sunday night it was reported stolen.

"How long?" Captain Largo asked at Monday afternoon's briefing. "Tommy Zah don't know how long. Nobody knows how long. Nobody seems to remember seeing it since about a month ago. It came in for maintenance. Motor pool garage fixed a bad wheel bearing. Presumably it was then parked out in the lot. But it's not in the lot now. Therefore it has to be stolen. That's because it makes Zah look less stupid to declare it stolen. Better'n admitting he just don't know what the hell they did with it. So we're supposed to find it for 'em. After whoever took it had time to haul it about as far as Florida."

Looking back on it, looking for the reason all of what followed came down on him instead of some other officer on the evening shift, Chee could see it was because he had not been looking alert. The captain had spotted it. In fact, Chee had been guilty of gazing out of the assembly room window. The globe willows that shaded the parking lot of the Shiprock subagency of the Navajo Tribal Police were full of birds that afternoon. Chee had been watching them, deciding they were finches, thinking what he would say to Janet Pete when he saw her again. Suddenly he became aware that Largo had been talking to him.

"You see it out there in the parking lot?"

"Sir?"

"The goddam trailer," Largo said. "It out there?"

"No sir."

"You been paying enough attention to know what trailer we're talking about?"

"Motor pool trailer," Chee said, hoping Largo hadn't changed the subject.

"Wonderful," Largo said, glowering at Chee. "Now from what Superintendent Zah said on the telephone, we're going to get a memo on this today and the memo is going to say that they called our dispatcher way back sometime and reported pilfering out there at night and asked us to keep an eye on things. Long before they mislaid their trailer, you understand. That's to cover the superintendent's ass and make it our fault."

Largo exhaled a huge breath and looked at his audience—making sure his night shift understood what their commanding officer was dealing with here.

"Now, just about now," Largo continued, "they're starting to count all their stuff out there. Tools. Vehicles. Coke machines. God knows what. And sure as hell they're going to find other stuff missing. And not know when they lost it, and claim it got stolen five minutes ago. Or tomorrow if that's handier for 'em. Anyway, it will be at some time after—I repeat, after—we've been officially informed and asked to watch out for 'em. And then I'm going to be spending my weekends writing reports to send down to Window Rock." Largo paused. He looked at Chee.

"So, Chee . . ."

"Yes sir." Chee was paying attention now. Too late.

"I want you to keep an eye on that place. Hang around there on your shift. Get past there every chance you get. And make chances. Call the dispatcher to keep it on record that you're watching. When they finish their inventory and find out they've lost other stuff, I don't want 'em in a position to blame us. Understand?"

Chee understood. Not that it helped.

That was Monday afternoon. Monday evening it got worse. Even worse than it might have been, because he didn't learn about it until Tuesday.

As instructed, Chee had been hanging close to the motor pool. He would coast out Highway 550 maybe as far as the Hogback formation, which marked the eastern edge of the Big Reservation. Then he would drift back past the motor pool fence and into Shiprock. Stopping now and then to check the gate. Noticing that the summer's accumulation of tumbleweeds piled along the chain-link fence was undisturbed. Drifting down 550 again. Drifting back. Keeping Farmington–Shiprock traffic holding nervously in the vicinity of the speed limit. Boring himself into sleepiness. Calling in now and then to have the dispatcher record that he was diligently watching the motor pool and that all there remained serene.

"Unit Eleven checking at the motor pool," Chee called. "All quiet. No sign of entry."

"Since you're there on five-fifty," the dispatcher said, "see what's going on at the Seven-Eleven. Just had a disturbance call."

Chee had done a quick U-turn, boredom replaced by the uneasiness that always preceded the probability of dealing with a drunk. Or two drunks. Or however many drunks it was taking to disturb the peace at the Shiprock 7-Eleven.

But the parking space in front of the convenience store had been quiet—empty except for an old Dodge sedan and a pickup truck. No drunks. Inside, no drunks either. The woman behind the cash register was reading one of those tabloids convenience stores sell. A green-ink headline proclaimed THE TRUTH ABOUT LIZ TAYLOR'S WEIGHT LOSS. Another declared SIAMESE TWINS BOTH PREGNANT. BLAME MINISTER. A teenaged boy was inspecting the canned soda pop in the cooler.

"What's the trouble?" Chee asked.

The teenager put down the Pepsi he'd selected, looking guilty. The cashier lowered her paper. She was a middle-aged Navajo woman. Towering House Clan, Chee remembered, named Gorman, or Relman, or something like that. Anglo-type name with six letters. Bunker. Walker. Thomas.

"What?" she asked.

"Somebody called in a disturbance here. What's the trouble?"

"Oh," the Towering House woman said. "We had a drunk in here. Where you been?"

"What'd he do? Any damages?"

"She," the woman said. "Old Lady George. She went away when she heard me calling the police."

The cashier's name was Gorman, Chee now remembered. But he was thinking of Old Lady George.

"Which way did she go?"

"Just went," Mrs. Gorman said. She gestured vaguely. "Didn't look. I was picking up the cans she knocked over."

So Chee had gone looking for Old Lady George. He knew her fairly well. She'd been a witness in an automobile theft case he'd worked on—a very helpful witness. Later, when he was looking for one of her grandsons on an assault warrant, she'd helped him again. Sent the boy down to the station to turn himself in. Besides, she was Streams Come Together Clan, which was linked to Chee's father's clan, which made her a relative. Chee had been raised knowing that you watch out for your relatives.

He had watched out for her, first up and down 550 and then up and down side streets. He found her sitting on a culvert, and talked her into the patrol car, and took her home and turned her over to a worried young woman who he guessed must be a granddaughter. Then he had gone back and established that the motor pool remained intact. At least it seemed to be intact as seen from the highway. But seen from the highway, it hadn't been possible to detect that someone had tinkered with the padlock securing the gate. He heard about that the next day when he reported for work.

Captain Largo's usually big voice was unusually quiet—an ominous sign.

"A backhoe," Largo said. "That's what they stole this time. About three tons. Bright yellow. Great big thing. I told Mr. Zah that I had one of my best men watching his place last night. Officer Jim Chee. I told Zah that it must be just another case of forgetting to put it down on the record when somebody borrowed it. You know what he said to me?"

"No sir," Chee said. "But nobody stole that on my shift. I was driving back and forth past there the whole time."

"Really," Largo said. "How nice." He picked up a sheet from the shift squeal report from his desk. He didn't look at it. "I'm pleased to hear that. Because you know what Zah said to me? He said"—Largo shifted his voice up the scale—" 'Oh, it was stolen last night all right. The guy that runs the service station across the street there told us about it.' " Largo's voice returned to normal. "This service station man stood there and watched 'em drive out with it."

"Oh," Chee said, thinking it must have been while he was at the 7-Eleven.

"This Zah is quite a comedian. He told me you'd think sneaking a big yellow backhoe out with one of my policemen watching would be like trying to sneak moonrise past a coyote."

Chee flushed. He had nothing to say to that. He had heard the simile before somewhere in another form. Hard as sneaking sunrise past a rooster, it had been. A moonrise without a coyote baying was equally impossible, and relating a coyote to Largo's police added a nicely oblique insult. You don't call a Navajo a coyote. The only thing worse is to accuse him of letting his kinfolks starve.

Largo handed Chee the squeal sheet. It confirmed what Zah had told Largo.

Subject Delbert Tsosie informed Officer Shorty that while serving a customer at the Texaco station at approximately 10 P.M. he noticed a man removing the chain from the gate of the motor pool maintenance yard across Highway 550. He observed a truck towing a flatbed trailer drive through the gate into the yard. Subject Tsosie said that approximately fifteen minutes later he noticed the truck driving out the gate towing a machine which he described as probably a backhoe or some sort of trenching machine loaded on the trailer. He said he did not report this to police because he presumed tribal employees had come to get the equipment to deal with some sort of emergency.

"That must have been while I was looking for Old Lady George," Chee said. He explained, hurrying through the last stages because of Largo's expression.

"Get to work," Largo said, "and leave this alone. Sergeant Benally will be chasing the backhoe. Don't mess with it."

That was Tuesday morning and should have been the very bottom of the week. The pits. It would have been, perhaps, had not Chee driven past the Texaco station on 550 and seen Delbert Tsosie stacking tires. Benally was handling it, but Chee sometimes bought gasoline from Tsosie. No harm in stopping to talk.

"No," Tsosie said. "Didn't see either one of them well enough to recognize 'em. But you could see one was Dineh—tall, skinny Navajo. Had on a cowboy hat. I know a lot of 'em that works at the motor pool. They come over here and use the Coke machine and buy candy. Wasn't none I knew and I was thinking it was a funny time to be coming to work. But I thought they must have forgotten something and was coming for it. And when I saw the backhoe I figured some pipe broke somewhere. Emergency, you know." Tsosie shrugged.

"You didn't recognize anybody?"

"Bad light."

"Guy in the truck. You see him at all?"

"Not in the truck," Tsosie said. "The skinny Navajo was driving the truck. This guy was following in a sedan. Plymouth two-door. About a '70, '71 maybe. Dark blue but they was doing some bodywork on it. Had an off-color right front fender. Looked white or gray. Maybe primer coat. And lots of patches here and there, like they was getting ready to paint it."

"Driver not a Navajo?"

"Navajo driving the truck. *Belagana* driving the Plymouth. And the white guy, I just barely got a look at him. They all sort of look alike anyway. All I notice is freckles and sunburn."

"Big or little?"

Tsosie thought. "About average. Maybe sort of short and stocky."

"What color hair?"

"Had a cap on. Baseball cap. With a bill."

None of which would have mattered since Benally was handling it, and Tsosie had already told Benally all of this, and probably more. But Saturday morning Chee saw the Plymouth two-door.

It was dark blue, about a '70 model. When it passed him going in the other direction—Shiprock-bound on 550—he saw the mismatched front fender and the patches of primer paint on its doors and the baseball cap on the head of the white man driving it. Without a thought, Chee did a U-turn across the bumpy divider.

He was driving Janet Pete's car. Not exactly Janet Pete's car. Janet had put down earnest money on a Buick Riviera at Quality Pre-owned Cars in Farmington and had asked Chee to test-drive it for her. She had to go to Phoenix Friday and when she got back Monday she wanted to close the deal.

"I guess I've already decided," Janet had told him. "It has everything I need and only fourteen thousand miles on it and the price seems reasonable and he's giving me a thousand dollars on my old Datsun and that seems fair."

To Chee the thousand for the Datsun seemed enough more than fair to arouse suspicion. Janet's Datsun was a junker. But it was clear that Janet was not going to be receptive to discouraging words. She described the Buick as "absolutely beautiful." As she described it, the lawyer in Janet Pete fell away. The girl emerged through the delight and enthusiasm, and Janet Pete became absolutely beautiful herself.

"It has the prettiest blue plush upholstery. Lovely color. Dark blue outside with a real delicate pinstripe down the side, and the chrome is just right." She looked slightly guilty at this. "I don't usually like chrome," she said. "But this . . ." She performed a gesture with shoulder and face that depreciated this lapse from taste. ". . . But this . . . well, I just love it."

She paused, examining Chee and transforming herself from girl to lawyer. "I thought maybe you would check it out for me. You drive all the time and you know all about mechanical things. If you don't mind doing it, and there's something seriously wrong with the engine, or something like that, then I could . . ."

She had left the awful statement unfinished. And Chee had accepted the keys and said sure, he'd be glad to do it. Which wasn't exactly the case. If there was something seriously wrong with the engine, telling her about it wasn't going to make him popular with Janet Pete. And Chee wanted to be popular. He wondered about her. He wondered about a woman lawyer. To be more precise, he wondered if Janet Pete, or any woman, could fill the gap Mary Landon seemed to be leaving in his life.

That was Friday evening. Saturday morning he drove the Buick down to Bernie Tso's garage and put it on the rack. Bernie was not impressed.

"Fourteen thousand miles, my ass," Bernie said. "Look at the tread on those tires. And here." Bernie rattled the universal joint. "Arizona don't have a law about running back the odometer, but New Mexico does," he said. "And she got this junker over in New Mexico. I'd say they fudged the first number a little. Turned her back from forty-four thousand, or maybe seventy-four."

He finished his inspection of the running gear and lowered the hoist. "Steering's slack, too," he said. "Want me to pull the head and take a look there?"

"Maybe later," Chee said. "I'll take it out and see what I can find and then I'll let her decide if she wants to spend any money on it."

And so he had driven Janet Pete's blue Buick out Highway 550 toward Farmington, glumly noting its deficiencies. Slow response to the gas pedal. Probably easy to fix with an adjustment. Tendency to choke on acceleration. Also fixable. Tendency to steer to the right on braking. Suspension far too soft for Chee, who was conditioned to the cast-iron springing of police cars and pickup trucks. Maybe she liked soft suspension, but this one was also uneven—suggesting a bad shock absorber. And, as Bernie had mentioned, slack steering.

He was measuring this slack, swaying down the Farmington-bound lanes of 550, when he saw the Backhoe Bandit. And it was the slack steering, eventually, that did him in.

He noticed the off-color fender first. He noticed that the car approaching him, Shiprock-bound, was a blue Plymouth sedan of about 1970 vintage. As it passed, he registered the patches of gray-white primer paint on its door. He got only a glimpse of the profile of the driver—youngish, long blond hair emerging from under a dark billed cap.

Chee didn't give it a thought. He did a U-turn across the bumpy divider and followed the Plymouth.

He was wearing his off-duty work clothes—greasy jeans and a Coors T-shirt with a torn armpit. His pistol was locked securely in the table beside the cot in his trailer at Shiprock. No radio in the Buick, of course. And it was no chase car. He would simply tag along, determine where the Backhoe Bandit was going, take whatever opportunity presented itself. The Plymouth was in no particular hurry. It did a left turn off 550 on the access road to the village of Kirtland. It crossed the San Juan bridge, did another turn onto a dirt road, and made the long climb up the mesa toward the Navajo Mine and the Four Corners Power Plant. Chee had fallen a quarter-mile back, partly to avoid eating the Plymouth's dust and partly to avoid arousing suspicion. But by the time he reached the escarpment the Backhoe Bandit seemed to have sensed he was being followed. He did another turn onto a poorly graded dirt road across the sagebrush, driving much faster now and producing a rooster tail of dust. Chee followed, pushing the Buick, sending it bouncing and lurching over the humps, fighting the steering where the road was rutted. Through the dust he became belatedly aware the Plymouth had made another turn—a hard right. Chee braked, skidded, corrected the skid, collected the slack in the steering, and made the turn. He was a little late.

Oops! Right wheel onto the rocky track. Left wheel in the sagebrush. Chee bounced painfully against the Buick's blue plush roof, bounced again, saw through the dust the rocks he should have been avoiding, frantically spun the slack steering wheel, felt the impact, felt something go in the front end, and then simply slid along—his hat jammed low onto his forehead by its kiss with the ceiling.

Janet Pete's beautiful blue Buick slid sideways, plowing a sedan-sized gash through the sage. It stopped in a cloud of dirt. Chee climbed out.

It looked bad, but not as bad as it might have been. The left front wheel was horizontal, the tie-rod that held it broken. Not as bad as a broken axle. The rest of the damage was, to Chee's thinking, superficial. Just scrapes, dents, and scratches. Chee found the chrome strip that Janet Pete had so admired about fifteen yards back in the brush, peeled off by a limb. He laid it carefully on the backseat. The plume of dust produced by the Plymouth was receding over the rim of the mesa. Chee watched it, thinking about his immediate problem—getting a tow truck out here to haul in the Buick. Thinking about the five or six miles he would have to walk to get to a telephone, thinking about the seven or eight hundred dollars it was going to cost to patch up the damaged Buick. Thinking about such things was far more pleasant than considering his secondary problem, which was how to break the news to Janet Pete.

"Absolutely beautiful," Janet Pete had said. "I fell in love with it," she'd said. "Just what I'd always wanted." But he would think about that later. He was staring into the diminishing haze of dust, but his vision was turned inward—imprinting the Backhoe Bandit in his memory. The profile, the suggestion of pockmarks on the jaw, the hair, the cap. This had become a matter of pride. He would find the man again, sooner or later.

By midafternoon, with the Buick back at Bernie Tso's garage, it seemed it would be sooner. Tso knew the Plymouth. Had, in fact, once towed it in. And he knew a little about the Backhoe Bandit.

"Everything that goes around comes around," Chee said, happily. "Everything balances out."

"I wouldn't say that," Tso said. "What's it going to cost you to balance out this Buick?"

"I mean catching the son of a bitch," Chee said. "At least I'm going to be able to do that. Lay that on the captain's desk."

"Maybe your girlfriend can take it back to the dealer," Tso said. "Tell 'em she doesn't like the way that front wheel looks."

"She's not my girlfriend," Chee said. "She's a lawyer with DNA. Tribal legal services. I ran into her last summer." Chee described how he had picked up a man who came to be Janet Pete's client, and had tried to have him kept in the Farmington jail until he had a chance to talk to him, and how sore Pete had been about it.

"Tough as nails," Chee said. "Not my type. Not unless I kill somebody and need a lawyer."

"I don't see how you're going to catch him with what little I know about him," Tso said. "Not even his name. All I remember is he works out in the Blanco gas field the other side of Farmington. Or said he did."

"And that you pulled him in when he had transmission troubles. And he paid you with two hundred-dollar bills. And he told you when you got it fixed to leave it at Slick Nakai's revival tent."

"Well, yeah," Tso said.

"And he said you could leave the change with Slick 'cause he saw Slick pretty often."

And now it was Saturday night. Slick Nakai's True Gospel had long since left the place near the Hogback where Tso had gone to tow in the Plymouth. But it was easy enough to locate by asking around. Nakai had loaded his tent, and his portable electric organ, and his sound system into his four-wheel trailer and headed southeast. He had left behind fliers tacked to telephone poles and Scotch-taped to store windows announcing that all hungering for the Word of the Lord could find him between Nageezi and the Dzilith-Na-O-Dith-Hie School.

4

FULL DARKNESS CAME LATE on this dry autumn Saturday. The sun was far below the western horizon but a layer of high, thin cirrus clouds still received the slanting light and reflected it, red now, down upon the ocean of sagebrush north of Nageezi Trading Post. It tinted the patched canvas of Slick Nakai's revival tent from faded tan to a doubtful rose and the complexion of Lieutenant Joe Leaphorn from dark brown to dark red.

From a lifetime of habit, Leaphorn had parked his pickup a little away from the cluster of vehicles at the tent and with its nose pointing outward, ready for whatever circumstances and duty might require of it. But Leaphorn was not on duty. He would never be on duty again. He was in the last two weeks of a thirty-day "terminal leave." When it ended, his application to retire from the Navajo Tribal Police would be automatically accepted. In fact he was already retired. He felt retired. He felt as if it were all far, far behind him. Faded in the distance. Another life in another world, nothing to do with the man now standing under this red October sunset, waiting for the sounds coming from the True Gospel revival tent to signal a break in the preaching.

He had come to Slick Nakai's revival to begin his hunt. Where had that hyphenated woman gone? Why had she abandoned a meal so carefully prepared, an evening so obviously anticipated? It didn't matter, and yet it did. In a way he couldn't really understand, it would say good-by to Emma. She would have prepared such a meal in anticipation of a treasured guest. Often had done so. Leaphorn couldn't explain it, but his mind made a sort of nebulous connection between Emma's character and that of a woman who probably was quite different. And so he would use the final days of his final leave to find that woman. That had brought him here. That, and boredom, and his old problem of curiosity, and the need for a reason to get away from their house in Window Rock and all its memories.

Whatever had moved him, he was here, on the very eastern fringe of the Navajo Reservation—more than a hundred miles from home. When circumstances allowed, he would talk to a man whose very existence annoyed him. He would ask questions the man might not answer and which might mean nothing if he did. The alternative was sitting in their living room, the television on for background noise, trying to read. But Emma's absence always intruded. When he raised his eyes, he saw the R. C. Gorman print she'd hung over the fireplace. They'd argued about it. She liked it, he didn't. The words would sound in his ears again. And Emma's laughter. It was the same everywhere he looked. He should sell that house, or burn it. It was in the tradition of the Dineh. Abandon the house contaminated by the dead, lest the ghost sickness infect you, and you died. Wise were the elders of his people, and the Holy People who taught them the Navajo Way. But instead, he would play this pointless game. He would find a woman. If alive, she wouldn't want to be found. If dead, it wouldn't matter.

Abruptly, it became slightly more interesting. He had been leaning on the door of his pickup, studying the tent, listening to the sounds coming from it, examining the grounds (another matter of habit). He recognized a pickup, parked like his own behind the cluster of vehicles. It was the truck of another tribal policeman. Jim Chee's truck. Chee's private truck, which meant Chee was also here unofficially. Becoming a born-again Christian? That hardly seemed likely. As Leaphorn remembered it, Chee was the antithesis of Slick Nakai. Chee was a *hataalii*. A singer. Or would be one as soon as people started hiring him to conduct their curing ceremonials. Leaphorn looked at the pickup, curious. Was someone sitting in it? Hard to tell in the failing light. What would Chee be doing here?

The sound of music came from the tent. A surprising amount of music, as if a band were playing. Over that an amplified male voice leading a hymn. Time to go in.

The band proved to be two men. Slick Nakai, standing behind what seemed to be a black plastic keyboard, and a thin guitarist in a blue checked shirt and a gray felt hat. Nakai was singing, his mouth a quarter-inch from a stand-mounted microphone, his hands maintaining a heavy rhythm on the keyboard. The audience sang with him, with much swaying and clapping of hands.

"Jesus loves us," Nakai sang. "That we know. Jesus loves us. Everywhere."

Nakai's eyes were on him, examining him, sorting him out. The guitarist was looking at him, too. The hat looked familiar. So did the man. Leaphorn had a good memory for faces, and for just about everything else.

"We didn't earn it," Nakai sang. "But He don't care. His love is with us. Everywhere."

Nakai emphasized this with a flourish at the keyboard, shifting his attention now from Leaphorn to an elderly woman wearing wire-rimmed glasses who was sway-dancing, eyes closed, too caught up with emotion to be aware she had danced into the tangle of electrical cables linking Nakai's sound system to a generator outside the tent. A tall man with a thin mustache standing by the speaker's podium noticed Nakai's concern. He moved quickly, steering the woman clear of the cables. Third member of the team, Leaphorn guessed.

When the music stopped, Nakai introduced him as "Reverend Tafoya."

"He's Apache. I tell you that right out," Nakai said. "Jicarilla. But that's all right. God made the Apaches, and the *belagana,* and the blacks, and the Hopis, and us Dineh and everybody else just the same. And he inspired this Apache here to learn about Jesus. And he's going to tell you about that."

Nakai surrendered the microphone to Tafoya. Then he poured water from a thermos into a Styrofoam cup and carried it back toward where Leaphorn was standing. He was a short man, sturdily built, neat and tidy, with small, round hands, small feet in neat cowboy boots, a round, intelligent face. He walked with the easy grace of a man who walks a lot.

"I haven't seen you here before," Nakai said. "If you came to hear about Jesus you're welcome. If you didn't come for that you're welcome anyway." He laughed, showing teeth that conflicted with the symphony of neatness. Two were missing, one was broken, one was black and twisted. Poor people's teeth, Leaphorn thought. Navajo teeth.

"Because that's about all you hear around me anyway . . . Jesus talk," Nakai said.

"I came to see if you can help me with something," Leaphorn said. They exchanged the soft, barely touching handshake of the Navajo—the compromise of the Dineh between modern convention and the need to be careful with strangers who might, after all, be witches. "But it can wait until you're through with your revival. I'd like to talk to you then."

At the podium, Reverend Tafoya was talking about the Mountain Spirits of the Apaches. "Something like your *yei*, like your Holy People. But some different, too. That's who my daddy worshiped, and my mother, and my grandparents. And I did too, until I got this cancer. I don't have to tell you people here about cancer. . . ."

"The Reverend will take care of it for a while," Nakai said. "What do you need to know? What can I tell you?"

"We have a woman missing," Leaphorn said. He showed Nakai his identification and told him about Dr. Eleanor Friedman-Bernal. "You know her?"

"Sure," Nakai said. "For maybe three years, or four." He laughed again. "But not very well. Never made a Christian out of her. It was just business." The laugh went away. "You mean seriously missing? Like foul play?"

"She went to Farmington for the weekend a couple of weeks ago and nobody's heard from her since," Leaphorn said. "What was the business you had with her?"

"She studied pots. That was her business. So once in a while she would buy one from me." Nakai's small, round face was registering concern. "You think something went wrong with her?"

"You never know about that with missing people," Leaphorn said. "Usually they come back after a while and sometimes they don't. So we try to look into it. You a pot dealer?"

Leaphorn noticed how the question sounded, but before he could change it to "dealer in pots," Nakai said, "Just a preacher. But I found out you can sell pots. Pretty big money sometimes. Had a man I baptized over near Chinle give me one. Didn't have any money and he told me I could sell it in Gallup for thirty dollars. Told me where." Nakai laughed again, enjoying the memory. "Sure enough. Went to a place there on Railroad Avenue and the man gave me forty-six dollars for it." He made a bowl of his hands, grinning at Leaphorn. "The Lord provides," he said. "Not too well sometimes, but he provides."

"So now you go out and dig 'em up?"

"That's against the law," Nakai said, grinning. "You're a policeman. I bet you knew that. With me, it's once in a long while people bring 'em in. Several times at revivals I mentioned that fella who gave me the pot, and how it bought gasoline for a week, and the word got around among the born-again people that pots would give me some gasoline money. So now and then when they got no money and want to offer something, they bring me one."

"And the Friedman-Bernal woman buys them?"

"Mostly no. Just a time or two. She told me she wanted to see anything I got when I was preaching over around Chinle, or Many Farms—any of that country over around Chinle Wash. And out around here in the Checkerboard, and if I get up into Utah—Bluff, Montezuma Creek, Mexican Hat. Up in there."

"So you save them for her?"

"She pays me a little fee to take a look at them, but mostly she doesn't buy any. Just looks. Studies them for a couple of hours. Magnifying glass and all. Makes notes. The deal is, I have to know exactly where they came from."

"How do you manage that?"

"I tell the people, 'You going to bring in a pot to offer to the Lord, then you be sure you tell me where you found it.' " Nakai grinned his small, neat grin at Leaphorn. "That way, too, I know it's a legal pot. Not dug up off of government land."

Leaphorn didn't comment on that.

"When's the last time you saw her?" The answer should be late September, or something like that. Leaphorn knew the date he'd seen on Friedman's calendar, but it wasn't something Nakai would be likely to remember.

Nakai extracted a well-worn pocket notebook from his shirt and fingered his way through its pages. "Be last September twenty-third."

"More than a month ago," Leaphorn said. "What did she want?"

Nakai's round face filled with thought. Behind him, the Reverend Tafoya's voice rose into the high tenor of excitement. It described an old preacher at a revival tent in Dulce calling Tafoya to the front, laying on his hands, "right there on the place where that skin cancer was eating into my face. And I could feel the healing power flowing. . . ."

"Well," Nakai said, speaking very slowly. "She brought back a pot she'd gotten from me back in the spring. A piece of a pot, really. Wasn't all there. And she wanted to know everything I knew about it. Some of it stuff I had already told her. And she'd written it down in her notebook. But she asked it all again. Who I'd got it from. Everything he'd said about where he'd found it. That sort of stuff."

"Where was it? I mean where you met. And what did this notebook look like?"

"At Ganado," Nakai said. "I got a place there. I got home from a revival over by Cameron and I had a note from her asking me to call, saying it was important. I called her there at Chaco Canyon. She wasn't home so I left a message when I'd be back at Ganado again. And when I got back, there she was, waiting for me."

He paused. "And the notebook. Let's see now. Little leather-covered thing. Small enough to go in your shirt pocket. In fact that's where she carried it."

"And she just wanted to talk to you about the pot?"

"Mostly where it came from."

"Where was that?"

"Fella's ranch between Bluff and Mexican Hat."

"Private land," Leaphorn said, his voice neutral.

"Legal," Nakai agreed.

"Very short visit then," Leaphorn said. "Just repeating what you had already told her."

"Not really. She had a lot of questions. Did I know where she could find the person who had brought it? Could he have gotten it from the south side of the San Juan instead of the north side? And she had me look at the design on it. Wanted to know if I'd seen any like it."

Leaphorn had discovered that he was liking Nakai a little, which surprised him. "And you told her he couldn't have found it south of the San Juan because that would be on the Navajo Reservation, and digging up a pot there would be illegal?" He was smiling when he said it and Nakai was smiling when he answered.

"Didn't have to tell Friedman something like that," Nakai said. "That sort of thing, she knew."

"What was special about this pot?"

"It was the kind she was working on, I guess. Anasazi pot, I understand. They look pretty much alike to me, but I remember this one had a pattern. You know, sort of abstract shapes painted onto its surface. That seemed to be what she was interested in. And it had a sort of mixed color. That's what she always had me watching out for. That pattern. It was sort of an impression of Kokopelli, tiny, repeated and repeated and repeated."

Nakai looked at Leaphorn quizzically. Leaphorn nodded. Yes, he knew about Kokopelli, the Humpbacked Flute Player, the Watersprinkler, the fertility symbol. Whatever you called him, he was a frequent figure in strange pictographs the Anasazi had painted on cliffs across the Colorado Plateau.

"Anytime anyone brought one in like that—even a little piece of the pot with that pattern on it—then I was to save it for her and she'd pay a minimum of fifty dollars."

"Who found that pot?"

Nakai hesitated, studied Leaphorn.

"I'm not out hunting pot hunters," Leaphorn said. "I'm trying to find this woman."

"It was a Paiute Clan man they call Amos Whistler," Nakai said. "Lives out there near south of Bluff. North of Mexican Water."

Suddenly Reverend Tafoya was shouting "Hallelujah," his voice loud and hoarse, and the crowd was joining him, and the thin man with the hat was doing something with the guitar.

"Anything else? I can talk to you later," Nakai said. "I need to help out now."

"Was that the last time you saw her? The last contact?"

"Yeah," Nakai said. He started toward the speaker's platform, then turned back. "One other contact," he said. "More or less. A man who works with her came by when I was preaching over at the Hogback there by Shiprock. Fella named . . ." Nakai couldn't come up with the name. "Anyway he was a *belagana.* An Anglo. He said he wanted to pick up a pot I had for her. I didn't have any. He said he understood I had one, or maybe it was some, from over on the San Juan, around Bluff. I said no." Nakai turned again.

"Was it a tall man? Blond. Youngish. Named Elliot?"

"That's him," Nakai said.

Leaphorn watched the rest of it. He unfolded a chair at the back of the tent and sat, studied Nakai's techniques, and sorted out what he had learned, which wasn't much.

Nakai's congregation here on the fringe of the Checkerboard Reservation included perhaps sixty people—all Navajos apparently, but Leaphorn wouldn't swear that a few of them weren't from the Jicarilla Reservation, which bordered on Navajo territory here. They were about sixty percent women, and most middle-aged or older. That surprised Leaphorn a little. Without really thinking about it, because this aspect of his culture interested Leaphorn relatively little, he had presumed that those attracted to fundamentalist Christianity would be the young who'd been surrounded by the white man's religion off the reservation. That wasn't true here.

At the microphone, Nakai was gesturing toward the north.

"Right up the highway here—you could see it from right here if it wasn't dark—right up here you have Huerfano Mesa. We been taught, us Navajos, that that's where First Woman lived, and First Man, and some of the other Holy People, they lived there. An' so when I was a boy, I would go with my uncle and we'd carry a bundle of *aghaal* up there, and we'd stick those prayer sticks up in a shrine we made up there and we'd chant this prayer. And then sometimes we'd go over to Gobernador Knob. . . ." Nakai gestured toward the east. "Over there across Blanco Canyon where First Woman and First Man found the Asdza'a' Nadleehe', and we would leave some of those *aghaal* over there. And my uncle would explain to me how this was a holy place. But I want you to remember something about Huerfano Mesa. Just close your eyes now and remember how that holy place looked the last time you saw it. Truck road runs up there. It's got radio towers built all over the top of it. Oil companies built 'em. Whole forest of those antennae all along the top of our holy place."

Nakai was shouting now, emphasizing each word with a downward sweep of his fist. "I can't pray to the mountain no more," he shouted. "Not after the white man built all over the top of it. Remember what the stories tell us. Changing Woman left us. She's gone away. . . ."

Leaphorn watched the thin man with the guitar, trying to find a place for him in his memory. He studied the audience, looking for familiar faces, finding a few. Even though he'd rarely worked this eastern Checkerboard side of the Big Reservation, this didn't surprise him. The reservation occupied more space than all of New England but it had a population of no more than 150,000. In a lifetime of policing it, Leaphorn had met, in one way or another, a lot of its inhabitants. And these fifty or sixty assembled under Nakai's old canvas to try the Jesus Road seemed approximately typical. Fewer children than would have been brought to a ceremonial of the traditional Navajo religion, none of the teenagers who would have been hanging around the fringes of a Night Chant playing the mating game, none of the drunks, and certainly no one who looked even moderately affluent. Leaphorn found himself wondering how Nakai paid his expenses. He'd collect whatever donations these people would make, but that wouldn't be much. Perhaps the church he represented paid him out of some missionary fund. Leaphorn considered the pots. What he'd seen in the Nelson's catalog made it clear that some of them brought far, far more than fifty-five dollars. But most of them would have little value and Leaphorn couldn't imagine Nakai getting many of them. Even if they were totally converted, still these were born Navajo. The pots came from burials, and Navajos were conditioned almost from infancy to avoid the dead and to have a special dread of death.

It was exactly what Nakai was talking about. Or, more accurately, shouting. He gripped the microphone stand with both of his small, neat hands, and thundered into it.

"The way I was taught, the way you were taught, when my mother died my uncles came there to the place where we lived out there near Rough Rock and they took the body away and put it somewhere where the coyotes and the ravens couldn't get to it." Nakai paused, gripped the microphone stand, looked down. "You remember that?" he asked, in a voice that was suddenly smaller. "Everybody here remembers somebody dying." Nakai looked up, recovering both composure and voice. "And then there's the four days when you don't do nothing but remember. And nobody speaks the name of the dead. . . . Because there's nothing left of them but the *chindi,* that ghost that is everything that was bad about them and nothing that was good. And I don't say my mother's name anymore—not ever again—because that *chindi* may hear me calling it and come back and make me sick. And what about what was good about my mother? What about what was good about your dead people? What about that? Our Holy People didn't tell us much about that. Not that I know about, they didn't. Some of the Dineh, they have a story about a young man who followed Death, and looked down into the underworld, and saw the dead people sitting around down there. But my clan, we didn't have that story. And I think it got borrowed from the Hopi People. It is one of their beliefs."

Early in this discourse, Leaphorn had been interested in Nakai's strategy. Methods of persuasion intrigued him. But there seemed to be nothing particularly unique in it, and he'd let his attention wander. He had reviewed what little he'd learned from Nakai, and what he might do next, if anything, and then simply watched the audience reaction. Now Leaphorn found himself attentive again. His own Red Forehead Clan had no such story either—at least he hadn't been told it in his own boyhood introduction into the Navajo Way. He had heard it often in his days as an anthropology student at Arizona State. And he'd heard it since from Navajos around Window Rock. But Nakai was probably right. Probably it was another of the many stories the Dineh borrowed from the cultures that surrounded them—borrowed and then refined into abstract philosophical points. The Navajo Way was devoted to the harmony of life. It left death simply terrifying black oblivion.

"We learn this story about how Monster Slayer corners Death in his pit house. But he lets Death live. Because without death there wouldn't be enough room for the babies, for young people. But I can tell you something truer than that." Nakai's voice had risen again to a shout.

"Jesus didn't let Death live. Hallelujah! Praise the Lord!" Nakai danced across the platform, shouting, drawing from the audience answering shouts. "When we walk through the Valley of Death, he is with us, that's what Jesus teaches. We don't just drift away into the dark night, a ghost of sickness. We go beyond death. We go into a happy world. We go where there ain't no hunger. There ain't no sorrow. Ain't no drunks. No fighting. No seeing relatives run over out here on the highway. We go into a world where last are first, and the poor are the rich, and the sick are well, and the blind, they see again. . . ."

Leaphorn didn't hear the last of it. He was hurrying out through the tent flap into the darkness. He stood for a while, allowing his eyes to adjust, breathing the cool, clean high-altitude air. Smelling dust, and sagebrush, shaken, remembering the day they brought Emma's body home from the hospital.

It had still been unreal to him, what had happened at Gallup, what the doctor had told him. It had left him stunned. Emma's brothers had come to talk to him about it. He'd simply told them that he knew Emma would want a traditional burial, and they'd left.

They'd taken the body to her mother's place over near Blue Gap Chapter House, on the edge of Black Mesa. Under the brush arbor her old aunt had washed her, and combed out her hair, and dressed her in her best blue velvet skirt, and her old squash-blossom necklace, put on her rings, and wrapped her in a blanket. He had sat in the hogan, watching. Her brothers had picked her up then, and put the body in the back of their truck, and driven down the track toward the cliffs. In about an hour they came back without her and took their cleansing sweat bath. He didn't know— would never know—where they'd left her. In a crevice somewhere, probably. High. Protected by deadwood from the predators. Hidden away. He had stayed for two days of the silent days of mourning. Tradition demanded four days, to give the dead time to complete their journey into the oblivion of death. Two days was all he could stand. He'd left them.

And her. But no more of this.

Chee's pickup was still there. Leaphorn walked to it.

"Ya te'eh," Chee said, acknowledging him.

"Ya te," Leaphorn said. He leaned on the truck door. "What brings you out to the Reverend Slick Nakai's revival?"

Chee explained about the backhoe loader, and the abortive chase, and what Tso had told him about where the Backhoe Bandit might be found.

"But I don't think he is going to show up tonight," Chee said. "Getting too late."

"You going to go in and ask Nakai who this fellow is?" Leaphorn asked.

"I'm going to do that," Chee said. "When he's through preaching and when I get a look at the people coming out of the tent."

"You think Nakai would tell you he didn't know this guy, and then tip him off you're looking for him?"

Long silence. "He might," Chee said. "But I think I'll risk it."

Leaphorn didn't comment. It was the decision he would have made. Handle it on Navajo time. No reason to rush in there.

There was no hurry for him either, but he went back into the tent. He'd hear the rest of Nakai's sermon, and see how much money he took in at his collection. And how many, if any, pots. Leaphorn was thinking that maybe he'd learned a little more than he'd first realized. Something had jogged his memory. The thin Navajo with the guitar was the same man he'd seen helping Maxie Davis at the excavation at Chaco Canyon. That answered one small question. A Christian Navajo wouldn't be worrying about stirring up the *chindi* of long-dead Anasazi. But it also made an interesting connection—a man who dug up scientific pots at Chaco worked for a man who sold theoretically legal pots. And a man who sold theoretically legal pots linked to a man who stole a backhoe. Backhoes were machines notoriously useful in uprooting Anasazi ruins and despoiling their graves.

It was just about then, as he walked out of the darkness into the tent, that he became aware of something in his attitude about all this.

He felt an urgency now. The disappearance of Dr. Eleanor Friedman-Bernal had been merely something curious—an oddity. Now he sensed something dangerous. He had never been sure he could find the woman. Now he wondered if she'd be alive if he did.

5

"REMEMBER, BOY," Uncle Frank Sam Nakai would sometimes tell Chee, "when you're tired of walking up a long hill you think about how easy it's going to be walking down." Which was Nakai's Navajo way of saying things tend to even up. For Chee this proved, as his uncle's aphorisms often did, to be true. Chee's bad luck was followed by good luck.

Early Monday a San Juan County sheriff's deputy, who happened to have read the paperwork about the stolen flatbed trailer and backhoe, also happened to get more or less lost while trying to deliver a warrant. He turned off on an access road to a Southern Union pump site and found the trailer abandoned. The backhoe apparently had been unloaded, driven about twenty yards on its own power, and then rolled up a makeshift ramp—presumably into the back of a truck. The truck had almost new tires on its dual rear wheels. The tread pattern was used by Dayton Tire and Rubber, with a single dealer in Farmington and none in Shiprock. The dealer had no trouble remembering. The only truck tires he sold for a month had been to Farmington U-Haul. The company had three trucks out at the moment with dual rear wheels. Two had been recently reshod with Daytons. One was rented to a Farmington furniture company. The other, equipped with a power winch, was rented to Joe B. Nails, P.O. Box 770, Aztec, using a MasterCard.

Farmington police had a record on Nails. One driving while intoxicated. It was enough to provide an employer's name. Wellserve, Inc., a contractor maintaining the Gasco collection system. But Wellserve was a former employer. Nails had quit in August.

Chee learned all of this good news secondhand. He'd spent the morning hanging around Red Rock, worrying about what he'd tell

Janet Pete when she got back from Phoenix, and waiting for a witness he was supposed to deliver to the FBI office in Farmington. With that done two hours behind schedule, he had stopped at the Shiprock headquarters and got the first half of the news about the trailer. He'd spent the afternoon hunting around Teec Nos Pos for a fellow who'd broken his brother-in-law's leg. No luck on that. When he pulled back into Shiprock to knock off for the day, he ran into Benally going off shift.

"I guess we got your Backhoe Bandit," Benally said. And he filled Chee in on the rest of it. "U-Haul calls us when he checks the truck in."

That struck Chee as stupid. "You think he'll have the backhoe in it when he returns it?" Chee said. "Otherwise, no proof of anything. What you charge him with?"

Benally had thought of that and so had Captain Largo.

"We bring him in. We tell him we have witnesses who saw him taking the thing out, and we can connect it to the truck he rented, and if he'll cooperate and tell us where it is so we can recover it, and snitch on his buddy, then we go light on him." Benally shrugged, not thinking it would work either. "Better than nothing," he added. "Anyway, the call's out on the U-Haul truck. Maybe we catch him with the backhoe in it."

"I doubt it," Chee said.

Benally agreed. He grinned. "The best plan would have been for you to have grabbed him when he was driving out of the yard with it."

Chee called Pete's office from the station phone. He'd break it by degrees. Tell her first that a lot of things were wrong with the Buick, sort of slip into the part about tearing it up. But Miss Pete wasn't in, wasn't back from Phoenix, had called in and said she'd be held over for a day.

Wonderful. Chee felt immense relief. He put the Buick out of his mind. He thought about the Backhoe Bandit, who was going to get away with it. He thought about what the preacher had told him Saturday night.

The preacher said he didn't know the name of the man who owned the patched-up car. He thought he'd heard him called Jody, or maybe Joey. He thought the man worked in the Blanco field—maybe for Southern Union Gas, but maybe not. The man sometimes brought him a pot which the preacher said he sometimes bought. The last time he saw him, the man had asked if the preacher would buy a whole bunch of pots if the man could get them. "And I told him maybe I could and maybe I couldn't. It would depend on whether I had any money."

"So maybe he'll come back again and maybe he won't."

"I think he'll be back," the preacher had said. "I told him if I couldn't handle it, I knew somebody who could." And he told Chee about the woman anthropologist, and that led him to Lieutenant Leaphorn. The preacher was a talkative man.

Chee sat now in his pickup truck beside the willows shading the police parking lot. He felt relief on one hand, pressure on the other. The dreaded meeting with Janet Pete was off, at least until tomorrow. But when it came, he wanted to conclude his story by telling Pete how he had nailed the man to blame for all this. It didn't seem likely that was going to happen. Largo's solution was sensible if you were patient, even though it probably wouldn't produce an indictment. Aside from what it had done to Chee, the crime was relatively minor. Theft of equipment worth perhaps $10,000 in its badly used condition. Hardly an event to provoke all-out deployment of police to run down evidence. So the Backhoe Bandit would get away with it. Unless the rent-a-truck could be found with the backhoe on it. Where would it be?

Chee shifted sideways in the seat, leaned a knee against the dashboard, thought. Nails was a pot hunter. Probably he wanted the backhoe for digging up burials to find a lot of them. With the teeth removed from the shovel to minimize breakage, they were a favorite tool of the professionals. And from what the preacher said, Nails must be going professional. He must have found a likely ruins. What Nails had told the preacher suggested he'd found a wholesale source. Therefore it was a safe presumption that he'd stolen the backhoe to dig them.

So far it was easy. The hard question was where?

The willow branches dangling around Chee's pickup had turned yellow with the season. Chee studied them a moment to rest the brain. Surely he must know something helpful. How about the trailer? Stolen. Then brought back to haul out the backhoe. Then abandoned in favor of the truck? The night the trailer was stolen the backhoe was still being repaired. Had the head off the engine, in fact. So they took the trailer, and brought it back when the backhoe was ready to roll. Pretty stupid, on the face of it. But Chee had checked and learned the trailer was scheduled to haul equipment to a job at Burnt Water the next day. The Backhoe Bandit knew a hell of a lot about what went on in that maintenance yard. Interesting, but it didn't help now.

The next answers did. The question was why steal the trailer at all? Why not simply rent the U-Haul truck earlier, and haul the backhoe out on that? And why not rent the backhoe, instead of stealing it? As Chee thought it through, the answers connected. Rental trucks were easy to trace, so the Backhoe Bandit avoided the risk of having the truck seen at the burglary. A rented backhoe would also be easy to trace. But there would be no reason to trace it if it was checked back in after it was used. So why . . . ? Chee's orderly mind sorted through it. The truck was needed instead of the trailer because the trailer couldn't be pulled where the backhoe was needed. Could it be the dig site was somewhere from which the backhoe couldn't be extricated? Of course. It would be at the bottom of someplace, and that would explain why Nails had rented a truck with a power winch. Running a backhoe down the steep slope of a canyon could well be possible where pulling it out wouldn't be.

Chee climbed out of the cab, trotted into the office, and called the Farmington office of Wellserve, Inc. Yes, they could provide the police with a copy of their well-service route map. Yes, the service superintendent could mark the route Nails had served.

When Chee left Wellserve with the map folded on the seat beside him he had three hours left before sundown. Then there would be a half-moon. A good night for a pot hunter to work, and a good night to hunt pot hunters. He stopped at the sheriff's office and found out who was patrolling where tonight. If Nails was off reservation land, he'd need a deputy along to make an arrest. Then he drove up the San Juan River valley through the little oil town of Bloomfield, and out of the valley into the infinity of sagebrush that covers the Blanco Plateau. He was remembering he'd read somewhere of somebody estimating more than a hundred thousand Anasazi sites on the Colorado Plateau—only a few of them excavated, only a few thousand even mapped. But it wouldn't be impossible. He would guess Nails had found sites along the service roads he traveled and would be looting them. Chee knew some of those sites himself. And he knew what attracted the Anasazi. A cliff faced to catch the winter sun and shaded in the summer, enough floodplain to grow something, and a source of water. That, particularly the water, narrowed it a lot.

He scouted Canyon Largo first, and Blanco Canyon, and Jasis Canyon. He found two sites that had been dug into fairly recently. But nothing new and no sign of the tire tread pattern he was looking for. He moved north then and checked Gobernador Canyon and

La Jara and the Vaqueros Wash eastward in the Carson National Forest. He found nothing. He skipped westward, driving far faster than the speed limit down New Mexico Highway 44. The light was dying now—a cloudless autumn evening with the western sky a dull copper glow. He checked out a couple of canyons near Ojo Encino, restricting himself always to the access roads gouged out to reach the gas wells and pump stations Nails had been serving.

By midnight he finished checking the roads leading from the Star Lake Pump Station, driving slowly, using his flashlight to check for tracks at every possible turnoff. He circled back past the sleeping trading post the maps called White Horse Lake. He crossed the Continental Divide, and dropped into the network of arroyos that drain Chaco Mesa. Again he found nothing. He circled back across Chaco Wash and picked up the gravel road that leads northwestward toward Nageezi Trading Post.

Beyond Betonnie Tsosie Wash he stopped the pickup in the middle of the road. He climbed out wearily, stretched, and turned on the flash to check the turnoff of an access trail. He stood in the light of the half-moon, yawning, his flash reflecting from the chalky dust. It showed, clear and fresh, the dual tracks of an almost new Dayton tire tread.

Chee's watch showed 2:04 A.M. At 2:56 he found the place where, maybe a thousand years ago, a little band of Anasazi families had lived, and built their cluster of small stone shelters and living spaces, and died. Chee had been walking for more than a mile. He had left his pickup by a pump site and followed the twin tracks on foot. The pump marked the dead end of this branch of the service road—if two ruts wandering through the sage and juniper could be called that. From here, the dual tires had made their own road. Away from the hard-packed ruts, they were easy to follow now—crushed tumbleweeds, broken brush, the sharp smell of bruised sage.

They led up a long slope, and Chee guessed they wouldn't lead far. He walked carefully and quietly, moon over his shoulder, flash off. The slow huffing of the pump motor diminished behind him. He stopped, listening for the sound the backhoe motor would be making. He heard a coyote, and then its partner. One behind him, one on the ridge to his left. It was work time for predators, with all the little nocturnal rodents out braving death to find a meal.

He didn't see the truck until he was within fifty feet of it. Nails had nosed it into a cluster of juniper just over the crest of the hill. The doors of its van box stood open, a square black shape with the ramp used to unload the backhoe still in place. Chee stared, listening, feeling a mixture of excitement, exultation, and uneasiness. He put his hand on the pistol in his jacket pocket. Chee did not like pistols in general, and the one he had carried since being sworn into the force was no exception. But now the heavy hard metal was reassuring. He walked to the truck, placing each step carefully, stopping to listen. The cab was empty, the doors unlocked. The wire cable from the winch spool extended down the steep slope, slack. If the backhoe was down there, as it must be, the engine wasn't running. The silence was almost total. From far behind him, he could hear the faint sound of the walking beam pump. No coyote sounds now. The air was moving up the slope past his face, a faint coolness.

Chee held the cable in his left hand and started down the slope, following the path broken by the backhoe, trying to keep his weight on his feet, trying to avoid the noise sliding would make.

The slope was too steep. He slid a few feet, regained control. Slid again as the earth gave way under his feet. Then he lay on his back, motionless, breathing dust, cursing under his breath at the noise he had made. He listened, hand gripping the cable. Down here under the ridge, he could no longer hear the distant pump motor. The coyote yipped somewhere off to his left and provoked an answering yip from its partner. He saw the backhoe, partially visible through the brush, its motor silent. The half-moon lit the roof of its cab, the shovel, and part of the jointed arm that controlled it. Nails apparently had been frightened away. It didn't matter. He had the backhoe. He had the truck that had hauled it here, and the record would show Nails had rented the truck.

Chee gripped the cable and shifted his free hand to push himself erect. He felt cloth under his fingers. And a button. And the hard bone and cold skin of a wrist. He scrambled away from it.

The form lay facedown, head upslope, in the deep darkness cast by a juniper—its left hand stretching out toward the cable. A man, Chee saw. He squatted, controlling the shock. And when it was controlled, he leaned forward and felt the wrist.

Dead. Dead long enough to be stiff. He bent low over the corpse and turned on his flash. It wasn't Nails. It was a Navajo. A young man, hair cut short, wearing a blue checked shirt with two stains on its back. Chee touched one of them with a tentative finger.

Stiff. Dried blood. The man had apparently been shot twice. In the middle of the back and just above the hip.

Chee snapped off the light. He thought of the Navajo's ghost, hovering nearby. He turned his mind away from that. The *chindi* was out there, representing all that was evil in the dead man's being. But one did not think of *chindis* out in the darkness. Where was Nails? Most likely, hours away from here. But why did he leave the truck? This Navajo must be the one seen with Nails when they'd stolen the backhoe. Maybe the Navajo had driven the truck, Nails had come in his own car. Odd, but possible.

Chee moved cautiously the few remaining yards to the bottom of the hill. It was full dark here, the moonlight blocked by the high ground. Just enough reflected light to guide his feet. A falling out of thieves, Chee thought. A fight. Nails pulls a gun. The Navajo runs. Nails shoots him. He didn't believe Nails would still be here, or anywhere near here. But he walked carefully.

Even so he almost tripped over the bag before he saw it. It was black plastic, the sort sold in little boxes of a dozen to line wastebaskets. Chee untwisted the wire securing its top and felt inside. Fragments of pottery, just as he'd expected. Between him and the backhoe, more such bags were clustered. Chee walked past them to look at the machine.

It had been turned off with the shovel locked high over the trench it had been digging into a low, brush-covered mound. Scattered along the excavation was a clutter of flat stones. Once they must have formed the wall of an Anasazi settlement. He didn't notice the bones until he turned on his flash.

They were everywhere. A shoulder blade, a thigh bone, part of a skull, ribs, four or five connected vertebrae, part of a foot, a lower jaw.

Jim Chee was modern man built upon traditional Navajo. This was simply too much death. Too many ghosts disturbed. He backed away from the excavation, flashlight still on, careful no longer. He wanted only to be away from here. Into the sunlight. Into the cleansing heat of a sweat bath. To be surrounded by the healing, curing sounds of a Ghostway ceremonial. He started up the slope, pulling himself up by the cable.

The panic receded. First he would check the backhoe cab. He trotted to it, guided by the flash. He checked the metal serial-number plate and the Navajo Nation Road Department number painted on its side. Then he flashed the light into the cab.

A man was sitting there, slumped sideways against the oppo-site door, his open eyes reflecting white in Chee's flash. The left side of his face was black with what must be blood. But Chee could see his mustache and enough of his face to know that he had found Joe Nails.

6

LEAPHORN CAME HOME to Window Rock long after midnight. He hadn't bothered to turn on the lights. He drank from his cupped palms in the bathroom and folded his clothing over the bedside chair (where Emma had so often sat to read or knit, to do the thousand small things that Emma did). He had turned the bed ninety degrees so that his eyes would open in the morning to the shock of a different view. That broke his lifelong habit, the automatic waking thought of "Where's Emma?" and what then followed. He had moved from his side of the bed to Emma's—which had eliminated that once-happy habit of reaching out to touch her when he drifted into sleep.

Now he lay flat on his back, feeling tired muscles relax, thinking about the food in Eleanor Friedman-Bernal's refrigerator, drifting from that to her arrangement with Nakai to inspect contributed pots and from that to the notebook Nakai had described. He hadn't noticed a pocket-sized leather notebook in her apartment—but then it might be almost anywhere in the room. Thatcher had made no real search. On the long drive homeward across the Checkerboard from Huerfano Mesa, he had thought of why Elliot hadn't mentioned being sent by Friedman to see Nakai and collect a pot. It must have seemed odd to Elliot, this abortive mission. Why not mention it? Before Leaphorn could come to any conclusion, he drifted off to sleep, and it was morning.

He showered, inspected his face, decided he could go another few days without a shave, made himself a breakfast of sausage and fried eggs—violating his diet with the same guilty feelings he always had when Emma was away visiting her family. He read the mail that Saturday had brought him, and the Gallup *Independent*.

He snapped on the television, snapped it off again, stood at the window looking out on the autumn morning. Windless. Cloudless. Silent except for a truck rolling down Navajo Route 3. The little town of Window Rock was taking Sunday off. Leaphorn noticed the glass was dusty—a condition Emma had never tolerated. He got a handkerchief from his drawer and polished the pane. He polished other windows. Abruptly he walked to the telephone and called Chaco Canyon.

Until recently telephone calls between the world outside and Chaco had traveled via a Navajo Communications Company telephone line. From Crownpoint northeast, the wire wandered across the rolling grassland, attached mostly to fence posts and relying on its own poles only when no fence was available going in the right direction. This system made telephone service subject to the same hazards as the ranch fence on which it piggybacked. Drifts of tumbleweeds, winter blizzards, dry rot, errant cattle broke down both fences and communications. When it was operating, voices sometimes tended to fade in and out with the wind velocity. But recently this system had been modernized. Calls were now routed two hundred miles east to Santa Fe, then beamed to a satellite and rebroadcast to a receiving dish at Chaco. The space age system, like the National Aeronautics and Space Administration which made it possible, was frequently out of operation. When it operated at all, voices tended to fade in and out with the wind velocity. Today was no exception.

A woman's voice answered, strong at first, then drifting away into space. No, Bob Luna wasn't in. No use ringing his number because she'd seen him driving away and she hadn't seen him return.

How about Maxie Davis?

Just a minute. She might not be up yet. It was, after all, early Sunday morning.

Maxie Davis was up. "Who?" she asked. "I'm sorry. I can hardly hear you."

Leaphorn could hear Maxie Davis perfectly—as if she were standing beside him. "Leaphorn," he repeated. "The Navajo cop who was out there a couple of days ago."

"Oh. Have you found her?"

"No luck," Leaphorn said. "Do you remember a little leather-covered notebook she used? Probably carried in her shirt pocket?"

"Notebook? Yeah. I remember it. She always used it when she was working."

"Know where she keeps it? When it's not with her?"

"No idea. Probably in a drawer somewhere."

"You've known her long?"

"Off and on, yes. Since we were graduate students."

"How about Dr. Elliot?"

Maxie Davis laughed. "We're sort of a team, I guess you'd say." And then, perhaps thinking Leaphorn would misunderstand, added: "Professionally. We're the two who are going to write the bible on the Anasazi." She laughed again, the sound fading in and out. "After Randall Elliot and me, no more need for Anasazi research."

"Not Friedman-Bernal? She's not part of it?"

"Different field," Davis said. "She's ceramics. We're people. She's pots."

They had decided, he and Emma, to install the telephone in the kitchen. To hang it on the wall beside the refrigerator. Standing there, listening to Maxie Davis, Leaphorn inspected the room. It was neat. No dishes, dirty or otherwise, were in sight. Windows clean, sink clean, floor clean. Leaphorn leaned forward to the full reach of the telephone receiver cord and plucked a napkin from the back of the chair. He'd used it while he'd eaten his eggs. He held the receiver against his ear with his shoulder while he folded it.

"I'm going to come back out there," he said. "I'd like to talk to you. And to Elliot if he's there."

"I doubt it," Maxie Davis said. "He's usually out in the field on Sunday."

But Elliot was there, leaning against the porch support watching Leaphorn as he parked his pickup in the apartment's courtyard.

"Ya tay," Elliot said, getting the pronunciation of the Navajo greeting almost right. "Didn't know policemen worked on Sunday."

"They don't tell you that when they recruit you," Leaphorn said, "but it happens now and then."

Maxie Davis appeared at the door. She was wearing a loose blue T-shirt decorated with a figure copied from a petroglyph. Short dark hair fell around her face. She looked feminine, intelligent, and beautiful.

"I'll bet I know where she keeps that notebook," Davis said. "Do you still have the key?"

Leaphorn shook his head. "I'll get one from headquarters." Or, he thought, failing that, it would be simple enough to get into the apartment. He'd noticed that when Thatcher had unlocked the door.

"Luna's away," Elliot said. "We can get in through the patio door."

Elliot managed it with the long blade of his pocketknife, simply sliding the blade in and lifting the latch.

"Something you learn in graduate school," he said.

Or in juvenile detention centers, Leaphorn thought. He wondered if Elliot had ever been in one of those. It didn't seem likely. Jail is not socially acceptable for prep school boys.

Everything seemed exactly as it had been when he'd been here with Thatcher—the same stale air, the same dustiness, the boxes of pots, the disarray. Thatcher had searched it, in his tentative way, looking for evidence that Dr. Eleanor Friedman-Bernal was a violator of the Federal Antiquities Act. Now Leaphorn intended to search it in his own way, looking for the woman herself.

"Ellie kept her purse in the dresser," Maxie Davis said. She opened a bottom drawer. "In here. And I remember seeing her drop that notebook in it when she came in from work."

Davis extracted a purse and handed it to Leaphorn. It was beige leather. It looked new and it looked expensive. Leaphorn unsnapped it, checked through lipstick, small bottles, package of sugarless gum, Tums, small scissors, odds and ends. No small leather notebook. Emma had three purses—a very small one, a very good one, and a worn one used in the workaday world of shopping.

"She had another purse?" Leaphorn said, making it half a question.

Davis nodded. "This was her good one." She checked into the drawer. "Not here."

Leaphorn's mild disappointment at not finding the notebook was offset by mild surprise. The wrong purse was missing. Friedman-Bernal had not taken her social purse with her for the weekend. She had taken her working purse.

"I want to take a sort of rough inventory," Leaphorn said. "I'm going to rely on your memory. See if we can determine what she took with her."

There were the disclaimers he expected, from both Maxie Davis and Elliot, that they really didn't know much about Ellie's wardrobe or Ellie's possessions. But within an hour, they had a rough list on the back of an envelope. Ellie had taken no suitcase. She had taken a small canvas gym bag. She'd probably taken no makeup or cosmetics. No skirt was missing. No dress. She had taken only jeans and a long-sleeved cotton shirt.

Maxie Davis sat on the bed, examining her jottings, looking thoughtful. "No way of knowing about socks or underwear or things like that. But I don't think she took any pajamas." She motioned toward the chest of drawers. "There's an old blue pair in there I've seen her wear, and a sort of worn-out checked set, and a fancy new pair. Silk." Davis looked at him, checking the level of Leaphorn's understanding of such things. "For company," she explained. "I doubt if she would have a fourth set, or bring it out here anyway."

"Okay," Leaphorn said. "Did she have a sleeping bag?"

"Yeah," Davis said. "Of course." She sorted through the things on the closet shelf. "That's gone too," she said.

"So she was camping out," Leaphorn said. "Sleeping out. Probably nothing social. Probably working. Who did she work with?"

"Nobody, really," Elliot said. "It was a one-woman project. She worked by herself."

"Let's settle down somewhere and talk about that," Leaphorn said.

They settled in the living room. Leaphorn perched on the edge of a sofa that looked and felt as if it would fold outward into a bed, Davis and Elliot on the Park Service Purchasing Office low-bid overstuffed couch. Much of what Leaphorn heard he already knew from his own studies a lifetime ago at Arizona State. He had considered telling the two about his master's degree and decided against it. The time that might have saved had no value to Leaphorn now. And sometimes something might be gained by seeming to know less than you did. And so Leaphorn listened patiently to basic stuff, mostly from Davis, about how the Anasazi culture had risen on the Colorado Plateau, almost certainly a progression from the small, scattered families of hunters and seed collectors who lived in pit houses, and somehow learned to make baskets, and then the rudiments of agriculture, and then how to irrigate their crops by controlling runoff from rain, and—probably in the process of caulking baskets with fire-dried mud to make them waterproof—how to make pottery.

"Important cultural breakthrough," Elliot inserted. "Improved storage possibilities. Opened a door to art." He laughed. "Also gave anthropology something a lot more durable than baskets to hunt, and measure, and study, and all that. But you already know a lot about this, don't you?"

"Why do you say that?" Leaphorn never allowed a subject to shift him from the role of interrogator unless Leaphorn wanted to be shifted.

"Because you don't ask any questions," Elliot said. "Maxie isn't always perfectly clear. Either you're not interested in this background, or you already know it."

"I know something about it," Leaphorn said. "You've said Friedman's interest was in pottery. Apparently she was interested mostly in one kind of pot. Pots which have a kind of corrugated finish. Probably some other revealing details. Right?"

"Ellie thought she had identified one specific potter," Elliot said. "A distinctive individual touch."

Leaphorn said nothing. That sounded mildly interesting. But—even given the intense interest of anthropologists in the Anasazi culture and its mysterious fate—it didn't seem very important. His expression told Elliot what he was thinking.

"One potter. Dead probably seven hundred and fifty years." Elliot put his boots on the battered coffee table. "So what's the big deal? The big deal is, Ellie knows where he lived. Out there at BC57, across the wash from Pueblo Bonito, because she found a lot of his pots there broken in the process of being made. Must have been where he worked. . . ."

"She," Maxie Davis said. "Where she worked."

"Okay, she." Elliot shook his head, regaining his chain of thought, showing no sign of irritation. It was part of a game they played, Leaphorn thought. Elliot's boots were dusty, scarred, flat-heeled, practical. A soft brown leather, perfectly fitted, extremely expensive.

Davis was leaning forward, wanting Leaphorn to understand this. "Nobody before had ever found a way to link the pot with the person who made it—not before Ellie began noticing this peculiar technique repeated in a lot of those BC57 pots. She had already noticed it in a couple of others from other places—and now she had found the source. Where they came from. And she was lucky in another way. Not only was this potter prolific, she was good. Her pots traded around. Ellie tracked one back to the Salmon Ruins over on the San Juan, and she thinks one came out of a burial near the White House Ruin in Canyon de Chelly, and . . ."

If Elliot had any objection to Maxie Davis's commandeering his story, his face hadn't showed it. But now he said: "Get to the important point."

Maxie looked at him. "Well, she's not sure about that," she said.

"Maybe not, but this BC57 site was one of the last ones built—just before everybody disappeared. They dated a roof beam to 1292, and some of the charcoal in what might have been a kiln fire to 1298. So she was working just about the time they turned out the lights here and walked away. And Ellie is beginning to think she might be able to pin down where she went."

"That's the really big deal out here." Davis waved her arms. "Where'd the Anasazi go? The big huge mystery that all the magazine writers write about."

"Among a couple of other big questions," Elliot said. "Like why they built roads when they didn't have wheels, or pack animals, and why they left, and why they lived in this place in the first place with so damn little wood, or water, or good land, and . . ." Elliot shrugged. "The more we learn, the more we wonder."

"This man who was coming out to see her the week after she disappeared, do you know who he was?"

"Lehman," Davis said. "He came." She smiled ruefully. "Plenty sore about it. He came on a Wednesday and it had rained Tuesday night and you know how that road gets."

"And he's . . ." Leaphorn began to ask.

"He's the hotshot in Ellie's field," Elliot said. "I think he was chairman of her dissertation committee when she got her doctorate at Madison. Now he's a professor at University of New Mexico. Two or three books on Mimbres, and Hohokam, and Anasazi pottery evolution. Top guru in the ceramics field."

"Ellie's equivalent of our Devanti," Davis said. "She pretty well had to persuade Lehman she knew what she was talking about. Like in migrations, Elliot and I have to deal with our top honcho."

"Doctor Delbert Devanti," Elliot said. "Arkansas's answer to Einstein." The tone was sardonic.

"He's proved some things," Maxie Davis said, her voice flat. "Even if he didn't go to Phillips Exeter Academy, or Princeton."

There was silence. Elliot's long, handsome face had become stiff and blank. Maxie glanced at him. In the glance Leaphorn read . . . what? Was it anger? Malice? She turned to Leaphorn. "Please note the blue blood's lofty contempt for the plebeians. Devanti is definitely a plebe. He sounds like corn pone."

"And is often wrong," Elliot said.

Davis laughed. "There is that," she said.

"But you give people the right to be wrong if they came out of the cotton patch," Elliot said. His voice sounded normal, or almost normal, but Leaphorn could see the tension in the line of his jaw.

"More of an excuse for it," Maxie said, mildly. "Maybe he overlooked something while he was working nights to feed his family. No tutors to do his digging in the library."

To that, Randall Elliot said nothing. Leaphorn watched. Where would this tension lead? Nowhere, apparently. Maxie had nothing more to say.

"You two work as a team," Leaphorn said. "That right?"

"More or less," Davis said. "We have common interests in the Anasazi."

"Like how?" Leaphorn asked.

"It's complicated. Actually it involves food economics, nutrition tolerances, population sizes, things like that, and you spend a lot more time working on programming statistical projections in the computer than you do digging in the field. Really dull stuff, unless you're weird enough to be into it." She smiled at Leaphorn. A smile of such dazzling charm that once it would have destroyed him.

"And Randall here," she added, "is doing something much more dramatic." She poked him with her elbow—a gesture that almost made what she was saying mere teasing. "He is revolutionizing physical anthropology. He is finding a way to solve the mystery, once and for all, of what happened to these people."

"Population studies," Elliot said in a low voice. "Involves migrations and genetics."

"Rewrites all the books if it works," Maxie Davis said, smiling at Leaphorn. "Elliots do not spend their time on small things. In the navy they are admirals. In universities they are presidents. In politics they are senators. When you start at the top you have to aim high. Or everybody is disappointed."

Leaphorn was uncomfortable. "It would be a problem," he said.

"But not one I had," Maxie Davis said. "I'm white trash."

"Maxie never tires of reminding me of the silver spoon in my crib," Elliot said, managing a grin. "It doesn't have much to do with finding Ellie, though."

"But you have a point," Leaphorn said. "Dr. Friedman wouldn't have missed that appointment with Lehman without a good reason."

"Hell, no," Maxie said. "That's what I told that idiot at the sheriff's office."

"Do you know why he was coming? Specifically."

"She was going to bring him up-to-date," Elliot said.

"She was going to hit him with a bombshell," Maxie said. "That's what I think. I think she finally had it put together."

There was something in Elliot's expression. Maybe skepticism. Or disapproval. But Davis was enthusiastic.

"What did she tell you?"

"Nothing much, really. But I could just sense it. That things were working out. But she wouldn't say much."

"It's not traditional," Elliot said. "Not among us scientists."

Leaphorn found himself as interested in what was going on with Elliot as in the thrust of the conversation. Elliot's tone now was faintly mocking. Davis had caught it, too. She looked at Elliot and then back at Leaphorn, speaking directly to him.

"That's true," she said. "Before one boasts, one must have done something to boast about."

She said it in the mildest of voices, without looking at Elliot, but Elliot's face flushed.

"You think she had found something important," Leaphorn said. "She didn't tell you anything, but something caused you to think that. Something specific. Can you think what it was?"

Davis leaned back on the couch. She caught her lower lip between her teeth. She laid her hand, in a gesture that looked casual, on Elliot's thigh. She thought.

"Ellie was excited," she said. "Happy, too. For a week, maybe a little longer, before she left." She got up from the couch and walked past Leaphorn into the bedroom. Infinite grace, Leaphorn thought.

"She'd been over in Utah. I remember that. To Bluff, and Mexican Hat and—" Her voice from the bedroom was indistinct.

"Montezuma Creek?" Leaphorn asked.

"Yes, all that area along the southern edge of Utah. And when she came back"—Davis emerged from the bedroom carrying a Folgers Coffee carton—"she had all these potsherds." She put the box on the coffee table. "Same ones, I think. At least, I remember it was this box."

The box held what seemed to Leaphorn to be as many as fifty fragments of pots, some large, some no more than an inch across.

Leaphorn sorted through them, looking for nothing in particular but noticing that all were reddish brown, and all bore a corrugated pattern.

"Done by her potter, I guess," Leaphorn said. "Did she say where she got them?"

"From a Thief of Time," Elliot said. "From a pot hunter."

"She didn't say that," Davis said.

"She went to Bluff to look for pot hunters. To see what they were finding. She told you that."

"Did she say which one?" Leaphorn asked. Here might be an explanation of how she had vanished. If she had been dealing directly with a pot hunter, he might have had second thoughts. Might have thought he had sold her evidence that would put him in prison. Might have killed her when she came back for more.

"She didn't mention any names," Davis said.

"Hardly necessary," Elliot said. "Looking for pot hunters around Bluff, you'd go see Old Man Houk. Or one of his friends. Or hired hands."

Bluff, Leaphorn thought. Maybe he would go there and talk to Houk. It must be the same Houk. The surviving father of the drowned murderer. The memories flooded back. Such tragedy burns deep into the brain.

"Something else you might need to know," Davis said. "Ellie had a pistol."

Leaphorn waited.

"She kept it in the same drawer with that purse."

"It wasn't there," Leaphorn said.

"No. It wasn't," Davis said. "I guess she took it with her."

Yes, Leaphorn thought. He would go to Bluff and talk to Houk. As Leaphorn remembered him, he was a most unusual man.

7

JIM CHEE SAT on the edge of his bunk, rubbed his eyes with his knuckles, cleared his throat, and considered the uneasiness that had troubled his sleep. Too much death. The disturbed earth littered with too many bones. He put that thought aside. Was there enough water left in the tank of his little aluminum trailer to afford a shower? The answer was perhaps. But it wasn't a new problem. Chee long ago had developed a method for minimizing its effects. He filled his coffeepot ready for perking. He filled a drinking glass as a tooth-brushing reserve and a mustard jar for the sweat bath he was determined to take.

Chee climbed down the riverbank carrying the jar, a paper cup, and a tarpaulin. At his sweat bath in the willows beside the San Juan, he collected enough driftwood to heat his rocks, filled the cup with clean, dry sand, started his fire, and sat, legs crossed, waiting and thinking. No profit in thinking of Janet Pete—that encounter represented a humiliation that could be neither avoided nor minimized. Any way he figured it, the cost would be $900, plus Janet Pete's disdain. He thought instead of last night, of the two bodies being photographed, being loaded into the police van by the San Juan County deputies. He thought of the pots, carefully wrapped in newspapers inside the garbage bags.

When the rocks were hot enough and the fire had burned itself down to coals, he covered the sweat bath frame with the tarp, slid under it. He squatted, singing the sweat bath songs that the Holy People had taught the first clans, the songs to force contamination and sickness from the body. He savored the dry heat, conscious of muscles relaxing, perspiration seeping from his skin, trickling behind his ears, down his back, wet against his flanks. He poured a palmful of water from the jar into his hand and sprinkled it onto the rocks, engulfing himself in an explosion of steam. He inhaled this hot fog deeply, felt his body slick with moisture. He was dizzy now, free. Concern for bones and Buicks vanished in the hot darkness. Chee was conscious instead of his lungs at work, of open pores, supple muscles, of his own vigorous health. Here was his *hozro*—his harmony with what surrounded him.

When he threw back the tarp and emerged, rosy with body heat and streaming sweat, he felt light of head, light of foot, generally wonderful. He rubbed himself down with the sand he'd collected, climbed back to the trailer, and took his shower. Chee added to the desert dweller's habitual frugality with water the special caution that those who live in trailers relearn each time they cover themselves with suds and find there's nothing left in the reservoir. He soaped a small area, rinsed it, then soaped another, hurried by the smell of his coffee perking. His Navajo genes spared him the need to shave again for probably a week, but he shaved anyway. It was a way to delay the inevitable.

That was delayed a bit more by the lack of a telephone in Chee's trailer. He used the pay phone beside the convenience store on the highway. Janet Pete wasn't at her office. Maybe, the receptionist said, she had gone down to the Justice building, to the police station. She had been worried about her new car. Chee dialed the station. Three call-back messages for him, two from Janet Pete of DNA, the tribal legal service, one from Lieutenant Leaphorn. Leaphorn had just called and talked to Captain Largo. The captain then had left the message for Chee to call Leaphorn at his home number in Window Rock after 6:00 P.M. Had Pete left any messages? Yes, with the last call she had said to tell him she wanted to pick up her car.

Chee called Pete's home number. He tapped his fingers nervously as the telephone rang. There was a click.

"Sorry I can't come to the phone now," Pete's voice said. "If you will leave a message after the tone sounds, I will call you."

Chee listened to the tone, and the silence following it. He could think of nothing sensible to say, and hung up. Then he drove over to Tso's garage. Surely the damage hadn't been as bad as he remembered.

The damage was exactly as he'd remembered. The car squatted on Tso's towing dolly, discolored with dust, the front wheel grotesquely misaligned, paint scraped from the fender, the little clips that once held Janet Pete's favorite chrome strip holding nothing. A small dent in the door. A large dent marring the robin's-egg blue of the rear fender. Looking crippled and dirty.

"Not so terrible," Tso said. "Nine fifty to eleven hundred dollars and it's good as it was. But she really ought to fix all those problems it had when you first drove it in." Tso was wiping the grease from his hands in a gesture that reminded Chee of greedy anticipation. "Grabby brakes, slack steering, all that."

"I'm going to need some credit," Chee said.

Tso thought about that, his face full of remembered debts, of friendships violated. Chee's thoughts of Tso, always warm, began turning cool. While they did, Janet Pete's motor pool sedan pulled up beside the building. The front door opened. Janet Pete emerged. She looked at the Buick, at two other cars awaiting Tso's ministrations, and gave Chee a dazzling smile.

"Where's my Buick?" she asked. "How did it run? Did you . . ."

The question trailed off. Janet Pete looked again at the Buick.

"My God," she said. "Was anybody killed?"

"Well," Chee said. He cleared his throat. "You see, I was driving down . . ."

"Bad shocks," Tso said. "Slack steering. But Chee here took it out anyway. Sort of a safety check." Tso shrugged, made a wry face. "Could have been killed," he said.

Which, if you thought about it right, was perhaps true, Chee thought. His displeasure with Tso was swept away by a wave of gratitude.

He made a depreciating gesture. "I should have been more careful," he said. "Tso warned me."

Janet was staring at the Buick, reconciling what she saw with what she had left. "They told me everything was fine," she said.

"Odometer set back," Tso said. "Brake lining unevenly worn. U-joint loose. Steering loose. Needed lots of work."

Janet Pete bit her lip. Thought. "Can I use your telephone?"

Chee overheard only part of it. Getting past the salesman to the sales manager to the general manager. It seemed to Chee that the general manager mostly listened.

"Officer Chee doesn't seem to be too badly hurt, but I haven't heard from his lawyer . . . mechanic's list of defects shows . . . that's a third-degree misdemeanor in New Mexico, odometer tampering is. Yes, well, a jury can decide that for us. I think the fine is five thousand dollars. You can pick it up at Tso's garage in Shiprock. He tells me he won't release it until you pay his costs. Towing, inspection, I guess. My lawyer told me to make sure that none of your mechanics worked on it until he decides . . ."

On the way to get a cup of coffee in Janet Pete's motor pool sedan, Chee said, "He'll have his mechanics fix everything."

"Probably," Janet said. "Wouldn't be much of a lawsuit anyway. Not worth it."

"Just letting him sweat a little?"

"You know, they wouldn't try that on you. You're a man. They pull that crap on women. They figure they can sell a woman on the baby blue paint and the chrome stripe. Sell us a lemon."

"Um," Chee said, which provoked a period of silence.

"What really happened?" Janet asked.

"Steering failed," Chee said, feeling uneasy.

"Come on," Janet said.

"Tried to make a turn," Chee said. "Missed it."

"How fast? Come on. What was going on?"

So Jim Chee explained it, all about the missing trailer, and the missing backhoe, and Captain Largo, and that led to what he had found last night.

Janet had heard about it on the radio. Over coffee she was full of questions, not all of them about the crime.

"I heard you were a *hataalii*," she said. "That you sing the Blessing Way."

"I'm still learning," Chee said. "The only one I performed was in the family. A relative. But I know it now. If anybody wants one done."

"How do you get time off? Isn't that a problem? Eight days, isn't it? Or do you sing the shorter version?"

"No problem yet. No customers."

"Another thing I hear about you—you have a *belagana* girl-friend. A teacher over at Crownpoint."

"She's gone away," Chee said, and felt that odd sensation of hearing, from some external point, his voice saying the words. "Gone away to be a graduate student in Wisconsin."

"Oh," Janet said.

"We write," Chee said. "I sent her a pregnant cat once."

Janet looked surprised. "Testing her patience?"

Chee tried to think how to explain it. A stupid thing to send to Mary Landon, stupid to mention it now.

"At the time I thought it had some symbolism," he said.

Janet let the silence live, Navajo fashion. If he had more he wanted to say about Mary Landon and the cat, he would say it. He liked her for that. But he had nothing more to say.

"It was that cat you told me about? Last summer when you'd arrested that old man I was representing. The cat the coyote was after?"

Chee was stirring his coffee, head down but conscious that Janet Pete was studying him. He nodded, remembering. Janet Pete had suggested he provide his stray cat with a coyote-proof home and they had gone to a Farmington pet store and bought one of those plastic and wire cages used to ship pets on airliners. He had used it, eventually, to ship the abandoned white man's cat back to the white man's world.

"Symbolism," Janet Pete said. Now she was stirring her coffee, looking down at the swirl the spoon made.

To the top of her head, Chee said: *"Belagana* cat can't adapt to the Navajo ways. Starves. Eaten by coyote. My stray cat experiment fails. I accept the failure. Cat goes back to the world of the *belaganas,* where there's more to eat and the coyote doesn't get you." It was more than Chee had intended to say. He was torn. He wanted to talk about Mary Landon, about the going away of Mary Landon. But he wasn't comfortable talking about it to Janet Pete.

"She didn't want to stay on the reservation. You didn't want to leave," Janet Pete said. "You are saying you understand her problem."

"Our problem," Chee said. "My problem."

Janet Pete sipped her coffee. "Mine was a law professor. Assistant professor, to be technical." She put the cup down and considered. "You know," she said, "maybe it was the same symbolic cat problem. Let me see if I can make it fit."

Chee waited. Like Mary Landon, Janet Pete had large, expressive eyes. Dark brown instead of blue. Now they were surrounded by frown lines as Janet Pete thought.

"Doesn't fit so well," she said. "He wanted a helpmate." She laughed. "Adam's rib. Something to hold back the loneliness of the young man pursuing his brilliant career at law. The Indian maiden." The words sounded bitter, but she smiled at Chee. "You remember. Few years ago, Indian maidens were in with the Yuppies. Like squash-blossom necklaces and declaring yourself to be part Cherokee or Sioux if you wanted to write romantic poetry."

"Not so much now," Chee said. "I gather you agreed to disagree."

"Not really," she said. "The offer remains open. Or so he tells me."

"Fits in a way," Chee said. "I wanted her to be my Navajo."

"She was a schoolteacher? At Crownpoint?"

"For three years," Chee said.

"But didn't want to make a career out of it. I can see her point."

"That wasn't exactly the problem. It was raising kids out here. More than that, too. I could leave. Had an offer from the FBI. Better money. Sort of a choice involved, as she saw it. Did I want her enough to quit being a Navajo?"

Outside the dusty front window of the Navajo Nation Café the dazzling late-day sunlight turned dark with cloud shadow. A Ford 250 pickup rolled past slowly, its front seat crowded with four Navajos, its rear bumper crowded by the van of an impatient tourist. Chee caught the eye of the waitress and got their coffees refilled. What would he say if Janet Pete pressed the question. If she said: "Well, do you?" what would he say?

Instead, she stirred her coffee.

"How has the professor's brilliant career developed?" Chee asked.

"Brilliantly. He's now chief legal counsel of Davidson-Bart, which I understand is what is called a multinational conglomerate. But mostly involved with the commercial credit end of export-import business. Makes money. Lives in Arlington."

Through the dusty window came the faint sound of thunder, a rumble that faded away.

"Wish it would rain," Janet Pete said.

Chee had been thinking exactly the same thing. Sharing a Navajo thought with another Navajo. "Too late to rain," he said. "It's October thirty-first."

Janet Pete dropped him at the garage. He stopped at the station to call Lieutenant Leaphorn on his way back to the trailer.

"Largo told me you found the bodies of those pot hunters," Leaphorn said. "He was a little vague about what you were doing out there."

He left the question implied and Chee thought a moment before answering. He knew Leaphorn's wife had died. He'd heard the man was having trouble coping with that. He'd heard—everybody in the Navajo Tribal Police had heard—that Leaphorn had quit the force. Retired. So what was he doing in this affair? How official was this? Chee exhaled, taking another second for thought. He thought, quit or not, this is still Joe Leaphorn. Our legendary Leaphorn.

"I was looking for that fellow who stole that backhoe here at Shiprock," Chee said. "I found out he was a pot hunter now and then, and I was trying to catch him out digging. With the stolen property."

"And you knew where to look?" Leaphorn, Chee remembered, never believed in coincidence.

"Some guessing," Chee said. "But I knew what gas company he worked for, and where his job would have taken him, and where there might be some sites in the places he would have been."

The word that spread among the four hundred employees of the Navajo Tribal Police was that Joe Leaphorn had lost it. Joe Leaphorn had a nervous breakdown. Joe Leaphorn was out of it. To Jim Chee, Leaphorn's voice sounded no different. Neither did the tone of his questions. A kind of skepticism. As if he knew he wasn't being told all he needed to know. What would Leaphorn ask him now? How he knew the man would be digging last night?

"You have anything else to go on?"

"Oh," Chee said. "Sure. We knew he rented a truck with new tires on double back wheels."

"Okay," Leaphorn said. "Good. So there were tracks to look for." Now his voice sounded more relaxed. "Makes a lot of difference. Otherwise you spend the rest of your life out there running down the roads."

"And I figured he might be out digging last night because of something he said to Slick Nakai. The preacher bought pots from him, now and then. And he sort of told the preacher he'd have some for him quick," Chee said.

Silence.

"Did you know I'm on leave? Terminal leave?"

"I heard it," Chee said.

"Ten more days and I'm a civilian. Right now, matter of fact, I guess I'm unofficial."

"Yes sir," Chee said.

"If you can make it tomorrow, would you drive out there to the site with me? Look it over with me in daylight. Tell me how it was before the sheriff's people and the ambulance and the FBI screwed everything up."

"If it's okay with the captain," Chee said, "I'd be happy to go."

8

LEAPHORN HAD BEEN AWARE of the wind most of the night, listening to it blow steadily from the southeast as he waited for sleep, awakening again and again to notice it shifting, and gusting, making *chindi* sounds around the empty house. It was still blowing when Thatcher arrived to pick him up, buffeting Thatcher's motor pool sedan.

"Cold front coming through," Thatcher said. "It'll die down."

And as they drove northward from Window Rock it moderated. At Many Farms they stopped for breakfast, Thatcher reminiscing about Harrison Houk, cattleman, pillar of the Church of Jesus Christ of Latter-day Saints, potent Republican, subject of assorted gossip, county commissioner, holder of Bureau of Land Management grazing permits sprawling across the southern Utah canyon country, legendary shrewd operator. Leaphorn mostly listened, remembering Houk from long ago, remembering a man stricken. When they paid their check, the western sky over Black Mesa was bleak with suspended dust but the wind was down. Fifty miles later as they crossed the Utah border north of Mexican Water, it was no more than a breeze, still from the southeast but almost too faint to stir the sparse gray sage and the silver cheat grass of the Nokaito Bench. The sedan rolled across the San Juan River bridge below Sand Island in a dead calm. Only the smell of dust recalled the wind.

"Land of Little Rain," Thatcher said. "Who called it that?"

It wasn't the sort of friendship that needed answers. Leaphorn looked upstream, watching a small flotilla of rubber kayaks, rafts, and wooden dories pushing into the stream from the Sand Island launching site. A float expedition down into the deep canyons. He and Emma had talked of doing that. She would have loved it, getting him away from any possibility of telephone calls. Getting him off the end of the earth. And he would have loved it, too. Always intended to do it but there was never enough time. And now, of course, the time was all used up.

"One of your jobs?" Leaphorn asked, nodding toward the flotilla below.

"We license them as tour boatmen. Sell 'em trip permits, make sure they meet the safety rules. So forth." He nodded toward the stream. "That must be the last one of the season. They close the river down just about now."

"Big headache?"

"Not this bunch," Thatcher said. "This is Wild Rivers Expeditions out of Bluff. Pros. More into selling education. Take you down with a geologist to study the formations and the fossils, or with an anthropologist to look at the Anasazi ruins up the canyons, or maybe with a biologist to get you into the lizards and lichens and the bats. That sort of stuff. Older people go. More money. Not a bunch of overaged adolescents hoping to get scared shitless going down the rapids."

Leaphorn nodded.

"Take great pride in cleaning up after themselves. The drill now is urinate right beside the river, so it dilutes it fast. Everything else they carry out. Portable toilets. Build their camp fires in fireboxes so you don't get all that carbon in the sand. Even carry out the ashes."

They turned upriver toward Bluff. Off the reservation now. Out of Leaphorn's jurisdiction and into Thatcher's. Much of the land above the bluffs lining the river would be federal land—public domain grazing leases. The land along the river had been homesteaded by the Mormon families who'd settled this narrow valley on orders from Brigham Young to form an outpost against the hostile Gentile world. This stony landscape south of the river had been Leaphorn's country once, when he was young and worked out of Kayenta, but it was too waterless and barren to support the people who would require police attention.

History said 250 Mormons had settled the place in the 1860s, and the last census figures Leaphorn had seen showed its current population was 240—three service stations strung along the highway, three roadside cafés, two groceries, two motels, the office and boathouse of Wild Rivers Expeditions, a school, a ward meeting-house, and a scattering of houses, some of them empty. The years hadn't changed much at Bluff.

Houk's ranch house was the exception. Leaphorn remembered it as a big, solid block of a building, formed of cut pink sandstone, square as a die and totally neat. It had been connected to the gravel road from Bluff by a graded dirt driveway, which led through an iron gate, curved over a sagebrush-covered rise, and ended under the cottonwoods that shaded the house. Leaphorn noticed the difference at the gate, painted then, rusted now. He unlatched it, refastened it after Thatcher drove through. Then he pulled the chain, which slammed the clapper against the big iron church bell suspended on the pole that took the electric line to the house. That told Houk he had visitors.

The driveway now was rutted, with a growth of tumbleweeds, wild asters, and cheat grass along the tracks. The rabbit fence, which Leaphorn remembered surrounding a neat and lush front yard garden, was sagging now and the garden a tangle of dry country weeds. The pillars that supported the front porch needed paint. So did the pickup truck parked beside the porch. Only the solid square shape of the house, built to defy time, hadn't been changed by the years. But now, surrounded by decay, it stood like a stranger. Even the huge barn on the slope behind it, despite its stone walls, seemed to sag.

Thatcher let the sedan roll to a stop in the shade of the cottonwood. The screen door opened and Houk appeared. He was leaning on a cane. He squinted from the shadows into blinding sunlight, trying to identify who had rung the yard bell. At first look, Leaphorn thought that Houk, like the pink sandstone of his house, had been proof against time. Despite the cane, his figure in the shadow of the porch had the blocky sturdiness Leaphorn remembered. There was still the round bulldog face, the walrus mustache, the small eyes peering through wire-rimmed glasses. But now Leaphorn saw the paunch, the slight slump, the deepened lines, the grayness, the raggedness of the mustache which hid his mouth. And as Houk shifted his weight against the cane, Leaphorn saw the grimace of pain cross his face.

"Well, now, Mr. Thatcher," Houk said, recognizing him. "What brings the Bureau of Land Management all the way out here so soon? Wasn't it only last spring you was out here to see me?" And then he saw Leaphorn. "And who . . ." he began, and stopped. His expression shifted from neutral, to surprise, to delight.

"By God," he said. "I don't remember your name, but you're

the Navajo policeman who found my boy's hat." Houk stopped. "Yes I do. It was Leaphorn."

It was Leaphorn's turn for surprise. Almost twenty years since he'd been involved in the hunt for Houk's boy. He had talked to Houk only two or three times, and only briefly. Giving him the wet blue felt hat, soggy with muddy San Juan River water. Standing beside him under the alcove in the cliff that tense moment when the state police captain decided they had Brigham Houk cornered. And finally, on this very porch when it was all over and no hope remained, listening to the man examine his conscience, finding in his own flaws the blame for his boy's murderous rage. Three meetings, and a long, long time ago.

Houk ushered them into what he called the parlor, a neat room that smelled of furniture polish. "Don't use this room much," Houk said loudly, and he pulled back the curtains, raised the blinds, and pushed up the sash windows to admit the autumn. But the room was still dim—its walls a gallery of framed photographs of people, of bookshelves lined mostly with pots. "Don't get much company," Houk concluded. He sat himself in the overstuffed armchair that matched the sofa, creating another faint puff of dust. "In just a minute the girl will be in here with something cold to drink." He waited then, his fingers tapping at the chair arm. It was their turn to speak.

"We're looking for a woman," Thatcher began. "Anthropologist named Eleanor Friedman-Bernal."

Houk nodded. "I know her." He looked surprised. "What she do?"

"She's been missing," Thatcher said. "For a couple of weeks." He thought about what he wanted to say next. "Apparently she came out here just a little while before she disappeared. To Bluff. Did you see her?"

"Let's see now. I'd say it was three, four weeks when she was out here last," Houk said. "Something like that. Maybe I could figure it out exactly."

"What did she want?"

It seemed to Leaphorn that Houk's face turned slightly pinker than its usual hue. He stared at Thatcher, his lip moving under the mustache, his fingers still drumming.

"You fellas didn't take long to get out here," he said. "I'll say that for you." He pushed himself up in the chair, then sat back down again. "But how the hell you connect it with me?"

"You mean her being missing?" Thatcher said, puzzled. "She had your name down in her notes."

"I meant the killings," Houk said.

"Killings?" Leaphorn asked.

"Over in New Mexico," Houk said. "The pot hunters. It was on the radio this morning."

"You think we're connecting those with you?" Leaphorn asked. "Why do you think that?"

"Because it seems to me that every time the feds start thinking about pot stealing, they come nosing around here," Houk said. "Those folks get shot stealing pots, stands to reason it's going to get the BLM cops, and the FBI, and all off their butts and working. Since they don't know what the hell they're doing, they bother me." Houk surveyed them, his small blue eyes magnified by the lenses of his glasses.

"You fellas telling me this visit hasn't nothing to do with that?"

"That's what we're telling you," Leaphorn said. "We're trying to find an anthropologist. A woman named Eleanor Friedman-Bernal. She disappeared the thirteenth of October. Some references in her notes about coming out here to Bluff to see Mr. Harrison Houk. We thought if we knew what she came out here to see you about, it might tell us something about where to look next."

Houk thought about it, assessing them. "She came to see me about a pot," he said.

Leaphorn sat, waiting for his silence to encourage Houk to add to that. But Thatcher was not a Navajo.

"A pot?"

"To do with her research," Houk said. "She'd seen a picture of it in a Nelson auction catalog. You know about that outfit? And it was the kind she's interested in. So she called 'em, and talked to somebody or other, and they told her they'd got it from me." Houk paused, waiting for Thatcher's question.

"What did she want to know?"

"Exactly where I found it. I didn't find it. I bought it off a Navajo. I give her his name."

A middle-aged Navajo woman came into the room, carrying a tray with three water glasses, a pitcher of what appeared to be ice water, and three cans of Hires root beer.

"Drinking water or root beer," Houk said. "I guess you knew I'm Latter-day Saints."

Everybody took water.

"Irene," Houk said. "You want to meet these fellas. This is Mr. Thatcher here. The one from the BLM who comes out here now and then worrying us about our grazing rights. And this fella here is the one I've told you about. The one that found Brigham's hat. The one that kept those goddam state policemen from shooting up into that alcove. This is Irene Musket."

Irene put down the tray and held her hand out to Thatcher. "How do you do," she said. She spoke in Navajo to Leaphorn, using the traditional words, naming her mother's clan, the Towering House People, and her father's, the Paiute Dineh. She didn't hold out her hand. He wouldn't expect it. This touching of strangers was a white man's custom that some traditional Navajos found difficult to adopt.

"You remember what day it was that anthropology woman was out here?" Houk asked her. "Almost a month ago, I think."

Irene considered. "On a Friday," she said. "Four weeks ago last Friday." She picked up the tray and left.

"Great friend of my wife, Irene was. After Alice passed on, Irene stayed on and looked after things," Houk said.

They sipped the cold water. Behind Houk's gray head, the wall was lined with photographs. Houk and his wife and their children clustered on the front porch. Brigham, the youngest, standing in front. The brother and sister he was destined to kill standing behind him, smiling over his shoulders. Brigham's mouth looked slightly twisted, as if he had been ordered to smile. Houk's face was happy, boyish. His wife looked tired, strain showing in the lines around her mouth. A wedding picture, the bride with the veil raised above her face, Houk with the mustache much smaller, older couples flanking them. A picture of Brigham on a horse, his smile strained and lopsided. A picture of the sister in a cheerleader's uniform. Of the brother in a Montezuma Creek High School football jacket. Of Brigham holding up a dead bobcat by its back legs, his eyes intense. Of Houk in an army uniform. Of the Houks and another couple. But mostly the pictures were of the three children. Dozens of them, at all ages. In most of them, Brigham stood alone, rarely smiling. In three of them, he stood over a deer. In one, over a bear. Leaphorn remembered Houk talking endlessly on the porch the day Brigham had drowned.

"Always outdoors," Houk had said. "From the very littlest. Shy as a Navajo. Wasn't happy around people. We shouldn't have made him go to school there. We should have gotten him some help."

Now Houk put down his glass. Thatcher asked, "When she left

here, was she going to see the Navajo? The one who found the pot?"

"I reckon," Houk said. "That was her intention. She wanted to know where he got it. All I knew is what he told me. That he didn't break any law getting it." Houk was talking directly to Thatcher. "Didn't get it off public domain land, or off the reservation. Got to be off private land or I won't have nothing to do with it."

"What was his name?" Thatcher asked.

"Fella named Jimmy Etcitty," Houk said.

"Live around here?"

"South, I think," Houk said. "Across the border in Arizona. Between Tes Nez Iah and Dinnehotso, I think he said." Houk stopped. It seemed to Leaphorn that it was to decide whether he had told them enough. And this time Thatcher didn't interrupt the silence. Houk thought. They waited. Leaphorn studied the room. Everything was dusty except the piano. It glowed with wax. Like most of the bookshelves, a shelf above the piano was lined with pots.

"I think I told her she should stop at the Dinnehotso Chapter House and ask how to get to the Mildred Roanhorse outfit," Houk added. "Etcitty's her son-in-law."

"I noticed in the Nelson catalog that they give the customer some sort of documentation on their artifacts," Leaphorn said. He left the question implied, and Houk let it hang a moment while he thought about how to answer it.

"They do," Houk said. "If I happen to find something myself— or sometimes when I have personal knowledge where it came from—then I fill out this sort of statement, time and place and all that, and I sign it and send it along. Case like this, I just give the documentation form to the finder—whoever I'm buying it from. I have them fill it in and sign it."

"You show that paper to the lady?" Leaphorn asked.

"Didn't have it," Houk said. "Usually I just have the finder send the letter directly to whoever is buying from me. This case, I gave Etcitty the Nelson form and told him to take care of it."

They sat and considered this.

"Cuts out the middleman on that," Houk said.

And, Leaphorn thought, insulates Harrison Houk from any charge of fraud.

"Might as well get it from the horse's mouth," Houk added, somberly. But he winked at Leaphorn.

There was still plenty of the day left to drive south to the Dinnehotso Chapter House and get directions to the Mildred Roanhorse outfit and find Jimmy Etcitty. On the porch Houk touched Leaphorn's sleeve.

"Always wanted to say something to you about what you did," he said. "That evening I wasn't in any condition to think about it. But it was a kindly thing. And brave too."

"It was just my job," Leaphorn said. "That highway patrolman was a traffic man. Green about that kind of work. And scared too, I guess. Somebody needed to keep it cool."

"Turned out it didn't matter," Houk said. "Brigham wasn't hiding up there anyway. I guess he was already drowned by then. But I thank you."

Thatcher was standing at the foot of the steps, waiting and hearing all this. Embarrassing. But he didn't bring it up until they were out of Bluff driving toward Mexican Water into the blinding noontime sun.

"Didn't know you were involved in that Houk case," he said. He shook his head. "Hell of a thing. The boy was crazy, wasn't he?"

"That's what they said. Schizophrenia. Heard voices. Unhappy around anyone but his dad. A loner. But Houk told me he was great at music. That piano in there, that was the boy's. Houk said he was good at it and played the guitar and the clarinet."

"But dangerous," Thatcher said. "Ought to been put in a hospital. Locked up until he was safe."

"I remember that's what Houk said they should've done. He said his wife wanted to, but he wouldn't do it. Said he thought it would kill the boy. Locking him up. Said he wasn't happy except when he was outdoors."

"What'd you do to make such an impression on Houk?"

"Found the boy's hat," Leaphorn said. "Washed up on the reservation side of the river. It was already pretty clear he'd tried to swim across."

Thatcher drove for a while. Turned on the radio. "Catch the noon news," he said. "See what they got to say about those pot hunters getting shot."

"Good," Leaphorn said.

"There was more to it than that," Thatcher said. "More than finding his goddamned hat."

Might as well get it over with. The memories had been flooding back anyway—another of those many things a policeman accumulates in the mind and cannot erase. "You remember the case," Leaphorn said. "Houk and one of his hired hands came home that night, and found the bodies, and the youngest boy,

Brigham, missing, with some of his stuff. And the shotgun he'd done it with was missing too. Big excitement. Houk was even more important then than he is now—legislator and all that. Bunches of men out everywhere looking. This Utah highway patrol officer—a captain or lieutenant or something—he and a bunch he was handling thought they had the boy cornered in a sort of alcove-cave up in a box canyon. Saw something or heard something, and I guess the kid had used the place before as a sort of hangout. Anyway, they'd called for him to come out, and no answer, so this dumb captain is going to have everybody shoot into there, and I said first I'd get a little closer and see what I could see, and turned out nobody was in there."

Thatcher looked at him.

"No big deal," Leaphorn said. "Nobody was there."

"So you didn't get shot with a shotgun."

"I happened to have a pretty clear idea of how far a shotgun will shoot. Not very far."

"Yeah," Thatcher said.

The tone irritated Leaphorn. "Hell, man," he said. "The boy was only fourteen."

Thatcher had no comment on that. The woman reading the noon news had gotten to the pot hunter shooting. The San Juan County Sheriff's Office said they had no suspects in the case as yet but they did have promising leads. Casts had been made of the tire tracks of a vehicle believed used by the killer. Both victims had now been identified. They were Joe B. Nails, thirty-one, a former employee of Wellserve in Farmington, and Jimmy Etcitty, thirty-seven, whose address was given as Dinnehotso Chapter House on the Navajo Reservation.

"Well now," Thatcher said. "I guess we can skip stopping at Dinnehotso."

9

"THIS IS JUST ABOUT where they'd left the U-Haul truck parked," Chee said. He turned off the ignition, set the parking brake. "Pulled up to the edge of the slope with the winch cable run out. Apparently they eased the backhoe down on the cable."

The front of Chee's pickup was pointed down the steep slope. Fifty feet below, the grassy, brushy hump where a little Anasazi pueblo had stood a thousand years ago was a chaos of trenches, jumbled stones, and what looked like broken sticks. Bones reflecting white in the sunlight.

"Where was the backhoe?"

Chee pointed. "See the little juniper? At the end of that shallow trench there."

"The sheriff hauled everything off, I guess," Leaphorn said. "After they got their photographs."

"That was the plan when I left."

Leaphorn didn't comment. He sat silently, considering the destruction below. This ridge was much higher than it had seemed to Chee in the darkness. Shiprock stuck up like a blue thumb on the western horizon seventy miles away. Behind it, the dim outline of the Carrizo Mountains formed the last margin of the planet. The sagebrush flats between were dappled with the shadow of clouds, drifting eastward under the noon sun.

"The bodies," Leaphorn said. "The *belagana* in the backhoe? Right? Named Nails. And the Navajo partway up this slope under us? Jimmy Etcitty. Which one was shot first?"

Chee opened his mouth, closed it. His impulse had been to say the coroner would have to decide. Or about the same time. But he realized what Leaphorn wanted.

"I'd guess the Navajo was running for his life," he said. "I'd say he'd seen the white man shot in the machine. He was running for the truck."

"Do much checking before you called it in to the sheriff?"

"Hardly any," Chee said.

"But some," Leaphorn said.

"Very little."

"The killer parked up here?"

"Down by the oil well pump."

"Tire tracks mean anything?"

"Car or pickup. Some wear." Chee shrugged. "Dusty dry and in the dark. Couldn't tell much."

"How about his tracks? Or hers?"

"He parked on the sandstone. No tracks right at the vehicle. After that, mostly scuff marks."

"Man?"

"Probably. I don't know." Chee was remembering how shaken he had been. Too much death. He hadn't been using his head. Now he felt guilty. Had he concentrated, he surely could have found at least something to indicate shoe size.

"Not much use going over it again," Leaphorn said. "Too many deputy sheriffs and paramedics and photographers been trampling around."

And so they scrambled down the hill—Leaphorn losing his footing and sliding twenty feet in a shower of dislodged earth and gravel. Standing there, amid the dislodged stones, amid the scattered bones, Chee felt the familiar uneasiness. Too many *chindi* had taken to the air here, finding freedom from the bodies that had housed them. Leaphorn was standing at a narrow trench the backhoe had dug beside a crumbled wall, looking thoughtful. But then Leaphorn didn't believe in *chindi,* or in anything else.

"You studied anthropology, didn't you? At New Mexico?"

"Right," Chee said. So had Leaphorn, if the word around the Navajo Tribal Police was true. At Arizona State. A BA and an MS.

"Get into the Anasazi much? The archaeological end of it?"

"A little," Chee said.

"The point is, whoever did this work knew something about what he was doing," Leaphorn said. "Anasazi usually buried their dead in the trash midden with the garbage, or right against the walls, sometimes inside the rooms. This guy worked the midden. . . . " Leaphorn gestured to the torn earth beyond them. "And he worked along the walls. So I'd guess he knew they buried pottery with their corpses, and he knew where to find the graves."

Chee nodded.

"And maybe he knew this was a late site, and that—rule of thumb—the later the site, the better the pot. Glazed, multicolored, decorated, so forth." He bent, picked up a shard of broken pottery the size of his hand and inspected it.

"Most of the stuff I've seen here is like this," he said, handing the shard to Chee. "Recognize it?"

The interior surface was a rough gray. Under its coating of dust the exterior glowed a glossy rose, with ghostly lines of white wavering through it. Chee touched the glazed surface to his tongue—the automatic reaction of a former anthropology student to a potsherd—and inspected the clean spot. A nice color, but his memory produced nothing more than a confused jumble of titles: Classical. Pueblo III. Incised. Corrugated, etc. He handed the shard to Leaphorn, shook his head.

"It's a type called St. John's Polychrome," Leaphorn said. "Late stuff. There's a theory it originated in one of the Chaco outlier villages. I think they're pretty sure it was used for trading."

Chee was impressed and his face showed it.

Leaphorn chuckled. "I can't remember stuff like that either," he said. "I've been doing some reading."

"Oh?"

"We seem to have a sort of overlap here," he said. "You were looking for a couple of men who stole our backhoe. I'm looking for an anthropologist. A woman who works at Chaco and took off one day three weeks ago to go to Farmington and never came back."

"Hadn't heard about that," Chee said.

"She prepared this big, elaborate dinner. Had a guest coming to visit. A man very important to her. She put it in the fridge and she didn't come back." Leaphorn had been looking out across the grassland toward the distant thunderheads. It must have occurred to him that this would sound strange to Chee. He glanced at him. "It's a San Juan County missing person's case," he said. "But I'm on leave, and it sounded interesting."

"You mentioned you were quitting," Chee said. "I mean resigning."

"I'm on terminal leave," Leaphorn said. "A few more days and I'm a civilian."

Chee could think of nothing to say. He didn't particularly like Leaphorn, but he respected him.

"But I'm not a civilian yet," he added, "and what we have here is peculiar. This overlap, I mean. We have Dr. Friedman-Bernal being a ferocious collector of this kind of pottery." Leaphorn tapped the potsherd with his forefinger. "We have Jimmy Etcitty killed here digging up this sort of pot. This same Jimmy Etcitty worked over at Chaco where Friedman-Bernal worked. This same Jimmy Etcitty found a pot somewhere near Bluff which he sold to a collector who sold it to an auction house. This pot got Friedman-Bernal excited enough a month ago to send her driving to Bluff looking for Etcitty. And on top of that we have Friedman-Bernal buying from Slick Nakai, the evangelist, and Nails selling to Slick, and Etcitty playing guitar for Nakai."

Chee waited, but Leaphorn seemed to have nothing to add.

"I didn't know any of that," Chee said. "Just knew Nails and a friend stole the backhoe when I was supposed to be watching the maintenance yard."

"Nice little tangle of strings, and right here is the knot," Leaphorn said.

And none of it any of Leaphorn's business, Chee thought. Not if he had resigned. So why was he out here, sitting on that stone wall with his legs in the sun, with almost two hundred miles of driving already behind him today? He must enjoy it or he wouldn't be here. So why has he resigned?

"Why did you resign?" Chee asked. "None of my business, I guess, but . . ."

Leaphorn seemed to be thinking about it. Almost as if for the first time. He glanced at Chee, shrugged. "I guess I'm tired," he said.

"But you're using leave time out here, chasing after whatever it is we have here."

"I've been wondering about that myself," Leaphorn said. "Maybe it's the fire horse syndrome. Lifelong habit at work. I think it's because I'd like to find this Friedman-Bernal woman. I'd like to find her and sit her down and say: 'Dr. Bernal, why did you prepare that big dinner and then go away and let it rot in your refrigerator?' "

To Chee, the answer to why Dr. Bernal let her dinner spoil was all too easy. Especially now. Dr. Bernal was dead.

"You think she's still alive?"

Leaphorn considered. "After what we have here, it doesn't seem likely, does it?"

"No," Chee said.

"Unless she did it," Leaphorn said. "She had a pistol. She took it with her when she left Chaco."

"What caliber?" Chee asked. "I heard this one was small."

"All I know is small," Leaphorn said. "Small handgun. She carried it in her purse."

"Sounds like twenty-two caliber," Chee said. "Or maybe a twenty-five or a small thirty-two."

Leaphorn rose, stiffly, to his feet. Stretched his back, flexed his shoulders. "Let's see what we can find," he said.

They found relatively little. The investigators from the county had taken the bodies and whatever else had interested them, which probably hadn't been much. The victims seemed to be clearly identified, and that would be checked with people who knew them for confirmation. The FBI would be asked to do a run on their fingerprints, just in case. The backhoe had been hauled away and would be gone over carefully for prints in the event the killer had been careless with his hands when he shot Nails. The rental truck would receive the same treatment. So would the two plastic sacks in which Chee had seen the pots carefully packed. And just in case, a cord had been run around the dig site, with the little tags dangling to warn citizens away from a homicide site. If some afterthought brought an investigator back to check on something, nothing would be disturbed.

What interested Chee was outside the cord—a new cardboard carton bearing the red legend SUPERTUFF and the sub-legend WASTE-BASKET LINERS, and several other messages: "Why Pay More For Something You'll Throw Away? Six free in this carton. Thirty for the price of twenty-four!"

The cardboard was smudged with white. Chee squatted beside it and recognized fingerprint powder. Someone had checked it and found the cardboard too rough to show prints. Chee picked it up, extracted the carefully folded plastic sacks. Counted them. Twenty-seven. Twenty-seven plus two filled with pots made twenty-nine. He slipped the sacks back into the box and replaced it. One sack unaccounted for. Filled with what? Had the killer taken one set of pots and left the other two? Had Nails's girlfriend, if he had a girlfriend, borrowed one? It was one of those imponderables.

He watched Leaphorn prowling along the trenches, inspecting digging procedures, or perhaps the human bones. Chee had been avoiding the bones without realizing it. Now almost at his foot he noticed the weathered flat surface of a scapula, broken off below the shoulder joint. Just beyond was a very small skull, complete except for the lower jaw. A child, Chee guessed, unless the Anasazi had been even smaller than he remembered. Beyond the skull, partly buried by the excavation dirt, were ribs, and part of a spinal column, the small bones of a foot, three lower jaws placed in a row.

Chee stared. Why had that happened? He strolled over and looked down at them. One was broken, a small jaw with part of its left side missing. The other two were complete. Adult, Chee guessed. An expert would be able to tell the sex of their owners, the approximate ages at death, something about their diet. But why had someone lined them up like this? One of the pot hunters, Chee guessed. It didn't seem the sort of thing one of the deputies would have done. Then Chee noticed another jawbone, and three more, and finally a total of seventeen within a few yards of the juniper where he was standing. He could see only three craniums. Someone—again surely the pot hunters—had sorted out the jaws. Why? Chee walked over to where Leaphorn was standing, studying something in the trench.

"Find anything?" Leaphorn asked, without looking up.

"Nothing much," Chee said. "One of those plastic bags seems to be missing."

Leaphorn looked up at him.

"The box said contents thirty. There were still twenty-seven folded in it. I saw two with pots in them."

"Interesting," Leaphorn said. "We'll ask about that at the sheriff's office. Maybe they took one."

"Maybe," Chee said.

"You notice anything about the skeletons?" Leaphorn was squatting now in the shallow trench, examining bones.

"Somebody seemed to be interested in the jawbones," Chee said.

"Yes," Leaphorn said. "Now why would that be?" He stood up, holding in both hands a small skull. It was gray with the clay of the grave, and the jaw was missing. "Why in the world would that be?"

Chee had not the slightest idea, and said so.

Leaphorn bent into the grave again, poking at something with a stick. "I think this is what they call a Chaco outlier site," he said. "Same people who lived in the great houses over in the canyon, or probably the same. I think there is some evidence, or at least a theory, that these outliers traded back and forth with the great-house people, maybe came into Chaco for their religious ceremonials. Nobody really knows. This was probably one of the sites being reserved for digging sometime in the future." He sounded, Chee thought, like an anthropology lecturer.

"You have anything pressing to do in Shiprock tonight?" Chee denied it with a negative motion of his head.

"How about stopping off at the Chaco Center on the way home then," Leaphorn said. "Let's see what we can find out about this."

FROM THE DESPOILED OUTLIER SITE to the eastern boundary of the Chaco Culture National Historic Park would be less than twenty-five miles if a road existed across the dry hills and Chaco Mesa. None did. By the oil company roads that carried Leaphorn and Chee back to Highway 44, thence northwest to Nageezi, and then southwest over the bumpy dirt access route, it was at least sixty miles. They arrived at the visitors' center just after sundown, found it closed for the day, and drove up to the foot of the bluff where employee housing was located.

FROM THE DESPOILED OUTLIER SITE to the eastern boundary of the Chaco Culture National Historic Park would be less than twenty-five miles if a road existed across the dry hills and Chaco Mesa. None did. By the oil company roads that carried Leaphorn and Chee back to Highway 44, thence northwest to Nageezi, and then southwest over the bumpy dirt access route, it was at least sixty miles. They arrived at the visitors' center just after sundown, found it closed for the day, and drove up to the foot of the bluff where employee housing was located.

The Luna family was starting supper—the superintendent, his wife, a son of perhaps eleven, and a daughter a year or two younger. Supper centered on an entrée involving macaroni, cheese, tomatoes, and things that Leaphorn could not readily identify. That he and Chee would eat was a foregone conclusion. Good manners demanded the disclaimer of hunger from the wayfarer, but the geography of the Colorado Plateau made it an obvious lie. Out here there was literally no place to stop to eat. And so they dined, Leaphorn noticing that Chee's appetite was huge and that his own had returned. Perhaps it was the smell of the home cooking—something he hadn't enjoyed since Emma's sickness reached the point where it was no longer prudent for her to be in the kitchen.

Bob Luna's wife, a handsome woman with a friendly, intelligent face, was full of questions about Eleanor Friedman-Bernal. After polite feelers established that questions were not out of order, she asked them. The Luna son, Allen, a blond, profusely freckled boy who looked like a small copy of his blond and freckled mother, put down his fork and listened. His sister listened without interrupting her supper.

"We haven't learned much," Leaphorn said. "Maybe the county has done better. It is their jurisdiction. But I doubt it. No sheriff ever has enough officers. In San Juan County it's worse than normal. You're worried to death with everything from vandalism of summer cabins up on Navajo Lake to people tapping distillate out of the gas pipelines, or stealing oil field equipment, things like that. Too much territory. Too few people. So missing persons don't get worked on." He stopped, surprised at hearing himself deliver this defense of the San Juan County Sheriff's Office. Usually he was complaining about it. "Anyway," he added, lamely, "we haven't learned anything very useful."

"Where could she have gone?" Mrs. Luna said. Obviously it was something she had often thought about. "So early in the morning. She told us she was going to Farmington, and got the mail we had going out, and our shopping lists, and then just vanished." She glanced from Chee to Leaphorn and back. "I'm afraid it isn't going to have a happy ending. I'm afraid Ellie got in over her head with a man we don't know about." She attempted a smile. "I guess that sounds odd—to say that about a woman her age—but at this place, it's so small—so few of us live here, I mean—that everybody tells everybody everything. It's the only thing we have to be interested in. One another."

Luna laughed. "It's pretty hard to have secrets here," he said. "You have experienced our telephone. You don't get any secret calls. And you don't get any secret mail—unless it happens to show up at Blanco the day you happen to pick it up." He laughed again. "And it would be pretty hard to have any secret visitors."

But not impossible, Leaphorn thought. No more impossible than driving out to make your calls away from here, or setting up a post office box in Farmington.

"You just get to know everything by accident even if people don't mention it," Mrs. Luna said. "For example, going places. I hadn't thought to tell anybody when I was going to Phoenix over the Fourth to visit my mother. But everybody knew because I got a postcard that mentioned it, and Maxie or somebody picked up the mail that day." If Mrs. Luna resented Maxie or somebody reading her postcard, it didn't show. Her expression was totally pleasant—someone explaining a peculiar, but perfectly natural, situation. "And when Ellie made that trip to New York, and when Elliot went to Washington. Even if they don't mention it, you just get to know." Mrs. Luna paused to sip her coffee. "But usually they tell you," she added. "Something new to talk about." At that she looked slightly abashed. She laughed. "That's about all we have to do, you know. Speculate about one another. TV reception is so bad out here we have to be our own soap operas."

"When was the trip to New York?" Leaphorn asked.

"Last month," Mrs. Luna said. "Ellie's travel agent in Farmington called and said the flight schedule had been changed. Somebody takes the message, so everybody knows about it."

"Does anyone know why she went?" Leaphorn asked.

Mrs. Luna made a wry face. "You win," she said. "I guess there are some secrets."

"How about why Elliot went to Washington?" Leaphorn added. "When was that?"

"No secret there," Luna said. "It was last month. A couple of days before Ellie left. He got a call from Washington, from his project director I think it was. Left a message. There was a meeting of people working on archaic migration patterns. He was supposed to attend."

"Do you know if Ellie's going to New York had anything to do with her pots? Is that logical?"

"Just about everything she did had something to do with her pots," Luna said. "She was sort of obsessive about it."

Mrs. Luna's expression turned defensive. "Well now," she said, "Ellie was about ready to make a really important report. As least she thought so. And so do I. She pretty well had the proof that would connect a lot of those St. John Polychromes from the Chetro Ketl site with Wijiji and Kin Nahasbas. And more important than all that, she was finding that this woman must have moved away from Chaco and was making pots somewhere else."

"This woman?" Luna said, eyebrows raised. "She tell you her potter was a woman?"

"Who else would do all that work?" Mrs. Luna got up, got the coffeepot, and offered all hands, including the children, a refill.

"She was excited, then?" Leaphorn asked. "About something she'd found recently? Did she talk to you about it?"

"She was excited," Mrs. Luna said. She looked at Luna with an expression Leaphorn read as reproach. "I really do believe that she'd found something important. To everybody else those people are just a name. Anasazi. Not even their real name, of course. Just a Navajo word that means . . ." She glanced at Chee. "Old Ones. Ancestors of our enemies. Something like that?"

"Close enough," Chee said.

"But Ellie has identified a single human being in what has

always just been statistics. An artist. Did you know that she'd arranged her pots chronologically . . . showing how her technique developed?"

The question was aimed at Luna. He shook his head.

"And it's very logical. You can see it. Even if you don't know much about pots, or glazing, or inscribing, or any of those decorative techniques."

Luna seemed to have decided about then that his self-interest dictated a change in posture on this issue.

"She's done some really original work, Ellie has," he said. "Pretty well pinned down where this potter worked, up Chaco Wash at a little ruins we call Kin Nahasbas. She did that by establishing that a lot of pots made with this potter's technique had been broken there before they were fully baked in the kiln fire. Then she tied a bunch of pots dug up at Chetro Ketl and Wijiji to the identical personal techniques. Trade pots, you know. One kind swapped to people at Chetro Ketl and another sort to Wijiji. Both with this man's—this potter's peculiar decorating strokes. Hasn't been published yet, but I think she has it pinned."

It gave Leaphorn a sense of déjà vu, as if he remembered a graduate student over some supper in a dormitory at Tempe saying exactly these same words. The human animal's urge to know. To leave no mysteries. Here, to look through the dirt of a thousand years into the buried privacy of an Anasazi woman. "To understand the human species," his thesis chairman liked to say. "To understand how we came to behave the way we do." But finally it had seemed to Leaphorn he could understand this better among the living. It was the spring he'd met Emma. When the semester ended in May he'd left Arizona State and his graduate fellowship and his intentions of becoming Dr. Leaphorn, and joined the recruit class of the Navajo Tribal Police. And he and Emma . . .

Leaphorn noticed Chee watching him. He cleared his throat. Sipped coffee.

"Did you have any clear idea of what she was excited about?" Leaphorn asked. "I mean just before she disappeared. We know she drove over to Bluff and talked to a man over there named Houk. Man who sometimes deals in pots. She asked him about a pot she'd seen advertised in an auction catalog. Wanted to know where it came from. Houk told us she was very intense about it. He told her how to get the documentation letter. Did she say why she was going to New York?"

"Not to me, she didn't," Mrs. Luna said.

"Or why she was excited?"

"I know some more of those polychrome pots had turned up. Several, I think. Same potter. Some identical and some with a more mature style. Later work. And it turned out they came from some-where else—away from the Chaco. She thought she could prove her potter had migrated."

"Did you know Ellie had a pistol?"

Luna and his wife spoke simultaneously. "I didn't," she said. Luna said: "It doesn't surprise me. I'd guess Maxie has one, too. For snakes," he added, and laughed. "Actually it's for safety."

"Do you know if she ever hired Jimmy Etcitty to find pots for her?"

"Boy, that was a shock," Luna said. "He hadn't worked here long. Less than a year. But he was a good hand. And a good man."

"And he didn't mind digging around graves."

"He was a Christian," Luna said. "A fundamentalist born-again Christian. No more *chindi*. But no, I doubt if he worked for Ellie. Hadn't heard of it."

"Had you ever heard he might be a Navajo Wolf?" Leaphorn asked. "Into any kind of witchcraft. Being a skinwalker?"

Luna looked surprised. And so, Leaphorn noticed, did Jim Chee. Not at the question, Leaphorn guessed. That fooling around with the bones they'd found at the ruins would suggest witchcraft to anyone who knew the Navajo tradition of skinwalkers robbing graves for bones to grind into corpse powder. But Chee would be surprised at Leaphorn's thinking. Leaphorn was aware that his contempt for the Navajo witchcraft business was widely known throughout the department. Chee, certainly, was aware of it. They had worked together in the past.

"Well," Luna said. "Not exactly. But the other men who worked here didn't have much to do with him. Maybe that was because he was willing to dig around the burials. Had given up the traditional ways. But they gossiped about him. Not to me but among themselves. And I sort of sensed they were wary of him."

"Davis told me Lehman came. The man she had the appoint-ment with."

"Her project supervisor? Yeah."

"Did he say what the meeting was about?"

"She'd told him she had one more piece of evidence to get and then she'd be ready to publish. And she wanted to show it all to him and talk it over. He stuck around the next day and then drove back to Albuquerque."

"I'll get his address from you," Leaphorn said. "Did he have any idea what that one piece of evidence was?"

"He thought she'd probably found some more pots. Ones that fit. He said she was supposed to have them when they met."

Leaphorn thought about that. He noticed Chee had marked it, too. It seemed to mean that when Ellie left Chaco it was to pick up those final pots.

"Would Maxie Davis or Elliot be likely to know any more about all this?"

Mrs. Luna answered that one. "Maxie, maybe. She and Ellie were friends." She considered that statement, found it too strong. "Sort of friends. At least they'd known each other for years. I don't think they'd ever worked together—as Maxie and Elliot sometimes do. Teamed."

"Teamed," Leaphorn said.

Mrs. Luna looked embarrassed. "Sue," she said. "Allen. Don't you two have any homework? Tomorrow is a school day."

"Not me," Allen said. "I did mine on the bus."

"Me either," Sue said. "This is interesting."

"They're friends," Mrs. Luna said, looking at Sue, but meaning Maxie and Elliot.

"When Mr. Thatcher and I talked to them it seemed pretty obvious that Elliot wanted it that way," Leaphorn said. "I wasn't so sure about Miss Davis."

"Elliot wants to get married," Mrs. Luna said. "Maxie doesn't." She glanced at her children again, and at Luna.

"Kids," Luna said. "Sue, you better see about your horse. And Allen, find something to do."

They pushed back their chairs. "Nice to have met you," Allen said, nodding to Leaphorn and to Chee.

"Great children," Leaphorn said, as they disappeared down the hallway. "They ride the bus? To where?"

"Crownpoint," Mrs. Luna said.

"Wow!" Chee said. "I used to ride a school bus about twenty-five miles and that seemed forever."

"About sixty miles or so, each way," Luna said. "Makes an awful long day for 'em. But that's the nearest school."

"We could teach them out here," Mrs. Luna said. "I have a teacher's certificate. But they need to see other children. Nothing but grown-ups at Chaco."

"Two young women and one young man," Leaphorn said.

"Was there any friction between the women over that? Any sort of jealousy?"

Luna chuckled.

Mrs. Luna smiled. "Eleanor wouldn't be much competition in that race," she said. "Unless the man wants an intellectual, and then it's about even. Besides, I think in Randall Elliot you have one of those one-woman men. He left a job in Washington and worked his way into a project out here. Just following her. I think he's sort of obsessive about it."

"Delete the 'sort of,' " Luna said. "Make it downright obsessive. And sad, too." He shook his head. "Elliot's a sort of macho guy most ways. Played football at Princeton. Flew a navy helicopter in Vietnam. Won a Navy Cross and some other decorations. And he's made himself a good name in physical anthropology for a man his age. Got stuff published about genetics in archaic populations. That sort of stuff. And Maxie refuses to take anything he does seriously. It's the game she plays."

From down the hall came the high, sweet sound of a harmonica—and then the urgent nasal whine of Bob Dylan. Almost instantly the volume was muted.

"Not a game," Mrs. Luna said, thoughtfully. "It's the way Maxie is."

"Reverse snob, you mean?" Luna asked.

"More to it than that. Kind of a sense of justice. Or injustice, maybe."

Luna looked at Leaphorn and Chee. "To explain what we're talking about, and maybe why we're doing this gossiping, there's no way Maxie would be jealous of Dr. Friedman. Or anybody else, I think. Maxie is the ultimate self-made woman from what I've heard about her. Off of some worn-out farm in Nebraska. Her father was a widower, so she had to help raise the little kids. Went to a dinky rural high school. Scholarship to University of Nebraska, working her way through as a housekeeper in a sorority. Graduate scholarship to Madison, working her way through again. Trying to send money home to help Papa and the kids. Never any help for her. So she meets this man from old money, Exeter Academy, where the tuition would have fed her family for two years. Where you have tutors helping you if you need it. And then Princeton, and graduate school at Harvard, all that." Luna sipped his coffee. "Opposite ends of the economic scale. Anyway, nothing Elliot can do impresses Maxie. It was all given to him."

"Even the navy career?"

"Especially the navy," Mrs. Luna said. "I asked her about that. She said, 'Of course, Randall has an uncle who's an admiral, and an aunt who's married to an undersecretary of the navy, and somebody else who's on the Senate Armed Services Committee. So he starts out with a commission.' And I said something like, 'You can hardly blame him for that,' and she said she didn't blame him. She said it was just that Randall has never had a chance to do anything himself." Mrs. Luna shook her head. "And then she said, 'He might be a pretty good man. Who knows? How can you tell?' Isn't that odd?"

"It sounds odd to me," Leaphorn said. "In Vietnam, he was evacuating the wounded?"

"I think so," Luna said.

"That was it," Mrs. Luna said. "I asked Maxie about that. She said, 'You know, he probably could have done something on his own if he had the chance. But officers give each other decorations. Especially if it pleases Uncle Admiral.' 'Uncle Admiral,' that's what she said. And then she told me her younger brother was in Vietnam, too. She said he was an enlisted man. She said a helicopter flew his body out. But no uncles gave him any decorations."

Mrs. Luna looked sad. "Bitter," she said. "Bitter. I remember the night we'd been talking about this. I'd said something about Randall flying a helicopter and she said, 'What chance do you think you or I would have had to be handed a helicopter to fly?' "

Leaphorn thought of nothing to say about that. Mrs. Luna rose, asked about coffee refills, and began clearing away the dishes. Luna asked if they'd like to spend the night in one of the temporary personnel apartments.

"We better be getting back home," Leaphorn said.

The night was dead still, lit by a half-moon. From the visitor camping area up the canyon there was the sound of laughter. Allen was walking up the dirt road toward his house. As he watched him, it occurred to Leaphorn how everyone knew Eleanor Friedman-Bernal had left so early on her one-way trip.

"Allen," Leaphorn called. "What time do you catch the bus in the morning?"

"It's supposed to get here about five minutes before six," Allen said. "Usually about then."

"Down by the road?"

Allen pointed. "At the intersection down there."

"Did you see Ellie drive away?"

"I saw her loading up her car," Allen said.

"You talk to her?"

"Not much," Allen said. "Susy said hello. And she said something about you kids have a good day at school and we said for her to have a good weekend. Something like that. Then we went down and caught the bus."

"Did you know she was going away for the weekend?"

"Well," Allen said, "she was putting her stuff in her car."

"Sleeping bag, too?" Maxie said she owned one, but he hadn't found it in her apartment.

"Yeah," Allen said. "Whole bunch of stuff. Even a saddle."

"Saddle?"

"Mr. Arnold's," Allen said. "He used to work here. He's a biologist. Collects rocks with lichens on them, and he used to live in one of the temporary apartments. Dr. Friedman had his saddle. She was putting it in her car."

"She'd borrowed it from him?"

"I guess so," Allen said. "She used to have a horse. Last year it was."

"Do you know where this Mr. Arnold lives now?"

"Up in Utah," Allen said. "Bluff."

"How'd she sound? Okay? Same as usual? Nervous?"

"Happy," Allen said. "I'd say she sounded happy."

FOR MOST OF HIS LIFE—since his early teens at least—knowing that he was smarter than most people had been a major source of satisfaction for Harrison Houk. Now, standing with his back pressed against the wall of the horse stall in the barn, he knew that for once he had not been smart enough. It was an unusual feeling, and chilling. He thought of that aphorism of southern Utah's hard country—if you want to be meaner than everybody else without dying young, you have to be smarter than everybody else. More than once Harrison Houk had heard that rule applied to him. He enjoyed the reputation it implied. He deserved it. He had gotten rich in a country where almost everybody had gotten poor. It had made him enemies, the way he had done it. He controlled grazing leases in ways that might not have stood grand jury scrutiny. He bought livestock, and sold livestock, under sometimes peculiar circumstances. He obtained Anasazi pots from people who had no idea what they were worth and sometimes sold them to people who only thought they knew what they were getting. He had arranged deals so lopsided that, when daylight hit them, they brought the high councilor of his Latter-day Saints stake down from Blanding to remind him of what was said about such behavior in the Book of Mormon. Even his stake president had written once exhorting him to make things right. But Houk had been smart enough not to die young. He was old now, and he intended to become very, very old. That was absolutely necessary. Things remained for him to do.

Now more than ever. Responsibilities. Matters of clearing his conscience. He hadn't stopped at much, but he'd never had a human life on his hands before. Not this directly. Never before.

He stood against the wall, trying to think of a plan. He should have recognized the car more quickly, and understood what it must mean. Should have instantly made the link between the killing of Etcitty and the rest of it. He would have when he was younger. Then his mind worked like lightning. Now the killings had made him nervous. They could have been motivated by almost anything, of course. Greed among thieves. Malice over a woman. God knows what. Almost anything. But the instinct that had served him so well for so long suggested something more sinister. An erasing of tracks. A gathering in of strings. That certainly would involve him, and he should have seen. Nor should he have thought so slowly when he saw the car turning through his gate. Maybe he would have had enough time then to hobble back to the house, to the pistol in his dresser drawer or the rifle in the closet. He could only wait now, and hope, and try to think of some solution. There could be no running for it, not with the arthritis in his hip. He had to think.

Quickly. Quickly. He'd left a note for Irene. He thought Irene would be coming back for her squash and she'd wonder where he'd gone. Pinned it on the screen door, telling her he'd be out in the barn working. It was right there in plain view. The worst kind of bad luck.

He looked around him for a hiding place. Houk was not a man subject to panic. He could climb into the loft but there was no cover there. Behind him bales of alfalfa were stacked head-high. He could restack some of them, leave himself a cave. Would there be time? Not without luck. He began a new stack against the wall, leaving a space just wide enough to hold him, groaning as he felt the weight of the heavy bales grinding his hip socket. As he worked, he realized the futility. That would only delay things a few minutes. There was really no place to hide.

He noticed the pitchfork then, leaning beside the door where he'd left it. He limped over, got it, limped back to the horse stall. Maybe there would be some chance to use it. Anyway, it was better than hiding and just waiting.

He gripped the fork handle, listening. His hearing wasn't what it once had been but he could detect nothing except, now and then, the breeze blowing through the slats. The smell of the barn was in his nostrils. Dust. Dry alfalfa. The faint acid of dried horse urine. The smell of a dry autumn.

"Mr. Houk," the voice called. "You in the barn?"

Add it all together, average it out, it had been a good enough life. The first fifty years, close to wonderful, except for Brigham being sick. Even that you could live with, given the good wife he'd been blessed with. Except for the downswings of the schizophrenia, Brigham had been happy enough, most of the time. The rages came and went, but when he was out in the wild country, hunting, living alone, he seemed full of joy. Thinking back, Houk was impressed again with the memory. He'd been pretty good himself outdoors as a kid. But not like The Boy. By the time he was ten, Brigham could go up a cliff that Houk wouldn't have tried with ropes. And he knew what to eat. And how to hide. That brought back a rush of memories, and of the old, old sorrow. The Boy, the summer he was seven, missing long after suppertime. All of them hunting him. Finding him in the old coyote den under the saltbush. He'd been as terrified at being found as if he had been a rabbit dug out by a dog.

That had been the day they no longer lied to themselves about it. But nothing the doctors tried had worked. The piano had helped for a while. He had a talent for it. And he could lose himself for hours just sitting there making his music. But the rages came back. And putting him away had been unspeakable and unthinkable.

"Houk?" the voice said. Now it was just beyond the barn wall. "I need to talk to you."

And now he could hear footsteps, the door with the draggy hinge being pulled open.

One thing he had to do. He couldn't leave it undone. He should have handled it yesterday, as soon as he found out about it. Yesterday—personally. It had to be taken care of. It wasn't something you went away and left—not a human life.

He took out his billfold, found a business card from a welldrilling outfit in it, and began writing on its back, holding the card awkwardly against the billfold.

"Houk," the voice said. It was inside the barn now. "I see you there, through the slats. Come out."

No time now. He couldn't let the note be found, except by the police. He pushed it down inside his shorts. Just as he did, he heard the stall door opening.

12

IT WAS RAINING IN NEW YORK. L. G. Marcy, the director of public affairs to whom Joe Leaphorn was referred, proved to be a slender, stylish woman with gray hair, and eyes as blue as blade steel. On drier days, the expanse of glass behind her desk looked out upon the rooftops of midtown Manhattan. She examined Leaphorn's card, turned it over to see if the back offered more information, and then glanced up at him.

"You want to see the documentation on an artifact," she said. "Is that correct?" She glanced down at the open catalog Leaphorn had handed her.

"That's all. Just this Anasazi pot," Leaphorn said. "We need to know the site it came from."

"I can assure you it was legal," Ms. Marcy said. "We do not deal in pots collected in violation of the Antiquities Preservation Act."

"I'm sure that's true," said Leaphorn, who was equally sure no sane pot hunter would ever certify that he had taken a pot illegally. "We presume the pot came from private land. We simply need to know which private land. Whose ranch."

"Unfortunately, that pot sold. All pots went in that auction. So we don't have the documentation. The documentation went to the buyer. Along with the pot," L. G. Marcy said. She smiled, closed the catalog, handed it to Leaphorn. "Sorry," she said.

"Who was the buyer?"

"We have a problem there," she said. "It is Nelson's policy to cooperate with the police. It is also Nelson's policy to respect the confidence of our customers. We never tell anyone the identity of buyers unless we have their advance clearance to do so." She leaned across the desk to return Leaphorn's card. "That rarely happens," she said. "Usually, none of the parties concerned wants publicity. They value privacy. On rare occasions, the object involved is so important that publicity is inevitable. But rarely. And in this case, the object is not the sort that attracts the news media."

Leaphorn put the card in the pocket of his uniform shirt. The shirt was damp from the rain Leaphorn had walked through from his hotel toward this office building before ducking for shelter into a drugstore. To his surprise, the store sold umbrellas. Leaphorn had bought one, the first he'd ever owned, and continued his journey under it—tremendously self-conscious—thinking he would own the only umbrella in Window Rock, and perhaps the only umbrella on the reservation, if not in all of Arizona. He was conscious of it now, lying wetly across his lap, while he waited silently for L. G. Marcy to add to her statement. Leaphorn had learned early in his career that this Navajo politeness often clashed with white abhorrence for conversational silences. Sometimes the resulting uneasiness caused *belagana* witnesses to blurt out more than they intended to say. While he waited, he noticed the prints on the wall. All, if Leaphorn could judge, done by female artists. The same for the small abstract sculpture on the Marcy desk. The silence stretched. It wasn't going to work with this *belagana.*

It didn't.

The pause caused L. G. Marcy's smile to become slightly bent. Nothing more. She outwaited him. About his own age, Leaphorn thought, but she looked like a woman in her mid-thirties.

Leaphorn stirred. Moved the umbrella off his lap. "I believe the FBI notified your company that we are investigating two homicides," he said. "This particular pot seems to figure into it. Your client won't be embarrassed. Not in any way. We simply . . ."

"I'm not sure the FBI exactly notified us of anything," Ms. Marcy said. "An FBI agent called from . . ." She examined a notebook. ". . . Albuquerque, New Mexico, and told us that a representative of the Navajo Tribal Police would call today about an artifact we had handled. He said our cooperation would be appreciated. The call was referred to me, and when I questioned him about what the federal government interest might be, this agent, this Mr. Sharkey, he, well . . ." Ms. Marcy hunted politely for a word politer than "weaseled." "He made it appear that his call was not official at all. It was intended as a sort of a personal introduction."

Leaphorn simply nodded. Sharkey hadn't wanted to make the call, had foreseen embarrassment, had been talked into it. Having been caught at it, Sharkey would be angry and hard to deal with. But then in a few more days, nothing like that would matter. Leaphorn would be a civilian. He nodded again.

"There's a system for dealing with problems like this, of course," Ms. Marcy said. "One petitions the appropriate court for an injunction. You then serve this order on us, and we provide you with the information. The requirement that we make available evidence needed in a judicial proceeding supersedes our own need to maintain a confidential relationship with our customers." Her expression was bland.

After a moment, Leaphorn said, "Of course that's a possibility. We'd like to avoid it if we could." He shrugged. "The paperwork. We'd like to avoid all the delay." And, he thought, the problem of persuading the court that an item circled in a Nelson's catalog has anything at all to do with anything.

"That's understandable," Ms. Marcy said. "I think you can also understand our position. Our clients rely on us to keep transactions confidential. For many good reasons." She made an inclusive gesture with small white hands. "Burglars," she said, "for one example. Former wives. Business reasons. So you must understand . . ."

Ms. Marcy began pushing back her chair. When she rises, Leaphorn thought, she will tell me that without a court order she cannot give me any information. He did something he almost never did. He interrupted.

"Our problem is time," he said. "A woman's life may be at stake."

Ms. Marcy lowered herself back into the chair. That little motion brought to Leaphorn's nostrils an awareness of perfume, and powder, and fine feminine things. It reminded him, with overpowering force, of Emma. He closed his eyes, and opened them.

"A woman who was very interested in this particular pot—the woman who drew the circle around it in your catalog—she's been missing for weeks," Leaphorn said. He took out his wallet, extracted his photograph of Dr. Eleanor Friedman-Bernal, the bride. He handed it to Ms. Marcy. "Did she come in to see you? This autumn? Or call?"

"Yes," Ms. Marcy said. "She was in." She studied the photograph, frowning. Leaphorn waited until she looked up.

"Dr. Eleanor Friedman-Bernal," he said. "An anthropologist. Published a lot of papers in the field of ceramics—and of primitive ceramic art. We gather that Dr. Friedman-Bernal believes she has discovered an Anasazi potter whose work she can specifically identify. Did she tell you all that?"

As he related this, Leaphorn was aware of how mundane and unimportant it must sound to a layman. In fact, it sounded trivial to him. He watched Ms. Marcy's face.

"Some of it," Ms. Marcy said. "It would be fascinating if she can prove it."

"From what we can find out, Dr. Friedman-Bernal identified a decorative technique in the finishing of a kind of pottery called St. John Polychrome—a kind made in the last stages of the Anasazi civilization. She found that technique was peculiar to one single specific Anasazi potter."

"Yes. That's what she said."

Leaphorn leaned forward. If his persuasion didn't work, he'd wasted two days on airplanes and a night in a New York hotel.

"I gather that this woman, this Anasazi potter, had some special talent which the doctor spotted. Dr. Friedman-Bernal was able to trace her work backward and forward in time through scores of pots, arranging them chronologically as this talent developed. The potter worked at Chaco Canyon, and her work turned up at several of the villages there. But recently—probably earlier this year—Friedman-Bernal began finding pots that seemed to come from somewhere else. And they were later pots—with the woman's style matured. Your spring auction catalog carried a photograph of one of these pots. We found the catalog in Dr. Friedman-Bernal's room, with the photograph circled."

Ms. Marcy was leaning forward now. "But those pots, they were so stylized," she said. "So much alike. How . . . ?" She didn't complete the question.

"I'm not sure," Leaphorn said. "I think she does it the way graphologists identify handwriting. Something like that."

"It makes sense," Ms. Marcy said.

"From what we know, from what Friedman-Bernal told other anthropologists, she seems to have believed that she could find the place to which this potter moved when the Chaco civilization collapsed," Leaphorn said.

"About right," Ms. Marcy said. "She said she thought this pot was the key. She said she had come across several shards, and one complete pot, which she was sure came from a late phase in this potter's work—an extension and refinement and maturing of her techniques. The pot she'd seen in our catalog seemed to be exactly identical to this work. So she wanted to study it. She wanted to know where she could go to see it, and she wanted to see our documentation."

"Did you tell her?"

"I told her our policy."

"So you didn't tell her who had bought it? Or how to contact the buyer?"

Ms. Marcy sighed, allowed her expression to show a flash of impatience.

"I told her the same thing I am telling you. One of the reasons people have been dealing with Nelson's for more than two hundred years is because of our reputation. They know they can depend, absolutely and without a qualm of doubt, on Nelson's keeping transactions in confidence."

Leaphorn leaned forward.

"Dr. Friedman-Bernal flew back to Albuquerque after she talked to you. Then she drove back to Chaco Canyon, where she lives and works. The following Friday she got up very early, put her sleeping bag into her car, and drove away. She'd told her friends she'd be gone for a day or two. We suspect that somehow she found out where this pot had come from and went to see if she could find something to prove it. Probably to see if there were other such pots, or potsherds, at the place."

He leaned back, folded his hands across his chest, wondering if this would work. If it didn't, he was near a dead end. There was Chee, of course. He'd asked Chee to find the Reverend Slick Nakai—to learn from Nakai everything the man knew about where those damned pots were coming from. Chee seemed interested. Chee would do his best. But how smart was Chee? He should have waited, done it himself, not risked having it all screwed up.

"She vanished," Leaphorn said. "No trace of the woman, or car, or anything. Not a word to anyone. As if Eleanor Friedman-Bernal had never existed."

Ms. Marcy picked up the photograph and studied it. "Maybe she just went away," she said, looking up at Leaphorn. "You know. Too much work. Too much stress. Suddenly you just want to say to hell with it. Maybe that was it." She said it as a woman who knows the feeling.

"Possibly," Leaphorn said. "However, the evening before she left she spent a lot of time fixing a dinner. Marinated the meat entrée, all that. The professor she had worked with was coming in from Albuquerque. She fixed this fancy dinner and put it in the refrigerator. And at dawn the next morning she put her sleeping bag and things like that in her car and drove away."

Ms. Marcy considered. She took the picture of Eleanor Friedman as a bride from the desk and looked at it again.

"Let me see what I can do," she said. She picked up the telephone. "Will you wait outside just a moment?"

The reception room had no view of the rain. Just walls displaying abstract prints, and a receptionist in whom Leaphorn's damp Navajo Tribal Police uniform had aroused curiosity. He sat against the wall, glancing through an *Architectural Digest,* aware of the woman staring at him, wishing he had worn civilian clothes. But maybe it wasn't the uniform. Maybe it was the damp Navajo inside it.

Ms. Marcy came out in a little less than ten minutes. She handed Leaphorn a card. It bore a name, Richard DuMont, and an address on East Seventy-eighth Street.

"He said he would see you tomorrow morning," she said. "At eleven."

Leaphorn stood. "I appreciate this," he said.

"Sure," she said. "I hope you'll let me know. If you find her I mean."

Leaphorn spent the rest of the afternoon prowling through the Museum of Modern Art. He sat, finally, where he could see the patio of sculpture, the rain-stained wall behind it, and the rainy sky above. Like all dry-country people, Leaphorn enjoyed rain—that rare, longed-for, refreshing blessing that made the desert bloom and life possible. He sat with his head full of thoughts and watched the water run down the bricks, drip from the leaves, form its cold pools on the flagstones, and give a slick shine to Picasso's goat.

The goat was Leaphorn's favorite. When they were young and he was attending the FBI Academy, he had brought Emma to see New York. They had discovered Picasso's goat together. He had already been staring at it when Emma had laughed, and plucked at his sleeve, and said: "Look. The mascot of the Navajo Nation."

He had an odd sensation as he remembered this, as if he could see them both as they had been then. Very young, standing by this glass wall looking out into the autumn rain. Emma, who was even more beautiful when she laughed, was laughing.

"Perfect for us Dineh," she'd said. "It's starved, gaunt, bony, ugly. But look! It's tough. It endures." And she had hugged his arm in the delight of her discovery, her face full of the joy, and the beauty, that Leaphorn had found nowhere else. And of course, it was true. That gaunt goat would have been the perfect symbol. Something to put on a pedestal and display. Miserable and starved, true enough. But it was also pregnant and defiant—exactly right to challenge the world at the entrance of the ugly octagonal Tribal Council meeting hall at Window Rock. Leaphorn remembered their having coffee at the museum café and then walking out and patting the goat. The sensation came back to him now—wet, cold metal slick under his palm—utterly real. He got up and hurried out of the museum into the rain, leaving the umbrella hanging forgotten on the chair.

Leaphorn took a cab to the Seventy-eighth Street address, got there a quarter of an hour early, and spent the time prowling the neighborhood—a territory of uniformed doormen and expensive dogs walked by persons who seemed to have been hired for the job. He rang the door chimes at eleven exactly. He waited on the steps, looking at the sky down the street. It would rain again, and soon—probably before noon. An old man, stooped and gray in a wrinkled gray suit, opened the door and stood silently, looking at him patiently.

"My name is Leaphorn," he said. "I have an appointment with Richard DuMont."

"In the study," the man said, motioning Leaphorn in.

The study was a long, high-ceilinged room down a long, high-ceilinged hall. A man in a dark blue dressing gown was sitting at the end of a long library table. Light from a floor lamp beside his chair reflected off the white of a breakfast cloth, and china, and silver.

"Ah, Mr. Leaphorn," the man said, smiling. "You are most punctual. I hope you will excuse me for not getting up to greet you." He tapped the arms of the wheelchair in which he was sitting. "And I hope you will join me for some breakfast."

"No thank you," Leaphorn said. "I've eaten."

"Some coffee, then?"

"I have never refused coffee. Never will."

"Nor I," DuMont said. "Another of my vices. But seat yourself." He gestured toward a blue plush chair. "The woman at Nelson's told me you are hunting a missing woman. An anthropologist. And that murder is involved." DuMont's small gray eyes peered at Leaphorn, avid with interest. Unusual eyes set in a pinched, narrow face under eyebrows almost identical in color to his pale skin.

"Murder," he repeated, "and a missing woman." His voice was clear, precise, easy to understand. But like his face it was a small voice. Any background noise would bury it.

"Two pot hunters were killed," Leaphorn said. Something about DuMont was unpleasant. Too much interest? But interest in such a man seemed natural enough. After all, he was a collector. "Including the man who found my pot," DuMont said, with what seemed to Leaphorn to be a sort of pleasure. "Or so that woman at Nelson's told me."

"We think so," Leaphorn said. "Ms. Marcy told me you would be willing to let me see the documentation he sent in. We want to know where he found the pot."

"The document," DuMont said. "Yes. But tell me how the man was killed. How the woman is missing." He raised his arms wide apart, his small mouth grinning. "Tell me all of that."

Behind DuMont, on both sides of a great formal fireplace, shelves formed the wall. The shelves were lined with artifacts. Pots, carved stone images, baskets, fetishes, masks, primitive weapons. Just behind the man, a pedestal held a massive stone head—Olmec, Leaphorn guessed. Smuggled out of Mexico in defiance of that country's antiquities act.

"Mr. Etcitty and a companion were digging up an Anasazi ruin, apparently collecting pots. Someone shot them," Leaphorn said. "An anthropologist named Friedman-Bernal was specializing in this sort of ceramics. In fact, she was interested in this pot you bought. She disappeared. Left Chaco Canyon—she worked there—for a weekend and hasn't come back."

Leaphorn stopped. He and DuMont looked at each other. The stooped, gray man who had admitted Leaphorn appeared at his elbow, placed a small table beside his chair, spread a cloth upon it, put a silver tray on the cloth. The tray held a cup of paper-thin china sitting on a translucent saucer, a silver pot from which steam issued, two smaller silver containers, and a silver spoon. The gray man poured coffee into Leaphorn's cup and disappeared.

"One doesn't buy merely the object," DuMont said. "One wants what goes with it. The history. This head, for example, came out of the jungles in northern Guatemala. It had decorated the doorway to a chamber in a temple. The room where captives were held until they were sacrificed. I'm told the Olmec priests strangled them with a cord."

DuMont covered the lower part of his small face with his napkin and produced a small cough, his avid eyes on Leaphorn.

"And this Anasazi pot of yours. Why is it worth five thousand dollars?" He laughed, a small, tinkling sound. "It's not much of a pot, really. But the Anasazi! Such mysterious people. You hold this pot, and think of the day it was made. A civilization that had grown a thousand years was dying." He stared into Leaphorn's eyes. "As ours is surely dying. Its great houses were standing empty. No more great ceremonials in the kivas. This is about when my pot was made—so my appraisers tell me. Right at the end. The twilight. In the dying days."

DuMont did something at the arm of his wheelchair and said: "Edgar."

"Yes sir." Edgar's voice seemed to come from under the table.

"Bring me that pot we bought last month. And the documents."

"Yes sir."

"So stories are important to me," DuMont said to Leaphorn. "What you could tell me has its value here. I show my new pot to my friends. I tell them not just of the Anasazi civilization, but of murder and a missing woman." He grinned a small, prim grin, showing small, perfect teeth.

Leaphorn sipped his coffee. Hot, fresh, excellent. The china was translucent. To the right of DuMont a row of high windows lined the wall. The light coming through them was dim, tinted green by the vines that covered them. Rain streamed down the glass.

"Did I make my point?" DuMont said.

"I think so," Leaphorn said.

"Tit for tat. You want information from me. In exchange it seems to me only fair that you give me my story. The story to go with my pot."

"I did," Leaphorn said.

DuMont raised two white hands, fluttered them. "Details, details, details," he said. "All the bloody details. The details to pass along."

Leaphorn told him the details. How the bodies were found. How the men had been killed. Who they were. He described the scene. He described the bones. DuMont listened, rapt.

". . . and there we are," Leaphorn concluded. "No leads, really. Our missing woman might be a lead to the killer. More likely she's another victim. But it's all vague. We know just that she was interested in the same pots. Just that she's missing."

Edgar had returned early in this account and stood beside

DuMont, holding a pot and a manila folder. The pot was small, about the size of a man's head. A little larger than DuMont's skull.

"Hand the pot to Mr. Leaphorn," DuMont said. "And the documents, please."

Edgar did so. And stood there, stooped and gray, his presence making Leaphorn edgy. Why didn't the man sit down? Leaphorn placed the pot carefully on the table, noticing the smooth feel of the glazing, aware that it had nothing to tell him. He opened the folder.

It contained what appeared to be two bills of sale, one from Harrison Houk to Nelson's and one from Nelson's to DuMont, and a form with its blanks filled in by an awkward hand. It was signed by Jimmy Etcitty.

Leaphorn checked the date. The previous June. He checked the space marked "Place of recovery." The entry read:

About eight or ten miles down San Juan from Sand Island. From mouth of canyon on north side of river go up the canyon about five and a half miles to the place where there are three ruins on the left side of the canyon at a low level. Right there by the lower ruin are a bunch of pictures of Anasazi *yei* figures and one looks like a big baseball umpire holding up a pink chest protector. On the north side of the canyon one of the ruins is built against the cliff on the shelf above the canyon bottom. Above it on the higher shelf there is a cave under the cliff with a ruin built in it, and above that in a smaller cave there is another ruin. All these ruins are on private land under lease to my friend Harrison Houk of Bluff, Utah. This pot came from a trench beside the south wall of the ruin against the cliff. It was faceup, with three other pots, all broken, and a skeleton, or part of a skeleton. When found, the pot had nothing but dirt in it.

Leaphorn was surprised at the intensity of his disappointment. It was exactly what he should have expected. He checked the other blanks and found nothing interesting. DuMont was watching him, grinning.

"A problem?"

"A little case of lying," Leaphorn said.

"Just what Dr. Friedman said." DuMont chuckled. "False, false, false."

"You talked to Dr. Friedman?"

"Just like this," DuMont said, delighted with Leaphorn's amazement. "Your missing lady was right here. In that same chair. Edgar, was she drinking from the same cup?"

"I have no idea, sir," Edgar said.

"Same questions, anyway." DuMont gestured. "Fascinating."

"How did she find you?"

"As you did, I presume. Through Nelson's. She called, and identified herself, and made an appointment."

Leaphorn didn't comment. He was remembering her note. "Call Q!" Ellie seemed to have had a pipeline into the auction house that got her past Ms. Marcy.

"She said the certification was false? The location?"

"She said that canyon isn't where Mr. . . . Mr. . . ."

"Etcitty," Edgar said.

"Where Mr. Etcitty said it was." DuMont laughed. "Running the wrong way, she said. Too far down the river. Things like that."

"She was right," Leaphorn said. If that false location had an effect on DuMont's five-thousand-dollar pot, it had no effect on his humor. He was grinning his small white grin.

"She was quite upset," he said. "Disappointed. Are you?"

"Yes," Leaphorn said. "But I shouldn't be. It's exactly what I should have expected."

"Edgar has made you a copy of that," DuMont said. "To take with you."

"Thank you," Leaphorn said. He pushed himself out of the chair. He wanted to get out of this room. Away. Out into the clean rain.

"And Edgar will give you my card," DuMont said from behind him. "Call me with all the details. When you find her body."

13

FINDING THE REVEREND SLICK NAKAI had not been easy. At the Nageezi site Chee found only the trampled place where the revival tent had stood, and the trash left behind. He asked around, learned that Nakai was known at the Brethren Navajo Mission. He drove to Escrito. The *belagana* at the mission there knew of Nakai but not his whereabouts. If he had scheduled a revival around there, they hadn't heard of it. Must be a mistake. Chee left, sensing that he wasn't alone in his disapproval of Slick Nakai. At Counselors Trading Post, where people tend to know what's happening on the north side of the Checkerboard Reservation, he hung around until he found someone who knew of a family not only fervently following the Jesus Road, but doing so as prescribed by the tenets of Nakai's sect. It was the family of Old Lady Daisy Manygoats. The Manygoats outfit, unfortunately, lived way over by Coyote Canyon. Chee drove to Coyote Canyon, stopped at the chapter house, got directions down a road that was bad even by reservation standards, and found nobody at home at the Manygoats place except a boy named Darcy Ozzie. Yes, Darcy Ozzie knew about the Reverend Slick Nakai, had in fact gone to his recent revival over at Nageezi.

"They say he was going to preach over between White Rock and Tsaya, over there by the mountains," the boy said, indicating west in the Navajo fashion by a twist of his lips. "And then when he was finished there, he was going way over into Arizona to have a revival over there by Lower Greasewood. Over there south of the Hopi Reservation."

So Chee drove up the Chuska Valley toward Tsaya, with the Chuska Range rising blue to his left and autumn asters forming two lines of color along the opposite sides of the cracked old asphalt of U.S. 666, and snakeweed and chamisa coloring the slopes mottled tan-yellow-gold and the November sky dark blue overhead.

He had quit thinking of Slick Nakai about halfway between Nageezi and Coyote Canyon, having exhausted every possible scenario their meeting might produce. Then he considered Mary Landon. She loved him, he concluded. In her way. But there was love, and then there was love. She would not change her mind about living her life on the reservation. And she was right. Lacking some very basic change in Mary, she would not be happy raising their children here. He wanted Mary to neither change nor be unhappy. Which led him back to himself. She would marry him if he left the reservation. And he could do that. He'd had offers. He could go into federal law enforcement. Work somewhere where their children could go to school with white kids and be surrounded by white culture. Mary would be happy. Or would she? He could still be a Navajo in the sense of blood, but not in the sense of belief. He would be away from family and the Slow Talking Dineh, the brothers and sisters of his maternal clan. He would be outside of Dineh Bike'yah—that territory fenced in by the four sacred mountains within which the magic of the curing ceremonials had its compulsory effect. He would be an alien living in exile. Mary Landon would not enjoy life with that Jim Chee. He could not live with an unhappy Mary Landon. It was the conclusion he always eventually reached. It left him with a sense of anger and loss. That, in turn, moved his thoughts to something else.

He thought of Janet Pete, trying to work what little he knew of her character into the solution she would find to her own problem. Would she allow her lawyer to convert her into an Indian maiden? Not enough data to be sure, but he doubted if Janet Pete would ever buy that.

Who killed Nails and Etcitty? Find the motive. There lies the answer. But there could be a dozen motives and he had no basis for guessing. Leaphorn, obviously, believed Slick Nakai somehow fit into that puzzle. But then Leaphorn knew a lot more about this business than Chee. All Chee knew was that Nakai bought pots from Etcitty—or perhaps was given them. That Etcitty was one of Nakai's born-again Christians. That Leaphorn believed Nakai sold pots to the woman missing from Chaco Canyon. That was the focus of Chee's assignment. Leaphorn's voice on the telephone had sounded tired. "You want to stick with me a little longer on this Friedman-Bernal business?" he asked. "If you do, I can arrange it with Captain Largo."

Chee had hesitated, out of surprise. Leaphorn had identified the pause as indecision.

"I should remind you again that I'm quitting the department," Leaphorn had interjected. "I'm on terminal leave right now. I already told you that. I tell you now so if you're doing me a favor, remember there's no way I can return it."

Which, Chee had thought, was a nice way of saying the reverse—I can't punish you for refusing.

"I'd like to stay on it," Chee had said. "I'd like to find out who killed those guys."

"That's not what we're working on," Leaphorn had said. "They're connected, I guess. They must be connected. But what I'm after is what happened to the woman missing from Chaco. The anthropologist."

"Okay," Chee had said. It seemed an odd focus. Two murders, apparently premeditated assassinations. And Leaphorn was devoting his leave time, and Chee's efforts, to a missing person case. Same case, probably, the way it looked now. But going at it totally backward. Well, Lieutenant Leaphorn was supposed to be smarter than Officer Chee. He had a reputation for doing things in weird ways. But he also had a reputation for guessing right.

At Tsaya, Chee found he'd missed Slick Nakai, but not by much. Nakai had canceled his planned revival there and headed north.

"Just canceled it?" Chee asked.

He was asking a plump girl of about eighteen who seemed to be in charge of the Tsaya Chapter—since she was the only one present in the chapter house.

"He sort of hurried in, and said who he was, and said he had to cancel a tent meeting that was supposed to be for tonight," she said. "It's over there on the bulletin board." She nodded toward the notices posted by the entrance.

"NOTICE!" Nakai had scrawled at the top of a sheet of notepaper:

> Due to an unexpected emergency Reverend Nakai
> is forced to cancel his revival for here.
> It will be rescheduled later if God wills it.
> —REVEREND SLICK NAKAI

"Well, shit!" said Jim Chee, aloud and in English, since Navajo lends itself poorly to such emotional expletives. He glanced at his watch. Almost four-thirty. Where the devil could Nakai have gone? He walked back to the desk where the girl was sitting. She had been watching him curiously.

"I need to find Nakai." Chee smiled at her, happy that he hadn't worn his uniform. A good many people her age looked upon Navajo Tribal Police as the adversary. "Did he say anything else? Like where he was going?"

"To me? Nothing. Just borrowed a piece of paper for his note. You one of his Christians?"

"No," Chee said. "Matter of fact, I'm a *hataalii*. I do the Blessing Way."

"Really?" the girl said.

Chee was embarrassed. "Just beginning," he said. "Just did it once." He didn't explain that the one time had been for a member of his own family. He fished out his billfold, extracted a business card, and handed it to her.

JIM CHEE

HATAALII

Singer of The Blessing Way
Available for other ceremonials

For consultation call _____
(P.O. Box 112, Shiprock, N.M.)

Since he had no telephone at his trailer, he'd left the number blank. His plan had been to list the Shiprock police station number, gambling that by the time Largo got wind of it and blew the whistle, he'd have a reputation and a following established. But the dispatcher had balked. "Besides, Jim," she'd argued, "what will the people think? They call for a singer to do a ceremonial and when the phone rings somebody says, 'Navajo Tribal Police.'"

"Give me some more," the girl said. "I'll stick one up on the board, too. Okay?"

"Sure," Chee said. "And give them to people. Especially if you hear of anybody sick."

She took the cards. "But what's a *hataalii* doing looking for a Christian preacher?"

"A minute ago, when I asked you if Nakai said anything about where he was headed, you said not to you. Did he tell somebody else?"

"He made a phone call," she said. "Asked if he could borrow the phone here"—she tapped the telephone on her desk—"and called somebody." She stopped, eyeing Chee doubtfully.

"And you overheard some of it?"

"I don't eavesdrop," she said.

" 'Course not," Chee said. "But the man's talking right there at your desk. How can you help it? Did he say where he was going?"

"No," she said. "He didn't say that."

Chee was smart enough to realize he was being teased. He smiled at her. "After a while you are going to tell me what he said," Chee said. "But not yet."

"I just might not tell you at all," she said, grinning a delighted grin.

"What if I tell you a scary story? That I'm not really a medicine man. I'm a cop and I'm looking for a missing woman, and Nakai is not really a preacher. He's a gangster, and he's already killed a couple of people, and I'm on his trail, and you are my only chance of catching him before he shoots everybody else."

She laughed. "That would fit right in with what he said on the phone. Very mysterious."

Chee managed to keep grinning. Just barely.

"Like what?"

She made herself comfortable. "Oh," she said. "He said, did you hear what happened to so-and-so? Then he listened. Then he said something like, it made him nervous. And to be careful. And then he said somebody-else-or-other was who he worried about and the only way to warn him was to go out to his hogan and find him. He said he was going to cancel his revival here and go up there. And then he listened a long time, and then he said he didn't know how far. It was over into Utah." She shrugged. "That's about it."

"About it isn't good enough."

"Well, that's all I remember."

Apparently it was. She was blank on both so-and-so and somebody-else-or-other. Chee left, thinking "over into Utah" was over into the country Leaphorn wanted Nakai cross-examined about— the source of Friedman-Bernal's pot obsession. He was also thinking that heading into the Four Corners would take him past Shiprock. Maybe he would take the night off, if he was tired when he got there. Maybe he would run Slick Nakai to earth tomorrow. But why had Nakai changed his plans and headed for the Utah border? Who knows? "So-and-so" was probably Etcitty. "Somebody-else-or-other" probably another of Nakai's converts who stole pots on the side. To Chee, Nakai was seeming increasingly odd.

He was driving through the Bisti Badlands, headed north toward Farmington, when the five o'clock news began. A woman reporting from the Durango, Colorado, station on the letting of a contract for range improvement on the Ute Mountain Reservation, and a controversy over the environmental impact of an additional ski run at Purgatory, and a recall petition being circulated to unseat a councilman at Aztec, New Mexico. Chee reached up to change the channel. He'd get more New Mexico news from a Farmington station. "In other news of the Four Corners country," the woman said, "a prominent and sometimes controversial Southeast Utah rancher and political figure has been shot to death at his ranch near Bluff."

Chee stopped, hand on the dial.

"A spokesman for the Garfield County Sheriff's Office at Blanding said the victim has been identified as Harrison Houk, a former Utah state senator and one of southern Utah's biggest ranch operators. The body of Houk was found in his barn last night. The sheriff's office said he had been shot twice.

"Some twenty years ago, Houk's family was the victim of one of the Four Corners' worst tragedies. Houk's wife and a son and daughter were shot to death, apparently by a mentally disturbed younger son who then drowned himself in the San Juan.

"Across the line in Arizona, a suit has been filed in federal district court at . . ."

Chee clicked off the radio. He wanted to think. Houk was the man to whom Nakai had sold pots. Houk lived at Bluff, on the San Juan. Maybe Etcitty was Nakai's "so-and-so." More likely it would be Houk. Could Nakai have heard of Houk's murder en route to Tsaya? Probably, on an earlier newscast. That would explain the abrupt change in plans. Or maybe Houk was "somebody-else-or-other"—the man Nakai wanted to warn. Too late for that now. Either way, it seemed clear that Nakai would be headed to somewhere very close to Bluff, to where Houk, his customer for pots, had been killed.

Chee decided he would work overtime. If he could find the elusive Nakai tonight, he would.

It proved to be surprisingly easy. On the road north toward Bluff, far enough north of Mexican Water so he was sure he'd crossed the Arizona border into Utah, Chee saw Nakai's tent trailer. It was parked maybe a quarter-mile up an old oil field road that wanders off U.S. 191 into the rocky barrens south of Caso del Eco Mesa.

Chee made an abrupt left turn, parked by the trailer, and inspected it. The tie-down ropes were in place, all four tires were aired, everything in perfect order. It had simply been unhooked and abandoned.

Chee jolted down the old road, past a silent oil pump, down into the bare stoniness of Gothic Creek, and out of that into a flatland of scattered sage and dwarf juniper. The road divided into two trails—access routes, Chee guessed, to the only two Navajo families who survived in these barrens. It was almost dark now, the western horizon a glowing, luminous copper. Which route to take? Far down the one that led straight ahead he saw Nakai's car.

He drove the five hundred yards toward it cautiously, feeling uneasy. He'd been joking with the girl at Tsaya when he cast Nakai in the role of gangster. But how did he know? He knew almost nothing. That Nakai had been preaching on the reservation for years. That he encouraged his converts to collect pots for him to sell to help finance his operation. Did he have a pistol? A criminal record? Leaphorn probably knew such things, but he hadn't confided in Chee. He slowed even more, nervous.

Nakai was sitting on the trunk of the massive old Cadillac, legs straight out, leaning against the rear window, watching him, looking utterly harmless. Chee parked behind the car, climbed out, stretched.

"Ya te'eh," Nakai said. And then he recognized Chee, and looked surprised. "We meet again—but a long way from Nageezi."

"Ya te," Chee said. "You are hard to find. I heard you were supposed to be"—he gestured southward—"first at Tsaya and then way down beyond the Hopi Country. Down at Lower Greasewood."

"Ran outta gas," Nakai said, ignoring the implied question. "This thing burns gas like a tank." He jumped down from the trunk, with the small man's natural agility. "Were you looking for me?"

"More or less," Chee said. "What brings you up here into Utah? So far from Lower Greasewood?"

"The Lord's business takes me many places," Nakai said.

"You planning a revival out here?"

"Sure," Nakai said. "When I can arrange it."

"But you left your tent," Chee said. And you're lying, he thought. Not enough people out here.

"I was on empty," Nakai said. "Thought I could save enough

gas to get where I was going. Then come back and get it." He laughed. "Waited too long to unhook. Burned too much gasoline."

"You forget to look at your gauge?"

"It was already broke when I bought this thing." Nakai laughed again. "Blessed are the poor," he said. "Didn't do no good to look at it. Before I got outta gas, I was outta money."

Chee didn't comment on that. He thought about how he could learn what Nakai was doing out here. Who he came to warn.

"Have a brother lives down there," Nakai explained. "Christian, so he's my brother in the Lord. And he's Paiute. My "born to" clan. So he's a brother that way, too. I was going to walk. And then I saw you coming."

"So you just got here?"

"Five minutes, maybe. Look, could you give me a ride? Maybe eight miles or so. I could walk it, but I'm in a hurry."

Nakai was looking down the trail, westward. Chee studied his face. The copper light gave it the look of sculpture. Metal. But Nakai wasn't metal. He was worried. Chee could think of no clever way to get him to talk about what he was doing here.

"You found out Harrison Houk was killed," Chee said. "And you headed out here. Why?"

Nakai turned, his face shadowed now. "Who's Houk?"

"The man you sold pots to," Chee said. "Remember? You told Lieutenant Leaphorn about it."

"Okay," Nakai said. "I know about him."

"Etcitty dealt with you, and with Houk, and with these pots, and he's dead. And now Houk. Both shot. And Nails, too, for that matter. Did you know him?"

"Just met him," Nakai said. "Twice, I think."

"Look," Chee said. "Leaphorn sent me to find you because of something else. He wants to locate this Eleanor Friedman-Bernal woman—find out what happened to her. He talked to you about her already. But now he wants more information. He wants to know what she said to you about looking for pots right out here in this part of the country. Along the San Juan. Up around Bluff. Around Mexican Hat."

"Just what I told him. She wanted those smooth polychrome pots. Those pinkish ones with the patterns and the wavy lines and the serration, or whatever you call it. Pots or the broken pieces. Didn't matter. And she told me she was particularly interested in anything that turned up around this part of the reservation." Nakai shrugged. "That was it."

Chee put his hands on hips and bent backward, eliminating a kink in his back. He'd spent ten hours in that pickup today. Maybe more. Too many. "If Joe Leaphorn were here," he said, "he'd say no, that wasn't quite it. She said more than that. You are trying to save time. Summarizing. Tell me everything she said. Let me do the summarizing."

Nakai looked thoughtful. An ugly little man, Chee decided, but smart.

"You're thinking that I am a cop, and that these pots came off the Navajo Reservation where they are *mucho, mucho* illegal. Felony stuff. You're thinking you are going to be careful about what you say." Chee slouched against the pickup door. "Forget it. We are doing one thing at a time and the one thing is finding this woman. Not figuring out who shot Etcitty. Not catching somebody for looting ruins on Navajo land. Just one single, simple thing. Just find Eleanor Friedman. Leaphorn seems to think she went looking for these pots. At least that's what I think he thinks. He thinks she told you where to find them. Therefore, I'd appreciate it, you'd win my gratitude and a ride to wherever you want to go, if you'll just tell me all of it. Whether or not you think it matters."

Nakai waited awhile, making sure Chee's outburst was finished.

"What matters isn't much," he said. "Let me remember a minute or two."

Behind Nakai the sunset had darkened from glowing pale copper to dark copper. Against that gaudy backdrop, two streaks of clouds were painted, blue-black and ragged. To the left, a three-quarter moon hung in the sky like a carved white rock.

"You want her words," Nakai said. "What she said, what he said, what she said. I don't remember that well. But I remember some impressions. One. She was thinking about very specific ruins. She'd been there. She knew what it looked like. Two. It was illegal. Better than that, it was on the Navajo Reservation. She good as said that. I remember I said something about it being illegal, and she said maybe it shouldn't be. I was a Navajo and it was Navajo land."

Nakai stopped. "How about the ride?"

"What else?"

"That's all I know, really. Did I say it was in a canyon? I'm sure it was. She said she'd been told about it. Didn't say who told her. Somebody she'd bought a pot from, I guess. Anyway, the way she described the place it had to be a canyon. Three ruins, she said. One down by the streambed in the talus, one on the shelf above it, and a third one out of sight in the cliff above the shelf. So that would have to be in a canyon. And that's all I know."

"Not the name of the canyon."

"She didn't know it. Said she didn't think it had one. Canyon *sin nombre.*" Nakai laughed. "She didn't tell me much, really. Just that she was very, very interested in pots, or potsherds, even little fragments, but only if they had this pinkish glaze with the wavy light lines and the serration. Said she'd triple her price for them. That she wanted to know exactly where they came from. I wondered why she didn't go try to find the place herself. I guess she didn't want to risk getting caught at it."

"Leaphorn thinks she went. Or, I think he does."

"Now," Nakai said, "I earned my ride."

Chee took him to a hogan built on the slope of a wash that drained into Gothic Creek—using three-quarters of an hour to cover less than eight jarring miles. It was almost full dark when they pulled onto the slick rock surface that formed the hogan yard, but the moon was bright enough to show why the site had been picked. A growth of cottonwoods, tamarisks, and rabbitbrush at the lip of the wash showed where a spring flowed. It was probably the only live water within thirty miles, Chee guessed, and it wasn't lively enough to support a family in the dry season. A row of rusty water barrels on a wooden rack told him that. Chee parked, raced the pickup engine to make sure the hogan's occupants had noticed their arrival, and turned off the engine. A dim light, probably from a kerosene lamp, showed through the side window. The smell of sheep, a smell that always provoked nostalgia in Chee, drifted down from a brush compound behind the house.

"You have another little problem now," Chee said.

"What?"

"This brother of yours who lives here. He steals pots for you. You want to tell him about Etcitty, and Nails, and Houk. You want to tell him to be careful—that somebody's shooting pot hunters. But I'm a cop so you don't want me to hear it."

Nakai said nothing.

"No car. No truck. At least I don't see one. Or see any place to put one on this flat rock where I couldn't see it. So somebody who lives here has gone off with the truck."

Nakai said nothing. He drew in a breath and exhaled it.

"So if I just leave you here, as you'd intended, then you're stuck. No gas and no ride to where you can get some."

"One of his sons probably has the truck," Nakai said. "He

probably keeps some gasoline here somewhere. At least a five-gallon can."

"In which case you walk that eight miles back to the Caddy with it," Chee said. "Or maybe he doesn't have any gas."

A blanket hanging over the hogan doorway swung aside. The shape of a man appeared, looking out at them.

"What do you have in mind?" Nakai said.

"You quit playing the game. I'm not going to arrest anyone for stealing pots. But I gotta find out where they came from. That's all I care about. If you don't know where that is, this Paiute Clan man here does. Let him tell me. No more games."

The Paiute Clan man was called Amos Whistler. A skinny man with four of his lower front teeth missing. He knew where the pots had come from. "Way over there, toward the west. Toward Navajo Mountain," he said, indicating the direction. "Maybe thirty miles across the Nokaito Bench." But there were no roads, just broken country, sandstone cut by one wash after another. Whistler said he had heard about the ruins years ago from an uncle, who told him to stay out of the place because the ghosts were bad in there. But he had learned about Jesus, and he didn't believe in ghosts, so he packed in with a couple of horses, but it was tough going. An ordeal. He'd lost a horse. A good one.

Chee owned an excellent U.S. Geological Survey map of the Big Reservation, a book in which each page showed everything in a thirty-two-mile square. "What's the name of the canyon?"

"I don't know if it has a name," Amos Whistler said. "Around here they say its name is Canyon Where Watersprinkler Plays His Flute." It was a long name in Navajo, and Whistler looked embarrassed when he said it.

"Would you take me in there? Rent the horses and lead me in?"

"No," Amos Whistler said. "I don't go there no more."

"I'd hire you," Chee said. "Pay you for using your horses. Good money."

"No," Whistler said. "I'm a Christian now. I know about Jesus. I don't worry about Anasazi ghosts like I did when I was a pagan. Before I walked on the Jesus Road. But I won't go into that place."

"Good money," Chee said. "No problems with the law."

"I heard him in there," Whistler said. He took two steps away from Chee, toward the hogan door. "I heard the Watersprinkler playing his flute."

14

LEAPHORN MANAGED a forward seat by the window when he changed planes in Chicago. There was nothing to see—just the topside of solid cloud cover over the great flat, fertile American heartland. Leaphorn looked down at this gray mass and thought of the river of wet air flowing up from the Gulf of Mexico, and of cold rain, and bleak, featureless landscapes closed in by a sky no more than six feet above one's forehead. At least Emma had saved them from that by holding him on the reservation.

He was depressed. He had done what he had gone to do and achieved nothing useful. All he knew that he hadn't known before was that Etcitty had been too smart to sign a pot documentation admitting a violation of federal law. Leaphorn was fairly sure that the physical description of the site must be accurate. He could think of no reason for Etcitty to have made up such a complicated description. It seemed to flow from memory. An unsophisticated man following the form's instructions, describing reality with the single lie to avoid incrimination. That helped very little. The Utah–Arizona–New Mexico border country was a maze of washes, gulches, draws, and canyons. Thousands of them, and in their sheltered, sun-facing alcoves, literally scores of thousands of Anasazi sites. He'd seen an estimate of more than a hundred thousand such sites on the Colorado Plateau, built over a period of almost a thousand years. What Etcitty had given him was like a description of a house in a big city with no idea of its street address. He could narrow it down some. Probably in southern Utah or extreme northern Arizona. Probably north of Monument Valley. Probably east of Nokaito Mesa. Probably west of Montezuma Creek. That narrowed it to an area bigger than Connecticut, occupied by maybe five thousand humans. And all he had was a site description that might be as false as its location obviously was.

Perhaps Chee had done better. An odd young man, Chee. Smart, apparently. Alert. But slightly . . . slightly what? Bent? Not exactly. It wasn't just the business of trying to be a medicine man—a following utterly incongruous with police work. He was a romantic, Leaphorn decided. That was it. A man who followed dreams. The sort who would have joined that Paiute shaman who invented the ghost dance and the vision of white men withering away and the buffalo coming back to the plains. Maybe that wasn't fair. It was more that Chee seemed to think an island of 180,000 Navajos could live the old way in a white ocean. Perhaps 20,000 of them could, if they were happy on mutton, cactus, and piñon nuts. Not practical. Navajos had to compete in the real world. The Navajo Way didn't teach competition. Far from it.

But Chee, odd as he was, would find Slick Nakai. Another dreamer, Nakai. Leaphorn shifted in the narrow seat, trying vainly for comfort. Chee would find Nakai and Chee would get from Nakai about as much information as Leaphorn would have been able to extract.

Leaphorn found himself thinking of what he would say to Emma about Chee. He shook his head, picked up a *New Yorker,* and read. Dinner came. His seatmate examined it scornfully. To Leaphorn, who had been eating his own cooking, it tasted great. They were crossing the Texas panhandle now. Below, the clouds were thinning, breaking into patches. Ahead, the earth rose like a rocky island out of the ocean of humid air that blanketed the midlands. Leaphorn could see the broken mesas of eastern New Mexico. Beyond, on the western horizon, great cloud-castle thunderheads, unusual in autumn, rose into the stratosphere. Leaphorn felt something he hadn't felt since Emma's death. He felt a kind of joy.

Something like that mood was with him when he awoke the next morning in his bed at Window Rock—a feeling of being alive, and healthy, and interested. He was still weary. The flight from Albuquerque to Gallup in the little Aspen Airways Cessna, and the drive from Gallup, had finished what reserves he had left. But the depression was gone. He cooked bacon for breakfast and ate it with toast and jelly. While he was eating the telephone rang.

Jim Chee, he thought. Who else would be calling him?

It was Corporal Ellison Billy, who handled things that needed handling for Major Nez, who was more or less Leaphorn's boss.

"There's a Utah cop here looking for you," Billy said. "You available?"

Leaphorn was surprised. "What's he want? And what kind of cop?"

"Utah State Police. Criminal Investigation Division," Billy said. "He just said he wants to talk to you. About a homicide investigation. That's all I know. Probably told the major more. You coming in?"

Homicide, he thought. The depression sagged down around him again. Someone had found Eleanor Friedman-Bernal's body. "Tell him ten minutes," he said, which was the time it took for him to drive from his house among the piñons on the high side of Window Rock to police headquarters beside the Fort Defiance Highway.

The desk had two messages for him. One from Jim Chee was short: "Found Nakai near Mexican Hat with a friend who says ruins is located in what the locals call Watersprinkler Canyon west of his place. I will stay reachable through the Shiprock dispatcher."

The other, from the Utah State Police, was shorter. It said: "Call Detective McGee re: Houk. Urgent."

"Houk?" Leaphorn said. "Any more details?"

"That's it," the dispatcher said. "Just call McGee about Houk. Urgent."

He put the message in his pocket.

The door to the major's office was open. Ronald Nez was standing behind his desk. A man wearing a blue windbreaker and a billed cap with the legend LIMBER ROPE on the crown sat against the wall. He got up when Leaphorn walked in, a tall man, middle-aged, with a thin, bony face. Acne or some other scarring disease had left cheeks and forehead pocked with a hundred small craters. Nez introduced them. Carl McGee was the name. He had not waited for a call back.

"I'll get right to it," McGee said. "We got a homicide case, and he left you a note."

Leaphorn kept his face from showing his surprise. It wasn't Friedman-Bernal.

McGee waited for a response.

Leaphorn nodded.

"Harrison Houk," McGee said. "I imagine you know him?"

Leaphorn nodded again, his mind processing this. Who would kill Houk? Why? He could see an answer to the second question.

And in general terms to the first one. The same person who had killed Etcitty, and Nails, and for the same reason. But what was that?

"What was the message?"

McGee looked at Major Nez, who looked back, expression neutral. Then at Leaphorn. This conversation was not going as McGee had intended. He extracted a leather folder from his hip pocket, took a business card from it, and handed it to Leaphorn.

BLANDING PUMPS

Well Drilling, Casing, Pulling
General Water System Maintenance
(We also fix your Septic Tanks)

The card was bent, dirty. Leaphorn guessed it had been damp. He turned it over.

The message there was scrawled in ballpoint ink.

It said:

Tell Leaphorn shes still alive up

Leaphorn handed it to Nez, without comment.

"I saw it," Nez said, and handed it back to McGee, who put it back in the folder, and the folder back in his pocket.

"What do you think?" he said. "You got any idea who the 'she' is?"

"A good idea," Leaphorn said. "But tell me about Houk. I saw him just the other day."

"Wednesday," McGee said. "To be exact." He looked at Leaphorn, expression quizzical. "That's what the woman who works for him told us. Navajo named Irene Musket."

"Wednesday sounds right," Leaphorn said. "Who killed Houk?"

McGee made a wry face. "This woman he wrote you about, maybe. Anyway, it looks like Houk quit trying to find a place to hide to tell you about her. Sounds like you two thought she was dead. Suddenly he sees her alive. He tries to tell you. She kills him."

Leaphorn was thinking that his terminal leave had five more days to run. Actually, only about four and two-thirds. He hadn't been in a mood to screw around like this for at least three months. Not since Emma got bad. He was in no mood for it today. In fact, he had never been tolerant of it. Nor for being polite to this *belagana,* who wanted to act as if Leaphorn was some sort of suspect. But he'd make one more effort to be polite.

"I've been away," he said. "Back east. Just got in last night. You're going to have to skip way back and tell me about it."

McGee told him. Irene Musket had come to work Friday morning and found a note on the screen door telling her that Houk was in the barn. She said she found his body in the barn and called the Garfield County Sheriff's Office, who notified Utah State Police. Both agencies investigated. Houk had been shot twice with a small-caliber weapon, in the center of the chest and in the lower back of the skull. There were signs that Houk had been rearranging bales of hay, apparently into a hiding place. Two empty .25 caliber cartridge casings were found in the hay near the body. The medical examiner said either of the bullets might have caused death. No witnesses. No physical evidence found in the barn except the shell casings. The housekeeper said she found the back screen door lock had been broken and Houk's office was in disarray. As far as she could tell, nothing had been stolen.

"But then, who knows?" McGee added. "Stuff could be gone from his office and she wouldn't know about it." He stopped, looking at Leaphorn.

"Where was the note?"

"In Houk's shorts," McGee said. "We didn't turn it up. The medical examiner found it when they undressed him."

Leaphorn found he was feeling a little better about McGee. It wasn't McGee's attitude. It was his own.

"I went Wednesday to see him about a woman named Eleanor Friedman-Bernal," Leaphorn said. He explained the situation. Who the woman was, her connection with Houk, what Houk had told him. "So I presume he was telling me she was still alive."

"You thought she was dead?" McGee asked.

"Missing two, three weeks. Leaves her clothes. Leaves a big dinner waiting to be cooked in her fridge. Misses important appointments. I don't know whether she's dead or not."

"Pretty fair bet she is," Nez said. "Or it was."

"You and Houk friends?" McGee asked.

"No," Leaphorn said. "I met him twice. Last Wednesday and about twenty years ago. One of his boys wiped out most of the family. I worked a little on that."

"I remember it. Hard one to forget." McGee was staring at him.

"I'm just as surprised as you are," Leaphorn said. "That he left me the note." He paused, thinking. "Do you know why he left the note in the screen door? About being in the barn?"

"Musket said she'd gone off and left some stuff—some squash—she was going to take home. He'd put it in the refrigerator and left the note. It said, 'squash in the icebox, I'm in the barn.' She figured he thought she'd come back for it."

Leaphorn was remembering the setting—the long, weedy drive, the porch, the barn well up the slope behind the house, a loading pen on one side of it, horse stalls on the other. From the barn, Houk would have heard a car coming. He might have seen it, watched its driver open the gate. He must have recognized death coming for him. McGee said he'd started preparing a hiding place—stacking bales with a gap behind them, to form a hidey-hole probably. And then he'd stopped to write the unfinished note. And put it in his shorts. Leaphorn imagined that. Houk, desperate, out of time, sticking the calling card under his belt line. The only possible reason would be to keep his killer from finding it. And that meant the killer would not have left it. And what did that mean? That the killer was Eleanor Friedman-Bernal, who would not want people to know she was alive? Or, certainly, that Houk knew she was alive.

"You have any theories yet?" he asked McGee.

"One or two," he said.

"Involving pot hunting?"

"Well, we know about Etcitty and Nails. They were hunting pots. Houk's been dealing with 'em for years and not particular where what he buys comes from," McGee said. "So, maybe somebody he cheated got tough about it. Houk screwed one person too many. He had a reputation for that. Or maybe it was this woman he was selling to." McGee got up stiffly, adjusted his hat. "Why else the note? He saw her coming. Back from the dead, so to speak. Knew she was after him. Figured she'd already bagged Nails and Etcitty. Started leaving you the note. Put it where she wouldn't find it and get off with it. I'd like you to tell me what you know about that woman."

"All right," Leaphorn said. "Couple of things I have to do and then I'll get with you."

He'd stayed away from his office since Emma's death and now it smelled of the dust that seeps gradually into everything in a desert climate. He sat in his chair, picked up the phone, and called Shiprock. Chee was in.

"This Watersprinkler Canyon," he asked. "Which side of the river?"

"South," Chee said. "Reservation side."

"No question of that?"

"None," Chee said. "Not if this Amos Whistler knew what he was talking about. Or where he was pointing."

"There isn't any Watersprinkler Canyon on my map. What do you think it is?"

"Probably Many Ruins," Chee said.

It was exactly what Leaphorn would have guessed. And getting into the north end of it was damn near impossible. It ran for its last forty miles through a roadless, jumbled stony wilderness.

"You knew Harrison Houk was shot?"

"Yes sir."

"You want to keep working on this?"

Hesitation. "Yes sir."

"Get on the telephone then. Call the police at Madison, Wisconsin. Find out if handguns are licensed there. They probably are. If they are, find out who does it and then find out exactly what kind of pistol was licensed to Eleanor Friedman-Bernal. It would have been . . ." He squeezed his eyes shut, recalling what Maxie Davis had told him about the woman's career. "Probably 1985 or '86."

"Okay."

"If she didn't license her gun in Madison, you're going to have to keep checking." He gave Chee other places he knew of where the woman had studied or taught, relying on his memory of his talk with Davis and guessing at the dates. "You may be spending all day on the phone," Leaphorn warned. "Tell 'em three homicides are involved. And then stay close to the phone where I can get you."

"Right."

That done, he sat a moment, thinking. He would go to Bluff and take a look at the barn where Harrison Houk had done the remarkable—written him a note while waiting for his killer. He wanted to see that place. The action jarred on him. Why would Houk care that much about a woman who was merely a customer? "Shes still alive up," the note had said. Up? Up to today? Up what? Up where? Up Watersprinkler Canyon? She had taken her sleeping bag. The boy had seen her loading a saddle. But back to Houk. Starting the note. At that point, almost certainly, Houk had been interrupted by the killer. Had run out of time. Had presumed the killer would destroy the note. Would not want the police to know that "she" was alive. So was "she" Eleanor hyphenated? Who else would care about the note? And yet Leaphorn had trouble putting into the picture the woman who marinated the beef and prepared the dinner so lovingly. He could not see her in that barn, firing her little pistol into the skull of an old man lying facedown in the hay. He shook his head. But that was sentiment, not logic.

Major Nez stood in his door, watching him. "Interesting case," Nez said.

"Yeah. Hard one to figure." Leaphorn motioned him in.

Nez simply leaned against the wall, holding a folded paper in his hand. He was getting fat, Leaphorn noticed. Nez had always been built like a barrel, but now his stomach sagged over his broad uniform belt.

"Doesn't sound like something you can get sorted out in less than a week," Nez said. He tapped the paper against the back of his hand, and it occurred to Leaphorn that it was his letter of resignation.

"Probably not," Leaphorn said.

Nez held out the letter. "You want this back? For now? You can always send it in again."

"I'm tired, Ron. Have been a long time, I guess. Just didn't know it."

"Tired of living," Nez said, nodding. "I get that way now and then. But it's hard to quit."

"Anyway, thanks," Leaphorn said. "You know where McGee went?"

Leaphorn found Detective McGee eating a late breakfast at the Navajo Nation Inn and told him everything he knew about Eleanor Friedman-Bernal that seemed remotely pertinent. Then he drove back to his house, dug his pistol belt out of the bottom drawer of his dresser, took out the weapon, and dropped it into his jacket pocket. That done, he drove out of Window Rock, heading north.

15

THE YOUNG WOMAN to whom Chee's call was referred at the Madison Police Department had a little trouble believing in the Navajo Tribal Police. But after that was settled, things became most efficient. Yes, handguns were licensed. No, it would be easy to check the record. Just a moment. It was not much more than that.

The next voice was male. Eleanor Friedman-Bernal? Yes, she had been issued a license for a handgun. She had registered a .25 caliber automatic pistol.

Chee noted the details. The pistol was a brand he'd never heard of. Neither had the clerk in Madison. "Portuguese, I think," he said. "Or maybe it's Turkish, or Brazilian."

Step two went almost as quickly. He called the San Juan County Sheriff's Office and asked for Undersheriff Robert Bates, who usually handled homicides. Bates was married to a Navajo, who happened to be "born to" the Kin yaa aanii—the Towering House People—which was linked in some way Chee had never understood to his grandfather's To' aheedlinii'—the Waters Flow Together Clan. That made Chee and Bates vaguely relatives. Just as important, they had worked together a time or two and liked each other. Bates was in.

"If you have the lab report back, I need to know about the bullets that killed Etcitty and Nails," Chee said.

"Why?" Bates asked. "I thought the FBI decided that killing wasn't on reservation land."

"Out on the Checkerboard, the FBI always decides that," Chee said. "We're just interested."

"Why?"

"Ah, hell, Robert," Chee said. "I don't know why. Joe Leaphorn is interested, and Largo has me working with him."

"What's going on with Leaphorn? We heard he had a nervous breakdown. Heard he quit."

"He did," Chee said. "But not yet."

"Well, it was a twenty-five-caliber pistol, automatic judging from the ejection marks on the empties. All the same weapon."

"You have a missing person's report on a woman who owns a twenty-five-caliber automatic pistol," Chee said. "Her name's Dr. Eleanor Friedman-Bernal. She worked out of Chaco Canyon. Anthropologist. Where Etcitty worked." He told Bates more of what he knew about the woman.

"I got her file right here on my desk," Bates said. "I just a minute ago got a call from a Utah State Policeman. They want us to do some checking up on her out at Chaco. Seems they had a fellow shot up at Bluff and he left a note to Leaphorn telling him this woman is still alive. You know about that?"

"Heard about the killing. Not about any note." He was thinking that a few years ago this weird roundabout communication would have surprised him. Now he expected it. He was remembering Leaphorn chewing him out for not passing along all the details. Well, there was no reason for Leaphorn not to have told him about this. Except that Leaphorn considered him merely an errand boy. Chee was offended.

"Tell me about it," he told Bates. "And don't leave anything out."

Bates told him what he'd been told. It didn't take long.

"So Utah State Police think Dr. Friedman showed up and offed Houk," Chee concluded. "Any theories about motive?"

"Big pot hunting conspiracy is what they seem to think. They've had a federal crackdown up there on pot thieves last year. Bunch of arrests. Grand jury sitting in Salt Lake handing down indictments. So they're thinking pots," Bates said. "And why not? Big money in it the way prices are now. Hell, when we was kids and used to go out and dig 'em up around here, you were lucky to get five bucks. Listen," he added, "how you coming on being a medicine man?"

"No clients." It was not a subject Chee wanted to discuss. It was November, already into the "Season When Thunder Sleeps," the season for curing ceremonials, and he hadn't had a single contact. "You going to Chaco now?"

"Soon as I get off the telephone."

Chee gave him a quick rundown on the people he should talk to: Maxie Davis, the Lunas, Randall Elliot.

"They're worried about the woman. Friends of hers. Be sure and tell them about the note."

"Why, sure," Bates said. He sounded slightly offended that Chee had even mentioned it.

There was nothing to do then but stick close to the telephone and wait for Leaphorn's call from Bluff. He dug into his paperwork. A little before noon, the phone rang. Leaphorn, Chee thought.

It was Janet Pete. Her voice sounded odd. Was Chee doing anything for lunch?

"Nothing," Chee said. "You calling from Shiprock?"

"I drove up. Really just went for a drive. Ended up here." She sounded thoroughly down.

"Lunch then," he said. "Can you meet me at the Thunderbird Café?"

She could. And did.

They took a booth by the window. And talked about the weather. A gusty wind was rattling the pane and chasing dust and leaves and now a section of the *Navajo Times* down the highway outside.

"End of autumn, I guess," Chee said. "You watch Channel Seven. Howard Morgan says we're going to get the first blast of winter."

"I hate winter," Janet Pete said. She hugged herself and shivered. "Dismal winter."

"The counselor has the blues," Chee said. "Anything I can do to cheer you up? I'll call Morgan and see if he can postpone it."

"Or call it off altogether."

"Right."

"Or there's Italy."

"Which is warm, I hear," Chee said, and then he saw she was serious.

"You hear from your Successful Attorney?"

"He flew all the way to Chicago, to Albuquerque, to Gallup. I met him at Gallup."

Not knowing what to say, Chee said: "Not exactly meeting him halfway." It sounded flippant. Chee didn't feel flippant. He cleared his throat. "Has he changed? Time does that with people. So I'm told."

"Yes," Janet Pete said. But she shook her head. "But no. Not really. My mother told me a long time ago: 'Don't ever expect a man to change. What you see is what you live with.' "

"I guess so," Chee said. She looked tired, and full of sadness. He reached out and took her hand in his. It was cold. "Trouble is, I guess you love him anyway."

"I don't know," Janet Pete said. "I just . . ." But the sympathy was too much for her. Her voice choked. She looked down, fumbling in her purse.

Chee handed her his napkin. She held it to her face.

"Rough life," Chee said. "Love is supposed to make us happy, and sometimes it makes us miserable."

Through the napkin he heard Janet sniff.

He patted her hand. "This sounds like a cliché, or whatever it is, but I know how you feel. I really do."

"I know," Janet said.

"But you know, I've decided. I'm giving up. You can't go on forever." As he heard himself saying that, he was amazed. When did he decide that? He hadn't realized it. He felt a surge of relief. And of loss. Why can't men cry? he wondered. Why is that not allowed?

"He wants me to go to Italy with him. He's going to Rome. Taking over their legal affairs for Europe. And Africa. And the Middle East."

"He speak Italian?" As he said it, it seemed an incredibly stupid question. Totally beside the point here.

"French," she said. "And some Italian. And he's perfecting it. A tutor."

"How about you?" he said. Why couldn't he think of something less inane. He would be asking her next about her passport. And packing. And airfares. That wasn't what she wanted to talk about. She wanted to talk about love.

"No," she said.

"What did he say? Does he understand now that you want to be a lawyer? That you want to practice it?"

The napkin was in her lap now. Her eyes dry. But they showed she'd been crying. And her face was strained.

"He said I could practice in Italy. Not with his company. It has a nepotism rule. But he could line something up for me after I got the required Italian license."

"He could line something up. For you."

She sighed. "Yeah. That's the way he put it. And I guess he could. At a certain level in law, the big firms feed on one another.

There would be Italian firms doing feed-out work. The word would go into the good-old-boy network. Tit for tat. I guess once I learned Italian I would be offered a job."

Chee nodded. "I'd think so," he said.

Lunch came. Mutton stew and fry bread for Chee. Janet was having a bowl of soup.

They sat looking at the food.

"You should eat something," said Chee, who had totally lost his appetite. He took a spoonful of the stew, a bite of fry bread. "Eat," he ordered.

Janet Pete took a spoonful of soup.

"Made a decision yet?"

She shook her head. "I don't know."

"You know yourself better than anyone," he said. "What's going to make you happy?"

She shook her head again. "I think I'm happy when I'm with him. Like dinner last night. But I don't know."

Chee was thinking about the dinner and how it had ended, and what happened then. Had she gone to his room with him? Had she spent the night there? Probably. The thought hurt. It hurt a lot. That surprised him.

"I shouldn't let things like this drag on," she said. "I should decide."

"We let ours drag on. Mary and I. And I guess she decided."

He had released her hand when lunch arrived. Now she reached over and put hers on his. "I have your napkin," she said. "Slightly damp but still"—she looked at it, a rumpled square of pale blue paper—"usable in case of emergency."

He realized instantly that this was her bid to change the subject. He took the napkin, dropped it in his lap.

"Have you realized how lucky you are to have been brought to the only café in Shiprock with napkins?"

"Noted and appreciated," she said. Her smile seemed almost natural. "And how are things going with you?"

"I told you about the Backhoe Bandit. And Etcitty?"

She nodded. "That must have been gruesome. How about finding the woman?"

"How much did I tell you about that?"

She reminded him.

He told her about Houk, about the note left for Leaphorn, about Eleanor Friedman-Bernal's pistol and how it was the same caliber used in the killings, about Leaphorn's obsessive interest in finding the Utah site to which Friedman's long-lost potter seemed to have moved.

"You know you have to file for a permit to dig sites like that on the reservation. We have an office in Window Rock that deals with it," Janet Pete said. "Did you check that?"

"Leaphorn might have," Chee said. "But apparently she was trying to find out where the stuff was coming from. You'd have to know that before you could file."

"I guess so. But I think they're all numbered. Maybe she would just guess at it."

Chee grinned and shook his head. "Back when I was an anthropology student, I remember Professor Campbell, or somebody, telling us there were forty thousand sites listed with New Mexico Laboratory of Anthropology numbers. That's in New Mexico alone. And another hundred thousand or so on other registries."

"I didn't mean just pick a number at random," she said, slightly irked. "She could describe the general location."

Chee was suddenly interested. "Maybe Leaphorn already looked into it," he said. He was remembering that probably he would be hearing from Leaphorn soon. He'd left word with the switchboard to relay the call here. "But would it take long to check?"

"I could call," she said, looking thoughtful. "I know the man who runs it. Helped him with the regulations. I think, to dig on the reservation, I think you have to apply to the Park Service and the Navajo Cultural Preservation Office both. I think you have to name a repository for whatever you recover, and get the archive system approved. And maybe . . ."

Chee was thinking how great it would be if, when Leaphorn called, he could tell him the map coordinates of the site he was looking for. His face must have showed his impatience. Janet stopped midsentence. "What?" she said.

"Let's go back to the station and call," he said.

The call from Leaphorn was waiting when they walked in. Chee gave him what he'd learned from the Madison police and from Bates at the San Juan County Sheriff's Office. "They're expecting a report from the Utah State Police," Chee added. "Bates said he would call when he gets it."

"I've got it," Leaphorn said. "It was twenty-five-caliber, too."

"Do you know if Friedman applied for a permit to dig that site you're looking for?"

Long silence. "I should have thought of that," Leaphorn said finally. "I doubt if she did. The red tape takes years and it's a double filing. Park Service clearance plus tribal clearance, and all sorts of checking and screwing around gets involved. But I should have checked it."

"I'll take care of it," Chee said.

The man to call, Janet Pete said, was T. J. Pedwell. Chee reached him just back from lunch. Had he had any applications from Dr. Eleanor Friedman-Bernal to dig on a reserved Anasazi site on the reservation?

"Sure," Pedwell said. "Two or three. On Checkerboard land around Chaco Canyon. She's that ceramics specialist working over there."

"How about over on the north side of the reservation? Up in Utah."

"I don't think so," Pedwell said. "I could check on it. Wouldn't know the site number, would you?"

" 'Fraid not," Chee said. "But it might be somewhere near the north end of Many Ruins Canyon."

"I know that place," Pedwell said. "Helped with the Antiquities survey all up through that part of the country."

"You know the canyon the local people call Watersprinkler?"

"It's really Many Ruins," Pedwell said. "It's full of pictographs and petroglyphs of Kokopelli. That's the one the Navajos call the Watersprinkler *yei.*"

"I have a description of the site, and it sounds unusual," Chee said. He told Pedwell what Amos Whistler had told him.

"Yeah," Pedwell said. "Sounds familiar. Let me check my files. I have photos of most of them."

Chee heard the telephone click against something. He waited and waited. Sighed. Leaned a hip against the desk.

"Trouble?" Janet Pete asked.

Pedwell's voice was in his ear before he could respond.

"Found it," Pedwell said. "It's N.R. 723. Anasazi. Circa 1280–1310. And there's two other sites right there with it. Probably connected."

"Great!" Chee said. "How do you get there?"

"Well, it ain't going to be easy. I remember that. We packed into some of them on horseback. Others we floated down the San Juan and walked up the canyon. This one I think we floated. Let's see. Notes say it's five point seven miles up from the mouth of the canyon."

"Dr. Friedman. She apply to dig that one?"

"Not her," Pedwell said. "Another of those people out at Chaco did. Dr. Randall Elliot. They working together?"

"I don't think so," Chee said. "Does the application say he was collecting St. John's Polychrome pots?"

"Lemme look." Papers rustled. "Doesn't sound like pots. Says he is studying Anasazi migrations." Mumbling sounds of Pedwell reading to himself. "Says his interest is tracing genetic patterns." More mumbling. "Studying bones. Skull thickness. Six-fingeredness. Aberrant jaw formation." More mumbling. "I don't think it has anything to do with ceramics," Pedwell said, finally. "He's looking at the skeletons. Or will be if your famous Navajo bureaucracy, of which I am a part, ever gets this processed. Six-fingeredness. Lot of that among the Anasazi, but hard to study, because hands don't survive intact after a thousand years. But it sounds like he's found some family patterns. Too many fingers. An extra tooth in the right side of the lower jaw. A second hole where those nerves and blood vessels go through the back of the jaw, and something or other about the fibula. Physical anthropology isn't my area."

"But he hasn't gotten his permit yet?"

"Wait a minute. I guess we weren't so slow on this one. Here's a carbon of a letter to Elliot from the Park Service." Paper rustled. "Turndown," Pedwell said. "More documentation needed of previous work in this field. That do it?"

"Thanks a lot," Chee said.

Janet Pete was watching him.

"Sounds like you scored," she said.

"I'll fill you in," he said.

"On the way back to my car." She looked embarrassed. "I'm normally the usual stolid, dull lawyer," she said. "This morning I just ran off in hysterics and left everything undone. People coming in to see me. People waiting for me to finish things. I feel awful."

He walked to the car with her, opened the door.

"I'm glad you called on me," he said. "You honored me."

"Oh, Jim!" she said, and hugged him around the chest with such strength that he caught his breath. She stood, holding him like that, pressed against him. He sensed she was about to cry again. He didn't want that to happen.

He put his hand on her hair and stroked it.

"I don't know what you'll decide about your Successful Attorney," he said. "But if you decide against him, maybe you and I could see if we could fall in love. You know, both Navajos and all that."

It was the wrong thing to say. She was crying as she drove away.

Chee stood there, watching her motor pool sedan speed toward the U.S. 666 junction and the route to Window Rock. He didn't want to think about this. It was confusing. And it hurt. Instead he thought of a question he should have asked Pedwell. Had Randall Elliot also filed an application to dig in that now-despoiled site where Etcitty and Nails had died?

He walked back into the station, remembering those jawbones so carefully set aside amid the chaos.

16

TO LEAPHORN, the saddle had seemed a promising possibility. She had borrowed it from a biologist named Arnold, who lived in Bluff. Other trails led to Bluff. The site of the polychrome pots seemed to be somewhere west of the town, in roadless country where a horse would be necessary. She would go to Arnold's place. If he could loan her a saddle, he could probably loan her a horse. From Arnold he would learn where Eleanor Friedman-Bernal had headed. The first step was finding Arnold, which shouldn't be difficult.

It wasn't. The Recapture Lodge had been Bluff's center of hospitality for as long as Leaphorn could remember. The man at the reception desk loaned Leaphorn his telephone to call Chee. Chee confirmed what Leaphorn had feared. Whether or not Dr. Friedman was killing pot hunters, her pistol was. The man at the desk also knew Arnold.

"Bo Arnold," he said. "Scientists around here are mostly anthropologists or geologists, but Dr. Arnold is a lichen man. Botanist. Go up to where the highway bends left, and take the right toward Montezuma Creek. It's the little red-brick house with lilac bushes on both sides of the gate. Except I think Bo let the lilacs die. He drives a Jeep. If he's home, you'll see it there."

The lilacs were indeed almost dead, and a dusty early-model Jeep was parked in the weeds beside the little house. Leaphorn parked beside it and stepped out of his pickup into a gust of chilly, dusty wind. The front door opened just as he walked up the porch steps. A lanky man in jeans and faded red shirt emerged. "Yessir," he said. "Good morning." He was grinning broadly, an array of white teeth in a face of weathered brown leather.

"Good morning," Leaphorn said. "I'm looking for Dr. Arnold."

"Yessir," the man said. "That's me." He stuck out a hand, which Leaphorn shook. He showed Arnold his identification.

"I'm looking for Dr. Eleanor Friedman-Bernal," Leaphorn said.

"Me too," Arnold said enthusiastically. "That biddy got off with my kayak and didn't bring it back."

"Oh," Leaphorn said. "When?"

"When I was gone," Arnold said, still grinning. "Caught me away from home, and off she goes with it."

"I want to hear all about that," Leaphorn said.

Arnold held the door wide, welcomed Leaphorn in with a sweep of his hand. Inside the front door was a room crowded with tables, each table crowded with rocks of all sizes and shapes—their only common denominator being lichens. They were covered with these odd plants in every shade from white through black. Arnold led Leaphorn past them, down a narrow hall.

"No place to sit in there," he said. "That's where I work. Here's where I live."

Where Arnold lived was a small bedroom. Every flat surface, including the narrow single bed, was covered with boards on which flat glass dishes were lined. The dishes had something in them that Leaphorn assumed must be lichens. "Let me make you a place," Arnold said, and cleared off chairs for each of them.

"Why you looking for Ellie?" he asked. "She been looting ruins?" And he laughed.

"Does she do that?"

"She's an anthropologist," Arnold said, his chuckle reduced again to a grin. "You translate the word from academic into English and that's what it means: ruins looter, one who robs graves, preferably old ones. Well-educated person who steals artifact in dignified manner." Arnold, overcome by the wit of this, laughed. "Somebody else does it, they call 'em vandals. That's the word for the competition. Somebody gets there first, gets off with the stuff before the archaeologists can grab it, they call 'em Thieves of Time." His vision of such hypocrisy left him in high good humor, as did the thought of his missing kayak.

"Tell me about that," Leaphorn said. "How do you know she took it?"

"She left a full, signed confession," Arnold said, fumbling in a box from which assorted scraps of papers overflowed. He extracted a small sheet of lined yellow notepaper and handed it to Leaphorn.

> Here's your saddle, a year older but no worse for wear. (I sold that damned horse.) To keep you caring about me, I am now borrowing your kayak. If you don't get back before I do, ignore the last part of this note because I will put the kayak right back in the garage where I got it and you'll never know it was gone.
>
> Don't let any lichens grow on you!
>
> Love,
>
> Ellie

Leaphorn handed it back to him. "When did she leave it?"

"I just know when I found it. I'd been up there on Lime Ridge collecting specimens for a week or so and when I got back, the saddle was on the floor in the workroom up front with this note pinned on it. Looked in the garage, and the kayak was gone."

"When?" Leaphorn repeated.

"Oh," Arnold said. "Let's see. Almost a month ago."

Leaphorn told him the date Eleanor Friedman-Bernal had made her early-morning departure from Chaco Canyon. "That sound right?"

"I think I got back on a Monday or Tuesday. Three or four days after that."

"So the saddle might have been sitting there three or four days?"

"Could have been." Arnold laughed again. "Don't have a cleaning lady coming in. Guess you noticed that."

"How did she get in?"

"Key's over there under the flower box," Arnold said. "She knew where. Been here before. Go all the way back to the University of Wisconsin." Abruptly Arnold's amusement evaporated. His bony, sun-beaten face became somber. "She's really missing? People worried about her? She didn't just walk off for a few days of humanity?"

"I think it's serious," Leaphorn said. "Almost a month. And she left too much behind. Where would she go in your kayak?"

Arnold shook his head. "Just one place to go. Downstream. I use it to play around with. Like a toy. But she'd have been going down the river. Plenty of sites along the river until you get into the deep canyon where there's nothing to live on. And then there's hundreds of ruins up the side canyons." There was no humor at all left in Arnold's face. He looked at least his age, which Leaphorn guessed at forty. He looked worn and worried.

"Ceramics. That's what Ellie would be looking for. Potsherds." He paused, stared at Leaphorn. "I guess you know we had a man killed here just the other day. Man named Houk. The son of a bitch was a notorious pot dealer. Somebody shot him. Any connection?"

"Who knows?" Leaphorn said. "Maybe so. You have any more specific idea where she took your kayak?"

"Nothing more than I said. She borrowed it before and went down into the canyons. Just poking around in the ruins looking at the potsherds. I'd guess she did it again."

"Any idea how far down?"

"She'd ask me to pick her up the next evening at the landing upstream from the bridge at Mexican Hat. Only place to get off the river for miles. So it would have to be between Sand Island and Hat."

Her car too could be found between Sand Island and Mexican Hat, Leaphorn was sure. She would have to have hauled the kayak within dragging distance of the river. But there was no reason now to look for the car.

"That narrows it down quite a bit," Leaphorn said, thinking Ellie's trips were into the area Etcitty had described in his falsified documentation, the area Amos Whistler had pointed to in his talk with Chee. He would find a boat and go looking for Arnold's kayak. Maybe, when he found it, he would find Eleanor Friedman, and what Harrison Houk meant in that unfinished note. ". . . shes still alive up." But first he wanted a look at that barn.

Irene Musket came to the door at Harrison Houk's old house. She recognized him instantly and let him in. She was a handsome woman, as Leaphorn remembered, but today she looked years older, and tired. She told him about finding the note, about finding the body. She confirmed that she had found absolutely nothing missing from the house. She told him nothing he didn't already know. Then she walked with him up the long slope toward the barn.

"It happened right in here," she said. "Right in that horse stall there. The third one."

Leaphorn looked back. From the barn you could see the driveway, and the old gate with its warning bell. Only the front porch was obscured. Houk might well have seen his killer coming for him.

Irene Musket stood at the barn door. Kept out, perhaps, by her fear of the *chindi* Harrison Houk had left behind him and the ghost sickness it would cause her. Or perhaps by the sorrow that looking at the spot where Houk had died would bring to her.

Leaphorn's career had made him immune to the *chindi* of the dead, immune through indifference to all but one of them. He walked out of the wind and into the dimness.

The floor of the third horse stall had been swept clean of the old alfalfa and prairie-hay straw that littered the rest of the place. That debris now formed a pile in one corner, where the Utah crime lab crew had dumped it after sorting through it. Leaphorn stood on the dirt packed by a hundred years of hooves and wondered what he had expected to find. He walked across the barn floor, inspected the piles of alfalfa bales. It did, indeed, seem that Houk might have been rearranging them to form a hiding place. That touched him oddly, but taught him nothing. Nothing except that Houk, the hard man, the scoundrel, had set aside a chance to hide to make time to leave him a message. "Tell Leaphorn shes still alive up"—up the canyon? That seemed likely. Up which canyon? But why would Houk have put his own life at greater risk to help a woman who must have been nothing more than one of his many customers? It seemed out of character. Not the Houk he knew about. That Houk's only weakness seemed to have been a schizophrenic son, now long dead.

Outside the barn the wind shifted direction slightly and howled through the cracks, raising a small flurry of straw and dust on the packed floor and bringing autumn smells to compete with the ancient urine. He was wasting his time. He walked back toward where Irene Musket was standing, checking the stalls as he passed. In the last one, a black nylon kayak was leaning against the wall.

Bo Arnold's kayak. Leaphorn stared at it. How could it have gotten here? And why?

It was inflated, standing on one pointed end in the stall corner. He walked in for a closer look. Of course it wasn't Arnold's kayak. He had described his as dark brown, with what he called "white racing stripes."

Leaphorn knelt beside it, inspecting it. It seemed remarkably clean for this dusty barn. He felt inside, between the rubber-coated nylon of its bottom and the inflated tubes that formed its walls, hoping to find something telltale left behind. His fingers encountered paper. He pulled it out. The crumpled, water-stained wrapper from a Mr. Goodbar. He ran his fingers down toward the bow.

Water.

Leaphorn pulled out his hand and examined his wet fingers. Whatever water had been left in the kayak had drained down into this crevice. How long could it have been there? How long would evaporation take in this no-humidity climate?

He walked to the door.

"The inflated kayak in there. You know when it was used?"

"I think four days ago," Irene Musket said.

"By Mr. Houk?"

She nodded.

"His arthritis didn't bother him?"

"His arthritis hurt all the time," she said. "It didn't keep him from that boat." She sounded as if this represented an argument lost, an old hurt.

"Where did he go? Do you know?"

She made a vague gesture. "Just down the river."

"Do you know how far?"

"Not very far. He would have me pick him up down there near Mexican Hat."

"He did this a lot?"

"Every full moon."

"He went down at night? Late?"

"Sometimes he would watch the ten o'clock news and then we would go down to Sand Island. We'd make sure nobody was there. Then we'd put it in." The wind whipped dust around Mrs. Musket's ankles and blew up her long skirt. She held it down, pressed back against the barn door. "We would put it in, and then the next morning, I would drive the pickup down to that landing place upstream from Mexican Hat and I'd wait for him there. And then . . ." She paused, swallowed. Stood a moment, silently. Leaphorn noticed her eyes were wet, and looked away. Hard as he was, Harrison Houk had left someone to grieve for him.

"Then we would drive back to the house together," she concluded.

Leaphorn waited awhile. When he had given her enough time, he asked: "Did he tell you what he did when he went down the river?"

The silence lasted so long that Leaphorn wondered if his question had been lost in the wind. He glanced at her.

"He didn't tell me," she said.

Leaphorn thought about the answer.

"But you know," he said.

"I think so," she said. "One time he told me not to guess. And he said, 'If you guess anyway, then don't ever tell anybody!' "

"Do you know who killed him?"

"I don't," she said. "I wish they would have killed me, instead."

"I think we will find the one who did it," Leaphorn said. "I really do."

"He was a good man. People talked about how mean he was. He was good to good people and just mean to the mean ones. I guess they killed him for that."

Leaphorn touched her arm. "Would you help me put the kayak in? And then tomorrow, drive my truck down to Mexican Hat and pick me up?"

"All right," Irene Musket said.

"First I have to make a telephone call. Can I use your telephone?"

He called Jim Chee from Houk's house. It was after six. Chee had gone home for the day. No telephone, of course. Typical of Chee. He left Houk's number for a call back.

They slid the kayak into the back of his truck, with its double-bladed paddle and Houk's worn orange jacket, tied it down, and drove south to Sand Island launch site. Bureau of Land Management signs there warned that the river was closed for the season, that a license was required, that the San Juan catfish was on the extinction list and taking it was prohibited.

With the kayak in the water, Leaphorn stood beside it, feet in the cold water, doing a last-minute inventory of possibilities. He wrote Jim Chee's name and the Shiprock police station number on one of his cards and gave it to her.

"If I don't meet you by noon tomorrow down at Mexican Hat, I hope you will call this man for me. Tell him what you told me about Mr. Houk and this kayak. And that I took it down the river."

She took it.

He climbed into the kayak.

"You know how to run that thing?"

"Years ago I did. I think I'll remember."

"Well, put on the life jacket and buckle it. It's easy to turn over."

"Right," Leaphorn said. He did it.

"And here," she said. She handed him a heavy canteen with

a carrying strap and a plastic bread sack. "I got something for you to eat out of the kitchen," she said.

"Well, thanks," Leaphorn said, touched.

"Be careful."

"I can swim."

"I didn't mean the river," Mrs. Musket said.

17

TRAILERS ARE POOR PLACES to sleep on those nights when seasons are changing on the Colorado Plateau. All night Jim Chee's narrow bed quivered as the gusts shook the thin walls of his home. He slept poorly, wrestling with the problem of Elliot's application while he was awake, dreaming of jawbones when he dozed. He rose early, made coffee, and found four Twinkies abandoned in his otherwise empty bread box to round out his breakfast. It was his day off, and time to buy groceries, do the laundry, check three overdue books back into the Farmington library. He'd refilled his water reservoir, but his butane supply was low. And he needed to pick up a tire he'd had repaired. And, come to think of it, drop by the bank and see about the $18.50 difference between his checkbook balance and their records.

Instead he looked in his notebook and found the number Dr. Pedwell had given him for the Laboratory of Anthropology in Santa Fe. "That would have an MLA number," Pedwell had told him when he'd asked if Elliot had also applied to excavate the site where Etcitty and Nails had been killed. "It's in New Mexico, and apparently on public land. If it's on a Navajo section, we record it. If it's not, Laboratory of Anthropology handles it."

"Sounds confusing," Chee had said.

"Oh, it is," Pedwell had agreed. "It's even more confusing than that." And he'd started explaining other facets of the numbering system, the Chaco numbers, the Mesa Verde, until Chee had changed the subject. Now he realized he should have asked for a name at Santa Fe.

He made the call from the station, drawing a surprised look from the desk clerk, who knew he was off. And it took three transfers before he connected with the woman who had access to the information he needed. She had a sweet, distinct middle-aged voice.

"It's easier if you know the MLA number," she said. "Otherwise I have to check through the applicant files."

And so he waited.

"Dr. Elliot has eleven applications on file. You want all of them?"

"I guess so," Chee said, not knowing exactly what to expect.

"MLA 14,751. MLA 19,311. MLA—"

"Just a moment," Chee said. "Do they have site locations? What county they're in. Like that?"

"On our map, yes."

"The one I'm interested in would be in San Juan County, New Mexico."

"Just a minute," she said. The minute passed. "Two of them. MLA 19,311 and MLA 19,327."

"Could you pin the location down any more?"

"I can give you the legal description. Range, township, and section." She read them off.

"Was he issued the permits?"

"Turned down," she said. "They're saving those sites to be dug sometime in the future when they have better technology. It's hard to get permission to dig them now."

"Thanks a lot," Chee said. "It's exactly what I need."

And it was. When he checked the legal description on the U.S. Geological Survey map in Captain Largo's office, MLA 19,327 proved to share range, township, and section with the oil well pump beyond which he'd found the U-Haul truck.

He had less luck trying to call Chaco Canyon. The phone was suffering some sort of satellite relay problem that produced both fade-out and echo. Randall Elliot was out of reach at one of the down-canyon ruins. Maxie Davis was somewhere. Luna was doing something, unintelligible to Chee, at Pueblo Bonito.

Chee glanced at his watch. He calculated the distance to Chaco. About a hundred miles. He remembered the condition of that last twenty-five miles of dirt. He groaned. Why was he doing this on his day off? But he knew why. Much as Leaphorn irritated him, he wanted the man to pat him on the head. To say, "Good job, kid." Might as well admit it. Also he might as well admit another fact. He was excited now. That grotesque line of lower jaws suddenly seemed to mean something. Perhaps something important.

The strange weather slowed him a little, rocking his truck when he stretched the limit on the fast pavement of N.M. 44 across the sagebrush flats of Blanco Plateau. End of autumn, he thought. Winter coming out of the west. Behind him over Colorado's La Plata range, the sky was dark, and when he left the pavement at Blanco Trading Post, he had a direct side wind to deal with—and the tiring business of steering against it as he fought chugholes and ruts. And tumbleweeds and blowing sand chased him across the parking lot at the Chaco visitors' center.

The woman he'd talked to was at the desk, looking trim in her park ranger uniform and glad to have Chee break the boredom of a day, and a season, that brought few visitors. She showed him on the Chaco map how to get to Kin Kletso, the site where Randall Elliot would be working today, "if he can work in this wind." Where Maxie Davis was seemed a mystery, "but maybe she'll be working with Randall." Luna had driven into Gallup and wouldn't be back until tonight.

Chee went back to his truck, leaning into the wind, squinching his eyes against the dust. At Kin Kletso, he found a Park Service truck parked and an employee sitting in the shelter of one of the walls.

"Looking for Dr. Randall Elliot," Chee said. "Did I miss him?"

"A mile," the man said. "He didn't show up today."

"You know where . . ."

The man waved a dismissive wave. "No idea," he said. "He's independent as a hog on ice."

Maybe he was home. Chee drove to the temporary housing. Nothing in the parking area. He knocked at the door marked Elliot. Knocked again. Walked around the building to the back. Randall Elliot hadn't pulled the drapes across his sliding-glass patio door. Chee peered into what must be the living room. Elliot seemed to have converted it into a work area. Sawhorses supported planks on which cardboard cartons were lined. Those that Chee could see into seemed to contain bones. Skulls, ribs, jawbones. Chee pressed his forehead against the cool glass, shading his eyes with both hands, straining to see. Against the wall, boxes were lined. Books on shelves against the kitchen partition. No sign of Elliot.

Chee glanced down at the lock that held the door. Simple enough. He looked around him. No one visible. He dug out his penknife, opened the proper blade, slipped the catch.

Once inside he closed the drapes and turned on the light. He hurried through a quick search of the bedroom, kitchen, and bath, touching hardly anything and using his handkerchief to avoid leaving prints. This made him nervous. Worse, it made him feel dirty and ashamed.

But back in the living room he lingered over the boxes of bones. They seemed to be arranged in groups, tagged by site. Chee checked the tags, looking for either N.R. 723 or MLA 19,327. On the makeshift table by the kitchen door he found the N.R. number.

The tag was tied through the eye socket of a skull, number on one side, notes on the other. They seemed to be in some sort of personal shorthand, with numbers in millimeters. Bone thickness, Chee guessed, but the rest of it meant nothing to him.

The N.R. 723 box contained four lower jaws, one apparently from a child, one broken. He examined them. Each contained an extra molar, or a trace of one, on the right side. Each had two of the small holes low in the bones through which Elliot's petition had stated nerves and blood vessels grow.

Chee put the jaws back in the box exactly as he had found them, wiped his fingers on his pants legs, and sat down to sort out the significance of this. It seemed clear enough. Elliot's genetic tracking had led him to the same site as had Eleanor Friedman-Bernal's pottery chase. No. That didn't state it accurately. In their mutual fishing expeditions, both had struck pay dirt in the same ruins. Perhaps, Chee thought, one of the jawbones belonged to the potter.

He thought about site MLA 19,327, the lined jawbones, the missing plastic sack from the box of thirty. Thinking about that, he made another search of the apartment.

He found a black plastic sack in the bottom of a wastebasket in the kitchen. He carefully set aside the table scraps and wadded papers that had buried it and put it on the counter beside the sink. The top was tied in a knot. Chee untied it and examined the plastic. SUPERTUFF was printed around the top. The missing sack.

Inside it were seven human mandibles, two of them child-sized, two broken. Chee counted teeth. Each had seventeen—one more than standard—and in each the superfluous molar was second from the back and out of line.

He put the sack back in the wastebasket, recovered it with waste, and picked up the telephone.

No, the woman at the visitors' center said, Elliot hadn't reported in. Nor had Luna or Maxie Davis.

"Can you get me Mrs. Luna?"

"Now that's easy," she said.

Mrs. Luna answered on the third ring and remembered Chee instantly. How was he? How was Mr. Leaphorn? "But this isn't what you called about."

"No," Chee said. "I came out to talk to Randall Elliot but he's away somewhere. I remembered you said he went to Washington last month. You said his travel agent called and you took the message. Do you remember the name of the agency?"

"Bolack's," Mrs. Luna said. "I think just about everybody out here uses Bolack's."

Chee called Bolack Travel in Farmington.

"Navajo Tribal Police," he told the man who answered. "We need to confirm the dates of an airline ticket. Don't know the airline, but the tickets were issued by your agency to Randall Elliot, address at Chaco Canyon."

"You know about when? This year? This month? Yesterday?"

"Probably late last month," Chee said.

"Randall Elliot," the man said. "Randall Elliot. Let's see." Chee heard the clacking sound of a computer keyboard. Silence. More clacking. More silence.

"That's funny," the man said. "We issued them, but he didn't pick them up. It was an October eleven departure, with an October sixteen return. Mesa from Farmington to Albuquerque, American from Albuquerque to Washington. You just need the dates?"

"The tickets weren't picked up? You're certain?"

"I sure am. Makes a lot of work for nothing."

Chee called Mrs. Luna again. Listening to the ring, he felt a sense of urgency. Randall Elliot wasn't in Washington that morning Eleanor Friedman-Bernal drove away to oblivion. He didn't go. But he pretended to go. He arranged it so that everyone in this gossipy place would think he was in Washington. Why? So they wouldn't be curious about where he'd actually gone. And where was that? Chee thought he knew. He hoped he was wrong.

"Hello," Mrs. Luna said.

"Chee again," he said. "Another question. Did a deputy sheriff come out here yesterday to talk to people?"

"He did. About a month late, I'd say."

"Did he tell you about the note left for Lieutenant Leaphorn? The one that sounded like Dr. Friedman might still be alive."

"Is alive," Mrs. Luna said. "He said the note said, 'Tell Leaphorn she is still alive.' "

"Does everybody here know about that? Does Elliot?"

"Of course. Because everybody was beginning to have their

doubts. You know, that's a long time to just disappear unless something bad has happened."

"You sure about Elliot?"

"He was right here when he told Bob and me."

"Well, thanks a lot," Chee said.

The wind had fallen now into something near a calm. Which was lucky for Chee. He drove back to Blanco Trading Post much faster than the rutted dirt roadbed made wise, and then much faster than the law allowed on N.M. 44 to Farmington. He was worried. He had told Undersheriff Bates to tell the people at Chaco about Houk's note. He should not have done that. But maybe these suspicions were groundless. He thought of a way he could check—a call he should have made before he left Chaco.

He pulled into the grocery store at Bloomfield and ran to the pay phone, then ran back to his truck for the supply of quarters he kept in the glove box. He called the Farmington airport, identified himself, asked the woman who answered who there rented helicopters. He jotted down the two names she gave him, and their numbers. The line was busy at Aero Services. He dialed Flight Contractors. A man who identified himself as Sanchez answered. Yes, they had rented a copter that morning to Randall Elliot.

"Pretty sorry weather for flying, even in a copter," Sanchez said. "But he's got the credentials and the experience. Flew for the navy in Nam."

"Did he say where he was going?"

"He's an anthropologist," Sanchez said. "We been renting to him for two, three years now. Said he was going down over the White Horse Lake country hunting one of them Indian ruins. If you're going to fly in this kind of weather, that's a good place to fly. Just grass and snakeweed down that way."

It was also just about exactly the opposite direction from where Elliot was really flying, Chee thought. Southeast instead of northwest.

"When did he leave?"

"I'd say maybe three hours ago. Maybe a little longer."

"Do you have another one to rent? With a pilot?"

"Have the chopper," Sanchez said. "Have to see about the pilot. When's it for?"

Chee made some instant calculations. "Thirty minutes," he said.

"I doubt it by then," Sanchez said. "I'll try."

It took Chee a little less than that, at considerable risk of a speeding ticket. Sanchez had found a pilot, but the pilot hadn't arrived.

"He's the substitute pilot for the air ambulance service," Sanchez said. "Man named Ed King. He didn't care much for this weather, but then the wind's been dying."

In fact the wind had moderated to a steady breeze. It seemed to be dying away as the weather front that brought it moved southeast. But now the sky to the north and west was a solid dark overcast.

While they waited for King, he'd see if he could get hold of Leaphorn. If he couldn't, he'd leave word for him. Tell him about finding the missing wastebasket liner hidden in Elliot's kitchen with the bones in it, and about Elliot's rejected applications to dig those sites. He'd tell Leaphorn that Elliot hadn't taken the flight to Washington the weekend that Friedman-Bernal disappeared. That provoked another thought.

"Mr. Sanchez. Could you check and see if Dr. Elliot took out a helicopter on, let's see, the thirteenth of October?"

Sanchez looked as doubtful as he had when Chee had said he should bill the copter rental to the Navajo Tribal Police. The look had hardened, and Chee had finally presented his MasterCard and waited while Sanchez checked his credit balance. It seemed to have reached the minimum guarantee. ("Now," said Sanchez, cheerful again, "if it's okay with the tribal auditors you can get your money back.")

"I don't know that I'm supposed to be telling all this stuff," Sanchez said. "Randall's a regular customer of ours. It might get back to him."

"It's police business," Chee said. "Part of a criminal investigation."

"About what?" Sanchez looked stubborn.

"Those two men shot out in the Checkerboard. Nails and Etcitty."

"Oh," Sanchez said. "I'll check."

"While you do, I'll call my office."

Benally was in charge of the shift. No, Benally knew no way to get in touch with Leaphorn.

"Matter of fact, you have a message from him. Woman named Irene Musket called from Mexican Hat. She said Leaphorn headed down the San Juan—" Benally paused, chuckling. "You know," he said, "this sounds just like the screwy stuff you get mixed up in, Jim. Anyway, she said Leaphorn took off down the San Juan yesterday evening in a boat, looking for a boat this anthropologist you're looking for took. She was supposed to pick him up this morning at Mexican Hat, and call you if he didn't show up. Well, he didn't show up."

And just then the door opened behind Chee, letting in the cold breeze.

"Somebody here want a chopper ride?"

A burly, bald-headed man with a great yellow mustache was standing holding it open, looking at Chee. "You the daredevil who wants to fly out into this weather? I'm the daredevil here to take you."

18

FINDING THE KAYAK Eleanor Friedman-Bernal had borrowed seemed simple enough to Leaphorn. She could have gone only downriver. The cliffs that walled in the San Juan between Bluff and Mexican Hat limited takeout places to a few sandy benches and the mouths of perhaps a score of washes and canyons. Since Leaphorn's reason and instincts told him her target ruin was on the reservation side of the river, his hunting grounds were further limited. And the description he had been given of the woman suggested she wouldn't be strong enough to pull the heavy rubber kayak very far out of the water. Therefore, finding it, even in the gathering darkness with only a flashlight, would be easy. Finding the woman would be the tough part.

Leaphorn had calculated without the wind. It treated Houk's little craft like a sail, pushing against its sides and forcing Leaphorn into a constant struggle to keep it in the current. About four miles below the Bluff bridge, he let the kayak drift into a sandbar on the north side of the river, as much to stretch cramping muscles and give himself a rest as in any hope of finding something. On the cliffs here he found an array of petroglyphs cut through the black desert varnish into the sandstone. He studied a row of square-shouldered figures with chevronlike stripes above their heads and little arcs suggesting sound waves issuing from their mouths. If they hadn't predated the time his own people had invaded this stone wilderness, he would have thought they represented the Navajo *yei* called Talking God. Just above them was the figure of a bird—an unambiguous representation of the snowy egret. Above that, Kokopelli played his flute, bent so far forward that it pointed at the earth. The ground here was littered with shards of pottery but Leaphorn found no sign of the kayak. He hadn't expected to.

Relaunched, he paddled the kayak back into the current. Twilight now, and he found himself relaxing. Someone had said that "the rush of the river soothes the mind." It did seem to, in contrast to the sound of wind, which always made him tense. But the wind was moderating now. He heard the call of a bird behind him, and a coyote somewhere on the Utah side, and the distant voice of rapids from the darkness ahead.

He checked two possible landing points on the reservation side, and spent more time than he'd planned looking at the mouths of Butler Wash and Comb Creek on the Utah side. When he pushed off again, it was into the light of the rising moon—a little past full. Leaphorn heard an abrupt flurry of sound. A snowy egret had been startled from its roosting place. It flew away from him into the moonlight, a graceful white shape moving against the black cliff, solitary, disappearing into the darkness where the river bent.

Egrets, he thought, were like snow geese and wolves and those other creatures—like Leaphorn himself—that mated only once and for life. That would explain its presence here. It was living out its loneliness in this empty place. Leaphorn's kayak slid out of the darkness under the cliff and into a moonlit eddy. His shadow streaked out from that of the kayak, making a strange elongated shape. It reminded him of the bird, and he waved the paddle to magnify the effect. As he rested with his arms relaxed, he became the stick figure of the *yei* Black God as Navajo shamans represented him in the dry painting of the Night Chant. Bent over the paddle, pulling his weight against the water, he was Kokopelli, with his hunched back full of sorrows. He was thinking that, as the current swept him around the cliff into the dark. Here, with all black except the stars directly overhead, the shout of the river drowned out everything.

As the San Juan drops toward its rendezvous with the mighty Colorado, its rapids are relatively mild. It is the goal of those who run rivers for joy to nose their tough little kayaks into the throats of these cataracts for the thrill of being buried under the white water. It was Leaphorn's goal to skirt the bedlam and keep dry. Even so, he emerged soaked from the waist down and well splashed elsewhere. The river here had cut through the Comb Ridge anticline—what millions of years of erosion had left of the Monument Upwarp. Here, eons ago, the earth's crust had bulged outward in a massive bubble of bending stone layers. Leaphorn drifted past slanting layers of stone which, even in this dim light, gave the eerie impression of sliding toward the center of the earth.

Beyond the anticline, he used his flashlight to check another sandy bench and the mouth of two washes. Then, around another bend and through another rapids, he guided the kayak into the eddy where Many Ruins Wash drained a huge expanse of the Navajo Reservation into the San Juan. If he had a specific destination when he left Sand Island, this was it.

Leaphorn had long since stopped trying to keep dry. He waded knee-deep through the eddy, pulled the kayak well ashore, and sat on the sand beside it, catching his breath. He was weary. He was wet. He was cold. Abruptly, he was very, very cold. He found himself shaking and unable to control the motion. His hands shook. So did his legs. His teeth chattered. Hypothermia. Leaphorn had suffered it before. It frightened him then and it frightened him now.

He pushed himself to his feet, staggered down the sand, the flashlight beam jittering erratically ahead of him. He found a place where a flash flood had left a tangle of twigs. He fumbled the lip balm tube in which he kept kitchen matches out of his jacket, managed to get his shaking fingers to open it, managed to stuff desiccated grass under a pile of twigs, managed on the third match to get the fire going. He added driftwood, fanned the fire into a blaze with his hat, and stood beside it, panting and shaking.

In his panic he had made the fire in the wrong place. Now, with his jeans steaming and some warmth returning to his blood, he looked around for a better place. He built this new fire where two walls of stone formed a sand-floored pocket, collecting enough heavy driftwood to keep it going until morning. Then he dried his clothing thoroughly.

This was where he'd expected to find the kayak. Up this canyon somewhere he expected to find the site that had drawn Eleanor Friedman-Bernal. When the river delayed him, he'd decided to wait for daylight to hunt the kayak. But now he couldn't wait. Tired as he was, he picked up the flashlight and walked back to the water.

She had hidden it carefully, dragging it with more strength than he credited her with far up under the tangled branches of a cluster of tamarisks. He searched, expecting to find nothing, and finding only a little nylon packet jammed under the center tube. It held a red nylon poncho. Leaphorn kept it. Back at the fire, he kicked himself a loosened place in the sand, spread the poncho as a ground cloth and lay down to sleep, leaving his boots close enough to the flames to complete the drying process.

The flames attracted flying insects. The insects attracted the bats. Leaphorn watched them fluttering at the margin of the darkness, darting to make their kill, flashing away. Emma had disliked bats. Emma had admired lizards, had battled roaches endlessly, had given names to the various spiders that lived around their house and—all too often—in it. Emma would have enjoyed this trip. He had always planned to take her, but there was never time, until now, when time no longer mattered. Emma would have been intensely interested in the affair of Eleanor Friedman-Bernal, would have felt a rapport with her. Would have asked him, if he'd forgotten to report, what progress was being made. Would have had advice for him. Well, tomorrow he would find that woman. A sort of gift, it would be.

He shifted himself into the sand. A chunk of driftwood fell, sending a shower of sparks up toward the stars. Leaphorn slept.

The cold awakened him. The fire had burned to dim embers, the moon was down, and the sky over him was an incredible dazzle of stars humans can see only when high altitude, clear, dry air, and an absence of ground light combine. Below these black thousand-foot cliffs, it was like looking into space from the bottom of a well. Leaphorn rebuilt the fire and dozed off again, listening to the night sounds. Two coyotes were on their nocturnal hunt now somewhere up the canyon and he could hear another pair very distant across the river. He heard a saw-whet owl high in the cliffs, a cry as shrill as metal rubbing metal. Just as he fell into sleep he heard the sound of a flute. Or perhaps it was just part of his dream.

When he awoke again, he was shivering with cold. It was late dawn, with the coldest air of night settled into this canyon slot. He got up, flinching against the stiffness, restarted the fire, drank from his canteen, and looked for the first time into the sack of food Irene Musket had sent with him—a great chunk of fry bread and a coil of boiled Polish sausage. He was hungry, but he would wait. He might need it much more later.

Despite their age, he found a fair set of Eleanor Friedman-Bernal's tracks pressed into the hard sand under the tamarisks— where the hanging vegetation had protected them from the moving air. Then he methodically searched the rest of this junction of canyons. He wanted to confirm that this was the place Houk had come, and he did. In fact, Houk seemed to have come here often. Probably it was his monthly destination. Someone, presumably Houk, had repeatedly slid a kayak up the sloping sand at the extreme upper end of the bench and left it under a broken-off cottonwood. From there a narrow trail took an unlikely course about five hundred yards through the brush, through the little dunes of blown sand, and down into the bottom of Many Ruins. It stopped at a little cul-de-sac of boulders.

Leaphorn spent a half-hour in that much-used spot, partly because he could find no sign that Houk had gone beyond it. This sheltered place seemed to be where Houk's moonlit journeys ended. Again, he was looking for confirmation of what he was now sure must be true. This damp and protected place held footprints well, and Houk's were everywhere. Many were fresh, evidence of the final visit before his murder. On these Leaphorn focused his attention, narrowing it finally to two prints. Both had been pressed upon by something heavy and partly erased. A soft, edgeless pressure. But not a moccasin. Something odd about it. Finally, looking at both prints from every possible angle, Leaphorn realized what caused the strange lines. Fur. But they weren't animal tracks. When patched together in Leaphorn's mind, the pressed places had the shape of a man's foot.

With nothing else to learn, Leaphorn started up-canyon. While he walked he considered what he was now almost certain were the facts. Brigham Houk probably had not drowned. Somehow he had managed to get across the river. Brigham Houk, the boy who had slaughtered his mother, his brother, and his sister, was somewhere in this canyon. Had been here almost twenty years, living away from people as he had longed to live. Houk had found the boy after the hue and cry of murder died away, had sustained him secretly all these years with whatever this born hunter had needed to stay alive. Nothing else seemed to explain Houk's note. Nothing else Leaphorn could think of would have motivated the man to stop an admittedly futile effort to build a hiding place to write a note. Houk didn't want this mad son of his abandoned here. He wanted him found by the same policeman who had once shown some awareness of the boy's humanity. He wanted him cared for, and he'd given up whatever minuscule chance he'd had of living to write his note. The writing had been tiny, Leaphorn remembered, and started at one end of the card. What would Houk have said had time allowed? Would he have explained about Brigham? He'd never know.

About two miles up the twisting canyon Leaphorn found the only sign of modern human occupancy. The bare poles of an old sweat bath stood on the broad shelf above the canyon floor. The ashes under it suggested it hadn't been used for years. If the canyon had ever been grazed, it hadn't been recently. He found no tracks of horses, sheep, or goats. The only hoofprints he found were mule deer, and there seemed to be plenty of rabbits, porcupines, and small rodents. He noticed three game trails leading to a deep spring-fed pothole at the canyon bottom. Four miles up, he stopped in a shady place and ate a small piece of the bread and a couple of inches of the sausage. There was heavy cloud cover over the northwest sky now. It was colder and yesterday's wind was back again now with a vengeance. It blew cross-canyon, forming powerful eddies of air that swirled this way here, and that way there. It made the odd sounds wind makes when it pours through stony crevices. It sent whirlwinds of fallen leaves sweeping around Leaphorn's legs. It blotted out all other sound.

The wind made walking difficult, and the crooked, erratic nature of the canyon bottom made estimating distance—even for one as experienced as Leaphorn—little more than guesswork. Double guesswork, he thought. He had to guess how much of this climbing over tumbled boulders and detouring around brush would have added to the five and a half miles Etcitty had estimated. It would be less than that, he was sure, and he'd been looking for the landmarks Etcitty had mentioned since about mile three. Just ahead, where the canyon bottom made a sharp bend, he saw a crevice in the cliff walled in with stones—an Anasazi storeroom. On the cliff below it, half obscured by tall brush, he saw pictographs. He climbed the soft earth to the floor of the bench and pushed his way through the heavy growth of nettles for a closer look.

The dominant shape was one of those broad-shouldered, pinheaded figures that anthropologists believe represented Anasazi shamans. It looked, as Etcitty had described it, "like a big baseball umpire holding up a pink chest protector." Leaphorn recrossed the canyon bottom and climbed the shelf on the other side. He saw what he had come to find.

Near its beginnings in the Chuska Mountains, Many Ruins Canyon is cut deep and narrow through the Chinle sandstone formation of that plateau. There its cliffs rise sheer and vertical almost a thousand feet above a narrow, sandy bottom. It is much shallower by the time it emerges into Chinle Valley and becomes a mere drainage wash as it meanders northward toward Utah through the Greasewood Flats. But the cut deepens again in its passage through the Nokaito Bench to the San Juan. Here the crazy mishmash geology of the earth's crust had given Many Ruins a different shape. One climbed out of it on a series of steps. First the low, sometimes earthen cliffs that crowded its narrow streambed, then a broken sandstone shelf hundreds of yards wide, then more cliffs, rising to another shelf, and still more cliffs rising to the flat top of Nokaito Mesa.

In the spring when the snowpack melts a hundred miles away in the Chuska Mountains, Many Ruins carries a steady stream. In the late-summer thunderstorm season it rises and falls between a trickle and booming flash floods, which send boulders tumbling like marbles down its bottom. In late autumn it dries. The life that occupied it finds water then only in spring-fed potholes. From where he stood on the sandstone shelf above such a pothole, Leaphorn could see the second of the ruins Etcitty had described. Two ruins, in fact.

Part of the wall of one was visible in an alcove in the second level of cliffs above him. Another, reduced to little more than a brushy hump, had been built along the base of the cliff not two hundred yards from the alcove.

All this day he had fought down his sense of excitement and urgency. He had a long ways to go and he went at a careful walk. Now he trotted across the sandstone bench.

He stopped when the alcove came in full view. Like those invariably picked as building sites by the Anasazi, it faced the low winter sun, with enough overhang to shade it in the summer. A cluster of brushy vegetation grew under it, telling him it was also the site of seep. He walked toward it, more slowly now. He didn't consider Brigham Houk particularly dangerous. Houk had called him schizophrenic—unpredictable but not likely to be a threat to a stranger. Still, he had killed once in an insane rage. Leaphorn unsnapped the flap that held his pistol in its holster.

Eons of water running down the inner face of the alcove had worn a depression several feet into the sandstone below it. Water stains indicated this held a pool about four feet deep in wetter seasons. Now only a foot or two was left—still fed by a tiny trickle from a mossy crevice in the cliff, and now green with algae. It was also the home of scores of tiny leopard frogs, which hopped away from Leaphorn's feet.

Only some of them hopped.

Leaphorn squatted, grunted with surprise. He studied the small scattered frog bodies, some already shriveled, some newly dead, each with a leg secured by a yucca thread to a tiny peg cut from a twig. He stood, trying to make sense of this. The pegs followed a series of faint concentric circles drawn around the pothole, the outside one perhaps four feet from the water. Some sort of game, Leaphorn guessed. He tried to understand the mind that would be amused by it. He failed. Brigham Houk was insane, probably dangerous.

He considered. Brigham Houk almost certainly would already know he was here.

Leaphorn made a megaphone of his hands. "Eleanor," he shouted. "Ellie. Ellie." Then he listened.

Nothing. Outside the alcove, the wind made whimpering sounds.

He tried again. Again, nothing.

The Anasazi had built their structure on a stone shelf above the pool. About a dozen small rooms once, Leaphorn estimated, with part of it at two levels. He skirted around the pool, climbed over the tumbled walls, peered into the still-intact rooms. Nothing. He walked back to the pool, puzzled. Where to look next?

At the edge of the alcove, a worn set of footholds had been cut into the sandstone—a climbway leading to the shelf above the alcove. Perhaps that led to another site. He walked out of the alcove around the cliff to the brushy hump. Immediately he saw it had been plundered. A ditch had been dug along the outside wall. Bones were scattered everywhere. The digging had been recent—hardly any rain since the earth was disturbed. Leaphorn inspected it. Was this why Eleanor Friedman-Bernal had slipped away from Chaco, slipped down the San Juan? To search this site for her polychrome pots? So it would seem. And what had happened then? What had interrupted her? He checked in the disturbed earth for shards and collected a handful. They might be the sort that interested her. He couldn't be sure. He looked down in the trench. Jutting from the earth was part of a pot. And another. In the bottom were a half-dozen shards, two of them large. Why had she left them there? Then he noticed an oddity. Among the bones littering the trench he saw no skulls. On the earth outside more than a dozen were scattered. None had jawbones. Natural, probably. The mandible would be attached only by muscle and gristle, which wouldn't survive an eight-hundred-year burial. Then where were the missing mandibles? He saw five of them together beside the trench, as if discarded there. It reminded him of the jawbones lined so neatly at the dig site where Etcitty and Nails had died.

But where was the woman who had dug the trench? He went back to the pool and inspected the footholds. Then he started climbing, thinking as he did that he was far too old for this. Fifty feet up the cliff, he was aware of two facts. These Anasazi footholds were in regular current use, and he was a damn fool to have attempted the climb. He clung to the stone, reaching blindly for the next handhold, wondering how many remained. Finally the slope eased. He looked up. He had done it. His head was almost even with the top. He pulled himself up, his upper body over the edge.

Standing there, watching him, was a man. He wore a beard cut straight across, a nylon jacket so new it still had the creases of its folds, a pair of tattered jeans, and moccasins that seemed to have been sewn together from deer hide.

"Mr. Leaphorn," the man said. "Papa said you coming."

19

AS HARRISON HOUK'S MESSAGE to him had promised, Dr. Eleanor Friedman-Bernal was still alive. She lay dozing under a gray wool blanket and a covering of sewn-together rabbit skins. She looked very, very ill.

"Can she talk?" he asked Brigham.

"A little," he said. "Sometimes."

It occurred to Leaphorn that Brigham Houk might have been describing himself. He talked very little and sometimes not at all. What you'd expect, Leaphorn thought, after twenty years of no one to talk to except once every full moon.

"How bad is it? Her injuries I mean?"

"Knee's hurt," he said. "Arm broken. Place in her side. Place in her hip."

And probably all infected, Leaphorn thought. Thin as her face was, it was flushed.

"You found her and brought her here?"

Brigham nodded. Like his father, he was a small man, tightly built, with short arms and legs and a thick, strong torso.

"Do you know what happened to her?"

"The devil came and hurt her," Brigham said in an odd, flat voice. "He hit her. She ran away. He chased. She fell down. He pushed her off. She fell into the canyon. Broke everything."

Brigham had made a bed for her by digging a coffin-shaped pit in the sand that had drifted into a room of the sheltered ruin. He'd filled it with a two- or three-foot layer of leaves. Open as it was to the air, it had the sickroom smell of urine and decay.

"Tell me about this," Leaphorn said.

Brigham was standing at what had been the entry door to the

little room—now a narrow gap into a roofless space. Behind him the sky was dark. The wind, which had fallen during the afternoon, was blowing again now. It blew steadily out of the northwest. Winter, Leaphorn thought. He kept his eyes locked with Brigham's. The young man's eyes were the same odd blue-gray as his father's. Had the same intensity about them. Leaphorn looked into them, searching for insanity. Looking for it, he found it.

"This devil came," Brigham said, speaking very slowly. "He dug up the bones, and sat on the ground there looking at them. One after another he would look at them. He would measure them with a tool he had. He was looking for the souls of people who never had been prayed for. He would suck the souls out of the skulls and then he would throw them away. Or some of them he would take away in his sack. And then one day the last time the moon was full—" He paused and his somber bearded face converted into an expression of delight. "When the moon is full, that's when Papa comes and talks to me, and brings me what I need." The smile drifted away. "A little after that, this woman came." He nodded at Friedman-Bernal. "I didn't see her come and I think maybe the angel Moroni brought her because I didn't see her come and I see everything in this place. Moroni left her to fight with that devil. She had come to the old cliff house down below here where I keep my frogs. I didn't know she was there. I was playing my flute and I frightened her and she ran away. But the next day, she came to where the devil was digging up the bones. I saw them talking."

Brigham's mobile face became fierce. His eyes seemed to glitter with the anger. "He knocked her down, and he was on top of her, fighting with her. He got up and was searching through her pack, and she jumped up and ran over to the edge where the cliff drops down to the streambed and then she fell down. That devil, he went over and pushed her over with his foot." Brigham stopped, his face wet with tears.

"He just left her there, where she fell?"

Brigham nodded.

"You kept her alive," Leaphorn said. "But now I think she is starting to die. We have to get her out of here. To a hospital where doctors can give her medicine."

Brigham stared at him. "Papa said I could trust you." The statement was reproachful.

"If we don't get her out, she dies," Leaphorn said.

"Papa will bring medicine. The next time the moon is full he will come with it."

"Too long," Leaphorn said. "Look at her."

Brigham looked. "She's asleep," he said, softly.

"She has fever. Feel her face. How hot. She has infections. She has to have help."

Brigham touched Eleanor Friedman-Bernal's cheek with the tips of his fingers. He jerked them away, looking frightened. Leaphorn thought of the shriveled bodies of the frogs and tried to square that image with this tenderness. How do you square insanity?

"We need to make something to carry her on," Leaphorn said. "If you can find two poles long enough, we can tie the blanket between them and carry her on that."

"No," Brigham Houk said. "When I try to move her, to clean her after she does number one or number two, she screams. It hurts too bad."

"No choice," Leaphorn said. "We have to do it."

"It's terrible," Brigham said. "She screams. I can't stand that, so I had to leave her dirty." He looked at Leaphorn for understanding. Houk had apparently given him a haircut and trimmed his beard on the last visit. The old man was no barber. He had simply left the hair about an inch long everywhere, and whacked the beard off a half-inch under Brigham's chin.

"It was better to leave her dirty," Leaphorn said. "You did right. Now, can you find me two poles?"

Brigham nodded. "Just a minute. I have poles. It's close." He disappeared, making no sound at all.

Here is how it must have been when man lived as predator, Leaphorn thought. He developed the animal skills, and starved with his children when the skill failed him. How had Brigham hunted? Traps, probably, and a bow to kill larger game. Perhaps his father had brought him a gun—but someone might have heard gunshots. He listened to the sound of Eleanor Friedman's shallow breathing, and over that, the wind sounds. Suddenly he heard a thumping. Steady at first, then louder. He leaped to his feet. A helicopter. But before he could get into the open there was only the wind. He stared into the grayness, frustrated. He had found her. He must get her out of here alive. The risk lay in carrying such a fragile load over such rough terrain. It would be difficult. It might be impossible. A helicopter would save her. Why hadn't Houk done more to get her out? No time, Leaphorn guessed. His son had told him of this injured woman, but perhaps not how near she was to death. Houk would have wanted a way to save the woman without giving up this mad son to life (or perhaps death) in a prison for the criminally insane. Even Houk needed time to solve such a puzzle. He was too crippled to bring her out himself. If he did, she would talk of the man who had nursed her, and Brigham would be found—an insane triple murderer in the eyes of the law. The only solution Leaphorn saw would be to find Brigham another hideaway. That would take time, and the killer had allowed Houk no time.

The woman stirred, moaned. He and Brigham would have to carry her to the canyon bottom, then five miles down to the river. They could tie the kayaks together, put her litter on one of them, and float her to Mexican Hat. Five or six hours at least, and then an ambulance would come for her. Or the copter would come from Farmington if the weather allowed. It hadn't been too bad for whatever had just flown over.

He walked out under the dark sky. He smelled ozone. Snow was near. Then he saw Randall Elliot walking toward him.

Elliot raised his hand. "I saw you from up there," he said, pointing past Leaphorn to the rim of the mesa. "Came down to see if you needed help."

"Sure," Leaphorn said. "Lots of help."

Elliot stopped a few feet away. "You find her?"

Leaphorn nodded toward the ruin, remembering Elliot was a copter pilot.

"How is she?"

"Not good," Leaphorn said.

"But alive at least?"

"In a coma," Leaphorn said. "She can't talk." He wanted Elliot to know that immediately. "I doubt if she'll live."

"My God," Elliot said. "What happened to her?"

"I think she fell," Leaphorn said. "A long ways. That's what it looks like."

Elliot was frowning. "She's in there?" he said. "How did she get here?"

"A man lives out here. A hermit. He found her and he's been trying to keep her alive."

"I'll be damned," Elliot said. He moved past Leaphorn. "In here?"

Leaphorn followed. They stood, Elliot staring at Friedman-Bernal, Leaphorn watching Elliot. He wanted to handle this just exactly right. Only Elliot could fly the helicopter.

"A hermit found her?" he said softly, posing the question to himself. He shook his head. "Where is he?"

"He went to get a couple of poles. We're going to make a litter. Carry her down to the San Juan. Her kayak's there, and mine. Float her down to Mexican Hat and get help."

Elliot was looking at her again, studying her. "I have a helicopter up on the mesa. We can carry her up there. Much quicker."

"Great," Leaphorn said. "Lucky you found us."

"Really, it was stupid," Elliot said. "I should have remembered about this place. She'd told me once she'd found the polychrome pattern she was chasing on potsherds in here. Back when she was helping inventory these sites. I knew she'd planned to come back." He turned away from the woman. His eyes locked with Leaphorn's.

"As a matter of fact, she said some things that made me think she had come here earlier. She didn't exactly say it, but I think she did some illegal digging in here. I think she found what she was looking for, and she came back to get some more."

"I think you're right," Leaphorn said. "She dug up that ruins on the shelf down below here. Dug up a bunch of graves."

"And got careless," Elliot added, looking at her.

Leaphorn nodded. Where was Brigham? He'd said just a minute. Leaphorn walked out of the ruin, looking along the talus slope under the cliff. Two poles leaned against the wall not ten feet away. Brigham had returned and seen his devil, and gone away. The poles were fir, apparently, and weathered. Driftwood, Leaphorn guessed, carried down Many Ruins all the way from the mountains by one of its flash floods. On the ground beside them was a loop of rawhide rope. He hurried back into the room with them.

"A very skittish man," Leaphorn said. "He left the poles and disappeared again."

"Oh," Elliot said. He looked skeptical.

They doubled the blanket, made lacing holes, and tied it securely to the poles.

"Be very careful," Leaphorn said. "Knee probably broken. Broken arm, all sorts of internal injuries."

"I used to collect the wounded," Elliot said, without looking up. "I'm good at this."

And Elliot seemed to be careful. Even so, Eleanor Friedman-Bernal uttered a strangled moan. Then she was unconscious again.

"I think she fainted," Elliot said. "Do you really think she's dying?"

"I do," Leaphorn said. "I'm giving you the heavy end because you're younger and stronger and not so exhausted."

"Fair," Elliot said. He picked up the end of the poles at the woman's head.

"You know the way back to your copter, so you lead the way."

They carried Eleanor Friedman-Bernal carefully down the talus, then toward a long rock slide which sloped down from the rim. Beyond the slide—probably the cause of it—was a deep erosion cut which carried runoff water down from the top. Elliot turned toward the cut.

"Rest a minute," Leaphorn said. "Put her down on this slab."

He was fairly sure now what Elliot planned. Somewhere between here and the helicopter, wherever that was, something fatal had to happen to Eleanor Friedman-Bernal. Elliot simply could not risk having her arrive at a hospital alive. Ideally, something fatal would also happen to Leaphorn. If Elliot was smart, he would wait until they had climbed a hundred feet or so up the cut. Then he would push the litter backward, tumbling Friedman-Bernal and Leaphorn down the jumble of boulders. Then he would climb back down and do whatever was needed, if anything, to finish them off. A bang of the head on a rock would do it and leave nothing to arouse the suspicion of a medical examiner. Figuring that out had been easy enough. Knowing what to do about it was another matter. He could think of nothing. Shooting Elliot was shooting the copter pilot. Pointing a gun at him to force him to fly them out wasn't practical. Elliot would know Leaphorn wouldn't shoot him once they were airborne. He'd be able to make the helicopter do tricks that Leaphorn couldn't handle. And he probably had the little pistol. And yet, once they started that steep climb, Elliot had simply to drop his end of the litter and Leaphorn would be helpless.

"Is this the only way up?" Leaphorn asked.

"Only one I could see," Elliot said. "It's not as bad as it looks. We can take it slow."

"I'll wait here with the lady," Leaphorn said. "You fly the copter down here, land it somewhere where we don't have to make the climb." You could land a copter on this shelf if you had to, Leaphorn guessed. You'd have to be good, but someone who'd flown evacuations in Vietnam would be very good.

Elliot seemed to consider. "That's a thought," he said.

He reached into his jacket, extracted a small blue automatic pistol, and pointed it at Leaphorn's throat. "Unbuckle your belt," he said.

Leaphorn unbuckled it.

"Pull it out."

Leaphorn pulled it out. His holster fell to the ground.

"Now kick the gun over here to me."

Leaphorn did.

"You make it tough," Elliot said.

"Not tough enough."

Elliot laughed.

"You'd rather not have a bullet hole in me," Leaphorn said. "Or her either."

"That's right," Elliot said. "But I don't have any choice now. You seem to have figured it out."

"I figured you were going to get us far enough up the rocks to make it count and then tumble us down."

Elliot nodded.

"I'm not sure of your motive for all this. Killing so many people."

"Maxie told you that day," Elliot said. The good humor was suddenly gone, replaced by bitter anger. "What the hell can a rich kid do to impress anyone?"

"Impress Maxie," Leaphorn said. "A truly beautiful young woman." And he was thinking, maybe I'm like you. I don't want this to go wrong now because of Emma. Emma put little value on finding people to punish them. But this would really have impressed her. You love a woman, you want to impress her. The male instinct. Hero finds lost woman. The life saved. He didn't want it to go wrong now. But it had. In a very little while, wherever and whenever it was most convenient, Randall Elliot would kill Eleanor Friedman-Bernal and Joe Leaphorn. He could think of nothing to prevent it. Except maybe Brigham Houk.

Brigham must be somewhere near. It had taken him only minutes to get the poles and return. He had seen his devil, recognized him, and slipped away. Brigham Houk was a hunter. Brigham Houk was also insane, and afraid of this devil. What would he do? Leaphorn thought he knew.

"We'll leave her here for now and we'll walk over there," Elliot said, pointing with the pistol toward the edge of the shelf. It was exactly the direction Leaphorn wanted to go. It was the only way that led to convenient shelter. It must be the way Brigham had gone.

"It's going to look funny if too many people fall off things," Leaphorn said. "Two is too many."

"I know," Elliot said. "Do you have a better idea?"

"Maybe," Leaphorn said. "Tell me your motive for all this."

"I think you guessed," Elliot said.

"I guess Maxie," Leaphorn said. "You want her. But she's a self-made, class-conscious woman with a lot of bad memories of being put down by the upper class. On top of that, she's a tough one, a little mean. She resents you, and everybody like you, because it's all handed to you. So I think you're going to do something that has nothing to do with being born to the upper, upper, upper class. Something that neither Maxie nor anybody else can ignore. From what you told me at Chaco it's something to do with tracing what happened to these Anasazi by tracking genetic flaws."

"How about that," Elliot said. "You're not as dumb as you try to act."

"You found the flaw you were hunting in the bones here, and over at the site on the Checkerboard, too, I guess. You were digging here illegally, and our friend here came in and caught you at it."

Elliot held up his empty hand. "So I tried to kill her and screwed it up."

"Curious about something," Leaphorn said. "Were you the one who called in the complaint about Eleanor being a pot hunter?"

"Sure," Elliot said. "You figured why?"

"Not really," Leaphorn said. Where the devil was Brigham Houk? Maybe he'd run. Leaphorn doubted it. His father wouldn't have run. But then his father wasn't schizophrenic.

"You can't get a permit to dig," Elliot said. "Not in your lifetime. These asshole bureaucrats are always saving it for the future. Well, if a site is being vandalized, that puts it in a different category. Not so tough then, after it's already been messed up. I was going to follow up later with some hints about where to find digs Eleanor was stealing from. They'd find her body, so they'd have their Thief of Time. They wouldn't have to be looking for one and maybe suspecting me. And then I'd get my dig permit." He laughed. "Roundabout way, but I've seen it work."

"You were getting your bones anyway," Leaphorn said. "Buying some, digging some up yourself."

"Wrong category, friend," Elliot said. "Those are unofficial bones. Not 'in site.' I was finding 'em unofficially, so I'd know where to find 'em officially when I got my permit. You understand that?" Elliot peered at him, grinning. He was enjoying this. "When I get my permit to excavate, I come back and the bones I find then are registered in place. Photographed. Documented." He grinned again. "Same bones, maybe, but now they're official."

"How about Etcitty," Leaphorn asked, "and Nails?" Over Elliot's shoulder, Leaphorn had seen Brigham Houk. He saw Houk because the man wanted Leaphorn to see him. He was behind a fallen sandstone slab, screened by brush. He held something that might have been a curved staff and he motioned Leaphorn toward him.

"That was a mistake," Elliot said.

"Killing them?"

Elliot laughed. "That was correcting the mistake. Nails was too careless. And too greedy. Once the silly bastards stole that backhoe they were sure to get caught." He glanced at Leaphorn. "And Nails was sure to tell you guys everything he knew."

"Which would have been bad for your reputation," Leaphorn said.

"Disastrous," Elliot said. He waved the pistol. "But hurry it up. I want to get out of here."

"If you're working on what I think," Leaphorn said, "there's something I want to show you. Something Friedman-Bernal found. You're interested in jaw deformities. Something like that?"

"Well, a little like that," Elliot said. "You understand how the human chromosome works? Fetus inherits twenty-three from its mother, twenty-three from its father. Genetic characteristics handed down in the genes. Once in a while polyploidy occurs in the genetic crossover points. Someone gets multiple chromosomes, and you get a characteristic change. Inheritable. But you need more than one to do a trace which has any real meaning. At Chaco, in some of the early Chaco burials, I found three that were passed along. A surplus molar in the left mandible. And that went along with a thickening of the frontal bone over the left eye socket, plus—" Elliot stopped. "You understanding this?"

"Genetics wasn't my favorite course. Too much math," Leaphorn said. What the devil was Brigham Houk doing? Was he still behind that slab up ahead?

"Exactly," Elliot said, pleased by this. "It's one percent digging and ninety-nine percent working out statistical models for your computer. Anyway, the third thing, which sort of mathematically proves the passalong genes, is that hole in the mandible through which the blood and nerve tissue passes. At Chaco, from about 650 A.D. until they turned out the lights, this family had two holes in the left mandible and the usual one in the right. Plus those other characteristics. And out here, I'm still finding it among these exiles. Can you see why it's important?"

"And fascinating," Leaphorn said. "Dr. Friedman must have known what you were looking for. She saved a lot of jawbones." He was almost to the great sandstone slab. "I'll show you."

"I doubt if she found anything I overlooked," Elliot said. He followed Leaphorn, keeping the pistol level. "But this is the way we were going anyway."

They were passing the sandstone now. Leaphorn tensed. If nothing happened here, he would have to try something else. It wouldn't work, but he wouldn't simply stand still to be shot.

"Right over here," Leaphorn said.

"I think you're just—"

The sentence ended with a grunt, a great exhalation of breath. Leaphorn turned. Elliot was leaning slightly forward, the pistol hanging at his side. About six inches of arrow shaft and the feathered tip protruded from his jacket.

Leaphorn reached for him, heard the whistle and thump of the second arrow. It went through Elliot's neck. The pistol clattered on the stone. Elliot collapsed.

Leaphorn retrieved the pistol. He squatted beside the man, turned him on his back. His eyes were open but he seemed to be in shock. Blood trickled from the corner of his mouth.

There was snow in the wind now, little dry flakes that skittered along the surface like white dust. Leaphorn tested the arrow. It was the sort of bow hunters buy in sporting goods stores and it was lodged solidly through Elliot's neck. Pulling it out would just make things worse. If they could be worse. Elliot was dying. Leaphorn stood, looking for Brigham Houk. Houk was standing beside the slab now, holding a great ugly bow of metal, wood, and plastic, looking upward. From somewhere Leaphorn heard the clatter of a helicopter. Brigham Houk had heard it earlier. He stood very close to cover, ready to vanish.

The helicopter emerged over the rim of the mesa almost directly overhead. Leaphorn waved, saw an answering wave. The copter circled and disappeared over the mesa again.

Leaphorn checked Elliot's pulse. He didn't seem to have one. He looked for Brigham Houk, who seemed never to have existed. He walked over to the litter where Dr. Eleanor Friedman-Bernal lay. She opened her eyes, looked at him without recognition, closed them again. He tucked the rabbit fur cloak around her, careful to apply no pressure. Now it was snowing harder, still blowing like dust. He walked back to Elliot. No pulse now. He opened his jacket and shirt and felt for a heartbeat. Nothing. The man was no longer breathing. Randall Elliot, graduate of Exeter, of Princeton, of Harvard, winner of the Navy Cross, was dead by arrow shot. Leaphorn gripped him under the arms and pulled him into the cover of the slab where Brigham Houk had hidden. Elliot was heavy, and Leaphorn was exhausted. By pulling hard and doing some twisting, he extracted the arrows. He wiped the blood off as well as he could on Elliot's jacket. Then he picked up a rock, hammered them into pieces, and put the pieces in his hip pocket. That done, he found dead brush, broke it off, and made an inefficient effort to cover the body. But it didn't matter. The coyotes would find Randall Elliot anyway.

Then he heard the clatter of someone scrambling down the cut. It proved to be Officer Chee, looking harassed and disheveled.

It took some effort for Leaphorn not to show he was impressed. He pointed to the litter. "We need to get Dr. Friedman to the hospital in a hurry," he said. "Can you get that thing down here to load her?"

"Sure," Chee said. He started back toward the cut at a run.

"Just a second," Leaphorn said.

Chee stopped.

"What did you see?"

Chee raised his eyebrows. "I saw you standing beside a man slumped down on the ground. I guess it was Elliot. And I saw the litter over there. And maybe I saw another man. Something jumping out of sight back there just as we came over the top."

"Why did you think it was Elliot?"

Chee looked surprised. "The helicopter he rented is parked up there. I figured when he heard she was still alive he'd have to come out here and kill her before you got here."

Leaphorn again was impressed. This time he made a little less effort to conceal it. "Do you know how Elliot knew she was alive?"

Chee made a wry face. "I more or less told him."

"And then made the connection?"

"Then I found out he had filed for permission to dig this site, and the site where he killed Etcitty. Turned down on both of them. I went out there to talk to him and found—you remember the box of plastic wastebasket liners at the Checkerboard site. One missing from it. Well, it was hidden in Elliot's kitchen. Had jawbones in it."

Leaphorn didn't ask how Chee had gotten into Elliot's kitchen.

"Go ahead, then, and get the copter down here. And don't say anything."

Chee looked at him.

"I mean don't say anything at all. I'll fill you in when we get a chance."

Chee trotted toward the cut.

"Thank you," Leaphorn said. He wasn't sure if Chee heard that.

It was snowing hard by the time they had the litter loaded and the copter lifted off the shelf. Leaphorn was jammed against the side. He looked down on a stone landscape cut into vertical blocks by time and now blurred by snow. He looked quickly away. He could ride the big jets, barely. Something in his inner ear made anything less stable certain nausea. He closed his eyes, swallowed. This was the first snow. They would come when the weather cleared to recover the copter and look for Elliot. But they wouldn't look hard because it was so obviously hopeless. Snow would have covered everything. After the thaw, they would come again. Then they would find the bones, scattered like the Anasazi skeletons he looted. There would be no sign of the arrow wounds then. Cause of death unknown, the coroner would write. Victim eaten by predators.

He glanced back. Chee was jammed in the compartment beside the litter, his hand on Dr. Eleanor Friedman-Bernal's arm. She seemed to be awake. I will ask him what curing ceremony he would recommend, Leaphorn thought, and knew at once that his fatigue was making him silly. Instead he said nothing. He thought of the circumstances, of how proud Emma would be of him tonight if she could be home to hear about this woman brought safely to the hospital. He thought about Brigham Houk. In just about twenty-four more days, the moon would be full again. Brigham would be waiting at the mouth of Many Ruins Canyon, but Papa wouldn't come.

I will go, Leaphorn thought. Someone has to tell him. And that meant that he would have to postpone his plan to leave the reservation, probably a long postponement. Solving the problem of what to do about Brigham Houk would take more than one trip down the river. And if he had to stick around, he might as well withdraw that letter. As Captain Nez had said, he could always write it again.

Jim Chee noticed Leaphorn was watching him.

"You all right?" Chee asked.

"I've felt better," Leaphorn said. And then he had another thought. He considered it. Why not? "I hear you're a medicine man. I heard you are a singer of the Blessing Way. Is that right?"

Chee looked slightly stubborn. "Yes sir," he said.

"I would like to ask you to sing one for me," Leaphorn said.

TALKING GOD

This book is dedicated to Delbert Kedelty, Terry Teller, David Charley, Donald Tsosie, and the other kids at Tsaile School who drew the Yeibichai pictures that started me thinking about Talking God.

And to Will Tsosie, Tsosie Tsinijinnie, Tribal Councilman Melvin Bigthumb, and the others who fight to preserve Hajiinei-Dine'tah and its ruins and pictographs for future generations.

The author is grateful to Caroline L. Rose, Martin Burke, Don Ortner, Jo Allyn Archambault, and other curators, conservators, and generally good people at the Smithsonian's National Museum of Natural History for putting up with me and giving me some insight into what goes on behind the exhibits at a great museum.

THROUGH THE DOORWAY which led from her receptionist-secretary's office into her own, Catherine Morris Perry instantly noticed the box on her desk. It was bulky—perhaps three feet long and almost as high. The legend printed on it said it had originally contained a microwave oven manufactured by General Electric. Strips of brown tape had been wrapped erratically around it. It was a crude box, incongruous amid the pale pastels and tasteful artifacts of Catherine Perry's stylish office.

"How was the weekend?" Markie said.

Catherine Morris Perry hung her raincoat on its peg, hung her rain hat over it, removed the transparent plastic from her shoes, and said, "Hello, Markie."

"How was Vermont?" Markie asked. "Wet up there, too?"

"Where'd that come from?" Catherine said, indicating the box.

"Federal Express," Markie said. "I signed for it."

"Am I expecting anything?"

"Not that you told me about. How was Vermont?"

"Wet," Catherine said. She did not wish to discuss Vermont, or anything else involving life outside this office, with Markie Bailey. What she did wish to discuss with Markie was taste. Or lack of taste. Putting the big box, brown and ugly, on her antique desk, as Markie had done, was typical of the problem. It squatted there, ugly, obscenely out of place. As out of place as Mrs. Bailey was in this office. But getting rid of her would be almost impossible. Certainly a huge amount of trouble under federal civil service rules. Mrs. Perry's specialty in law was not personnel, but she had learned something from the efforts to get rid of Henry Highhawk, that troublemaking conservator in the Museum of Natural History. What an unending fiasco that had been.

"You had a call," Markie said. "The cultural attaché's office at the Chilean embassy. He wanted an appointment."

"Later," Catherine Morris Perry said. "I'll return it later." She knew what that problem would be. Another Indian giver problem. General Something-or-Other wanting artifacts returned. He claimed his great-grandfather had only loaned them to some big shot in United Fruit, and he had no right to give them to the Smithsonian, and they were national treasures and must be returned. Incan, as she remembered. Gold, of course. Gold masks, encrusted with jewels, and the general would probably decide they were the general's personal treasure, if he could get his hands on them. And seeing that he didn't meant a huge amount of work for her, research into documents and into international law, which she should get working on right away.

But there sat the box taking up desk space. It was addressed to her as "Museum Spokesperson." Catherine Morris Perry didn't like being addressed as "Spokesperson." That she was so addressed probably stemmed from the statement she'd given the *Washington Post* on museum policy. It had been more or less an accident, the whole thing. The reporter's call had been referred to her only because someone was sick in the public affairs office, and someone else was away from his desk, and whoever had handled the call had decided a lawyer should deal with it. It concerned Henry Highhawk again, obliquely at least. It concerned the trouble he was stirring up about returning aboriginal skeletal remains. And the *Post* had called and identified her incorrectly as spokesperson, and quoted her when they should have quoted the museum board of directors. The policy on skeletons was, after all, official policy of the board. And a sound policy.

The Federal Express shipping order attached to the box was correct except for the erroneous title. She was "Temporary Assistant Counsel, Public Affairs" on loan from the Department of the Interior. She sat and flipped quickly through the remainder of her mail. Nothing much. What was probably an invitation from the National Ballet Guild to an upcoming fund-raiser. Something from the American Civil Liberties Union. A memo from the museum maintenance director telling her why it was impossible for him to deal with a personnel complaint as the law required him to. Another letter concerning insurance for borrowed items going into an exhibit opening next month, and three letters which seemed to be from private outside sources, none familiar.

Catherine Morris Perry put all the envelopes aside unopened, looked at the box, and made a wry face. She opened her desk drawer and extracted her letter opener. Then she buzzed Mrs. Bailey.

"Yes'um."

"Mrs. Bailey. When packages arrive like this, don't bring them in and put them on my desk. Open them and get the contents out."

"Okay," Mrs. Bailey said. "I'll open it now. It's a heavy thing." She paused. "Mrs. Paterson always wanted all the mail put in on her desk."

"I'll open it," Catherine said. "I meant from now on. And Mrs. Paterson is on leave. She is not in charge now."

"Okay," Mrs. Bailey said. "Did you notice the telephone messages? Two of them? On your desk, there?"

"No," Catherine said. They were probably under the box.

"Dr. Hebert called and just said he wanted to congratulate you on the way you handled the skeleton thing. On what you said in the *Post*."

With her free hand Catherine Perry was slicing the tape away with the letter opener. She thought that this box was probably a result of that story in the *Washington Post*. Any time the museum got into the news, it reminded a thousand old ladies of things in the attic that should be saved for posterity. Since she was quoted, one of them had sent this trash to her by name. What would it be? A dusty old butter churn? A set of family albums?

"The other one was somebody in the anthropology division. I put her name on the slip. Wants you to call. Said it was about the Indians wanting their skeletons back."

"Right," Catherine said. She pulled open the top flaps. Under them was a copy of the *Washington Post*, folded to expose the story that had quoted her. Part of it was circled in black.

MUSEUM OFFERS COMPROMISE
IN OLD BONE CONTROVERSY

The headline irritated Catherine. There had been no compromise. She had simply stated the museum's policy. If an Indian tribe wanted ancestral bones returned, it had only to ask for them and provide some acceptable proof that the bones in question had indeed been taken from a burial ground of the tribe. The entire argument was ridiculous and demeaning. In fact, even dealing with that Highhawk man was demeaning. Him and his Paho Society. A museum underling and an organization which, as far as anybody knew, existed only in his imagination. And only to create trouble. She glanced at the circled paragraph.

"Mrs. Catherine Perry, an attorney for the museum and its spokesperson on this issue, said the demand by the Paho Society for the reburial of the museum's entire collection of more than 18,000 Native American skeletons was 'simply not possible in light of the museum's purpose.'

"She said the museum is a research institution as well as a gallery for public display, and that the museum's collection of ancient human bones is a potentially important source of anthropological information. She said that Mr. Highhawk's suggestion that the museum make plaster casts of the skeletons and rebury the originals was not practical 'both because of research needs and because the public has the right to expect authenticity and not to be shown mere reproductions.' "

The clause "the right to expect authenticity" was underlined. Catherine Morris Perry frowned at it, sensing criticism. She picked up the newspaper. Under it, atop a sheet of brown wrapping paper, lay an envelope. Her name had been written neatly on it. She opened it and pulled out a single sheet of typing paper. While she read, her idle hand was pulling away the layer of wrapping paper which had separated the envelope from the contents of the box.

"Dear Mrs. Perry:

"You won't bury the bones of our ancestors because you say the public has the right to expect authenticity in the museum when it comes to look at skeletons. Therefore I am sending you a couple of authentic skeletons of ancestors. I went to the cemetery in the woods behind the Episcopal Church of Saint Luke. I used authentic anthropological methods to locate the burials of authentic white Anglo types—"

Mrs. Morris Perry's fingers were under the wrapping paper now, feeling dirt, feeling smooth, cold surfaces.

"Mrs. Bailey!" she said. "Mrs. Bailey!" But her eyes moved to the end of the letter. It was signed "Henry Highhawk of the Bitter Water People."

"What?" Mrs. Bailey shouted. "What is it?"

"—and to make sure they would be perfectly authentic, I chose two whose identities you can personally confirm yourself. I ask that you accept these two skeletons for authentic display to your clients and release the bones of two of my ancestors so that they may be returned to their rightful place in Mother Earth. The names of these two authentic—"

Mrs. Bailey was standing beside her now. "Honey," she said. "What's wrong?" Mrs. Bailey paused. "There's bones in that box," she said. "All dirty, too."

Mrs. Morris Perry put the letter on the desk and looked into the box. From underneath a clutter of what seemed to be arm and leg bones a single empty eye socket stared back at her. She noticed that Mrs. Bailey had picked up the letter. She noticed dirt. Damp ugly little clods had scattered on the polished desk top.

"My God," Mrs. Bailey said. "John Neldine Burgoyne. Jane Burgoyne. Weren't those— Aren't these your grandparents?"

2

ON THE LAST THURSDAY in August, the doctor treating Agnes Tsosie in the Public Health Service hospital at Fort Defiance told her she was dying and there was nothing he could do about it.

"I knew that," Agnes Tsosie said. And she smiled at him, and patted his hand, and asked him to call the chapter house at Lower Greasewood and leave word there for her family to come and get her.

"I won't be able to release you," the doctor said. "We have to keep you on medications to control the pain, and that has to be monitored. You won't be able to go home. Not yet."

"Not ever," Agnes Tsosie said, still smiling. "But you leave the message for me anyway. And don't you feel bad about it. Born for Water told Monster Slayer to leave Death alive to get rid of old people like me. You have to make some room for the new babies."

Agnes Tsosie came home from the hospital at Fort Defiance on the last Monday of August—overriding the objections of her doctor and the hospital establishment by force of the notorious Agnes Tsosie willpower.

In that part of the Navajo Reservation west of the Chuska mountain range and north of the Painted Desert, just about everybody knew about Agnes Tsosie. Old Woman Tsosie had twice served her Lower Greasewater Chapter on the Navajo Tribal Council. *National Geographic* had used her picture in an article about the Navajo Nation. Her iron will had a lot to do with starting tribal programs to get water wells drilled and water supplies available at every chapter house where hauling drinking water was a problem. Her stubborn wisdom had been important for years among her clansmen, the Bitter Water People. On the Bitter Water Dinee she imposed her rigid rules of peace. Once, she had kept a meeting of two Bitter Water families in session for eleven days until—out of hunger and exhaustion—they settled a grazing rights feud that had rankled for a hundred years.

"Too many people come out of these *belagana* hospitals dead," Agnes Tsosie had told her doctor. "I want to come out alive." And no one was surprised that she did. She came out walking, helped by her daughter and her husband. She sat in the front seat of her daughter's pickup, joking as she always did, full of teasing and funny stories about hospital behavior. But on the long drive through the sagebrush flats toward Lower Greasewood the laughter died away. She leaned heavily against the pickup door and her face was gray with sickness.

Her son-in-law was waiting at her hogan. His name was Rollie Yellow and Agnes Tsosie, who liked almost everyone, liked Yellow a lot. They had worked a way around the Navajo taboo that decreed sons-in-law must avoid mothers-in-law. Agnes Tsosie decided that role applied only to mean mothers-in-law with bad sons-in-law. In other words, it applied to people who couldn't get along. Agnes Tsosie and Yellow had gotten along wonderfully for thirty years and now it was Yellow who half carried her into her summer hogan. There she slept fitfully all afternoon and through the night.

The next morning, Rollie Yellow made the long bumpy drive around the mesa to the Lower Greasewood Chapter House and used the telephone. He called the chapter house at Many Farms and left word that Nancy Yabenny was needed.

Nancy Yabenny was a clerk-typist in the office of the Navajo Timber Industries and a crystal gazer—one of the category of Navajo shamans who specialize in answering hard questions, in finding the lost, in identifying witches, and in diagnosing illnesses so that the proper curing ceremonial can be arranged.

Nancy Yabenny arrived Thursday afternoon, driving a blue Dodge Ram pickup. She was a plump, middle-aged woman wearing a yellow pantsuit which had fit her better when she was slimmer. She carried her crystal, her four-mountains bundle, and the other paraphernalia of her profession in a briefcase. She placed a kitchen chair in the shade beside Agnes Tsosie's bed. Yellow had moved the bed out of the hogan into the brush arbor so that Agnes Tsosie could watch the thunderclouds form and blow away above the Hopi Buttes. Yabenny and Old Woman Tsosie talked for more than an hour. Then Nancy Yabenny arranged her slab of crystal on the earth, took her *jish* of sacred things out of her purse, and extracted from it a prescription bottle filled with corn pollen. She dusted the crystal with that, chanted the prescribed blessing song, held it so that the light from the sky illuminated it, and stared into it.

"Ah," she said, and held the crystal so that Agnes Tsosie could see what she was seeing. Then she questioned Agnes Tsosie about what they had seen.

It was sundown when Nancy Yabenny emerged from the brush arbor. She talked to Tsosie's husband and daughter and to Rollie Yellow. She told them Agnes Tsosie needed a Yeibichai to be restored to harmony and beauty.

Rollie Yellow had half expected that, but still it was a blow. White men call it the Night Chant, but the ceremonial was named for its principal participant—Yeibichai, the great Talking God of Navajo metaphysics. As the maternal grandfather of all the other gods, he often serves as their spokesman. It is an expensive ceremony, nine days and nights of feeding the audience of clansmen and friends, and providing for the medicine man, his helpers, and as many as three teams of *yei* dancers. But much worse than the expense, in the mind of Rollie Yellow, was that what Yabenny had told them meant the *belagana* doctor was probably right. Agnes Tsosie was very, very sick. No matter the cost, he would have to find a singer who knew how to do the Night Chant. Not many did. But there was time. The Yeibichai can be performed only after the first frost, after snakes have hibernated, only in the Season When Thunder Sleeps.

3

"I HEARD YOU DECIDED not to quit," Jay Kennedy said. "That right?"

"More or less," Lieutenant Joe Leaphorn said.

"Glad to hear it. How busy are you?"

Leaphorn hesitated, his eyes flicking over the pile of paperwork on his desk, his mind analyzing the tone of Kennedy's voice on the telephone.

"Nothing unusual," he said.

"You heard about this body out east of Gallup?"

"I heard a something-or-other," Leaphorn said—which meant a secondhand report of what had been overheard by the radio dispatcher downstairs. Just enough to know it wasn't a routine body find.

"It may not be Agency business," Kennedy said. "Except technically. But it's interesting."

Which was Kennedy's way of saying he thought it soon would be his business. Kennedy was Gallup area Federal Bureau of Investigation, and had been a friend of Leaphorn's long enough so that such things no longer had to be exactly said.

"The way I heard it, they found him beside the railroad," Leaphorn said. "That would be off the reservation. None of our business either."

"No, but it might get to be," Kennedy said.

Leaphorn waited for an explanation. None came.

"How?" he asked. "And is it a homicide?"

"Don't know the cause of death yet," Kennedy said. "And we don't have an identification. But it looks like there's some sort of connection between this bird and a Navajo." He paused. "There was a note. Well, not really a note."

"What's the interesting part? Is that it?"

"Well, that's peculiar. But what interests me is how the body got where it is."

Leaphorn's face relaxed slightly into something like a smile. He looked over the work on the desk. Through the window of his second-floor office in the Navajo Tribal Police Building he could see puffy white autumn clouds over the sandstone formation which gave Window Rock, Arizona, its name. A beautiful morning. Beyond the desk, out through the glass, the world was cool, clear, pleasant.

"Leaphorn. You still there?"

"You want me to look for tracks? Is that it?"

"You're supposed to be good at it," Kennedy said. "That's what you always tell us."

"All right," Leaphorn said. "Show me where it is."

The body was under the sheltering limbs of a clump of chamisa, protected from the slanting morning sun by an adjoining bush. From where he stood on the gravel of the railroad embankment, Leaphorn could see the soles of two shoes, their pointed toes aimed upward, two dark gray pant legs, a white shirt, a necktie, a suit coat, still buttoned, and a ground's-eye view of a pale narrow face with oddly pouched cheeks. Under the circumstances, the corpse seemed remarkably tidy.

"Nice and neat," Leaphorn said.

Undersheriff Delbert Baca thought he meant the scene of the crime. He nodded.

"Just luck," he said. "A fellow running a freight engine past here just happened to notice him. The train was rolling so he couldn't get down and stomp around over everything. Jackson here—" Baca nodded to a plump young man in a McKinley County deputy sheriff's uniform who was standing on the tracks "—he was driving by on the interstate." Baca gestured toward Interstate Highway 40, which was producing a faint rumble of truck traffic a quarter-mile to the west. "He got out here before the state police could mess everything up."

"Nobody's moved the body then?" Leaphorn asked. "What about this note you mentioned? How did you find that?"

"Baca here checked his pockets looking for identification,"

Kennedy said. "Reached under him to check hip pockets. He didn't find a billfold or anything, but he found this in the handkerchief pocket of his coat." Kennedy held out a small folded square of yellow paper. Leaphorn took it.

"You don't know who he is then?"

"Don't know," Kennedy said. "The billfold is missing. There wasn't anything in his pockets except some change, a ballpoint pen, a couple of keys, and a handkerchief. And then there was this note in his coat pocket."

Leaphorn unfolded the note.

"You wouldn't think to look in that coat pocket if you were stripping somebody of identification," Baca said. "Anyway, that's what I think was happening."

The note was written with what might have been a ballpoint pen with a very fine point. It said:

"Yeabechay? Yeibeshay? Agnes Tsosie (correct). Should be near Windowrock, Arizona."

Leaphorn turned the square over. "Stic Up" was printed across the top, the trade name of the maker of notepads which stick to bulletin boards.

"Know her?" Kennedy asked. "Agnes Tsosie. It sounds familiar to me."

"Tsosie's like Kennedy in Boston," Leaphorn said. He frowned. He did know one Agnes Tsosie. Just a little and from way back. An old lady who used to serve on the tribal council a long time ago. Elected from the Lower Greasewood district, if he remembered it right. A good woman, but probably dead by now. And there must be other Agnes Tsosies here and there around the reservation. Agnes was a common name and there were a thousand Tsosies. "Maybe we can find her, though. We can easy enough, if she's associated with a Yeibichai. They're not having many of those any more."

"That's the ceremony they call the Night Chant, isn't it?" Kennedy asked.

"Or Nightway," Leaphorn said.

"The one that lasts nine days," Kennedy said. "And they have the masked dancers?"

"That's it," Leaphorn said. But who was this man with the pointed shoes who seemed to know an Agnes Tsosie? Leaphorn moved past the chamisa limbs, placing his feet carefully to erase nothing not already erased in Baca's search of the victim's pockets. He squatted, buttocks on heels, grunting at the pain in his knees.

He should exercise more, he thought. It was a habit he'd dropped since Emma's death. They had always walked together—almost every evening when he got home from the office. Walked and talked. But now—

The victim had no teeth. His face, narrow as it was, had the caved-in, pointed-chin look of the toothless old. But this man wasn't particularly old. Sixty perhaps. And not the sort to be toothless. His suit, blue-black with an almost microscopic gray stripe, looked old-fashioned but expensive, the attire of that social class with the time and money to keep its teeth firmly in its jaws. At this close range, Leaphorn noticed that the suit coat had a tiny patch by the middle button and the narrow lapel looked threadbare. The shirt looked threadbare, too. But expensive. So did a simple broad gold ring on the third finger of his left hand. And the face itself was an expensive face. Leaphorn had worked around white men for almost forty years, and Leaphorn studied faces. This man's complexion was dark—even with the pallor of death—but it was an aristocratic face. A narrow, arrogant nose, fine bones, high forehead.

Leaphorn shifted his position and examined the victim's shoes. The leather was expensive, and under the day's thin film of dust it glowed with a thousand polishings. Handmade shoes, Leaphorn guessed. But made a long time ago. And now the heels were worn, and one sole had been replaced by a shoemaker.

"You noticed the teeth?" Kennedy asked.

"I noticed the lack of them," Leaphorn said. "Did anyone find a set of false teeth?"

"No," Baca said. "But nobody really looked. Not yet. It seemed to me that the first question to consider was how this guy got here."

Leaphorn found himself wondering why the sheriff's office had called the FBI. Had Baca sensed something about the death of this tidy man that suggested a federal crime? He looked around him. The track ran endlessly east, endlessly west—the Santa Fe main line from the Midwest to California. North, the red sandstone ramparts of Iyanbito Mesa; south, the piñon hills which rose toward the Zuni Mesa and the Zuni Mountains. And just across the busy lanes of Interstate 40 stood Fort Wingate. Old Fort Wingate, where the U.S. Army had been storing ammunition since the Spanish-American War.

"How did he get here? That's the question," Kennedy said. "He wasn't thrown off the Amtrak, that's obvious. He doesn't look the type to be riding a freight. So I'd guess that probably somebody carried him here. But why the hell would anybody do that?"

"Could this have anything to do with Fort Wingate?" Leaphorn asked. A half-mile or so up the main line he could see the siding that curved away toward the military base.

Baca laughed, shrugged.

"Who knows?" Kennedy said.

"I heard they were going to shut the place down," Leaphorn said. "It's obsolete."

"I heard that too," Kennedy said. "You think you can find any tracks?"

Leaphorn tried. He walked down the railroad embankment some twenty paces and started a circle through the sage, snakeweed, and chamisa. The soil here was typical of a sagebrush flat: loose, light, and with enough fine caliche particles to form a crust. An early autumn shower had moved over this area about a week ago, making tracking easy. Leaphorn circled back to the embankment without finding anything except the marks left by rodents, lizards, and snakes and confident there had been nothing to find. He walked another dozen yards down the track and started another, wider circle. Again, he found nothing that wasn't far too old or caused by an animal. Then he crisscrossed the sagebrush around the body, slowly, eyes down.

Kennedy, Baca, and Jackson were waiting for him on the embankment above the body. Behind him, far down the track, an ambulance had parked with a white sedan behind it—the car used by the pathologist from the Public Health Service hospital in Gallup. Leaphorn made a wry face. He shook his head.

"Nothing," he said. "If someone carried him in from this side, they carried him up from way down the tracks."

"Or down from way up the tracks," Baca said, grinning.

"What were you looking for?" Kennedy asked. "Besides tracks."

"Nothing in particular," Leaphorn said. "You're not really looking for anything in particular. If you do that, you don't see things you're not looking for."

"So you think he got brought in from way down the track?" Kennedy said.

"I don't know," Leaphorn said. "Why would anyone do that? That's lots of hard work. And the risk of being seen while you're doing it. Why is this sagebrush better than any other sagebrush?"

"Maybe they hauled him in from the other side," Kennedy said.

Leaphorn stared across the tracks. There was no road over there either. "How about lifting him off a train?"

"Amtrak is going about sixty-five miles an hour here," Kennedy said. "Doesn't start slowing for Gallup for miles. I can't see that man on a freight, and they don't stop out here either. I checked with the railroad on all that."

They stood then on the embankment above the man with the pointed shoes, with nothing to say in the presence of death. The ambulance crew came down the track, carrying a stretcher, trailed by the pathologist carrying a satchel. He was a small young man with a blond mustache. Leaphorn didn't recognize him and he didn't introduce himself.

He squatted beside the body, tested the skin at the neck, tested the stiffness of the wrists, bent finger joints, looked into the toothless mouth.

He looked up at Kennedy. "How'd he get here?"

Kennedy shrugged.

The doctor unbuttoned the suit coat and the shirt, pulled up the undershirt, examined the chest and abdomen. "There's no blood anywhere. No nothin'." He unbuckled the belt, unzipped the trouser fly, felt. "You guys know what killed him?" he asked nobody in particular.

"What?" Baca said. "What killed him?"

"Hell, I don't know," the doctor said, still intent on the body. "I just got here. I was asking you."

He rose, took a step back. "Put him on the stretcher," he ordered. "Face down."

Face down on the stretcher the man with the pointed shoes looked even smaller. The back of his dark suit was floured with gray dust, his dignity diminished. The doctor ran his hands over the body, up the spine, felt the back of the head, massaged the neck.

"Ah," he said. "Here we are."

The doctor parted the hair at the back of the man's head at the point where the spine joins the skull. The hair, Leaphorn noticed, was matted and stiff. The doctor leaned back, looking up at them, grinning happily. "See?"

Leaphorn could see very little—only a small place where neck became skull and where there seemed to be the blackness of congealed blood.

"What am I seeing?" Kennedy asked, sounding irritated. "I don't see a damned thing."

The pathologist stood, brushed off his hands, and looked down at the man in the pointed shoes.

"What you see is where somebody who knows how to use a knife can kill somebody quick," he said. "Like lightning. You stick it in that little gap between the first vertebra and the base of the skull. Cut the spinal cord." He chuckled. "Zap."

"That what happened?" Kennedy asked. "How long ago?"

"Looks like it," the doctor said. "I'd say it was probably yesterday. But we'll do an autopsy. Then you'll have your answer."

"One answer," Kennedy said. "Or two. How and when. That leaves who."

And why, Leaphorn thought. Why was always the question that lay at the heart of things. It was the answer Joe Leaphorn always looked for. Why did this man—obviously not a Navajo—have the name of a Navajo woman written on a note in his pocket? And the misspelled name of a Navajo ceremonial? The Yeibichai. It was the ceremonial in which the great mystical, mythical, magical spirits who formed the culture of the Navajos and created their first four clans actually appeared, personified in masks worn by dancers. Was the murdered man headed for a Yeibichai? As a matter of fact, he couldn't have been. It was weeks too early. The Yeibichai was a winter ceremonial. It could be performed only after the snakes had hibernated, only in the Season When Thunder Sleeps. But why else would he have the note? Leaphorn pondered and found no possible answers. He would find Agnes Tsosie and ask her.

The Agnes Tsosie Leaphorn remembered proved to be—apparently—the right one. At least when Leaphorn inquired about her as the first step in what he feared would be a time-consuming hunt he learned the family was planning a Yeibichai ceremonial for her. He spent a few hours making telephone inquiries and decided he had struck it lucky. There seemed to be only three of the great Night Chant ceremonials scheduled so far. One would be held at the Navajo Nation Fair at Window Rock for a man named Roanhorse and another was planned in December over near Burnt Water for someone in the Gorman family. That left Agnes Tsosie of Lower Greasewood as the only possibility.

The drive from Leaphorn's office in Window Rock to Lower Greasewood took him westward through the ponderosa forests of the Defiance Plateau, through the piñon-juniper hills which surround Ganado, and then southeast into the sagebrush landscape that falls away into the Painted Desert. At the Lower Greasewood Boarding School those children who lived near enough to be day students were climbing aboard a bus for the trip home. Leaphorn asked the driver where to find the Agnes Tsosie place.

"Twelve miles down to the junction north of Beta Hochee," the driver said. "And then you turn back south toward White Cone about two miles and take the dirt road past the Na-Ah-Tee trading post, and about three-four miles past that, to your right, there's a road that leads off toward the backside of Tesihim Butte. That's the road that leads up to Old Lady Tsosie's outfit. About two miles, maybe."

"Road?" Leaphorn asked.

The driver was a trim young woman of perhaps thirty. She knew exactly what Leaphorn meant. She grinned.

"Well, actually, it's two tracks out through the sage. But it's easy to find. There's a big bunch of asters blooming along there—right at the top of a slope."

The junction of the track to the Tsosie place was easy to find. Asters were blooming everywhere along the dirt road past Na-Ah-Tee trading post, but the place where the track led off from the road was also marked by a post which the bus driver hadn't mentioned. An old boot was jammed atop the post, signaling that somebody would be at home. Leaphorn downshifted and turned down the track. He felt fine. Everything about this business of learning why a dead man had Agnes Tsosie's name in his pocket was working well.

"I don't have no idea who that could be," Agnes Tsosie said. She was reclining, thin, gray haired, propped up by pillows on a metal bed under a brush arbor beside her house, holding a Polaroid photograph of the man with the pointed shoes. She handed it to Jolene Yellow, who was standing beside the bed. "Daughter, you know this man?"

Jolene Yellow examined the photograph, shook her head, handed the print back to Leaphorn. He had been in the business too long to show disappointment.

"Any idea why some stranger might be coming out here to your Yeibichai?"

"No." She shook her head. "Not this stranger."

Not this stranger. Leaphorn thought about that. Agnes Tsosie would explain in good time. Now she was looking away, out across the gentle slope that fell away from Tesihim Butte and then rose gradually toward the sharp dark outline of Nipple Butte to the west. The sage was gray and silver with autumn, the late afternoon sun laced it with slanting shadows, and everywhere there was the yellow of blooming snakeweed and the purple of the asters. Beauty before her, Leaphorn thought. Beauty all around her. But Agnes Tsosie's face showed no sign she was enjoying the beauty. It looked strained and sick.

"We have a letter," Agnes Tsosie said. "It's in the hogan." She glanced at Jolene Yellow. "My daughter will get it for you to look at."

The letter was typed on standard bond paper.

September 13

Dear Mrs. Tsosie:

I read about you in an old issue of *National Geographic*—the one with the long story about the Navajo Nation. It said you were a member of the Bitter Water Clan, which was also the clan of my grandmother, and I noticed by the picture they had of you that you two look alike. I write to you because I want to ask a favor.

I am one-fourth Navajo by blood. My grandmother told me she was all Navajo, but she married a white man and so did my mother. But I feel I am a Navajo, and I would like to see what can be done about becoming officially a member of the tribe. I would also like to come out to Arizona and talk to you about my family. I remember that my grandmother told me that she herself was the granddaughter of Ganado Mucho and that she was born to the Bitter Water People and that her father's clan had been the Streams Come Together People.

Please let me know if I can come and visit you and anything you can tell me about how I would become a Navajo.

Sincerely,
Henry Highhawk

I am enclosing a stamped, self-addressed envelope.

Leaphorn reread the letter, trying to connect these words, this odd plea, with the arrogant face of the man with the pointed shoes.

"Did you answer it?"

"I told him to come," Agnes Tsosie said. She sighed, shifted her weight, grimaced.

Leaphorn waited.

"I told him there would be a Yeibichai for me after the first frost. Probably late in November. That would be when to come. There would be other Bitter Water people there for him to talk to. I said he could talk to the *hataalii* who is doing the sing. Maybe it would be proper for him to look through the mask and be initiated like they do with boys on the last night of the sing. I said I didn't know about that. He would have to ask the *hataalii* about that. And then he could go to Window Rock and see about whether he could get on the tribal rolls. He could find out from the people there what proof he would need."

Leaphorn waited. But Agnes Tsosie had said what she had to say.

"Did he answer your letter?"

"Not yet," she said. "Or maybe he did and his letter is down at Beta Hochee. That's where we pick up our mail."

"Nobody has been by the trading post there for a while," Jolene Yellow said. "Not since last week."

"Do you think you know who this man's grandmother was?" Leaphorn asked.

"Maybe," Agnes Tsosie said. "I remember they said my mother had an aunt who went away to boarding school and never did come back."

"Anyway," Jolene Yellow said, "he's not the same man."

Leaphorn looked at her, surprised.

"He sent his picture," she said. "I'll get it."

It was about two inches square, a color photograph of the sort taken by machine to be pasted in passports. It showed a long, slender face, large blue eyes, and long blond hair woven into two tight braids. It was a face that would always look boyish.

"He certainly doesn't look like a Navajo," Leaphorn said. He was thinking that this Henry Highhawk looked even less like the man with the pointed shoes.

4

FROM BEHIND HIM in the medicine hogan, Officer Jim Chee could hear the chanting of the First Dancers as they put on their ceremonial paint. Chee was interested. He had picked a spot from which he could see through the hogan doorway and watch the personifiers preparing themselves. They were eight middle-aged men from around the Naschitti Chapter House in New Mexico, far to the east of Agnes Tsosie's place below Tesihim Butte. They had painted their right hands first, then their faces from the forehead downward, and then their bodies, making themselves ready to represent the Holy People of Navajo mythology, the *yei,* the powerful spirits. This Night Chant ceremonial was one that Chee hoped to learn someday himself. Yeibichai, his people called it, naming it for Talking God, the maternal grandfather of all the spirits. The performance was nine days long and involved five complicated sand paintings and scores of songs. Learning it would take a long, long time as would finding a *hataalii* willing to take him on as student. When the time came for that, he would have to take leave from the Navajo Tribal Police. But that was somewhere in the distant future. Now his job was watching for the Flaky Man from Washington. Henry Highhawk was the name on the federal warrant.

"Henry Highhawk," Captain Largo had said, handing him the folder. "Usually when they decide to turn Indian and call themselves something like Whitecloud, or Squatting Bear, or Highhawk, they decide they're going to be Cherokees. Or some dignified tribe that everybody knows about. But this jerk had to pick Navajo."

Chee was reading the folder. "Flight across state lines to avoid prosecution," he said. "Prosecution for what?"

"Desecration of graves," Largo said. He laughed, shook his head, genuinely amused by the irony. "Now ain't that just the ideal criminal occupation for a man who decides to declare himself a Navajo?"

Chee had noticed something that seemed to him even more ironic than a white grave robber declaring himself to be a Navajo—a tribe which happened to have a fierce religious aversion to corpses and everything associated with death.

"Is he a pot hunter?" Chee asked. "Is the FBI actually trying to catch a pot hunter?" Digging up graves to steal pre-Columbian pottery for the collector's market had been both a federal crime and big business on the Colorado plateau for generations, and the FBI's apathy about it had been both unshakable and widely known. Chee stood in front of Largo's desk trying to imagine what would have stirred the federals from such historic and monolithic inertia.

"He wasn't hunting pots," Largo said. "He's a politician. He was digging up *belagana* skeletons back East." Largo explained what Highhawk had done with the skeletons. "So not only were they white skeletons, they were Very Important People *belagana* skeletons."

"Oh," Chee said.

"Anyway, all you need to know about it is that you go out to the Lower Greasewood Chapter House and you find out where they're holding this Yeibichai. It will probably be at Agnes Tsosie's place. She's the one they're doing the Night Chant for. Anyway, this Highhawk nut is supposed to come to it. Probably he's already there. The FBI says he rented a Ford Bronco from Avis in Washington. A white one. They think he drove it out here. So you get yourself to Old Woman Tsosie's place. If he's there, bring him in. And if he's not there yet, then stick around and wait for him."

"Nine days?"

"Tonight's the last night of the Yeibichai," Largo said. "That's when Mrs. Tsosie said she told him to come."

"What makes us think this guy is coming all the way out here for a Yeibichai? Sounds strange to me." Chee had been looking at the sheet in the folder when he said it. When he looked up, Captain Largo was glowering at him.

"You don't get paid to make decisions on whether the feds know what the hell they're doing," the captain said. "You get paid for doing what I tell you to do. But if it makes you happier, we're told that this Highhawk told it around back in Washington that he was coming out to the Navajo Reservation to attend this specific

Agnes Tsosie Yeibichai. Is that good enough for you?"

It had been good enough. And so for the past four hours Chee had been at the Agnes Tsosie place waiting for Henry Highhawk to arrive at this Yeibichai ceremonial so that he could arrest him. Chee was good at waiting. He waited at his favorite lurking point near Baby Rocks Mesa for the endless empty miles of U.S. 160 to provoke drivers into speeding. He waited at the fringe of rodeo crowds for unwary bootleggers, and in the hallways outside the various Navajo Nation Department of Justice courtrooms to be called in to testify. Deputy Sheriff Cowboy Dashee, his good friend who had tagged along on this venture, complained endlessly about the waiting their jobs required. Chee didn't mind. He had one of those minds in which curiosity is constantly renewed. Wherever he waited, Chee's eyes wandered. They always found something that interested him. Here, waiting for the white Ford Bronco to appear (or fail to appear), Chee was first fascinated with the ceremonial itself. And then he'd noticed the Man with Bad Hands.

Bad Hands was curious indeed.

He had arrived early, as had Chee, a little before sundown in that recess between the afternoon singing in the medicine hogan and the dancing of the *yeis,* which would begin only when the night was totally dark. He was driving a green four-door Jeep Cherokee which bore a Farmington car rental company's sticker. Chee had identified him at first as a *belagana,* that grab bag of social-ethnic types which included whites plus all those who were neither fellow members of the Dineh (Navajos), nor Nakai (Mexicans), nor Zunis, nor Hopis, nor Apaches, nor Utes, nor members of any of the other Indian tribes who lived near enough to the Navajos to have earned a name in the Navajo language—which had no noun for "Indian." Thus Bad Hands was *belagana* by default. Bad Hands wasn't the only white attracted by this ceremonial, but he was the only one who defied Chee's personal classification system.

The handful of other whites standing around the bonfires or keeping warm in their vehicles fit neatly enough. Two were "friends." They included a lanky, bald-headed man from whom Chee sometimes bought hay at a Gallup feed store, and Ernie Bulow, a towering, gray-bearded desert rat who'd been raised on the Big Reservation and had written a book about Navajo taboos. Bulow spoke coherent Navajo and had developed close personal relationships with Navajo families. He had brought with him today in his dusty station wagon a fat Navajo man and three middle-aged white women, all of whom stood beside the vehicle look-ing cold, nervous, and uncomfortable. Chee put the women in his "tourist" category. The remainder of the *belagana* delegation were mostly "Lone Rangers"—part of the liberal/intellectual covey. They had flocked into the Navajo Mountain territory and declared themselves spokesmen for, and guardians of, the Navajo families facing eviction from their lands in what had become the Hopi part of the old Joint Use Reservation. Lone Rangers were a nuisance, but also a source of anecdotes and amusement. There were three of these, two males not much older than Chee and a pretty young blonde woman with her hair rolled atop her head. All wore the ragged jeans, jean jacket, and horse-blanket uniform of their clique.

Bad Hands' necktie, his neatly fitted business suit, his white shirt, his gloves of thin black leather, his snap-brim felt hat, his fur-collared overcoat, all disqualified him as a Lone Ranger. Like them he was a city person, but without the disguise. Total dis-interest in the ceremonial ruled him out as tourist, and he seemed to know no one here—most of them Bitter Water People of the patient's maternal clan. Like Jim Chee, Bad Hands was simply waiting. But for Bad Hands, waiting was a joyless matter of endur-ing. He showed no sign of pleasure in it.

Chee had first noticed him when he emerged from the Jeep Cherokee. He'd parked it amid a cluster of shabbier vehicles a polite distance from the dance grounds. He had stretched, rotated his shoulders in his overcoat, bent his knees, bowed his back, went through those other movements of people who have been confined too long in a car. He gave no more than a glance to the men who were unloading sawmill waste from the tribe's lumbermill to help fuel the fires which would warm the spectators and illuminate the dancing tonight. He was more interested in the parked vehicles. These he inspected carefully, one after another. He had noticed Chee noticing him, and he had noticed Chee's police uniform, but he showed no special interest. After stretching his muscles he climbed back into his vehicle and sat. It was then that Chee noticed his hands.

He had opened the door by grasping the handle with two fin-gers of his left hand, then pressing in the release button with a finger of his right hand. It was obviously a practiced motion. Still it was clumsy. And as he did it, Chee noticed that the thumb and little finger of the right glove jutted out stiffly. The man was either missing that thumb and finger, or they were immobilized. Why then didn't he open the door with the other hand? Chee couldn't get a look at it.

But now Chee's curiosity was clicked up a notch. He prowled the dance ground the Tsosie family had cleared, he chatted with people, he watched the fire builders build the stacks of logs and waste wood which would line the dancing area with flames. He talked to the husband of the woman whose mother was the patient. Yellow was his name. Yellow was worrying about everything going right.

Chee helped Yellow check the wiring from the little generator he'd rented to provide the electric lighting he'd rigged up behind the medicine hogan. Chee kept an eye on five boys wearing Many Farms football jackets who might become trouble if their group became large enough to reach teenage critical mass. Chee prowled among the parked vehicles on the lookout for drunks or drinking. He stopped where Cowboy Dashee was parked in his Apache County Sheriff's Department patrol car to see if Cowboy was still asleep. ("Wake me when your criminal gets here, or wake me when the dancing gets going," Dashee said. "Otherwise, I need my rest.") But always he wandered back to where he could see the Jeep Cherokee and its driver.

The man was sometimes sitting in it, sometimes leaning against it, sometimes standing beside it.

He's nervous, Chee decided, but he's not the sort who allows himself to show his nerves in the usual ways. When the light of an arriving car lit his face, Chee noticed that he might be part Indian. Or perhaps Asiatic. Certainly not Navajo, or Apache, or a Pueblo man. In the same light he saw his hands again, gloved, both of them this time resting lightly on the steering wheel. The thumbs and little fingers of both hands jutted out stiffly as if their joints were frozen.

Chee was standing beside the medicine hogan thinking of these odd hands and what might have happened to them when Henry Highhawk arrived. Chee noticed the vehicle coming over the rim of the mesa and jolting toward the parking area. In the reflected light from the fires it seemed to be small and white. As it parked he saw it was the white Ford Bronco he had been waiting for.

". . . Wind Boy, the holy one, paints his form," the voices behind him chanted in rhythmic Navajo.

"With the dark cloud, he paints his form.
With the misty rain, he paints his form. . . ."

The vehicle disappeared from sight in an irregular row of mostly pickup trucks. Chee strolled toward it, remaining out of the firelight when he could. It was a Bronco, new under its heavy coating of dust. Its only occupant seemed to be the driver. He opened the door, lighting the overhead bulb. He swung his legs out, stretched, emerged stiffly, and closed the door behind him. In no hurry, apparently.

Neither was Jim Chee. He leaned against the side of an old sedan and waited.

The cold breeze moved through the sage around him, whispering just loud enough to obscure the ceremonial chanting. The fires that lined the sides of the dance ground between the hogan and the little brush-covered medicine lodge were burning high now. The light reflected from the face of Henry Highhawk. Or, to be more accurate, Chee thought, the man I presume to be Henry Highhawk. The man, at least, who drove the prescribed white Bronco. He wore a shirt of dark blue velvet with silver buttons—the shirt a traditional Navajo would have proudly worn about 1920. He wore an old-fashioned black felt hat with a high crown and a band of silver conchas—a "reservation hat" as old-fashioned as the shirt. A belt of heavy silver conchas hung around his waist, and below it he wore jeans and boots—the left boot, Chee now noticed, reinforced with a metal brace and thickened sole. He stood for a long time beside the car in his shirt sleeves, oblivious of the cold, engrossed in what he was seeing. In contrast to Bad Hands, this visitor was obviously fascinated by this ceremonial event. Finally, he reached inside, pulled out a leather jacket, and put it on. The jacket had leather fringes. Of course it would have fringes, Chee thought. Hollywood's Indian.

Chee strolled past him to Cowboy's patrol car and rapped on the window.

Cowboy sat up, looked at him. Chee opened the door and slid in.

"They ready to dance?" Cowboy asked, the question muffled by a yawn.

"Any minute now," Chee said. "And our bandito has arrived."

Cowboy felt around for his gun belt, found it, straightened to put it on. "Okay," he said. "Away we go."

Deputy Sheriff Cowboy Dashee climbed out of his patrol car and followed Navajo Tribal Policeman Jim Chee toward the crowd gathering around the fires. Dashee was a citizen of Mishhongnovi on the Hopi Second Mesa, born into the distinguished Side Corn Clan, and a valuable man in the ancient Hopi Antelope Society. But he was also a friend of Jim Chee from way back in their high school days.

"There he is," Chee said. "The cat with the reservation hat, leather jacket with the Buffalo Bill fringes."

"And the braids," Dashee said. "He trying to set a new style for you guys? Replace buns with braids?"

The driver of the Bronco was standing very close to a squat, elderly man in a red plaid coat, leaning over him as he first talked, then listened attentively. Chee and Dashee edged through the crowd toward him.

"Not now," Plaid Coat was saying. "Old Lady Tsosie she's sick. She's the patient. Nobody can talk to her until this sing is over."

Why would this *belagana* grave robber want to see Agnes Tsosie? Chee had no idea. That irritated him. The big shots never told working cops a damned thing. Captain Largo certainly didn't. Nobody did. Someday he would walk into something and get his head shot off because nobody had told him something. There was absolutely no excuse for it.

Bad Hands walked past him, approached Highhawk, waited for the polite moment, touched the man's shoulder. Highhawk looked startled. Bad Hands seemed to be introducing himself. Highhawk offered a hand, noticed Bad Hands' glove, listened to what might have been an explanation, shook the glove gingerly. "Let's get him," Dashee said. "Come on."

"What's the hurry?" Chee said. "This guy's not going anyplace."

"We arrest him, we put him in the patrol car, and we don't have to worry about him," Dashee said.

"We arrest him, and we have to baby-sit him," Chee said. "We have to haul him down to Holbrook and book him into jail. We miss the Yeibichai dance."

Dashee yawned a huge yawn, scrubbed his face with both palms, yawned again. "To tell the truth," he said, "I forget how you talked me into coming out here anyway. It's us Hopi that have the big tourist-attraction ceremonials. Not you guys. What am I doing here, anyway?"

"I think I told you something about all the Miss Navajo and the Miss Indian Princess contestants always coming to these Yeibichais," Chee said. "They haul them in from Albuquerque and Phoenix and Flagstaff on buses."

"Yeah," Dashee said. "You did say something about girls. Where the hell are they?"

"Be here any minute," Chee said.

Dashee yawned again. "And speaking of women, how you doing with your girlfriend?"

"Girlfriend?"

"That good-looking lawyer." Dashee created curves in the air with his hands. "Janet Pete."

"She's not my girlfriend," Chee said.

Dashee put on his skeptical expression.

"I'm her confidant," Chee said. "The shoulder upon which she weeps. She's got a boyfriend. In Washington. Her old law professor down at the University of Arizona decided to quit teaching and be a millionaire. Now she's back there working for him."

Dashee's disappointment showed. "I liked her," he said. "For a Navajo, that is. And for a lawyer, too. Imagine liking a lawyer. But I thought you two had something going."

"No," Chee said. "She tells me her troubles. I tell her mine. Then we give one another bad advice. It's one of those things."

"Your troubles? You mean that blue-eyed little schoolteacher. I thought she'd kissed you off and moved back to Milwaukee or some place. Is she still your trouble?"

"Mary Landon," Chee said.

"That sure has dragged along," Dashee said. "Is she back out here again?"

"She did move back to Wisconsin," Chee said, thinking he really didn't much want to talk about this. "But we write. Next week, I'm going back there to see her."

"Well," Dashee said. The breeze had shifted now and was moving out of the north, even colder than it had been. Dashee turned up his coat collar. "None of my business, I guess. It's your funeral."

The screen of blankets had been dropped over the doorway of the patient's hogan now and all the curing activities were going on in privacy. The bonfires that lined the cleared dance ground burned high. Spectators huddled around them, keeping warm, gossiping, renewing friendships. There was laughter as a piñon log collapsed and the resulting explosion of sparks routed a cluster of teenagers. Mr. Yellow had built a kitchen shelter behind the hogan, using sawed telephone poles as roof posts, two-by-fours and particle board for its walls. Through its doorway, Chee could see dozens of Mrs. Tsosie's Bitter Water clansmen drinking coffee and helping themselves from stacks of fry bread and a steaming iron pot of mutton stew. Highhawk had drifted that way too, with Bad Hands trailing behind. Chee and Dashee followed Highhawk into the kitchen shelter, keeping him in sight. They sampled the stew and found it only fair.

Then the curtain drew back and the *hataalii* backed out through it. He walked down the dance ground to the *yei* hogan. A moment later he made the return trip, walking slowly, chanting. Old Woman Tsosie emerged from the medicine hogan. She was bundled in a blanket, her hair bound in the traditional fashion. She stood on another blanket spread on the packed earth and held out her hands toward the east. The kitchen shelter emptied as diners became spectators. The socializing at the bonfires quieted. Then Chee heard the characteristic call of Talking God.

"Huu tu tu. Huu tu tu. Huu tu tu. Huu tu tu."

Talking God led a row of masked *yei,* moving slowly with the intricate, mincing, dragging step of the spirit dancers. The sound of the crowd died away. Chee could hear the tinkle of the bells on the dancers' legs, hear the *yei* singing in sounds no human could understand. The row of stiff eagle feathers atop Talking God's white mask riffled in the gusty breeze. Dust whipped around the naked legs of the dancers, moving their kilts. Chee glanced at Henry Highhawk, curious about his reaction. He noticed the man with the crippled hands had moved up beside Highhawk.

Highhawk's lips were moving, his expression reverent. He seemed to be singing. Chee edged closer. Highhawk was seeing nothing but Talking God dancing slowly toward them. "He stirs. He stirs," Highhawk was singing. "He stirs. He stirs. Now in old age wandering, he stirs." The words were translated from the ceremony called the Shaking of the Masks. That ritual had been held four days earlier in this ceremonial, awakening the spirits which lived in the masks from their cosmic dreams. This white man must be an anthropologist, or a scholar of some sort, to have found a translation.

Talking God and his retinue were close now and Highhawk was no longer singing. He held something in his right hand. Something metallic. A tape recorder. *Hataalii* rarely gave permission for taping. Chee wondered what he should do. This would be a terrible time to create a disturbance. He decided to let it ride. He hadn't been sent here to enforce ceremonial rules, and he was in no mood to be a policeman.

The hooting call of the Yeibichai projected Chee's imagination back into the myth that this ceremony reenacted. It was the tale of a crippled boy and his compact with the gods. This was how it might have been in those mythic times, Chee thought. The fire-light, the hypnotic sound of the bells and pot drum, the shadows of the dancers moving rhythmically against the pink sandstone of the mesa walls behind the hogan.

Now there was a new smell in the air, mixing with the perfume of the burning piñon and dust. It was the smell of dampness, of impending snow. And as he noticed it, a flurry of tiny snowflakes appeared between him and the fire, and as quickly disappeared. He glanced at Henry Highhawk to see how the grave robber was taking this.

Highhawk was gone. So was Bad Hands.

Chee looked for Cowboy Dashee. But where was Cowboy when you needed him? Never in sight. There he was. Talking to a young woman bundled in a down jacket. Grinning like an ape. Chee jostled his way through the crowd. He grabbed Dashee's elbow.

"Come on," he said. "I lost him."

Deputy Sheriff Dashee was instantly all business.

"I'll check Highhawk's car," he said. And ran.

Chee ran for Bad Hands' car. The two men were standing beside it, talking.

No more waiting, Chee thought. He could see Dashee approaching.

"Mr. Highhawk," Chee said. "Mr. Henry Highhawk?"

The two men turned. "Yes," Highhawk said. Bad Hands stared, his lower lip clenched nervously between his teeth.

Chee displayed his identification.

"I'm Officer Chee, Navajo Tribal Police. We have a warrant for your arrest and I'm taking you into custody."

"What for?" Highhawk said.

"Flight across state lines to avoid prosecution," Chee said. He sensed Dashee at his elbow.

"You have the right to remain silent," Chee began. "You have the right to—"

"It's for digging up those skeletons, isn't it?" Highhawk said. "It's okay to dig up Indian bones and put 'em on display. But you dig up white bones and it's a felony."

"—can and will be used against you in a court of law," Chee concluded.

"I heard the law was looking for me," Highhawk said. "But I wasn't sure exactly why. Is it for sending those skeletons through the mail? I didn't do that. I sent them by Federal Express."

"I don't know anything about it," Chee said. "All I know is

you're Henry Highhawk and I got a warrant here to arrest you on. As far as I know you shot eighteen people in Albuquerque, robbed the bank, hijacked airplanes, lied to your probation officer, committed treason. They don't tell us a damned thing."

"What do you do to him?" Bad Hands asked. "Where do you take him?"

"Who are you?" Dashee asked.

"We take him down to Holbrook," Chee said, "and then we turn him over to the sheriff's office and they hold him for the federals on the fugitive warrant, and then he goes back to somewhere or other. Wherever he did whatever he did. Then he goes on trial."

"Who are you?" Dashee repeated.

"My name is Gomez," Bad Hands said. "Rudolfo Gomez."

Cowboy nodded.

"I'm Jim Chee," Chee said. He held out his hand.

Bad Hands looked at it. Then at Chee.

"Pardon the glove, please," he said. "I had an accident."

As he shook it, Chee felt through the thin black leather an index finger and, perhaps, part of the second finger. All else inside the glove felt stiff and false.

That was the right hand. If his memory was correct, the right hand was Bad Hands' better hand.

5

LEROY FLECK ENJOYED having his shoes shined. They were Florsheims—by his standards expensive shoes—and they deserved care. But the principal reason he had them shined each morning at the little stand down the street from his apartment was professional. Fleck, who was often after other people, felt a need to know if anyone was after him. Sitting perched these few minutes on the Captain's shoeshine throne gave him a perfect opportunity to rememorize the street. Each morning except Sunday Fleck examined every vehicle parked along the shady block his apartment house occupied. He compared what he saw with what he remembered from previous days, and weeks, and months of similar studies.

Still, he enjoyed the shine. The Captain had gradually grown on him as a person. Fleck no longer thought of him as a nigger, and not even as one of Them. The Captain had gradually become— become what? Somebody who knew him? Whatever it was, Fleck found himself looking forward to his shoeshine.

This morning, though, Fleck had other things on his mind. Things to do. A decision to make. He examined the street through habit. The cars were familiar. So was the bakery truck making its delivery to the coffee shop. The old man limping down the sidewalk had limped there before. The skinny woman was another regular walking her familiar dog. Only the white Corvette convertible parked beside the Texaco station down the street and the dark green Ford sedan immediately across from the entrance to the apartments were strangers. The Corvette was not the sort of car that interested Fleck. The Ford he would check and remember. It was one of those nondescript models that cops liked to use.

Fleck glanced down at the top of the head of the shoeshine man. The hair was a thick mass of tight gray curls. Darky hair, Fleck thought. "How you doing there, Captain?"

"About got 'em."

"You notice that green Ford yonder? Across the street there? You know who belongs to that?"

The man glanced up, found the Ford, examined it. Once his face had been a shiny, coffee black. Age had grayed it, broken it into a wilderness of lines. "I don't know it," the Captain said. "Never noticed it before."

"I'll get a check on the license number down at headquarters," Fleck said. "You tell me if you see it around here again."

"Sure," the Captain said. He whipped his shine cloth across the tip of Fleck's right shoe. Snapped it. Stood up and stepped back. "Done," he said.

Fleck handed him a ten-dollar bill. The Captain folded it into his shirt pocket.

"See if you can get a look at who gets into it," Fleck said.

"Your man, maybe?" the Captain said, his expression somewhere between skeptical and sardonic. "You think it's that dope dealer you been after?"

"Maybe," Fleck said.

He walked the five blocks down to the telephone booth he was using today, thinking about that expression on the Captain's face, and about Mama, and about what he was going to tell The Client. The Captain's expression made it clear that he didn't really believe Fleck was an undercover cop. The old man had seemed convinced enough last summer when Fleck had first taken this job and moved into the apartment. He'd shown the Captain his District of Columbia police detective credentials the third morning he had his shoes shined. The man had seemed properly impressed then. But weeks ago—how many weeks Fleck couldn't quite decide—Fleck's subconscious began registering some peculiarities. Now he was pretty sure the old man didn't believe Fleck was a cop. But he was also fairly sure the Captain didn't give a damn. The old man was playing lookout partly because he enjoyed the game and partly because of the money. The Captain was a neutral. He didn't give a damn whether Fleck was part of the law, or outside it, or the Man from Mars.

At that point, Fleck had even considered talking to the Captain about Mama. He was a nigger, but he was old and he knew a lot about people. Maybe he'd have some ideas. But talking about

Mama was complicated. And painful. He didn't know what to do about her. What could he do? She hadn't been happy out there at Bluewater Home outside Cleveland, and she wasn't happy at this place he'd put her when he came to D.C.—Eldercare Manor. Maybe she wouldn't be happy anywhere. But that wasn't the point right now. The point was Eldercare wanted to be shut of her. And right away.

"We just simply can't put up with it," the Fat Man had told him. "Simply cannot tolerate it. We have to think of our other clients. Look after their welfare. We can't have that woman harassing them."

"Doing what?" Fleck had asked. But he knew what Mama was doing. Mama was getting even.

"Well," the Fat Man had said, trying to think how to put it. "Well, yesterday she put out her hand and tripped Mrs. Oliver. She fell right on the floor. Might have broken her bones." The Fat Man's hands twisted together at the thought, anxiously. "Old bones break easily, you know. Especially old ladies'."

"Mrs. Oliver has done something to Mama," Fleck said. "I can tell you that right now for dead certain." But he knew he was wasting his breath when he said it.

"No," Fat Man said. "Mrs. Oliver is a most gentle person."

"She did something," Fleck had insisted.

"Well," Fat Man said. "Well, I hadn't meant to say anything about this because old people do funny things and this isn't serious and it's easy to deal with. But your mother steals the silverware at the table. Puts the knives and forks and such things up her sleeve, and in her robe, and slips them into her room." Fat Man smiled a deprecatory smile to tell Fleck this wasn't serious. "Somebody collects them and brings them back when she's asleep, so it doesn't matter. But Mrs. Oliver doesn't know that. She tells us about it. Maybe that was it."

"Mama don't steal," Fleck had said, thinking that would be it all right. Mama must have heard the old woman telling on her. She would never tolerate anybody snitching on her, or on anybody in the family. Snitching was not to be tolerated. That was something you needed to get even for.

"Mrs. Oliver fell down just yesterday," Fleck had said. "You called me before then."

"Well," Fat Man said. "That was extra. I told you on the phone about her pulling out Mr. Riccobeni's hair?"

"She never did no such thing," Fleck had said, wearily, wondering what Mr. Riccobeni had done to warrant such retribution, wondering if pulling out the old man's hair would be enough to satisfy Mama's instinct for evening the score.

But there was no use remembering all that now. Now he had to think of what he could do with Mama, because the Fat Man had been stubborn about it. Get Mama out of there by the end of next week or he would lock her out on the porch. The Fat Man had meant it, and he had gotten that much time out of the son of a bitch only by doing a little very quiet, very mean talking. The kind of talk where you don't say a lot, and you don't say it loud, but the other fellow knows he's about to get his balls cut off.

With the phone booth in view ahead, Fleck slowed his brisk walk to a stroll, inspecting everything. He glanced at his watch. A little early, which was the way he liked it. The booth was outside a neighborhood movie theater. There was a single car in the lot, an old Chevy which Fleck had noticed before and presumed was owned by the morning cleanup man. Nothing unusual on the street, either. Fleck went into the booth, felt under the stand, found nothing more sinister than dried chewing gum wads. He checked the telephone itself. Then he sat and waited. He was thinking he would just have to be realistic about Mama. There was simply no way he could keep her with him. He'd have to just give up on that idea. He'd tried it and tried it, and each time Mama had gotten even with somebody or other, things had gone to hell, and he'd had to move her. The last time, the police had come before he'd gotten her out, and if he hadn't skipped they probably would have committed her.

The phone rang. Fleck picked it up.

"This is me," he said, and gave The Client his code name. He felt silly doing it—like kids playing with their Little Orphan Annie code rings.

"Stone," the voice said. It was an accented voice which to Fleck's ear didn't match an American name like Stone. A Spanish accent. "What do you have for me today?"

"Nothing much," Fleck said. "You gotta remember, there's one of me and seven of them." He paused, chuckled. "I should say six now."

"We're interested in more than just six," the voice said. "We're interested in who they're dealing with. You understand that?"

Fleck didn't like the tone of voice. It was arrogant. The tone of a man used to giving orders to underlings. Mama would call The Client one of Them.

"Well," Fleck said. "I'm doing the best I can, just being one man and all. I haven't seen nothing interesting though. Not that I know of."

"You're getting a lot of money, you know. That's not just to pay for excuses."

"When we get right down to it," Fleck said, "you're owing me some money. There was just two thousand in that package Monday. You owed me another ten."

"The ten is if the job was done right," The Client said. "We don't know that yet."

"What the hell you mean? It's been almost a month and not a word about anything in the papers." Fleck was usually very good at keeping his emotion out of his voice. It was one of the skills he prided himself on, one of the tricks he'd learned in the recreation yards of detention centers and jails and, finally, at Joliet. But now you could hear the anger. "I need that money. And I'm going to get it."

"You will get it when we decide nothing went wrong with that job," The Client said. "Now shut up about it. I want to talk to you about Santero. We still don't know where he went when he left the District. That worries us."

And so the man who called himself Stone talked about Santero and Fleck half listened, his mouth stiff and set with his anger. Stone outlined a plan. Fleck told him the number of the pay phone where he would be next Tuesday, blurting it out because he had some things to say to this arrogant son of a bitch. Some rules to lay down, and some understanding that Fleck was nobody's nigger.

"So that'll be the number and now I want you to listen—" Fleck began, but he heard the line disconnect. He stared at the phone. "You son of a bitch," he said. "You dirty son of a bitch." His voice squeaked with the anger. The rage. This was what Mama had told them about. Him and Delmar. About the ruling class. The way they put you down if you let them. Treated you like niggers. Like dogs. And the only way you kept your head up, the only way to keep from being a bum and a wino, was by getting even. Always keeping things even. Always keeping your pride.

He walked back toward his apartment thinking about how he would go about it. Lot of work to be done. They knew who he was, he'd bet a million dollars on that. The shyster pretended otherwise. Elkins pretended that what he called "protective insulation" worked both ways. But lawyers lied. Lawyers were part of Them. Leroy Fleck would be expendable, something to be thrown to the police when he wasn't useful. Safer for everybody to have Fleck dead, or back in lockup. But The Client was where the money came from, so The Client would know everything he wanted to know.

There would be plenty of time to even that up, Fleck thought, because there was nothing he could do until he had Mama taken care of. He had to have another place for her, and that always meant a big advance payment. While he was hunting a place for Mama, he'd find out just who The Client was and where he could find him. Now he was almost certain The Client was an embassy. Spanish-speaking. Some country that had revolution problems, judging from the work they had him doing.

6

THE TROUBLE WAS nobody was interested. November had become December and the man with the pointed shoes remained nameless, an unresolved problem. Somewhere someone worried and waited for him. Or, if they had guessed his fate, they mourned him. The man had taken on a personality in Joe Leaphorn's mind. Once he would have discussed him with Emma, and Emma would have had something sensible to say.

"Of course no one is interested," Emma would have said in that small, soft voice. "The Agency doesn't have to take jurisdiction so it's not an FBI problem. And McKinley County has had about five bodies since then to worry about and these bodies are local with relatives who vote. And it didn't happen on the reservation, and it wouldn't be your problem even if it had because it's clearly a homicide, and reservation homicides are the FBI's problem. You're just interested because it's an interesting puzzle." To which he would have said: Yes. You're right. Now tell me why he was put under those chamisa bushes when it was so tough to get him there, carrying him all the way down the railroad tracks, and explain the Yeibichai note. And Emma would have said something like, They wanted the body seen from the train and reported and found, or they stopped the train and put him off.

But Leaphorn couldn't imagine what Emma would have said about the Yeibichai and Agnes Tsosie. He felt the old, painful, overwhelming need to talk to her. To see her sitting in that old brown chair, working on one of those endless making-something-for-somebody's-baby projects which always kept her hands busy while she thought about whatever problem he'd presented her. A year now, a little more than a year, since she had died. This part of it seemed to get no better.

He turned off the television, put on his coat and walked out on the porch. It was still snowing a little—just an occasional dry flake. Enough to declare the end of autumn. Inside again, he got his winter jacket from the closet, dropped it on the sofa, turned on the TV again, and sat down. Okay, Emma, he thought, how about the missing dentures? They don't just pop out when one is struck. They're secured. He'd told the pathologist he was curious about those missing false teeth and the man had done some checking during the autopsy. There was not just one question, the doctor had said, but two. The gums showed the victim secured his teeth with a standard fixative. Therefore either the fellow had been killed while his teeth were out, or they had been removed after his death. In light of the way the man was dressed the first seemed improbable. So why remove the teeth? To avoid identification of the victim? Possibly. Would Emma have any other ideas? The second question was exactly the sort which intrigued Leaphorn.

"I didn't find any sign of any of those gum diseases, or those jawbone problems, which cause dentists to remove teeth. Everything was perfectly healthy. There was some sign of trauma. The upper right molars, upper left incisor, had been broken in a way that caused some trauma to the bone and left resulting bone lesions." That's what the pathologist had said. He had looked up from his report at Leaphorn and said: "Do you know why his teeth are missing?"

So tell me, Emma, Leaphorn thought. If you're so smart, you tell me why such a high-class gentleman got his teeth extracted. And why.

As he thought it, he heard himself saying it aloud. He pushed himself out of the chair, embarrassed. "Crazy," he said, also aloud. "Talking to myself."

He switched off the TV again and retrieved the coat. It was colder but no longer snowing. He brushed the feathery deposit from the windshield with his sleeve, and drove.

Eastbound through Gallup, he saw Kennedy's sedan parked at the Zuni Truck Stop Cafe. Kennedy was drinking tea.

"Sit," Kennedy said, indicating the empty bench across the booth table from him. He extracted the tea bag from his cup and held it gingerly by its string. "Peppermint," he said. "You ever drink this stuff?"

Leaphorn sat. "Now and then," he said.

"What brings you off the reservation on such an inclement Saturday evening?"

What, indeed? Old friend, I am running from Emma's ghost, Leaphorn thought. I am running from my own loneliness. I am running away from craziness.

"I'm still curious about your man with the pointed shoes," Leaphorn said. "Did you ever get him identified?"

Kennedy gazed at him over the cup. "Nothing on the fingerprints," he said. "I think I told you that. Nothing on anything else, either."

"If you found his false teeth, could you identify him from that?"

"Maybe," Kennedy said. "If we knew where he was from, then we could find out who made that sort of denture. Probably we could."

The waitress appeared with a menu. "Just coffee," Leaphorn said. He had no appetite this evening.

"My wife tells me coffee is giving me the night sweats. The caffeine is making me jumpy," Kennedy said. "She's got me off on tea."

Leaphorn nodded. Emma used to do such things to him.

"That guy's sheriff's office business anyway," Kennedy said. "I had a hunch he'd be my baby if he was identified. Just by the looks of him. He looked foreign. Looked important." He grinned. "Kinda nice, not having him identified."

"How hard did you try?"

Kennedy glanced at him over the teacup, mildly surprised at Leaphorn's tone.

"The usual," he said. "Prints. Clothes were tailor-made. So were the shoes. We sent them all back to Washington. Sent photographs, too. They didn't match anyone on the missing list." He shook his head. "Nothing matched anywhere. *Nada.* Absolutely nothing."

"Nothing?"

"Lab decided the clothes were foreign made. European or South American probably. Not Hong Kong."

"That's a big help," Leaphorn said. He sipped the coffee. It was fresh. Compared to the instant stuff he'd been drinking at home it was delicious.

"It confirmed my hunch, I think," Kennedy said. "If we ever get that sucker identified, it will be a federal case. He'll be some biggie in drugs, or moving money illegally. Something international."

"Sounds like it," Leaphorn said. He was thinking of a middle-aged woman sitting somewhere wondering what had happened to Pointed Shoes. He was wondering what circumstances brought a man in old, worn, lovingly polished custom-built shoes to die amid the chamisa, sage, and snakeweed east of Gallup. He was wondering about the fatal little puncture at the base of his skull. "Anything new about the cause of death? The weapon?"

"Nothing changed. It's still a thin knife blade inserted between the first vertebra and the base of the skull. Still a single thrust. No needless cuts or punctures. Still a real pro did it."

"And what brings a real pro to Gallup? Does the Agency have any thoughts on that?"

Kennedy laughed. "You caught me twenty-eight years too late, Joe. When I was on the green side of thirty and still bucking for J. Edgar's job, then this one would have worried me to death. Somewhere back there about murder case three hundred and nine it dawned on me I wasn't going to save the world."

"You ran out of curiosity," Leaphorn said.

"I got old," Kennedy said. "Or maybe wise. But I'm curious about what brings you off the reservation in this kind of weather."

"Just feeling restless," Leaphorn said. "I think I'm going to drive out there where the body was."

"It'll be dark by the time you could get out there."

"If the pathologist is right, it was dark when that guy got knifed. The night before we found him. You want to come along?"

Kennedy didn't want to come along. Leaphorn cruised slowly down Interstate 40, his patrol car causing a brief bubble of uneasy sixty-five-mile-an-hour caution in the flood of eastbound traffic. The cold front now was again producing intermittent snow, flurries of small, feathery flakes which seemed as cold and dry as dust, followed by gaps in which the western horizon glowed dully with the dying day. He angled off the highway at the Fort Wingate interchange and stopped where the access road met the old fort's entrance route. He sat a moment, reviving the question he raised when he'd seen the body. Any link between this obsolete ammunition depot—long on the Pentagon's list for abandonment—and a corpse left nearby wearing clothing cut by a foreign tailor? Smuggling out explosives? From what little Leaphorn knew about the mile after mile of bunkers here, they held the shells for heavy artillery. There was nothing one would sneak out in a briefcase—or find a use for if one did. He restarted the car and drove under the interstate to old U.S. Highway 66, and down it toward the Shell Oil Company's refinery at Iyanbito. The Santa Fe railroad had built the twin tracks of its California-bound main line here, paralleling the old highway with the towering pink ramparts of Nashodishgish Mesa walling in this corridor to the north. Leaphorn parked again, pulling the car off in the snakeweed beside the pavement. From this point it was less than four hundred yards to the growth of chamisa where the body of Pointed Shoes had been laid. Leaphorn checked the right-of-way fence. Easy enough to climb through. Easy enough to pass that small body over. But that hadn't been done. Not unless whoever did it could cross four hundred yards of soft, dusty earth without leaving tracks.

Leaphorn climbed through the fence and walked toward the tracks. A train was coming from the east, creating its freight train thunder. Its locomotive headlight made a dazzling point in the darkness. Leaphorn kept his eyes down, the brim of his uniform hat shading his face, walking steadily across the brushy landscape. The locomotive flashed past, pushed by three other diesels and trailing noise, towing flatcars carrying piggyback truck trailers, and then a parade of tank cars, then hopper cars, then cars carrying new automobiles stacked high, then old slab-side freight cars, and finally a caboose. Leaphorn was close enough now to see light in the caboose window. What could the brakeman in it see? Could some engineer have seen two men (three men? four men? The thought was irrational) carrying Pointed Shoes along the right of way to his resting place?

He stood watching the disappearing caboose lights and the glare of an approaching eastbound headlight on the next track. The snow was a little heavier now, the wind colder on his neck. He pulled up his jacket collar, pulled down the hat brim. What he didn't know about this business had touched something inside Leaphorn—a bitterness he usually kept so submerged that it was forgotten. Under this dreary cold sky it surfaced. If Pointed Shoes had been something different than he was, someone too important to vanish unmissed and unreported, someone whose tailored suit was not frayed, whose shoe heels were not worn, then the system would have answered all these questions long ago. Train schedules would have been checked, train crews located and interviewed. Leaphorn shivered, pulled the jacket tighter around him, looked down the track trying to get a reading on what an engineer could see along the track in the glare of his headlight. From the high vantage point of the cabin, he could see quite a lot, Leaphorn guessed.

The freight rumbled past, leaving silence. Leaphorn wandered down the track, and away from it back toward the road. Then he heard another train coming from the east. Much faster than the freights. It would be the Amtrak, he thought, and turned to watch it come. It whistled twice, probably for the crossing of a county road up ahead. And then it was roaring past. Seventy miles an hour, he guessed. Not yet slowing for its stop at Gallup. He smiled, remembering the suggestion he had put into Emma's voice—that maybe they stopped the Amtrak and put him off. He was close enough to see the heads of people at the windows, people in the glass-roofed observation car. People with a fear of flying, or rich enough to afford not to fly. Maybe they stopped the Amtrak and put him off, he thought. Well, maybe they did. It seemed no more foolish than his vision of a platoon of men carrying Pointed Shoes down the tracks.

Bernard St. Germain happened to be the only railroader who Leaphorn knew personally—a brakeman-conductor with the Atchison, Topeka and Santa Fe Railroad Company. Leaphorn called him from the Fina station off the Iyanbito interchange and got the recording on St. Germain's answering machine. But while he was leaving a message, St. Germain picked up the receiver.

"I have a very simple question," Leaphorn said. "Can a passenger stop an Amtrak train? Do they still have that cord that can be pulled to set the air brakes, like you see in the old movies?"

"Now there's a box in each car, like a fire alarm box," St. Germain said. "They call it the 'big hole lever.' A passenger can reach in there and pull it."

"And it stops the train?"

"Sure. It sets the air brakes."

"How long would it be stopped?"

"That would depend on circumstances. Ten minutes maybe. Or maybe an hour. What's going on?"

"We had a body beside the tracks east of Gallup last month. I'm trying to figure out how it got there."

"I heard about it," St. Germain said. "You think somebody stopped the Amtrak and took the body off?"

"Just a thought. Just a possibility."

"What day was it? I can find out if somebody pulled the big hole lever."

Leaphorn gave him the date of the death of Pointed Shoes.

"Yeah. All that stuff has to be reported," St. Germain said. "Any time a train makes an unscheduled stop for any reason you have to turn in a delay report. And that has to be radioed in immediately. I'll find out for you Monday."

ONE IS NOT supposed to deal with one's personal mail while on duty in the Navajo Tribal Police Office at Shiprock. Nor is one supposed to receive personal telephone calls. On Monday, Officer Jim Chee did both. He had a fairly good reason.

The post office would not deliver mail to Chee's little aluminum house trailer parked under the cottonwoods beside the San Juan River. Instead, Chee picked it up at the post office each day during his lunch break. On Monday his portion was an L. L. Bean catalog for which he had sent off a coupon, and a letter from Mary Landon. He hurried back to the office with them, put the catalog aside, and tore open the letter.

"Dearest Jim," it began. From that excellent beginning, it went downhill fast.

When your letter arrived yesterday, I was thrilled at the thought of your visit, and seeing you again. But now I have had time to think about it and I think it is a mistake. We still have the same problem and all this will do is bring all the old pain back again. . . .

Chee stopped reading and stared at the wall across from his desk. The wall needed painting. It had needed painting for years. Chee had stuck a calendar to it, and an eight-by-ten photograph of Mary Landon and himself, taken by Cowboy Dashee with the two of them standing on the steps of the little "teacherage" where she had lived when she taught at the Crownpoint Elementary School. Like many of Cowboy's photographs it was slightly out of focus but Chee had treasured it because it had managed to capture Mary's key ingredient: happiness. They had been out all night, watching the final night of an Enemy Way ceremonial over near the Whippoorwill Chapter House. Looking back on it, Chee had come to realize that it was that night he decided he would marry Mary Landon. Or try to marry her.

He read the rest of the letter. It was short—a simple recitation of their problem. She wouldn't want her children raised on the reservation, bringing them up as strangers to her own culture. He wouldn't be happy away from the reservation. And if he made the sacrifice for her, she would be miserable because she had made him miserable. It was an impossible dilemma, she said. Why should they revive the pain? Why not let the wound heal?

Why not, indeed? Except it wasn't healing. Except he couldn't seem to get past it. He put the letter aside. Think of something else. What he had to do today. He had pretty well cleaned up everything pending, getting ready for this vacation. There was a man he was supposed to find out behind Toh-Atin Mesa, a witness in an assault case. The trial had been postponed and he'd intended to let that hang until he came back from Wisconsin and seeing Mary. But he would do it today. He would do it right now. Immediately.

The telephone rang. It was Janet Pete, calling from Washington.

"Ya et eeh," Janet Pete said. "You doing all right?"

"Fine," Chee said. "What's up?"

"Our paths are crossing again," she said. "I've got myself a client and it turns out you arrested him."

Chee was puzzled. "Aren't you in Washington?"

"I'm in Washington. But you arrested this guy on the rez. Out at a Yeibichai, he tells me."

Henry Highhawk. "Yeah," Chee said. "Guy with his hair in braids. Like a blond Kiowa."

"That's him," Janet said. "But he noticed he wasn't in style on the reservation. He changed it to a bun." There was a pause. "You doing all right? You sound sort of down."

"Even Navajos get the blues," Chee said. "No. I'm okay. Just tired. Tomorrow my vacation starts. You're supposed to be tired just before vacation. That's the way the system's supposed to work."

"I guess so," Janet said. She sounded tired, too. "When you arrested him, do you remember if there was another man with him? Slender. Latin-looking."

"With crippled hands? He said his name was Gomez. I think it was Gomez. Maybe Lopez."

"It was Gomez. What did you think of him?"

The question surprised Chee. He thought. "Interesting man. I wondered how he managed to lose so many fingers."

There was a long silence.

"How did he lose those fingers?"

"I don't know," Janet said. "I'm just trying to get some sort of handle on this man. On my client, really. I like to understand what I'm getting into."

"How did you manage to get involved with this Highhawk bird anyway?" Chee asked. "Are you specializing in really weird cases?"

"That's easy. Highhawk is part Navajo and very proud of it. He wants to be whole Navajo. Anyway, he talks like he does. So he wants a Navajo attorney."

"Totally his idea then," Chee said, sounding skeptical. "You didn't volunteer?"

Janet laughed. "Well, there's been a lot about the case in the papers here. Highhawk's a conservator at the Smithsonian and he'd been raising hell about them keeping a million or so Native American skeletons in their warehouse, and last year they tried to fire him. So he went and filed a suit and won his job back. It was a First Amendment case. First Amendment cases get a lot of space in the *Washington Post*. Then he pulls this caper you arrested him for. He dug up a couple of graves up in New England, and of course he picked a historically prominent couple, and that got him a lot more publicity. So I knew about him, and I had read about the Navajo connection . . ." Her voice trailed off.

"I think you have a strange one for a client," Chee said. "Any chance to get him off?"

"Not if he gets his way. He wants to make it a political debate. He wants to put the *belagana* grave robbers on trial for robbing Indian graves while he's on trial for digging up a couple of whites. It might work in Washington, if I could pick the right jury. But the trial will be up in New Haven or someplace up in New England. Up in that part of the country everybody's happy memories are of hearing great-granddaddy tell about killing off the redskins."

Another pause. Chee found himself looking at the picture. Mary Landon and Jim Chee on the doorstep, clowning. Mary's hair was incredibly soft. Out on the malpais that day they went on the picnic, it had blown around her face. He had used his first finger to brush it away from her forehead. Mary's voice saying: "You have a choice. You know if you go to the FBI Academy, then you'll do well, and you know they'll offer you a job. They need some Navajo agents. It's not as if you didn't have any choice." And he had said, you have a choice, too, or something like that. Something inane.

"You're probably supposed to be working," Janet Pete was saying, "and I don't know what I called about exactly anyway. I think I just hoped you could tell me something helpful about Gomez. Or about Highhawk."

Or wanted to hear a friendly voice, Chee thought. It was his own feeling, exactly. "Maybe I'm overlooking something," Chee said. "Maybe if I understood the problem better—"

"I don't understand the problem myself," Janet said. She exhaled noisily. "Look. What would you think if you're talking to your client and it went like this. This guy's going on trial for desecrating a grave. You are being very cool, trying to talk some sense into him about how to handle it if he actually did what they accuse him of, and all of a sudden he says: 'Of course I did it. I'm proud I did it. But would you be my lawyer for another crime?' And I say, 'What crime?' And he says, 'It hasn't been committed yet.' And I don't know what to say to that so I say something flippant. If you're going to dig up another grave, I don't want to hear about it, I say. And he says, 'No, this one would be something better than that.' And I look at him, surprised, you know. I'm thinking it's a joke, but his face is solemn. He's not joking."

"Did he tell you what crime?"

"I said, What crime? How serious? And he said *we* can't talk about it. And, if *we* told you, you would be an accessory before the fact. He was smiling when he said that. Notice, he said *we.*"

"We," Chee repeated. "Any idea who? Is he part of some sort of Indian Power organization? Is somebody working with him on this 'free the bones' project?"

"Well, he's always talking about his 'Paho Society' but I think he's the only member. This time I think he meant Gomez."

"Why Gomez?"

"I don't know. Gomez brings him to my office. I call Highhawk at Highhawk's place, and Gomez answers the telephone. Gomez always seems to be around. Did you know Gomez bonded him out after you picked him up in Arizona?"

"I didn't," Chee said. "Maybe they're just friends."

"I wanted to ask you about that," Janet said. "Did they come to the Yeibichai together? Did you get the feeling they were friends? Old friends?"

"They were strangers," Chee said. "I'm sure of that." He remembered the scene, described it to Janet—Gomez arriving first, waiting in the rental car, disinterested, making contact with Highhawk. He described the clear, obvious fact that Highhawk didn't know Gomez. "I'd say that Gomez came to the Yeibichai just to find Highhawk. But how could he have known Highhawk was coming, if they were really strangers?"

"That's easy. The same way the FBI knew where to arrest him," Janet said. "He told everybody, the woman he rents his apartment from, his neighbors, his drinking buddies, the people he works with at the Smithsonian, told everybody, that he was coming out to Arizona to attend a Yeibichai for his *shima'sa'ni'.*"

"He used that word? Maternal grandmother?"

"Well, he told them he had found this old woman in his Bitter Water Clan. He claims his maternal grandmother was a Bitter Water Dineh. And he claims the old woman had invited him to her Yeibichai."

Chee found he was getting interested in all this. "Well, whatever, when I saw them, Gomez was trying to get acquainted with a stranger. Either that, or they're both good actors. And who would they be trying to fool?" Chee didn't wait for an answer to that rhetorical question. He was thinking about what Janet had said about the crime not yet committed. Something serious. Something *"we"* couldn't talk about.

"I'd say you have a very flaky client," Chee added. "Any reason to think this isn't just some neurotic Lone Ranger trying to impress a pretty lawyer?"

"There's a little bit more," Janet Pete said. "His telephone is tapped."

"Oh," Chee said. "He tell you that?"

"I heard the click. The interference on the line. I called him just before I called you. In fact, that's what actually motivated me to make this call."

"Oh," Chee said. "I thought maybe you were missing me."

"That too," Janet said. "That, and somebody's been following me."

"Ah," Chee said. He was remembering Janet Pete. How she had handled him when she thought he was mishandling one of her clients the first time they had met; how she had dealt with the situation when he'd damaged a car she was buying. Janet Pete was not a person who would be easy to spook.

"If not exactly following me, then keeping an eye on my place. And on me. I see this guy outside my apartment. I see him in the newsstand below where we work. I see him too often. And I never saw him until I got tied up with this Highhawk business."

Chee had been holding Mary Landon's letter in his left hand, folding and unfolding it between his fingers. Now he dropped it into his out-basket on top of the little folder which held his round-trip Continental Airlines ticket to Milwaukee. He thought he might go to Washington, drop in at the J. Edgar Hoover Building in Washington. See what it looked like. Talk to a couple of people he knew back there. See what it would feel like to work for the Agency.

"Tell you what," he said. "I'm coming to Washington anyway. Next day or two. I have some business at the FBI office. I'll let you know exactly when and you set it up for me to talk to Highhawk. And Gomez, too, if you can. That is, if you want to see what I think of it."

"I do." A long pause. "Thanks, Jim."

"It'll be good to see you," he said. "And I want to meet your boyfriend, the rich and famous attorney."

At least it would be better than two weeks lying around the trailer. And he had detected something in Janet Pete's voice that he'd never heard before. She sounded frightened.

8

SUNDAY LIEUTENANT JOE LEAPHORN had felt a lot better about the man with pointed shoes. His sense of the natural order of things had been restored. While in many ways Joe Leaphorn had moved into the world of the whites, his Navajo requirement for order and harmony remained. Every effect must have its cause, every action its necessary result. Unity existed, universal and eternal. And now it seemed that nothing violating this natural order had happened in the sagebrush plain east of Gallup. Apparently Pointed Shoes had flashed his bankroll in the wrong place, perhaps at a poker game in the observation car. The man with the knife had killed him, stopped the train, put the body under a convenient cover of chamisa brush, and gotten back on with the victim's wallet.

There were some holes in that theory, some unanswered questions. For example, what the devil had happened to the false teeth? What was the connection with the Agnes Tsosie Yeibichai? But basically much of the disharmony had seeped out of this homicide. Leaphorn could think of other things. He thought about cleaning his house, and getting ready for his vacation. As with most Navajo Tribal Policemen, vacation time for Leaphorn came after the summer tourist season ended and before winter brought its blizzards with their heavy work load of rescue operations. If Leaphorn wanted to take his vacation, now was the time. He had already postponed it once, simply because in the absence of Emma he could think of nothing he would enjoy doing. But he should take it. If he didn't, his friends would notice. He would see more of those subtle little indications of their kindness and their pity that he had come to dread. So he would think of someplace to go. Something to do. And he would think of it today. Just as soon as he got the dishes done, and the dirty clothes down to the laundromat.

But when the phone rang just as he was getting ready to go to lunch Monday he still hadn't thought of anything. Lunch was going to be with Kennedy. Kennedy was in Window Rock on some sort of Agency records-checking business and was waiting for him at the coffee shop of the Navajo Nation Motor Inn. He had decided he would ask Kennedy for suggestions about what to do with eighteen days off. Leaphorn picked up the receiver and said "Leaphorn," in a tone which he hoped expressed hurry.

The voice was Bernard St. Germain's. Leaphorn had time for this call.

"Pretty good guess you made," St. Germain said. "Not perfect, but close."

"Good," Leaphorn said. Now, he thought, Pointed Shoes becomes a homicide committed in interstate commerce. A federal case. Now the Agency would be involved. More than eleven thousand FBI agents, well dressed, well trained, and highly paid, would be unleashed to attach an identity to the man with pointed shoes. The world's most expensive crime lab would be involved. And if Pointed Shoes was important and a solution seemed imminent, law enforcement's best-funded and most successful public relations machinery would spring into action. Kennedy, his old friend, with whom he was about to have lunch, would have to get to work.

"What do you mean, close but not perfect?" Leaphorn asked.

"Close because the Amtrak did stop that evening, and right about where your body was found. But nobody pulled the big hole lever," St. Germain said. "The ATS system malfunctioned and stopped it."

"ATS?"

"They used to call it the dead man's switch," St. Germain said. "If the engineer doesn't push the button periodically, it automatically applies the air brakes. It's just in case the engineer has a heart attack or a stroke or something. Or maybe goes to sleep. Then he doesn't push the button and the ATS stops the train automatically."

"That means it was just an accident? A passenger couldn't cause that? No question about it?"

"No question at all. Such things have to be reported in writing. It's all there on the delay report. The Amtrak was seven minutes behind schedule. Then, a few miles east of the Fort Wingate spur, the ATS shorted out or something and put on the brakes."

Leaphorn stared at the map on the wall behind his desk, re-thinking his theory.

"How long was it stopped?"

"I knew you'd ask that," St. Germain said. "It was stopped 38 minutes. From 8:34 until 9:12 P.M. That would be about average, I think. The engineer has to get the air pressure up and the brakes have to be reset. So forth."

"Could passengers get off?"

"Not supposed to."

"But could they?"

"Sure. Why not?"

"And get back on again?"

"Yep."

"Would anybody see if someone did? Anybody on the train crew?"

"You mean at night? After dark? It would depend. But probably not. Not if the guy didn't want to be seen. It would be simple enough. You'd just have to wait until everybody was busy. Nobody looking."

"Bernard, what happens to the luggage if a passenger gets off before his destination and leaves it?"

"They take it off at the end of the line—the turnaround point when they're cleaning out the cars. It goes into the claims office. The Lost and Found. Or, if it comes out of a reserved compartment on the sleeper, or a roomette, then they'd do a tracer on it and send it back to the point of origin. So the passenger could pick it up there."

"This Amtrak that comes through here, would the turnaround point be Los Angeles?"

"Not exactly. There's an eastbound and a westbound each day. West is Number 3. East is Number 4."

"Who would I call there to find out about left-behind luggage?"

St. Germain told him.

Kennedy could wait a minute to have lunch with him. He called the Amtrak claims office in Los Angeles, and told the man who answered who he was, what he needed, and why he needed it. He gave the man the train and the date. Then he waited. It didn't take long.

"Yeah. There was a suitcase and some personal stuff left in a roomette on that train. We held it here to see if somebody would claim it. But now it's gone back to Washington," the man said.

"Washington?"

"That's where the passenger boarded. He transferred to Number 3 in Chicago."

Leaphorn took the cap off his ballpoint, pulled his note pad toward him.

"What was his name?"

"Who knows? I guess you could get it from the claims office in Washington. Or from the reservations office. Wherever they keep that sort of records. That's not my end of the business."

"How about locating the train crew? That possible?"

"That's Washington, too. That's where that crew is based. I'd think it would be easy enough to get their names out of Washington."

Kennedy had already ordered when Leaphorn reached his table. He was eating a club sandwich.

"You running on Navajo time?" he asked.

"Always," Leaphorn said. He sat, glanced at the menu, ordered green chili stew. He felt great.

"I've learned a few things about that body," he said. He told Kennedy about the Amtrak being stopped that night at the place where the body was left, and about what St. Germain had told him, and about the passenger's baggage being left in the roomette.

Kennedy chewed, looking thoughtful. He grinned, but the grin was faint. "If you don't quit this, you know, you're going to make a federal case out of it," he said. "What do you want me to do?"

"Do your famous FBI thing," Leaphorn said.

Kennedy swallowed, took a sip of water, nodded. "Okay. I'll get somebody in Washington to go down and take a look at the luggage. We'll see if they can get an identification. We'll see where that leads us."

"What more could anyone ask?"

"I can think of a few more things you're going to ask," Kennedy said. "Based on our past experiences with you. It'll turn out this luggage belongs to an alcoholic who has a habit of falling through cracks. So we will sensibly decide he's not the body, but you won't be happy with that." Kennedy held up a hand, all fingers extended. He bent down one. "One. You'll want some sort of latent fingerprint check on the luggage." He bent down another. "Two. You'll want identification of the eighty-two people who have handled it since the owner." He bent down a third. "Three. You'll want a rundown on everybody who was on that particular Amtrak trip." Kennedy bent down the surviving finger. "Four. You'll want interviews with the train crews. Five—" Kennedy had exhausted his supply of fingers. He extended his thumb. "In summation, you'll want the same sort of stuff we'd do if the Emperor of Earth had been kidnapped by the Martians. Cost eighty-six billions in overtime and then it turns out that your body is a car dealer who got in an argument with somebody in the bar of the train and it's not the business of the Agency."

Leaphorn nodded.

"It's none of your business, either," Kennedy added. "You know that, don't you?"

Leaphorn nodded again. "Not my business yet." He took a spoonful of the stew, ate it. "But I wonder why he was going to the Yeibichai," he said. "Don't you?"

"Sure," Kennedy said. "That seems strange."

"And if he was going, why was he almost a month early?"

"I wonder about a lot of things," Kennedy said. "I wonder why George Bush picked what's-his-name for vice president. I wonder why the Anasazis walked away from all those cliff dwellings. I wonder why the hell I ever got into law enforcement. Or had lunch with you when I knew you'd be wanting a favor."

"And I wonder about that guy's false teeth," Leaphorn said. "Not so much where the false ones went as what happened to his original teeth."

Kennedy laughed. "I'm not that deeply into the wondering game," he said.

"There was nothing wrong with his gums, or his jawbone," Leaphorn said. "That's what the autopsy showed. And that's why people have their teeth pulled."

Kennedy sighed, shook his head. "You get the check," he said. "I'll get somebody to check on the luggage in Washington."

He did. Leaphorn got the call Tuesday.

"Here's what they found," Kennedy said. "The reservation was made in the name of Hilario Madrid-Peña. Apparently it was a bogus name. At least both the address and the telephone number were phony and the name isn't in any of the directories."

"That puts us back to square one," Leaphorn said, trying to keep the disappointment out of his voice. "Unless they found something in the luggage."

"Just a second," Kennedy said. "One large suitcase and one briefcase," he read. "Suitcase contained the expected articles of underwear, shirts, socks, one pair trousers, ceramic pottery, toilet articles. Briefcase contained magazines and newspapers in Spanish, books, small notebook, stationery, envelopes, stamps, fountain pen, package Tums, incidentals. Nothing in notebook appeared helpful in establishing identity." Kennedy paused. "That's it. That's all she wrote."

Leaphorn thought about it. "Well," he said, "I don't know what to think."

"I'm waiting for you to say 'Thank you, Mr. Kennedy,'" Kennedy said.

"Do you know the agent who checked?" Leaphorn asked.

"You mean personally? Or what was his name? No to both. It could have been anybody."

"You think it would have been somebody who knew what he was doing?"

"I wouldn't think so," Kennedy said. "Some rookie you'd want to get out of the office. A deal like this one wouldn't be high priority." Kennedy laughed. "Neither am I."

"What's the chance of getting the Agency to run down the train crew, find out who picked up the luggage, cleaned up the roomette, that sort of thing?"

"I don't know. Probably about the same as you pitching the opening game of the World Series next year."

"I'm told that train crew works out of Washington."

"So what?" Kennedy said. "Before they put a man on something like that, they have to have a reason."

"I guess so," Leaphorn said. He was thinking that he knew a man in Washington who might do it for him. Out of friendship. If Leaphorn was willing to impose on the friendship. He said, "Well, thank you, Mr. Kennedy," and hung up, still thinking about it. P. J. Rodney would do it out of friendship, but it would be a lot of work for him—or at least it might be. And maybe Rodney was retired by now. Leaphorn tried to remember what year it had been when Rodney left the Duluth Police Department and signed on at Washington. He must have enough years in to qualify for retirement, but when Leaphorn had written Rodney to tell him about Emma, he had still been on the District of Columbia force.

Leaphorn glanced at his watch. Time for the news. He walked into the living room, turned on the television, flicked it to channel seven, turned off the sound to avoid the hysterical screaming of the Frontier Ford commercial, then turned it up to hear the newscast. Nothing much interesting seemed to be happening and he found his thoughts returning to Rodney. A good man. They had become friends when they were both country-cousin outsiders attending the FBI Academy. One of those all-too-rare cases when you know almost at first glance that you're going to like someone, and the liking is mutual. And when Rodney had stopped off at Window Rock to visit them on his way to California, he'd had the same effect on Emma. "You make good friends," Emma had told him.

Rodney was a good friend. Leaphorn watched Howard Morgan warning about a winter storm moving across southern Utah toward northeastern Arizona and New Mexico. "Watch out for blowing snow," Morgan said.

Leaphorn thought it would be good to see Rodney again. He knew what he would do with his vacation time.

9

JANET PETE MET HIM at the Continental gate at National Airport, looking trim, efficient, tense, and happy to see him. She hugged him and shepherded him through the mob to the taxi stands.

"Wow," Chee said. "Is it always this crowded?"

"Anthill East," Janet said. She's tired, he thought. But pretty. And very sophisticated. The suit she wore was pale gray and might have been made out of silk. Whatever it was made of it reminded Chee that Janet Pete had a very nice shape. It also reminded him that his town jeans, leather jacket, and bolo tie did not put him in the mainstream of fashion in Washington, D.C., as they did in Farmington or Flagstaff. Here every male above the age of puberty wore a dark three-piece suit, a white shirt, and a dark tie. To Chee, the suits seemed to be identical. His eyes shifted back to Janet, studying her.

"Nobody ever looks at anyone," Chee said, who had been caught by Janet staring at her. "You notice that?"

"Avoid eye contact," Janet said. "That's the first rule of survival in an urban society. I hear it's even worse in Tokyo and Hong Kong and places like that. And for the same reason. Too damn many people crowded together." She gave the driver the address of Chee's hotel. "It was nice of you to come," she said, and her tone told Chee she meant it.

It was a gray, chilly, drizzling day, a "female rain" in Chee's Navajo vocabulary. Janet asked about the reservation, about tribal politics, about their very few mutual acquaintances. Chee answered, wondering now why he had come, wondering if he should have gone to Wisconsin despite Mary's letter. He'd told the travel agency at Farmington to get him a hotel in the "moderate to economical" range. The one where the cab stopped looked economical at best. He checked in. The price was seventy-six dollars per day— approximately triple a good room in the Four Corners country. This room was tiny, with a small double bed, a single chair, a TV set mounted on a wall bracket with one of the control knobs missing, a single narrow window looking out at the windows of a building across the street. Chee motioned Janet to the chair and sat on the bed.

"Here I am," Chee said. "What can I do?"

Janet made a wry face. "The trouble is I don't know what's going on. Or even if *anything* is going on."

"You said someone was following you. Tell me about that."

"That doesn't take long," Janet said. "The first time I went to see Henry Highhawk, I couldn't find his place at first. I walked right past it, and then back again. There was a car parked up the block a ways with a man sitting in it. He was staring at me, so I noticed him. Medium to small apparently. Maybe forty-five or so. Red hair, a lot of freckles, sort of a red face." She paused and glanced at Chee with an attempt at a smile. "Do you ever wonder why they call *us* redskins?" she asked.

"Go on," Chee said. "I'm interested."

"Highhawk lives out on Capitol Hill, in a neighborhood they call Eastern Market. It's easy to get there on the Metro. That's the subway. So I took the Metro and walked to his house. About seven or eight blocks, maybe. I happened to walk past this guy twice sitting in his parked car, so I noticed him. Then when—"

"Hold it," Chee said. "You mean he'd moved the car after you passed him the first time? He moved it up ahead of you?"

"Apparently. And then, when I left Highhawk's place, he was still there. Still sitting in that car. Again, I noticed him twice more while I was walking back to the subway. He was walking the second time. Like he wanted to know where I was going and he left his car parked and followed me on foot. But he didn't get on the subway. Or if he did, I didn't see him."

She paused, looked at him for reaction.

"Hmm," Chee said, trying to sound thoughtful. He was thinking there were plenty of nonsinister reasons a man might follow Janet Pete.

"Since then, three or four times, I've seen him," she added.

Chee apparently didn't looked sufficiently impressed by this. Janet flushed.

"This isn't Shiprock," she said. "You don't just keep seeing a stranger in Washington. Not unless you work in the same place. Or eat in the same place. Millions of people. But I saw this man outside the building where we have our law offices. Once in the parking lot and once outside the lobby. And not counting the Eastern Market Metro business, I saw him out at the Museum of Natural History. Too much to be a coincidence."

"The very first time was at Highhawk's place," Chee said. "Is that right? And again out in his neighborhood. Maybe he's interested in Highhawk. And you're Highhawk's lawyer. Maybe he's interested in you because of that."

"Yes," Janet said. "I thought of that. That's probably it."

"I'd offer you some refreshments if I had any," Chee said. "In Farmington, in a seventy-five-dollar hotel, if they had anything that expensive, you'd have a little refrigerator with all those snacks and drinks in it. Or you'd have room service."

"In Washington that comes in the three-hundred-dollar-per-day hotels," Janet said. "But I don't want anything. I want to know what you think of Highhawk. What do you think of all of this?"

"He struck me as slightly bent," Chee said. "Big, good-looking *belagana,* but he wants to be a Navajo. Or that's the impression I got. And I guess he dug up those bones he's accused of digging up to be a militant Indian."

Janet Pete looked at him, thoughtfully. "Do you know anything that connects him with the Tano Pueblo?"

"Tano? No. Really, I know damned little. I just got stuck with the job of taking the federal warrant and going out to the Yeibichai and arresting the guy. They don't tell you a damn thing. If they don't give you the 'armed and dangerous' speech, then you presume he's not armed or dangerous. Just pick him up, take him in, let the federals handle the rest of it. It was a fugitive warrant. You know, flight to avoid. But I heard he was wanted somewhere East for desecrating a graveyard, vandalism. So forth."

Janet sat with her lower lip caught between her teeth, looking troubled.

"Jim," she said, "I think I'm being used."

"Oh?"

"Maybe it's just I'm the token Navajo and Highhawk wanted a Navajo lawyer. That would make sense. Washington is lousy with lawyers but not with Navajo lawyers."

"Guess not."

"But I've got a feeling," she added. She shook her head, got up, tried to pace. The room was, by Chee's quick estimate, about nine feet wide and sixteen feet long, with floor space deleted for a bathroom and a closet. Pacing was not just impractical, it was impossible. Janet sat down again. "This Highhawk, he's a publicity hound. Oh, that's not really fair. Just say he knows how to make his point with the press and he knows the press is important to him and the press loves him. So when he waived extradition and came back here, he said he wanted a Navajo lawyer and that made the *Post.*" She paused, glanced at Chee. "You know me," she said.

Chee had known her on the reservation as a lawyer on the staff of the Dinebeiina Nahiilna be Agaditahe, which translated loosely into English as "People Who Talk Fast and Help the People Out" but was more often called the DNA or Tribal Legal Aid, and which had earned a hard-nosed reputation for defending the underdog. In fact, Chee had gotten to know her when she nailed him for trying to keep one of her clients locked up in the San Juan County jail longer than Janet thought was legal or necessary.

"Knowing you, I bet you volunteered," Chee said.

"Well, I called him," she said. "And we talked. But I didn't make any commitments. I thought the firm wouldn't like it."

"Let's see," Chee said. "It's Dalman, MacArthur, Fenix, and White, isn't it? Or something like that. They sound like they'd be a little too dignified to be representing somebody who vandalizes graveyards."

"Dalman, MacArthur, White, and Hertzog," Janet said. "And yes, it's a dignified outfit. And it doesn't handle criminal defense cases. I thought they'd want to avoid Highhawk. Especially when the case is going to make the *Post* every day and the client is a notorious grandstander. And I didn't think John would like it either. But it didn't work that way."

"No," Chee said. John was John McDermott. Professor John McDermott. Ex-professor. Ex-University of Arizona law faculty. Janet Pete's mentor, faculty advisor, boss, lover, father figure. The man she'd quit her job with the Navajo Tribe to follow to Washington. Ambitious, successful John. "It doesn't sound like John's sort of thing."

"It turned out I was wrong about that," Janet said. "John brought it up. He asked me if I'd like to represent Highhawk."

Chee made a surprised face.

"I said I didn't think the firm would like it. He said it would be fine with the firm. It would demonstrate its social consciousness."

Chee nodded.

"Bullshit," Janet said. "Social consciousness!"

"Why then?"

Janet started to say something but stopped. She got up again and walked to the window and looked out. Rain streaked the glass. In the office across the street the lights were on. A man was standing at his window looking across at them. Chee noticed he had his coat off. Vest and tie but no coat. It made Chee feel more cheerful.

"You have an idea why, don't you?" Chee said.

"I don't know," Janet said to the window.

"You could guess," Chee said.

"I can guess," she agreed. "We have a client. The Sunbelt Corporation. It's a big factor in real estate development, apartment complexes, that sort of thing. They bought a ranch outside Albuquerque. From what little I know about it, I think they have some sort of big development planned there." She turned away from the window, sat down again, stared at her hands. "Sunbelt is interested in where an interstate bypass is located. It makes a lot of difference in their land values. From what I hear the route Sunbelt favors runs across Tano Pueblo land. The Tano tribal council is split on whether to sell the right of way. The traditionals say no; the progressives see economic development, money." She glanced up at Chee. "The old familiar story."

"It does sound familiar," Chee said. When she got around to it, Janet Pete would explain to him how all this involved Henry Highhawk, and her being followed. It was still raining outside. He looked at the man in the tie and vest in the window across the street who seemed to be looking at him. Funny town, Washington.

"They're having their tribal election some time this winter," Janet said. "Youngish guy named Eldon Tamana is a contender against one of the old guard. Tamana favors granting the right of way." There was another long pause.

"Good chance of winning?" Chee asked.

"I'd guess not," Janet said. She turned and looked at him.

"I'm getting to be like a white man," Chee said. "I'm getting in a hurry for you to tell me what this is all about."

"I'm not sure I know myself. What I know is that the Smithsonian seems to have in its collection a Tano fetish. It's a figure representing one of their Twin War Gods. Somehow Tamana found out about it, and I think he knew John at Arizona, and he came to John to talk about how to get it returned."

Janet hesitated, looked down at her hands.

"I'd think that would be fairly simple," Chee said. "You'd have the Tano tribal council adopt a resolution asking for it back—or maybe have it come from the elders of the kiva society that owned the fetish. Then you'd ask the Smithsonian to return it, and they'd take it under advisement, and do a study to find out where they'd got their hands on it, and after about three years you'd either get it back or you wouldn't."

"I don't think that would work. Not for Tamana," Janet said, still studying her hands.

"Oh?"

Janet sighed. "Did I tell you he's running for a position on the tribal council? I guess he wants to just walk in and present the War God, sort of prove he's a young man who can get things done while the old-timers just talk about it. I doubt if the council knows the museum has the fetish."

"Ah," Chee said. "Are you representing Sunbelt interests in this? I guess Sunbelt has an interest in getting Tamana elected."

"I'm not," Janet said. "John is. John is the law firm's Southwestern expert. He gets the stuff which involves public land policy, Indians, uranium, water rights, all the cases like that."

"Did he tell you all this?"

"Mostly he was asking me. I'm the firm's Indian. Indians are supposed to know about Indians. All us redskins are alike. Mother Earth and Father Sun and all that Walt Disney crap." She smiled a wan smile. "That's really not fair to John. He's not as bad as most. Mostly he understands the cultural differences."

"But you think he's using you?"

"I think the law firm would like to use me," Janet corrected. "John works for them. So do I."

The gray rain outside, the form of the shirt-sleeved man standing in the window across from them, the narrow, shabby room, all of it was depressing Chee. He got off the bed and tried to pull the drape fully across the window. It helped some.

"I'm going to wash up," Chee said. "Then let's get out of here and get some coffee somewhere." He wanted to think about what Janet had told him. He could understand her suspicion. The firm wanted her to represent Highhawk because Highhawk worked in a sensitive position for the museum which held Tano sacred objects. Why? Did they want Highhawk to steal the War Twin? Was Janet, as his lawyer, supposed to talk him into doing that?

"Fine," Janet said. "We have an appointment with Highhawk.

I don't think I told you about that. Out at his place in Eastern Market."

There were two bare bulbs above the wash-basin mirror, one of which worked. Chee rinsed his face, looked at himself in the mirror, wondered again what the hell he was doing here. But in some subconscious way he knew now. He was looking forward to another conversation with the man who wanted to be a Navajo.

10

LEAPHORN HAD LEFT his umbrella. He'd thought of it as he boarded the plane at Albuquerque—the umbrella lying dusty in the trunk of his car and the plane flying eastward toward Washington and what seemed to Leaphorn to be inevitable rain. The umbrella had never experienced rain. He'd bought it last year in New York, the second of two umbrellas he'd purchased on the same trip—the first one having been forgotten God knows where. He'd tossed the second one into the trunk of his car with his luggage on his return to the Albuquerque airport. There it had rested for a year.

Now, with the rain drumming down on his neck, he paid the cabby. He pulled his hat lower over his ears, and hurried across the sidewalk to the Amtrak office. He had an appointment with Roland Dockery, who was the person in the Amtrak bureaucracy stuck with handling such nondescript problems as Leaphorn represented.

Dockery was waiting for him, a plump, slightly bald, and slightly disheveled man of perhaps forty. He examined Leaphorn's Navajo Tribal Police identification through bifocal glasses with obvious curiosity and invited Joe to sit with a wave of his hand. He pointed to the luggage on his desk—a shabby leather suitcase and a smaller, newer briefcase.

"The FBI's already been through them," Dockery said. "Like I told you on the phone. I guess they would have told you if they found anything."

"Nothing useful," Leaphorn said. "What we're looking for is anything that might connect the bags to a homicide we have out in New Mexico. I hope you won't mind me going over some questions the FBI probably already covered."

"No problem," Dockery said. He laughed. "No trouble about keys. The FBI already opened them." He flipped open both cases with a flourish. Dockery was obviously enjoying this. It represented something unusual in a job that must be usually routine.

Leaphorn sorted through the big case first. It held a spare suit, dark gray and of some expensive fabric, but looking much used. A sweater. Two dark blue neckties. White, long-sleeved shirts, some clean and neatly folded, some used and folded into a laundry sack. Eight altogether. Three used. Five clean. Leaphorn checked his notes. The neck and arm sizes matched the shirt on the corpse. Shorts and undershirts, also white. Same total, same breakdown. Same with socks, except the color now was black. He thought about the numbers and the timetable. He'd check but it seemed about right. If this was indeed the luggage of Pointed Shoes, then he had in fact been about three shirts west of Washington by the time he reached Gallup. Wearing shirt four when he was stabbed, with five clean ones to take him to where he was going. Or—if he was simply going to see Agnes Tsosie—home again to Washington.

The smaller bag contained a jumble of things. Leaphorn glanced up from it but Dockery didn't give him a chance to ask the question.

"One of the cleanup crew packed it," Dockery said. "Just dumped all the stuff that was around the roomette into the bag. I've got his name somewhere. The FBI had him in and talked to him when they checked on it."

"So this would be everything left lying around?" Leaphorn asked. And Dockery nodded his agreement. But it wasn't everything, of course, Leaphorn knew. Odds and ends that seemed to have no value would have been discarded. Old newspapers, notes, empty envelopes, just the sort of stuff that might be most helpful would have been thrown away.

But what hadn't been thrown away was also helpful. First, Leaphorn noticed an almost empty tube of Fixodent and a small can of denture cleaner. He had expected to find them. If he hadn't he would have doubted that this was the luggage of a man who wore false teeth. Three books, all printed in Spanish, added another bit of support. The clothing Pointed Shoes had been wearing had looked old-fashioned and foreign. So did the clothing in the suitcase. He found a thin little notebook, covered in black plastic, glanced at it, and set it aside. Under a sweater in the bag he found two pots, each wrapped in newspaper. He examined them. They were the sort Pueblo Indians made to sell to tourists—small, one with a black-on-white lizard design, the other geometric. Probably they had been purchased as gifts at the Amtrak station in Albuquerque, where such things were sold beside the track. But the pots interested Leaphorn less than the newspaper pages in which the purchaser had cushioned them.

Spanish again. Leaphorn unfolded a wad of pages, looking for the name and the date. The name was *El Crepúsculo de Libertad.* Something-or-other of Liberty. Leaphorn's working vocabulary in Spanish was mostly the Gallup-Flagstaff wetback variety. Now he ransacked his memory of the twelve credit hours he'd taken at Arizona State. He came up with "sunrise," or perhaps "twilight." Dawn seemed more likely. The Dawn of Liberty. The date on the page was late October, about two weeks before Pointed Shoes had been knifed. Leaphorn glanced at the headlines, getting only a word or two, but enough to guess the subject was politics. Neither of the crumpled pages included a place of publication.

Leaphorn folded them into his pocket and sorted through the odds and ends in the bottom of the bag. He extracted a sheet of white notepaper, folded vertically as if to fit into a pocket. On it, someone had written what seemed to be a checklist.

Pockets

Prescription bottles

eyeglasses (check case, too)

dentures (if any)

labels in coats

address books, etc.

letters, envelopes

book plats (plates?) stuff written in books

addresses on mags, etc.

Leaphorn stared at the list, thinking. He showed it to Dockery. "What do you think of this?"

Dockery looked at it. "Looks like some sort of shopping list," Dockery said. "No, it's not that. Reminders, maybe. Things to do."

Leaphorn put the list on the desk. He picked up the notebook he'd set aside, opened it. Several pages had been torn out. The writing in it was in Spanish, done with blue ink in a small, careful hand. He got out his wallet, extracted the note he'd found in the dead man's shirt pocket. The handwriting matched the small, neat penmanship in the notebook. And it looked nothing at all like the handwriting on the list.

"Do you happen to know if that fellow had a roommate?" he asked.

"Just the single occupant," Dockery said.

"Any sign somebody broke in?"

"Not that I know of," Dockery said. "And I think I would have heard. I'm sure I would have. That's the sort of thing that would get around." He fished a pack of Winstons from his desk drawer, offered one to Leaphorn.

"I finally managed to quit," Leaphorn said.

Dockery lit up, exhaled a blue cloud. "What are you fellows looking for, anyway?"

"What did the FBI tell you?"

Dockery laughed. "Not a damned thing. It was some young fella. He didn't tell me squat."

"We found the body of a man beside the tracks east of Gallup. Stabbed. All identification gone. False teeth missing." Leaphorn tapped the Fixodent with a finger. "Turns out the Amtrak had an emergency there at the right time. Turns out the baggage unclaimed from this roomette has also been stripped of all identification. The clothing we have here in this bag is the same size and type the corpse was wearing. So we think it's likely that the man who reserved this roomette under the phony name was the victim."

"Hey, now," Dockery said. "That's interesting."

"Also," Leaphorn added slowly, looking at Dockery, "we think that someone—probably the person who knifed our victim—got into this roomette, searched through his stuff, and took out everything that would help identify the corpse."

"Have you talked to the attendant?" Dockery asked.

"I'd like to," Leaphorn said. "And whoever it was who cleaned up the room, and packed up the victim's stuff."

"He saw somebody in that roomette," Dockery said.

Leaphorn stopped leafing through the notebook and stared at Dockery. "He told you that?"

"Conductor on that run's a guy named Perez, an old-timer. He used to be our chapter chairman in the Brotherhood of Railroad Trainmen. He told me he and the guy traveling in that roomette would chat in Spanish now and then. You know, just polite stuff. He said the guy was a nice man, and kind of sickly. Had some sort of heart condition and the altitude out there had been bothering him. So when they had that nonscheduled stop there in New Mexico, after they got the train rolling again, Perez checked at the roomette to see if this guy needed any help getting off at Gallup." Dockery paused, ashed his cigarette into something invisible in his desk drawer, inhaled more smoke. Through the window behind him Leaphorn noticed it was raining hard now.

"There was a man in there. Perez said that he tapped on the door and when nobody answered it, he was uneasy about this sick passenger so he unlocked it. And he said there was a man in there. He asked Perez what he wanted, and Perez told him he was checking to see if the passenger needed any help. The man said 'no help needed' and shut the door." Dockery blew a smoke ring. "Seemed funny to Perez because he said he couldn't see his passenger back in the roomette and he'd never seen the passenger and this guy together. So he was watching for the passenger when they made the Gallup stop. Didn't see him get off so he tapped at the door again and nobody answered. So he unlocked the door and went in and all this stuff was in there but no passenger." Dockery stopped, waiting for reaction.

"Odd," Leaphorn said.

"Damn right," Dockery agreed. "It's the sort of thing you remember."

"You tell the FBI agent about this?"

"Didn't really get a chance. He just wanted to look at the bags and be on his way."

"Could I talk to Perez?"

"He's on the same run," Dockery said. He fished a timetable out of his drawer and handed it to Leaphorn. "Call some station a stop ahead where they stop long enough to get him to the telephone. He'll call you back. He'd be damned interested in what happened to his passenger."

Leaphorn was thumbing his way through the notebook a second time, making notes in his own notebook. Most of the pages were blank. Some contained only initials and what seemed to be telephone numbers. Leaphorn copied them off. One page contained only two letter-number combinations. Most of the notations seemed to concern meetings. The one Leaphorn was looking at read, "Harrington. *Cuarto* 832. 3 p."

"Harrington," Leaphorn said. "Would that be a hotel?"

"It's downtown," Dockery said. "Over on E Street and not far from the Mall. Sort of lower middle class. They let it run down.

Usually when that happens somebody buys it and turns it into offices."

Leaphorn wrote the address and room number in his notebook. At the top of the next page "AURANOFIN" was written in capital letters, followed by "W1128023." He jotted that down, too. Below, on the same page, a notation touched a faint chord in Joe Leaphorn's excellent memory. It was a name, slightly unusual, that he'd seen somewhere before.

The man with the pointed shoes had written: "Natl. Hist. Museum. Henry Highhawk."

JANET PETE DECIDED they would take the Metro from the Smithsonian Station up to Eastern Market. It cost only eighty cents a ticket, and was just as fast as a taxi. Then, too, it would give Jim Chee a chance to see the Washington subway. As Chee was wise enough to guess, Janet wanted to play city mouse to his country mouse. That was okay with Chee. He could see that Janet Pete's self-esteem could use a little burnishing.

"Not like New York," Janet said. "It's clean and bright and fast and you feel perfectly safe. Not at all like New York." Chee, who had only heard rumors of the New York subway, nodded. He'd always wanted to ride the New York subway. But maybe this trip would be interesting, too.

It was. The soaring waffled ceiling, the machines which dispensed paper slips as tickets along with the proper change, the gates which accepted those paper slips, opened, and then returned the slips, the swarm of people conditioned to avoid human contact—eye, knee, or elbow. Chee clung to the bracket by the sliding door and inspected them. It surprised him, at first, that he wasn't being inspected in return. He must look distinctly different: his best felt reservation hat with its silver band, his best leather jacket, his best boots, his rawboned, weather-beaten, homely Navajo face. But the only glances he drew were quick and secretive. He was politely ignored. That seemed odd to Chee.

And there were other oddities. He'd presumed the subway would be used by the working class. The blue-collar people were here, true enough, but there was more than that. He could see three men and one woman in navy uniforms, with enough stripes on their sleeves to indicate membership in the privileged class. Since rank had come young for them, they would be graduates of the Naval Academy. They would be people with political connections and old family money. At least half the white men, and about that mix of blacks, wore the inevitable dark three-piece suit and dark tie of the Eastern Establishment, or perhaps here it was the Federal Bureaucracy. The women wore mostly skirts and high heels. Chee's study of anthropology at the University of New Mexico had led him into sociology courses. He remembered a lecture on those factors which condition humans and thereby form culture. He felt detached from this subway crowd, an invisible entity looking down on a species that had evolved to survive overcrowding, to endure aggression, to survive despite what old Professor Ebaar called "intraspecies hostility."

On the long ride up the escalator to what his own Navajo Holy People would have called the Earth Surface World, Chee mentioned these impressions to Janet Pete.

"Will you ever feel at home here?" he asked. She didn't answer until they reached the top and walked out into the dim twilight, into what had become something between drizzle and mist.

"I don't know," she said. "I thought so once. But it's hard to handle. A different culture."

"And you don't mean different from Navajo?"

She laughed. "No. I don't mean that. I guess I mean different from the empty West."

Henry Highhawk's place was about seven blocks from the Metro station—a narrow, two-story brick house halfway down a block of such narrow houses. Tied to the pillar just beside the mailbox was something which looked like a paho. Chee inspected it while Janet rang the bell. It was indeed a Navajo prayer stick, with the proper feathers attached. If Highhawk had made it, he knew what he was doing. And then Highhawk was at the door, inviting them in. He was taller than Chee remembered him from the firelight at Agnes Tsosie's place. Taller and leaner and more substantial, more secure in his home territory than he had been surrounded by a strange culture below the Tsosies' butte. The limp, which had touched Chee with a sense of pity at the Tsosie Yeibichai, seemed natural here. The jeans Highhawk wore had been cut to accommodate the hinged metal frame that reinforced his short leg. The brace, the high lift under the small left boot, the limp, all of them seemed in harmony with this lanky man in this crowded little house. He had converted his Kiowa-Comanche braids into a tight Navajo bun. But nothing would convert his long, bony, melancholy face into something that would pass for one of the Dineh. He would always look like a sorrowful white boy.

Highhawk was in his kitchen pouring coffee before he recognized Chee. He looked at Chee intently as he handed him his cup.

"Hey," he said, laughing. "You're the Navajo cop who arrested me."

Chee nodded. Highhawk wanted to shake hands again—a "no hard feelings" gesture. "Policeman, I mean," Highhawk amended, his face flushed with embarrassment. "It was very efficient. And I appreciated you getting that guy to drive that rent-a-car back to Gallup for me. That saved me a whole bunch of money. Probably at least a hundred bucks."

"Saved me some work, too," Chee said. "I would have had to do something about it the next morning." Chee was embarrassed, too. He wasn't accustomed to this switch in relationships. And Highhawk's behavior puzzled him a little. It was too deferential, too—Chee struggled for the word. He was reminded of a day at his uncle's sheep camp. Three old dogs, all shaggy veterans. And the young dog his uncle had won somewhere gambling. His uncle lifting the young dog out of the back of the pickup. The old dogs, tense and interested, conscious that their territory was being invaded. The young dog walking obliquely toward them, head down, tail down, legs bent, sending all the canine signals of inferiority and subjection, deferring to their authority.

"I'm Bitter Water Dinee," Highhawk said. He looked shy as he said it, tangling long, slender fingers. "At least my grandmother was, and so I guess I can claim it."

Chee nodded. "I am one of the Slow Talking Dineh," he said. He didn't mention that his father's clan was also Bitter Water, which made it Chee's own "born for" clan. That made him and Highhawk related on their less important paternal side. But then, after two generations under normal reservation circumstances, that secondary paternal link would have been submerged by marriages into other clans. Chee considered it, and felt absolutely no kinship link with this strange, lanky man. Whatever his dreams and pretensions, Highhawk was still a *belagana*.

They sat in the front room then, Chee and Janet occupying a sofa and Highhawk perched on a wooden chair. Someone, Chee guessed it had been Highhawk, had enlarged the room by removing the partition which once had separated it from a small dining alcove. But most of this space was occupied by two long tables, and the tables were occupied by tools, by what apparently had been a section of tree root, by a roll of leather, a box of feathers, slabs of wood, paint jars, brushes, carving knives—the paraphernalia of Highhawk's profession.

"You had something to tell me," Highhawk said to Janet. He glanced at Chee.

"Your preliminary hearing has been set," Janet said. "We finally got them to put it on the calendar. It's going to be two weeks from tomorrow and we have to get some things decided before then."

Highhawk grinned at her. It lit his long, thin face and made him look even more boyish. "You could have told me that on the telephone," he said. "I'll bet there was more than that." He glanced at Chee again.

Chee got up and looked for a place to go. "I'll give you some privacy," he said.

"You could take a look at my kachina collection," Highhawk said. "Back in the office." He pointed down the hallway. "First door on the right."

"It's not all that confidential," Janet said. "But I can imagine what the bar association would say about me talking about a plea bargain with a client right in front of the arresting officer."

The office was small and as cluttered as the living area. The desk was a massive old roll top, half buried under shoeboxes filled with scraps of cloth, bone fragments, wood, odds and ends of metal. A battered cardboard box held an unpainted wooden figure carved out of what seemed to be cottonwood root. It stared up at Chee through slanted eye sockets, looking somehow pale and venomous. Some sort of fetish or figurine, obviously. Something Highhawk must be replicating for a museum display. Or could it be the Tano War God? Another box was beside it. Chee pulled back the flaps and looked inside. He looked into the face of Talking God.

The mask of the Yeibichai was made as the traditions of the Navajos ruled it must be made—of deerskin surmounted by a bristling crown of eight eagle feathers. The face was painted white. Its mouth protruded an inch or more, a narrow tube of rolled leather. Its eyes were black dots surmounted by painted brows. The lower rim of the mask was a ruff of fox fur. Chee stared at it, surprised. Such masks are guarded, handed down in the family only to a son willing to learn the poetry and ritual of the Night Chant, and to carry the role his father kept as a Yeibichai dancer.

Keepers of such masks gave the spirits that lived within them feedings of corn pollen. Chee examined this mask. He found no sign of the smearing pollen would have left on the leather. It was probably a replica Highhawk had made. Even so, when he closed the cardboard flaps on the box, he did so reverently.

Three shelves beside the only window were lined with the wooden figures of the kachina spirits. Mostly Hopi, it seemed to Chee, but he noticed Zuni Mudheads and the great beaked Shalako, the messenger bird from the Zuni heavens, and the striped figures of Rio Grande Pueblo clown fraternities. Most of them looked old and authentic. That also meant expensive.

Behind him in the front room, Chee heard Janet's voice rise in argument, and Highhawk's laugh. He presumed Janet was telling her client during this ironic gesture at confidentiality what she had already told Chee on the walk from the subway. The prosecutor with jurisdiction over crime in Connecticut had more important things on his mind than disturbed graves, especially when they involved a minority political gesture. He would welcome some sort of plea-bargain compromise. Highhawk and attorney would be welcome to come in and discuss it. More than welcome.

"I don't think this nut of mine will go for it," Janet had told Chee. "Henry wants to do a Joan of Arc with all the TV cameras in sharp focus. He's got the speech already written. 'If this is justice for me, to go to jail for digging up your ancestors, where then is the justice for the whites who dug up the bones of my ancestors?' He won't agree, not today anyway, but I'll make the pitch. You come along and it will give you a chance to talk to him and see what you think."

And, sure enough, from the combative tone Chee could hear in Highhawk's voice, Janet's client wasn't going for it. But what the devil was Chee supposed to learn here? What was he supposed to think? That Highhawk was taller than he remembered? And had changed his hairstyle? That wasn't what Janet expected. She expected him to smell out some sort of plot involving her law firm, and a fellow following her, and a big corporation developing land in New Mexico. He looked around the cluttered office. Fat chance.

But it was interesting. Flaky as he seemed, Highhawk was an artist. Chee noticed a half-finished Mudhead figure on the table and picked it up. The traditional masks, as Chee had seen them at Zuni Shalako ceremonials, were round, clay-colored, and deformed with bumps. They represented the idiots born after a daughter of the Sun committed incest with her brother. Despite the limiting conventions of little round eyes and little round mouth, Highhawk had carved into the small face of this figurine a kind of foolish glee. Chee put it down carefully and reinspected the ka-chinas on the shelf. Had Highhawk made them, too? Chee checked. Some of them, probably. Some looked too old and weathered for recent manufacture. But perhaps Highhawk's profession made him skilled in aging, too.

It was then he noticed the sketches. They were stacked on the top level of the roll-top desk, done on separate sheets of heavy artist's paper. The top one showed a boy, a turkey with its feathers flecked with jewels, a log, smoke rising from it as it was burned to hollow it into a boat. The setting was a riverbank, a cliff rising behind it. Chee recognized the scene. It was from the legend of Holy Boy, the legend reenacted in the Yeibichai ceremony. It showed the spirit child, still human, preparing for his journey down the San Juan River with his pet turkey. The artist seemed to have captured the very moment when the illness which was to paralyze him had struck the child. Somehow the few lines which suggested his naked body also suggested that he was falling, in the throes of anguish. And above him, faintly in the very air itself, there was the blue half-round face of the spirit called Water Sprin-kler.

The sound of Highhawk's laugh came from the adjoining room, and Janet Pete's earnest voice. Chee sorted through the other sketches. Holy Boy floating in his hollow log, prone and paralyzed, with the turkey running on the bank beside him—neck and wings outstretched in a kind of frozen panic; Holy Boy, partially cured but now blind, carrying the crippled Holy Girl on his shoulders; the two children, hand in hand, surrounded by the towering figures of Talking God, Growling God, Black God, Monster Slayer, and the other *yei*—all looking down on the children with the relentless, pitiless neutrality of the Navajo gods toward mortal men. There was something in this scene—something in all these sketches now that he was aware of it—that was troubling. A sort of surreal, off-center dislocation from reality. Chee stared at the sketches, trying to understand. He shook his head, baffled.

Aside from this element, he was much impressed both by Highhawk's talent and by the man's knowledge of Navajo meta-physics. The poetry of the Yeibichai ceremonial usually used didn't include the role of the girl child. Highhawk had obviously done his homework.

The doorbell rang, startling Chee. He put down the sketch and went to the office door. Highhawk was talking to someone at the front door, ushering him into the living room.

It was a man, slender, dark, dressed in the standard uniform of Washington males.

"As you can see, Rudolfo, my lawyer is always on the job," Highhawk was saying. The man turned and bowed to Janet Pete, smiling.

It was Rudolfo Gomez, Mr. Bad Hands.

"I've come at a bad time," Bad Hands said. "I didn't notice Miss Pete's car outside. I didn't realize you were having a conference."

Jim Chee stepped out of the office. Bad Hands recognized him instantly, and with a sort of controlled shock that seemed to Chee to include not just surprise but a kind of dismay.

"And this is Jim Chee," Highhawk said. "You gentlemen have met before. Remember? On the reservation. Mr. Chee is the officer who arrested me. Jim Chee, this is Rudolfo Gomez, an old friend."

"Ah, yes," Bad Hands said. "Of course. This is an unexpected pleasure."

"And Mr. Gomez is the man who put up my bail," Highhawk said to Chee. "An old friend."

Bad Hands was wearing his gloves. He made no offer to shake hands. Neither did Chee. It was not, after all, a Navajo custom.

"Sit down," Highhawk said. "We were talking about my preliminary hearing."

"I've come at a bad time," Bad Hands said. "I'll call you tomorrow."

"No. No," Janet Pete said. "We're finished. We were just leaving." She gave Chee the look.

"Right," Chee said. "We have to go."

A cold wind out of the northwest had blown away the drizzle. They walked down the steps from Highhawk's porch and passed a blue Datsun parked at the sidewalk. It wasn't the car Bad Hands had been driving at the Agnes Tsosie place, but that had been three thousand miles away. That one was probably rented. "What'd you think?" Janet Pete asked.

"I don't know," Chee said. "He's an interesting man."

"Gomez or Highhawk?"

"Both of them," Chee said. "I wonder what happened to Gomez's hands. I wonder why Highhawk calls him an old friend. But I meant Highhawk. He's interesting."

"Yeah," Janet said. "And suicidal. He's flat determined to go to jail." They walked a little. "Stupid son-of-a-bitch," she added. "I could get him off with some community service time and a suspended sentence."

"You know anything about this Gomez guy?" Chee asked.

"Just what I told you and what Highhawk said. Old friends. Gomez posted his bail."

"They're not old friends," Chee said. "I told you that. I saw them meet at that Yeibichai where I arrested him. Highhawk had never seen the guy before."

"You sure of that? How do you know?"

"I know," Chee said.

Janet put her hand on his arm, slowed. "There he is," she said in a tiny voice. "That car. That's the man who's been following me."

The car was parked across the street from them. An aging Chevy two-door, its medium color hard to distinguish in the shadows.

"You sure?" Chee said.

"See the radio antenna? Bent like that? And the dent in the back fender? It's the same car." Janet was whispering. "I really looked at it. I memorized it."

What to do? His inclination was to ignore this situation, to simply walk past the car and see what happened. Nothing would happen, except Janet would think he was a nerd. He felt uneasy. On the reservation, he would have simply trotted across the street and confronted the driver. But confront him with what? Here Chee felt inept and incompetent. This entire business seemed like something one saw on television. It was urban. It seemed dangerous but it was probably just silly. What the devil would the Washington Police Department recommend in such a circumstance?

They were still walking very slowly. "What should we do?" Janet asked.

"Stay here," Chee said. "I'll go see about it."

He walked diagonally across the street, watching the dim light reflecting from the driver's-side window. What would he do if the window started down? If he saw a gun barrel? But the window didn't move.

Beside the car now, Chee could see a man behind the steering wheel, looking at him.

Chee tapped on the glass. Wondering why he was doing this. Wondering what he would say.

Nothing happened. Chee waited. The man behind the wheel appeared to be motionless.

Chee tapped on the window again, rapping the glass with the knuckles of his right hand.

The window came down, jerkily, squeaking.

"Yeah?" the man said. He was looking up at Chee. A small face, freckled. The man had short hair. It seemed to be red. "Whaddaya want?"

Chee wanted very badly to get a better look at the man. He seemed to be small. Unusually small. Chee could see no sign that he was armed, but that would be hard to tell in the darkness of the front seat.

"The lady I'm with, she thinks you've been following her," Chee said. "Any reason for her to think that?"

"Following her?" The man leaned forward toward the window, looking past Chee at Janet Pete waiting across the street. "What for?"

"I'm asking if you've been following her," Chee said.

"Hell, no," the man said. "What is this anyway? Who the hell are you?"

"I'm a cop," Chee said, thinking as he said it that it was the first smart thing he'd said in this conversation. And it was more or less true. A good thing to have said as long as this guy didn't ask for identification.

The man looked up at him. "You sure as hell don't look like a cop to me," he said. "You look like an Indian. Let's see some identification."

"Let's see your identification," Chee said.

"Ah, screw this," the man said, disappearing from the window. The glass squeaked as he rolled it up. The engine started. The headlights came on. The car rolled slowly away from the curb and down the street. It made a careful right turn and disappeared. Absolutely no hurry.

Chee watched it go. Through the back window he noticed that only the top of the driver's head protruded above the back of the seat. A very small driver.

12

SINCE BOYHOOD Fleck had been one of those persons who like to worry about one thing at a time. This morning he wanted to worry only about Mama. What the devil was he going to do about her? He was up against the Fat Man's deadline. Get her out of that nursing home. *"Get her out now!"* the Fat Man had shouted it at him. "Not one more day!" The only place he'd found to put her wanted first month and last month in advance. With all those so-called incidental expenses they always stuck you with for the private room, that added up to more than six thousand dollars. Fleck had most of it. Plus he had ten thousand coming, and overdue. But that didn't help him right now. He'd scared the Fat Man enough to hold him a day or two. But he couldn't count on much more than that. The son of a bitch was the kind who just might call the cops in on him. That wasn't something Fleck wanted to deal with. Not with Mama involved. He had to get the ten thousand.

There was another problem. He had to give some thought to that cowboy who'd walked over to his car last night and tapped at the window. What the hell did that mean? The guy looked like an Indian, and he was with that Indian woman who'd been visiting Highhawk. But what did it mean to Fleck? Fleck smelled cop. He sensed danger. There was more going down here than he knew about. That worried him. He needed to know more, and he intended to.

Fleck pulled into the Dunkin' Donuts parking area. He was a little early but he noticed that the Ford sedan with the telephone company symbol was already parked. His man was on a stool, the only customer in the place, eating something with a fork. Fleck took the stool next to him.

"You got it?" Fleck asked.

"Sure. You got fifty?"

Fleck handed the man two twenties and a ten and received a folded sheet of paper. He felt foolish as he did it. If he was smart, he could probably have found a way to get this information free without paying this creep in the telephone company. Maybe it was even in the library. He unfolded the paper. It was a section torn from a Washington Convention and Visitors Bureau map of the District of Columbia.

"I circled the area where they use the 266 prefix," the man said. "And the little x marks are where the public phone booths are."

Only a few x's, Fleck noticed. Less than twenty. He commented on it.

"It's mostly a residential district," the man explained, "and part of the embassy row. Not much business for pay phones out there. You want a doughnut?"

"No time," Fleck said, getting up.

"Haven't heard much from you lately," the man said. "You going out of business?"

"I'm in a little different line of work right now," Fleck said, walking toward the door. He stopped. "Would you happen to know of any good nursing homes? Where they take good care of old people?"

"Don't know nothing about 'em," the man said.

Fleck hurried, even though he had until two P.M. He started on Sixteenth Street, because that's where the countries without enough money to build on Massachusetts Avenue mostly located their embassies. None of the numbers matched there, although he found two booths with 266 numbers The Client had used earlier. He moved to Seventeenth Street and then Eighteenth. It was there he found the number he was scheduled to call at two P.M. Fleck backed out of the booth and looked up and down the street. No other pay booths in sight. He'd have to rent the car equipped with a mobile telephone. He'd reserved one at Hertz last night, just in case it worked out this way.

Fleck spent the next two hours driving out to Silver Spring and checking on a rest home he'd heard about out there. It was a little cheaper but the linoleum on the floors was cracked and streaked with grime and the windows hadn't been washed and the woman who ran the place had a mean-looking mouth. He picked up the rent-a-car a little after one, a black Lincoln town car which was too big and too showy for Fleck's taste but which would look natural enough in Washington. He made sure the telephone worked, put his Polaroid camera on the front seat beside him, and drove back to Eighteenth Street. He parked across the street and a little down the block from the phone booth, called it, left his receiver open, and walked down the sidewalk far enough to hear the ringing in the booth. Then he sat behind the wheel, slumped down to be less visible. He waited. While he waited, he thought.

First he went over his plan for this telephone call. Then he thought about the cowboy walking across the street and rapping at his window. If he was an Indian—and he looked like one—it might tie back to the killing. He'd left the train at the little town in New Mexico. Gallup, it was. Indians everywhere you looked. Probably they even had Indian cops and maybe one of them was looking into it. If that was true it meant they had tracked him back to Washington and somehow or other tied something together with that silly-looking bastard who wore his hair in a bun. That meant they must know a hell of a lot more about what Fleck was involved with than Fleck knew himself.

That thought made him uneasy. He shifted in the seat and looked out the window at the weather, getting his mind off what would happen to him if the police ever had him in custody, with his fingerprints matched and making the circuit. If it ever got that far, he could kiss his ass good-bye. He could never, ever let that happen. What would Mama do if it did?

If he could only find someplace where her always getting even didn't get Mama into trouble. She was too old for that now. She couldn't get away with it like when she was healthy. Like that time when they were living down there near Tampa when Mama was young and the landlord got the sheriff onto them to make them move out. He remembered Mama down on her stomach behind the stove loosening up something or other on the gas pipe with Delmar standing there handing her the tools. "You can't let the bastards get up on you," she was saying. "You hear that, Delmar? If you don't even it up, they grind you down even more. They spit on you ever' living time if you don't teach them you won't let them do it."

And they had almost spit on them that time, if Mama hadn't been so smart. Some of the neighbors had seen Delmar down there that night just before the explosion and the big fire. And they told on him, and the police came there to the Salvation Army shelter where Mama was keeping them and they took Delmar off with them. And then he and Mama had gone down to the sheriff's office and he told them it was him, not Delmar, the neighbors had seen. And it had worked out just like Mama had said it would. They had to go easy on him because he was only thirteen and it was a first offense on top of that, and they'd have to handle him in juvenile court. But with Delmar being older, and with shoplifting and car theft and assault already on his books, they would try him as an adult. Fleck had only got sixty days in the D Home and a year's probation out of that one. Mama had always been good at handling things. But now she was just too old and her mind was gone.

Fleck's reverie was ended by a woman hurrying around the corner toward him. She wore a raincoat, something shiny and waterproof over her head, and was carrying a plastic sack. She walked past Fleck's Lincoln without a glance. While he watched her in the rearview mirror, another figure appeared at the corner ahead of him. A man in a dark blue raincoat and a dark gray hat. He carried an umbrella and as he hesitated at the curb, looking for traffic, he opened it.

It had started to rain, streaking the car windows, pattering against the windshield. Fleck glanced at his watch. Seventeen minutes until two. If this was his man, the man was early. He crossed the street, slanting the umbrella against the rain, and hurried down the sidewalk toward the telephone booth. He walked past it.

Fleck slumped down in the seat, too low to see or be seen. He waited. Then he pushed himself up. He used the electric control to adjust the side mirror, found the man just as he turned the corner behind the car. Probably someone with nothing to do with this business, Fleck thought. He relaxed a little. He glanced at his watch again. Waited.

What Mama had always taught Delmar and him had saved him there in the Joliet State Penitentiary, that was certain enough. It had been hard to do it. Things are always hard when you're a little man, and you're young. He thought they'd kill him if he tried it. But it had saved him. He couldn't have lived through those years if he'd let them spit on him. He'd have died. Or worse than that, been like the little pet animals they turned their baby dolls into. Three of them had been after him. Cassidy, Neal, and Dalkin, those were their names. Cassidy had been the biggest, and the one Fleck had been the most afraid of, and the one he'd decided he had to kill first. But looking back on it, knowing what he knew now, Dalkin was really the dangerous one. Because Dalkin was smart. Cassidy had made the move on him first, and when he got away from that, the three of them had got him into a corner in the laundry. He'd never forget that. Never tried to in fact, because that had been the black, grim, hard-rock bottom of his life and he needed to think of it whenever things were tough, like today. They'd held him down and raped him, Cassidy first. And when they were all finished with him, he had just laid there a moment, not even feeling the pain. He remembered vividly exactly what he had thought. He'd thought: Do I want to stay alive now? And he absolutely didn't want to. But he remembered what Mama had taught him. And he thought, I'll get even first. I'll get that done before I die. And he'd got up and told them all three they were dead men. Three or four other cons had been in the laundry by then. He hadn't noticed them. He wouldn't have noticed anyone then, but they got the word out in the yard. Cassidy had beaten him after that, and Dalkin had beaten him, too. But getting even had kept him alive.

It was raining harder now. Fleck turned on the ignition and started the windshield wipers. As he did, the man with the umbrella turned the corner again. He'd circled the block and was walking again down the opposite sidewalk toward the telephone booth. Fleck turned off the wipers and glanced at his watch. Five minutes until two. The Client was punctual. He watched him enter the booth, close the umbrella and the door. Cassidy had been punctual, too. Fleck had gotten the note to him. Printed on toilet paper. "I'll have something just for you five minutes into the work break. Behind the laundry."

He gambled that Cassidy would think only of sex. He gambled that a macho two-hundred-and-forty-pounder who could bench press almost four hundred pounds wouldn't be nervous about a hundred-and-twenty-pounder, the kid the yard called Little Red Shrimp. Sure enough, Cassidy wasn't nervous. He came around the corner, grinning. He had walked out of the sunlight into the shadow, squinting, reaching out for Fleck when he saw Fleck smiling at him, walking into the shank.

Fleck dialed all but the final digit of the 266 number, glanced at his watch. Almost a minute early. Fleck could still remember the sensation. Holding the narrow blade flat, just as he'd practiced it, feeling it slide between the ribs, flicking the handle back and forth and back again as it penetrated to make certain it cut the artery and the heart. He hadn't really expected it to work. He expected Cassidy to kill him, or the thing to end with him on trial for premeditated murder and getting nothing better than life and probably the gas chamber. But there was no choice. And Eddy had told him it would be like Cassidy was being struck by lightning if he did it right.

"Do it right, he shouldn't make a sound," Eddy had said. "It's the shock that does it."

Now it was time. Fleck punched the final digit, heard the beginning of the ring, then The Client's voice.

Fleck brought him up to date, told him about checking on Highhawk, about the woman lawyer showing up there with the cowboy, about Santero driving up and going in and the woman and the cowboy coming out a minute later. He told him about the cowboy walking right up and tapping on his window. "I circled the block and followed them back to the Eastern Market Metro station, and then I dropped it. There's just one of me. Now I want to know who that cowboy is. He's tall. Slender. Dark. Looks like an Indian to me. Narrow face. Leather jacket, boots, cowboy hat, all that. Who the hell is he? Something about him smells like cop to me."

"What did he say?"

"He said the woman thought I was following her. I told him he was crazy. Told him to screw off."

"Amateurs!" The Client's voice was full of scorn. It took a moment for Fleck to realize he meant Fleck.

Fleck pressed it. "You know anything at all about the cowboy? Know who he is?"

"God knows," The Client said. "This is the product of you letting Santero slip away from you. We don't know where he went or who he talked to and we don't know what he did. I warned you about that."

"And I told you about it," Fleck said. "Told you there's just one of me and seven of them, not counting the womenfolk. I can't watch them all all the time."

"Seven?" The Client said. "Was that a slip? You told us you had subtracted one. The old man. You're expecting us to pay you for that."

"Six is the correct number," Fleck said. "Old Man Santillanes is definitely off the list. Did you send the ten thousand?"

"We wait for the full month. Now I wonder if we should also ask to see a little more proof."

"I sent you the goddamn billfold. And the false teeth." Fleck sighed. "You're just stalling," he said. "I can see that now. I want that money by tomorrow night."

There was a period of silence from the other end. Fleck noticed the rain had stopped. With his free hand he rolled down the window beside him. Then he picked up the camera and checked the settings.

"The deal is no publicity, no identification for one full month. Then you get the money. After a month. Now I want you to think about Santero. I think he needs to go. The same deal. But remember it can't happen in the District. We can't risk that. It should be a long way outside the Beltway. A long way from here. And no chance of identification. No chance at all of identification."

"I have got to have the ten thousand now," Fleck said. Never lose your temper, Mama had said. Never show them a thing. About all we got going for us, Mama had always told Delmar and him, is they never expect us to do anything at all but crawl there on the ground on our bellies and wait to get stepped on again.

"No," The Client said.

"Tell you what. If you'll have three thousand of it delivered to me tomorrow, then I can wait for the rest of it."

"You can wait anyway," The Client said. And hung up.

Fleck put down the telephone and picked up the camera. It rattled against the door, making him aware that he was shaking with rage. He took a deep breath. Held it. Through the rangefinder he saw The Client emerge from the telephone booth, umbrella folded. He stood with hand outstretched, looking around, confirming that the rain had stopped. Fleck had taken four shots before he walked down the sidewalk away from him.

Fleck let The Client get well around the corner before he left the car to follow. He kept a block behind him down Eighteenth Street, and then east to Sixteenth. There The Client turned again. He walked down the row of second-string embassies and disappeared down a driveway.

Fleck walked past it with only a single sidelong glance. It was just enough to tell him who he was working for.

13

SINCE JOE LEAPHORN and Dockery had arrived a little early, and the Amtrak train had arrived a little late, Leaphorn had been given the opportunity to answer a lot of Dockery's questions. He'd presumed that Dockery had volunteered to come down to Union Station on his day off because Dockery was interested in murder. And clearly Dockery was interested in that. And he was interested in what Perez might have seen in the roomette of his doomed passenger. But Dockery seemed even more interested in Indians.

"Sort of a fascination with me ever since I was a kid," Dockery began. "I guess it was all those cowboy and Indian movies. Indians always interested me. But I never did know any. Never had the opportunity." And Leaphorn, not knowing exactly what to say to this, said: "I never knew any railroad people, either."

"They have this commercial on TV. Shows an Indian looking at all this trash scattered around the landscape. There's a tear running down his cheek. You seen that one?"

Leaphorn nodded. He had seen it.

"Are Indians really into that worshiping Mother Earth business?"

Leaphorn considered that. "It depends on the Indian. The Catholic bishop at Gallup, he's an Indian."

"But in general," Dockery said. "You know what I mean."

"There are all kinds of Indians," Leaphorn said. "What religion are you?"

"Well, now," Dockery said. He thought about it. "I don't go to church much. I guess you'd have to say I'm a Christian. Maybe a Methodist."

"Then your religion is closer to some Indians' than mine is," Leaphorn said.

Dockery looked skeptical.

"Take the Zunis or the Hopis or the Taos Indians for example," said Leaphorn, who was thinking as he spoke that this sort of conversation always made him feel like a complete hypocrite. His own metaphysics had evolved from the Navajo Way into a belief in a sort of universal harmony of cause and effect caused by God when He started it all. Inside of that, the human intelligence was somehow intricately involved with God. By some definitions, he didn't have much religion. Obviously, neither did Dockery, for that matter. And the subject needed changing. Leaphorn dug out his notebook, opened it, and turned to the page on which he'd reproduced the list from the folded paper. He asked Dockery if he'd noticed that the handwriting on that paper was different from the fine, careful script in the passenger's notebook.

"I didn't take a really close look at it," Dockery said.

About what Leaphorn had expected. But it was better than talking religion. He turned another page and came to the place he had copied "AURANOFIN W1128023" from the passenger's notebook. That had puzzled him. The man apparently spoke Spanish, but it didn't seem to be a Spanish word. *Aura* meant something more or less invisible surrounding something. Like a vapor. *No fin* in Spanish, if it held such a phrase, would mean something like "without end." No sense in that. The number looked like a license or code designation. Perhaps that would lead him to something useful.

He showed it to Dockery. "Can you make any sense out of that?"

Dockery looked at it. He shook his head. "Looks like the number off an insurance policy, or something like that. What's the word mean?"

"I don't know," Leaphorn said.

"Sounds like a medicine my wife used to take. Former wife, that is. Expensive as hell. I think it cost about ninety cents a capsule."

The sound of the train arriving came through the wall. Leaphorn was thinking that in a very few minutes he would be talking to a conductor named Perez, and that there was very little reason to believe Perez could tell him anything helpful. This was the final dead end. After this he would go back to Farmington and forget the man who had kept his worn old shoes so neatly polished.

Or try to forget him. Leaphorn knew himself well enough to recognize his weakness in that respect. He had always had difficulty leaving questions unanswered. And it had become no better with the age that, in his case, hadn't seemed to have brought any wisdom. All he had gotten out of Dockery was more evidence of how careful the killer of Pointed Shoes had been. That catalog of things on the folded paper must have been intended as a checklist, things to be checked off to avoid leaving behind any identification. The dentures were gone. So were the glasses, and their case, which might have contained a name and address, and prescription bottles which would certainly have a name on them. Prescription bottles were specifically mentioned on the checklist. And judging from the autopsy report the man must have taken medications. But no prescription bottles were in the luggage. He didn't need more evidence of the killer's cleverness. What he needed was some clue to the victim's identity. He would talk to Perez but it would be more out of courtesy—since he had wasted everyone's time to arrange this meeting—than out of hope.

Perez didn't think he'd be much help.

"I just got one look at him," the attendant said, after Dockery had introduced them and led them back to a cold, almost unfurnished room, where the passenger's luggage sat on a long, wooden table. "I'd noticed this passenger wasn't feeling all that great so I went by his compartment to see if he needed any help. I heard somebody moving in there but when I tapped on the door, nobody answered. I thought that was funny."

Perez pushed his uniform cap back to the top of his head and looked at them to see if that needed explanation. It didn't seem to.

"So, I unlocked it. There's this man in there, standing over a suitcase. I told him I'd come by to see if my passenger needed a hand and he said something negative. Something like he'd take care of it, or something like that. I remember he looked sort of hostile."

Perez stopped, looking at them. "Now when I think about that I think I was talking to the guy who had already knifed my passenger to death. And what he was probably thinking about right that moment was whether he should do it to me, too."

"What'd you do then?" Dockery asked.

"Nothing. I said, Okay. Or let me know if he needs a hand, or something like that. And then I got out." Perez looked slightly resentful. "What was I supposed to do? I didn't know anything was wrong. Far as I know this guy really is just a friend."

"What did he look like?" Leaphorn asked. He had remembered now why the name Henry Highhawk scribbled in the notebook struck a chord. It was the name of the man who had written Agnes Tsosie about coming to the Yeibichai. The man who had sent his photograph. He felt that odd sort of relief he had come to expect when unconnected things that troubled him suddenly clicked together. Perez would describe a blond man with braided hair and a thin, solemn face—the picture Agnes Tsosie had shown him. Then he'd have another lead away from this dead end.

"I just got a glance at him," Perez said. "I'd say sort of small. I think he had on a suit coat, or maybe a sports coat. And he had short hair. Red hair. Curly and close to his head. And a freckled face, like a lot of redheads have. Sort of a round face, I think. But he wasn't fat. I'd say sort of stocky. Burly. Like he had a lot of muscles. But small. Maybe hundred and thirty pounds, or less."

The good feeling left Leaphorn.

"Any other details? Scars? Limp? Anything like that? Anything that would help identify him?"

"I just got a glance at him," Perez said. He made a wry face. "Just one look."

"When did you check the room again?"

"When I didn't see the passenger get off at Gallup. I sort of was watching for him, you know, because Gallup was his destination. And I didn't see him. So I thought, well, he got off at another door. But it seemed funny, so when we was ready to pull out west, I took a look." He shrugged. "The roomette was empty. Nobody home. Just the luggage. So I looked for him. Checked the observation car, and the bar. I walked up and back through all the cars. And then I went back and looked in the room again. Seemed strange to me. But I thought maybe he had got sick and just got off and left everything behind."

"Everything was unpacked."

"Unpacked," Perez agreed. "Stuff scattered around." He pointed to the bags. "I took it and put it in the bags and closed them."

"Everything?"

Perez looked surprised, then offended.

"Sure, everything. What'd ya think?"

"Newspapers, magazines, empty candy wrappers, paper cups, everything?" Leaphorn asked.

"Well, no," Perez said. "Not the trash."

"How about some magazine that might have been worth saving?" Leaphorn phrased the question carefully. Perez was obviously touchy about the question of him taking anything out of the passenger's room. "Some magazine, maybe, that might have something interesting in it and shouldn't be thrown away. If it was something he had subscribed to, then it would have an address label on it."

"Oh," Perez said, understanding. "No. There wasn't anything like that. I remember dumping some newspapers in the waste container. I left the trash for the cleaners."

"Did you leave an empty prescription bottle, or box, or vial, or anything?"

Perez shook his head. "I would have remembered that," he said. He shook his head again. "Like I'm going to remember that red-headed guy. Standing there looking at me and he had just killed my passenger a few minutes before that."

In the taxi heading back for his hotel, Leaphorn sorted it out. He listed it, put it in categories, tried to make what little he knew as neat as he could make it. The final summation. Because this was where it finished. No more leads. None. Pointed Shoes would lie in his anonymous grave, forever lost to those who cared about him. If such humans existed, they would go to their own graves wondering how he had vanished. And why he had vanished. As for Lieutenant Joe Leaphorn of the Navajo Tribal Police, who had no legitimate interest in any of this anyway, he would make a return flight reservation from the room. He would return the call of Rodney, who had missed him returning Leaphorn's call, and take Rodney out to dinner tonight if that was possible. Then he would pack. He would get to the airport tomorrow, fly to Albuquerque, and make the long drive back home to Window Rock. There would be no Emma there waiting for him. No Emma to whom he would report this failure. And be forgiven for it.

The cab stopped at a red light. The rain had stopped now. Leaphorn dug out his notebook, flipped through it, stared again at "AURANOFIN" and the number which followed it. He glanced at the license of the cab driver posted on the back of the front seat. Susy Mackinnon.

"Miss Mackinnon," he said. "Do you know where there's a pharmacy?"

"Pharmacy? I think there's one in that shopping center up in the next block. You feeling okay?"

"I'm feeling hopeful," Leaphorn said. "All of a sudden."

She glanced back at him, on her face the expression of a

woman who is long past being surprised at eccentric passengers. "I've found that's better than despair," she said.

The pharmacy in the next block was a Merit Drug. The pharmacist was elderly, gray-haired, and good-natured. "That looks like a prescription number all right," he said. "But it's not one of ours."

"Is there any way to tell from this whose prescription it is? Name, address, so forth?"

"Sure. If you tell me where it was filled. If it was ours, see—any Merit Drug anywhere—then we'd have it on the computer. Find it that way."

Leaphorn put the notebook back in his jacket pocket. He made a wry face. "So," he said. "I can start checking all the Washington, D.C., drugstores."

"Or maybe the suburbs. Do you know if it was filled in the city?"

"No way of guessing," Leaphorn said. "It was just an idea. Looks like a bad one."

"If I were you, I'd start with Walgreen's. There was a *W* at the start of the numbers, and that looks like their code."

"You know where the nearest Walgreen's might be?"

"No. But we'll look that sucker up," the pharmacist said. He reached for the telephone book. It proved to be just eleven blocks away.

The pharmacist at Walgreen's was a young man. He decided Leaphorn's request was odd and that he should wait for his supervisor, now busy with another customer. Leaphorn waited, conscious that his cab was also waiting, with its meter running. The supervisor was a plump, middle-aged black woman, who inspected Leaphorn's Navajo Tribal Police credentials and then the number written in his notebook.

She punched at the keyboard of the computer, looking at Leaphorn over her glasses.

"Just trying to get an identification? That right? Not a refill or anything?"

"Right," Leaphorn said. "The pharmacist at another drugstore told me he thought this was your number."

"It looks like it," the woman said. She examined whatever had appeared on the screen. Shook her head. Punched again at the keyboard.

Leaphorn waited. The woman waited. She pursed her lips. Punched a single key.

"Elogio Santillanes," she said. "Is that how you pronounce it? Elogio Santillanes." She recited a street address and a telephone number, then glanced at the computer screen again. "And that's apartment three," she added. She wrote it all on a sheet of note paper and handed it to Leaphorn. "You're welcome," she said.

Back in the cab Leaphorn read the address to Miss Susy Mackinnon.

"No more going to the hotel?" she asked.

"First this address," Leaphorn said. "Then the hotel."

"Your humor has sure improved," Miss Mackinnon said. "They selling something in Walgreen's that you couldn't get in that other drugstore?"

"The solution to my problem," Leaphorn said. "And it was absolutely free."

"I need to remember that place," Miss Mackinnon said.

The rain had begun again—as much drizzle as rain—and she had the wipers turned to that now-and-then sequence. The blades flashed across the glass and clicked out of sight, leaving brief clarity behind. "You know," she said, "you're going to have a hell of a tab. Waiting time and now this trip. I hope you're good for about thirty-five or forty dollars when you finally get where you're going. I wouldn't want to totally tap you out. My intention is to leave you enough for a substantial tip."

"Um," Leaphorn said, not really hearing the question. He was thinking of what he would find at apartment number three. A woman. He took that for granted. And what he would say to her? How much would he tell her? Everything, he thought, except the grisly details. Leaphorn's good mood had been erased by the thought of what lay ahead. But in the long run it would be better for her to know everything. He remembered the endless weeks which led to Emma's death. The uncertainty. The highs of hope destroyed by reality and followed by despair. He would be the destroyer of this woman's hope. But then the wound could finally close. She could heal.

Miss Mackinnon seemed to have sensed he no longer wanted conversation. She drove in silence. Leaphorn rolled a window down an inch in defiance of the rain, letting in the late-autumn smell of the city. What would he do next, after the awful interview ahead? He would notify the FBI. Better to call Kennedy in Gallup, he thought, and let him initiate the action. Then he would call the McKinley County Sheriff's office and give them the identification. Not much the sheriff could do with such information but professional courtesy required it. And then he would go and call Rodney. It would be good to have some company this evening.

"Here you are," Miss Mackinnon said. She slowed the cab to avoid an old Chevy sedan which was backing into a parking space, and then stopped the cab in front of a two-story brick building with porches, built in a U shape around a landscaped central patio. "You want me to wait? It's expensive."

"Please wait," Leaphorn said. When he had broken the news here, he didn't want to wait around.

He walked down the pathway, following the man who had disembarked from the Chevy. Apartment one seemed to be vacant. The driver of the Chevy unlocked the door of apartment two and disappeared inside after a backward glance at Leaphorn. At apartment three, Leaphorn looked at the doorbell button. What would he say? I am looking for the widow of Elogio Santillanes. I am looking for a relative of Elogio Santillanes. Is this the residence of Elogio Santillanes?

From inside the apartment Leaphorn heard voices, faintly. Male and then female. Then he heard the sound of music. He rang the bell.

Now he heard only music. Abruptly that stopped. Leaphorn removed his hat. He stared at the door, shifting his weight. From the eaves of the porch behind him there came the sound of water dripping. On the street in front of the apartment a car went by. Leaphorn shifted his feet again. He pushed the doorbell button again, heard the ringing break the silence inside. He waited.

Behind him, he heard the door of apartment two opening. The man who had parked the Chevy stood in the doorway peering out at him. He was a small man and on this dim, rainy afternoon his form was backlit by the lamps in his apartment, making him no more than a shape.

Leaphorn pushed the button again and listened to the ring. He reached into his coat and got out the folder which held his police credentials. He sensed that behind him the man was still watching. Then he heard the sound of a lock being released. The door opened about a foot. A woman looked out at him, a middle-aged woman, slender, a thin face with glasses, black hair pulled severely back.

"Yes," she said.

"My name is Leaphorn," he said. He held out the folder, letting it drop open to reveal his badge. "I am looking for the residence of Elogio Santillanes."

The woman closed her eyes. Her head bent slightly forward.

Her shoulders slumped. Behind her, from some part of the room beyond Leaphorn's vision, came the sound of a sharp intake of breath.

"Are there relatives of Mr. Santillanes living here?" Leaphorn asked.

"Yo soy," the woman said, her eyes still closed. And then, in English: "Yes." She was pale. She reached out, felt for the door, clutched it.

Leaphorn thought, the news I am bringing her is not news. It is something she anticipated. Something her instincts told her was inevitable. He knew the feeling. He had lived with it for months, knowing that Emma was dying. It was a fate already faced. But that didn't matter. There was still no humane way to tell her even though her heart had already given her the warning.

"Mrs. Santillanes?" he said. "Is there someone here with you? Some friend or relative?"

The woman opened her eyes. "What do you want?"

"I want to tell you about your husband." He shook his head. "It's bad news."

A man wearing a loose blue sweater appeared beside the woman. He was as old as Leaphorn, gray and stocky. He stood rigidly erect and peered at Leaphorn through the thick lenses of dark-rimmed glasses. A soldier, Leaphorn thought. "Sir," he said, in a loud, stern voice. "What can I do for you?"

The woman put her hand on the man's arm. She spoke in Spanish. Leaphorn didn't catch her words. The man said *"Callate!"* sharply, and then, more gently, something that Leaphorn didn't understand. The woman looked at Leaphorn as if remembering his face would be terribly important to her. Then she nodded, bit her lip, bowed, and disappeared from the room.

"You asked about a man named Santillanes," the man said. "He does not live here."

"I came looking for his relatives," Leaphorn said. "I'm afraid I bring bad news.

"We do not know him," the man said. "No one of that name lives here."

"This was the address he gave," Leaphorn said.

The man's expression became totally blank—a poker player staring at his cards. "He gave an address to you?" he asked. "And when was that?"

Leaphorn didn't hurry to answer that. The man was lying, of course. But why would he be lying?

"He gave this address to the pharmacist where he buys his medicine," Leaphorn said.

"Ah," the man said. He produced a slight smile. "Then he has been sick. I trust this man, this Santillanes, is feeling better now."

"No," Leaphorn said. They stood there in the doorway, both of them waiting. Leaphorn had sensed some motion behind him. He shifted his weight enough to see the entrance of apartment two. The door was almost closed now. But not quite. Through it he could see the shadow of the small man, listening.

"He is not better? Then he is worse?"

"I should not be wasting your time with this," Leaphorn said. "Did Elogio Santillanes live here once and move away? Do you know where I might find any of his relatives? Or a friend?"

The gray man shook his head.

"I will go then," Leaphorn said. "Thank you very much. Please tell the lady I am sorry I disturbed her."

"Ah." The man hesitated. "You have made me curious. What happened to this fellow, this Santillanes?"

"He's dead," Leaphorn said.

"Dead." There was no surprise. "How?"

"He was stabbed," Leaphorn said.

"When did this happen?" Still there was no surprise. But Leaphorn could see the muscle along his jaw tighten. "And where did it happen?"

"Out in New Mexico. About a month ago." Leaphorn put his hand on the man's arm. "Listen," he said. "Do you know why this man Santillanes would have gone to New Mexico? What interest did he have in going to see a woman named Agnes Tsosie?"

The man pulled his arm away. He swallowed, his eyes misty with grief. He looked away from Leaphorn, toward his feet. "I don't know Elogio Santillanes," he said. And he carefully shut the door.

Leaphorn stood for a moment staring at the wood, sorting this out. The puzzle that had brought him here was solved. Clearly solved. No doubt about it. Or only the shadow of a doubt. The man with the worn, pointed shoes was Elogio Santillanes, the husband (perhaps brother) of this dark-haired woman. The brother (perhaps friend) of this gray-haired man. No more question of the identity of Pointed Shoes. Now there was another puzzle, new and fresh.

He walked down the porch, noticing that the door to apartment two was now closed but the light still illuminated the drapery. A dark afternoon, the kind of weather Leaphorn rarely saw on the Arizona–New Mexico border, and which quickly affected his mood. His taxi was waiting at the curb. Miss Mackinnon sat with a book propped on the steering wheel, reading.

Leaphorn turned and walked back to apartment two. He pushed the doorbell button. This one buzzed. He waited, thinking that people in Washington are slow to come to their doors. The door opened and the small man stood in it, looking at him.

"I need some information," Leaphorn said. "I'm looking for Elogio Santillanes."

The small man shook his head. "I don't know him."

"Do you know those people in that apartment over there?" Leaphorn nodded toward it. "I understand Santillanes lives in this building."

The man shook his head. Behind him in the apartment Leaphorn could see a folding card table with a telephone on it, a folding lawn chair, a cardboard box which seemed to contain books. A cheap small-screen television set perched on another box. The sound was turned off but the tube carried a newscast, in black and white. Otherwise the room seemed empty. A newspaper was on the floor beside the lawn chair. Perhaps the man had been reading there when the doorbell rang. Leaphorn suddenly found himself as interested in this small man as he was in the slim chance of getting information that had brought him here.

"You don't know the names of the people?" Leaphorn asked. He asked it partly to extend this conversation and see where it might lead. But there was a note of disbelief in his voice. Old as he was, Leaphorn still found it incredible that people could live side by side, see each other every day, and not be acquainted.

"Who are you?" the small man asked. "Are you an Indian?"

"I'm a Navajo," Leaphorn said. He reached for his identification. But he thought better of that.

"From where?"

"Window Rock."

"That's in—" The man hesitated, thinking. "Is it in New Mexico?"

"It's in Arizona," Leaphorn said.

"What are you doing here?"

"Looking for Elogio Santillanes."

"Why? What do you want with him?"

Leaphorn's eyes had been locked with the small man's. They were a sort of greenish blue and Leaphorn sensed in them, in the man's tone and his posture, a kind of hostile resentment.

"I just need information," Leaphorn said.

"I can't help you," the man said. He closed the door. Leaphorn heard the security chain rattle into place.

Miss Mackinnon started the motor as soon as he climbed into the backseat of the taxi. "I hope you got a lot of money," she said. "Back to the hotel now? And get your traveler's checks out of the safe-deposit box."

"Right," Leaphorn said.

He was thinking of the small man's strange, intent eyes, of his freckles, of his short, curly red hair. There must be thousands of short men in Washington who fit the Perez description of the man searching the roomette of Elogio Santillanes. But Leaphorn had never believed in coincidence. He had found the widow of Santillanes. He was sure of that. The widow or perhaps a sister. Certainly, he had found someone who had loved him.

And almost as certainly, he had found the man who had killed him. Going back to Window Rock could wait a little. He wanted to understand this better.

14

OVER LUNCH, the day after their visit to Highhawk's house, Chee and Janet Pete had discussed the man waiting in the sedan. "I think he was watching Highhawk, not you," Chee had said. "I think that's why he was parked out there." And Janet had finally said maybe so, but he could tell she wasn't persuaded by his logic. She was nervous. Uneasy about it. So he didn't tell her something else he had concluded—that the little man was one of the sort policemen call "freaks." At least the desert-country cops with whom Chee worked called them that—those men who have been somehow damaged beyond fear into a species that is unpredictable, and therefore dangerous. Finding a strange man tapping at his window in the darkness hadn't shaken the small man in the slightest. That was obvious. It had only aroused curiosity, and then provoked a sort of aggressive macho anger. Chee had seen that in such men before.

He had given Janet his analysis of Highhawk. ("He's nuts. Perfectly normal in some ways, but his sketches, they show you he's tilted about nine degrees. Slightly crazy.") And he told her of the carving of the fetish he'd seen in Highhawk's office-studio.

"He was carving it out of cottonwood root—which is what the Pueblo people like to use, at least the ones I know. The Zunis and the Hopis," Chee had said. "No reason to believe Tano would be any different. Maybe he was making a copy of the Twin War God."

And Janet, of course, was way ahead of him. "I've thought about that," she said. "That maybe John would hire him to make a copy of the thing. Maybe I guessed right about that." She looked sad as she said it, not looking at Chee, studying her hands. "Then I guess we would give it to our man in the Tano Pueblo. And he'd use it to get himself elected."

"Tell him it's the real thing?"

"Depending on how honest our Eldon Tamana is," Janet said glumly. "If he's honest, then you lie to him. If he's not, then you tell the truth and let him do the lying."

"I wonder if anyone at the Pueblo could tell the copy from the real thing," Chee said. "How long has the thing been missing?"

"Since nineteen three or four, I think John said. Anyway, a long time."

"You'd probably be safe with a substitute then," Chee said. He was thinking about Highhawk. It didn't seem within the artist's nature to use his talent in a conspiracy to cheat an Indian Pueblo. But perhaps Highhawk would be another one considered honest enough to require that he be lied to. Maybe he didn't know why he was making the replica. In fact, maybe that carving wasn't a replica at all. Maybe that cottonwood fetish in his office was something else. Or maybe it was the genuine fetish itself. Or maybe this whole theory was nonsense.

"Jim," Janet said. "What do you think? Do you think they're sort of being—that I'm getting sort of led into something?" She was looking down at her hands, gripped tightly in her lap. "What do you think?"

Jim Chee thought the way she had changed that question was interesting. He thought it was interesting that she didn't ever actually pronounce the name of John McDermott. He wanted to say "Led by whom?" and force her at least to put some sort of name to it—if only the name of the law firm.

"I think something's going on," Chee said. "And I think we should go somewhere quiet, and eat dinner and talk it over." He glanced at her. "Maybe even hold hands. I could use a little hand-holding."

She had been looking down at her hands. Now she gave him a quick sidelong glance, and then turned away. "I can't tonight," she said. "I promised John I would meet him. Him and the man from Tano."

"Well, then," Chee said. "I'll ask you another question. Has Highhawk said anything more to you about this crime that hasn't been committed yet? You remember that? You mentioned it when you called me at Shiprock. I think it was sort of vague. Some reference to needing a lawyer in the future for something that hadn't yet happened. Do you remember?"

"Of course I remember," Janet said, looking at her hands again. "And tonight it's really law firm business. John arranged to have Tamana come. He said he wants to get me involved in how to handle the problem. He wants me to talk to Tamana. So I could hardly get out of it."

"Of course not," Chee said. He was disappointed. He had counted on this evening stretching on. But it was more than disappointment. There was resentment, too.

Janet sensed it. "I guess I could," she said. "I don't know how long this man's going to be in Washington. But I can try to call John and cancel it. Or leave a message for him at the restaurant."

"No, no," Chee said. "Business is business." But he didn't want to think about Janet and John McDermott having dinner and about what would happen after dinner. If I was honest with her, he thought, I would tell her that of course McDermott was using her. That he had probably used her when she was his student in law school, and ever since, and would always use her. He had never seen McDermott, but he knew professors who used their graduate students. Used them for slave labor to do their research, used them emotionally.

"Back to my question," Chee said. "Did you ever ask High-hawk what he meant by that reference to the uncommitted crime? Did he ever explain what he meant by that?"

Janet seemed happy to shift the subject. "I said something like I hoped he wasn't intending to dig up any more old bones. And he just laughed. So I said—frankly, this whole thing bothered me, so I said I didn't think it was laughable if he was planning to commit a felony. Something stuffy-sounding like that. And he laughed again and said he didn't intend to be guilty of making his attorney a co-conspirator. He said the less I knew the better."

"He seems to know something about the law."

"He knows a lot about a lot of things," Janet agreed. "Nothing wrong with the man's mind."

"Except for being crazy."

"Except for that," Janet agreed.

"Can you arrange for me to see him again?" Chee said. "And I'd like to get a look at that genuine Tano fetish figure. You think that's possible?"

"I'm sure there's no problem seeing Highhawk. About the fetish, I don't know. It's probably stored somewhere in a basement. And the Smithsonian must be pretty selective about who has access to what."

"Maybe because I'm a cop," Chee said, wondering as he said it what in the world he could say to make anyone believe the

Navajo Tribal Police had a legitimate interest in a Pueblo Indian artifact.

"More likely because you're a shaman," Janet Pete said. "You still are, aren't you?"

"Trying to be," Chee said. "But being a medicine man doesn't fit very well with being a policeman. Don't get much business." Even that was an overstatement. The curing ceremonial Chee had learned was the Blessing Way. In the four years since he had declared himself a *hataalii* ready to perform that most popular ceremonial he'd had only three customers. One had been a maternal cousin, whom Chee had suspected of hiring him only as an act of family kindness. One had been the blessing of a newly constructed hogan owned by the niece of a friend, and one had been for a fellow policeman, the famous Lieutenant Joe Leaphorn. "Did I tell you about singing a Blessing Way for Joe Leaphorn?"

Janet looked shocked. "The famous Leaphorn? Grouchy Joe? I thought he was—" She searched for the word to define Lieutenant Joe Leaphorn. "Agnostic. Or skeptical. Or—what is it? Anyway, I didn't think he believed in curing ceremonials and things like that."

"He wasn't so bad," Chee said. "We had worked together on a case. People were digging up Anasazi graves and then there were a couple of homicides. But I think he asked me to do it because he wanted to be nice."

"Nice," Janet said. "That doesn't sound like the Joe Leaphorn I always used to hear about. Seems like I was always hearing Navajo cops bitching about Leaphorn never being quite satisfied with anything."

But it had, in fact, been nice. More than nice. Beautiful. Everything had gone beautifully. Not many of Leaphorn's relatives had been there. But then the old man was a widower and he didn't think Leaphorn had much family. Leaphorn was a Red Forehead Dinee and that clan was pretty much extinct. But the curing itself had gone perfectly. He had forgotten nothing. The sand paintings had been exactly correct. And when the final singing had been finished Old Man Leaphorn had, in some way difficult for Chee to define, seemed to be healed of the sickness that had been riding him. The bleakness had been gone. He had seemed back in harmony. Content.

"I think he just always wants things to be better than they naturally are," Chee said. "I got used to him after a while. And I've got a feeling that all that talk about him being a smart son-of-a-bitch is pretty much true."

"I used to see him in court there at Window Rock now and then, and in the police building, but I never knew him. I heard he was a real pragmatist. Not a traditional Navajo."

And how about you, Janet Pete? Chee thought. How traditional are you? Do you believe in what Changing Woman taught our ancestors about the power we are given to heal ourselves? How about you leaving Dinetah and the Sacred Mountains because a white man wants you to keep him happy in Washington? But that was none of his goddamn business. That was clear enough. His role was to be a friend. No more. Well, why not? For that matter, he could use a friend himself.

"What did you mean about getting to see the fetish as a shaman?" he asked.

"Highhawk would be very impressed if he knew you were a Navajo *hataalii*," she said. "Tell him you're a singer and let him know you would like to see his work. He's setting up a mask exhibition, you know. Tell him you'd like to see the Navajo part of the show."

"And then ask to see the fetish," Chee said.

Janet looked at him, studying his expression. "Why not?" she asked, and the question sounded a little bitter. "You think I'm thinking too much like a lawyer?"

"I didn't say that."

"Well, I am a lawyer."

He nodded. "You think I could see Highhawk tonight?"

"He's working tonight," she said. "On that exhibit. I'll call him at the museum and see if I can set something up. Will you be at your hotel?"

"Where else?" Chee said, noticing as Janet glanced at him that his tone, too, sounded a little bitter.

"I'll try to hurry it up," she said. "Maybe you can do it tomorrow."

It proved to be quicker than that.

Janet had shown him the Vietnam Memorial wall, the Jefferson Memorial, and the National Air and Space Museum, and then dropped him off at his hotel. Chee ate a cheese omelet in the hotel coffee shop, took a shower in his bathroom tub (which, small as it was, was huge compared to the bathing compartment in Chee's trailer home), and turned on the television. The sound control was stuck somewhere between loud and extremely loud and Chee spent a futile five minutes trying to adjust the volume. Failing that, he found an old movie in which the mood music was lower-decibel and sprawled across the pillow to watch it.

The telephone rang. It was Henry Highhawk.

"Miss Pete said you wanted to see the exhibit," Highhawk said. "Are you doing anything right now?"

Chee was available.

"I'll meet you at the Twelfth Street entrance to the Museum of Natural History building," Highhawk said. "It's just about five or six blocks from your hotel. I hate to rush you but I have another appointment later on."

"I'll be there in twenty minutes," Chee said. He turned off the TV and reached for his coat.

Perhaps Janet's idea of being followed had made him edgy. He looked for the car and he saw it almost as soon as he left the hotel entrance. The old Chevy sedan with the bent antenna was parked across the street and down the block. He stood motionless studying it, trying to see if the small man was in it. Reflection from the windshield made it impossible to tell. Chee walked slowly down the sidewalk, thinking that the small man hadn't made any effort at concealment. What might that mean? Did he want Chee to know he was being watched? If so, why? Chee could think of no reason for that. Perhaps it was simply carelessness. Or arrogance. Or perhaps he wasn't watching Chee at all.

His route to the Museum of Natural History would take him the other way, but Chee detoured to walk past the sedan. It was empty. He leaned against the roof, looking in. On the front seat there was a folded copy of today's *Washington Post* and a paper cup. A street map of the District of Columbia was on the dash. The backseat was empty except that an empty plastic bag with a Safeway logo was crumpled on the floor. The car was locked.

Chee looked up the street and down it. Two teenaged black girls were walking toward him, laughing at something one had said. Otherwise, no one was in sight. The rain had stopped now but the streets and sidewalks still glistened with dampness. The air was damp too, and chill. Chee pulled his jacket collar around his throat and walked. He listened. He heard nothing but occasional traffic sounds. He was on Tenth Street now, the gray mass of the Department of Justice building beside him, the Post Office building looming across the street. Justice seemed dark but a few of the windows in the postal offices were lit. What did post office bureaucrats do that kept them working late? He imagined someone at a drafting table designing a stamp. He stopped at the intersection of Constitution Avenue waiting for the Don't Walk signal to change. Two men and a woman, all wearing the Washington uniform, were walking briskly down the sidewalk toward him. Each held a furled umbrella. Each carried a briefcase. The little man was nowhere in sight. Then, under the shrubbery landscaping the corner of the Justice building to Chee's left, he saw a body.

Chee sucked in his breath. He stared. It was a human form, drawn into the fetal position and partially covered by what seemed to be a cardboard box. Near the head was a sack. Chee made a tentative step toward it. The trio walked past the body. The man nearest glanced at it and said something unintelligible to Chee. The woman looked at the body and looked quickly away. They walked past Chee. ". . . at least GS 13," the woman was saying. "More likely 14, and then before you know it . . ." Probably a wino, Chee thought. Chee had seen a thousand or so unconscious drunks since his swearing-in as an officer of the Navajo Tribal Police, seen them sprawled in Gallup alleys, frozen in the sagebrush beside the road to Shiprock, mangled like jackrabbits on the asphalt of U.S. Highway 666. But he could see the floodlit spire of the Washington Monument just a few blocks behind him. He hadn't expected it here. He walked over the dead autumn grass, knelt beside the body. The cardboard was damp from the earlier rain. The body was a man. The familiar and expected smell of whiskey was missing.

Chee reached his hand to the side of the man's throat, feeling for a pulse.

The man screamed and scrambled into a crouching position, trying to defend himself. The cardboard box bounced to the sidewalk.

Chee jumped back, totally startled.

The man was bearded, bundled in a navy peacoat many sizes too large for him. He struck at Chee, feebly, screaming incoherently. Two men in the Washington uniform hurrying down Constitution Avenue glanced at the scene and hurried even faster.

Chee held out empty hands. "I thought you needed help," he said.

The man fell forward to hands and knees. "Get away, get away, get away," he howled.

Chee got away.

Highhawk was waiting for him at the employees' entrance on Twelfth Street. He handed Chee a little rectangle of white paper with the legend VISITOR printed and Chee's name written on it.

"What do you want to see first?" he asked. Then paused. "You all right?"

"There's a man out there. Sick, I guess. Lying out there under the bushes across the street."

"Drunk maybe," Highhawk said. "Or stoned on crack. Usually there's three or four of them. That Department of Justice building grass is a favorite spot."

"This guy wasn't drunk."

"On crack probably," Highhawk said. "These days it's usually crack if they're dopers, or it can be anything from heroin to sniffing glue. But sometimes they're just mental cases." He considered Chee's reaction to all this. "You have them too. I saw plenty of drunks in Gallup."

"I think we have more drunks per capita than anybody," Chee said. "But on the reservation we try to pick them up. We try to put them somewhere. What's the policy here?"

But Highhawk was already limping hurriedly down the hallway, not interested in this subject, the braced leg dragging but moving fast. "Let me show you this display first," he said. "I'm trying to get it to look just like it would if it was really happening out there in your desert."

Chee followed. He still felt shaken. But now he was thinking again, and he thought that he hadn't looked for the small man around the Twelfth Street entrance to the Natural History Museum. And he thought that possibly the reason he hadn't seen the small man following him was because the small man might not have needed to follow. He might have known where Chee was going.

Henry Highhawk's exhibit was down a side hall on the main floor of the museum. It was walled off from the world of museumgoers by plywood screens and guarded by signs declaring the area TEMPORARILY CLOSED TO THE PUBLIC and naming the display THE MASKED GODS OF THE AMERICAS. Behind the screen was the smell of sawdust, glue, and astringent cleaning fluids. There was also an array of masks, ranging from grotesque and terrible to calm and sublimely beautiful. Some were displayed in groups, one group representing the varying concept of demons in Yucatán villages, and another Inca deities. Some stood alone, accompanied only by printed legends explaining them. Some were displayed on costumed models of the priests or personifiers who wore them. Some were mounted in settings illustrative of the ceremonies in which they were used. Highhawk limped past these to a diorama protected by a railing. In it stood Yeibichai himself, Talking God, the maternal grandfather of all the great and invisible *yei* who made up the gallery of the Navajo supernatural powers.

Talking God's gray-white mask, with its bristle of eagle feathers and its collar-ruff of animal fur, formed the head of a manikin. Chee had just walked past dozens of such human forms in other Smithsonian displays—of Laplanders mending reindeer harnesses, of Aztec musicians in concert, of a New Guinea hunter stalking a pig, of a Central American tribeswoman finishing a pot. But this manikin, this wearer of the Yeibichai mask, seemed alive. In fact, he seemed more than alive. Chee stood and stared at him.

"This one is mine, of course," Highhawk said. "I did some of the others, too, and helped on some. But this one is mine." He glanced at Chee, waiting a polite moment for a comment. "If you see anything wrong, you point it out," he added. He stepped across the railing to the figure and adjusted the mask, moving his fingers under the leather, tilting it slightly, then readjusting it. He stepped back and looked at it thoughtfully.

"You see anything wrong?" he asked.

Chee could see nothing wrong. At least nothing except trivial details in some of the decoration. And that was probably intended. Such a sacred scene should not be reproduced exactly except for its purpose—to cure a human being. Talking God was frozen in that shuffling dance step the *yeis* traditionally used as they approached the patient's hogan. In this display, the patient was standing on a rug spread on the earth in front of the hogan door. He was wrapped in a blanket and held his arms outstretched. Talking God's short woven kilt seemed to flow with the motion, and in each hand he carried a rattle which looked genuine. And, Chee thought, probably was. Behind Talking God in this diorama the other gods followed in identical poses, seeming to dance out of the darkness into the firelight. Chee recognized the masks of Fringed Mouth, of Monster Slayer, of Born for Water, and of Water Sprinkler with his cane and humped back. Other *yei* figures were also vaguely visible moving across the dance ground. And on both sides, the fires illuminated lines of spectators.

Chee's eyes lingered on the mask of Talking God. It seemed identical to the one he'd seen in Highhawk's office. Naturally it would. Probably it was the same one. Probably Highhawk had taken it home to prepare it for mounting. Or, if he was copying it, he would be making the replica look as much like the original as he could.

"What do you think?" Highhawk asked. His voice sounded anxious. "You see anything wrong?"

"It looks great to me. Downright beautiful," Chee said. "I'm impressed." In fact, he was tremendously impressed. Highhawk had reproduced that moment in the final night of the ceremonial called the Yei Yiaash, the Arrival of the Spirits. He turned to look at Highhawk. "Surely you didn't get all this from that little visit out to Agnes Tsosie's Night Chant. If you did you must have a photographic memory." Or, Chee thought, a videotape recorder hidden away somewhere, like the audio recorder he had hidden in his palm.

Highhawk grinned. "I guess I read about a thousand descriptions of that ceremonial. All the anthropologists I could find. And I studied the sketches they made. And looked at all the materials we have on it here in the Smithsonian. Whatever people stole and turned over to us down through the years, I studied it. Studied the various *yei* masks and all that. And then Dr. Hartman—she's the curator who's in charge of setting up this business—she called in a consultant from the reservation. A Navajo shaman. Guy named Sandoval. You know him?"

"I've heard of him," Chee said.

"Partly we wanted to make sure we aren't violating any taboos. Or misusing any religious material. Or anything like that." Highhawk paused again. He started to say something, stopped, looked nervously at Chee. "You sure you don't see anything wrong?"

Chee shook his head. He was looking at the mask itself, wondering if there was an artificial head under it with an artificial face with an artificial Navajo expression. No reason there should be. The mask looked ancient, the gray-white paint which covered the deerskin patterned with the tiny cracks of age, the leather thongs which laced up its sides darkened with years of use. But of course those were just the details Highhawk would not have overlooked in making a copy. The mask he'd seen in the box in Highhawk's office was either this one, or an awfully close copy—that was obvious from what he had remembered. The tilt of the feathered crest, the angle of the painted eyebrows, all of those small details which went beyond legend and tradition that had lent themselves to the interpretation of the mask maker, they all seemed to be identical. Except in its ritual poetry and the sand paintings of its curing ceremonials, the Navajo culture always allowed room for poetic license. In fact it encouraged it—to bring whatever was being done into harmony with the existing circumstances. How much such license would Highhawk have if he was copying the Tano effigy? Not much, Chee guessed. The kachina religion of the Pueblo Indians, it seemed to Chee, was rooted in a dogma so ancient that the centuries had crystallized it.

"How about the basket?" Highhawk asked him. "On the ground by his feet? That's supposed to be the basket for the Yei Da'ayah. According to our artifact inventory records, anyway."

Highhawk's pronunciation of the Navajo word was so strange that what he actually said was incomprehensible. But what he probably meant was the basket which held the pollen and the feathers used for feeding the masks after the spirits within them were awakened. "Looks all right to me," Chee said.

A woman, slender, handsome, and middle-aged, had walked around the screen into the exhibit area.

"Dr. Hartman," Highhawk said. "You're working late."

"You too, Henry," she said, with a glance at Chee.

"This is Jim Chee," Highhawk said. "Dr. Carolyn Hartman is one of our curators. She's my boss. This is her show. And Mr. Chee is a Navajo shaman. I asked him to take a look at this."

"It was good of you to come," Carolyn Hartman said. "Did you find this Night Chant authentic?"

"As far as I know," Chee said. "In fact, I think it's remarkable. But the Yeibichai is not a ceremonial that I know very well. Not personally. The only one I know well enough to do myself is the Blessing Way."

"You're a singer? A medicine man?"

"Yes, ma'am. But I am new at it."

"Mr. Chee is also Officer Chee," Highhawk said. "He's a member of the Navajo Tribal Police. In fact, he's the very same officer who arrested me out there. I thought you'd approve of that." Highhawk was smiling when he said it. Dr. Hartman was smiling, too. She likes him, Chee thought. It was visible. And the feeling was mutual.

"Good show," she said to Chee. "Running down the grave robber. Sometime I must come out to your part of the country with time enough to really see it. I should learn a lot more about your culture. I'm afraid I've spent most of my time trying to understand the Incas." She laughed. "For example, if I were your guide here, I wouldn't be showing you that Night Chant display. I'd be showing you my own pets." She pointed to the diorama immediately adjoining. In it a wall of great cut stones opened onto a courtyard. Beyond, a temple rose against a mountain background. This display also offered its culturally attired manikins. Men in sleeveless tunics, cloaks of woven feathers, headbands, and leather sandals, women in long dresses with shawls fastened across their breasts with jeweled pins and their hair covered with cloths. But the centerpiece of all of this was a great metal mask. To Chee it seemed to have been molded of gold and decorated with a fortune in jewels.

"I'd been admiring that," he said. "Quite a mask. It looks expensive."

"It's formed of a gold-platinum alloy inset with emeralds and other gems," she said. "It represents the great god Viracocha, the creating god, the very top god of the Inca pantheon. The smaller mask there, that one represents the Jaguar god. Less important, I guess. But potent enough."

"It looks like it would be worth a fortune," Chee said. "How did the museum get it?" As he said it, he wished he hadn't. In his ears the question seemed to imply the acquisition might be less than honorable. But perhaps that was a product of the way he'd been thinking. No honorable Navajo could have sold the museum that mask of Talking God he had been admiring. Not if it was genuine. Such masks were sacred, held in family custody. No one had a right to sell them.

"It was a gift," Dr. Hartman said. "It had been in the hands of a family down there. A political family, I gather. And from them it went to some very important person in the United Fruit Company, or maybe it was Anaconda Copper. Anyway, someone like that. And then it was inherited, and in the 1940s somebody needed to offset a big income tax problem." Dr. Hartman created a flourish with an imaginary wand, laughing. "Shazam! The Smithsonian, the attic of America, the attic of the world, obtains another of its artifacts. And some good citizen gets a write-off on his income tax bill."

"I guess no one can complain," Chee said. "It's a beautiful thing."

"Someone can always complain," Dr. Hartman laughed. "They're complaining right now. They want it back."

"Oh," Chee said. "Who?"

"The Chilean National Museum. Although of course the museum never actually had its hands on it." Dr. Hartman leaned against a pedestal which supported, according to its caption, the raven mask used by shamans in the Carrier tribe of the Canadian Pacific Coast. It occurred to Chee that she was enjoying herself.

"Actually," she continued, "the fuss is being raised by someone named General Huerta. General Ramon Huerta Cardona, to be formal. It was his family from which the American tycoon, whoever he was, got the thing in the first place. Or so I understand. And I imagine that if their national museum manages to talk us out of it, the good general would then file a claim to recover it for his family. And being a very, very big shot in Chilean politics, he'd win."

"Are you going to give it back?"

Highhawk laughed.

"I'm not," Dr. Hartman said. "I wouldn't give it back under the circumstances. I would be happy enough to give Henry here his bones back in the name of common sense, or maybe common decency. But I wouldn't return that mask." She smiled benignly at Henry Highhawk. "Romantic idealism I can approve. But not greed." She shrugged and made a wry face. "But then I don't make policy."

"He's coming to see it at the opening," Highhawk said. "General Huerta is. Did you notice that story about it the other day in the *Post*?"

"I read that," Dr. Hartman said. "I gather from what he told the reporter that the general is coming to Washington for some more dignified purpose, but I noticed he said he would also visit us to see"—Dr. Hartman's voice shifted into sarcasm—" 'our national treasure.' "

"That'll be a pain," Highhawk said. "Special security always screws things up."

"He's not a head of state," Dr. Hartman said. "Just the head secret policeman. We'll give him a couple of guides and a special 'meet him at the front door with a handshake.' After that, he's just another tourist."

"Except the press will flock in after him. And the TV cameras," said Highhawk, who knew a lot about such affairs.

Chee found himself liking Dr. Hartman. "He'll be seeing quite a display here," he said.

"No false modesty," Dr. Hartman said. "I think so, too. I would be good at this if I didn't have to spend so much time being a museum bureaucrat." She smiled at Highhawk. "For example, trying to figure out how to keep peace between an idealistic young conservator and the people over in the Castle who make the rules."

Chee noticed that Henry Highhawk did not return the smile.

▾   ▾   ▾

"We have to be going," Highhawk said.

"Well," Dr. Hartman said. "I hope you're enjoying your visit, Mr. Chee. Is Mr. Highhawk showing you everything you want to see?"

This seemed to be an opportunity. "I wanted to see this," Chee said, indicating the Night Chant and the world of masks around it. "And I was hoping to see that Tano War God that I've heard about. I heard somewhere that someone at the Pueblo was hoping to get that back, too."

Dr. Hartman's expression was doubtful. "I haven't heard of that," she said, frowning. She looked at Highhawk. "A Tano fetish. Do you know anything about that? Which fetish would they mean?"

Highhawk glanced from Dr. Hartman to Chee. He hesitated. "I don't know."

"I guess you could look it up in the inventory," she said.

Highhawk was looking at Chee, examining him. "Why not?" he said. "If you want to."

They went up the staff elevator to the sixth floor, to Highhawk's airless cubicle of an office. He punched the proper information into his computer terminal and received, in return, a jumble of numbers and letters.

"This tells us the hallway, the room, the corridor in the room, the shelf in the corridor, and the number of the bin it's in," Highhawk said. He punched another set of keys and waited. "Now it tells us that it is out of inventory and being worked on. Or something."

He turned off the computer, glanced at Chee, looked thoughtful.

He knows where it is, Chee thought. He knew from the beginning. He's deciding whether to tell me.

"It should be in the conservation lab," Highhawk said. "Let's go take a look."

The telephone rang.

Highhawk looked at it, and at Chee.

It rang again. Highhawk picked it up. "Highhawk," he said. And then: "I can't right now. I have a guest."

He listened, glanced at Chee. "No, I couldn't make the damn thing work," Highhawk said. "I'm no good with that stuff." He listened.

"I tried that. It didn't turn on." Listened again. "Look. You're coming down anyway. I'll leave it for you to fix." Listened. "No.

That's a little early. Too much traffic then." And finally: "Make it nine thirty then. And remember it's the Twelfth Street entrance."

Highhawk listened, and hung up.

"Let's go," he said to Chee.

Highhawk made his limping way down a seemingly endless corridor. It was lined on both sides with higher-than-head stacks of wooden cases. The cases were numbered. Some were sealed with paper stickers. Most wore tags reading CAUTION: INVENTORIED MATERIALS or CAUTION: UNINVENTORIED MATERIALS.

"What's in all this?" Chee asked, waving.

"You name it," Highhawk said. "I think in here it's mostly early agricultural stuff. Tools, churns, hoes, you know. Up ahead we have bones."

"The skeletons you wanted returned?"

"*Want* returned," Highhawk said. "Still. We've got more than eighteen thousand skeletons boxed up in this attic. Eighteen goddamn thousand Native American skeletons in the museum's so-called research collection."

"Wow," Chee said. He would have guessed maybe four or five hundred.

"How about white skeletons?"

"Maybe twenty thousand black, white, and so forth," Highhawk said. "But since the white-eyes outnumber the redskins in this country about two hundred to one, to reach parity I have to dig up three-point-six million white skeletons and stack them in here. That is, if the scientists are really into studying old bones—which I doubt."

Old bones was not a subject which appealed to Chee's traditional Navajo nature. Corpses were not a subject for polite discussion. The knowledge that he was sharing a corridor with thousands of the dead made Chee uneasy. He wanted to change the subject. He wanted to ask Highhawk about the telephone conversation. What was he trying to fix? What was it that wouldn't turn on? Who was he meeting at nine thirty? But it was none of his business and Highhawk would tell him so or evade the question.

"Why the seals?" he asked instead, pointing.

Highhawk laughed. "The Republicans used the main gallery for their big inaugural ball," Highhawk said. "About a thousand Secret Service and FBI types came swarming in here in advance to make sure of security." The memory had converted Highhawk's bitterness to high good humor. His laugh turned into a chortle.

"They'd unlock each case, poke around inside to make sure

Lee Harvey Oswald wasn't hiding in there, and then lock it up again and stick on the seal so nobody could sneak in later."

"My God," Chee exclaimed, struck by a sudden thought. "How many keys would it take to unlock all of these?"

Highhawk laughed. "You're not dealing with the world's heaviest key ring here," he said. "Just one key, or rather copies of the same key, fits all these box locks. They're not intended to keep people from stealing stuff. Who'd want to steal a section of a Civil War rowboat, for example? It's to help with inventory control. You want in one of these cases, you go to the appropriate office and get the key off a hook by the desk and sign for it. Anyway, it all worried the Secret Service to death. About eighty million artifacts in this building, and maybe a hundred thousand of them could be used to kill somebody. So they wanted everything tied down."

"I guess it worked. Nobody got shot."

"Or harpooned, or crossbowed, or beaned with a charro lasso, or speared, or arrowed, or knitting needled, or war clubbed," Highhawk added. "They wanted all that stuff to come out too. Anything that might be a weapon, from Cheyenne metate stones to Eskimo whale-skinning knives. It was quite an argument."

Highhawk did an abrupt turn through a doorway into a long, bright, cluttered room lit by rows of fluorescent tubes.

"The conservatory lab," he said, "the repair shop for decaying cannonballs, frayed buggy whips, historic false teeth and so forth, including—if the computer was right—one Tano War God."

He stopped beside one of the long tables which occupied the center of the room, rummaged briefly, extracted a cardboard box. From it he pulled a crudely carved wooden form.

He held it up for Chee to inspect. It was shaped from a large root, which gave it a bent and twisted shape. Bedraggled feathers decorated it and its face stared back at Chee with the same look of malice that he remembered on the fetish he'd seen in Highhawk's office. Was it the same fetish? Maybe. He couldn't be sure.

"This is what the shouting's about," he said. "The symbol of one of the Tano Twin War Gods."

"Has somebody been working on it?" Chee asked. "Is that why it's here?"

Highhawk nodded. He looked up at Chee. "Where did you hear the Pueblo was asking for it back?"

"I can't remember," Chee said. "Maybe there was something in the *Albuquerque Journal* about it." He shrugged. "Or maybe I'm getting it confused with the Zuni War God. The one the Zunis finally got back from the Denver Museum."

Highhawk laid the fetish gently back in the box. "Anyway, I guess that when the museum got the word that the Pueblo was asking about it, somebody over in the Castle sent a memo over. They wanted to know if we actually had such a thing. And if we did have it, they wanted to make damn sure it was properly cared for. No termites, moss, dry rot, anything like that. That would be very bad public relations." Highhawk grinned at Chee. "Folks in the Castle can't stand a bad press."

"Castle?"

"The original ugly old building with the towers and battlements and all," Highhawk explained. "It sort of looks like a castle and that's where the top brass has offices." The thought of this wiped away Highhawk's good humor. "They get paid big money to come up with reasons why the museum needs eighteen thousand stolen skeletons. And this—" He tapped the fetish. "—this stolen sacred object."

He handed it to Chee.

It was heavier than he'd expected. Perhaps the root was from some tree harder than the cottonwood. It looked old. How old? he asked himself. Three hundred years? Three thousand? Or maybe thirty. He knew no way to judge. But certainly nothing about it looked raw or new.

Highhawk was glancing at his watch. Chee handed him the fetish. "Interesting," he said. "There's a couple of things I want to ask you about."

"Tell you what," Highhawk said. "I have a thing I have to do. We'll go back by my office and you wait there and I'll be right back. This is going to take—" He thought. "—maybe ten, fifteen minutes."

Chee glanced at his own watch when Highhawk dropped him at the office. It was nine twenty-five. He sat beside Highhawk's desk, heels on the wastebasket, relaxing. He was tired and he hadn't realized it. A long day, full of walking, full of disappointments. What would he be able to tell Janet Pete that Janet Pete didn't already know? He could tell her of Highhawk's coyness about the fetish. Obviously it was Highhawk who had brought the War God up to the conservancy lab to work on it. Obviously he'd known exactly where to find it. Obviously he didn't want Chee to know of his interest in the thing.

Chee yawned, and stretched, and rose stiffly from his chair to prowl the office. A framed certificate on the wall declared that his host had successfully completed studies in anthropological conservation and restoration at the London Institute of Archaeology. Another certified his completion with honors of a materials conservation graduate program at George Washington University. Still another recognized his contribution to a seminar on "Conservation Implications of the Structure, Reactivity, Deterioration, and Modification of Proteinaceous Artifact Material" for the American Institute of Archaeology.

Chee was looking for something to read and thinking that Highhawk's few minutes had stretched a bit when he heard the sounds—a sharp report, a clatter of miscellaneous noises with what might have been a yell mixed in. It was an unpleasant noise and it stopped Chee cold. He caught his breath, listening. Whatever it was ended as abruptly as it had started. He walked to the door and looked up and down the hallway, listening. The immense sixth floor of the Museum of Natural History was as silent as a cave. The noise had come from his right. Chee walked down the hallway in that direction, slowly, soundlessly. He stopped at a closed door, gripped the knob, tested it. Locked. He put his ear to the panel and heard nothing but the sound his own blood made moving through his arteries. He moved down the hallway, conscious of the rows of wooden bins through which he walked, of the smells, of dust, of old things decaying. Then he stopped again and stood absolutely still, listening. He heard nothing but ringing silence and, after a moment, what might have been an elevator descending in another part of the building.

Then steps. Rapid steps. From ahead and to the left. Chee hurried to the corridor corner ahead, looked around it. It was empty. Simply another narrow pathway between deep stacks of numbered bins. He listened again. Where had the hurrier gone? What had caused those odd noises? Chee had no idea which way to look. He simply stood, leaning against a bin, and listened. Silence rang in his ears. Whoever, whatever, had made the noise had gone away.

He walked back to Highhawk's office, suppressing an urge to look back, controlling an urge to hurry. And when he reached it, he closed the door firmly behind him and moved his chair against the wall so that it faced the door. When he sat in it he suddenly felt very foolish. The noise would have some perfectly normal explanation. Something had fallen. Someone had dropped something heavy.

He resumed his explorations of the documents on Highhawk's untidy desk, looking for something interesting. They tended toward administrative documents and technical material. He selected a photocopy of a report entitled

ETHICAL AND PRACTICAL CONSIDERATIONS IN CONSERVING ETHNOGRAPHIC MUSEUM OBJECTS

and settled down to read it.

It was surprisingly interesting—some twenty-five pages full of information and ideas mostly new to Chee. He read it carefully and slowly, stopping now and then to listen. Finally he put it back on the desk, put his heels back on the wastebasket, and thought about Mary Landon, and then about Janet Pete, and then about Highhawk. He glanced at his watch. After ten. Highhawk had been gone more than thirty minutes. He walked to the door and looked up and down the corridor. Total emptiness. Total silence. He sat again in the chair, feet on the floor, remembering exactly what Highhawk had said. He'd said wait here a few minutes. Ten or fifteen.

Chee got his hat and went out into the corridor, turning off the light and closing the door behind him. He found his way through the labyrinth of corridors to the elevator. He pushed the button and heard it laboring its way upward. Highhawk obviously had not returned by this route. On the ground floor he found his way to the Twelfth Street exit. There had been a security guard there when he came in, a woman who had spoken to Highhawk. She would know if he'd left the building. But the woman wasn't there. No one was guarding the exit door.

Chee felt a sudden irrational urge to get out of this building and under the sky. He pushed the door open and hurried down the steps. The cold, misty air felt wonderful on his face. But where was Highhawk? He remembered the last words Highhawk had said as he left him at Highhawk's office:

"I'll be right back."

15

LEAPHORN CALLED Kennedy from his hotel room and caught him at home.

"I've got him," Leaphorn said. "His name is Elogio Santillanes. But I need you to get a fingerprint check made and see if the Agency has anything on him."

"Who?" Kennedy said. He sounded sleepy. "What are you talking about?"

"The man beside the tracks. Remember? The one you got me out into the weather to take a look at."

"Oh," Kennedy said. "Yeah. Santillanes, you say. A local Hispano then, after all. How'd you get a make on him?"

Leaphorn explained it all, from St. Germain to Perez to the prescription number, including the little red-haired man who might (or might not) be watching the Santillanes apartment.

"Nice to be lucky," Kennedy said. "Where the hell you calling from? You in Washington now?"

Leaphorn gave him the name of his hotel. "I'm going to stay here—or at least I'll be here for message purposes. Are you going to call Washington?"

"Why not?" Kennedy said.

"Would you ask 'em to let me know what they find out? And since they probably won't do it, would you call me as soon as they call you back?"

"Why not?" Kennedy said. "You going to stick around there until we know something?"

"Why not?" Leaphorn said. "It shouldn't take long with the name. Either they have prints on him or they don't."

It didn't take long. Leaphorn watched the late news. He went out for a walk in what had now transformed itself into a fine, damp, cold mist. He bought an edition of tomorrow's *Washington Post* and read it in bed. He woke late, had breakfast in the hotel coffee shop, and found his telephone ringing when he got back to the room.

It was Kennedy.

"Bingo," Kennedy said. "I am sort of a hero with the Agency this morning—which will last until about sundown. Your Elogio Santillanes was in the Agency print files. He was one of the relatively few surviving leaders of the substantially less than loyal left-wing opposition to the Pinochet regime in Chile."

"Well," Leaphorn said. "That's interesting." But what the devil did it mean? What would call a Chilean politician to Gallup, New Mexico? What would arouse in such a man an interest in a Night Chant somewhere out beyond Lower Greasewood?

"They wondered what had happened to him," Kennedy was saying. "He wasn't exactly under close surveillance, but the Agency tries to keep an eye on such folks. It tries to keep track of them. Especially this bunch because of that car bombing awhile back. You remember about that?"

"Very vaguely. Was it Chilean?"

"It was. One of this bunch that Santillanes belongs to got blown sky-high over on Sheridan Circle, near where the very important people live. The Chilean embassy crowd didn't make enough effort to hide their tracks and the Department of State declared a bunch of them *persona non grata* and sent them home. There was a big protest to Chile, human rights complaints, the whole nine yards. Terribly bad publicity for the Pinochet gang. Anyway after that the Agency seems to have kept an eye on them. And things cooled down."

"Until now," Leaphorn said.

"It looks to me like Pinochet's thugs waited until they figured they wouldn't get caught at it," Kennedy said. "But how do I know?"

"That would explain all the effort to keep Santillanes from being identified."

"It would," Kennedy agreed. "If there's no identification, there's no static from the Department of State."

"Did you ask your people here to give me a call? Did you tell them about Santillanes' neighbor? And did you pass along what I told you about Henry Highhawk's name being in Santillanes' notebook?"

"Yes, I told them about the little man in apartment two, and yes I mentioned Henry Highhawk, and yes I asked them to give Joe Leaphorn a call. Have they called?"

"Of course not," Leaphorn said.

Kennedy laughed. "Old J. Edgar's dead, but nothing ever changes."

But they did call. Leaphorn had hardly hung up when he heard knocking at his door.

Two men waited in the hall. Even in Washington, where every male—to Leaphorn's casual eye—dressed exactly like every other male, these two were obviously Agency men.

"Come in," Leaphorn said, glancing at the identification each man was now holding out for inspection, "I've been sort of expecting you."

He introduced himself. Their names were Dillon and Akron, both being blond, Dillon being bigger and older and in charge.

"Your name is Leaphorn? That right?" Dillon said, glancing in his notebook. "You have identification?"

Leaphorn produced his folder.

Dillon compared Leaphorn's face with the picture. He examined the credentials. Nothing in his expression suggested he was impressed by either.

"A lieutenant in the Navajo Tribal Police?"

"That's right."

Dillon stared at him. "How did you get involved in this Santillanes business?"

Leaphorn explained. The body beside the tracks. Learning the train had been stopped. Learning of the abandoned luggage. Learning of the prescription number. Going to the apartment on the prescription address.

"Have you checked on the man in apartment two?" Leaphorn asked. "He fit the description of the man the attendant saw in Santillanes' roomette. And he was curious."

Akron smiled slightly and looked down at his hands. Dillon cleared his throat. Leaphorn nodded. He knew what was coming. He had worked with the Agency for thirty years.

"You have no jurisdiction in this case," Dillon said. "You never had any jurisdiction. You may have already fouled up a very sensitive case."

"Involving national security," Leaphorn added, thoughtfully and mostly to himself. He didn't intend any sarcasm. It was simply the code expression he'd been hearing the FBI use since the 1950s. It was something you always heard when the Agency was covering up incompetence. He was simply wondering if the Agency's current screwup was considered serious by Dillon's superiors. Apparently so.

Dillon stared at him, scenting sarcasm. He saw nothing on Leaphorn's square Navajo face but deep thought. Leaphorn was thinking about how he could extract information from Dillon and he had reached some sort of conclusion. He nodded.

"Did Agent Kennedy mention to you about the slip of paper found in Santillanes' shirt pocket?"

Dillon's expression shifted from stern to unpleasant. He took his lip between his teeth. Released it. Started to say something. Changed his mind. Pride struggled with curiosity. "I am not aware of that at this point in time," he said.

So there was no purpose in talking to Dillon about it. But he wanted Dillon's goodwill. "Nothing was written on it except the name Agnes Tsosie—Tsosie is a fairly common Navajo name, and Agnes is prominent in the tribe—and the name of a curing ceremonial. The Yeibichai. One of those had been scheduled to be held for Mrs. Tsosie. Scheduled about three or four weeks after the Santillanes body was found."

"What is your interest in this?" Dillon asked.

"The agent-in-charge at Gallup is an old friend," Leaphorn said. "We've worked together for years."

Dillon was not impressed with "agent-in-charge at Gallup." As a matter of fact, an agent stationed in Washington wasn't easy to impress with an agent stationed anywhere else, much less a small Western town. In earlier days agents were transferred to places like Gallup because they had somehow offended J. Edgar Hoover or one of the swarm of yeasayers with which he had manned the upper echelons of his empire. In J. Edgar's day, New Orleans had been the ultimate Siberia of the Agency. J. Edgar detested New Orleans as hot, humid, and decadent and presumed all other FBI employees felt the same way. But since his demise, his camp followers usually exiled to smaller towns agents considered unduly ambitious, unacceptably intelligent, or prone to bad publicity.

"It's still not your case," Dillon said. "You don't have any jurisdiction outside your Indian reservation. And in this case, you wouldn't have jurisdiction even there."

Leaphorn smiled. "And happy I don't," he said. "It looks too complicated for me. But I'm curious. I've got to get with Pete

Domenici for lunch before I go home, and he's going to want to know what I'm doing here."

Agent Akron had sat down in a bedside chair just out of Leaphorn's vision but Leaphorn kept his eye on Dillon while he said this. Obviously, Dillon recognized the name of Pete Domenici, the senior senator from New Mexico, who happened to be ranking Republican on the committee which oversaw the Agency's budget. Leaphorn smiled at Dillon again—a conspiratorial one-cop-to-another smile. "You know how some people are about homicides. Pete is fascinated by 'em. I tell Pete about Santillanes and he's going to have a hundred questions."

"Domenici," Dillon said.

"One thing the senator is going to ask me is why Santillanes was killed way out in New Mexico," Leaphorn said. "Out in his district."

Leaphorn watched Dillon making up his mind, imagining the process. He would think that probably Leaphorn was lying about Domenici, which he was, but Dillon hadn't survived in Washington by taking chances. Dillon reached his decision.

"I can't talk about what he was doing out there," Dillon said. "Agent Akron and I are with the antiterrorist division. And I can say Santillanes was a prominent member of a terrorist organization."

"Oh," Leaphorn said.

"Opposed to the regime of President Pinochet." Dillon looked at Leaphorn. "He's the president of Chile," Dillon added.

Leaphorn nodded. "But you can't tell me why Santillanes was out in New Mexico?" He nodded again. "I can respect that." In the code the FBI had developed down the years, it meant Dillon didn't know the answer.

"I cannot say," Dillon said. "Not at this moment in time."

"How about why he was killed?"

"Just speculation," Dillon said. "Off the record."

Leaphorn nodded, agreeing.

"The effort that was made to avoid identification suggests that it was a continuation of the Pinochet administration's war against the Communists in Chile," Dillon said. He paused, studying Leaphorn to see if this needed explanation. He decided that it did.

"Some time ago, a Chilean dissident was blown up here in Washington. A car bomb. The State Department deported several Chilean nationals and delivered a warning to the ambassador. Or so I understand." Dillon returned the same cop-to-cop smile he had received a few moments earlier from Leaphorn. "Therefore, the Chilean security people at the embassy seem to have decided they would wait until one of their targets was as far from Washington as possible before eliminating him. They would try to make sure the connection was never made."

"I see," Leaphorn said. "I have two more questions."

Dillon waited.

"What will the Agency do about the little man in apartment two?"

"I can't discuss that," Dillon said.

"That's fair enough. Does the name Henry Highhawk mean anything to you?"

Dillon considered. "Henry Highhawk. No."

"I think Kennedy mentioned him when he called the Agency," Leaphorn prompted.

"Oh, yeah," Dillon said. "The name in the notebook."

"How does this Henry Highhawk fit in? Why would Santillanes be interested in him? Why was he interested in Agnes Tsosie? Or the Yeibichai ceremonial?"

"Yeibichai ceremonial?" Dillon said, looking totally baffled. "I am not free to discuss any of that. At this point in time I cannot discuss Henry Highhawk."

But Henry Highhawk stuck in Leaphorn's mind. The name had been somehow familiar the first time he'd seen it written in the Santillanes notebook. It was an unusual name and it had rung some sort of dim bell in his memory. He remembered looking at the name in Santillanes' careful little script and trying to place it, without any luck. He remembered looking at Highhawk's photograph at Agnes Tsosie's place. He knew he had never seen the man before. When Dillon and Akron had gone away to wherever FBI agents go, he tried again. Clearly the name had meant nothing to Dillon. Clearly, Leaphorn himself must have run across it before any of this business had begun. How? What had he been doing? He had been doing nothing unusual. Just routine police administration.

He reached for the telephone and dialed the Navajo Tribal Police building in Window Rock. In about eleven minutes he had what he wanted. Or most of it.

"A fugitive warrant? What was the original offense? Really? What date? No, I meant the date of the arrest? Where? Give me his home address off the warrant." Leaphorn jotted down the Washington address. "Who handled the arrest for us? I'll wait." Leaphorn waited. "Who?"

The arresting officer was Jim Chee.

"Well, thanks," Leaphorn said. "Is Chee still stationed up at Shiprock? Okay. I'll call him there."

He dialed the number of the Shiprock subagency police station from memory. Office Chee was on vacation. Had he left an address where he might be reached? Navajo Tribal Police rules required that he would, but Chee had a reputation for sometimes making his own rules.

"Just a second," the clerk said. "Here it is. He's in Washington, D.C. I'll give you his hotel."

Leaphorn called Chee's hotel. Yes, Chee was still registered. But he didn't answer his telephone. Leaphorn left a message and hung up. He sat on the bed, asking himself what could have possibly drawn Officer Jim Chee from Shiprock to Washington. Lieutenant Joe Leaphorn had never, never believed in coincidence.

16

LEROY FLECK SIMPLY couldn't get his mind relieved. He sat on the folding lawn chair in his empty apartment with the telephone on the floor beside him. In about an hour it would be time to go out to the phone booth and put in his once-a-month check-in call to Eddy Elkins. What he was going to say to Elkins was part of the problem. He was going to have to ask Elkins to wire him enough money to get Mama moved, enough to tide him over for the two or three days it would take The Client to pay up. He dreaded asking, because he was almost sure Elkins would just laugh and say no. But he had to get enough to move Mama.

Fleck had on his hat and his coat. It was cold in the apartment because he was trying to save on the utility bill. What he was doing while he was doing all this thinking normally brought him pleasure. He was hunting through the classified ad section of the *Washington Times,* looking for somebody to talk to. Normally that relieved his mind. Not tonight. Even with talking to people he couldn't get Mama out of his thoughts. The worst of it was he'd had to hurt the Fat Man. He'd had to threaten to kill the son-of-a-bitch and twisted his arm while he was doing it. There just wasn't any other way to make him keep Mama until he could find another place. But doing that had opened things up to real trouble—or the probability of it. He'd warned the man not to call the police and the bastard had looked scared enough so maybe he wouldn't. On the other hand, maybe he would. And when the police checked his address and found it was phony—well, who knows what then? They'd be interested. Fleck couldn't afford to have the police interested.

The tape recorder on the box against the wall made a whispering sound. Fleck glanced at it, his thoughts elsewhere. It whispered, and fell silent. The microphone he'd installed in the crawlspace above the ceiling of the Santillanes apartment was supposed to be voice activated. That really meant "sound activated." A lot of what Fleck was recording was Mrs. Santillanes, or whoever that old Mexican woman was, running her vacuum cleaner or clattering around with the dishes. At first, he had sometimes played the tape before sending it off to the post-office-box address Elkins had given him. He'd heard a lot of household noises, and now and then people talking. But the talking was in Spanish. Fleck had picked up a little of that in Joliet from the Hispanos. Just enough to understand that most of what he was taping was family talk. What's for dinner? Where's my glasses? That sort of stuff. Not enough for Fleck to guess why Elkins' clients wanted to keep track of this bunch. It had seemed to Fleck from very early in this assignment that these folks next door were smart enough to do their serious talking somewhere else.

He found an ad that sounded promising. It offered an Apple computer complete with twelve video games for sale by owner. Fleck knew almost nothing about computers, and cared less. But this sounded like a family where the kids had grown up and the item for sale was expensive enough so the owner wouldn't mind talking for a while. Fleck dialed the number, listened to a busy signal, and picked up the paper again. This time he selected a gasoline-powered trash shredder. A man answered on the second ring.

"I'm calling about the shredder," Fleck said. "What are you asking for it?"

"Well, we paid three hundred and eighty dollars for it, and it's just like new." The man had a soft, Virginia Tidewater voice. "But we ain't got no use for it anymore. And I think we'd come down to maybe two hundred."

"No use for it?" Fleck said. "Sounds like you're moving or something. Got anything else you're selling? Several things I need."

"Not moving," the man said. "We're just getting out of gardening. My wife's developed arthritis." He laughed. "And she's the one that did all the work."

From there, Leroy Fleck led the conversation into personal affairs—first the affairs of the owner of the item offered, and then Fleck's own. It was something he had done for years and had become very good at doing. It was his substitute for hanging out in a bar. Keeping Mama in a rest home had made bars too expensive and the people you talked to there tended not to be normal anyway. Fleck had discovered more or less by accident that it was pleasant and relaxing to talk to regular people. It happened when he decided that it would be nice for Mama to have one of those little refrigerators in her room. He'd noticed one in the want ads, and called, and got into a good-natured conversation with the lady selling it. Mama had thrown the little refrigerator on the floor and broke it, but Fleck had remembered the chat. And it had become a habit. At first he did it only when he needed to relieve his mind. But for the last few years he'd done it almost every night. Except Saturday. People didn't like to be called on Saturday night. With practice he had learned which ads to call, and how to keep the conversation going. After three or four such calls Fleck found he could usually sleep. Talking to somebody normal relieved the mind.

Usually, that is. Tonight, it didn't work. After a while the man selling the trash shredder just wanted to talk about that—what Fleck would pay for it and so forth. Fleck had then called about a pop-up-top vacation trailer which would sleep four. But this time he found himself getting impatient even before the woman who was selling it did.

After that call he just sat there on the lawn chair. To keep from worrying about Mama, he worried about those two Indians— and especially about the one who had come to his door here. Both of those men had really smelled like cops to him. Fleck didn't like having cops know where to find him. Normally in a situation like that he would have moved right out of here and got lost. But now he couldn't move. This job Eddy Elkins had got him into this time kept him tied here. He was stuck. He had to have the money. Absolutely had to have it. Absolutely had to wait two more days until the month was up. Then he'd get the ten thousand the bastards were making him wait for.

He went into the kitchen and checked the refrigerator. He had a little bit of beef liver left and two hamburger buns, but no ground beef and only two potatoes. That would handle his needs tonight. But he'd need food tomorrow. He didn't even have enough grease to fry the potatoes for breakfast. Fleck put on his hat and his coat and went out into the misty rain.

He returned with a plastic grocery sack and an early edition of the *Washington Post.* Fleck knew how to stretch his dollars. The bag contained two loaves of day-old bread, a dozen grade B eggs, a half-gallon of milk, a carton of Velveeta, and a pound of margarine. He put the frying pan on the gas burner, dumped in a spoonful of margarine and the liver. Fleck's furniture consisted of stuff he could fold into the trunk of his old Chevy, which meant nothing in the kitchen except what was built in. He leaned against the wall and watched the liver fry. As it fried he unfolded the *Post* and read.

There was nothing he needed to know on the front page. On page two, the word *Chile* caught his eyes.

TOP CHILEAN POLICE BRASS VISITS; ASKS MUSEUM TO RETURN GOLDEN MASK

He scanned the story, mildly interested in the affairs of his client. It told him that General Ramon Huerta Cardona, identified as "commander of Chilean internal security forces," was in Washington on government business and planned to deliver a personal appeal tomorrow to the Smithsonian Institution for the return of an Inca mask. According to the story, the mask was "golden and encrusted with emeralds," and the general described it as "a Chilean national treasure which should be returned to the people of Chile." Fleck didn't finish the story. He turned the page.

The picture caught his eye instantly. The old man. It was on page four, a single-column photograph halfway down the page with a story under it. Old man Santillanes.

"Oh, shit!" Fleck said it aloud, in something close to a shout. The headline read:

KNIFE VICTIM PROVES TO BE CHILEAN REBEL

Fleck slammed the paper to the floor and stood against the wall. He was shaking. "Ah, shit," he repeated, in something like a whisper now. He bent, retrieved the paper, and read:

"The body of a man found beside a railroad track in New Mexico last month has been identified as Elogio Santillanes y Jimenez, an exiled leader of the opposition to the Chilean government, a spokesman for the Federal Bureau of Investigation announced today.

"The FBI spokesman said Santillanes had been killed by a single stab wound in the back of the neck and his body removed from an Amtrak train.

" 'All identification had been removed from his body—even

his false teeth,' the spokesman said. He noted that this made identification difficult for the agency.

"The FBI declined comment on whether any suspects were
being investigated. Two years ago, another opposition leader to the
Pinochet regime was assassinated in Washington by the detona-
tion of a bomb in his car. Following that incident, the Department
of State issued a sharply worded protest to the Chilean embassy
and two members of the embassy staff were deported as *personae
non gratae* in the United States."

The story continued, but Fleck dropped the paper again. He
felt sick but he had to think. He had guessed right about the embassy, and about why they had wanted him to kill Santillanes a
long way from Washington, and why all that emphasis had been
placed on preventing identification. How the hell had the FBI
managed to make the connection? But what difference did that
make? His problem was what to do about it.

They weren't going to send him the ten thousand now. No
identification and no publicity for a month. That was the deal. A
month without anything in the papers was going to be proof
enough he hadn't screwed it up. And now, what was it? Twenty-
nine days? For a moment he allowed himself to think that they
would agree that this was close enough. But that was bullshit
thinking. All they needed to screw him was the slightest excuse.
They looked down on him like trash. Like dirt. Just like Mama had
always told Delmar and him.

He smelled the liver burning in the frying pan, moved it off
the burner, and fanned away the smoke. Elkins had told him that
Mama was right. He hadn't remembered telling Elkins anything
about Mama, certainly wouldn't have normally, but Elkins said he
talked about it when he was coming out from under the sodium
pentothal—the stuff they'd given him when they fixed him up
there at the prison infirmary. Right after the rape.

Elkins had been standing beside his bed when he came to,
holding a pan in case he threw up the way people sometimes do
when they come up from sodium pentothal. "I want you to listen
now," Elkins had told him in a whisper right by his face. "They're
going to be coming in here as soon as they know you can talk and
asking you questions. They're going to ask you which ones did you."
And he guessed he had mumbled something about getting the
score evened with the sons of bitches because Elkins had put his
hand over Fleck's mouth—Fleck remembered that very clearly
even now—and said: "Get even. But not now. You got to do it your-

self. You tell the screws that you don't know who did you. Tell 'em you didn't get a look at anybody. They hit you from behind. If you want to stay alive in here, you don't talk to the screws. You do your own business. Like your Mama told you."

"Like your Mama told you!" So he must have been talking about Mama when he was still under the anesthesia. It was all still so very vivid.

He'd asked Elkins if they had really raped him the way he seemed to remember, and Elkins said they truly had.

"Then I got to kill 'em."

"Yes," Elkins said. "I think so. Unless you want to live like an animal."

Elkins was a disbarred lawyer with some seniority in Joliet and he understood about such things. He was doing four to eight on an Illinois State felony count. Something to do with fixing up some witnesses, or maybe it was jurors, for somebody important in the Chicago rackets. Fleck understood that Elkins had kept his mouth shut and taken the fall for it, and that seemed to be the way it worked out. Because now Eddy Elkins was important again with some Chicago law firm, even if he couldn't practice law himself.

For that matter, Elkins had been important even in the prison. He was just a trustee working as a male nurse and orderly in the prison hospital. But he had money. He had connections inside and out and everybody knew it. When Fleck came out of isolation, he found he had a job in the infirmary. Elkins had done that. And Elkins had helped him with the big problem—how to kill three hard cases. All bigger than him. All tougher. First he'd started him pumping iron. Fleck had been skinny then as well as small. But at nineteen you can develop fast if you have direction. And steroids. Elkins got him them, too. And then Elkins had showed him how a knife can make a small man equal to a big one if the small man is very, very fast and very cool and knows what to do with the blade. Fleck had always been fast—had to be fast to survive. Elkins used the life-size body chart in the infirmary office and the plastic skeleton to teach him where to put the shank.

"Always flat," Elkins would say. "Remember that. What you're after is behind the bones. Hitting the bones does you no good at all and the way past them is through the crevices." Elkins was a tall, slender man, slightly stooped. He was a Dartmouth man, with his law degree from Harvard. He looked like a teacher and he liked to teach. In the empty, quiet infirmary he would stand there in front of the skeleton with Fleck sitting on the bed, and Elkins would tutor Fleck in the trade.

"If you have to go in from the front"—Elkins recommended against going in from the front—"you have to go between the ribs or right below the Adam's apple. Quick thrust in, and then the wiggle." Elkins demonstrated the little wiggle with his wrist. "That gets the artery, or the heart muscle, or the spinal column. A puncture is usually no damn good. Any other cut is slow and noisy. If you can go in from the back, it's the same. Hold it flat. Hold it horizontal."

Elkins would demonstrate on the plastic skeleton. "The very quickest is right there"—and he would point a slender, manicured finger—"above that first vertebra. You do it right and there's not a motion. Not a sound. Very little bleeding. Instant death."

When it was time for him to go into the yard again, he went with a slender, stiff little shank fashioned of surgical steel and as sharp as the scalpel it had once been. Elkins had given him that along with his final instructions.

"Remember the number for you is three. There are three of them. If you get caught with the first one you don't do the last two. Remember that, and remember to hold it flat. What you're after is behind the bone."

He had been twenty when he did it. A long time ago. He had yearned to tell Mama about it. But it wasn't the sort of thing you could say in a letter, with the screws reading your mail. And Mama hadn't ever been able to get away to come on visiting days. He felt badly about that. It had been a hard life for her and not much he'd done had made it any easier.

The liver had that burned taste. And the hamburger buns were pretty much dried out. But he didn't like liver anyway. He only bought it because it was about half the price of hamburger. And it satisfied what little appetite he had tonight. Then he put on his hat and his still-damp coat and went out to make his call to Elkins.

"There's not a damn thing I can do for you," Elkins said. "You know how we work. After twenty years you ought to know. We keep insulated. It's got to be that way."

"It's been more than twenty years," Fleck said. "Remember that first job?"

The first job had been while he was still in prison. Elkins was out, thanks to a lot of good time and an early parole. And the visitor had come to see him. As a matter of fact, it was the only visitor he'd ever had. A young lawyer. Elkins had sent him to give Fleck a name. It had been a short visit.

"Elkins just said to tell you to make it four instead of three. He wants you to make it Cassidy and Dalkin and Neal and David Petresky. He said you'd understand. And to tell you you'd be represented by a lawyer at the parole hearing and that he had regular work for you after that." The lawyer was a plump, blond man with greenish-blue eyes. He was not much older than Fleck and he looked nervous—glancing around all the time to see if the screw was listening. "He said for me to bring back a yes or a no."

Fleck had thought about it a minute—wondering who Petresky was and how to get to him. "Tell him yes," he said.

And now Elkins remembered it.

"That one was sort of a test," Elkins said. "They said you couldn't handle Petresky. I said I'd seen your work."

"All these years," Fleck said. "Now I need help. I think you owe me."

"I was always business," Eddy Elkins said. "You know that. It couldn't be any other way. It would just be too damned dangerous."

Dangerous for you, Fleck thought, but he didn't say it. Instead he said: "I simply got to have three thousand. I've got to have enough to get my Mama moved." Fleck paused. "Man, I'm desperate."

There was a long silence. "You say this involves your mother?"

"Yeah." In Joliet he had talked to Elkins a lot about Mama. He thought Elkins understood how he felt about her.

Another silence. "What's your number there?"

Fleck told him.

"Stay there. I'll make a contact and see what I can do."

Fleck waited almost an hour, huddled in his damp coat in the booth and, when he felt the chill stiffening him, pacing up and down the sidewalk close enough to hear the ring.

When it rang, it was The Client.

"You dirty little *hijo de puta*," he said. "You want money? You bring us nothing but trouble and you want us to pay you money for it?"

"I got to have it," Fleck said. "You owe me." He thought: *hijo de puta;* the man had called him son of a whore.

"We ought to break your dirty little neck," The Client said. "Maybe we do that. Yes. Maybe we cut your dirty little throat. We give you a simple little job. What do you do? You screw it up!"

Fleck felt the rage rising within him, felt it like bile in his throat. He heard Mama's voice: "They treat you like niggers. You let 'em, they treat you like dogs. You let 'em step on you, they'll treat you like animals."

But he choked back the rage. He couldn't afford it. He had to pick her up right away. He had to get her to a place they'd take care of her.

"I know who you are," Fleck said. "I followed you back to your embassy. I get paid or I can cause you some trouble." Then he listened.

What he heard was a stream of obscenities. He heard himself called the filthy, defecation-eating son of a whore, the son of an infected dog. And the click of the line disconnecting.

Standing in the drizzle outside the booth, Fleck spit on the sidewalk. He let the rage well up. He'd get the money another way, somehow. He'd done it in the past. Mugging. A lot of mugging to come up with three thousand dollars unless he was lucky. It was dangerous. Terribly dangerous. Only the ruling class carried big money, and some of them carried only plastic. And the police protected the ruling class. And now there was something else he had to do. It involved getting even. It involved using his shank again. It involved getting the blade in behind the bone.

17

"WHAT I WANT to know, for starters," Joe Leaphorn said, "is everything you know about this Henry Highhawk."

They had met in what passed for a coffee shop in Jim Chee's hotel, surrounded by blue-collar workers and tourists who, like Chee, had asked their travel agents to find them moderately priced housing in downtown Washington. Leaphorn had donned the Washington uniform. But his three-piece suit was a model sold by the Gallup Sears store in the middle seventies, and its looseness testified to the pounds Leaphorn had lost eating his own cooking since Emma's death.

With the single exception of his Blessing Way ceremonial, Jim Chee had never seen the legendary Leaphorn except in a Navajo Tribal Police uniform. He was having psychological trouble handling this inappropriate attire. Like a necktie on a herd bull, Chee thought. Like socks on a billy goat. But above the necktie knot Leaphorn's eyes were exactly as Chee remembered them—dark brown, alert, searching. As always, something in them was causing Chee to examine his conscience. What had he neglected? What had he forgotten?

He told Leaphorn about Highhawk's job, his educational background, the charge against him for vandalizing graves, his campaign to cause the Smithsonian to release its thousands of Native American skeletons for reburial. He described how he and Cowboy Dashee had arrested Highhawk. He reported how Gomez had shown up, how Gomez had agreed to post Highhawk's bond. How yesterday Gomez had appeared at Highhawk's house. He described Highhawk's limp, his leg brace, and how Janet Pete had come to be his attorney. He touched on Janet Pete's doubts about

the Tano Pueblo fetish and what he had seen in Highhawk's office-studio. But he said nothing at all about Janet Pete's doubts and
problems. That was another story. That was none of Leaphorn's
business.

"What do you think he was doing at the Yeibichai?" Leaphorn
asked.

Chee shrugged. "He doesn't look it but he's one-fourth Navajo.
One grandmother was Navajo. I guess she made a big impression
on him. Janet Pete tells me he wants to be a Navajo. Thinks about
himself as a Navajo." Chee considered that some more. "He
wanted to be sort of initiated into the tribe. And he knew enough
about the Yeibichai to show up on the last night." He glanced at
Leaphorn. Did this Navajo version of pragmatist-agnostic know
enough about the Yeibichai himself to know what that meant? He
added: "When the *hataalii* sometimes initiates boys—lets them
look through the mask. Highhawk wanted to do that."

Leaphorn merely nodded. "Did he?"

"We arrested him," Chee said.

Leaphorn thought about that answer. "Right away?"

"Well, no," Chee said. "We watched him awhile. And then
when we did arrest him he asked if we could stick around a little
longer. He wanted to see the part where Talking God and Humpback and the Fringed Mouth *yei* appear. So we stuck around for
that." Chee shrugged. He had been enjoying this role of knowing
more than Lieutenant Leaphorn. "That's about it," he said.

Leaphorn picked up his coffee cup, examined it, looked across
it at Chee, took a small sip, put it back in the saucer, and waited.
"Stuck around about two hours," he said. "Right?"

"About," Chee agreed.

"You didn't just stand around. You talked. What did Highhawk talk about?"

Chee shrugged. What had they talked about?

"It was cold as hell—wind out of the north. We talked about
that. He thought the people wearing the *yei* masks must get awful
frostbitten with nothing on but leggings and kilts. And he asked a
lot of questions. Did the paint on their bodies insulate them from
the cold? Which mask represented which *yei*? Questions about the
ceremonial. And he knew enough about it to ask smart questions."
Chee stopped. Finished.

"About anything else?"

Chee shrugged.

Leaphorn stared at him. "That won't get it," he said. "I need to know."

Chee was not in the mood for this. He felt his face flushing. "Highhawk was taping some of it," Chee said. "He had this little tape recorder palmed. Then he'd pull it up his sleeve if anyone noticed it. You're not supposed to do that unless you square it with the *hataalii*. I let that go. Didn't say anything. And once I heard him singing the words of one of the chants. What else? He and this Gomez went into the kitchen shed once and ate some stew. And when Dashee and I arrested him, Gomez came up and wanted to know what was going on."

"If he knew as much as he seemed to know, then he knew he shouldn't be taping without the singer's permission," Leaphorn said. "And it looked to you like he was being sneaky about it?"

"It was sneaky," Chee said. "Hiding the recorder in his palm. Up his sleeve."

"Not very polite," Leaphorn said. "Not as polite as his letter sounded." He said it mostly to himself, thinking out loud.

"Letter?" Chee said, louder than he intended. The edge in his voice was enough so that at the next table two men in Federal Express delivery uniforms looked up from their waffles and stared at him.

"He wrote a letter to Agnes Tsosie," Leaphorn said. "Very polite. Tell me about this Gomez. Describe him."

Chee was aware that his face was flushed. He could feel it, distinctly.

"I'm on vacation," Chee said. "I'm off duty. I want you to tell me about this letter. When did that happen? How did you know about it? How did you know about Highhawk? What the hell's going on?"

"Well, now," Leaphorn began, his face flushing. But then he closed his mouth. He cleared his throat. "Well, now," he said again, "I guess you're right." And he told Chee about the man with pointed shoes.

Leaphorn was unusually good at telling. He organized it all neatly and chronologically. He described the body found beside the tracks east of Gallup, the cryptic note in the shirt pocket, the visit to the Agnes Tsosie place, the letter from Highhawk with Highhawk's photograph included, what the autopsy showed, all of it.

"This little man in the next apartment, he fit the description of the man in Santillanes' compartment on the train. No question he was interested in the Santillanes bunch. Any chance he and Gomez are the same?"

"Not the way you describe him," Chee said. "Gomez had black hair. He's younger than your man sounds, and taller and slender— none of those weightlifter muscles. And I think he lost several fingers."

Leaphorn's expression shaded from alert to very alert. "Several? What do you mean?"

"He was wearing leather gloves, but on both hands some of the fingers were stiff—as if the gloves were stuffed with cotton or maybe there was a finger in it that didn't bend. I took a look every chance I got because it seemed funny. Strange I mean. Losing fingers off both hands."

Leaphorn thought. "Any other scars? Deformities?"

"None visible," Chee said. And waited. He watched Leaphorn turning these mangled fingers over in his mind. Chee reminded himself that he was on vacation and so was Leaphorn. By God, he was simply not going to let the lieutenant get away with this.

"Why?"

Leaphorn, his thoughts interrupted, looked startled. "What?"

"I can tell you're thinking those missing fingers are important. Why are they important? How does that fit with what you know?"

"Probably they're not important," Leaphorn said.

"Not good enough," Chee said. "Remember, I'm on vacation."

Leaphorn's expression shifted into something that might have been a grin. "I have some bad habits. A lot of them involve doing things to save time. A strange habit for a Navajo, I guess. But you're right. You're on vacation. So am I, for that matter." He put down his coffee cup.

"Where do I start? Santillanes didn't have any teeth. All pulled. But the pathologist who did the autopsy said there was no sign of any reason to have them pulled. No jawbone problems, no traces left by the gum diseases that cause you to lose your teeth. I wondered how Santillanes lost his teeth. You wondered how Gomez lost his fingers." Leaphorn took the final sip of his coffee, signaled the waiter. "You see a connection?"

Chee hesitated. "You mean like they both might have been tortured?"

"It occurs to me. I guess they're Chilean leftists. The right wing's in power. There's been a lot of reporting of the secret police, or maybe the army, knocking people off. People disappearing. Political prisoners. Murder. Torture. Some really hideous stuff causing investigations by Amnesty International."

Chee nodded.

"I think we should go talk to Highhawk," Leaphorn said. "Okay?"

"If we can find him," Chee said. "I called this morning. Called his house. Called his office. No answer. So I called Dr. Hartman. She's the curator he's working for at the museum. She hadn't seen him either. She was looking for him."

"Let's go try to find him anyway," Leaphorn said. He picked up the check.

"I didn't tell you about last night," Chee said. He described how Highhawk had taken the telephone call, then left saying he'd be right back, and never returned.

"I think we should go on out there. See if we can find the man. Try his house and if he's not there, we'll try the Smithsonian."

Chee put on his hat and followed.

"Why not?" he said, but even as he said it he had a feeling they weren't going to find Henry Highhawk.

They took a cab to Eastern Market.

"Stick around a minute until we see if our party is home," Leaphorn said.

The cabby was a plump young man with a mass of curly brown hair and fat, red lips. He pulled a paperback copy of *Passage to Quivera* off the dashboard and opened it. "It's your money," he said. "Spend it any way you like."

Leaphorn punched the doorbell. They listened to it buzz inside. He punched it again. Chee walked back down the porch steps and rescued the morning paper from where it had been thrown beside the front walk. He showed it to Leaphorn. He nodded. Punched the doorbell again. Chee walked to the window, shaded the glass with his hands. The blinds were up, the curtains open. The room was empty and dark on this dreary, overcast morning.

"What do you think?" Chee said.

Leaphorn shook his head, rang the bell again. He tried the doorknob. Locked.

"Curtains open, blinds up," Chee said. "If he came home last night, maybe he didn't turn on the lights."

"Maybe not." Leaphorn tried the door again. Still locked. "I know a cop here," he said. "I think we'll give him a call and see what he thinks."

"FBI?" Chee asked.

"A real cop," Leaphorn said. "A captain on the Washington police force."

They took the cab to the public phone booths at the Eastern Market Metro station. Leaphorn made his call. Chee waited, watching the cabby read and trying to decide what the hell Highhawk was doing. Where had he gone? Why had he gone? How was Bad Hands involved in this? He thought of Bad Hands in the role of revolutionary. He thought of how it would feel to have your fingers removed by a torturer trying to make you talk. Leaphorn climbed back into the cab.

"He said he would meet us at a little coffee place in the old Post Office building."

The cabby was awaiting instructions. "You know how to find it?" Leaphorn asked.

"Is the Pope a Catholic?" the cabby said.

They found Captain Rodney awaiting them just inside the coffee shop door, a tall, bulky black man wearing bifocals, a gray felt hat, and a raincoat to match. The sight of Leaphorn provoked a huge, delighted, white-toothed grin.

"This is Jim Chee," Leaphorn said. "One of our officers."

They shook hands. Rodney's craggy, coffee-colored face usually registered expression only when Rodney allowed it to do so. Now, just for a moment, it registered startled surprise. He removed the fedora, revealing kinky gray hair cropped close to the skull.

"Jim Chee," he said, memorizing Chee's face. "Well, now."

"Rodney and I go way back," Leaphorn said. "We survived the FBI Academy together."

"Two misfits," Rodney said. "Back in the days when *all* FBI agents had blue eyes instead of just most of them." Rodney chuckled, but his eyes never left Chee. "That's when I first learned that our friend here—" he indicated Leaphorn with a thumb—"has this practice of just telling you what he thinks you have to know."

They were at a table now and Leaphorn was ordering coffee. Now he looked surprised. "Like what?" he said. "What do you mean by that?"

Rodney was still looking at Chee. "You work for this guy, right? Or with him, anyway."

"More or less," Chee said, wondering where this was leading. "Now I'm on vacation."

Rodney laughed. "Vacation. Is that a fact. You just happen to be three thousand miles east of home at the same time as your boss.

I think maybe I was blaming Joe for something that's a universal Navajo trait."

"What are we talking about here?" Leaphorn asked.

"About the Navajo Tribal Police sending two men"—he pointed a finger at Leaphorn and then at Chee—"two men, count 'em, to Washington, Dee, Cee, which is several miles out of their jurisdiction, to look for a fellow which us local cops didn't even yet know there was a reason to be looking for."

"Nobody sent us here," Leaphorn said.

Rodney ignored the remark. He was staring at Chee.

"What time did you leave the Smithsonian last night?"

Chee told him. He was baffled. How did this Washington policeman know he had been at the museum last night? Why would he care? Something must have happened to Highhawk.

"Which exit?"

"Twelfth Street."

"Nobody checked you out?"

"Nobody was there."

Surprise again registered on Rodney's face.

"Ah," he said. "No guard? No security person? How did you get out?"

"I just walked out."

"The door wasn't locked."

Chee shook his head. "Closed, but unlocked."

"You see anything? Anybody?"

"I was surprised no one was there. I looked around. Empty."

"You didn't see a young woman in a museum guard's uniform? A black woman? The guard who was supposed to be keeping an eye on that Twelfth Street entrance?"

Chee shook his head again. "Nobody was around," he said. "Nobody. What's the deal?" But even as he asked the question, he knew the deal. Highhawk was dead. Chee was just about the last person who'd seen him alive.

"The deal is"—Rodney was looking at Leaphorn now—"that I get a call from my old friend Joe here to check on whether there's any kind of report on a man named Henry Highhawk and I find out this Highhawk is on a list of people Homicide would like to talk to." Rodney shifted his gaze back to Chee. "So I come down here to talk to my old friend Joe, and he introduces me to you and, what do ya know, you happen to be another guy on Homicide's wish list. That's what the deal is."

"Your homicide people want to talk to Highhawk," Chee said. "That means he's alive?"

"You have some reason to think otherwise?" Rodney asked.

"When you said you had a homicide I figured he was the one," Chee said. He explained to Rodney what had happened last night at the Smithsonian. "Back in just a minute, he said. But he never came back. I went out and wandered around the halls looking for him. Then finally I went home. I called him at home this morning. No soap. I called his office. The woman he works for was looking for him too. She was worried about him."

Rodney had been intent on every word.

"Went home when?"

"I told you," Chee said. "I must have left the Twelfth Street entrance a little before ten thirty. Very close to that. I walked right back to my hotel."

"And when did Highhawk receive this telephone call? The call just before he left?"

Chee told him.

"Who was the caller?"

"No idea. It was a short call."

"What about? Did you hear it?"

"I heard Highhawk's end. Apparently he had been trying to tell Highhawk how to fix something. Highhawk had tried and it hadn't worked. I remember he said it 'didn't turn on,' and Highhawk said since he was coming down anyway the caller could fix it. And then they set the nine-thirty time and Highhawk told him to remember it was the Twelfth Street entrance."

"Him?" Rodney said. "Was the caller a man?"

"I should have said him or her. I couldn't hear the other voice."

"I'm going to make a call of my own," Rodney said. He rose, gracefully for a man of his bulk. "Pass all this along to the detective handling this one. I'll be right back." He grinned at Chee. "Quicker than Highhawk, anyway."

"Who's the victim?" Leaphorn asked.

Rodney paused, looking down on them. "It was the night shift guard at the Twelfth Street entrance."

"Stabbed?" Leaphorn asked.

"Why you say stabbed?"

Now Leaphorn's voice had an impatient edge in it. "I told you about what brought me here," he said. "Remember? Santillanes was stabbed. Very professionally, in the back of the neck."

"Oh, yeah," Rodney said. "No. Not stabbed this time. It was skull fracture." He made another move toward the telephone.

"Where did they find the body?" Chee asked. "And when?"

"A couple of hours ago. Whoever hit her on the head found the perfect place to hide her." Rodney looked down at them, the tale teller pausing to underline his point. "They laid her out on the grass there between the shrubbery and the sidewalk, and got some old newspapers out of the trash bin there and threw them over her."

Chee understood perfectly the sardonic tone in Rodney's voice, but Leaphorn said: "Right by the sidewalk and nobody checked all morning?"

"This is Friday," Rodney said. "In Washington, the Good Samaritan comes by only on the seventh Tuesday of the month." And he walked away to make his telephone call.

The only remaining sign that a corpse had been on display under the shrubbery adjoining the Twelfth Street entrance to the Smithsonian Museum of Natural History was a uniformed policeman who stood beside a taped-off area. He was whistling idly, and he glanced at Rodney without a sign of recognition. Probably too young.

Inside, Rodney's badge got them through the STAFF ONLY doorway. They took the elevator to the sixth floor and found that Dr. Hartman was not in. A young woman who seemed to be her assistant said she was probably down on the main floor at her mask exhibition. And no, the young woman said, Henry Highhawk had not showed up for work.

"Did you hear what happened?" she asked. "I mean about the guard being killed?"

"We heard," Rodney said. "Do you know where we can get the key to Highhawk's office?"

"Dr. Hartman would probably have one," she said. "But wasn't that dreadful? You don't expect something like that to happen to someone you know."

"Did you know her?" Rodney said.

The young woman looked slightly flustered. "Well I saw her a lot," she said. "You know. When I worked late she would be standing there."

"Her name was Alice Yoakum," Rodney said, mildly. "Mrs. Alice Yoakum. Is there a way we can page Dr. Hartman? Or call down there for her somehow?"

There was, but Dr. Hartman proved to be either unreachable or too busy to come to the telephone.

"It might not be locked," Chee said. "It wasn't when I left. If he didn't come back who would lock it?"

"Maybe some sort of internal security," Rodney said.

But nobody had locked it. The door opened under Rodney's hand. The room was silent, lit by an overhead fluorescent tube, the blinds down as Chee remembered them. Highhawk's gesture at keeping his light from leaking out into the night was now holding out the daylight.

"You leave the light on last night?" Rodney asked.

Chee nodded. "He said he was coming back. I thought he might. I just pulled the door closed."

They stood inside the doorway, inspecting the room.

"Everything look like you left it?" Rodney asked.

"Looks like it," Chee said.

Rodney picked up the telephone, dialed, listened. "This is Rodney," he said. "Get hold of Sergeant Willis and tell him I'm calling from Henry Highhawk's office on the sixth floor of the Smithsonian Museum of Natural History. He's not here. Nobody's seen him. Tell him I have Jim Chee with me. We're going to look around up here and if I don't hear from him before then, I'll call back in—" he glanced at his watch "—about forty-five minutes." He cradled the telephone, sat in Highhawk's chair, looked at Leaphorn who was leaning against the wall, then at Chee by the window.

"Either one of you have any creative thoughts?" he asked. "This isn't my baby—nor yours either for that matter—but here we are knee deep in it."

"I'm asking myself some questions," Leaphorn said. "We have this Highhawk vaguely connected to the knifing of a terrorist, or whatever you want to call him, out in New Mexico. Just the name in the victim's notebook. Now we have him disappearing, I guess, the same night this guard is killed here. But do we know when the guard was killed?"

"Coroner said the first glance looked like it was before midnight," Rodney said. "He may get closer when they have the autopsy finished."

Leaphorn looked thoughtful. "So it might have been either shortly before, or shortly after, Highhawk walked out of here. Either way?"

"Sounds like it," Rodney said. He glanced at Chee. "How about you?"

"I'm thinking that this is the world's best place to hide a body," Chee said, slowly. "Tens of thousands of cases and containers lining the halls. Most of them big enough for a body."

"But locked," Rodney said. "And some of them, I noticed, were sealed, too."

"They all use the same simple little master key," Chee said. "At least most of them must use the same key, or you'd need a truck to haul your keys around. I think you just pick up a key, sign for it, and keep it until you're finished with it. Something like that."

"You know if Highhawk had a key?"

"I'd guess so," Chee said. "He was a conservator. He would have been working with this stuff all the time."

Leaphorn put his forefinger on a hook which had been screwed into the doorjamb. "I'd been wondering what this was for," he said. "I'd guess it was where Highhawk hung his key."

No key hung there now, but the white paint below the hook was discolored with years of finger marks.

"Let's go look around," Rodney said. He got up.

"He took it when he left," Chee said. "And before we go looking, why not make a telephone call first? Call maintenance, or whoever might know, and ask them if they found anything unusual this morning."

Rodney paused at the doorway, looking interested. "Like what?"

Chee noticed that Leaphorn was looking at him, smiling slightly.

"Chee's a pessimist," Leaphorn said. "He thinks somebody killed Highhawk. If somebody did, it would be tough to drag him out of the building—even with the guard dead. Not many people around at night in here, I'd guess, but it would only take one to see you."

Rodney still looked puzzled. "So?"

"So this place is jammed with bins and boxes and cases and containers where you could hide a body. But they're probably all full of things already. So the killer empties one out, puts in the body, and then he relocks it. But now he's stuck with whatever came out of the bin. So he looks for a place and dumps it somewhere."

Rodney picked up the telephone again. He dialed, identified himself, and said: "Give me the museum security office, please." Judging from the Rodney end of the conversation, Museum Security had no useful information. The call was transferred to maintenance. Chee found himself watching Leaphorn, thinking how quickly his mind had worked. Leaphorn was still standing beside the open door and as Chee watched, he shifted his weight from one foot to the other, grimacing slightly. He was wearing black wing-tip shoes burnished to a high gloss. Leaphorn's feet, as was true of Chee's, would be accustomed to boots and more breathing space. Chee guessed Leaphorn's hurt and that made him conscious of the comfort of his own feet, at home in the familiar boots. He felt slightly superior. It served Leaphorn right for trying to look like an Easterner.

"A what?" Rodney was saying. "Where did they find it?" He listened. "How large is it?" Listened again. "Where did it come from?" Listened. "Okay. We'll check. Thanks." He hung up, looked at Chee.

"They found a fish trap," he said. "Thing's made out of split bamboo by somebody-or-other. They said it had just sort of been pushed up into a passage between two stacks of containers."

"How big?" Leaphorn asked.

Rodney was dialing the telephone again. He glanced up at Leaphorn and said: "Big as a body."

18

FIRST, LEROY FLECK called his brother. It was something he rarely did. Delmar Fleck had made it very clear that he couldn't afford to have contacts with a convict—particularly one known to be his relative. Delmar's wife answered the telephone. She didn't recognize his voice and Leroy didn't identify himself to her because if he did, he was pretty sure she would hang up on him.

"Yeah," Delmar said and Leroy got right to the point.

"It's me. Leroy. And I got to have some help with Mama. They're kicking her out of the home here in the District and the one I found to move her into wants more advance money down than I can handle."

"I told you not to call me," Delmar said.

"I just got to have some help," Leroy said. "I was supposed to get a payment today, but something held it up. Ten thousand dollars. When I get it next week, I'll pay you right back."

"We been over this before," Delmar said. "I don't make hardly anything at the car lot, and Faye Lynn just gets tips at the beauty shop."

"If you could just send me two thousand dollars I could come up with the rest. Then next week I'll send it back to you. Western Union." Next week would take care of itself. He would think of something by then. Elkins would have another job for him. Elkins always had jobs for him. And until Elkins came through with something bigger, he'd just have to go on the prowl for a few days.

"No blood in this turnip," Delmar said. "It's already squeezed. I couldn't raise two thousand dollars if my life depended on it. We got two car payments, and rent, and the credit card, and medical insurance and—"

"Delmar. Delmar. I just got to have some help. Can you borrow something? Just for a week or so?"

"We been all over this. The government takes care of people like Mama. Let the government do it."

"I used to think that, too," Leroy said. "But they don't actually do it. There's no program for people like Mama." Silence on the other end. "And, Delmar, you need to find a way to come and visit with her. It's been years and she's asking about you all the time. She told me she thought the Arabs had you a hostage somewhere. She thinks that to keep her feelings from being hurt. Her mind's not what it used to be. Sometimes she don't even recognize me."

There was still only silence. Then he heard Delmar's voice, sounding a long ways off, talking to someone. Then he heard a laugh.

"Delmar!" he shouted. "Delmar!"

"Sorry," Delmar said. "We got company. But that's my advice. Just call social services. I'd help you if I could, but I'm pressed myself. Got to cut it off now."

And he cut it off, leaving Fleck standing at the telephone booth. He looked at the telephone, fighting down first the despair and then the anger, trying to think of who else he could call. But there wasn't anyone.

Fleck kept his reserve money in a child's plastic purse tucked under the spare tire in the trunk of his old Chevy—a secure enough place in a society where thieves were not attracted to dented 1976 sedans. He fished it out now, and headed across town toward the nursing home, counting it while he waited for red lights to turn green.

He counted three hundreds, twenty-two fifties, eleven twenties, and forty-one tens. With what he had in his billfold it added up to $2,033. He'd see what he could do with that with the Fat Man at the rest home. He didn't like going back there like this. It sure as hell wasn't the way he had it planned, or would plan anything for that matter. He normally would have been smart enough not to make an enemy of a man when you were going to have to ask him a favor. But maybe a combination of paying him and scaring him would work for a little while. Until he could pull something off. He could make a hit out at National Airport. In the men's room. The blade and then off with the billfold. People going on planes always carried money. It would be risky. But he could see no choice. He'd try that, and then work on the tourists around the Capitol Building. That was risky, too. In fact, both places scared him. But he had made up his mind. He would fix something up with the Fat Man to buy a little time and then start collecting enough to get Mama someplace safe and decent.

The Fat Man wasn't in.

"He went out to get something. Down to the Seven-Eleven, I think he said," the receptionist told him. "Why don't you just come on back later in the day? Or maybe you better call first." She was looking at the little sack Fleck was carrying, looking suspicious, as if it was some sort of dope. Actually it was red licorice. Mama liked the stuff and Fleck always brought her a supply. The receptionist was some kind of Hispanic—probably Puerto Rican, Fleck guessed. And she looked nervous as well as suspicious while she talked to him. That made Fleck nervous. Maybe she would call the police. Maybe she had heard something the last time he was here when he told the Fat Man he would kill him if he didn't hold onto Mama until he could find her another place. But he hadn't seen her that day, and he'd kept his voice low when he explained things to the fat bastard. Maybe she was around somewhere listening. Maybe she wasn't. There was nothing he could do about it. He didn't have any options left.

"I'll just go on back there to the parlor and visit with Mama until he gets back," Fleck said.

"Oh, she's not there any more," the receptionist said. "She fights with the other ladies all the time. And she hurt poor old Mrs. Endicott again. Twisted her arm."

Fleck didn't want to hear any more of that kind of talk. He hurried down the hallway to Mama's room.

Mama was sitting in her wheelchair looking at the little TV Fleck had bought for her, watching some soap opera which Fleck thought might be "The Young and the Restless." They had her tied in the chair, as they did all the old people, and it touched Fleck to see her that way. She was so helpless now. Mama had never been helpless until she'd had those strokes. Mama had always been in charge before then. It made Fleck unhappy when he came to see her. It filled him with a kind of dreary sorrow and made him wish he could get far enough ahead so that he could afford a place somewhere and take care of her himself. And he always started trying to think again how he could do it. But there was simply no way. The way Mama was, he would have to be with her all the time. He couldn't just go off and leave her tied in that chair. And that wouldn't leave him with any way to make a living for them.

Mama glanced at him when he came through the door. Then

she looked back at her television program. She didn't say anything.

"Hello," Fleck said. "How are you feeling today?"

Mama didn't look up.

"I brought you some licorice, Mama," Fleck said. He held out the sack.

"Put it down on the bed there," Mama said. Sometimes Mama spoke normally, but sometimes it took her a while to form the words—a matter of pitting indomitable will against a recalcitrant, stroke-damaged nervous system. Fleck waited, remembering. He remembered the way Mama used to talk. He remembered the way Mama used to be. Then she would have made short work of the Fat Man.

"You doing all right today, Mama?" he asked. "Anything I can do for you?"

Mama still didn't look at him. She stared at the set, where a woman was shouting at a well-dressed man in poorly feigned anger. "I was," Mama said, finally. "People keep coming in and bothering me."

"I guess I could put a stop to that," Fleck said.

Mama turned then and looked at him, her eyes absolutely without expression. It occurred to him that maybe it was him she meant. He studied her, wondering if she recognized him. If she did, there was no sign of it. She rarely did in recent years. Well, he would stay and visit anyway. Just keep her company. All her life, as far back as Fleck could remember into his childhood, Mama had had pitifully little of that.

"That girl there's got on a pretty dress," Fleck said. "I mean the one on TV."

Mama ignored him. Poor woman, Fleck thought. Poor, pathetic old woman. He stood beside the open door, examining her profile. She had been a good-sized woman once—maybe 140 pounds or so. Strong and quick and smart as they come. Now she was skinny as a rail and stuck in that wheelchair. She couldn't hardly talk and her mind was not working well.

"How about me giving you a push?" Fleck asked. "Would you like to go for a ride? It's raining outside but I could push you around inside the building. Give you a little change."

Mama still stared at the TV. The angry woman on "The Young and the Restless" had left, slamming the door behind her. Now the man was talking on the telephone. Mama hitched herself forward in the chair. "I had a boy once who had a four-door Buick," she said in a clear voice that sounded surprisingly young. "Dark blue and that velvety upholstery on the seats. He took me to Memphis in that."

"That would have been Delmar's car," Fleck said. "It was a nice one." Mama had talked of it before but Fleck had never seen it. Delmar must have bought it while Fleck was doing his time in Joliet.

"Delmar is his name, all right," Mama said. "The A-rabs got him hostage in Jerusalem or someplace. Otherwise he'd come to see me, Delmar would. He'd take care of me right. He was all man, that one was."

"I know he would," Fleck said. "Delmar is a good man."

"Delmar was all man," Mama said, still staring at the TV set. "He wouldn't let nobody treat him like a nigger. Do Delmar and he'd get you right back. He'd make you respect him. You can count on that. That's one thing you always got to do, is get even. If you don't do that they treat you like a goddamn animal. Step right on your neck. Delmar wouldn't let anybody not treat him right."

"No Mama, he wouldn't," Fleck said. Actually, as he remembered it, Delmar wasn't much for fighting. He was for keeping out of the way of trouble.

Mama looked at him, eyes hostile. "You talk like you know Delmar."

"Yes Mama. I do. I'm Leroy. I'm Delmar's brother."

Mama snorted. "No you ain't. Delmar only had one brother. He ended up a damn jailbird."

The room smelled stale to Leroy. He smelled something that might have been spoiled food, and dust and the acidic odor of dried urine. Poor old lady, he thought. He blinked, rubbed the back of his hand across his eyes.

"I think it would be nice for you to get out in the halls at least. Get out of this room a little bit. See something different just for a change."

"I wouldn't be in here at all if the A-rabs hadn't got to Delmar. He'd have me someplace nice."

"I know he would," Fleck said. "I know he'd come to visit you if he could."

"I had two boys, actually," Mama said. "But the other one he turned out jailbird. Never amounted to shit."

It was just then that Leroy Fleck heard the cop. He couldn't make out the words but he recognized the tone. He strained to listen.

But Mama was still talking. "They said that one turned fairy up there in the prison. He let them use him like a girl."

Leroy Fleck leaned out into the hallway, partly to see if the voice which sounded like a cop really was a cop. It was. He was standing beside the receptionist and she was pointing down the hall. She was pointing right at Leroy Fleck.

Elkins had always told him he was naturally fast. He could think fast and he could move like lightning. "It's partly in your mind, and it's partly in your reflexes," Elkins had told him. "We can get your muscles built up, build up your strength, by pumping iron. But anybody can do that. That quickness, that's something you gotta be born with. That's where you got the edge if you know how to use it."

He used it now. He knew instantly that he could not let himself be arrested. Absolutely not. Maybe he'd come clear on the Santillanes affair. Probably not. Why else were those two Indian-looking cops dogging him? But even if they didn't make him on that one, as soon as they matched his prints, they'd make him on something else. He'd worked for Elkins on too many jobs, and been on the prowl in too many airports and nightclubs, to ever let himself be arrested. He'd survived only by being careful not to be. But now the Fat Man, that fat bastard, had put an end to that. He'd have to get even with the Fat Man. But there was no time to think of that now. Within what was left of the same second, Fleck had decided how he would talk his way out of this. It would help that the Fat Man wasn't here to press his case. The receptionist apparently had orders to call the law anytime he showed up, but she was minimum-wage help. She wouldn't care what happened next.

Fleck moved back into the room and sat on the bed. "Mama," he said softly, "you're going to have some more company in just a minute. It's a policeman. I want to ask you to just keep calm and be polite."

"Policeman," Mama said. She spit on the floor by the television set.

"It's important to me, Mama," Fleck said. "It's awful important."

And then the policeman was at the door, looking in.

"You Dick Pfaff?"

It took Fleck the blink of an eye to remember that was the name he'd used when he'd checked Mama in here.

Fleck stood. "Yes sir," he said. "And this here is my Mama."

The policeman was young. He had smooth, pale skin and a close-cropped blond mustache. He nodded to Mama. She stared at him. Where was his partner? Fleck wondered. He would be the old hand on this team. If Fleck was lucky, the partner would be resting out in the patrol car, letting the rookie handle this pissant, nothing little complaint. If they thought there was any risk at all of it being serious they would both be in here. In fact, Fleck suspected the police rules probably required it. Somebody was goofing off.

"We have a complaint that you caused a disturbance here," the policeman said. "We have a statement that you threatened to kill the manager."

Fleck produced a self-deprecatory laugh. "I'm ashamed of that. That's the main reason I came today—to apologize for the way I behaved." As he said it, Fleck became aware that Mama was no longer watching the television set. Mama was watching him.

"That's a pretty serious offense," the officer said. "Telling a man you're going to kill him."

"I doubt if I really quite said that," Fleck said. "But you notice how it smells in here? My Mama here, she hadn't been properly cleaned up. She had bedsores and all that and I just lost my temper. I had told him about it before."

Clearly the policeman was aware of the smell. Fleck could tell from his face that he'd switched from cautiously hostile to slightly sympathetic.

"If he's got back yet, I'll go out there and apologize to him. I'm sorry for whatever I said. Just got sore about the way they was treating Mama here."

The policeman nodded. "I don't think he's here anyway," he said. "That woman said he was off somewhere. I'll just check you for weapons." He grinned at Fleck. "If you didn't come in here armed, I'd say it's a pretty good argument on your side since he's about four times your size."

"Yes sir," Fleck said. He resisted the prison-learned instinct to spread his legs and raise his arms. The cop would never find his shank, which was in the slot he'd made for it inside his boot, but getting into the shakedown stance would tip off even this rookie that he was dealing with an ex-con.

"What do you want me to do?" Fleck asked.

"Just turn around. And then lock your hands over the back of your neck," the policeman said.

"Get down—" Mama began. Then it broke off into a sort of incoherent stammer. But she kept trying to talk and Fleck looked away from the policeman and looked at her instead. Her face was filled with an expression of such fierce contempt that it took Leroy Fleck back to his childhood.

"—and lick his goddamn shoes," Mama said.

He had made his decision even before she forced it out. "Now, Mama," he said, and bending down, he slid the blade out of his boot into his palm. He gripped it flat-side horizontal and as he stepped toward the policeman he was saying: "Mama had a stroke—" and with the word "stroke" the blade was driving through the uniform shirt.

It sank between the policeman's ribs with the full force of Fleck's weightlifter muscles behind it. And there, in that terribly vulnerable territory Elkins had called "behind the bone," Fleck's weightlifter's wrist flicked it, and flicked it and flicked it. Cutting artery. Cutting heart. The officer's mouth opened, showing white, even teeth below the yellow mustache. He made a kind of a sound, but not very loud because the shock was already killing him. It was hardly audible above the shouting that was going on in "The Young and the Restless."

Fleck released the knife handle, grabbed the policeman's shoulders, and lowered him to his knees. He removed the knife and wiped it on the uniform shirt. (If you do it all properly, Elkins would say, the bleeding is mostly inside. No blood all over you.) Then Fleck let the body slide to the floor. Face down. He put the knife back in his boot and turned toward Mama. He intended to say something but he didn't know what. His mind wasn't working right.

Mama was looking at the policeman, then she looked up at him. Her mouth was partly open, working as if she was trying to say something. Nothing came out but a sort of an odd sound. A squeaking sound. It occurred to him that Mama was afraid. Afraid of him.

"Mama," Leroy Fleck said. "I got even. Did you see that? I didn't let him step on me. I didn't kiss any boot."

He waited. Not long but more time than he could afford under the circumstances, waiting for Mama to win her struggle to form words. But no words came and Fleck could read absolutely nothing in her eyes except fear. He walked out the door without a glance toward the reception desk, and down the narrow hallway toward the rear exit, and out into the cold, gray rain.

19

MUSEUM SECURITY had located Dr. Hartman, and Dr. Hartman had located possible sources of the fish trap. It was a matter of deciding in what part of the world the trap had originated (obviously in a place which produced both bamboo and good-sized fish) and then knowing how to retrieve data from the museum's computerized inventory system. The computer gave them thirty-seven possible bamboo fish traps of appropriate antiquity. Dr. Hartman knew almost nothing about fish and almost everything about primitive construction methods and quite a bit about botany. Thus she was able to organize the hunt.

She pushed her chair back from the computer terminal, and her hair back from her forehead.

"I'm going to say this Palawan Island tribe is the best bet, and then we should check, I'd say, this coastal Borneo collection, and then probably Java. If none of those collections is missing a fish trap, then it's back to the drawing board. That must be a Smithsonian fish trap and if it is then we can find out where it was stored."

She led them down the hallway, a party of five now with the addition of a tired-looking museum security man. With Hartman and Rodney leading the way, they hurried past what seemed to Leaphorn a wilderness of branch corridors all lined with an infinity of locked containers stacked high above head level. They turned right and left and left again and stopped, while Hartman unlocked a door. Above his head, Leaphorn noticed what looked like, but surely wasn't, one of those carved stone caskets in which ancient Egyptians interred their very important corpses. It was covered with a sheet of heavy plastic, once transparent but now rendered translucent with years of dust.

"I have a thing with locks," Dr. Hartman was saying. "They never want to open for me."

Leaphorn considered whether it would be bad manners to lift the plastic for a peek. He noticed Chee was looking too.

"Looks like one of those Egyptian mummy cases," Leaphorn said. "What do you call 'em? But they wouldn't have a mummy here."

"I think it is," Chee said, and lifted the sheet. "Yeah, a mummy coffin." His expression registered distaste. "I can't think of the name either."

Dr. Hartman had solved the lock. "In here," she said, and ushered them into a huge, gloomy room occupied by row after row of floor-to-ceiling metal shelving racks. As far as Leaphorn could see in every direction every foot of shelf space seemed occupied by something—mostly by what appeared to be locked canisters.

Dr. Hartman examined her list of possible fish trap locations, then walked briskly down the central corridor, checking row numbers.

"Row eleven," she said, and did an abrupt left turn. She stopped a third of the way down and checked bin numbers.

"Okay, here we are," she said, and inserted her key in the lock.

"I think I had better handle that," Rodney said, holding his hand out for the key. "And this is the time to remind everyone that we may be interested in fingerprints in here. So don't be touching things."

Rodney unlocked the container. He pulled open the door. It was jammed with odds and ends, the biggest of which was a bamboo device even larger than the fish trap found by the janitor. It occupied most of the bin, with the remaining space filled with what seemed to be a seining net and other such paraphernalia.

"No luck here," Rodney said. He closed and locked the door. "On to, where was it? Borneo?"

"I'm having trouble with making this seem real," Dr. Hartman said. "Do you really think someone killed Henry and left his body in here?"

"No," Rodney said. "Not really. But he's missing. And a guard's been killed. And a fish trap was located out of place. So it's prudent to look. Especially since we don't know where else to look."

The Borneo fisherman's bin, Dr. Hartman's second choice, happened to be only two aisles away.

Rodney unlocked it, pulled open the door.

They looked at the top of a human head.

Leaphorn heard Dr. Hartman gasp and Jim Chee suck in his breath. Rodney leaned forward, felt the man's neck, stepped aside to give Chee a better view. "Is this Highhawk?"

Chee leaned forward. "That's him."

Some of the homicide forensic crew was still out at the Twelfth Street entrance and got there fast. So did the homicide sergeant who'd been working the Alice Yoakum affair. Rodney gave him the victim's identification. He explained about the fish trap and how they had found the body. Dr. Hartman left, looking pale and shaken. Chee and Leaphorn remained. They stood back, away from the activity, trying to keep out of the way. Photographs were taken. Measurements were made. The rigid body of Henry Highhawk was lifted out of the bin and onto a stretcher.

Leaphorn noticed the long hair tied into a Navajo-style bun, he noticed the narrow face, sensitive even in the distortion of death. He noticed the dark mark above the eye which must be a bullet hole and the smear of blood which had emerged from it. He noticed the metal brace supporting the leg, and the shoe lift lengthening it. Here was the man whose name was scrawled on a note in a terrorist's pocket. The man who had drawn a second terrorist all the way to Arizona, if Leaphorn was guessing correctly, to a curing ceremonial at the Agnes Tsosie place. Here was a white man who wanted to be an Indian—specifically to be a Navajo. A man who dug up the bones of whites to protest whites digging up Indian bones. A man important enough to be killed at what certainly must have been a terrible risk to the man who killed him. Leaphorn looked into Highhawk's upturned face as it went past him on the police stretcher. What made you so important? Leaphorn wondered. What made Mr. Santillanes polish his pointed shoes and pack his bags and come west to New Mexico looking for you? What were you planning that drew someone with a pistol into this dusty place to execute you? And if you could hear my questions, if you could speak, would you even know the answer yourself? The body was past now, disappearing down the corridor. Leaphorn glanced at Chee. Chee looked stricken.

Chee had found himself simultaneously watching what had been Henry Highhawk emerge from the container and watching his own reaction to what he was seeing. He had been a policeman long enough to have conditioned himself to death. He had handled an old woman frozen in her hogan, a teenaged boy who had hanged himself in the restroom at his boarding school, a child backed over by a pickup truck driven by her mother. He had been investigating officer of so many victims of alcohol that he no longer tried to keep them sorted out in his memory. But he had never been involved with the death of someone he'd known personally, someone who interested him, someone he'd been talking to only a matter of minutes before he died. He had rationalized his Navajo conditioning to avoid the dead, but he hadn't eliminated the ingrained knowledge that while the body died, the *chindi* lingered to cause ghost sickness and evil dreams. Highhawk's *chindi* would now haunt this museum's corridors. It would haunt Jim Chee as well.

Rodney had been inspecting the items removed from the container where Highhawk's body had rested. He held up a flat, black box with something round connected to it by wires. "This looks a little modern for a Borneo fishing village," he said, showing the box to all of them. The box was a miniature Panasonic cassette tape recorder.

"I think it's Highhawk's tape recorder," Chee said. "He had one just like that when he was at Agnes Tsosie's place. And I saw it again in the office at his place." Chee could see now that the tape recorder was wired to one of those small, battery-operated watches. It was much like the nine-dollar-and-ninety-nine-cent model he was wearing except it used hands instead of digital numbers.

"I think it's wired to turn on the recorder," Leaphorn said. "Possibly that's what Highhawk was talking about on that telephone call. Getting that thing fixed."

Rodney inspected it carefully. He laughed. "If it was, it wasn't fixed very well," he said. "If Highhawk did this he doesn't know any more about electricity than my wife. And she thinks it leaks out of the telephone." He unwound the wires and removed the watch. Holding it carefully by the edges he opened the recorder and popped out the miniature tape. He weighed it in his hand, examined it, and put it back in the machine. "Let's see what we have on this," he said. "But first, let's see what else we have in this container."

Rodney sorted gingerly among the fish nets, bamboo fish spears, canoe paddles, clothing, and assorted items that Chee couldn't identify. Pressed against the side of the bin, partly obscured by folded twine of fish netting, was something white. It looked like leather. In fact, to Chee it looked like it might be a *yei* mask.

"I guess that's it," Rodney said. "Except your team will come along and do a proper search and find the murder weapon in there, and the killer's photograph, fingerprints, and maybe his business card."

"We'll catch that later," the sergeant said. "We'll get somebody from the museum who knows what's supposed to be in there and what isn't."

Chee leaned past Rodney and turned the white leather between his fingers. The mask of Talking God stared up at him. "This is the mask Highhawk had been working on," Chee said. "Or one of them."

The sergeant retrieved it, turned it over in his hands, examined it. "What'd you say it was?" he asked Chee, and handed it to him.

"It's the Yeibichai mask. A Navajo religious mask. Highhawk was working on this one, or one just like it, for that mask display downstairs."

"Oh," the sergeant said, his curiosity satisfied and his interest exhausted. "Let's get this over with."

They followed Highhawk's body into the bright fluorescent lighting of the conservancy laboratory. When the sergeant finished whatever he wanted to do with him, Henry Highhawk would go from there to the morgue. Now the cause of death seemed apparent. The blackened round mark of what must be a bullet hole was apparent above the left eye. From it a streak of dried blood discolored the side of Highhawk's face.

The sergeant went through Highhawk's pockets, spreading the contents on a laboratory table. Wallet, pocketknife, a half-used roll of Tums, three quarters, two dimes, a penny, a key ring bearing six keys, a crumpled handkerchief, a business card from a plumbing company, a small frog fetish carved out of a basaltic rock.

"What the hell is this?" the sergeant said, pushing the frog with his finger.

"It's a frog fetish," Leaphorn said.

The sergeant had not been happy to have two strangers and Rodney standing around while he worked. The sergeant had the responsibility, but obviously Rodney had the rank.

"What the hell is a frog fetish?" the sergeant asked.

"It's connected with the Navajo religion," Leaphorn said. "Highhawk was part Navajo. He had a Navajo grandmother. He was interested in the culture."

The sergeant nodded. He looked slightly less hostile.

"No bin key?" Chee asked.

The sergeant looked at him. "Bin key?"

"When he left his office last night, he took the key that unlocks all these bins off a hook beside his door and put it in his pocket," Chee said. "It was on a little plain steel ring." The killer probably had taken Highhawk's key to open the bin and to relock it. Unless of course the killer was another museum employee with his (or her) own key.

"You saw him put the key in his pocket?"

Chee nodded. "He took it off the hook. He put it in his right front pants pocket."

"No such key in his pocket," the sergeant said. "What you see here is everything he had on him. From the car keys he was carrying, it looks like he was driving a Ford. You know about that? You know the license number?"

"There was a Ford Mustang parked in the driveway by his house. I'd say about five or six years old. I didn't notice the license. And I don't know if it was his," Chee said.

"We'll get it from Motor Vehicle Division. It's probably parked somewhere close to here."

Rodney put the tape recorder beside Highhawk's possessions on the laboratory table. "I unwired the recorder from the watch. Just in case," he said. "You want to hear it?"

He removed a pencil from his inside coat pocket, held it over the PLAY key, and glanced up at the sergeant, awaiting a response.

The sergeant nodded. "Sure."

The first sounds Chee heard sent him back into boyhood, into the winter hogan of Frank Sam Nakai on the west slope of the Chuska Mountains. Bitter cold outside, the cast-iron wood stove under the smoke hole glowing with heat. Frank Sam Nakai, brother of his mother, teaching the children how the Holy People saved the Holy Boy and his sister from the lightning sickness. His uncle sitting on the sheepskin, legs crossed, head back against the blanket hung against the log wall, eyes closed, singing. At first, the voice so low that Cousin Emmett and little Shirley and Chee would have to lean forward to hear them:

"Huu tu tu. Huu tu tu," Frank Sam Nakai would sing, the sound of night birds, the sound of Talking God summoning the *yei* to attend to the affair at hand. And the voice rising: *"Ohohoho, hehehe heya haya—"* The sound of his fellow spirits answering. And by now the children would know that these were not words in any human language. They were the words of the gods.

From the tiny speaker of the tiny recorder Chee was hearing

the same chant. Talking God summoning the *yei* to the Naakhai ceremony on the final night of the Yeibichai, calling them for the ritual which would heal Mrs. Agnes Tsosie and restore her to harmony. Not cure her, because Agnes Tsosie was dying of liver cancer. But heal her, return her to *hozro,* to harmony with her fate. As he listened, Chee became aware that Henry Highhawk had been recording a long time before Chee had caught him at it. Chee remembered the moment. Highhawk had been standing beside one of the rows of bonfires which lined the dance ground. Through the chant Chee heard the crackle of burning sage and piñon, and the startled exclamation of a woman who had suddenly found her blanket smoldering from a spark. And then came the voices of Water Sprinkler, and the male *yeis,* forming sounds which—being the sounds gods make—would not produce any meaning mere humans could understand.

Chee noticed that both Rodney and the sergeant were looking at him, awaiting an explanation.

"It's chanting from the Yeibichai," Chee said. "The Night Chant." That, obviously, explained nothing. "Highhawk was at this ceremonial the night I arrested him," Chee said. "He was recording it."

As he said it, the sound of the chanting was replaced by the voice of Henry Highhawk.

"The song you have been hearing is the beginning of one of hundreds of songs which make up the poetry of a Navajo curing ceremony," the voice of Highhawk said. "White people call it the Night Chant. Navajos call it the Yeibichai—or Talking God. Talking God is one of the powerful supernatural spirits of that great tribe, one of the connections between the Navajo and the great all-powerful Creating God. We could compare him with the figure of the Archangel Raphael in Jewish/Christian creation mythology."

There was silence. Chee glanced up. Rodney said: "Well, now—" and then Highhawk's voice resumed:

"I, I being Talking God, ask you who have come to look at this display of masks to look around you in this exhibition, and throughout this museum. Do you see a display of the masks of the gods of the Christian, or of the Jew, or of Islam, or of any other culture strong enough to defend its faith and to punish such a desecration? Where is the representation of the Great God Jehovah who led the Jews out of their bondage in Egypt, or the Mask of Michael the Archangel, or the Mother of the Christian God we call

Jesus Christ, or a personification of Jesus himself? You do not see them here. You have here in a storage room of this museum the Tano Pueblo's representation of one of its holy Twin War Gods. But where is a consecrated Sacred Host from the Roman Catholic cathedral? You will not find it here. Here you see the gods of conquered people displayed like exotic animals in the public zoo. Only the overthrown and captured gods are here. Here you see the sacred things torn from the temples of Inca worshippers, stolen from the holy kivas of the Pueblo people, sacred icons looted from burned tepee villages on the buffalo plains."

Highhawk's voice had become higher, almost shrill. It was interrupted by the sound of a great intake of breath. Then a moment of silence. The ambulance crew picked up Highhawk's stretcher and moved out—leaving only his voice behind. The forensic crew sorted his possessions into evidence bags.

"Do you doubt what I say?" Highhawk's voice resumed. "Do you doubt that your privileged race, which claims such gentility, such humanity, would do this? Above your head, lining the halls and corridors of this very building, are thousands of cases and bins and boxes. In them you find the bones of more than eighteen thousand of your fellow humans. You will find the skeletons of children, of mothers, of grandfathers. They have been dug out of the burials where their mourning relatives placed them, reuniting them with their Great Mother Earth. They remain in great piles and stacks, respected no more than the bones of apes and . . ."

Rodney hit the OFF button and looked around him in the resulting silence.

"What do you think? He was going to broadcast this somehow with that mask display he was working on? Was that the plan?"

"Probably," Chee said. "He seems to be speaking to the audience at the exhibition. Let's hear the rest of it."

"Why not?" Rodney said. "But let's get out of here. Down to Highhawk's office where I can use the telephone."

The items from Highhawk's pockets were in evidence bags now, except for the recorder.

"I've got to get moving," the sergeant said. "I still have some work to do on the Alice Yoakum thing."

"I'll bring in the recorder," Rodney said. "I'll clean up here."

"I'll need to talk to—" The sergeant hesitated, searching for the name. "To Mr. Chee here, and Mr. Leaphorn. I'll need to get their statements on the record."

"Whenever you say," Leaphorn said.

"I'll bring them in," Rodney said.

In Highhawk's office, Rodney put the recorder on the desk top and pushed the PLAY button. Rodney, too, was anxious to hear the rest of it.

"—antelopes. Their children have asked that these bones be returned so that they can again be reunited with their Mother Earth with respect and dignity. What does the museum tell us? It tells us that its anthropologists need our ancestral bones for scientific studies. Why doesn't it need the ancestral bones of white Americans for these studies? Why doesn't it dig up your graves? Think of it! Eighteen thousand human skeletons! Eighteen thousand! Ladies and gentlemen, what would you say if the museum looted your cemeteries, if it dug up the consecrated ground of your graveyards in Indianapolis and Topeka and White Plains and hauled the skeletons of your loved ones here to molder in boxes and bins in the hallways? Think about this! Think about the graves of your grandmothers. Help us recover the bones of our own ancestors so that they may again be reunited with their Mother Earth."

Silence. The tape ran its brief miniature-recorder course and clicked off. Rodney pushed the REWIND button. He looked at Chee. "Quite an argument."

Chee nodded. "Of course there's another side to it. An earlier generation of anthropologists dug up most of those bones. And the museum has given a few of them back. I think it sent sixteen skeletons to the Blackfoot Tribe awhile ago, and it says it will return bones if they were stolen from regular cemeteries or if you can prove a family connection."

Rodney laughed. "Get those skeletons in the lineup," he said. "Get the kinfolks in and see if they can pick their grannie out from somebody's auntie." About a millisecond before he ended that jest, Rodney's expression shifted from amused to abashed. In the present company, maybe this was no laughing matter. "Sorry," Rodney said. "I wasn't thinking."

Now Chee looked amused. "We Navajos aren't into this corpse fetish business," he said. "Our metaphysics turns on life, the living. The dead we put behind us. We avoid old bones. You won't find Navajos asking for the return of their stolen skeletons."

It was now Leaphorn's turn to look amused. "As a matter of fact, we are. The Navajo Tribe is asking the museum to send us our skeletons, if the museum has any of them. I think somebody in the tribal bureaucracy decided it was a chance to make a political point. A little one-upmanship on Washington."

"Any reason to hear this again?" Rodney asked. He slipped the recorder into an evidence bag, sealed it, leaned heavily against the edge of the table, and sighed. He looked tired, Chee thought, and unhappy.

"I don't enjoy being involved in things I don't understand," Rodney said. "I don't have the slightest goddamn idea why somebody killed this Highhawk bird, or whether it ties in with that guard being killed, or whether this tape has a damned thing to do with anything. That tape sounds like the Smithsonian Museum might have a motive to knock him off." Rodney rubbed the back of a hand across his forehead and made a wry face. "But I gather that museums tend to wait until you're dead and then go after your skeleton. So I'd guess that tape doesn't have much to do with this. And—"

"I'd guess it does," Chee said.

Leaphorn studied him. He nodded, agreeing. "How?"

"I haven't thought it through," Chee said. "But think about it a minute. Highhawk goes to a lot of trouble to get to that Yeibichai to make this tape." He glanced at Leaphorn. "He wrote to Old Lady Tsosie, didn't he? He'd have to find a way to run down her address."

"She was in that big Navajo Reservation article *National Geographic* ran," Leaphorn said. "That's where he got her name."

"Then he goes all the way out there from Washington, and finds out how to find Lower Greasewood, and the Tsosie place, dreams up that bullshit story about wanting to be a Navajo, and—"

"Maybe not bullshit," Leaphorn said. "From what you told me about him."

"No," Chee said, thoughtfully, "I think maybe not. I think now that might have been part of the genuine Highhawk package. But anyway, it involved a lot of trouble. He must have written that oration he gave we just heard, and then got it dubbed in on the tape. Now why? What's he going to do with it? I think it's obvious he was planting it in that mask exhibit, in his Talking God exhibit. The tape practically says that. And Highhawk has a track record of knowing how to get publicity. The kind to put the heat on the Smithsonian. That tape was sure well designed to do that. Zany enough to make the front page."

"Yeah," Rodney said. "The Talking God actually talking."

"Did he have it with him when he left you in his office?" Leaphorn asked.

"He had a cardboard box. About three times the size of a

shoebox. Anyway, it was big enough for the mask and all. He picked it up just as he was leaving."

"And that tells us what?" Rodney asked. He shook his head, thinking about it.

Silence in the room. Rodney now slouched in Highhawk's swivel chair; Chee leaning against the wall in the practiced slouch of a man who had done a lot of leaning against things, a lot of waiting for his age; Joe Leaphorn sitting on the edge of the desk, looking uncomfortable in his three-piece suit, his gray, burr-cut head bowed slightly forward, his expression that of a man who is listening to sounds inside his own head. The quiet air around them smelled of dust and, faintly, of decay.

"Officer Chee here, he and I, we have a problem," Leaphorn said—half to Rodney and half to the desk. "We are like two dogs who followed two different sets of tracks to the same brush pile. One dog thinks there's a rabbit under the brush, the other thinks it's a bobcat. Same brush pile, different information." He glanced at Chee. "Right?"

Chee nodded.

"As for my end of it, I see the body of a worn-out, toothless man who keeps his old shoes polished. His body is under a chamisa bush in New Mexico. And in the shirt pocket is a note mentioning Agnes Tsosie's Yeibichai ceremony. When I get out to Agnes Tsosie's place, I run into the name of Henry Highhawk. He's coming out. I follow those pointed shoes back to Washington and I find a little den of Chilean terrorists—or, maybe more accurately, the victims of Chilean terror. And right in the next apartment to this den is a little man with red hair and freckles and the torso of a weightlifter who just happens to fit the description of the guy who probably killed Pointed Shoes with his knife. But I've come to a dead end. Good idea who killed my man, now. I think that surely the man's widow, his family, they'll tell me why. No such luck. Instead of that, they act like they never heard of him."

Leaphorn sighed, tapped his fingers on the desk top, and continued without a glance at either of his listeners. "I get a make on Mr. Pointed Shoes' identity from the FBI. It turns out he's one of the big ones in one of the factions that's sort of at war with the right-wing government in Chile. Turns out the ins have already killed one of his bunch earlier. So now the mystery is solved. I know who Pointed Shoes is. His name is Santillanes. I know who killed him—or I think I do—and I think I know why. But now I've got a new problem. Why were Santillanes' kinfolks acting that way? It looked like they didn't want anyone to know the man had been killed."

Leaphorn's droning voice stopped for several seconds. "Now why in the world would that be?" he said. He was frowning. He shook his head, looked at Rodney and Chee. "Either one of you want to break in here?"

Neither one did.

"So," Leaphorn said. "So, I'm almost to the brush pile. Now my question is what the hell is going on here? And for some reason I can't get Highhawk out of my head. He doesn't seem to fit anywhere. I think I know how Santillanes found out he should go to the Navajo Reservation to find Highhawk. But I don't understand why."

Leaphorn paused again, looked at Chee. "Do you know about this? Right after Highhawk pulled that business of digging up the graves and mailing the bones to the museum, he got the big splash of publicity he wanted. But before anybody could serve a warrant on him, he had dropped out of sight. All his friends and his neighbors could tell anybody looking for him that he was going to Arizona to attend a Yeibichai ceremonial for some relative named Agnes Tsosie. I think Santillanes probably read about his exploits in the paper and went looking for him about the same time the police did. Santillanes got the word that Henry was heading west for the Yeibichai. But he didn't know it was a month in the future."

Leaphorn stopped again, inhaled hugely, exhaled, drummed his fingers against the desk top, thinking. Rodney made a sentence-opening sound but cut it off without actually saying anything. But he looked at his watch.

"Why would Chilean politicians want to meet with Henry Highhawk?" Leaphorn asked himself the question. "They had to want to contact him badly enough to send someone three thousand miles, and get him killed, and then send somebody else to complete the mission. And post his bail." He glanced up at Chee. "That's right, isn't it? And Highhawk called that guy with the missing fingers his friend, didn't he? Any idea how long they'd known each other?"

"They didn't," Chee said. "Highhawk was lying. They hadn't met until the Yeibichai."

"You sure?" Leaphorn asked.

"I watched them meet," Chee said. "I'm sure."

Rodney held up a hand. "Friends, I've got to go and do some things. Two or three in fact. I was going to be back at the office about an hour ago. Stick around. I'll be back." He slipped off the desk and disappeared into the hallway.

"Every effect has its cause," Leaphorn said to Chee. "Once in a while, maybe, a star just falls at random. But I don't believe in random. The Santillanes bunch had a hell of a good reason to chase after Highhawk. What was it?"

"I don't know," Chee said. "All I know about the Santillanes bunch is from seeing Bad Hands a couple of times. I got here by a totally different route. And I've got a different question under your brush pile." He sat on the desk about where Rodney had been leaning, thinking, deciding how to explain this premonition, this hunch that had been making him uneasy.

"I keep remembering Highhawk at the Yeibichai," Chee said. "I was curious about him so I was watching him, standing just a little off to the side where I could see his face. He was cold—" He laughed, glanced at Leaphorn. "Of course he was cold. Everybody's cold at a Night Chant, but he was colder than most of us because, you know, if you come from the East you think desert country is supposed to be hot, so he wasn't dressed like us. Just had on a leather jacket. Anyway, he was shivering." Chee stopped. Why was he telling Leaphorn all this? Highhawk standing, shaking with cold, hugging himself, the wind blowing dust across the dance ground around his ankles, the wavering light from the bonfires turning his face red. His expression had been rapt, and Chee had noticed his lips were moving. Highhawk was singing to himself. Agnes Tsosie had been standing on a blanket spread on the packed earth in front of the medicine hogan attended by the *hataalii.* Talking God, Humpback God, and Water Sprinkler had been making their slow, stately approach. Chee had edged closer, close enough to hear what Highhawk was chanting. "He stirs. He stirs. He stirs. He stirs," Highhawk had been singing. "Now in old age wandering, he stirs." It had been words from the "Song of Waking" which the *hataalii* would have sung on the first midnight of the ceremonial, summoning the spirit in the mask from its cosmic sleep to take its part in the ritual. He remembered noticing as Highhawk sang that while some of the words were wrong, the man's expression was deeply reverent.

Now he noticed that Leaphorn's expression was puzzled. "He was cold," Leaphorn said. "Yes, but you haven't made your point."

"He was a believer," Chee said. "You know what I mean. Some people come to a ceremonial out of family duty, and some come out of curiosity, or to meet friends. But to some it is a spiritual experience. You can tell by their faces."

Leaphorn's expression was still puzzled. "And he was one of those? He believed?"

Yes, Chee thought, Highhawk was one of those. You're not one, lieutenant. You don't believe. You see the Navajo Way as a harmless cultural custom. You would be one of those who go only as a family duty. But this crazy white man believed. Truly believed.

"He did," Chee said. "He was moved. He even knew words to the song that awakens the spirit of Talking God in the mask. He was singing it at the wrong time, but he knew the words. And the point I'm trying to make with all this—the point is I'm puzzled about this mask we found."

Leaphorn waited for that to be explained.

"Maybe I'm wrong but I don't think so. I don't think Highhawk would use the *yei* mask like that. I don't think he would put it on the head of a manikin in a public display. I don't think the museum would approve of that either. Despite what Highhawk said. For example, they brought in a *hataalii,* a man named Sandoval, brought him in to check out the exhibit and make sure Henry wasn't doing anything sacrilegious. So—" Chee paused, thinking about it.

"Go on," Leaphorn said.

"So Highhawk was making a duplicate mask. A replica of the genuine Yeibichai mask in the museum's collection. A copy. He must have had both of them here last night." Chee picked up the *yei* mask by its fur collar ruff and held it up, facing Leaphorn.

"This mask we have here, it's not the genuine Yeibichai mask," Chee said. "It's just about an exact replica. Highhawk made it because he wouldn't use the real one in a public display, and he certainly wouldn't have rigged up his tape player inside of it."

"It looks old as the mountains to me," Leaphorn said. "Cracked and worn."

"He's good at that," Chee said. "But take a look at it. Up close. Look for pollen stains, along the cheeks where the medicine man puts it when he feeds the mask, and on the end of the mouthpiece. And down into the leather tube that forms the mouth. It's not there. No stains. He dried the buckskin somehow, or got an old piece, and dried out the paint, but why bother with the pollen stains? Nobody would notice it."

"No," Leaphorn said slowly. "Nobody would. So the mask on exhibit downstairs is the genuine Yeibichai mask."

"What else could it be? And there has to be a mask on the Talking God manikin. Dr. Hartman was down there this morning checking everything. She couldn't find Highhawk so she must have checked his display carefully. You naturally would. If Talking God didn't have his mask on, she sure as hell would have noticed that. But she wouldn't be able to tell the genuine mask from Highhawk's counterfeit."

"So who put it there?" Leaphorn mused. "Whoever killed Highhawk must have put it there, wouldn't you say? But—" Leaphorn stopped, midsentence. "Where is that Yeibichai display?"

"It's sort of off to one side, to the left of the center of the mask exhibition. Right across from it is an exhibition of Andean stuff, Incan and so forth. The high point is a gold and emerald mask which some Chilean general is trying—" Now it was Chee's turn to halt, midthought. "My God!" he said. "Dr. Hartman said this Chilean general—I think he's the head of their political police—was supposed to come in to today to look at the thing."

"Is this Chilean exhibit right across from Talking God?" Leaphorn asked. "Is that it?"

He moved toward the door while he was still asking the question, amazingly fast for a man of his age in a three-piece suit. And Jim Chee was right behind him.

20

LEROY FLECK WALKED the block and a half to where he'd parked the old Chevy sedan. He walked briskly, but without breaking into a trot, without any sign of urgency that anyone who saw him might remember. The important point was to keep any connection from being made between the crime and the car. If that happened he was a goner. If it didn't, then he had time to do the things he had to do.

He drove just at the speed limit, careful at the lights, careful changing lanes, and as he drove he listened to the police scanner on the seat beside him. Nothing much exciting except for a multi-vehicle, multi-injury accident on the Interstate 66 exit ramp at the Theodore Roosevelt Bridge. He was almost downtown before the call came. A slight strain showed in the laconic voice of the dispatcher and Fleck recognized the address of the nursing home and the code. It meant officer down. It meant nothing else would matter much for a while in D.C. law enforcement. A policeman had been killed. Within fifteen minutes, probably less, Fleck's description would be broadcast to every police car in the district. The noon newscasts would carry it big. But nobody had his picture and he still had time.

His first stop was at Western Union. The message he sent to Delmar was short: TAKE CARE OF MAMA. TELL HER I LOVE HER. AM SENDING MONEY ORDER.

He gave the girl at the desk the message and then opened the plastic purse and counted out $2,033. He thought for a moment. He had almost half a tank of gasoline but he might need to make a telephone call, or pay an admission fee somewhere. He saved the three ones, stuffed them in his shirt pocket. He asked the girl to subtract the transmission fees and make out a money order for the rest. Then he drove to the Chilean embassy.

He parked down the street at a place where he could watch the entrance gate. Then he walked through the drizzle to the pay booth, dialed the embassy, and gave the woman who answered the word that The Client had given him for emergencies.

"I need Stone," he said. He always wondered why the man used that for a code name. Why not something in Spanish?

"Ah," the woman said. "One little moment, please."

Then he waited. He waited a long time. The rain was mixed with snow now, big wet flakes which stuck to the glass of the booth for a second and then slid down the pane. Fleck went over his plan, but there was nothing much to go over. He would try to lure The Client out where he could reach him. If The Client wouldn't come out, he would wait. He would get him eventually. He would get as many as he could. He would get ones as important as possible. It was all he could do. He knew The Client wasn't his own man. He was taking his orders from somebody up the ladder. But it didn't matter to Fleck. Like Mama said, they were all the same.

"Yes," the voice said. It was not The Client's voice.

"I got to talk to Stone," Fleck said.

"He is not available. Not now."

"When then?" Fleck asked.

"Later today."

Perhaps, Fleck thought, he could get someone else. Someone more important. That would be as good. Even better.

"Let me talk to his superior then."

"Just a moment." Fleck could hear a distant-sounding voice, asking questions.

"They are getting ready to go," the man said. "They have no time now."

"I have to talk to somebody. It's an emergency."

"No time now. You call back. This evening."

The line went dead.

Fleck looked at it. Hung it up gently. Walked back to his car. It made no difference at all really. He could wait.

He had waited less than five minutes when the iron driveway gate creaked open and the limousine emerged. After it came another, equally black. They turned downtown, toward Capitol Hill.

Leroy Fleck trailed them in his rusty Chevy.

The limos did left turns on Constitution Avenue, rolled past the National Gallery of Art, and pulled to a stop at the Tenth Street entrance to the Museum of Natural History. Fleck pulled his Chevy into a No Parking zone, turned off the ignition, and watched.

Seven men emerged from the two limos. Fleck recognized The Client. Of the others, one carried cameras and a camera bag, and two more were burdened by a movie camera, tripods, and what Fleck guessed must be sound-recording equipment. The remaining three were a short, plump man in a fur-collared coat; a tall, elegantly dressed man with a mustache; and a burly, hard-looking weightlifter type with a crooked nose. The driver from the front limo held a black umbrella over Mustache, protecting him from the wet snowflakes until the entourage reached the shelter of the museum entrance. Fleck sat a moment, sorting them out in his mind. The plump man would probably be the ambassador himself, or at least someone high on the power ladder. The elegant man would be a visiting Very Important Person, the one he'd read about in the *Post*. Judging from who got the umbrella, the visitor outranked the ambassador and rated the personal attention of The Client. The weightlifter type would be the VIP's personal muscle. As for The Client, Fleck had pegged him long ago as the man in charge of security at the embassy. In all they made a formidable bunch.

Fleck climbed out of the Chevy without bothering to take the key out of the ignition or to lock the door. He was finished with the Chevy now. No more need for it. He trotted up the museum steps and into the entrance foyer. The last two cameramen from the limo delegation were disappearing through a doorway into the central hall. They hurried into a side hallway to his right, under a banner which read THE MASKED GODS OF THE AMERICAS. Fleck followed.

There were perhaps fifty or sixty people in the exhibit of masks. Two-thirds of them looked to Fleck like a mixture of standard tourists. The rest were reporters and television cameramen and museum functionaries who must have been here waiting for Big Shot and his followers to appear. Now they were clustered around the elegant man. The Client stood a little aside from the central knot. He was doing his job. He was watching, his eyes checking everyone. They rested a moment on Fleck, then dismissed him and moved on.

The Client would have to be first, Fleck decided. He was the professional. Then he would go for the VIP. Fleck was conscious that he held two advantages. None of them had ever seen him and they wouldn't be expecting an attack. He would have total surprise on the first one he hit, and maybe a little surprise left on number two if there was enough confusion. He would need more luck than he could expect to take out the third one, but it was worth a try.

A cameraman's strobe flash lit the scene. Then another one. They were setting up some sort of filming apparently, with the VIP over by the display of South American stuff. Beside Fleck was an exhibit of masked dancers, big as life. Apparently some sort of American Indians. Fleck stooped, slipped the shank out of his boot, and held it in his palm, the honed blade hidden by his sleeve. Then he waited. He wanted the crowd to be exactly big enough. He wanted the time to be exactly right.

21

"THIS MIGUEL SANTERO, was that his name? This guy with the mutilated hands, did you see any sign of him around here last night?"

Leaphorn was standing exactly in front of the vertical line formed by the junction of the elevator doors, staring at the crack as he asked the question. It seemed to Chee that the elevator was barely moving. Why hadn't they looked for the stairs? Six flights. They could have run down six flights while this incredibly slow elevator was dropping one.

"I didn't see him," Chee said. "I just had a feeling that it was Santero on the telephone."

"I wish we knew for sure how he connects," Leaphorn said, without relaxing his stare at the elevator door. "Three slim threads is all we have—or maybe four—tying him to the Santillanes bunch. The FBI connects him, but the FBI has a bad habit of buying bad information. Second, after Santillanes was killed going to find Highhawk, Santero went out and found him. Maybe that was just a coincidence. Third, the little red-headed man who killed Santillanes seems to have been following Santero too."

The elevator's floor indicator passed three and sank toward two. Leaphorn watched it. He got Chee to explain how the displays were arranged. He told Chee what he'd seen in the *Post* about General Huerta Cardona demanding return of the Incan mask. If he felt any of the anxiety which was causing Chee to chew relentlessly on his lower lip, he didn't allow it to show.

"What's the fourth?" Chee said.

Leaphorn's mind had left this part of the puzzle to explore something else. "Fourth?"

"You said maybe four thin threads."

"Oh. The fourth. Santero's mangled hands and Santillanes' teeth. They were broken out, I think. The pathologist said there was nothing wrong with the man's gums." He looked at Chee. "I think that's what decides me. Santero is one of the Santillanes people. The FBI had this one right. Describe him to me again."

Chee described Bad Hands in detail.

"What do you think we're dealing with here?"

"I'd guess a bomb," Chee said.

Leaphorn nodded. "Probably," he said. "Plastic explosive in the mask, and someone there to detonate it when the general is in exactly the right place."

The elevator creaked to a halt at the ground floor.

"I'll get the mask," Chee said. "You look for Santero."

Finding Santero proved to be no problem.

They rushed out of the elevator, through the door into the museum's main-floor public display halls and down the corridor toward the MASKED GODS OF THE AMERICAS banner—Chee leading, Leaphorn puffing along behind. Chee stopped.

"There he is," he said.

Santero had his back to them. He was standing beside an exhibit of Toltec masks, watching the crowd, which was watching television crews at another exhibit. Bright lights flashed on—a television crew preparing for action.

Chee turned his hurried walk into a run, dodging through the spectators, staggering a teenaged girl who backed into his path, being staggered in turn by a hefty woman whose shoulder grazed him as he passed. The Yeibichai itself had drawn only a few lookers. Curiosity about the television crews and the celebrity at the Incan display was the magnet but Chee had to push his way through the overflow to reach the exhibit. He was forcing himself not to think two terrible, unthinkable thoughts. He would reach the mask and there would be a bomb under it and Bad Hands would detonate it in his face. He would reach the mask and tear it off and there would be nothing under it. Only the molded plastic head of the manikin. In the first thought he would be instantly dead. In the second he would be hideously, unspeakably, terminally humiliated—living out his life as a public joke.

Chee pushed aside a boy and vaulted over the guardrail into the Yeibichai display. Up close, the manikin representing Talking God seemed even larger than he'd remembered. He gripped the fur ruff at the throat of the mask. Behind him he heard a voice shouting: "Hey! You! Get out of there." He pulled up on the leather. (It will explode, he thought. I will be dead.) Through his fingers, the mask and head seemed to be one—a single entity. The stiff leather wouldn't pull loose.

"Hey!" he heard behind him. "Get away from that. What the hell are you doing!" A security guard was climbing over the railing.

Chee jerked at the mask, tilting the manikin against him. He jerked again. The mask, the head, all of it came off in his arms. The headless manikin toppled with a crash. "Hey!" the guard shouted.

Leroy Fleck had several terrible weaknesses and several terrible strengths. One of his strengths was in stalking his prey, attaining the exact place, the exact time, the exact position, for using his shank exactly as Eddy Elkins—and his own subsequent experience—had taught him to use it. The secret of Leroy Fleck's survival had been finding a way to make his kill instant and silent. And Fleck had managed to survive seventeen years since his release from prison.

He was stalking now. While he watched the crowd and waited for the moment, he slipped the shank out of his sleeve and an envelope out of his pocket. He put the shank in the envelope, and carried it in his right hand, deep in his right coat pocket where it would be ready. The envelope had been Elkins' idea. "If witnesses see an envelope, they react like they're seeing somebody handing somebody a letter. Same with the victim. But if people see a knife coming, it's a totally different reaction." That had been proved true. And the paper didn't get in the way at all, or slow things down. With the handle of the shank ready between his thumb and forefinger, he watched The Client carefully, and the VIP, and the VIP's muscleman, and the ambassador, and the rest of them. He concluded from the way the man moved, and the way he watched, that the still photographer was also the ambassador's bodyguard. Partially on the basis of that he had changed his strategy. The VIP would go first. The Client second. The VIP was the one that mattered, the one who would best demonstrate that Leroy Fleck was a man, and not a dog that could be spit on without retribution.

He could do it right now, he thought, but the situation was improving. It became clear to Fleck what was happening. The VIP had called some sort of press conference here at the Incan display. That brought in the television cameras, and TV crews attracted the curious. The bigger the crowd got, the better the odds for Fleck. It would multiply the confusion, improve his chances of getting two, and maybe even three.

Then he saw Santero—the man who always wore gloves. It was clear to Fleck almost immediately that Santero was also stalking. Fleck watched. Santero seemed to have two objectives. He was keeping out of the line of vision of The Client, and he was keeping the VIP in sight. Fleck considered this. It didn't seem to matter. Santero was no longer the enemy. The man had probably come here to try something. But if he did, it could only be helpful to Fleck. He could see no problem in that.

Just as he had decided that, he saw the two Indian cops. They hurried into the exhibit hall together. Then the tall one broke into a run toward him, and the older one headed for Santero. Here Fleck could definitely see a problem. Both of these men had seen him, the older one clearly and in good light. No more time to wait for a bigger crowd. Fleck pushed his way past a man in a raincoat, past a television light technician, toward the VIP. The VIP was standing with a well-dressed fat man wearing bifocal glasses. They were studying a sheet of paper, discussing it. Probably, Fleck thought, they were looking at notes for the statement he intended to make. If he could handle it, Fleck decided he would take the VIP from the back. He slipped his right hand from his pocket, crumpling one end of the envelope as he gripped the shank handle. Then he moved, Fleck fashion, like lightning.

Leaphorn always thought things through, always planned, always minimized the opportunity for error. It was a lifelong habit, it was the source of his reputation as the man to handle impossible cases. Now he had only a few seconds to think and no time at all to plan. He would have to presume that there was a bomb, that Santero held the detonator, that Santero was working alone because only one person would be needed. Santero's presence, lurking where he could watch the general, seemed to reinforce some of that thinking. The man was waiting until the general moved up to the position closest to the bomb. And the detonator? Probably something like the gadget that turned his television on and changed the channels. Grabbing him wouldn't work. He'd be too strong and agile for Leaphorn to handle, even with surprise. He'd simply point the thing and push the button. Leaphorn would try confusion.

Santero heard him rushing up and whirled to face him. His right hand was in his coat pocket, the arm rigid.

"Señor Santero," Leaphorn said, in a loud, hoarse, breathless whisper. *"Venga conmigo! Venga! Pronto! Pronto! Venga!"*

Santero's face was shocked, bloodless. The face of a man interrupted at the moment of mass murder.

"Come with you?" he stammered. "Who are you?"

"Los Santillanes sent me," Leaphorn said. "Come. Hurry."

"But what—" Santero became aware that Leaphorn had gripped his right arm. He jerked it away, pulled out his right hand. He wore a black glove on it, and in the glove he held a small, flat plastic box. "Get away from me," Santero said, voice fierce.

There was a clamor of voices from the crowd. Someone was shouting: "Hey! You! Get out of there." Santero turned from Leaphorn, backing away, starting at the sound of a second shout: "Hey! Get away from that."

Santero took another step backward. He raised the box.

"Santero," Leaphorn shouted. *"El hombre ahí no esta el general. No esta El General Huerta Cardona. Es un—"* Leaphorn's Arizona–New Mexico Spanish included no Castilian noun for "stand-in" or even "substitute." *"Es un* impostor," he concluded.

"Impostor?" Santero said. He lowered the box a little. "Speak English. I can't understand your Spanish."

"I was sent to tell you they were using a stand-in," Leaphorn said. "They heard about the plot. They sent someone made up to look like the general."

Santero's expression shifted from doubtful to grim. "I think you're lying," he said. "Stop trying to get between me and—"

From the crowd at the display came the sound of a woman screaming.

"What the devil—?" Santero began. And then there were shouts, another scream, and a man's voice shouting: "He's fainted! Get a doctor!"

Leaphorn's move was pure reflex, without time to think. His only advantages were that Santero was a little confused, a little uncertain. And the hand in which Santero held the control box had only two fingers left inside that glove. Leaphorn struck at the hand.

Leroy Fleck said, "Excuse me. Excuse me, please," and pushed past the woman he had been using as a screen and went for the general's back. But he did it just as the general was turning. Fleck saw the general staring at him, and the general's bodyguard making a quick-reflex move to block him. His instincts told him this was not going well.

"A letter—" he said, striking at the general's chest. He felt the paper of the envelope crumple against his fist as the steel razor of the shank slit through the general's vest, and shirt, and the thin muscle of the chest, and sank between the ribs.

"—from an admirer," Fleck said, as he slashed back and forth, back and forth, and heard the general gasp, and felt the general sag against him. "He's fainted!" Fleck shouted. "Get a doctor!"

The Muscle had grabbed him by the shoulder just as he shouted it, and struck him a terrible blow over the kidneys. But Fleck hugged the general's sagging body, and shouted again, "Help me!"

It caused confusion, exactly as Fleck had hoped. The Muscle released Fleck's arm and tried to catch the general. The Client was there now beside them, bending over the slumping body. "What?" he shouted. "What happened? General!"

Fleck withdrew the shank, letting the crumpled envelope fall. He stabbed The Client in the side. Stabbed him again. And again.

The bodyguard was no longer confused. He shot Fleck twice. The exhibit echoed with the boom of the pistol, and the screams of panicking spectators.

Chee was only dimly aware of the shouts, the screams, the general pandemonium around him. He was numb. He turned the mask in his hands and looked into it, with no idea what to expect. He saw two dangling wires, one red, one white, a confusing array of cop-per-colored connections, a small square gray box, and a heavy com-pact mass of blue-gray dough.

The security officer clutched his arm. "Come on!" he shouted. "Get out of here!" The security officer was a plump young black man with heavy jowls. The screams were distracting him. "Look," Chee said, turning the open end of the mask toward him. "It's a bomb." While he was saying it, Chee was tearing at the wires. He dropped them to the floor, and sat on the back of the fallen mani-kin, and began carefully peeling the Yeibichai mask from the mass of blue-gray plastic which had been pressed into it.

"A bomb," the guard said. He looked at Chee, at the mask, and at the struggle at the adjoining Incan exhibit. "A bomb?" he said again, and climbed the railing and charged into the Incan melee. "Break it up," he shouted. "We have a bomb in here."

And just then General Huerta Cardona's bodyguard shot Leroy Fleck.

Chee looked up to see what was happening. And then he finished brushing the fragments of plastic out of the mask of Talking God, and straightening the bristling row of eagle feathers and the fox-fur ruff. He picked it up in one hand, and the ball of plastic explosive in the other, and climbed over the railing and out of the exhibit. He wanted to show Leaphorn they'd guessed right.

Joe Leaphorn's hand knocked the control box out of Santero's grip. It clattered to the marble floor between them. Santero reached for it. Leaphorn kicked it. It went skittering down the corridor, spinning past the feet of running people. Santero pursued it, running into the crowd stampeding out of the exhibition hall. Leaphorn followed.

A man with a camera collided with him. "He killed the general," the photographer shouted to someone ahead of him. "He killed the general." On the floor near the wall Leaphorn saw fragments of black plastic and an AA-size battery. Someone had trampled the detonator. He stopped, backed out of the stampede. Santero had disappeared. Leaphorn leaned against the wall, gasping. His chest hurt. His hip hurt where the heavy camera had slammed into it. He would go and see about Jim Chee. But first he would collect himself. He was getting too damned old for this business.

22

JIM CHEE SAT on his bed, leaned back on his suitcase, and tried to cope with his headache by not thinking about it. He was wearing the best shirt and the well-pressed trousers he had hung carefully in the closet when he unpacked to save in the event he needed to look good. No need now to save them. He would wear them on the plane. It was a bitch of a headache. He had slept poorly—partly because of the strange and lumpy hotel mattress (Chee being accustomed to the hard, thin padding on the built-in bed of his trailer home), and partly because he had been too tense to sleep. His mind had been too full of horrors and terrors. He would doze, then jerk awake to sit on the edge of the mattress, shaking with the after-effects of shallow, grotesque dreams in which Talking God danced before him.

Finally, about a half-hour before the alarm was scheduled to rescue him from the night, he had given up. He had taken a shower, packed his stuff, and checked again with the front desk to see if he had any messages. There was one from Leaphorn, which simply informed him that Leaphorn had returned to Window Rock. That surprised Chee. It was a sort of courtly thing for the tough old bastard to have done. There was a message from Janet Pete, asking for a call back. He tried and got no answer. By then the headache was flowering and he had time to kill. Downstairs he drank two cups of coffee—which usually helped but didn't this morning. He left the toast he'd ordered on the plate and went for a walk.

The mild early-winter storm which had been bringing Washington rain mixed with snow yesterday had drifted out over the Atlantic and left behind a grim gray overcast with a forecast for high broken clouds and clearing by late afternoon. Now it was cold and still. Chee found that even in this strange place, even under these circumstances, he could catch himself up in the rhythm of the fast, hard motion, of heart and lungs hard at work. The nightmares faded a little, coming to seem like abstract memories of something he might have merely dreamed. Highhawk had never really existed. There were not really eighteen thousand ancestors in boxes lining hallways in an old museum. No one had actually tried to commit mass murder with the mask of Talking God. He walked briskly down Pennsylvania Avenue, and veered northward on Twelfth Street, and strode briskly westward again on H Street, and collapsed finally on a bench in what he thought, judging from a sign he'd noticed without really attending, might be Lafayette Square. Through the trees he could see the White House and, on the other side, an impressive hotel. Chee caught his breath, considered the note from Leaphorn, and decided it was a sort of subtle gesture. (You and I, kid. Two Dineh among the Strangers.) But maybe not. And it wasn't the sort of thing he would ever ask the lieutenant about.

A dove-gray limousine pulled up under the hotel's entryway roof, and after it a red sports car which Chee couldn't identify. Maybe a Ferrari, he thought. Next was a long black Mercedes which looked like it might have been custom built. Chee was no longer breathing hard. The damp low-country cold seeped up his sleeves and around his socks and under his collar. He got up, inspired half by cold and half by curiosity, and headed for the hotel.

It was warm inside, and luxurious. Chee sank into a sofa, removed his hat, warmed his ears with his hands, and observed what his sociology teacher had called "the privileged class." The professor admitted a prejudice against this class but Chee found them interesting to observe. He spent almost forty-five minutes watching women in fur coats and men in suits which, while they tended to look almost identical to Chee's untrained eye, were obviously custom made. He saw someone who looked exactly like Senator Teddy Kennedy, and someone who looked like Sam Donaldson, and a man who was probably Ralph Nader, and three others who must have been celebrities of some sort, but whose names eluded him.

He left the hotel warm but still with the headache. The material splendors, the fur and polished leather of the hotel's guests, had replaced his nightmares with a depression. He hurried through the damp cold back to his own hotel room.

The telephone was ringing. It was Janet Pete.

"I tried to call you last night," she said. "How are you? Are you all right?"

"Fine," Chee said. "We had trouble down at the museum. The FBI got involved and—"

"I know. I know," Janet said. "I saw it on television. The paper is full of it. There's a picture of you, with the statue."

"Oh," Chee said. The final humiliation. He could see it in the Farmington *Times:* Officer Jim Chee of Shiprock, New Mexico, seen above wrestling with a representation of Talking God, from which he has removed the head, in the Smithsonian Museum in Washington, D.C.

"On television, too. On the ABC morning news. They had some footage of you with the mask. But I'm not sure people who didn't know how you were dressed would know it was you."

Chee could think of nothing to say. His head still ached. He wished with a fervent longing to be back in New Mexico. In his trailer under the cottonwood on the bank above the San Juan River. He would take two aspirin and sprawl out on his comfortable, narrow bed and finish reading *A Yellow Raft on Blue Water.* He'd left it opened to page 158. A hard place to stop.

"They said Henry Highhawk was dead," Janet Pete said in a small voice.

"Yes. The police think Santero killed him," Chee said. "It seems fairly obvious that it must have been Santero."

"Henry was a sweet man," Janet said. "He was a kind man." She paused. "He was, wasn't he, Jim? But if he was, how did they talk him into being a part of this—of this horrible bomb thing?"

"I don't think they did," Chee said. "We'll never know for sure, I guess. But I think they conned him, and used him. Probably they saw the story in the *Post* about Highhawk digging up the skeletons. They needed a way to kill the general and they had a way of knowing their target would be visiting the Smithsonian, so they went out and made friends with Henry."

"But that doesn't explain why he would help them."

"I think Highhawk thought Santero was sympathetic to what Henry was trying to do. In fact, I'd be willing to bet that planting the tape recorded message in the mask was dreamed up by the Santillanes bunch. Maybe they knew he'd need technical help with the timer on the tape recorder and all that."

"I'd like to think you're right," Janet said. "I'd like to think I wasn't a complete fool. Wanting to help him when he was helping murder a lot of innocent people." But her tone was full of doubt.

"If I wasn't right— If you weren't they wouldn't have had to kill him," Chee said. "But they did kill him. Maybe he noticed something and caught on. Maybe they just couldn't leave him around to tell all to the police."

"Sure," Janet said. "I didn't think of that. I feel better. I guess I needed to keep believing Henry just wanted to do good."

"I think that's right," Chee said. "It took me a while, but I've decided that, too."

"What are you going to do now?"

"I have a flight this afternoon back to Albuquerque. Then I catch the Mesa Airlines flight to Farmington, and pick up my car and drive back to Shiprock," Chee said.

Janet Pete correctly read the tone of that.

"I'm sorry," she said. "I had no idea what I was getting you into. I never would have—"

Chee, a believer in the Navajo custom of never interrupting anyone, interrupted her.

"I wanted to come," he said. "I wanted to see you."

"Do you still want to see me? I'll come over and take you to the airport." A long pause. "If you really do have to go. You're on vacation, aren't you?"

"I'd like that," Chee said. "A ride to the airport."

So now he waited again. He was able now to think about what had happened yesterday. The D.C. police would probably catch Santero sooner or later. He found he had no interest in that. But he wondered what Leaphorn had done to keep Santero from pushing the button. Chee retraced it all in his memory. Handing the museum guard the ball of plastic explosive. ("Here. Be careful with this. It was a bomb. Give it to the cops.") He'd walked back to the STAFF ONLY elevator carrying Talking God's mask. He had pushed his way through the uproar of scurrying and shouting. He'd gotten off at the sixth floor and walked back to Highhawk's office. He'd emptied an assortment of leather, feathers, and bones out of a box beside Highhawk's chair. He placed the mask gently in the box and closed it. Then he searched the office, quickly and thoroughly, without finding what he wanted. That left two places to look.

He picked up the replica mask Highhawk had made, laid it atop the box, and carried it down the elevator to the exhibit hall.

By then the spectators were gone and two D.C. policemen were guarding the corridor. He saw Rodney, and Rodney let him through. Rodney was holding the plastic explosive.

"What the hell happened?" Rodney had asked. "Joe tells me this bomb was under the mask and you pulled it off. That right?"

"Yes," Chee said. He handed the replica to Rodney. "Here," he said. "Whoever did it sort of molded the plastic into the mask. Jammed it in."

Leaphorn was standing there, his face gray. "You all right?" he asked.

"I'm fine," Chee said. "But you don't look so hot."

On the floor between the Yeibichai exhibit and the Incan display three men were sprawled in that totally careless attitude that only the dead can manage. One of them matched Leaphorn's description of the little redhead with the shape of a weightlifter. Sooner or later he would wonder about what the redhead was doing here, and what had happened. When he did, he'd ask Leaphorn. Now it didn't seem to matter. And then the morgue crew began arriving. And more plainclothes cops, and men who had to be, by their costume, the feds.

Chee had not been in the mood for the Federal Bureau of Investigation. He walked out of the Tenth Street entrance and around the building. He checked parked cars. A wrecker was hauling an old Chevy sedan away from the towaway fire zone, but Chee was looking for Highhawk's Ford Mustang. He finally found it in a staff parking lot.

It was locked. What he was looking for wasn't visible inside, and it was too large to fit under the seat and out of sight. If it wasn't in the car, he'd have to take a cab out to Highhawk's place and look for it there. But first he'd check the trunk. Locked, of course. Chee found a slab of broken concrete near the sidewalk. He slammed it down on the trunk lid, springing it open. There was a box inside, wrapped in an old pair of coveralls. Chee took off the lid and looked in. The fetish representing the Tano War Twin smiled its sinister, malicious smile up at him. He took Talking God's mask out of the box from Highhawk's office, packed it carefully in with the fetish, put the empty box in the trunk, and closed it.

Two young men, each holding a briefcase, were standing beside a nearby car watching him break into the Mustang. Chee nodded to them. "Had to get this fetish out," he said, and walked back to the Natural History Museum. He had left the box in the checkroom and went back to the exhibit.

There the FBI had taken over. Chee had unchecked his box and walked to his hotel.

Now, in his room, he was coming to terms with yesterday when the telephone rang again.

"Jim?"

It was Mary Landon's voice.

"Yes," he said. "It's me, Mary."

"You weren't hurt? On the news they said you weren't hurt."

"No. Not at all."

"I'm coming to Washington. To see you," she said. "I called you yesterday. At the police station in Shiprock. They said you were in Washington and told me your hotel. I was going to call you and come. And then last night— That was terrible."

Jim Chee was having trouble analyzing his emotions. They were turbulent, and mixed.

"Mary. Why do you want to see me?" He paused, wondering how to phrase it. "I got your letter," he said.

"That was why," she said. "I shouldn't have said that in a letter. It's the sort of thing that you say in person. That was wrong. It was stupid, too. I know how you feel. And how I feel."

"How do you feel about living on the reservation? About the reservation being home?"

"Oh, Jim," she said. "Let's not—" She left it unfinished.

"Not get into that? But that's always been our problem. I want you to come and live with me. You know how I am. My people are part of me. And you want me to come out to the world and live with you. And that's only fair. But I can't handle it."

A moment passed before she spoke again, and her voice was a little different. "I wish I hadn't told you in a letter. That's all. That was cruel. I just didn't think. Or, I did think. I thought it would hurt too much to see you like that, and I would be all confused about it again. But I should have told you in person."

There was not much to say after that, and they said good-bye. Chee washed his face, and looked out his window into the window of the office across the narrow street. The man into whose office Chee's window looked was looking down at the passing cars, still with his vest and tie neatly in place. The man and Chee were looking at each other when Janet Pete tapped at his half-opened door and came in.

He offered her the chair, and she took it.

"You don't look like you feel like doing a lot of talking," she said. "Would you like to just check out now, and drive on out to the airport?"

"No hurry," he said. She was not exactly a beautiful woman,

he thought. She did not have the softness, the silkiness, the dark blue, pale yellow feminine beauty of Mary Landon. Instead she had a kind of strong, clean-cut dignity. A classy gal. She was proud, and he identified with that. She had become his friend. He liked her. Or he thought he did. Certainly, he pitied her. And he was going to do something for her. What was happening to her here in Washington was nothing but miserable. He hated that.

"And before we go," Chee added, "there's something I want to give to you."

Chee got off the bed and unsnapped the suitcase. He took out the hotel laundry sack in which he'd wrapped it and extracted the fetish.

He handed it to her. "The Tano War God," he said. "One of the twins."

Janet Pete stared at it, and then at Chee. She made no move to accept it.

"I didn't think he should be so far away from home," Chee said. "He has a twin somewhere, and people who miss him. It seemed to me that the Smithsonian has plenty of other gods, stolen from other people, and they could keep the replica Highhawk made and get along without this one. I thought this one should go back to its kiva, or wherever the Tanos keep him."

"You want to give it to me?" Janet asked, still studying his face.

"That way he will get home," Chee said. "You can turn him over to John McDermott, and John gives him to what's-his-name— Eldon Tamana, wasn't it? That lawyer from Tano. And Tamana, he takes it home."

Janet Pete said nothing. She looked down at her hands, and then up at him again.

"Or," Chee added softly, "whatever you like."

Janet held out her hands. Chee laid the Twin War God in them.

"I guess we should go now," Chee said, and he relocked the suitcase. "I think I've been in this town long enough for a country boy Navajo."

Janet Pete was rewrapping the Twin War God in the laundry sack. "Me too," she said. "I have been here for months and months and months. So long it seems like a lifetime." She put her hand on Chee's sleeve.

"I will take this little fellow home myself," she said.